Premashram

Premashram

Premchand

Translated by
Sonali Garg

GYAN

Published, 2020

Published by

Gyan Publishing House
5, Ansari Road
Daryaganj, New Delhi-110002
Phone: 011-47034999, 9811692060
www.gyanbooks.com
E-mail: books@gyanbooks.com

Printed at: G. Print Process, Delhi.

Cataloging in Publication Data--DK

Courtesy: D.K. Agencies (P) Ltd. <docinfo@dkagencies.com>

Premacanda, 1881-1936, **author.**
[Premāśrama. English]
The abode of love / [translated] by Dr. Sonali Garg.
pages cm
Novel.
Translated from Hindi.
Translation of: Premāśrama.
ISBN 9788121219426 (PB)

1. Hindi fiction--Translations into English. I. Garg, Sonali, translator. II. Title.

LCC PK2098.S7P74 2020 | DDC 891.4335 23

For

Dr. Anand Prakash

for showing me the way

to

Premchand and Premashram

Contents

Acknowledgements

This work has seen the light of the day primarily due to the initiative and encouragement of Sh. B.P. Garg of Gyan Books, whose motivation has made me pen down this new chapter of my writing career successfully.

I humbly acknowledge the guidance and contribution of all my teachers who have helped me to sustain my love for both history and literature, in the absence of which, I wouldn't have been able to comprehend *Premashram*, the way I am able to, today. I sincerely hope that many of them would be able to read it, and enrich me further with their valuable critiques and suggestions.

I also invoke the blessings of some people who are not with me today, but ever present in my thought and spirit.

My parents, late Sh. Satpal Bansal and Smt. Meena Bansal, to whom I may acknowledge just about everything that has gone into my making as a person of literature.

My mother-in-law, late Smt. Manjula Garg, to whom I owe many moments of love and wisdom.

To my husband, Rajiv, I acknowledge the task of breaking my lull of imagination and goading me to put my thoughts into practice.

My two sons, Pulkit and Vedant, who have broken the monotony of an academic project in various loving ways, deserve a heartfelt mention.

Thank you everyone.

A Note on the Translation

Translation is, before anything else, an attempt at opening a window – into a world hitherto impeded by practical problems of language. The historicity and contemporaniety of *Premashram* is its most attractive aspect; also the main idea behind translating it and making it accessible to the non-Hindi knowing Indian reader.

The challenges involved in translating the novel began with the title itself. The kind of 'prem' or love which the novel posits as its final ideal is a holistic, community-oriented feeling for which no exact word could be located in the English language. Added to this was the problem of locating a corresponding word for 'ashram'; again, a cultural connotation far different from a mere 'home' or 'abode'. For these particular reasons, the original title has been retained, the symbolic meaning of which, hopefully, should be clear to all by the end of the text.

Coming to the language used in the dialogues, Premchand's particular style comprises of short sentences, with little scope for clauses or other elaborations that allow the translator some space to convert the source language suitably. In English, these sentences might seem literal or compressed due to the same reason. It is hoped that instead of the limitation, focus would be drawn to the meanings captured through them.

To maintain the flow and transparency of language, the indigenous terms as well as certain religious and mythological references have been retained, to understand which, a detailed glossary has been provided at the end. Needless to say, Google translator has been a major help in the area, along with my basic knowledge of Hindi and Urdu, the latter being an intrinsic part of Premchand's novels and stories of the times.

Premashram is, primarily, a world belonging to the North Indian peasant of the 1920s. If this translation succeeds in providing a glimpse into that world of the struggling peasantry, the effort may be counted successful.

Preface

Premashram has traditionally been received as a novel dealing with the ideas of peasant struggle and land reform, most notably in the light of the Awadh Peasant Movement. The only novel by Premchand which depicts an actual murder by a peasant seems ideologically influenced by the unprecedented violent character of the Kisan Sabhas that took millions of farmers in Eastern Uttar Pradesh in its sweep. That struggle was definitely about to emerge, as it did in the oncoming years of the 1920's. Before that, however, Premchand had already completed both the Urdu and the Hindi versions of *Premashram*, publishing his novel in 1922 (Talwar 101).

The novel represents symptoms of a deep economic unrest boiling under the suppressed cover of a changed land situation. Along with the reasons behind that unrest, it also tries to suggest an ideological solution which has often been put to critical scrutiny in terms of its practical viability. The resolution at the end cannot be seen as an easy outcome of what the novel has depicted in its erstwhile pages. It needs to be understood in terms of a rationalist consciousness trying to emerge out of a realist socio-economic consciousness, which was indeed disturbing, and badly needed to change.

Before analyzing that ideology and its suggestions, one needs to return to the text and see where it stood – in its own years of publication, as well as today, where it raises more questions than it answers.

The composition and the context

If one looks at the precise dates of the composition of *Premashram* (1918-20), one finds that the original Urdu version of the novel was complete before the outbreak of the Awadh Peasant Movement. In August 1920, when Premchand was busy translating the novel into Hindi, Jawaharlal Nehru had already joined the struggle, and by November, the scenario had grown violent enough for leaders like Mahatma Gandhi, Muhammad Ali and Shaukat Ali to visit Awadh and intervene. The emergent wave of the Non-Cooperation movement was more on their agenda and they could not immediately resolve the situation. By January 1921, the movement assumed a violent character and peasants started attacking the fields and godowns owned by the talukedars. The attacks took many places like Raibareli, Sultanpur and Faizabad in their fold; yet, by July 1921, the movement had been completely quelled.

The important thing to note is that Jawaharlal Nehru, who had joined the movement in June 1920 consciously tried to divert the flow of the peasant concerns into the broader concerns of the Non-cooperation movement (the resolution for it having been passed in the Calcutta session of the INC in Sep' 1920). In Jan' 1921, Motilal Nehru was made the President of the Kisan Sabha, much against the wishes of its primary leader, Baba Ramchandra. By July 1921, the peasant movement had got completely merged with the overall agenda of the INC; there seemed no particular difference between the meetings of the peasants and those of the Congress (Talwar 109).

What do these developments suggest? That there is no direct relation between the events of *Premashram* and the real events of the Awadh Peasant Movement. The novel is definitely inspired by the historical context wherein the north Indian peasant faced an extremely unjustifiable pressure on his land and life, but it does not show that pressure evolving into any planned struggle or resolution.

The violent outburst in the novel that leads to the death of the zamindar's henchman and its tragic repercussions on the village of Lakhanpur seems to be a sudden and fatalistic uprising that is led to a desirable, yet not a logical or sequential end. Premshankar, the radical agricultural reformer, accused of belonging to a Kisan Sabha in Premashram is not any radical activist. His entire focus seems to be on an economic kind of reform which might enable the peasants to lead a decent life within the set parameters of their agricultural professions. He does not really wish to intervene or stop the exploitative tactics of his zamindar brother; he can only leave his share of the profit from the zamindari and eke out a livelihood on the basis of his communist lifestyle. He constantly debates the non-viability of the institution of zamindari, but is not shown opposing it in any practical way except distancing himself from it. Also, the final inspiration that leads to the emergence of 'Premashram' – the egalitarian heaven for peasants - is a personal and unprecedented choice attempted by Mayashankar. He is a historically absent character, as is Balraj - the futuristic pillars on whose shoulders the edifice of the "ashram" may stand and survive.

Premshankar, along with the benevolent peasant Qadir, are souls lending solace to the strife-ridden Lakhanpur. They do not lead the villagers into any organized revolt or a long-term solution to their woes. Even Sukhu Chaudhary, who gets agitated on the seizure of the village pond by the zamindar, finally turns into an ascetic who only visits Lakhanpur periodically; also helps in paying the land rent, but is not able to inspire anybody into an open opposition against the atrocities of the zamindar.

The novel is a literary response to the conditions that were about to create an open unrest very soon; a testimony to the prophetic ideology of an author engaged with the economic realities confronting the peasant around him. The two historical events that do seem to have inspired it were the Bolshevik Revolution of Russia (1917) and the Champaran movement in India, which also took place in 1917 (Talwar 118-119).The Gandhian intervention in Champaran and the scrutiny of the troubles of the indigo farmers had taken the nationalist agenda to a new level. The peasant suddenly seemed to occupy a space that disturbed the steady flow of the agenda leading on to swaraj.

Almost simultaneously, Pdt. Madan Mohan Malviya organized the U.P. Kisan Sabha in 1918, under the aegis of the Home Rule League. The Sabha led on to the spreading of the movement in an unprecedented way. However, the unfortunate merger that was to occur between its particular goals and the wider goals of the nationalist movement did not allow the former to last long. The middle-class bourgeois leadership of the INC absorbed the radical peasant leaders into its fold (Nehru being the most prominent) and the concerns of the farmers became confined to discussions and brainstorming amidst the educated intelligentsia of the times. Premchand was one of them, and his writings deeply reflect the disturbed radical consciousness which could not see a profitable relationship between the interest of the peasant and the 'alleged' interest of the swaraj that was being posited as the primary aim of the nationalist movement.

The writer's response to his times

The compatibility between the economic superstructure proposed by the British (in which, the zamindar played a very important role – that of the revenue collector) and the basic, agricultural economy of the Indian peasant was a matter of great concern for Premchand. The essays and editorials that he consistently wrote from the beginning of his career (1907) till the very end (1936) stand testimony to his evolving ideology about the nation and its professed goals. The most important of these is – 'Purana Zamana: Naya Zamana '(Old Age: New Age), Published in the February 1919 issue of the Urdu monthly, *Zamana* which clearly stipulates new goals for the emerging Indian nation.

Here, Premchand highlights how the developments in Europe and America have erased the evils of class differences in these nations. He also lauds the establishment of the League of Nations which sought an equal footing between the developed and the developing blocks of the world; the utopian nature of its goals notwithstanding. Coming to the 'new' nation that was emerging in the India of the early 1920s, he strongly questions the predominance of lawyers and landlords in the nationalist struggle and points out the disturbing absence of the peasant in the proposed face of the 'swaraj':

> Isn't it a matter of shame that a country which boasts of a 90% peasant population should have no Kisan Sabha, no movement for peasant welfare, no agricultural college, and no organized effort for the upliftment of the peasant? You opened thousands of schools and colleges … but for whom? Only for your own self; for increasing your own power … The age that is to come belongs to the peasants and the labourers… Hindustan cannot remain immune to the effects of these winds. (PR 7 197)[1]

The last lines of the essay draw a neat indictment on the kind of swaraj that the early nationalist leaders were endorsing and clearly warn them to beware of the vested nature of their struggle. He strongly urges them to win over the hearts of the people before they win any kind of political independence. This 'winning' clearly entails making the life of the peasant easy and tolerable; abstenance from the practices of 'ijafa' and 'bedakhli' (rent-increase and land confiscation) and an overall humanitarian approach towards the land tillers.[2]

For Premchand, the very perception of *swaraj* and its proposed goals meant a total, independent control over one's life and its resources, the political part being just one of them. An extremely important essay in this regard is 'Swarajya ke Fayade' (pub. 1921); an essay which sets in context almost all the aspects that a politically independent nation might focus on. After deliberating on the kind of state that might be termed as 'independent', he professes his anticipation of the effects of the worldwide revolutionary climate on the emerging Indian state:

> One can see the auspicious symptoms of a soldierless world emerging very soon. Therefore, the savings that will be left due to lesser expenditure on the army and the administration might be spent on

---

1. See the list of Works Cited; *Premchand Rachnavali* (Vols. 7-9); abbreviated in the Preface as *PR*.
2. The peasants in *Premashram* begin their discussion in the opening pages with these very ills that are currently bothering them; ever since the new master (Gyanshankar) has taken over as the new zamindar. Sukhu Chaudhary mentions how they keep witnessing "ijafa, bedakhli, akhraj" all around; the last word 'akhraj' referring to the increased expenditure, whether on agriculture or otherwise, which they have to bear. (See *Premashram*, p.10).

> healthcare and education. After this, it seems quite possible that the tax on land might become very less and that other taxes might be removed. Our leaders have always requested the government to lessen the burden of land-tax. When the entire management would be transferred in their hands, they will certainly follow their own principle and our peasants will be relieved of the heavy burden of lagaan. (PR 7, 222)

It is important to remember that the time period when these essays were written was one which was strongly influenced by the Gandhian ideology. Premchand's personal allegiance to Gandhi's insistence on an economic kind of independence from the trap of British-manufactured goods is evident not only in these essays, but in the very text of *Premashram*. Rai Kamlanand is a rich landowner in the novel, who is seen pursued by a company agent to buy some of its shares. The grounds on which Rai Saheb refuses to do so entails a long discussion on the tussle between an agricultural and an industrial, urban way of life, centering on the Indian peasant. Rai Saheb openly derides the rise of industrial capitalism and insists that a peasant, who is able to earn a decent livelihood on the basis of his land, would never prefer a slavery-ridden employment in the factories. He should be supported by the cottage industries in the village in case he does not have sufficient land, and that alone can serve the true interests of the nation (*Premashram* 87).

That a conventional landowner like Rai Saheb should advocate the winds of change is a reflection of the changing flow of thought in the intelligentsia of the India of the 1920s, which Premchand captures decidedly in the novel. He shows this symbol of the old zamindari as acutely perceptive of the fact that its days are numbered, and once the peasants are educated enough, 'zamindars would lose all chances' to rob and exploit them (*Premashram* 87). Rai Saheb ends up being poisoned by Gyanshankar, the more ruthless and selfish zamindar who has now replaced aging feudals like him and his uncle. Though he survives the assault, his life undergoes a complete change wherein he becomes an ascetic and distances himself from all the erstwhile luxuries that he had flaunted and advocated. Gyanshankar, who temporarily feels elated on his property manipulations, is himself led to commit suicide in the end – only because Lakhanpur's radical and self-renouncing talukedar – Mayashankar (Gyanshankar's own son) has not left any space for rotten ideals centred in his father to breathe.

These deaths are not merely accidental or idealistic (as numerous critics have debated) but are significantly related to the historical assaults that Premchand was witnessing on the old rubric of feudalism all over the world. True, that in the Indian context, the emergence of the benevolent zamindar (which Mayashankar seems to embody) did seem a complicated premise, but it cannot be refuted that this was indeed the wishful goal of many a Kisan Sabhas which were not really aiming at any eradication of the zamindari in their protests (Talwar 161)[3].

It is therefore important to first have a brief look at the state of agrarian relations beginning from late eighteenth century up to the early decades of the twentieth century in order to understand the changed nature of the peasant consciousness. One discovers two strategies that the British government had evolved after 1857, in form of the clash between the old feudal structure of the zamindari (landholdings) and its new metamorphosis in the shape of landlords (like Gyanshankar) and their new scheme of systematic exploitation.[4]

The history of land relations and the changes introduced after1793

Ever since the East India Company obtained the diwani rights for Bengal, Bihar and Orissa in 1765, the collection of land revenue became their major concern. Agriculture being the major source of livelihood for the vast majority, it also became the main source of state income. For a foreign company to understand and operate the channels of the native agrarian system, a need was soon felt to constitute a local body of landlords who would assist both in land assessment as well as in the collection of land tax.[5] By the time Lord Cornwallis arrived as the Governor General of India around 1786, the company had already infused the prevailing set of zamindars with a new set of revenue farmers, who paid revenue directly to the state or through bigger zamindars. The old order of assessment was ignored and arbitrary rates of tax were fixed, resulting in a complete chaos in terms of tax appropriation and collection.[6]

---

3. Vir Bharat Talwar clearly states that the peasants who were involved in the Uttar Pradesh peasant movement during the period 1918-22, were not demanding an abolition of the zamindari or the talukedari. The peasants wanted a restoration of the pre-British land order which did not include confiscation or disownership of land and had no provisions for 'nazranas' or gifts which were just a glorified form of bribery. Their basic opposition was not towards the old benevolent feudal order where the landlord operated as atrustee of their land as well as interests. (See Talwar's *Kisan, Rashtriya Aandolan aur Premchand*: 1918-22; pp. 161-162)
4. Thomas R. Metcalf has talked about the change in land revenue policies of the British after 1857 in his *Forging the Raj: Essays on British India in the Heydey of Empire* (New Delhi: OUP, 2005). See the essay "The Influence of the Mutiny of 1857 on Land Policy in India" pp. 25-40.
5. See Bernard S. Cohn's *An Anthropologist among Historians and Other Essays* (Delhi: OUP, 1987).
6. Sekhar Bandyopadhyay's *From Plassey to Partition: A History of Modern India* (New Delhi: Orient Blackswan, 2008) contains a useful survey of the changes in land revenue administration introduced by the British. See pp. 82-95.

The Permanent Settlement of Land (1793) sought to resolve most of these issues by fixing every piece of land in Bengal, Bihar and Orissa. All land was distributed among zamindars who had to collect the tax from the farmers and pay a fixed amount to the state. This ensured their direct ownership/properitership of land. Conversely, any failure to make payments on time led to the confiscation of land by the government and its sale by auction. The important thing to note about the scope and method of the plan is that its conceptualization and adoption was not simply a matter of land revenue policy.

The most important departure that the **Settlement** made with respect to the source of land revenue was the introduction of proprietorship or private ownership of land. The condition of private property was felt to be crucial for ensuring public revenue, and the zamindars were deemed as the new owners of land and its related significance, in relation to the ruling power (Guha 1963, 98). A most obvious and direct result of this kind of settlement was felt by the peasants, who now lost their traditional right on land, and were actually reduced to the status of revenue farmers or tenants. The entire onus of this new system of farming was held on the extraction of revenue or 'lagaan', where neither the new proprietors nor the state government felt any direct responsibility for the problems or welfare of the peasants.

Three major changes could be seen in the following years with respect to peasant interests:

(a) Collapse of the ancient feudal structure that existed between the erstwhile landlord and his raiyat (subjects).

(b) The entry of new social groups in land ownership due to open transfers of land enabled by bidding; notably the mahajan and the baniya.

(c) The rising pressure of debt on the tenant farmer due to increased money lending and the constant pressure of lagaan or land rent.

The new system now caused a pronounced polarization of the rural community. The crucial economic divide was actually not between the landlord and the tenant but between the absentee rent-receiver and the cultivating landholder, whose holding was made up of plots held during various tenures ranging from full proprietary right to tenancy at will. These small landlords turned out to be much harsher and notorious in their tactics of revenue collection, so much so that it is officially estimated that by 1893, the widespread use of unauthorized cesses (nazrana) as a means of evading rent control was highly prevalent and a matter of concern for the Revenue Board. Further more, the increased rates of revenue demand –

between 1858 and 1871 – confounded the entire balance of revenue payments and gave rise to agrarian disturbances in a number of places (Stokes 67)[7]. The situation was further complicated by the governmental insistence to grow cash crops such as jute and indigo, leading to further exploitation of the local peasants and deterioration of an economy focused on the growth of food crops. These internal troubles manifested in the form of the Indigo Rebellion in 1859-60, and the history of peasant discontent can be traced as far back as these years.[8]

Effects of the First World War

The First World War which broke out in 1914 added to the woes of the Indian farmers in an unprecedented way. Increased rates of inflation, famine and epidemics, plus forceful war donations that were extracted from the peasants made life extremely difficult. The national budget of 1917-18 records an amount of one and a half arab rupees to be given to Britain as part of India's contribution to the war. This money had to be derived from the hapless peasantry. Apart from money numerous peasant families had to forcefully deploy their young men as British soldiers in the war. Once they came back, they lost their earlier claim on land as well as confronted the empty promises of extra land being allotted as war compensation. The absolute loss of all means of survival culminated into a series of revolts such as the Akali Andolan in Punjab, the Mopla Revolt in Malabar and the peasant movement in the United Provinces. These movements which rose in the years 1919-23 extended the scope of the concurrent nationalist movement from the urban to the rural areas; thereby helping it to assume the mass character that it finally did in the nineteen thirties and the forties (K. Singh 51).[9] During the war itself, the farmers had risen against the commercial policies of the British in Champaran, against the forceful

---

7. See Eric Stokes' "Agrarian Relations: Northern and Central India" in Dharma Kumar (ed.) *The Cambridge Economic History of India*, Vol. 2. Stokes discusses how the administrative changes introduced by the British government around the late eighteenth century steadily changed the equation between the actual tillers of land and the revenue collectors, even though the upper and middle agricultural castes were to remain rooted to their cultivating systems, even uptil and after independence.
8. Bandyopadhyay discusses how the commercialization of agriculture did not really benefit the majority of the peasants, even if total national income increased, as the rising rural capitalist class concentrated the major part of the economic benefits in their hands. See *From Plassey to Partition*, pp. 122-134.
9. Kunwarpal Singh, in "Bhoomi-Sambandh, Kisan-Aandolan aur Premchand" in Shashibhushan Shitanshu Pandey (Ed.) *Premchand: Hamaare Samkaleen* (Amritsar: Guru Nanak Dev University, 1986) tries to locate Premchand's focus on peasant issues in the precise domain of the changes brought about in the early twentieth century Indian context. See pp. 47-63. The author's name hereby abbreviated as K. Singh.

cultivation of indigo (1917). In 1918, the Bijolia formers of Rajasthan had revolted against the Jagirdari system. From 1920 to 1922, the peasant movement in Awadh swept over twelve districts like Raibareli, Sultanpur, Faizabad etc.[10] Though the movement was completely quelled by 1922, it changed forever, the futuristic character of the nationalist movement.The nationalist leadership, from this point onwards, became divided along the lines of bourgeois socialism, and a different kind of Bolshevik ideology championed by the peasants and workers.

Premchand shows, right in the initial pages of *Premashram*, the hapless peasant who has an understanding of what ails the new system under the 'new' zamindar, his musclemen (the 'karinda' sahib) and British lord. Glancing through their typical rustic vision, one finds a sharp criticism of the new education which has only taught its exponents to be cruel to the 'raiyat' (the tenant; peasant) as opposed to an earlier, more sympathetic feudal system:

> Sukhu - Yes, you are right that education teaches you how to snatch wealth from others. Till the time our elder master was there, even if we had two years of rent unpaid, he would simply scold us and leave the matter. Ever since the young master has taken over, haven't you noticed the kind of tyranny he has let loose! Day and night, we hear of disownment, capturing and coercion of all sorts! (*Premashram* 10)[11]

These overtaxed peasants are the protagonists of *Premashram*. The peasant community depicted in Lakhanpur is situated within the landholding of Gyanshankar, about twelve miles north of Banaras, in eastern Uttar Pradesh. Besides Balraj and Manohar, there are Rajputs like Dapatsingh and Jhapat Singh, the Muslim peasant Qadir, the baniya Bisesar Sah, Dukhran Bhagat and Rangi chamar. They are not a united group in themselves, but together confront a unified nexus between the landlord and the colonial government.

It is precisely in their resistance that one can locate echoes of the historical and the contemporary events that were surrounding the location

---

10. See Gyan Pandey's "Peasant Revolt and Indian Nationalism: The Peasant Movement in Awadh, 1919-22" in Ranajit Guha (Ed.) *Subaltern Studies: Writings on South Asian History and Society,* Vol. I (Delhi: Oxford, 1982) pp. 143-191. The essay discusses how, despite being seen as the harbinger of change and leadership, the Congress did not pursue any serious commitment to peasant interests. In fact, the Congress' insistence in 1921-22 "on a united front of landlords as well as peasants and others, was a statement in favour of the *status quo* and against any radical change in the social set-up when the British finally handed over the reins of power" (Pandey 187).
11. The textual references are from Premchand's *Premashram* (Allahabad: Saraswati Press, 1962). The translations, if not indicated otherwise, are mine.

and composition of *Premashram*. The question is in fact, far more deep than the precedence or follow-up of the novel as a text chasing real, contemporary events. The real issue at hand is the authorial belief in a radical solution led by an enlightened consciousness; both of which were, so to say, historically absent at the moment. Where does one find and interpret a farmer like Balraj, who is absolutely ready to defy almost every coercive tactic that Gyanshankar and his karindas seem to come up with? Perhaps in that slowly evolving radical consciousness, which had taken many parts of the globe in its sweep in the 1920s, and which writers like Premchand were hoping to have some influence on the lives of the suffering masses in India.

The Progressive landowning farmer

It is indeed interesting that Premchand places his vision of the progressive landowning farmer within the loosely united group of peasants in Lakhanpur whom he endows with an increasing sense of awareness about not just their own deterioration, but also about what is happening elsewhere in the world. Balraj (Manohar's son) reads a Marxist newspaper, talks of the working class in the cities and represents a new kind of fighting spirit that had evolved in the post-First World War rural India among the farmers of eastern Uttar Pradesh. As he tells his compatriots:

> Balraj- You people mock what I say, as if the peasant is nothing,... but in the paper that I get, it is written that in Russia, there is the rule of peasantry; they do as they like. Near Russia there is a country called Bulgaria. There the peasants have made the king abdicate the throne, and now the farmers and labourers have formed a 'panchayat' which governs the nation. (Premashram 51-52)

Hearing his inspiring words Qadir immediately says: "Let's go in that country, we would not be required to pay land rent there" (*Premashram* 52). Manohar retorts that if those peasants can rule themselves, aren't the Indian ones capable of even reporting their grievances to the lord? A revolution that takes place thousands of miles away from Benaras instills in these peasants a powerful hope of changing the conditions of their life. They feel inspired that their tribe can even dethrone the reigning king to establish their own rule based on their own norms of justice. This new-found confidence becomes a strong motive for struggle against the hegemonic environment bred by colonial factors, and results in a situation which shows the deprived farmers of Lakhanpur moving towards a redefinition of the circumstances controlling their life. It is precisely here that Premchand situates his progressive landowning farmer, who is about to arrive as a formidable challenge to the forces that have made life unbearable for him.

The plot of the novel thus shows two parallel strands of development - the life of Gyanshankar, the landlord, and the stages of struggle which the farmers of Lakhanpur undergo in their bid to save their lives and marjaad or self-respect. Gyanshankar is the new feudal master pitted against Premshankar, a Western educated Gandhian, who openly defies the entire institution of landlordism as fake and unjust:

Premshankar - ... I just don't want to hear that I am the landlord of that village. I want to eat the bread earned by my own hard work. I do not want to become a broker in between. If my name has been registered [as a landlord] in the official papers then I am ready to resign. The burden of the upkeep of your sister-in-law shall be upon you. I shall keep on helping you in whatever way I can ...

Gyanshankar - ... In my narrow vision this very zamindari (smiling) which you consider nothing but a sort of brokerage is the best possible version of life. Though, it is possible that I may cultivate a holier thought process in the future, under your holy influence and companionship.

Prem - You think about it in your mind. Is it just that someone else does all the hard work, the burden of his protection falls on yet another, and we extract all the money?

Gyan - There is truth in what you say but the system has been prevalent since long as per convention. No one thinks of modifying it in any way.

Prem - So when do you plan to leave for Gorakhpur? (Premashram 140-141)

Premchand thus depicts, very clearly, the binding limits of a Gandhian, non-violent approach to the complex problems of rent-extraction and land-confiscation – the two major weapons which the British government had placed in the hands of the Indian zamindar. In taking up the issue of lagaan, *Premashram* almost predicts in a new historicist fashion, the upcoming aggravated economic confrontation that took the northern half of India by storm during 1930-1932. At the time when a later novel, *Karmabhoomi* was being written (1931-32), the peasant movement in Awadh assumed an almost violent character. Thousands of peasants were robbed of their land due to non-payment of rent. In Allahabad alone, more than twelve thousand peasants turned landless and the number of cases dealing with land confiscation in the whole of Awadh had reached up to one lac sixty thousand in 1931. In countries all over the globe, this was a period of economic depression (except Soviet Russia) and it was virtually impossible for the peasant to pay the increased land-rent (Ravibhushan 67).[12]

Beginning with *Premashram*, Premchand consistently tries to depict, through the novels and short stories that followed, how the middle-class peasant gradually gets subsumed in a vicious economic circle of debt and confiscation, and is finally reduced to being a landless farm-labourer. In *Premashram*, Manohar has around twenty acres of land, Qadir Khan has twenty bighas, Dukhran Bhagat has around fifteen and Kallu six. In *Karmabhoomi* (1931-32), Saloni has just three-four bighas. *Godan* (written 1932-36) shows Hori, Shobha and Hira sharing a single plough on their divided fields and by the end of the novel the three brothers do not remain peasants anymore. In Premchand's works, the number of landless farm-workers can be seen on a constant increase.

The climactic murder of Ghaus Khan, a karinda employed by Gyanshankar to extract lagaan pushes the developing discontent of the villagers to its extreme, and further involves each one of them to join the bandwagon of resistance led by Manohar's family.The insult heaped on Bilasi (Manohar's wife) by Faizu and Ghaus Khan incites Manohar to murder the latter in the dead of the night. When Balraj gets confused just before the act can be performed, Manohar quickly resolves his moral dilemma by justifying the murder as an attempt to save his 'marjaad'. Significantly, Balraj does not agree with his father that murdering Ghaus Khan would be the best solution; he would rather have a perceptive fight with him the next morning; something open and daring for everyone to see.

The progression in the novel that takes place from a hidden murder to an open defiance of the orders of the zamindar is the development of that radical consciousness which will enable these peasants to build their final 'Premashram'. Manohar's personal sense of marjaad (self respect) becomes the mission of the entire village; not a single peasant pays lagaan after the murder of Ghaus Khan. Despite repeated threats of confiscation, nobody pays any attention to the summons of Gyanshankar, not even to the dying

12. Ravibhushan in "Premchand Ke Kisan" in Shashibhushan Shitanshu Pandey (Ed.) *Premchand: Hamaare Samkaleen* talks about the deep and significant relation between Premchand's authorial concern for the Indian peasant and his particular life experiences which fostered this concern. See pp. 64-90.

crop in the fields (*Premashram* 239). Sukhu Chaudhary pays the two-year rent on behalf of the villagers, which ultimately saves their situation. The murder, its investigation, the impending court case as well as the harsh judgements not only show the peasants in a different light, they also reveal how the landowning class perceives its position vis-a-vis the farmers who have suddenly learnt the language of opposition.

But the real anti-climactic situation occurs when Dr. Priyanath, an erstwhile greedy physician decides to take on a mercy petition on the behalf of the peasants of Lakhanpur. In the actual hearing that occurs from pages 357 to 361 of the novel, the entire onus of Ghaus Khan's murder is transferred from the shoulders of Manohar to the corrupt nexus between the landlord, the officials and the police. Dr.Priyanath cleverly attributes Ghaus Khan's death to a silent heart attack, and does not let the government advocate make unnecessary use of the proximity between him and Premshankar.

The final judgment itself is an open document of criticism levelled on the police department and its paradoxically criminal ways of functioning:

> This accusation is a brilliant example of the functioning of the police. In order to deliberate the true or false aspects of any issue, it is important to think about the witnesses in an unbiased manner and to affirm any kind of notions on their basis, but the officers of the police operate precisely in the reverse direction; they first ascertain a notion, and then to prove it right begin their search of witnesses and evidences. It is evident that in such a situation, they proceed from the deed to its cause, and instead of doing any modification in their mental notion of it, rather distort the entire range of evidences to suit their imagination. Why is this reverse move enacted? It is difficult to surmise about it but not in the present case. The kind of burden that a group can undertake collectively is practically impossible for a single individual to bear. (*Premashram* 368-369)

This sudden twist in what could have been a straight case of murder and punishment makes the psychological weight of this conflict supersede the legal one. The phenomenon of violence in the novel raises the question as to whether "satyagraha (the insistence upon truth) can destroy injustice," or if it's simply a misthought (*Premashram* 239). What is the authorial motive behind representing happenings in this way? Is Premchand with or against the Gandhian way of resisting coercion? There have been endless debates on the question of Premchand's allegiance to Gandhism and its associated ramifications. Critics either see him as an extreme champion or as a thorough opponent of Gandhism. The answer perhaps lies in the evolutionary nature of Gandhism that Premchand both justified and opposed on different grounds. As Manager Pandey testifies:

> ... He endorsed Gandhi's political aim - independence of the nation, but was disillusioned with the mode of satyagraha ... He was convinced with Gandhi's criticism of the capitalist civilization to a great extent, but did not agree to an imposing of India's past on its future. He had initially experimented with the Gandhian principles of heart-transformation and trusteeship and had later abandoned them. (253)

The benevolent socialism propagated in *Premashram* thus lands the reader into similar confusions, except that the role of its leaders seems especially designed by an author deeply involved with the tragedy of people in Lakhanpur. The contrast between what eventually happens in the novel and its relevance to the north Indian agricultural scene of the 1920s has raised many critical questions about the viability of the ideal proposed in the end.

The ending and the possibilities

Critics like Nand Dulare Vajpayee feel that a kind of over-emphasis on the ideal "Premashram" (the harmonious abode of community living) puts Premchand in the category of writers who only "sermonize."[13] As he says:

> In *Premashram* the ideal village has been created in the latter half of the novel. This can be seen as objectivism in Premchand. The rife-torn depiction of the rural circumstances has been done in the former part of the novel. An idealist character has been created in the form of Premshankar; yet in order to clarify the ultimate goal, the ideal village has been built as the final objective...an extreme prominence of this objective puts Premchand in the category of sermonizing writers. (192)

Yet one can clearly see the difference between the Russian version of socialism resulting from a prolonged class-struggle and the way it has been visualized in the Indian colonial situation depicted in *Premashram*. Premchand seems to be suggesting here that the dominant political angle has to be a democratic one, wherein the community must reform its mode of operations on Bolshevik lines to make universal, happy living possible based on classlessness. Gopal Krishan Kaul seems to be wrestling with similar ideas when he says:

> Premchand was a progressive humanist writer. He cannot be called a progressive, since he did not agree with the principles of progressivism's

---

13. See Nanddulare Vajpaayi's "Hindi Upanyas Parampara" in Murli Manohar Prasad Singh and Rekha Avasthi (Eds.) *Premchand: Vigat Mahatta aur Vartamaan Arthvatta*, pp. 187-197.

basic foundation, which is communism. Yet he was very much a progressive writer, since he had propagated the humanist tradition through his writings, had opposed all forms of exploitation, and looked forward to the development of life's reality in all his works. (193-4)[14]

The problem with the "reality" of the ideal village celebrated at the end of *Premashram* arises due to its achievement without the obvious reversal of the feudal structures that have been opposed so vehemently in the earlier pages. Two important dimensions are brought to light as one discusses the ideal inherent in Mayashankar's ascension as the "reformed" zamindar or the "swami" whose sole interest in land lies for the sake of his subject's welfare. The first of these issues pertains to the very possibility of achieving a desired change through collective (and here, bloodless) struggle. Why does Premchand appear so keen to reinvent Lakhanpur along socialist lines, even if it means putting the entire onus of change on a potentially weak character (Premshankar) and his equally weak prodigy?

The ending, when analyzed from a postcolonial perspective, suggests how the author's keen involvement in the social scene depicted in Lakhanpur made him shift the entire onus of change from the shoulders of the contemporary bourgeois leadership to those of the people themselves. The ideal village witnessed in the final pages of the novel has grown in the authorial as well as textual consciousness before becoming the utopian 'ashram', as it were. The inter-connections between *Premashram* and Premchand's socialist thought are quite elaborately interspersed in the story of Lakhanpur. It could be imagined that a transitional phase shall soon witness its turning point with a novel like Rangabhoomi that shall depict a fight to the finish - a fight initiated by the common man against bourgeois forces. It is here that Premchand's ideology as a writer shall turn away from mere reformism to the need for fundamental social change, or "Aamool samajik badlaav", as Shiv Kumar Mishra puts it.[15]

The marriage between the 'real' and the 'ideal' was later explained as *Adarshonmukhi Yatharthvaad* or 'realism looking upto idealism' by the writer himself. Premchand had consciously tried to distance his writing from any hasty impositions of Western realism or idealism on his works.

---

14. Gopalkrishan Kaul in "Gandhivaad: Pragativaad aur Premchand" in Shachirani Gurtu (Ed.) *Premchand Aur Gorky* (Bombay: Rajkamal, 1955) tries to analyze how Premchand's ideology as a writer cannot be tied down to any one particular aspect of a predominant theory. It can only be understood as an evolving facet of his critical thought, developing new ideas with every critical development of the age.
15. See Shivkumar Mishra's "Premchand: Sudhaarvaad se Aamool Samajik Badlaav Tak" in his *Premchand: Virasat ka Sawaal*, (1994) pp. 17-24.

While he was deeply influenced by Russian humanist writers like Gorky and Tolstoy, he sought to propound his own understanding of the ills plaguing the Indian society and its plausible solutions.[16] Shiv Kumar Mishra attributes it to Premchand's personal ideological evolution as a creative writer. He also discusses how, for a very long period in his career, Premchand continued to impose an idealist resolution on the most 'real', or socially relatable plots in his works; especially *Premashram, Sevasadan, Karmabhoomi, Rangabhoomi,* and many other stories (S. Mishra 2002, 30).

Conclusion

These problems attest the challenges that progressive radicalism faces in the colonial context, making the very notion of social change a problematic one. In fact, as later economic studies of the period have testified, despite the 50 percent increase in population between 1851 and 1951 (from 45 to 63 million) the grip of the dominant minority (the zamindars) among the cultivating classes had not weakened. According to the figures of the Zamindari Abolition Committee, two-thirds of the cultivating body were confined to some one-fifth of the land, while just over one million cultivators, or a mere nine per cent of the total occupied as much as 43 per cent and cultivated an average of 16 acres each.[17] This was the peasant elite which found its way into the throes of political power even after the dissolution of the British raj, working itself free of the crushing burden of taxation that it had once been given to bear. Further, as Eric Stokes notes:

> As the main beneficiary of zamindari abolition the peasant elite became the principal upholder of the Congress raj in the countryside and the most formidable obstacle to radical agrarian and fiscal change. (86)

The abolition of the institution of zamindari, as one can see, could not, and did not prove as a one-time solution to peasant woes. One must note the usage of the phrase "Congress raj" instead of the earlier 'British raj'. It does not seem that the real *swaraj* or self-rule ever became a reality for the Indian peasant.

---

16. Premchand, in his *Kuch Vichaar* (New Delhi: Bhartiya Granth Niketan, 1990) has put forward his ideas on various critical issues pertaining to his work and literature in general. See pp. 49-63. The name of the compilation, hereafter abbreviated as *KV*.
17. As a prelude to the extensive programmes of land reform to be carried out after independence, a Zamindari (Landlord) Abolition Committee was appointed even before independence, in 1946, and its report formed the basis of legislation, enacted in 1951, which took back the large estates from the landlords to return it to the actual tillers. See "Landlords without Land" in Thomas R. Metcalf's *Forging the Raj: Essays on British India in the Heydey of Empire* (2005) pp. 71-87.

What Premchand seems to be suggesting is that real *swaraj* has to include a reformed zamindar as well as a reformed peasant. The 'ashram' in *Premashram* appears idealistic as it indicates reformation at all levels. The zamindar (Mayashankar) has given up the land, but is still concerned about the well-being of the present landholders, who still address him as 'swami' or master. The new peasant, symbolized by Balraj is not a passive recipient of governmental orders and regulations; he plays an active role in opinion-making and opinion-mobilizing, so that those in power get to know the interests of the peasants from the grass root level and can act accordingly. Honesty and compassion - these are the pillars that are needed for any human institution to survive; difficult, but indeed desirable.

In an overall analysis, one can see how *Premashram* depicts a comprehensive aspect of this implicit radical suggestion: that a village can possibly change its future with the power of resistance is a decided faith in the power of humane enterprise. Lakhanpur's decision to oppose tyranny in the first place is the basic cause behind its final prosperity, however utopian it might seem. This process in the novel, when read together with the historical documentation of what was actually happening on the political and agricultural scene depicts how changes in the social and psychological rubric of the nineteen twenties have disturbed the rigidities of the exploitative structure imposed by the foreign rule in India. They almost stand testimony to the writers' involvement in the complexities of the society's tryst with a changing situation. They further encapsulate within their literary canvas ample suggestions about locating and following a progressive route despite the prevalent pressures. Resistance, one might conclude, is just the first step.

WORKS CITED

Primary Source

Premchand. *Premashram*. Allahabad: Saraswati Press, 1962. Print.

Secondary Sources

Bandyopadhyay, Sekhar. *From Plassey to Partition: A History of Modern India*. New Delhi: Orient Blackswan, 2008. Print.

Cohn, Bernard S. *An Anthropologist among Historians and Other Essays*. Oxford: OUP, 1987. Print.

Gandhi, M. K. *Hind Swaraj: And Other Writings*. Ed. Anthony J. Parel. New Delhi: Cambridge University Press India Pvt. Ltd., 1997. Print.

Guha, Ranajit. *Elementary Aspects of Peasant Insurgency In Colonial India*. New Delhi: OUP, 1983. Print.

———. *A Rule of Property for Bengal*. Paris: Mouton & Co., 1963. Print.

Kaul, Gopalkrishan. "Gandhivaad: Pragativaad Aur Premchand." *Premchand Aur Gorky*. Ed. Shachirani Gurtu. Bombay: Rajkamal, 1955. 186-194. Print.

Kumar, Dharma, ed. *The Cambridge Economic History of India*. Vol. 2. New Delhi: Orient Blackswan Private Limited, 2010. Print.

Metcalf, Thomas. R. *Forging the Raj: Essays on British India in the Heyday of Empire*. New Delhi: Oxford University Press, 2005. Print.

Mishra, Shivkumar. *Kahanikar Premchand: Rachna Drishti aur Rachna-shilp*. Allahabad: Lokbharti Prakashan, 2002. Print.

———. *Premchand: Virasat Ka Sawal*. New Delhi: Vani Prakashan, 1994. Print.

Pandey, Manager. "Rashtravaad Aur Upanyas." Premchand: *Vigat Mahatta aur Vartmaan Arthvatta*. Eds. Murli Manohar Prasad Singh and Rekha Avasthi. New Delhi: Rajkamal, 2006. 247-258. Print.

Premchand. *Kuchh Vichaar*. New Delhi: Bhartiya Granth Niketan, 1990. Print.

———. *Premchand Rachnavali*. Ed. Ram Anand. 7-9 Vols. Delhi: Janvaani Prakashan Pvt. Ltd., 1996. Print.

Ravibhushan. "Premchand Ke Kisan." *Premchand: Hamare Samkaleen.* Ed. Dr. Pandey Shashibhushan Shitanshu. Amritsar: Guru Nanak Dev University Press, 1986. 64-90. Print.

Sherlock, Stephen. "Berlin, Moscow & Bombay: The Marxism that India inherited." *South Asia 21.1* (June 1988): 63-76. Print.

Singh, Kunwarpal. "Bhoomi Sambandh, Kisan-Andolan Aur Premchand." *Premchand: Hamare Samkaleen.* 47-73. Print.

Talwar, V. B. *Kisan, Rashtriya Aandolan Aur Premchand: 1918-22.* New Delhi: Vani Prakashan, 2008. Print.

Vajpayee, Nand Dulare. "Hindi Upanyas Parampara." *Premchand: Vigat Mahatta aur Vartamaan Arthvatta.* Eds. Murli Manohar Prasad Singh and Rekha Avasthi. New Delhi: Rajkamal, 2006. 187-197. Print.

PREMASHRAM

1

The evening has fallen. The oxen, tired after a day's labour have returned from the fields. Black ringlet clouds of smoke are rising from homes. In Lakhanpur, there was an inspection of the district haakim today. The leaders of the village had been running after his horse all day long. At present they are sitting near the fire, smoking hookahs and giving their opinion on the character of the district collectors. Lakhanpur is a big village in the north, about twelve miles away from Benaras. It is mostly populated by the kurmis and thakurs; about a handful of houses belong to other castes also.

Manohar said – Brothers, there is no master like the British; had they not been there, our own haakims would have chewed us to death.

Dukhran agreed to his opinion – The sense of honour that they have has been blessed by a similar character. They alone know how to do justice; they can separate milk from water, and have no concern with bribes or gifts. Look at chhote sahib today; he got on the horseback at the crack of dawn and inspected for the entire day. The tehsildar, peshkar or the kanungo; there was none who could match steps with him.

Sukhu kurmi said – How can these people compete with the British? All they know is to abuse the subjects and shout on them. They don't even get out of their homes. Whatever the chaprasi or patwari tell them they accept it. They have turned lazy lying on bed the whole day long.

Manohar – They say the Britishers don't take ghee.

Sukhu – Who says they don't? How can one survive without ghee or milk? They actually toil too hard, so they are able to digest all that. Our native officers eat a lot, but they keep lying down for long hours. That's why they end up with bloated bellies.

Dukhran Bhagat – The Tehsildar Sahib almost resembles a fat mill. When he first came, he used to be so thin, but has ended up accumulating so much fat in just two years.

Sukhu – It is the money from bribes which fattens you up.

Manohar – This is all hearsay. The Tehsildar doesn't take a penny.

Sukhu – You cannot grow fat without eating up illegal money.

Manohar (with a laugh) – Why doesn't the patwari swell up; he looks like a sucked up mango.

Sukhu – The patwari doesn't eat up a bag of hundreds or thousands himself. After all sorts of haggling he might get a couple of rupees. His salary is snatched by the kanungo. When he's surviving on such leftovers how can he grow fat? Didn't you see during the extortion; Tehsildar Sahib gobbled up thousands of rupees.

Dukhran – They say that education reforms a man's understanding but what one gets to see is entirely the opposite. The collector and his men are educated enough, but do not seem to bother about kindness or human values in the least.

Sukhu – When the country is going through a bad fortune, everything turns upside down. When it is time for a sick person to die, the medicine too starts harming him.

Manohar – It is we alone who have spoiled their habits by bribing them. If we don't give them anything, how can they pile up! It's we who are degraded and fallen. How can a person refuse money that falls his way? We keep harming each other in the process. You are ready to rob me; I am ready to destroy you. What else can be the result?

Dukhran – Well, if we happen to be foolish, backward and uneducated, they are educated enough. Shouldn't they think that the poor folk are their own brethren! If the lord has blessed them with knowledge, then they should take care of us. We foolish men are perhaps better than these knowledgeable ones. To tolerate injustice is of course better than to do injustice.

Sukhu – It is not the fault of education; it is the nation's misfortune.

Manohar – It is neither a fault of education nor the bad luck of the nation; it's just an outcome of our own petty divisions. If education does not cause anything else, it does indeed enable one to extract the wealth belonging to others. If one remains foolish, one has to lose one's own money.

Sukhu – Yes, you are right indeed that education enables you to extract wealth from others. Till the time our senior master was there, he would condone even two years of unpaid tax by a mere scolding! Ever since the young master has arrived; can't you see what kind of disruption is taking place? Day and night, one hears of nothing except tax-increase, dismissal of ownership and all kinds of hard measures!

Dukhran – The karinda sahib was saying yesterday that it's now the turn of our village; let's see what happens?

Manohar – What else can happen, you shall ride high on the extortion in my fields, I will do the same to yours; the young master shall mint money in the process. The government would have known the truth only if none of us would have bid for each others' fields. We should have arrived at an understanding amongst ourselves. But this will never happen. Sukhu Mahto will be the fastest runner in the race for bidding.

Sukhu – Who can tell that Manohar will not?

Manohar – You can make me swear on the waters of the Ganga; I will not go towards the fields, and how can I when there's no money left with me. There are months to go for the rabi harvest, and there isn't a grain to eat in the house. I have jaggery worth only a little above hundred, but my bull has given up. I will have to spend about a hundred and fifty to get a new one.

Dukhran – God knows what times have come about that agriculture has not remained prosperous anymore. I cultivated around five bighas with rabi, but I do not hope to get beyond ten man and you know very well about the condition of jaggery. Bisesar Shah got it weighed in the oil-mill itself. Not a bit of sweet syrup was left for the kids. Let me see how God makes me bear these days.

These talks were still going on when Girdhar Maharaj was seen coming. He was tall in appearance; stout, with a puffed-up chest, and was wearing a turban and a tight vest. He was carrying a heavy stick on his shoulders. On seeing him, all the peasants got down from their seats and took places on the ground. This man was the peon of the zamindar. He appeared to be a friend of all by way of words, but was an enemy of all in heart of hearts. He agreed with the zamindar on his face, and he also agreed with the tenants while talking to them. Perhaps this was the reason why no one said anything controversial to him directly, even if they criticized him behind his back.

Sukhu asked – Well Maharaj; where are you coming from?

Girdhar replied in a manner as if he was dissatisfied with life – 'Where do I begin? Gyan Babu has made me so fed up! He has now ordered to pay the tenants for ghee at the rate of a rupee per seer. I have been running the whole day long.'

Manohar – At what price did you get the ghee?

Girdhar – I have been told just to distribute money as of now. They are about to celebrate the death anniversary of our senior master. That's why the preparations. I have distributed around fifty rupees.

Manohar – But the market rate is usually calculated at ten chataanks.

Girdhar – Bhai, we can do only what we're told to. They can sell a chataank in the market; we have been ordered to purchase a seer. We have to give fifty rupees in this village also. Say, Sukhu Mahto; how much will you take?

Sukhu replied with his head bowed down – You can give as much as you please; we stay on your land; where can we run away?

Girdhar – You are a big landholder; take ten rupees. And Dukhran Bhagat; how much do we give you?

Dukhran – Give me five.

Manohar – I just have one buffalo at home, and her milk gets consumed by the children; there is no scope to make ghee. If anyone can claim in the village that I have sold ghee worth even a single penny, I am ready to take fifty rupees.

Girdhar – You won't take even five? At least take as much as Bhagat has.

Manohar – Bhagat has a buffalo at home; he even sells ghee so he can take as much as he wants. If I take money, I will have to buy at least ten chataanks from the market and give.

Girdhar – You can do what you please, but you will have to obey the master's orders. I have given thirty rupees in Lalganj; there isn't a single buffalo in that village. People shall buy from the market only and give. In the settlement too I have given twenty rupees. You very well know that there isn't any buffalo there also.

Manohar – If they don't have a buffalo, they must be having money. I don't have a single penny in my pocket.

Girdhar – When you plough the zamindar's land you cannot disobey his orders.

Manohar – We don't plough the land as an obligation! We pay tax on the same. If a single instalment is left unpaid, our land gets auctioned.

Girdhar – Manohar, you will run and get the ghee, but only after hearing some abuses. You cannot stay in the zamindar's village and have your own will. When the karinda sahib calls you, you will pay the money and apologize as well; I tell you in simple words and you show me different colours.

Manohar got angry and said – The karinda is not a swine; nor is the zamindar a threat. I won't be suppressed by anyone. When I pay every penny of the land rent, why should I tolerate this undue pressure?

Girdhar – You don't know the master as yet. The days of the elder master are over. If you fall in the hands of the present one, you won't be able to escape.

Manohar got angrier than ever. He said – 'Well, go and blow me up at the gunpoint.' Girdhar Maharaj also got up. Sukhu and Dukhran didn't deem fit to sit with Manohar after this exchange. They too left along with Girdhar. Manohar gave a sharp look to the leaving trio and started smoking his hookah.

2

The house of the Lakhanpur zamindars was near Aurangabad in Kashi. The two portions of the house stood facing each other. One portion was meant for women; the other was meant for the men. The ground in between the two portions was decorated with plant motifs and tall walls stood on each side, but both the parts were broken at many places. At some points, the railing had cracked and was now supported by sticks; at other places, the wall had split and the roof was almost falling down – just like an old, sick patient who walks with the help of a stick. At one point in the past, the family was quite established and respected in the city, but a false pride of its wealth and the upkeep of family conventions had steadily led to a fall of its honour to an extent that the baniya of the locality did not give credit worth a single penny in their name. Lala Jatashankar was catching the last of his leftover breaths, but still never left home except on a palanquin. He married his sons and daughters with a similar sense of honour and grandeur. On the occasion of a festival, his heart wanted to splurge like a flowing river; if a guest came over, he was treated with utmost respect and he felt a hearty sense of happiness in entertaining holy men and guests alike. A large part of his assets was sacrificed in the upkeep of this kind of honour; some of it had been mortgaged, and now, all that was left besides Lakhanpur were four tiny villages that earned a profit of about four thousand rupees per annum.

Lala Jatashankar had a younger brother. He was known as Prabhashankar. He was responsible for all the positive and negative aspects of the family. The senior Lala Sahib was very fond of his Bhagvad Gita. The management of household affairs was in the hands of the younger brother only. There was such an affection between the two brothers that no bitter exchange ever occurred in their midst. The women did quarrel at times, but its effect was never seen upon the brothers. However troubled Prabhashankar might have been, he never complained about it to his brother. Jatashankar too never interfered in any sphere under his purview.

Lala Jatashankar had left for his heavenly abode a year ago. His wife had expired before him. He had left behind two sons, Premshankar and Gyanshankar. Both had got married. Premshankar had gone missing since four-five years. His wife Shraddha wept for him but to no avail. Gyanshankar had been awarded a B.A. degree the previous year and now kept himself busy with the harmonium. He had a son, Mayashankar. Lala Prabhashankar's wife was alive. They had three sons and two daughters. His eldest son, Dayashankar was a sub-inspector in the police. He was married. The remaining two boys studied English at a local school. Both the daughters were still unmarried. Premshankar, after completing his B.A., wanted to go to America for higher studies, but when he saw his uncle protesting against it, he slipped out of the house one day. He even stopped corresponding with the family. In his absence, Gyanshankar started fighting with his father and uncle. He used to criticize their expensive ways, accusing them of squandering away the family wealth – 'Will you people leave nothing for us? Do you want us to run short of decent meals also?' But all he got as an answer was – 'Well, we shall keep following our tradition as we have done all these years. If you can manage in a better way, please do so; we would also like to see.' Gyanshankar used to be a college student at that time, so he kept quiet whenever he was challenged thus. But when he attained a degree, his father had already expired and he started intervening in home affairs, which resulted in harming that sense of unity and brotherhood which had been the hallmark of the family since six decades. The nephew didn't like the uncle's management, nor did the uncle approve of the nephew's. The battle of words thus kept occurring in their midst quite often. Gyanshankar said – 'You have destroyed the entire wealth of the family, and did not think about us at all. You spent your entire life resting on bed and squandering the money of our ancestors. Real honour would have been protected if you had done something on your own, or saved the family assets. What heroism is there in selling the house and enjoying the outcome?' Lala Prabhashankar used to remember his elder brother on hearing these bitter accusations and lament his demise. He could not bear these painful assaults.

For celebrating the death anniversary of Lala Jatashankar, Prabhashankar had made a budget of about two thousand rupees. About one thousand Brahmins were to be fed. He had thought of inviting all the well-known personalities in the city. Apart from these, silver utensils, carpets, bed and clothes etc. were also ordered for the purpose of donation. Gyanshankar deemed all this as a waste of money. He opined that two hundred rupees were sufficient for the cause. When the condition of the house was so worrisome it was totally unfair to spend so much, but

Prabhashankar replied that he could make his father's soul hanker after drops of water when he would be gone, but till the time he was alive, he won't cause any sorrow to his late brother's soul. The latter was celebrated for his magnanimity in the entire city; well-known people used to bow before him. Such a man's death anniversary should be appropriate to his name – this alone shall be a proof of their respect and love.

Gyanshankar harboured in his heart, grand desires of his future progress. He wanted to take his family back to the peak of prosperity and fame. Deep within, he had a craving for a horse-drawn carriage. He wanted to go for grand drives in the carriage so that people were forced to notice him and recognize him as Lala Jatashankar's son. He also wanted to decorate his drawing room with various artifacts. For this, he also wanted to extend the boundaries of the house. He used to sit for hours, concentrating deeply on these thoughts. He wanted to spend his life in utter peace; this alone was his aim. In the present state of affairs this peace could be bought only by curtailing the expenses. He didn't want to get employed in sundry jobs, had no interest in practicing law, and had no access to any higher avenues. His family might have been a respected one, but was now counted nowhere in the eyes of senior officers which alone could have earned him valuable rights. Lala Jatashankar had already grown passive to all this and Prabhashankar felt that the generosity of the District Collectors was all that he needed. Whatever could be gained from such relations had already been acquired. His eldest son, Dayashankar had become a sub-inspector in the police. Gyanshankar used to fight upon this idle thought with his uncle very often – 'You have spoilt your entire life. You blew up the entire family income on your own pleasures. You kept sacrificing yourself on entertaining the visitors and on the upkeep of honour. Had you spent even a tiny bit of this enthusiasm on pleasing the higher officials, I would have been a Deputy Collector today. People came, ate up our money and left. Now they don't even remember that you once feasted them. The family doesn't progress by feeding kachories and gold-laced paans to people; it happens through other ways.' Poor Prabhashankar used to listen to these indictments and reply in a sad tone, 'Son, do not burn our hearts by saying such things. You pine after a horse-drawn carriage, tables and chairs, mirrors and paintings. You want that we should have the best to eat, best to wear, but how will the others gain by our great eating and dressing ways? How will they profit from your money and assets? We didn't spend our lives in enjoying material comforts. That was actually a means to protect the family honour. Whatever we did, we did for the sake of a good name. The family might have had to fast, but if a guest arrived, he was treated with utmost respect. You are simply concerned with filling your own belly, and fulfilling your own desires.

These are symptoms of destruction; not of building the family's wealth. The only difference is that we spoilt it for others; you will spoil it for your own sake.'

The trouble was that Gyanshankar's wife, Vidyavati too, did not support her husband in his views. She rather agreed with Lala Prabhashankar. She had more faith in helping others than in promoting any selfish ends. She used to feel bad when she saw Babu Gyanshankar arguing with his uncle and tried to drive sense into him very often. But he, though educated, did not respect women more than the respect he accorded to his shoes. Therefore their married life, which is a prime channel of bringing solace to the human heart, was not very peaceful.

3

Manohar had said bitter words in a fit of anger, but when he calmed down, he realized that he had made a big mistake. He thought, 'All the village people are my enemies. They must be criticizing me at the moment, sitting in the chaupal. God knows what hell the karinda might break loose. He has destroyed Durjan in a few blows; he can do the same to me in no time. I am helpless due to my tongue. However much I wish to keep it under control, I just fail. I could have tolerated a burden of ten more rupees along with other expenses, and shouldn't have given in to a false pride.'

Yet, these thoughts were upturned in a moment. If a man doesn't deem something bad from the core of his heart, he takes shelter under an honourable sense of patience, even when afraid of its dire repercussions. Manohar kept calming his worried self in a similar way; 'I may be harmed, but I won't tolerate suppression by anyone, and I won't bow my head before anyone. Let the zamindar also know that all men are not jokers out here. If they create trouble for me I will also expose them in the court; let me see what happens.'

Lost in such thoughts, he sat down to eat. A kerosene lamp was burning in the kitchen, but the roof was filled with smoke to an extent that the lamp appeared too dim. His wife, Bilasi served him a curry of green leafy vegetables and thick chapatis of jowar in a brass plate. Manohar started putting bites in his mouth in a manner as if he was eating a medicine. Maybe, he could have eaten grass in a similar spirit. Bilasi asked –'Isn't the saag to your liking? Shall I give you some gur?'

Manohar – No, the curry is good.

Bilasi – Aren't you hungry then?

Manohar – Why not? That's why I am eating.

Bilasi – This is no way to eat; you are just out of spirit. Have you had a tiff with someone?

Manohar – No; who's there to quarrel with?

Just then a young man came and stood in the room. He had a well-built, healthy body and a broad, full chest. His eyes were shining bright with intelligence. He was wearing a gold locket in his neck and a silver amulet in his right arm. He was Manohar's son, Balraj.

Bilasi – Where are you roaming about? Come, have food; shall I serve?

Balraj rubbed his eyes due to smoke and said, 'Why, Dada, why was Girdhar Maharaj getting angry with you? People are saying that he was quite angry.'

Manohar – It's nothing; who told you?

Balraj – Just about everyone. He was demanding ghee from you; you refused, that's why he lost his temper.

Manohar – It wasn't really a quarrel. Girdhar Maharaj said, 'You'll have to give ghee', I said, 'When I have, I shall give it; right now I have none'. What was there to fight about?

Balraj – Why not? Why should anyone ask ghee from us? Do we survive on anyone's charity or do we go and beg in other people's homes? They don't leave a single penny of theirs; why should we bow under them unnecessarily? I wasn't there or else I would have shown him. Does he take us to be weak like Durjan?

Manohar's heart swelled with pride as he listened to all this, but he was also worried lest Balraj should strike a foolish squabble. He said – 'Sit quietly and eat; it's not good to lose your head. If someone gets to hear this, he might inflate the whole thing. Nobody is a friend out here.'

Balraj – Let them hear; I am not hiding behind anyone. Whosoever is swelled with pride can come and see for himself. I can break the heads of one and all. Worst come worst; I shall be arrested and will have to leave. Who's afraid of that? Even Mahatma Gandhi has come after serving a sentence.

Bilasi gave a reprimanding look to Manohar and said, 'What irritating habit you've acquired that you always get embroiled in one mess or the other. When the entire village is giving ghee, are we outside its purview? We shall manage somehow and give. This does not make us lesser than anyone. God himself has placed us on a lower position. Can mere pride take us to a higher level? I have some ghee in the pot; I shall gather some more in a few days; you can get it weighed then.'

Balraj – Why should we give at all? Are we subordinate to anyone?

Bilasi – Not at all; you are the Governor General indeed. There's no extra grain in the house; on top of it, you swell so much.

Balraj – We might be poor, but we don't go and beg from anyone?

Bilasi – You please go and sit; stop behaving like a great warrior. Unless a camel climbs a mountain he feels he is the tallest. It's not easy to antagonize the zamindar and yet survive in the village. (To Manohar) You listen, O great one, go and make amends with the karinda tomorrow.

Manohar – I will not go now.

Bilasi – Why?

Manohar – Why do you ask; it's my own sweet will. Why should I go and bend myself before him?

Bilasi – Well, will you let me go then?

Manohar – No, I won't. What can the karinda do to us after all? At best, he can take away his ploughable land; let only one plough run, instead of two.

Although Manohar was talking at the top of his voice, but actually, his refusal was akin to a defeated argument. If the wrongdoing could have been amended without appearing little in other people's eyes, he had no objection to it. But he thought himself belittled if he had to apologize himself. To bow again, once you have stood straight was quite shameful in his eyes. Balraj's rough behaviour had succeeded in calming him even more than a fear of any particular loss.

The next morning Bilasi got ready to go to the chaupal, but neither Manohar nor Balraj were ready to go with her. She couldn't find enough courage to go alone. Just then Qadir Mian entered the house. He was an old man; short in height, long bearded, wearing a loincloth over his knees and a vest made of rough cloth. He was related to Manohar as an elder brother according to village relations. Bilasi drew a veil over her face as soon as she saw him.

Qadir said in a worried tone – Manohar, what came upon you yesterday? Please go and make amends with the karinda sahib, or else there won't be time to do anything else. I've heard he's about to complain against you to the masters. Sukhu is also ready to accompany him. God knows what has transpired between the two.

Bilasi – Bhaiji, he has grown old, but is still so immature in his ways. I keep driving sense into him, but he does what he pleases. Our only son has also started following him, and appears to be going out of hands. He keeps fighting with one and all. Just ask him; when the whole village had taken money for the ghee, what made him say no?

Qadir – He is simply at fault, what else? I too had to take ten rupees; what else could I have done? And this is not anything new. When our elder master was there, then also some or the other form of forced labour kept bothering us.

Manohar – Brother, do not talk about those days. We used to keep the taxes pending even for a year or two. But the master never auctioned or dismissed us from the land. We were invited properly on all occasions. At the weddings of our daughters, there was wood, fodder and twenty-five rupees fixed from his side. Don't you know all this? When he used to care for his men like his own children then they too did all kinds of labour for him happily. Now all this is a thing of the past, and we are caught in one or the other matter all the time. So when they are treating us roughly, we too aren't balls of clay?

Qadir – Let bygones be bygones; take care of what lies before you. Come, hurry up, that's why I have come to you. My oxen are standing in the fields.

Manohar – Dada, I won't go.

Bilasi – Maybe his bangles will get soiled; come, I shall go with you.

Qadir and Bilasi started off for the chaupal. There was a huge crowd of men there at this moment. Some had come to deposit the land rent, some to take money for the ghee, and some others only to have fun and flatter the important people. The karinda was known as Ghulam Ghaus Khan. He was a huge man, wheatish in complexion, long bearded, and having a rough demeanour. He had served in the army in his youth, and had reached the position of the havaldaar. When there was some unrest in the frontier provinces he had escaped home taking sick leave and had sent his resignation from there. He still used to narrate the anecdotes of his soldier life with great interest. At present he was smoking a hookah, sitting on a wooden plank. Sukhu and Dukhran were sitting on the ground.

Sukhu said – We are the labour class; if we act haughtily, it's our fault. We stay on the land of the zamindar; we eat what's given by him, how can we annoy him? What do you say, Dukhran?

Dukhran – Yes, that's right.

Sukhu – If God gives us a little money or ten quintals of foodgrain, then should we fight with our masters, and start floating in the air due to pride?

Dukhran – Man gets destroyed due to such intoxicated ways. This alone wiped out Ravana and this alone was the reason behind the destruction of Jarasandh and Duryodhana. Where do you and I count?

Just then Qadir Mian reached the chaupal. He was followed by Bilasi.

Qadir said – Khan Sahib, Manohar's wife has come to see you; you can give as many rupees for ghee as you wish. Poor thing, she was too scared to come.' Ghaus Khan replied bitterly – 'And where is Manohar? Was he too ashamed to come here?' Bilasi said politely – 'Sarkar, please don't mind his words. I am ready to slave for you.'

Qadir – Normally he's as mild as a cow, but God knows what ghost came over him today. Why, Sukhu Mahto, has he ever fought with anyone in the village?

Sukhu replied, looking here and there – Not at all, why should anyone tell a lie?

Qadir – Now he's sitting and repenting. I insisted a lot; just go and beg pardon for your faults, but he's too ashamed to come.

Ghaus Khan – This is not shame, this is a prank. I know how to overpower the ghost riding his head. He is swollen with pride.

Qadir – Khan Sahib, the poor labourer has nothing to be proud of. Foolish, unpolished man; doesn't know how to talk.

Ghaus Khan – You don't need to advocate his cause. I know my job very well. If I get cowered down like this, I won't be able to serve as a karinda. Today one man is showing his colours; tomorrow more of his brothers shall gain courage to do so. Then who'll care for the zamindar? Had anyone done this in the army he would've been shot dead. To turn away one's eyes from the zamindar is not child's play.

After saying this, Ghaus Khan got up to board his carriage. Bilasi followed him crying and stood before him with folded hands, saying – 'Sarkar, I shall be destroyed. You can fix whatever fine you want, whatever punishment you deem fit, but please don't report this to the masters.' But Khan Sahib had already fixed up everything with Sukhu Mahto. He didn't want any empathy to disrupt his cruel game. He got on the horseback at once and ordered Sukhu to walk in the front. Qadir slowly whispered in Girdhar's ears – 'Why, Maharaj, will you rest only after destroying Manohar?'

Girdhar replied in a voice laden with pride – When you stare into our eyes, we shall also do what we please. If someone bows down an inch before us, we are also ready to bow ten inches before him. But if someone opposes us even to the length of a grain, we shall oppose him by the length of a foot.

Qadir – This is of course a well known dictum, but if you start giving away your rights, who will give you importance? Well, now think of a way out for Manohar. You know his nature very well. He's a short tempered fellow; first he loses his head, then sits and weeps about it. Poor thing; he shall be totally destroyed.

Girdhar – Bhai, now the arrow has left the bow.

Qadir – Manohar's death will be upon you.

Girdhar – I can think of one solution. You go and tell Manohar to go to the master and beg for forgiveness. There I will also say something in his favour. I really don't wish to do any favours to you; you come and plead when there's a vested interest; once that is fulfilled, you don't even see eye to eye. But one's deeds always pay one in the long run. Go and send him.

Qadir and Bilasi went to Manohar. He, looking like a statue of doubt and worry was staring in the direction from which they arrived. Qadir immediately reported all that had happened and also what Girdhar Maharaj had ordered. Manohar thought for a moment and replied – 'I shall be further insulted on going there. Now I have been caught in the net; whatever happens, I shall see for myself.'

Qadir – No, you must go. I will also come with you.

Manohar – You will also have to face the music because of me.

Bilasi looked at Qadir with an extremely gentle look and said – Dadaji, he won't go; I will go with you.

Qadir – What shall you do, one has to speak to high officials out there.

Bilasi – I may not be able to speak, but I can surely cry.

Qadir – Will he let you go?

Bilasi – Why not; do I ask anything from him? He cannot decide what is good or bad for him. I at least know the difference between the two.

Qadir – Then we must not delay our going or else those people will surely complain against us to the masters.

Manohar kept sitting in the same position like a statue. Bilasi went inside the house, wore her ornaments, took a shawl and came and stood outside. Qadir Mian was lost in hesitation. He still hoped that Manohar would rise to go but when he didn't stir at all from his position, he started walking ahead; slowly Bilasi started following him. But she kept staring at Manohar, again and again, with a pained look in her eyes. When the two got out of the village boundary, Manohar thought of something and leapt up to Qadir Mian's side, and said to Bilasi – 'Go, sit in the house, I shall go.'

4

The day had entered its last quarter. Gyanshankar was sitting in his drawing room, reading a book when a servant came and asked – 'Babu Sahib is asking; what's the time?'

Gyanshankar got annoyed and said – 'Go and tell him he's being called downstairs. Shall he keep on sleeping the whole day?

This Babu Sahib was none other than Babu Jwalasingh. He was an ex-classmate of Gyanshankar and had just arrived as the Deputy Collector of the area. The two friends had been talking to each other till late afternoon. Jwalasingh had been awake since the previous night hence he had gone to sleep. Gyanshankar could not sleep a wink. At present he was burning with jealousy and anger. 'All these men are emerging as winners and I have been left nowhere.' Sometimes, he felt angry with himself; sometimes with his father and uncle. The old camaraderie was slowly turning into contempt. Had he got the news of Jwalasingh's joblessness at that moment, his heart would have probably been at peace. Yet, he didn't want this degrading thought to settle in his mind. He tried to pacify himself, thinking that it was all a matter of fate. If one's own friend reaches a high position one must feel happy, but his anxiety could not be dispelled by these positive thoughts and despite his best efforts, they revealed their meanness in mutual dialogue. Jwalasingh could sense that his promotion was making him jealous, but this was not merely the result of Gyanshankar's mean nature. Jwalasingh's words and attitude did not carry the affectionate simplicity of the early years, but had now been replaced by an unexplained sense of magnanimity; an artificial love and a pride-laden goodness, which added salt to the wounds of Gyanshankar. It cannot be doubted that Jwalasingh's nature did not stem from any personal will; he wasn't a man of low attributes, but his success had indeed made him a bit intoxicated. On the other hand Gyanshankar wasn't so generous that he could have used the opportunity to happily analyze an aspect of human character.

Jwalasingh got down as soon as the servant left and said – 'Friend, just tell me what's the time? I have to go and meet the Sahib.'

Gyanshankar replied – Oh! See him in a while; where's the hurry?

Jwalasingh – No brother, I have to see him once; I need to find out what kind of a man he is; what really makes him happy?

Gyan – He is happy if you go and rub your nose at his doorstep thrice a day.

Jwalasingh laughed and replied – That's not difficult; I shall offer prayers at his altar five times a day.

Gyan – And he also becomes happy if you forget about rules and regulations, and only deem his will to be the law.

Jwalasingh – I'll do just that.

Gyan – You'll have to raise the income-tax. If you leave an accused even by mistake, he will take you to task very badly.

Jwala – Bhai, you must be joking, how can it be like that?

Gyan – No, believe me, he's a strange creature.

Jwala – Then it would be difficult for me to cope up with him.

Gyan – Not the least. Today you are talking thus; tomorrow you will run according to his instructions. You must not be proud that you have attained any right; actually, you have got slavery written in for yourself. Here, you will have to sacrifice the freedom of your soul and strangle out truth and justice; these measures alone can ensure your progress and respect. I just give a damn to such a position. Even if God descends from the skies and ask me to do injustice, I won't obey His orders.

Jwalasingh understood that these arguments were mere blisters of a heart burning with jealousy. He said – 'You are claiming too much; if you get nominated tomorrow, you too will forget all this.'

Gyanshankar – Yeah, it's quite possible, since I am also a human being; yet there isn't any fateful chance of me getting caught in such a situation and even if there is, I would give topmost priority to the protection of my soul.

Jwalasingh got angry and said, 'What right do you have to anticipate that others do not respect their souls as much as you do? I think that to the extent a man can guard his soul while fulfilling worldly demands; he can't be deterred from doing so. If you think that the practice of law or medicine is especially congenial to the idea of self-protection, you are seriously mistaken. My uncle is a lawyer, and my elder brother is a doctor but they are simply money-making machines. I have never found them caught in the moral tussle between right and wrong.

Gyanshankar – They can protect their souls if they wish to.

Jwalasingh – Yes, but only to an extent that a government servant can. Take a lawyer, for instance; if he listens to his mind he can fill up his belly but cannot be prosperous. He will need to become a favourite of the higher officials if he needs to rise in his profession, and doctors are dependent on rich men for their very lives; what shall they gain from the poor? Many poor patients linger at their door, but as soon as they are summoned by a rich man they leave them and get on to their carriage. I cannot term it as any independence of the soul.

Just then Ghaus Khan, Girdhar Maharaj and Sukhu entered the room. Ghaus sat on the floor after paying respects; the other two men kept standing. Lala Prabhashankar was sitting in the verandah. He asked – 'Did you distribute the money for ghee among the tenants?'

Ghaus Khan – Yes Sir, with the good word of the lord all money has been distributed, but there are some men in the area who have turned so rebellious that I can only think of God while handling them. If they are not controlled, my reputation might be harmed and don't be surprised if I also happen to lose my life.

Gyanshankar (surprised) – Have such winds started blowing in the countryside also?

Ghaus Khan made a tearful face and said, 'Huzoor, don't you ask; if Girdhar Maharaj hadn't run away, his life too would have been in danger.

Gyan – Why didn't you get hold of those men and get them beaten up?

Ghaus – From where I'd have managed money for the thanedar, had I done so?

Gyan – You people know so many ways out; you could have caught them in any trap.

Ghaus – Huzoor, they are mauroosi tenants. They think nothing of the zamindar. One of them is Manohar. He ploughs around twenty bighas and pays only Rs fifty as land tax. Today, if we rent out his land to any other tenant we could easily get a hundred rupees.

Gyanshankar looked at his uncle and asked - Why have most of your tenants turned rebellious?

Prabhashankar passively replied – Whatever has happened these karindas must have done it; how can I tell?

Gyanshankar (tauntingly) – That's why the region has been ruined.

Prabhashankar irritatingly replied – Now with God's grace you've come of age; why don't you manage the land affairs?

Gyan – I can do that, but am helpless before you.

Prabha – I swear if I ever interfere in your affairs; I've been doing this job since ages; I'm not hankering after it anymore.

Gyan – Then I will also show you what proper management can achieve.

Just then Qadir Khan and Manohar came and stood at the door. Ghaus Khan said, 'Huzoor, he's the man about whom I was telling you just now.'

Gyanshankar looked at Manohar angrily and said – Why, you drill holes in the very plate that you eat from? You are farming on land worth a hundred rupees at the cost of just fifty; on top of it, when you were asked to squeeze a little, you went out of limits?

Manohar stood dumbstruck. He forgot just about everything that Qadir Khan had taught him on the way!

Gyanshankar said in the same voice – You evil fellow, you must have thought that you are the whole sole master, what can the zamindar do to you? But I'll show you what the zamindar can do. You have the guts to raise your hands on my men?

Manohar was trembling with a helpless sort of anger and was thinking– 'I didn't take money for ghee but that's no sin. I should have taken the money not due to fear of oppression, but only because the elder master used to treat us with such kindness.' He felt ashamed that he didn't remain true to the soul of such a kind man, but its punishment was not abuse and insult. His sense of hurt started getting anxious to reply back! But Qadir did not give him any chance to speak. He said – 'Huzoor, we can never dare to raise our heads before sarkar's men. Yes, we are foolish and uneducated, we don't know the proper way to talk; we end up uttering uncivilized words. Don't we know that if Huzoor wills, he may uproot us today itself! All we can do is to pray that whatever has been our fault, it may be condoned.'

Lala Prabhashankar felt kindness for Manohar; he was a simple man. He said, 'You people are our old tenants; don't you know that we don't have any convention of being tough on you all? When there's a particular occasion like the one at present only then you are asked to put in extra labour, and you've been doing it happily ever since. You should keep up the same tradition. Or else, now the times are sensitive; we took the good and bad equally in our stride, but these boys won't be able to take it in the same spirit. They are hot-blooded, hence you must take care; you should tolerate few things; go for now, don't do this again. You must have arrived without eating anything. The sun is at its peak, take rest after eating something; you can leave after sunset.'

Prabhashankar tried to do away with the matter according to his peaceful nature, but Gyanshankar looked at him sharply and said – 'Why do you interfere in my affairs? Your soft dealing has caused these men to grow out of their skins. If you keep meddling in my job like this, this whole management would be impossible. You just promised not to have any concern with land affairs. Now you have no right to speak.'

Prabhashankar couldn't bear this insult. He said angrily – Why do you say that? Am I dead?

Gyanshankar – No, you don't have any rights. You have ruined the whole region; now do you want to spoil whatever little is left?

Prabhashankar felt the assault deeply on his heart. He said – 'Son, why do you hurt me with these words? Your honourable father is no more, but he never ignored my words. Now you wish to shut my mouth, but it just can't happen that I keep witnessing injustice and yet keep mum. You cannot take away this right from me till the time I'm alive.'

Jwalasingh consoled him, saying – No Sahib, you are the master of the house; he's been brought up in your lap; please ignore his innocent talk. He is mistaken if he says that you don't have any right. You have a right over everything; you are the lord of the house.

Ghaus Khan said – Huzoor is absolutely right. You are the caretaker of the family and its well-wisher. How can anyone go against your wishes?

Gyanshankar understood that Jwalasingh had had his revenge; he repented immediately for his high-headedness. The guilt in his heart, however, arose only from the fact that Jwalasingh was sitting there and he shouldn't have misbehaved in front of him.

He said – By rights, I didn't mean what you have understood. I just wanted to say that if you have put the land management under my purview, so let me handle it by myself. I just happened to utter what I did. I am really ashamed about that. Bhai Jwalasingh, I respect my uncle to a degree that I didn't even respect my father. I myself am opposed to acting tough on these poor men. You are well-versed with my thoughts on the issue. But this doesn't mean that in the process of protecting the poor, we lose our land itself? The old times were different. Back then, life and its struggles were not so terrible. Our wants were limited, the social condition was not so complex and the biggest fact is that the cost of land had not risen so much. Many other villages owned by me that were sold at two thousand, may have fetched twenty thousand today. Those days, it was difficult to find tenants. Today there are hundreds hankering after a tiny plot. How's it possible for the zamindar to remain unaffected by this economic condition?

Lala Prabhashankar felt very sad at his hurtful words; he regarded his elder brother like a god, he was very ashamed of getting angry with his son. He said – 'Bhai, how can an old man like me understand these things as well as you can? You are the master of the house. I made a mistake to have spoken in between. All I need is a morsel of bread daily. You can look after the house the way you want.'

Everyone kept sitting quietly for a while. In the end, Ghaus Khan asked – 'Huzoor, what do you order for Manohar?'

Gyanshankar – Increase the land rent.

Qadir – Sarkar, he's very poor, he'll die.

Gyanshankar – If there's (shikmi) land under his tenancy then take it back.

Qadir – Sarkar, it'll surely be the end of him.

Gyanshankar – I don't care, there's no dearth of tenants.

Qadir – Huzoor…

Gyanshankar – Keep quiet, I don't want to argue with you.

Qadir – Sarkar, please…

Gyanshankar – That's all; didn't I ask you to shut your mouth?

Manohar had been standing quietly uptil now. After hearing Prabhashankar's words he had been assured that his visit to the place had not been in vain. He had been overwhelmed by his gentility. As compared to Gyanshankar's bitter tirade, Prabhashankar's politeness seemed almost godlike to him. His heart was filled up with a desire to put his entire self before him and offer it as a gift to the elder master. But Gyanshankar's last words destroyed all such sentiments. Especially Qadir Mian's insult became unbearable to him. He changed his tone a little and said, 'Dada, now kindness and its dharma have vanished from this court. Let's see, whatever God wills will surely happen. Whoever has given us mouths shall give us to eat also. If we can't even beg, we can surely go somewhere else, can't we?'

Saying so, he took Qadir's hand and forcefully led him out of the drawing room. Gyanshankar was feeling so angry at the moment that had he not been afraid of the law, he would have got him fixed up alive in a wall. Had a part of this anger been spent on scolding Manohar, the flame might have been calmed a little, but now there was no way for it to spend itself except boiling within his heart. He seemed like a child whose playmate had run away after giving him a painful bite. His awareness that he was the lord of this man's fate could not bring him to rest, nor could the fact that he could destroy him under his feet. Anger has a special relation with evil words.

Jwalasingh was sitting all quiet. He was surprised as to how did Gyanshankar acquire such heartless sense of selfishness? Just a moment ago the fellow was describing in such an important tone, the value of justice and social service. He proved to be a turncoat in such a short time? So much of a difference in his thoughts and actual practice? When Manohar left, he said to Gyanshankar – 'If you file a claim to increase the land rent, won't he retaliate? Also, you can't do that only to a single tenant.'

Gyanshankar – Yes, you're right. Khan Sahib, please make a list of all such tenants on whom the rent can be increased according to the regulations. What's the harm if we're able to do it for the whole village?

Jwalasingh had voiced this doubt in order to save Manohar. When he saw the opposite being achieved, he lost the heart to say anything else. He got up and went upstairs.

5

Almost one month passed; Ghaus Khan did not prepare any list of the tenants and Gyanshankar did not remind him again about it. There was a tussle going on between Ghaus Khan's self- interest and that of his master. Gyanshankar was thinking that the whole family would benefit from the tax increase; why should he get into a headache for no special reason? 'I shall be blamed for strangling so many poor and the profit shall be enjoyed by everyone in the house.' He wanted to benefit alone from this unjust affair; he couldn't accept that others too should have a share in it. Now his whole concern was focussed upon the evil thought of separating from his uncle. The idea was perfectly in accordance with his personal interests. He was burdened with the upkeep of just three people – he himself, his wife and his sister-in-law. His son was still a baby surviving on milk. A large part of the area's income was spent by Prabhashankar who had three sons, two daughters, a daughter-in-law, a grandson and he along with his wife to support. Gyanshankar was often annoyed with his father's convention of family upkeep. Had he himself got separated from his brother three years ago, his (Gyanshankar's) condition wouldn't have been so bad now. 'The uncle would have minded his own concerns; would have eaten or fasted, we'd not have been troubled, rather had we helped him a little in such a state he would have deemed it as a debt. Or else, what have we achieved by spending so much except soiled hands?' Prabhashankar had seen the ways of the world. He kept quiet seeing such intentions on part of his nephew and ignored all unseemly talk even though it often fell upon his ears. Dayashankar kept asking for monetary help rather than assisting his father, hence Prabhashankar thought it best to tolerate everything for his own good.

Gyanshankar now got carried away in a current of false pride and enmity. If one servant worked for Prabhashankar, he kept the other engaged in his personal jobs without any purpose. He kept calculating that his family of three should spend as much as his uncle's eight members did. Whenever he ate, he left a lot on his plate. When he wasn't satisfied even after doing all this, he kept two pet dogs. He made them sit with him and fed them. It all went to an extent that in case Prabhashankar got some medicine from the doctor; he too bought a medicine for the same amount even if he had to throw it later on. His heart still couldn't rest even after all these unfair acts. He wanted the women of the house to get into quarrels. He couldn't stand Vidya's polite manners and often incited her, saying – 'You are just not bothered about your own good or bad. Men don't have the time to get into the nitty-gritties of everything. This is actually the job of women; they are usually blamed for causing trouble in the house, but you just don't care about anything. You see with your own eyes that ghee has started flowing from the pot, but you don't open your mouth.' Vidyavati was resistant towards such education even after getting it often from her husband.

In the meanwhile something took place which added fuel to the fire of this separatism. Dayashankar had already caused much trouble in his station, but when Jwalasingh became the area magistrate, the former started behaving like a king. He already knew that the Deputy Collector was a friend of Gyanshankar's. This little knowledge was enough for him to initiate a relationship with the former. Sometimes he used to send poultry to him as a gift; at other times, fish, milk or ghee. Whenever he went to see him he tried to behave in a friendly way. His sense of haughtiness increased and led to a decrease in caution; he openly started looting the area and its people. Jwalasingh got many complaints against him but he still refrained from discussing them with either Dayashankar or his family members. When people found that the Deputy Collector wasn't listening to their appeal, they kept quiet with a sense of defeat. Dayashankar grew all the more rowdy. Earlier he used to look for an opportunity to do something unlawful; now he grew absolutely sure of his deeds. There was no stopping to what he did now. Once there occurred an incident of robbery in his area. He went to investigate the case. One of the zamindars came under scrutiny; his house was searched and some stolen goods were seized. He immediately went on to arrest him. The zamindar got free after offering some bribe to him. But he was also hit upon his honour; he couldn't bear the insult. The next day he filed a case in Jwalasingh's court against the daroga (Dayashankar). The region was already simmering with sparks of revolt. This led to a further hottening up of the issue. There were all kinds of true and false allegations from various quarters. In the end, Jwalasingh was forced to look into all these matters. Everything was exposed. He sent a report to the higher officials of the police. Dayashankar was suspended and was charged with the crimes of taking bribes and creating false cases. The tables were turned; he had earlier arrested the zamindar, now he himself went behind the bars. His bail was accepted due to efforts of Lala Prabhashankar, but the charges against him were supported by such concrete evidences that there were little chances of his getting free. He himself had lost all hope. He even lost the power to think; as if all reason and rationale had disappeared. The voice that earlier made the walls of the police station tremble in fear, was now powerless to even utter a word. The brain that used to build castles in the air had no solution to this complicated affair. If someone asked him anything, he just kept staring in the vacuum. He had no sense of repentance or shame; only a sense of astonishment as to how he had got caught in this quagmire. Silently, he only sat and thought, 'I made a mistake; had this incident not gone overboard I would never have been caught.' The heart that refuses to admit self-knowledge even in times of trouble is just like a dry tree which does not flourish even after getting water; rather gets infected and dies. Gyanshankar thought it his duty to help his relatives in such a sorry state, yet in this case, he was not just hesitant to say anything about it, but also started agreeing with anyone who criticized Dayashankar's behaviour, instead of opposing him.

Lala Prabhashankar left no stone unturned to get his son exonerated from the court. He was lost in this tussle all day and night. This was surely due to his love for his son, but probably more due to a fear of social criticism. The fall of a household that was held in respect all over the city was indeed heartrending. When he lost hope after lots of running about in all directions, he went to Gyanshankar and said – 'Please go and see Jwalasingh in this regard; he's your friend, he might give us some concession.'

Gyanshankar replied with a sense of dismay, 'I think it would be highly improper of me to go to him at this moment.'

Prabhashankar – I know, and I didn't speak to you about it for this very reason. But now I think there's no other way out. Let the Deputy Collector release him from his court, we shall see what lies ahead. If he wants, he can very well weaken the evidences.

Gyan – But how can you expect that he would be ready to kill his sense of justice merely due to what I say.

Prabhashankar insisted, 'When friends insist upon something it's very effective. What old people think often goes against the conventions of the present civilization. Young men get impatient with such talk; they deem this ignorance on part of the old as an unpardonable offence.'

Gyanshankar irritatingly replied – When you have no understanding of the matter what can I say or do? I don't want to belittle myself in the eyes of others.

Prabhashankar said – Does one get belittled by advocating the cause of one's own brother?

Gyanshankar bitterly replied – Advocacy is a lowly affair, be it for any cause; especially in a case like this.

Prabhashankar said – Then it actually implies that one must not hope for any help from one's own brother in times of trouble.

'Trouble refers to those problems that are caused by supernatural and essential causes; it does not imply jumping into the fire knowingly.'

'Shouldn't one try to save the life of one who has indeed jumped into the fire knowingly?'

Just then his wife came to the door and said – 'Why don't you come and console Lallu (Dayashankar) a bit? He didn't have his dinner last night and hasn't washed his face or hands uptil now.'

Prabhashankar was annoyed at listening to this, and said – To what extent can I console him? I am now fed up. Son (to Gyanshankar), I cannot explain to you the state of my heart. Whatever you have said is absolutely right, but have some mercy on me; please go to the Deputy Collector today. I have a feeling that some good can surely be achieved by your going there.

Gyanshankar was thinking what to say when the old lady said – 'He will never go. Lallu was telling me that even if Gyanu goes and reports something false the whole matter would be solved but he won't be bothered even if someone is ruined. If he had wanted to get him trapped he would have run about a lot; how can he go to save him; won't that belittle him?'

Prabhashankar said with a tinge of reprimand – What nonsense are you talking about? Why don't you go and sit inside?

The lady looked at Gyanshankar with demeaning eyes and said – 'Whatever I say, I say clearly; whether anyone feels good or bad. I can obviously see the intention that is hidden in his mind.'

Gyanshankar felt assaulted and said – 'Chacha Sahib! Do you listen to that? She takes me to be so mean.'

The old lady made a face and said, 'What shall he listen to; does he have any ears? His whole life has been spent in slaving for others; he is still used to that. I know your true nature very well.'

Prabhashankar got very upset and said, 'Keep quiet for God's sake.'

The lady got further angry and replied, 'Why should I; do I fear anyone? Our lives are at stake and this man is lost in his pride. It is a sin to even look at his face.'

Prabhashankar looked at his nephew with a poor expression and said, 'Son, she's not in her senses right now. Please don't mind her words.'

But Gyanshankar did not listen to these words; his heart was reeling under the bitter taunts of his aunt. He said, 'Well, even I am not enjoying the pleasures of heaven by staying with you people.'

The lady – Please state clearly whatever you have in mind. When there's no fellow-feeling amongst us, we cannot become one merely by staying in the same house!

Gyan – If you wish it like that, let it be; please turn me out.

The lady – Our wish? I have been noticing your ways since months. God has blessed me with eyes; my hair hasn't turned white just by soaking the sun. We appear to you like grains of sand fallen in one's eyes. You think that we survive by consuming your assets. If your heart is housing such mean sentiments then …

Prabhashankar let out a sigh and said 'O God, why don't I die?'

The old lady looked at her husband with angry eyes and said – If you are so fond of these people go and lick their feet. The fellow who does not stand with you in times of trouble is an enemy and one must distance oneself from him.

Gyan – Whom are you trying to threaten? Why wait for tomorrow; divide the shares today itself!

The lady – Do you think I survive on your alms?

Gyan – What exactly do you mean by this?

The lady – You are simply too proud.

Gyan – Even if I am, what's unfair about that? I just don't spend as much as you do.

The lady looked tauntingly at her husband and said – Do you listen to what your worthy son is saying! Why don't you speak up? Is there curd set in your mouth? His father used to feed the hermits and beggars in thousands every year. Till his last breath, twelve palanquin bearers never left our door. He is today bothered about our poor meals? Lala, be grateful to us that you are enjoying life like the rich, or else flies would have been sitting and dirtying your face.

Prabhashankar could not bear these words. He got up and went outside. The elder lady could not keep fighting all alone, so she too went inside the house. But Gyanshankar kept sitting there. His heart was blazing with a burning fire; 'So much of coldness! Such ungratefulness! I am mean, I am an enemy; it's a sin to see my face! For their entire lives they kept eating from our pockets and today such talk! Such pride! Let me see how long it continues? If I don't break it, I am not a man of my word! These people must be thinking that they are the masters; they possess the keys; whatever they give me, I'll take. I shall make them divide every single object in halves. This old woman must be having lots of money. My father had left everything to them. She must have gathered ten or twenty thousand by hook or by crook. Yes, that's the reason behind her pride, that's all.' There's is a strong tendency in jealousy to think that others are more prosperous.

Lost in such evil thoughts, Gyanshankar came outside and found his uncle talking to Munshi Ijaad Hussain in the drawing room. He was the ahalmad in the court of Jwalasingh; very talkative and extremely clever. He was saying – 'You don't worry, if God wills, Babu Dayashankar shall be released with all charges cleared. I have contacted his (Jwalasingh's) wife through my maid and have impressed her to an extent that she will not leave the Deputy Collector without getting Darogaji (Dayashankar) released. A hundred or two will have to be spent, but what's the harm; our honour shall be saved.' Suddenly, on seeing Gyanshankar there, he felt a bit embarrassed.

Prabhashankar said, 'You can take as much money as is needed; if the matter is resolved due to your efforts, I will ever be grateful to you.'

Ijaad Hussain looked at Gyanshankar and said – Babu Jwalasingh will surely take care of his friendly ties. He might appear unconcerned in what he says, but he really respects you a lot. I too keep promoting this sentiment. Yesterday, while talking about you, I said, 'He hasn't had food or water since two or three days.' He started thinking something after hearing this, and went inside after the call came for namaz.

Prabhashankar looked at the Munshi with grateful eyes but Gyanshankar stared at him demeaningly and went upstairs. Vidyavati was waiting for him; she said – 'How come you are late today? Food has been ready since long.'

Gyanshankar passively replied –How can I eat in such a scenario; nothing seems to be left. The master and his lady both closed up my case today. They think it sinful to even look at my face. It is better to die than to stay with such people.

Listening to his tirade, Vidyavati grew doubtful and asked, 'What happened?'

Gyanshankar replied to this question in great detail. He was hopeful that his words shall affect Vidya's peace-loving nature, but he was very depressed when, after listening to the entire story she only said, 'You ought to have gone to Jwalasingh. In this way, you could have kept Chachaji's word. One gets to know the real face of one's own people only on occasions like these. Those people must have got angry at this denial from your side. One doesn't really voice one's real thoughts in a fit of anger. One only wishes to hurt the sentiments of others.'

Gyanshankar got very upset and said, 'After listening to you, I really wish to break my own head and even yours. You deem their bitter words as sweet as flowers, and are now trying to preach to me. I am rather worried that this idiot Ijaad Hussain must have told all false things from my side, and you tell me to plead their case. I want to communicate to Jwalasingh that I am absolutely detached from the issue. I don't want to be a favour-seeker and appear little in his eyes.'

Vidya was surprised and said – Will you go to him to say all this?

Gyanshankar – Yes, of course. Why should I lose my honour in a bid to save someone else's?

Vidya – What shall he think in his mind? Won't this express your ill-feeling towards Chachaji's family?

Gyanshankar – I am not as stupid as you think. I know which point should be put across in which manner.

Vidya started staring at the ground with worried eyes. She was very upset at her husband's narrow-mindedness but she was afraid to say anything else lest his evil thoughts got all the more strengthened. Just then Dayashankar's wife came to call them for dinner. On the other side, Shraddha went to talk to the senior lady. Vidya sent Tejshankar to plead to Lala Prabhashankar, but none of them came to have dinner. Prabhashankar was guilty that his wife had talked rudely to Gyanshankar. The old lady was sorrowful that none was a well-wisher of her son. And Gyanshankar burnt with a feeling that these people ate from his pocket and yet dared to show him angry eyes. The fire of hunger burning in his stomach ran parallel to the fire of his anger.

In an argumentative situation, we often turn very principled, but actually by doing so, our sole purpose is to shut the mouth of our opponent. In these few hours Gyanshankar's sense of principles had got transmuted into a fire of jealousy. Whereas earlier he was hesitant to go to Jwalasingh to help out Dayashankar, he immediately got ready to approach the former to harm the latter. He had sorted out all the points related to the matter in his mind; he wanted to raise the question in a manner that his true intentions shouldn't be exposed.

The next day, as soon as the clock struck nine, Gyanshankar took his bicycle and got out of the house. At the door, Lala Prabhashankar was having a walk with his two sons. Gyanshankar thought in his mind, 'The old fellow has turned sixty, but has the same haughtiness of his youth. He's walking in such a proud manner! Now I'll see how he gets butter and sugar to eat! The boys are staring at me as if they'd eat me up.'

The rainy season had already arrived; the clouds were cast in a manner as if the sea had taken over the sky. The streets had grown so muddy that Gyanshankar's bicycle couldn't get on without trouble; his clothes were soon soiled with mudstains. He was feeling angry with the municipal members that all of them were selfish, sycophants and robbers. 'At the time of elections, they roam from door to door like beggars, but as soon as they become members, they start behaving like kings. All the previous running about is rewarded by this great seat of enlightenment. It's really a mistake that these members are kept for a fixed period. The voters should have the right to impeach a member if they see him ignoring his duties. This is just a myth that no dutiful member would be found suddenly in such a situation. Whosoever is concerned about national progress will be ready to serve the people in every situation. In my opinion those who really wish to work with true dedication shall be delighted with this clause. This way, they'll find a way out of their own idleness. And if we are not dedicated to the service of people, then why should we crave to sit in the municipal hall. What respect can be earned from this? If someone is a soldier and tries to avoid fighting, it is rather his insult, not a matter of pride.'

Gyanshankar was lost in these thoughts when Jwalasingh's bungalow arrived. He was going for an outing on his horse. He met Gyanshankar in an affectionate manner and started talking randomly. He was under the impression that the latter must have arrived to plead his brother's case. He therefore wished to occupy him in such talk so that the case would not be discussed at all. He had not got any concrete evidence against Dayashankar. He knew very well that Dayashankar was not clean in his ways, but the charge couldn't be proved merely with this knowledge. He had decided to let him go free. In this state he didn't want anyone to doubt that he had been improperly biased. Gyanshankar's coming to see him would have strengthened such doubts on part of the public. People get such news quite easily. Helpers and peons distribute such rumours with great alacrity to propagate their sense of goodness. Jwalasingh asked – 'Tell me if your tenants have been taught a lesson.'

Gyanshankar - Not at all; it's not easy to control them. My uncle has pampered them a lot. I was busy with other affairs so I couldn't do anything about it.

Jwalasingh was scared lest he was trying to introduce the topic. He immediately changed his stance and said, 'Bhai Sahib, I have really taken up a headache by taking up this job. From morning to night I get no time for myself. Very often I keep working till ten or eleven at night. Had only this been the issue I'd have borne it, but I also need to worry about the good temper of the higher officials. You know very well that it has rained a lot this year; lots of villages in my area have been flooded. What to talk of fields, even the huts of farmers have got drowned. The zamindars have appealed for the concession in half of the land rent and it is quite justifiable. But I guess that the masters want these applications to be submitted to the official process. Although they don't do it openly but it hinders the survey of the losses to such an extent that the survey goes waste. If I pretend to remain ignorant even after knowing these things and try to do an independent enquiry, then it's me who'll have to face the music. People will end up doubting my intentions. The whole scenario has been spoiled to an extent that no one can escape this injustice in any way. When I see the condition of my colleagues, I just wish to resign and go home. To what extent a man can become a self-loving and a sycophantic individual, there can be no better example than this place. If the Sahib bahadur even slightly indicates that the tax on the income should be levied properly then believe me, our learned friends shall increase the tax twice or thrice in just two days. If an indication comes that the extortion should be done with restraint, then assume that it will be stopped. When I listen to the words of these great men I don't feel like seeing their faces for a lifetime. There's no scientific outlook, no political or economic thought, no literary discussion. Just an account of 'what I did, what the Sahib said; when he said this I replied this way.' I tell you the truth; even a rogue would not boast about his exploits in such a way. I am really sorry that this disease engulfs not just the old men belonging to a dated thought, but also our newly-educated class to a great extent. Marlow, Mill and Spenser, all are suppressed below this self-oriented principle. I tell you; there are such sophisticated men here who worship cooks and servants merely so that the latter should praise them before the Sahib. If someone gets even a little authority he takes himself to be the master, and starts thinking that he has no relation to the general public or his countrymen. When they go before the British officials, they become exponents of politeness and gentleness, as if they are standing in the court of God but when they go on a tour they treat the tenants and the landlords with such haughtiness as if they are the devisors of their fate.'

Jwalasingh exaggerated the situation a lot because he was aware of Gyanshankar's thoughts on the issue. His only intention was to avoid any discussion of the charge levied on Dayashankar.

Gyanshankar happily replied, 'I told you all this the first day itself but you didn't believe me. Till now, you have only become aware of the clever nature of your colleagues. After a few days you'll be surprised to see the ways of your subordinate employees. They will make you dance like a puppet. To avoid this bad name, there's no other way except to avoid them totally. Your ahlmad Ijaad Hussain is an evil fellow; please beware of him. He will try to catch you by multiple means. Only today I heard such talk from his mouth which implies that he's trying to deceive you. He has probably pleaded to you for Dayashankar from my side. Although I have that kind of sympathy for Dayashankar, which only a brother can have for his brother, yet I am not so fallen that I should hinder the process of justice by taking undue advantage of my friendship. I will never support the wrong means even if it concerns my own son. I deem humanity to be on a higher pedestal than brotherhood. I belong to such a group of men that if I see you leaning towards some empathy in the matter then I would prevent you from it.'

Jwalasingh was well-versed with human psychology. He understood that Gyanshankar was upset with his uncle. This whole talk about principles was actually a result of that annoyance. Ill-feeling and enmity cannot be hidden beyond a point, and he experienced it just then. The honour associated with Gyanshankar disappeared completely in his eyes. If a brother pleads for his brother it's perfectly natural and in accordance with human character. He didn't think it to be so bad, but to take the garb of moral principles in order to harm one's brother was totally inhuman in his eyes. He got a nice opportunity to assault such evil men who keep flaunting their sense of justice and truth.

He said, 'You are mistaken. Ijaad Hussain didn't talk to me about this matter at all. And it wasn't even required because I have already declared Dayashankar guilt-free in my report. And everyone knows very well that I don't listen to anybody unnecessarily. I have arrived at this understanding without taking any sides and I hope that you'll be happy after hearing this.'

Gyanshankar turned pale, as if someone had told him that his house was on fire. His heart felt as if pierced by an arrow. He was completely taken aback.

Jwalasingh – The witnesses were weak. The case was totally made up.

Gyanshankar – I am delighted to hear this. A million thanks to you. My uncle will turn mad with joy upon hearing this.

Jwalasingh was hurt at this comment, and said – It's just a point of law.

Gyanshankar – Whatever you might say, I will take it to be your kindness. Friendship extends the limits of law in an unknown fashion. Besides, you people have to cope up with the police pressure too. If you go against them, your way shall be obstructed in multiple ways; you have to think about that as well.

Jwalasingh couldn't bear this taunt. He proudly replied – Whatever I do, I do upon the strength of law. What to talk of the police, even God cannot pressurize me. I can smell some enmity in your words. I doubt that you're not pleased with Dayashankar's release.

Gyanshankar got agitated and replied – 'If you have any such doubt then pardon me, you haven't yet understood me even after staying with me for so many days. My nature might be feeble, but hasn't yet deteriorated to the extent that it might attack my brother. But I am not hesitant to insist that in my opinion, the interest of the nation is far superior to brotherly interest, and if they ever stand in contest to each other, I will lean towards the former. If you deem it to be my enmity or jealousy it's your greatness. My principled education has taught me this and I think it my duty to follow it as far as I can. If the public is harmed by a particular person, it's our duty to boycott him and bring him back on the right path, even if he's one of our close allies. Such examples aren't rare in world history where national interest has won over familial interest. When you blame me with a vested interest in such a situation what else can I say except that your education and ethics haven't benefitted you the least.'

After saying this, Gyanshankar left the place. The intention which had brought him here so early in the morning had been defeated and was causing great disturbance in his heart. 'Yes, this is sure that I have defeated this fellow; now he'd never dare to talk in such a manner to me.' Jwalasingh too, didn't try to stop him. He was thinking about the rare combination of wisdom and evil nature in Gyanshankar. When cleverness combines with evil intentions, it almost becomes a wine having twice the effect it could have ordinarily had. 'He might have come to his senses after my reprimand. He must have understood that the perceivers of conspiracy haven't yet vanished from the world.'

When Gyanshankar left the place, his condition was similar to that of a gambler who'd lost the game and was now wondering what object to put on stake so that he ends up winning. His heart was overwhelmed with anxiety. Though he had answered the charges of Jwalasingh in a befitting manner, yet he felt that he could not make any impressive assault on him. He could now remember many such topics with which he could have hurt Jwalasingh. He could have charged him with bribery if not anything else. 'Well, let me keep it for some other day,' he thought. At present, he felt the example of nationalist love and humanity to be quite laughable on whose basis he'd tried to shame Jwalasingh. Gradually, as he thought critically about the whole situation, he felt Jwalasingh's behaviour wholly improper.

'Even if he got to know of my secret jealousy his generosity and manners lay in the fact that he should have empathized with me and should've wiped my tears. Jealousy is very much a part of human nature, however abhorrent it might be. If someone insults me only because of this, then the reason behind it is not his purity of soul but a false sense of self-pride. Jwalasingh is no ascetic or god himself, nor is it possible that his own heart has never known the currents of jealousy. His proud principled nature and duty-loving tendency is itself the result of that particular jealousy which has errupted due to an awareness of his mental smallness.'

As he reached home thinking about all this he saw both his cousins ruffling some books in his room. Though this wasn't anything unusual, but Gyanshankar was suffering from mental agony at the moment. He immediately lost his temper and chased the boys out. 'These people must have sent these ruffians to disturb me,' he thought. 'There is such a huge sitting room downstairs; plus two other rooms, isn't that enough for them; can't they bear to see this one small room with me? Do they spite me for this? Do they want to turn me out of the house? This matter needs to be resolved right away. It just cannot happen that people keep oppressing me and I don't let out a whisper.' Having decided upon this he immediately wrote a letter to his uncle.

'Sir, it is just unbearable that your sons should trespass into my room in my absence, make a mess there and destroy my things. I want that we should divide the house amongst us, and the boys should be instructed not to step into my part even by mistake; or else if I scold them for it then you and my aunt won't have any right to complain against it. Please take care that the part allotted to me should be according to the needs of a householder, and the topmost condition is that it should be separate enough for me to call it my own and not become an eyesore and a subject of taunts while coming and going, or using it.'

He gave the letter to a servant and started waiting for the reply. He was wondering, 'Let's see, what response the old man gives?' The servant brought the answer in an instant and gave it to him –

'Son, my boys are your boys. You have every right to punish them. I don't have any objection to it, neither in the past or in the future. Rather it would be an obligation to me on your part if you keep reprimanding them from time to time. As regards the division of the house I leave it to you. The house is yours, and so am I; you can give me whatever corner you deem fit, I will never object to it. Well, just take care that I am used to sitting in the outskirts, so please give me a place to sit in the verandah of the sitting room. Yes, I wanted that the division shouldn't have occurred in my lifetime, but if this is what you want and it makes you happy then I don't think I can do anything about it.'

Gyanshankar kept the letter in his pocket and smiled. 'How clever is the old man; he had fooled my father with a similar show of politeness, and is using the same ploy with me but I am not such an idiot. He must have thought that by softening himself he'll soften me automatically! I haven't learnt such complex lessons of gentility. When one is forced to comply, it is understandable, but to comply simply due to appeasement and become a puppet at the hands of politeness is just sentimentalism, nothing else!'

Gyanshankar sat down and began to think – 'How should I solve this problem; this one room cannot compete with the sitting room and the two rooms adjoining it. The two rooms in the upper portion are with Dayashankar. But the three rooms upstairs should be mine. The three rooms below can go to him. This is easy to divide; but the women's portion will be difficult to separate. Two walls will have to be raised for the division. An opening will have to be created in the east for ventilation, and that's a real mess. The municipality will delay it by months. What's the harm if I take two portions above and below the sitting room? Let the women's portion be on their side. Here, the women can stay properly. The ladies wing is large enough but was constructed so long ago. In a few days it will need to be reconstructed. The walls have already started falling; there are repairs going on every other day. The roof also keeps leaking. The sitting room is perfect for me. My uncle cannot be accommodated there; he will have to take the ladies wing. Good that I thought of this. My purpose will be solved and I would get the credit too, for being generous.'

He decided all this in his mind and went inside to consult the ladies. He used to ask their opinion for the sake of convention but kept the right to 'veto' with himself and by using it on all occasions strangled every other opinion that was offered in its sway. We he came in he saw something very heartrending. Dayashankar was going to the court and the old lady was bidding him goodbye with tears in her eyes. Both the sisters were crying at his feet. His wife was sadly standing at her doorstep, covered with a veil. She couldn't have come and stood near her husband due to a conventional sense of shyness. Shraddha also stood there crying. Today, the decision was to be taken on the charge against him. God knows what was about to happen. No one knew whether he would come home or would not see the face of his house ever. Dayashankar appeared very sorrowful. As soon as he saw Gyanshankar, his eyes were filled with tears; he came near him and said, 'Brother, my heart is trembling with all sorts of doubts. I am afraid I won't be able to see you all again. Please forgive my sins; who knows whether we meet again or not; what is to become of Dayashankar? This house is now under your care.'

Gyanshankar got emotional after hearing this. He was momentarily ashamed of his narrow-mindedness and smallness. He consoled him saying, 'Don't talk like that; no one can harm you in the least. Jwalasingh might be ruthless, but he can never forget my obligations. And the truth of the matter is that I am just returning after seeing him regarding your case; you will surely get free. He has clearly assured me of this. I would have accompanied you now as well but it would only spoil the matter.'

Dayashankar looked at him with an unbelievable sense of gratefulness and said, 'How can one trust the word of an officer?'

Gyanshankar – Jwalasingh is not one of those officers.

Dayashankar – Don't say that; he is rather ruthless.

Gyanshankar tried to break the distrust lodged in his heart by saying – 'This mental weakness is the actual punishment for our crimes, or else you wouldn't have suffered such a lack of trust.'

Dayashankar felt ashamed and left the place. Gyanshankar too didn't say anything further; he had tried to win a lost game, but had not proved successful. He also was annoyed at the fact that those people did not deem him fit for such high-ranging thoughts. 'I am just a poisonous snake in their eyes. If they do not trust me, I am free to do what I wish in an open manner. It's useless to keep pretending closeness to them. These people won't be impressed with such tactics now.' The single seed of goodness that had blossomed in his heart for a second was destroyed by these evil desires. When he went to Vidya, she asked, 'Where did you go in the morning?'

Gyanshankar – I had gone to see Jwalasingh.

Vidya – I do not like such acts of yours.

Gyan – Which ones?

Vidya – These very acts, whereby you complain against your own family members to the officials. Everywhere brothers have tiffs with each other, but no one uproots one's own brother like you.

Gyanshankar bit his lips (in anger) and asked – You really think that I am so mean and wicked?

Vidya replied in a determined tone, 'Okay, then swear upon me that you didn't go to Jwalasingh for what I said just now.'

Gyanshankar replied in a stern voice, 'I do not think I need to justify myself before you.'

Saying thus, he sat down on the charpoy. Vidya had said something pointingly right and this had touched his heart and had hurt him. He suddenly became aware that his entire family, even his wife thought too low of him.

Vidya again asked, 'There's no other person out here who shall hear us.'

Gyan – Just keep quiet, I can feel the heat in your words. God knows when will you learn to talk properly? What's up; won't I get any food now? It's almost noon time.

Vidya – No one prepared any food today. You alone wrote to your uncle about the division of the house. He has been crying ever since.

Gyan – If he wishes to cry, he can! Does he want us to starve and die?

Vidya gave a stern look to her husband and said – When there is so much turmoil in the house, who can hope to sit down and eat? Who will be able to swallow food after seeing Chachaji in such a state? On one hand his son is in such trouble, and on the other hand, this sense of enmity! Ever since he's got your letter, he hasn't raised his head! What has come upon you that you're hankering after this division?

Gyan – Only because I wish to save that little land lest it should burn in this all-engulfing fire. We had land worth six thousand of annual income in the past. Now it has been reduced to just two thousand. These people have eaten up and wasted everything.

Vidya – These people are not outsiders.

Gyan – When you start talking in such a great manner, it almost seems as if you're the daughter of a millionaire. Your father has wealth equal to lakhs; why doesn't he give us something out of it; he doesn't care for you and you seem to be flowing in a sea of rupees.

Vidya – Hardworking men do not look up to other people's wealth. They have faith in the power of their own muscle.

Gyan – Instead of feeling ashamed you keep boasting unnecessarily. Why don't you admit that one's wealth is dearer to one than one's own life and thus one cares for it more than life itself? Or else, someone who has an annual income of about two and a half lacs shouldn't mind spending a few thousands on his daughter and son-in-law. Lala Sahib is such a miser, and you try to be so generous, as if this entire wealth means nothing to you.

Just then Shraddha arrived and Gyanshankar started talking to her about the division of the house.

6

As soon as Lala Prabhashankar's anger cooled off, he felt quiet ashamed of his bitter words. He also remembered his wife's sharp assaults which further added on to his guilt. The brother for whom his heart still overflowed with love and affection; whose death was a wound still unhealed, and in whose memory tears would start flowing from his eyes; to have behaved in such a way with his son seemed an act of sheer ungratefulness. He did not eat anything at night. He kept lying on bed feigning a headache. There was a dim light in the room. He almost felt as if Lala Jatashankar was standing at his door, giving him a stern look. He got up feeling upset, and his pulse started beating fast. He had a strong impulse to go and apologize to Gyanshankar that very moment, but just let out a sigh and lay down again. 'Oh! The brother who had never ever looked at me with a stern eye should be caused such grief by me! How cruel, how narrow-minded and wicked I am!'

In the morning he asked his wife, 'Did Gyanu eat something at night?'

The old lady – We didn't even light up the stove; so no one ate.

Prabhashankar – You may eat or not but why do you force him to remain hungry? What must Gyanu be thinking of me? He would have thought that I am so mean!

The lady – Why! As if he thought of you as a god till now. Your eyes are perhaps blindfolded but I am seeing his attitude for the past one year. I am rather surprised as to why he remained silent uptil now? What exactly are his intentions behind dividing the house! Only this that we are outsiders! He is just not bothered as to how we shall manage our living. He is simply hankering after money; whether his uncle, brothers and nephews live or die. It's a sin to see the face of such a man.

Prabhashankar – You have started repeating the same thing. If he has asked for his share what's wrong in it? This is the way of the world nowadays.

The lady – You have lost your head. How can one make you understand! As if you don't know anything. Our son's very life is on stake, the house is almost falling down, it's hard to swallow food or water, and there, someone's playing the harmonium till midnight! I almost take him to be a dark serpent whose poison is unbeatable. Even if someone slices our throats he won't let out a single tear from his eyes. You are sitting here repenting your words and he's roaming around in the village giving you a bad name. Everybody's criticizing you.

Prabha – This is all your false imagination; his heart is not so mean.

The lady – You will keep dreaming paradisical dreams and one fine day, he'll gather all the relatives and talk of dividing everything; then you'll be at a loss. He is also corresponding with Rai Kamlanand. Listen to me; just warn our own relatives. It's better to beware right from the beginning.

Prabhashankar replied with a sense of pride, 'I won't do that till my last breath. I am not so shameless that I keep flaunting the quarrels of my own house. Gyanshankar can show whatever attitude he wants but I always think of him as my own. We brothers kept vouching our lives for each other. Today, after my brother's death should I turn so shameless as to invite others to decide matters for me? I do not expect such enmity from Gyanshankar but even if he ends up harming me, I won't feel sad even a bit. Had our burden not been on my brother he would have led a prosperous life. He is his very son. If we have to undergo a little trouble for his convenience and peace then we should not mind it; his debt is already heavy on heads. I don't deem it proper to keep fighting with him over petty issues.'

The old lady did not answer back; she just got up and left his side. Prabhashankar wanted to bring her further to a realization. He kept sitting there for a while, thinking to pour his heart out once she came back but when a few hours passed, he got bored and went out. He had complained to his wife about Gyanshankar many a times in the past. He had never sanctioned money happily for his fashion and pomp, but whenever he saw his wife or any other family member opposing Gyanshankar, his sense of justice suddenly came to life, and he started flaunting a sense of goodness and generosity with such a vigour which he could never have championed himself in reality.

Once he came out, he started strolling in the verandah and sent Tejshankar to find out what Gyanshankar was doing. He wanted to apologize to him but when he saw him going somewhere on a bicycle he couldn't say anything. Gyanshankar was in a different mood and his eyes seemed to be flashing angrily. Prabhashankar thought, 'Where is he going so early in the morning; there must be something fishy about it.'

He took down the bird cages and started feeding the birds. He often used to forget all cares listening to hymns sung by the mountain canaries. After that he took a bath and started reading the Ramayana. All this continued till ten o' clock, and the servant brought him Gyanshankar's letter. He immediately took it and started reading. His prayers always went uninterrupted along with practical chores. On reading the letter, his whole body was almost set ablaze with anger. Every single word of the letter seemed to be adding sparks to his heart. He could now guess how proud and envious a man Gyanshankar was. He also understood that the delineation of his character by his wife was absolutely true. 'Such daring! How could he afford to pen such a letter! Had he actually sliced me with a sword, I wouldn't have been so hurt. He is so narrow-minded despite his cleverness and wisdom. Real education should promote tolerance and peace in a man; destroy petty meanness and make his heart generous rather than making him intoxicated with selfishness and brashness. If the boys had played a prank he could have scolded them and the matter could have ended there. Why did he make a mountain of a molehill! It is quite clear now that we won't be able to cope up together. To what extent shall I bend myself or bow down my head? Well, he can do as he pleases. He wants to divide the house. What can be more disastrous than this? The house and its secrets shall be exposed; people shall talk about us in all ways. Oh my ill-fortune! The house will have two kitchens now! What had never ever happened will now take place! There will be only a neighbour-like relation between me and my dear brother's son. Those who were together all their lives, played together and laughed together will now go their separate ways. But there is no other solution now! Should I write that he can divide the house as he wants? Why should I say that I will take this portion or that? If we must separate then we must avoid all confrontation.' Thus thinking Lala Prabhashankar replied to Gyanshankar. He was still hopeful that his polite reply will surely have some positive effect on Gyanshankar. 'What's the surprise if he leaves altogether the thought of being separate?' With these thoughts he wrote a reply to the letter and began waiting for his answer.

There was no letter till eleven. Dayashankar got up to go to the court. His mother came to Prabhashankar and said, 'You must go with Lallu. The decision will be read out today; God knows which side the tables will turn.' Prabhashankar had never stepped inside a court. Both the brothers had pledged that whatever might happen they would never see the face of the court. Though they had had to face many losses due to this pledge and even had to eat a humble pie before their opponents sometimes yet they had followed it strictly uptil now. Prabhashankar was at a loss upon hearing his wife. He could neither make up his mind to go nor refuse. He started looking here and there. Dayashankar sensed his dilemma and said passively, 'If you do not wish to go then please don't; I shall bear whatever comes upon me.'

The old lady – No, he will go; what's the harm?

Dayashankar – When he has never gone to the court, how will he go now? Won't it break his resolve then?

The lady – Well, I've seen many such resolves. Shall I get your clothes?

Dayashankar – No, I will go alone, you don't need to come.

Saying so, Dayashankar left. The old lady also went inside the house looking at her husband with disrespect. Prabhashankar was annoyed with her as to why she had raised the issue of his going to the court. 'What could I have done by going there,' he thought, 'I couldn't have held the pen of the judge, nor could I have pleaded before him. And when I have never gone there why should I go now? Let the person who has sowed such thorns eat their fruit. How far can I sacrifice myself in this anxiety?'

He was sitting in this disturbed state when Gyanshankar's second letter arrived. He had decided to take the entire sitting room. Prabhashankar had thought his politeness would be able to cool off his nephew's anger. But when he received this proposal against his hopes, he became all the more upset. The decisive words of the letter made him numb. He almost lost his cool. Instead of anger, he now felt a sense of helplessness. Anger is actually a sign of the power of retaliation. He had lost that power now. The mammoth picture of the proposal wiped out all intentions of a conflict. He seemed like a child who was scared upon seeing an elephant, was weeping with fear and had forgotten even to run away and save his skin. His entire life had been spent beneath the soothing shade of brotherly love. He couldn't bear the piercing rays of enmity and opposition now! He went like a poor suppliant to Gyanshankar and said in a sad tone, 'Gyanu, for God's sake don't be so heartless. Please have mercy on my old age. Do not attack so hard upon my soul. You take the entire house, just lend me a little space for me and my children, I will manage within that. You can do as you please after I die. Do not eat from the same plate, but stay in the same house at least; keep this little bond alive. I do not need the sitting room. Just think, if you go on to stay there what will our other relatives say? What will the city people say? Whatever might have happened, our family has had its good name intact. We brothers were referred to as the classical pair of Ram and Lakshman. The city used to quote our love and unity as an example to be followed. Please don't give anybody a chance to say that the moment one of the brothers died, there was such a quarrel that they could't even stay in the same house. Please accept this prayer of mine.'

Gyanshankar wasn't affected the least by these gentle words. This stance was a distorted sentiment in his eyes which also indicated mental fragility, though it could not be doubted as something artificial. He could believe that his uncle was passing through genuine stress at the moment. 'Old people have a soft heart in general. He has worshipped the family honour and personal dutifulness all his life. He is getting upset at the thought of the family getting defamed.' He said, 'I have complete respect for your wishes but please think as to how two families can manage in this old house? There is only one kitchen, that too, only in one portion. There are three bedrooms upstairs. There is a verandah, so to say, but wind and sunlight come in one part of it only. The bathroom is also just one. One cannot bear these troubles daily. We are not blessed with such long lives that we end up sacrificing a part of it only to problems. Your gentle soul will be saddened by these changes and I have full sympathy with you, but I don't approve of sacrificing my personal comfort and peace for the sake of mere sentiments. If you too think about the matter in an unbiased manner, you'll also agree with me.'

Prabhashankar – I do not deem these discomforts as anything before the problem of defamation that faces us. We can manage in the same way as we have been doing till now.

Gyanshankar – There's a world of difference between your life principles and mine. You worship your emotions and I follow my thoughts. You will bow before every trouble simply for fear of a bad word. I don't give a damn to the public opinion before my own freedom of thought! Our sole aim is that life should be spent in happiness. If the world calls this selfishness and makes fun of me or criticizes me, I will destroy its opinion below my feet. The entire basis of your value-system is self-destruction. You might be fasting in your own house, but in case a guest arrives you will entertain him by taking a loan. I would bid goodbye to such a guest from a distance. People often come to your place in winters without any warm bedding. You shiver yourself but manage good bedding for these guests. I just can't bear such a situation. No person, even if he's personally related to us has any right to put us in such an awkward position. I myself don't expect this from anybody. I actually think it improper for anyone to arrive at my house at an improper time, that too without informing me in advance, even if he's my own brother. At your place a few idle relatives have always been lying about; all your assets went down the drain but you never ignored their needs in the least. I would never let such seeds crop up that may end up destroying the plant of my life. Old traditions have now turned obsolete.

This is an age of life-struggle, and if we wish to survive we must adapt ourselves to new and manly principles.

Gyanshankar did not himself follow these conventions of the new age that he had mentioned. He just believed in them mentally. He had no power to erase the old traditions. He may not have been afraid of them at the level of criticism or mockery but could not ignore them openly. He might have thought of hospitality and family upkeep as unnecessary expenditure but his friends and relatives had no complaints against him in this regard. But usually, his dialogue used to take form of a debate and he used to support such principles in its wake which he could never dare to follow in reality. Lala Prabhashankar understood that he won't have any say in the matter now. He will end up doing what he has decided to do. One who doesn't care about the family tradition can't be expected to show any kind of generosity. He sadly said, 'Son, I am an old-fashioned man; I don't understand these modern thoughts of yours. We actually took our honour and name to be more valuable than our lives. We could have cut each others heads in the house but wouldn't have ever thought of getting separate. But if you are facing any loss, then do as you please; I have no objection to it. But I would still insist that you wait for a few days. If you have faced trouble for so long, please bear with us for some more days. Today Lallu's case will be decided. We are very scared; we can't even eat or drink anything; please let this fire cool down.'

Gyanshankar's nature had a high degree of self-importance. He had a natural hatred for lowliness. But his sense of self-love occasionally inspired him to resort to wicked means; especially where it concerned his honour and respect. He said in a sympathetic tone, 'Rest assured in this regard; Dayashankar will not just be released, he'll also be exonerated from the case. The other party has wooed the witnesses, as you know, due to which everyone doubted that Jwalasingh would succumb before pressure. How could I rest in such a situation? I went to him today morning, and God has shown me the right path. I don't wish to brag about it, but I made him write his decision right before me, read it myself and only then left the place. Initially he was trying to avoid me but I reprimanded him in such a way that he had no choice but to write his decision. I told him, 'Sir, it's because of me that you've earned your B. A. degree; just don't forget this. If you don't grant me this little favour, I'll think that you've forgotten my obligation.'

Prabhashankar looked at Gyanshankar with respectful eyes. He almost felt as if his brother was standing before him in person and had kept a protecting hand on his head. Had age not been an obstruction, he would have fallen on Gyanshankar's feet and washed them with his tears. He felt utterly ashamed that he had insulted such a duty-conscious, just, kind and godlike man! 'It was my sheer rudeness that I requested him to plead on Dayashankar's behalf. It was highly improper. The educated youth of today are quite aware of their duties and fulfill them according to their ways, that's why they find any external direction abhorrent.' He further said, 'Son, I cannot express how happy I am on hearing this news. You have saved my life as well as the honour of our family. I am grateful to you up to the tiniest pore of my body! I am now assured that my brother is protecting me even while sitting in heaven. I am extremely sorry that I said bitter things to you; may God punish me for this; please forgive my faults. Old men are often irritating in their behaviour; one must not take their chidings to heart. I had not seen your real self uptil now; I was unaware of your high ideals. I am sorry to admit that that I had started thinking of you as my enemy. But now I am experiencing your honesty, your love for your brother and generosity. I will forever regret this misconception of mine.'

Thus saying, Lala Prabhashankar's throat became full. The ice covering his heart melted away and started falling from his eyes in the form of teardrops. But Gyanshankar could not utter a single word of sympathy. He couldn't even darken the effect of his false act. In the face of Prabhashankar's simplicity, reverence and purity, his own self-centredness, wickedness and meanness started appearing most blackened and guilt-ridden. He fell in his own eyes and could not enjoy his false narrative. An educated soul can't remain weak beyond a point; Prabhashankar's pure and affectionate voice awakened it for a second. It opened its eyes and found that the mind was dragging it in the midst of thorns. It hardened its feet, stood firmly on the ground and decided that it'll not go any further.

Suddenly Syed Ijaad Hussain entered smilingly in the drawing room. Prabhashankar looked at him with hopeful eyes and asked, 'Please tell us if everything is fine?'

Ijaad – God is very benevolent. Please get sweets for a celebration. I swear upon God; I haven't taken a single drop of water since morning. God has kept my word; we've won the game; he was released without any charges, and with no other after-effects. The fact is that we achieved a greater success than we had ever expected. I had no hopes from Jwalasingh.

Prabhashankar – Gyanu, all this is the fruit of your inspired efforts. May God add many more years to your life.

Ijaad – Of course, of course, this success belongs to you alone. Whatever I have done, I've been able to do because of you. I think your morning visit proved much effective. Yesterday, I had drafted the verdict with these very hands. That was totally against us. Today what he read out was a different thing altogether; this is indeed a result of your meeting. What transpired amongst the two of you and the way you brought him to your side is known to me. Had you not acted with such clarity, this fellow would not have favoured us at all.

Prabhashankar – Son, had Bhaiya been alive today, he would have been immensely proud of your well-meaning efforts. You have done him proud today.

Gyanshankar saw clearly that Ijaad Hussain was trying to play games with his uncle and was trying to shut his mouth with his shrewd ways. But he could not afford to say anything right now. One thief gets compulsorily related to the other. He was getting angry with himself that he was feeling bound to cooperate with such a mean fellow in the enterprise of serving his vested interests. 'I have stepped into a muddy pit and am slipping downwards every single moment,' he thought.

7

As long as Lala Prabhashankar took care of the land and its management, he used to keep obstructing Ghaus Khan and his cruel means. Now Gyanshankar was its whole sole master and manager. His selfish interests had provided an opportunity to Khan Sahib to fulfill his own desires. At the end of the year, he extorted the land rent with extreme ruthlessness. He didn't leave a single penny pending. Whosoever didn't pay or could not pay; his land was auctioned, and about one and a half were earned where only one was pending. He uprooted the earlier tenants and leased their lands to others on an increased rate of rent. He started thinking of ways to increase rent on other independent tenants as well. He very well knew that an increase in rent was wholly dependent on the yielding power of land, and one needed only a bit of glib-talking to increase or decrease its power. There was deep unrest in the entire region. In order to calm the devil of rent increase, people got into various endeavours. From morning till evening, Khan Sahib had to attend to his court! He himself used to sit there against round pillows. Munshi Maujilal patwari sat on his right side and Sukhu Chaudhary sat on the left. The latter was the village headman, an eminent farmer and a man of powerful means. He had a lot of control over the tenant farmers, so Khan Sahib, in his clever ways, had made him a sort of personal minister. This trio of the patwari, Khan Sahib and Sukhu was the destiny-maker of the entire region.

Earlier, Khan Sahib used to spend his leisure time in pleasurable ways. Nowadays he had started reading the Quran. Earlier, no beggar was even allowed to stand near his door; now all visitors were treated with great respect. They were also given clothes occasionally. His worldly successes had engendered a desire to achieve transcendental victory as well.

Now Khan Sahib got to know that he had erred in understanding this region as rebellious. There was rarely a tenant who had not paid his respects at his door. There were about ten or twelve houses belonging to thakurs in this village. They used to pay the rent after much coaxing. But the news of rent-increase had managed to curb them also; Dapatsingh was their leader.

He used to come and greet Khan Sahib almost ten times in a day. Dukhran Bhagat used to come to the chaupal even before he went to the temple to worship lord Shiva. If there was really a rebel left in the area, he was Manohar and the only friend left to him was Qadir. As soon as he returned from the fields, he used to go to Qadir's house and mourn his bad days. When Sukhu Chaudhary saw these two men sitting together, he used to burn with envy. He wanted to find out what these people talked about. He thought that they must be talking ill of him. They used to keep quiet as soon as they saw him; hence Chaudhary's doubts were all the more strengthened. Khan Sahib had named Qadir as Satan and called Manohar as the black serpent. He was not really afraid of the serpent, because he could suppress him with a single blow, but he was really scared of the Satan because it was quite impossible to hurt him in any way. Qadir was a respectable man in the area. He was quite clever, generous and kind. Besides, he had a good knowledge of medicinal herbs. He was the sole doctor, or rather, medicine-man in the area. He was quite skilled in relieving people from diseases also. That is why people respected him a lot. Once, Lala Jatashankar was suffering from a painful eye disease. He took many medicines but to no avail; Qadir's herbs quelled the problem in just one week. His potion had once saved Khan Sahib from plague. Still, the latter was not grateful, but rather sceptical of his popularity. He kept thinking of ways and means to trap this devil.

Qadir, on the other hand, kept busy with his work, absolutely without any doubts or worry. He didn't fear for a moment that the village zamindar and karinda could possibly be his enemies, and the enmity could destroy him. If, by any godsent chance, Khan Sahib had fallen sick, he would have busied himself with his treatment and care at a single sign from him. His heart had no place for envy and enmity; nor was he bothered as to what false rumours were being spread about him. He could have ignited a revolt in the village; he could also have taken Khan Sahib and his men to task. There were many such rough youth in the village who were eager to do the job, but Qadir used to keep them under control. His aim was to safeguard the poor, not through encouraging anger and quarrels, but by camaraderie and truthfulness.

Manohar's situation was quite opposed to all this. The day he had returned after listening to Gyanshankar's rough words, negative feelings kept echoing in his heart and mind since then. He was like a poor, wounded bird, who was suffering the pain of his injuries! He could not forget those abusive words even for a second. He wanted to give a befitting answer to that assault. He knew that he would be destroyed by increasing enmity with such powerful men, but he was like that poor man at the moment, whose hut was on fire, and being unable to quell it, he put the other parts of the house on fire also, just in order to bring an end to his misery. When a sick person finds his disease uncurable, he tries to break the barriers between a beneficial and a harmful diet, to meet his approaching death. When Manohar used to pass through the chaupal, he started walking in a proud manner. While sitting on his charpoy, if he happened to see Khan Sahib or Girdhar Maharaj coming, he used to lie down at once, instead of getting up and greeting them. During the rainy season, when his mango trees bore fruit, he kept the entire produce with himself; did not pay the customary one-fourth part to the zamindar, as had been happening since ages, and when Girdhar Maharaj came to demand it, he rebuked him and sent him away. He wanted to prove that he was least bothered about their threats. Sometimes, people used to sing and enjoy till around ten in the night at his door, the sole purpose of which was to instigate Khan Sahib and Sukhu Chaudhary. The kind of behaviour which earlier made Balraj earn rebukes now became easily accessible to him. His mischievous friends were entertained a lot more now; they used to drink bhang, play all kinds of games, sing folk songs and play on the drums. Manohar participated in all these activities with the vigour of a young man. The site was a medium of communication for both the parties. Khan Sahib got to know every small thing through this group. His every single word was communicated here. These secret ways kept fanning the flames of animosity.

Khan Sahib said one day, ‘Nowadays, these people are enjoying themselves to the hilt; when they get the news of their land being usurped, they will come to their senses.’

Manohar replied, ‘This threat can be given to someone else; if anyone comes near the boundary of our fields, his children shall weep for his life.’

One particular evening, Manohar was sitting at his door, sorting out fodder for his oxen, and Balraj was polishing his stick with oil, when Thakur Dapatsingh came and sat on the mat, saying, ‘One hears that Jwalasingh is an old friend of our Babu Sahib. Our younger master’s (Prabhashankar’s) son is the thanedar; his case was held in his court. He got released today.’

Manohar – The allegation of bribery had been proved, I guess?

Dapatsingh – Yes, it had been proved. No one had any hopes of his release. But Babu Gyanshankar pleaded in such a way that the Deputy Sahib had to dismiss the case.

Manohar – The same Deputy is the authority in our area as well.

Dapat – Yes, that's the reason for worry. The matter of rent increase will also be taken up in his court and Gyan Babu will put optimum pressure on him.

Manohar – What shall we do then?

Dapat – I cannot say anything.

Manohar – Why can't such a law be made that rent increase matters shouldn't be held in the court of such judges. These people are zamindars themselves; hence they take the side of the zamindar. One hears there's a panchayat in the office of the Governor General. Does no one talk about these matters in that panchayat?

Dapat – There too, all are zamindars only; who will appeal on behalf of the peasants?

Manohar – We are determined not to pay a single penny extra.

Balraj kept his stick on his shoulders and said – Let me see who increases the rent; I shall break his head.

Manohar – Why do you interfere for nothing? We don't ask your opinion. Why don't you think that it's dusk time; the buffaloes have to be milked, the oxen have to be given water. You just keep ranting uselessly. (To Thakur) – This lad does not lift a finger in his house; he's here only to eat and loiter away.

Dapat – What is that to me; I have three such idlers to bear.

Manohar – I will neither pay a penny extra, nor will I leave my fields. My life shall go along with my fields and will take with it the lives of some more.

Balraj – If anyone looks at our fields with an evil eye, it won't be good for him.

Manohar – You are again poking your nose in the matter?

Balraj – Why shouldn't I; you are there for only a few years, whatever happens will have to be borne by us only. The zamindar is not an emperor that he can do endless tyranny and we keep bearing it silently. Nowadays even emperors do not have such powers; what to talk of zamindars! If no one listens to us in the court (showing his stick) this hasn't gone anywhere.

Dapat – If Khan Sahib gets to hear this; hell might break loose.

Balraj – You may fear the Khan Sahib; there's no one he can oppress here. Whether or not there's enough produce, the land rent goes on increasing; why's there such an injustice? The government must act with some sense of fairness; on what basis will the increase be sanctioned?

Dapat – Hasn't the rate of foodgrains been raised?

Balraj – If the rate has risen, so has the rate of wages, as also the rate of oxen, and even the price of wood and iron; who will give us these for free?

Meanwhile, Qadir Mian came carrying a bundle of grass on his head. When he listened to Balraj, he smiled and said, 'Even the price of bhang has risen. Charas is also costlier, katha-supari is also selling for double the price; why leave these out of the list!'

Manohar – Yes, Qadir Dada, you said what we couldn't.

Balraj – Haven't you people smoked or drunk bhang in your younger days? Or have you always survived on chanas for breakfast and roti-saag for dinner? And if you keep slaving for the zamindar what else could you have done? Had you not worked in your own fields, you would have laboured elsewhere. Nowadays, labourers are in demand in the sites; they get a rupee daily to eat, and a pucca house to live. Then why should we bear the suppression of the zamindars; why should we keep craving for a stomachful of food?

Qadir – Why, Manohar; don't you give him enough to eat?

Balraj – Is it proper that only one person gets to eat and the rest of the family have to fast? Except for Sukhu Chaudhary there's no house in the village where food is cooked twice a day. Some get to eat once in a day; others just make do with a bit of sattu. There isn't enough to eat a second time.

Qadir – Bhai, what Balraj says is quite true. There's nothing left in farming, one can't even recover the cost of labour. For instance, in my house, we are about ten people; even if we had earned around five rupees per person, it would have come to six hundred in a year. We could have saved nearly fifty rupees even after fulfilling all expenses. But we keep slogging it out in agriculture day and night, yet no one gets enough to eat.

Dapat – The only consolation is that our honour is still intact; we are not fit to do labour for others. Somehow we are able to manage. Or else, in Balraj's age, we never used to visit the fields. God knows what took away the prosperity of the earth. Whereas earlier, there used to be twenty quintals of yield per bigha, now it doesn't go any further than four or five.

Manohar – If the government knew this, it must have done something for the farmers.

Qadir – Who says it doesn't? They get to know every tiny bit of the news.

Dapat – (laughing) Tell Balraj to go and appeal on our behalf in the government office.

Balraj – You people mock what I say, as if the farmer is just a nobody. He is just born to slave for the zamindar all his life, but in the newspaper that I get, it's written that in Russia the farmers are rulers themselves; they do as they please. There's another country, Balgari (Bulgaria) near it. Just recently, the farmers have dethroned the king and now it is ruled by a panchayat of farmers and labourers.

Qadir – (With enthusiasm) Then Thakur! Let's go and settle down there; we won't be forced to pay such rents there.

Dapat – Their farmers must be very wise that they can handle the matters of ruling.

Qadir – I cannot believe this.

Manohar – Our newspaper does not report false matters.

Balraj – If they tell lies, they will be punished.

Manohar – When farmers in that country can handle the matters of governance, can't we even plead our grievances before the Lord Governor?

Qadir – You don't have the guts to talk to the tehsildar, who shall talk to the Laat Sahib?

Balraj – You can keep quiet if you wish; if I get to talk to the Lord Governor, I will tell him the entire story.

Qadir – Well, now when the officers come for a visit, we shall make you stand before them.

Thus saying Qadir took the road to his house. Balraj too, kept his stick on his shoulders and followed him. When both had crossed some distance Balraj said, 'Dada, if you allow me (rolling up his sleeves); I can teach Khan Sahib a lesson.'

Qadir got baffled and said – Do you wish to get the whole village arrested? Do not do that even by mistake.

Balraj – Everything is set; only an order from your side is needed.

Qadir – (Touching his ears) No, I won't advise you to jump into flames. When God wills he will leave this place himself.

Balraj – That means you won't interfere in the matter?

Qadir – Do you people really wish to do all that beating about? If you don't listen to us I shall go and inform the police. I can't bear to see you putting the village on fire, and won't bear that silently.

Balraj – So your real advice is that we should keep bearing this injustice day in and day out!

Qadir – When God listens to us, he'll surely give us a solution, all by itself.

8

After sunset, a particular type of creatures, who are neither animals nor birds, get out in search of livelihood, and cover the expanse of the sky with their long queues. In the same way, with the onset of the month of Kartik, another breed of creatures swarm the countryside and light it up with their tents and belongings. In the beginning of the monsoon, a royal breed of insects start emerging and by its end, another type of parasites come about. The moment they start rising, the villages are shaken by an earthquake of sorts and people start hiding themselves for fear of their lives.

It is doubtless that these official tours occur due to generous objectives. Their aim is to know about people's actual situation, reach the door of the justice-seeker, listen to the woes of the public, look into their requirements, estimate the nature of their troubles, and be acquainted with their thoughts. If such aims had actually been fulfilled, these tours would have been more fruitful than the spring season and people would have welcomed them with various musical instruments. But the way in which rays of light get deflected in water, in the same way positive aims too usually get corrupted after getting in touch with human weaknesses. Truth and justice get trampled below the feet; greed and selfishness often prove victorious! The officers and their juniors keep counting the days for the arrival of this blissful period like a maiden separated from her love. No one bothers about them in cities; and even if someone does, it's to little avail! There they have to spend on everything from their own pocket but in the villages, their hand rests more on the stick or on a poor peasant's neck than in their pockets. The kind of ghee, vegetables, meat or fish which are scarce in the cities; which one can't even crave in one's dreams are available in plenty just by the virtue of muscle power or power of the tongue. They eat whatever they can, and whatever they can't they send home. Truckloads full of ghee-pots, milk cans, fuel, wood, fodder and hay start arriving in the cities. Their families are full of joy; they start praising their fate as their days of woe are gone and ones of bliss have arrived. They are thus nurtured after the rainy season is over, for in these dry days lies their river of plenty. But for the villagers, these days are full of trouble; they pray for their skins, get beaten up and do all kinds of forced labour; the cruel assaults of slavery deteriorates the element of their souls as well.

It was the month of December, and evening had fallen. There was a fire burning at Qadir Khan's door. Many people were sitting around it and chatting. Qadir derided the tobacco sold in the market and Dukhran Bhagat seconded him. After that, Dapatsingh started analyzing the pros and cons of stone quarries versus mills using iron; it was iron that was declared victorious over stone in the end.

Dukhran said, 'Nowadays, during the night, wolves and deer cause great noise in the pea-fields; I can't get up due to cold.'

Qadir – It will be really cold this time. Cold winds blow even during the day. I don't even have a blanket; I just keep lying wrapped up in a double sheet. Had it not been for hay, I would have frozen in the night. Dapat – Who has a proper blanket here? I just have an old and tattered sheet. There isn't enough wood too, so that one might warm oneself by a fire.

Manohar – You got a tamarind tree cut during your daughter's wedding. Have you burnt it all?

Dapat – No, a lot was left, but was sent to Deputy Jwalasingh's party yesterday. I requested Khan Sahib not to take it, but who listens? He showed the wood stock to his peons. They took it all in no time.

Manohar – Didn't you say anything to the peons?

Dapat – What could I have said; would I have risked my life upon a few quintals of wood? I would have been abused, got arrested and beaten up, and you wouldn't have even got near me. My two boys and Jhapat had got agitated, but I rebuked them. One cannot fight a lonely fight.

Qadir – This is not an official tour; it is actually our death warrant. I had kept a male goat to be sacrificed on Bakrid; it was taken away in the official party yesterday. Rabbi butcher had offered five rupees for him but I hadn't agreed. It would have fetched nothing less than seven rupees now.

Manohar – These people are into all sorts of corruption. Apparently, they come to manage our affairs and do justice; in reality they end up slicing our throats. It would have been far better if these tours were banned. At best, the people fighting the cases would have been forced to go to court, but we would have been saved from this traumatic experience.

Qadir – Actually the officers aren't to be blamed. Their subordinates who camp around cause this corruption. They end up giving a bad name to the former as well.

Manohar – Dada, what do you say? All this is a joint conspiracy. If the officer doesn't approve, no subordinate can dare to usurp someone else's belongings. It all happens with official approval and why not? Anything that comes for free is always welcome.

Dapat – That's perfectly true. The more a person gets; the more he gets hungry for.

Dukhran – God sees this gross injustice, yet makes no effort to resolve it. Let's see what befalls Bisesar Sah this time.

Dapat – Last year, he was robbed of about three hundred rupees. The same shall happen this year too. If it was mere ration, the loss wouldn't be too much, but they want cardamoms, betelnuts, dry fruits and what not - all at the price of peanuts. They pretend to be so fond of eating good stuff, but forget to keep these things while on tour.

Manohar – The same stuff costs a pocketful in the cities; here they may or may not pay.

Qadir – Yesterday, a peon from the touring party was asking for sago at Bisesar's shop, he was pleading badly that there's none at the shop, but the peon wasn't ready to listen; he was saying that he should be supplied with it at all costs. He was abusing and threatening Bisesar with his stick. By chance, Balraj came there. When he showed his rough side, the peon cooled down and went away annoyed.

Dukhran – It would have been better if Bisesar had got beaten up. He troubles the entire village; this is his apt punishment.

Dapat – And who is troubled by you or me?

Manohar said in a worried tone, 'Balraj has started confronting government officers. I have forbidden him to do that so many times but he refuses to listen.'

Qadir – This age is like that only.

Such talk was going on in their midst when a traveller came and stood near the fire. Behind him, an old woman came walking on her stick and sat at a distance from the fire; her head bent low.

Qadir asked – Tell us brother, where do you come from?

The traveller said – My house is across the Dewri; I was going with my old mother to the hospital. But when I reached the Deputy Sahib's party which is camping in the garden near the roads, the peons stopped my cart and threw away our clothes from the cart to load it with wood. I pleaded that my old mother is sick; I have been travelling since night; if I don't reach the hospital God knows what will become of her tomorrow. I kept pleading before them but they loaded my cart forcibly. They then told me to drive the cart. Now I am going to the court. I left my oxen and the cart in their care. When I get the wood unloaded I shall go to the hospital. If you people can do something for me please give a cot for my mother and a place for her to lie down. Please oblige me; I am in great trouble.

Dukhran – This is serious injustice. These men are not humans but devils who have no thought of kindness or duty.

Dapat – Your oxen seem so tired due to the day-long travel; God knows what more distance you will have to cover and when you will come back. Till then, will the old woman keep lying all alone? God knows what might befall her. We may be more in number, but are unknown to her; she can't do without a person of her own family.

Manohar – I really wish to go to Deputy Sahib this very instant and state the facts so bluntly that he comes to his senses. What kind of an officer is he? Instead of doing justice, he is torturing the poor in every way. A cot is very much available, and there's no dearth of space too, but how shall your mother fend alone?

Traveller – What can I say? Whatever is written in her fate will happen.

Manohar – If someone else takes and drives this cart of yours, what's the harm?

Traveller – If this can be arranged it'll be very nice. Is anyone available?

Manohar – Lots of men; any of them will go.

Qadir – Your ploughman is free; send him.

Manohar – I don't know if he can handle the oxen, I shall go myself.

Qadir – I find it hard to trust you. If you get into a quarrel it'll be a greater mess. Dukhran Bhagat, if you can go it would be better.

Dukhran made a face and said, 'You know me well, I don't go anywhere at night. This is the time to remember God.'

Qadir – I would have gone, but I have a feeling that the credit for treating this old woman shall go to me. Who knows if Allah has willed it such? I will take her home. I shall do whatever I can. I'll tell Hasnu to take the cart. I've got to feed my oxen; send Balraj for a while.

The old woman's cot was laid in Qadir's verandah. Qadir's son Hasnu went to the camp to take the card. Meanwhile, Sukhu Chaudhary and Ghaus

Khan were seen coming on the spot with two peons. Balraj also came from the other side and stood there.

Ghaus Khan said, 'You people are sitting here and chatting; do you have any news of the camp? See, these peons have come for milk; arrange for the same.'

Qadir – How much milk do you need?

A Peon – At least ten seers.

Qadir – Ten! So much milk won't be available in the entire village. Only a few men have buffaloes and they too are not the milch ones. I don't get even a seer, twice a day.

Peon – Get the buffaloes to us; our man shall milk them. We can get milk even from a stone. We can get thieves to unravel things hidden in their stomach; you are talking of buffaloes. Our stick is so magical; it can make a deserted place full of life. Go and get the buffaloes here.

Ghaus Khan – Why do you get into these arguments? Milk will be arranged for. Sukhu has promised about two seers; Manohar and Dapatsingh can also give two seers each. That's it.

Qadir – I cannot ensure two or four seers. These two buffaloes are here. Whatever milk they are able to give can be taken.

Dukhuran – My two buffaloes are pregnant. At best, they can yield half a seer. They just get hay to eat and that too half a stomach. There are no good pastures for them to graze; where shall milk come from?

Dapatsingh – You can take from me half of what Sukhu Chaudhary is giving. Please don't look at my ability or status.

Ghaus Khan – You people have a most uncivilized habit of arguing in every matter. If one asks politely, you won't even give half but if one gets stern, you will be ready to pay the full amount. I've told you to give two seers. This much you'll have to give.

Dapat – You are the masters of everything; you can take my buffaloes away but two seers of milk are not possible for me.

Ghaus Khan – Manohar, you do have milch buffaloes?

Manohar had not replied as yet when Balraj spoke up, 'My buffaloes give a lot of milk, but will not give even a little if milked forcefully.'

Manohar – Why don't you stay quiet? Who is asking you? We shall give whatever we can; why do you bother?

The peon looked at Balraj with an anger incited by insult and said, 'Mahto, you haven't been caught in our trap till now. Once that happens, you will know the real tenacity of the situation. You will turn speechless.'

Second peon — It seems as if the heat has gone to his head, that's why he's so puffed up. Take him to the camp, he'll cool down there.

Balraj felt attacked and said, 'Mian, our anger is not like that of the peons who keep hankering after a few rupees; go and lick your Sahib Bahadur's feet, which is your real job; don't bother about our anger or you will get a taste of our hands. You are paying for the sins of your previous birth, and you still haven't learnt a lesson?'

Balraj uttered these words with such serious pride that both the peons felt a little embarrassed. It was very hard to return this gross insult. It was almost a challenge to pull out one's words from the limits of voice and place it in the arena of action. The assault of sarcasm is the final limit in a verbal fight. It is returned not via mouth but via hands. But seeing Balraj's broad chest and strong pair of arms, the peons couldn't muster enough courage to enter into a duel with him. One of them told Ghaus Khan, 'Khan Sahib, do you see this lad; how he advances without fear? Please tell him not to meddle with us. Or else he might get into trouble and rot up behind the bars for six months. We treat you people with respect, or we would have taught him a lesson for exhibiting such pride.'

Ghaus Khan – Do you listen to your son's rattle, Manohar? Just think, if Deputy Sahib gets to know this what will become of you? No one will offer even a tiny leaf to cover you.

Manohar looked at Khan Shaib with a poor expression and said, 'Khan Sahib, I have tried to made him understand, but to no avail. God knows what he wants to do? (To Balraj) - Will you go from here or not?'

Balraj - Why should I; I am not afraid of anyone. These people are threatening me of filing a complaint against me to the Deputy Sahib; I will go there myself. He must never have given such a tyrannous order as to put a village on fire. And even if we suppose he had, these people ought to think that the poor farmers are their own brethren, they must not torture them unnecessarily. But they have been so blinded by the greed for money and the intoxication of official power that they can't see anything. What shall become of that old woman; God knows whether she'll live or die. The real salary of these men is just five rupees; their real job is to carry luggage, wipe the tables, and follow the Sahib like retainers, but they behave like millionaires.

Manohar – Will you keep quiet or not?

A Peon – No, let him abuse us a lot, so that his heart cools down. He will get a taste of his actions tomorrow. Khan Sahib, you have listened to all this, so you'll have to be a witness. We have tolerated you people enough. Come; can you arrange for the milk, or should we leave?

Ghaus Khan – No, please; take your milk, and more than ten seers. These people will have to provide it. I am sorry; we had to cut a sorry figure before you due to this chap. The whole scenario in this village is quite disturbed. I understand the situation very well. These people who are sitting like scared cats have incited this boy or else he wouldn't have dared to rant so much. A calf jumps on the strength of its anchor. Well, if I am true to my name I shall see everyone.

This rebuke had its expected effect. Everyone was terrified. The roughness that was reflecting on everybody's faces suddenly disappeared. Manohar was so baffled as if he had been beaten up badly. This tiff brought everyone to their senses.

Qadir Khan said – Manohar, go send whatever milk you have.

Ghaus Khan – We don't need any milk from Manohar.

Balraj – Who's giving you, by the way?

Manohar felt embarrassed. He got up and said, 'Okay, you alone can speak now; do whatever you please. I am going. Take care of your house; I will not be able to cope up with you. You can either keep the house, or burn it if you please.'

After saying this, he left the place full of anger. Balraj too, slowly started walking towards the wrestling ring. There was no one there at this time. Exercising equipment was kept in a corner of the ring. A stone nail was dug in the ground, and a belt was hanging from the mango branch. Balraj took off his clothes and got into the ring, wearing a loincloth but he didn't feel like exercising. The peon's taunts were hurting him like an open wound. Though he had answered the peons fearlessly he didn't have any doubt that the men of the village, and even his own father had found his talk very rude. 'Everyone kept sitting without a murmur. It almost seemed as if they had no tongues in their mouths. That's why they have been brought to such a poor state. Had they shown courage, they wouldn't have been tortured like this. What's more, Dada also scolded just me. God knows why so much fear has entered their minds. Earlier, they were not so timid. Perhaps they are now worried about me. But if I find an opportunity I will tell him clearly not to worry on my behalf. God has given me hands and feet. I can work hard and earn enough to feed some more. If you are so fond or your fields that you are willing to tolerate tyranny and insults for their sake; do it, but I don't care for such land. I shall eat the bread earned by my sweat and walk with pride. If someone tries to threaten me, I will threaten him back. This old chap Ghaus Khan was looking at me with bloodshot eyes; I guess his death is going to be upon me. He has attacked me twice. Let me see what he does now. He's going to make me a victim of his anger. No worries, I shall see what comes next. Both the peons must be happily thinking that they have been able to control the entire village; everyone's ready to serve them. The villagers also must have flattered them. I don't care. What can they do to me? But I must report everything to the Deputy Sahib tomorrow morning. He is a learned man. He will certainly have mercy on the poor. If he forbids these men to stop our carts it'll be just perfect. He would never approve of such tyranny.'

'These peons engage in all this behind his back. But what if he turns me out of his court without listening to me? These great men are generally very proud. There's no harm if I stand on the road and guard against these men stopping the carts. Either I'll break their heads or end up dying myself. One can't do without the language of force now. Dada seems to be calling me.'

Balraj reached home behind his father. They didn't talk on the way. Bilasi saw Balraj and said, 'Where were you? Your Dada has been looking for you since long. Come, food is ready.'

Balraj – I had gone to the ring.

Bilasi – Stop going there.

Balraj – Why?

Bilasi – Why, can't you see; no one can bear to see you. The people who appear as your well-wishers are hunting for your life. They will push you inside a fire and stand outside to watch the result. Today itself, didn't they incite you to quarrel with the government servants and went to hide themselves?

Balraj didn't say anything in reply to this sermon. He went and sat on his stool in the kitchen. On one side, Manohar was sitting and on the other, at a distance, sat his ploughman Rangi chamar. Bilasi served them thick chapatis made of oats, green curry and arhar dal. Then she kept a brass bowl full of milk near Balraj.

Balraj – Isn't there more milk in the house?

Bilasi – Not at all; didn't we have to pay it as begaar to the official party?

Balraj – Fine, keep this bowl near Rangi.

Bilasi – You can have it; if Rangi doesn't take milk for one day, he won't thin down.

Balraj was already fuming with anger at the mention of 'begaar'. He picked up the bowl and threw it forcefully towards the verandah. The bowl hit the tulsi pot and broke into pieces. Bilasi ran to pick the bowl and said regretfully, 'What's wrong with you? Ram! Ram! What a beautiful bowl you've destroyed. Have you gone mad?'

Balraj – Yes indeed, I have gone mad.

Bilasi – Why did you throw away the bowl?

Balraj – Only because the person who works harder than us should get to eat more. I have told you repeatedly that whatever is cooked in the kitchen should be brought before everybody. Whether it's good or bad, it must be shared by everyone; but why do you always seem to forget it? Now you'll remember. Rangi is not a forced employee, he's a family member. He may not say it openly, but must be thinking in his mind that he does the most tiring work of all and others get to eat better meals for nothing. It's a curse to crave after such milk or ghee.

Rangi said – Bhaiya, I have milk daily; doesn't matter if I don't have it for a day. You just became angry for nothing.

After this, the three men started eating quietly. After their dinner, Balraj and Rangi went to the fields to guard their crops of sugarcane. There Balraj took charas and smoked heavily. When both lied down on a bed of sugarcane peels, taking their blankets, Rangi asked, 'Why bhaiya, did you get into a duel with the peons of the official camp?'

Balraj – Yes, there was a tiff. Had Dada not stopped me I would have beaten up both of them.

Rangi – That's why they were going around talking ill of you. I was watering the fields then. When they saw me they became quiet. I just heard, 'If this chap makes any noise tomorrow while the carts are being stopped, arrest him on the basis of theft. If he gets some fifty sticks on his back, he will lose all his pride.'

Balraj – Oh! These men are plotting such schemes against me! Good that you warned me; I'll go to the Deputy Sahib tomorrow morning.

Rangi – What shall you do there, brother? He is not a good man. He gives very severe punishments. He doesn't know how to spare anyone. Why do you want to interfere? Whosoever gets his carts stopped will deal with him himself.

Balraj – Well, if these people were so powerful then their carts wouldn't have been stopped in the first place. Even a dog can trouble a simple man. These peons are also human beings.

Rangi – Then why do you get into other people's affairs? Your father was so sad today and mother kept weeping.

Balraj – God knows why Rangi, ever since I've started understanding the ways of the world a bit, I cannot bear to see injustice. When I see a powerful man oppressing a poor soul my whole being starts burning. I just want to show him his true face, whether I'm able to survive or not. I get taken up by that madness. I know very well that a single man can't win the battle alone; but my will goes out of my control.

Thus chatting they dozed off to sleep. In the morning Balraj went home, did some exercise, had milk, wore a loose kurta with a turban, and set off for the Deputy Sahib's camp. Manohar had not been talking to him till now, but couldn't help asking, 'Where are you going?'

Balraj – I am going to see the Deputy Sahib.

Manohar – What has come over you? Why don't you mind your own business?

Balraj – I just want to see the temper of educated people.

Manohar – You will end up hurting yourself, that's all.

Balraj – We get hurt even by the peons; I don't mind. We shall see the true colours of this breed of men.

Manohar looked at him with a hopeless stare and started for the fields, taking his spade with him. Balraj understood that his father had taken him to be a senseless bull, but he was happy with his own self. Manohar had thought that instead of arguments, a passive response will bring him back to his senses, but he was proved wrong. As soon as he left the house, Balraj too kept his stick on his shoulders and left for the camp. This was his first occasion of seeing an authority. Many thoughts were teeming in his mind. 'God knows whether he will see me or not; he might get angry on my words; he might turn me out as the peons must have complained against me. He is also a friend of Babu Gyanshankar. He too must have talked a lot against us. He might get utterly upset on seeing my face. Doesn't matter, it'll be a new experience. These educated men are those who keep talking about our emancipation in meetings and in Lord Governor's court, and pretend to be our leaders. Let me see how true they are to their own words.'

When Balraj reached the camp, he found camp fires burning at many places; there was water getting heated and tea being made. On one side, the butcher was chopping pieces of goat for meat; on the other side, Bisesar Sah was weighing rations. On all sides, pots and pans were lying in broken pieces. Under the shade of a tree, many men whose cases were to be heard were squatting all huddled up. Balraj passed through the trees and reached Jwalasingh's tent. He was afraid lest the peons got to see him. He stood there thinking of ways to approach the Deputy Sahib. He was taken up by the aura surrounding his authority. His feet were trembling at the thought of entering the camp. Suddenly he saw Ghaus Khan and Sukhu Chaudhary warming themselves near a fire under a tree. Now he couldn't remain standing behind the tent. He couldn't bear to be pushed rudely or be rebuked in front of these men. With a brave resolve, he went in front of the tent and after paying respects to Jwalasingh, stood quietly on a side.

Babu Jwalasingh was a justice-loving and a kind fellow, but in his tours of the past few months, he had experienced that he could not do his duty successfully without being harsh. Politeness and good manners may be appreciable in personal life, but in the work of administration these good qualities became bad ones; people start taking undue advantage of these and make them a means to fulfill their vested interests. Thus there occurs a mutual opposition between justice and gentility. In the matters of rationing and labour too, the flattering ways of his subordinate officers had emerged victorious over his principles of justice and unknowingly, he had been appropriated by the ways of these unruly officers. He was already proud of his wisdom. Now it had assumed a sense of superiority complex. Whatever he said or did; he didn't want to listen to a single word against it. Nobody could influence his opinion now. He was a stern man and didn't waver a bit from the path of justice. He had a natural feeling that no one should have any issues with him. He had complete faith in his sense of dutifulness and a confidence bred by personal pride made him unkind towards plaintiffs. When he saw Balraj, he asked, 'Who are you? Why are you standing here?'

Balraj bent down and greeted him. His rudeness had vanished. Feeling afraid, he said, 'I want to say something to huzoor. I am a resident of this very village Lakhanpur.'

Jwalasingh – What do you have to say?

Balraj – Nothing, I just wanted to ask as to how many carts will be needed by you today?

Jwalasingh – Are you the supervisor of carts?

Balraj – No sir, these peons go to the road and stop the travelling carts and trouble the passengers. I want that I should get the required number of carts for Your Lordship from the nearby villages. Whatever is the government rent for them can be paid, so that the travellers may not be stopped.

Jwalasingh had employed camels to carry his own luggage but he knew that his subordinates and peons did need carts to carry their belongings. They did not get any expenses paid by the government. If they did not stop the carts, they wouldn't be able to manage their luggage. This practice may put the common man in trouble, but was quite pardonable. It his opinion, it wasn't an intolerable offence. Possibly, had the petition been made by some respectable man, he would have thought to resolve it, but the fact that an unpolished, foolish rustic should dare to complain to him, and try to teach him a thing or two about justice, was intolerable for his self-pride. Annoyingly, he said – 'Go and ask the supervisor.'

Balraj – Sir, you can call him and ask; he won't tell me anything.

Jwalasingh – I don't have time for such headaches.

Balraj's face broke into frowns on hearing this. His entire reverence for the dutifulness and goodness of the educated sections collapsed in a second. Instead of these positive values, he saw a mountain full of pride fed by authority and licentiousness. He didn't know how to bow before pride. He decided that a man who was so haughty and who looked down upon him, was not worthy of his respect. What was the difference between him and Ghaus Khan or those ordinary peons? Where was the flame of knowledge and justice? He said in a clear voice – 'Our respected sir deems it a headache and there, it's a question of life and death for us. Huzoor is sitting here on the seat of justice, and there, the peons are robbing the poor public. I could gather the courage to complain to you, due to the reason that I thought you'll protect the poor. I now got to know that there's no one to protect unfortunate men like us except the almighty.'

Thus saying he left the place without paying any respects. He was almost intoxicated with his depressed feelings. He had expressed himself in a tone of disrespect, but his voice had been full of self-respect and fellow-feeling. Jwalasingh's generosity had not died a complete death as yet. Anger was suddenly replaced by compassion in his mind. Till now, his company had been full of selfish and sychophantic men. He had not met any clear-voiced man till date. The way in which one gets tired of eating sweetmeats and craves for something bitter; in the same way, Jwalasingh found these bitter words very attractive. They were able to tear the curtain of official pride that had hitherto covered his eyes. He initially felt like calling Balraj back and talking to him at length, but was stopped by the limitations of his position. He kept thinking about the matter for quite some time. His last words had given a jolt to his soul, and it had awakened as a result. He decided upon a resolve in his mind and called the ahlmad. Syed Ijad Hussain had seen Balraj leaving. He already knew about yesterday's proceedings. He could sense that the lad must have come to appeal to the Deputy Sahib. At first, he suspected whether the officer had been taken in by his talk. But when he found that Deputy Sahib had actually scolded him, he was consoled. He started reprimanding Balraj himself. He was actually a servant of his officers' will and determined his sense of duty according to their wishes.

Balraj was so depressed at the moment that he initially kept listening to Ijaad Hussain's harsh words quietly. In the end, he asked in a serious tone, 'Do you want that we should simply tolerate injustice without pleading against it?'

Ijaad Hussain – You have had a taste of your appeal. Now if action is taken against you, let's see where it goes. It's no joke to argue with government officials. Deputy Sahib has complete information about your rebellious ways. Babu Gyanshankar has described the entire rotten state of affairs to him. He was just looking for an opportunity. By today evening probably the entire village will be under arrest. Ghaus Khan is not that dangerous, which is why you have become so bold. Now you will have to pay the price. You will receive so many canes that nothing will be left of you.

Balraj – Are these such unlawful times that the officers can punish anyone without any fault?

Ijaad Hussain – Yes indeed, the times are very anarchic. The government officers have always received free service and will keep getting it in future. If you don't provide carts, will they carry their luggage on their heads? Whatever things we require shall be taken from you only; whether you give them happily or sadly. Got it …!

Just then, a peon came and said, 'Please come, Sir is calling you.' Ijaad Hussain was chewing paan. He immediately gargled his mouth, tied his turban, and went in and greeted Jwalasingh.

Jwalasingh said, 'Mir Sahib, please instruct the peons that from now onwards, they must not stop the carts for the purposes of the camp. You people can keep your luggage on my carts. You might have to face some inconvenience in this, but it is thoroughly improper that others should be tortured for one's own convenience.'

Ijaad Hussain – Huzoor is absolutely right. Form today itself, the stopping of carts will be strictly forbidden. Indeed, it is very cruel.

Jwalasingh – Tell the peons that they can sleep in the encampment of my area. They must not extort hay for the purpose. The poor farmers cut this hay to feed their animals, which is why they resent giving it for our use.

Ijaad Hussain – Huzoor's views on the matter are absolutely correct. The officers should be kind and generous to the poor. People are already troubled with the cruelties of the zamindaar; on top of it, this forced service to the officers makes their lives unbearable.

Jwalasingh was still tortured by Gyanshankar's taunts in heart of hearts. If by tolerating a little trouble one could get a chance to answer him back, it would be very nice. Jwalasingh couldn't control this tide of enmity. He decided to go to the village and see its condition with his own eyes.

It was eight o' clock in the morning, but a fog was still spread all around. Lakhanpur's farmers were almost enjoying a holiday today. At many places people were warming themselves near a fire and talking about yesterday's incident. They were also commenting on Balraj's impudence. Just then, Jwalasingh arrived in the village with his peons and subordinates. Ghaus Khan and his two peons were following him from behind. As soon as they were seen, the womenfolk left their soiled utensils and ran to their houses. The children and the old men also hid themselves. Someone started cleaning the garbage at his door; someone else started picking the cot lying on the way. Jwalasingh roamed across the village, and came to Sukhu Chaudhary's oil mill. Sukhu ran to get a charpoy. Ghaus Khan sent a man to the chaupal to fetch a chair. People came and surrounded Jwalasingh on all sides. They all seemed too worried with a fear of impending trouble.

Jwalasingh – How's your yield this year?

Sukhu Chaudhary had assumed the role of a leader for the villagers. He used to come to the forefront on such occasions. But he was still engaged in getting the charpoy out of his house, which being large, could not be taken out easily from the small door. Therefore, Qadir Khan had to assume the position of the villagers' representative. He politely replied, 'Huzoor, it's been good uptil now; the rest is in God's hands.'

Jwalasingh – I have seen very few wells for irrigation out here; doesn't the zamindar arrange for those?

Qadir – Our zamindar cares for us a lot; may God bless him. We ourselves do not bother much out of laziness.

Jwalasingh – Munshi Ghaus Khan complains a lot about your rebellious ways. Babu Gyanshankar is also not happy with you; what's all this? You people don't pay the land rent on time, and when the officers ask you to pay, you make a hue and cry about it. Do you know that the zamindar can actually force you to pay double the amount if he so wants?

Gajadhar ahir said in a low voice, 'Who's saying that he leaves the unpaid rent?'

Jwalasingh – What are you saying? Come out in the open and say it.

Qadir – Nothing huzoor, he's just saying that we cannot dare to raise our heads against our master. We are his suppliants, we feed on his charity, we stay on his land; if we revolt against him, we won't be able to face God with a clean face. As for our pending tax; we try to pay every penny till the end of the year by all means. Yes, if things go beyond our control, a part of it does remain pending.

Jwalasingh asked many such questions, but his motive could not be fulfilled. No one uttered a single word against Ghaus Khan or Babu Gyanshankar. He admitted a defeat and left for his camp.

9

After proving himself as an excellent upholder of family goodwill, Gyanshankar was now impeded by nothing in the way of the division of the house. Lala Prabhashankar decided to follow his nephew's will in the matter. He vacated the drawing room for him, the entire village of Lakhanpur went to his share, and he also divided the rest of the possessions according to his desire. He feared an opposition in the matter from his wife, but the recent obligation had not just quitened her up, but also wiped out all the ill-feelings from her heart. Prabhashankar now praised Gyanshankar openly in front of his wife, servants, friends and relatives and often expressed his affection in the form of a gift. He gifted the latter with a shawl, a silver plate, many beautiful pictures, a very expensive woollen carpet and many such things. He was very fond of tasty dishes. He used to make various kinds of sauces, sweets and pickles very often. He was well versed in this art. He enjoyed eating good food himself, and felt happy feeding others.

He used to send a tasty dish daily for Gyanshankar. This went on to the extent that Gyanshankar became fed up of his generosity. His soul used to keep shaming him for his shrewd games. Such affectionate services from his uncle kept reminding him of his own meanness and he used to feel sorry about it. In the face of his uncle's simplicity and goodness, his own wickedness and corrupt nature appeared too atrocious to him.

Lakhanpur was the ultimate paradise of Gyanshankar's long-term ambitions. In the entire range of the family's assets, there was no such village which was as fertile or prosperous and had an easy access to the city; was near a pucca road, and had such a wonderful climate. There was plenty of land which could be ploughed, a kutcha but a beautiful house and the best part was that there was enough scope to increase the land rent. A little industriousness could double the profit. By getting a few kutcha wells dug, one could fulfill the legal requirements for increasing the rent. Hardly a week had passed after the house division that Gyanshankar called Ghaus

Khan, inspected the land affairs, drafted a proposal for rent increase and ordered a case to be filed against the tenants. Till now, there was no extra farming done on the land. He made arrangements for that as well. He wanted to keep his own ploughs and oxen, ploughmen, and do systematic farming. But Khan Sahib said, 'There's no need for all these efforts, you can very well order free labour to do the farming. It is well within the rights of the zamindar; why leave it?'

But in the midst of all this wonderful set-up, there was a bitter streak, which spoilt the pleasure totally. This was non-cooperation on part of Vidyavati. She didn't like her husband's selfish attitude at all. Sometimes this opposition took the form of debate and quarrels.

It was the month of Phagun. Lala Prabhashankar used to celebrate Holi with great pomp and show. He got new clothes for himself and and his family members, and also for Gyanshankar's family. He was used to buying new clothes for the entire house since past fifty years. He wanted to keep up the tradition even after the division of the house. It was very painful for him to keep fostering the feelings of separation even on this occasion of joy. Vidya kept those clothes, but also arranged new sets for Prabhashankar's sons, daughters and daughter-in-law from her side. Gyanshankar got annoyed with the proposal and said, 'If you plan to do all this, why don't you return their clothes?'

Vidya – If you return the clothes, what will he think? The poor man keeps craving to meet you and you keep avoiding him. It's the money you're bothered about, isn't it? Don't give anything; I shall give everything from my side.

Gyan – When you start talking like rich people, I feel absolutely lost! He has not obliged us by sending these clothes. He has already eaten up the advance rent from our shops. It is his way to quieten me up and keep up his sense of greatness. Had he spent from his own pocket, he would have known where it bites.

Vidya – You sometimes try to wipe out other people's goodwill in a way that I feel sad at your meanness. He gave me a gift out of affection and you're deeming it as his shrewdness.

Gyan – Had I also received items of pleasure merely by sitting idle at home, I'd also be more generous than you. You have no idea of the difficulties I'm facing in providing for the upkeep of the house. We're managing with whatever we've got from Lakhanpur. If I'd not tightened my fist, I'd have incurred debts in thousands. I need a lot of money just to go to the court. I have the papers ready for tax-increase and auction, but have nothing in hand to file a case. On the other hand, the villagers are also upset. In his recent tour, Jwalasingh has pampered them so much that they're no more bothered about me. I am sick with these worries and you keep thinking of ways to bother me further.

Vidya – I never ask you for money!

Gyan – I don't differenciate between your money and mine. Well, if Rai Sahib leaves you an inheritance, then I might.

Vidya – I don't want a single penny from you!

Gyan – Agreed, but you don't get any money from you father also. You might be getting about fifty or hundred rupees in a year and you keep flaunting them with foolish pride. This is nothing but a hollow sense of satisfaction.

Vidya – Do you expect him to hand over all his possessions to you?

Gyan – Let him enjoy them himself first; what can he really give me? In my opinion, a man who spends millions on his own pleasures and does not bother a bit about his close relatives is no more than an animal. I won't shed a tear even if he happens to die.

Vidya – Your soul is so mean; I got to know this only today.

Gyan – Go and thank God that you happened to get married to me or no one would have cared for you. Your father may have been flaunting his millions for years, but no one really bothered about him.

Vidyawati could not bear this assault and her face turned red with anger. She got up at once to go from there when a maid brought a telegram and handed it to Gyanshankar. It was written -

"Son expired, come soon." — Kamlanand.

Gyanshankar threw the telegram on the floor and took a long breath saying – 'Oh God! How sad! What did you do?'

Vidya suddenly stopped. Gyanshankar said to Vidya, 'Vidya, we have been struck with tragedy; our…'

Vidya looked at him with fearful eyes and asked, 'Is everything alright at my house?'

Gyanshankar – Oh dear, how can I say that everyone is fine! That house is destroyed; its light is gone! Babu Ramanand is no more. Oh God!'

Vidya let out a scream. Terrified, she fell on the ground and started crying, beating her breast. Shraddha came running upon hearing this. The maids of the house gathered around her. When Prabhashankar's wife heard her wails, she too arrived with her daughter and daughter-in-law. The room was full of women. Mayashankar started shouting when he saw his mother crying. All the women present there had a look of pain and water of sympathy in their eyes. Some cursed the ways of God; others criticized the power of time. In our eyes, an unnatural death is the greatest injustice that God can do. Such a blow destroys our reverence and devotion and makes us an atheist. We have to tolerate the will of God. But our terror-stricken eyes cannot tolerate the tragic scenes that it entails. This kind of death is the sternest kind of divine assault on our hearts. It is a terrible violation of our entire concept of justice.

But greater still are the pulls of vested interests! This ruthless blow of fate appeared to Gyanshankar as pleasant as a shower of flowers. He did feel sad for a moment, but his heart was immediately swept with a rush of new aspirations. His life had lacked a goal uptil now. It was suddenly given a great ambition to strive for. He was assured of a way to acquire unlimited wealth. It was akin to a fertile land coming to its full fruition. Rai Kamlanand didn't have any other son. Of his two daughters, one was a widow and that too, childless. It was Vidya alone who had a child and thus Mayashankar was now the only heir of Rai Sahib. It is therefore not surprising that Gyanshankar saw this entire tragic set of events as a godly arrangement of his good fortune. He took Mayashankar in his arms, came downstairs to the drawing room and started thinking of ancient arrangements with regard to the question of inheritance. He wanted to affirm his hopes and dispel his doubts. He had studied law for some years and had a good collection of law books. He opened Manusmriti first, but wasn't satisfied. He looked into the suggestions of Mitakshara, but his doubts increased. Even Yagyavalakya hadn't explained anything satisfactorily. He felt the need for consulting a lawyer. He was so impatient about it that he immediately got ready to go out and do so. He told the servant, 'Take Maya, and go to the market for a stroll.' He had just got out of the room that he remembered he'd forgotten to send a reply to the telegram. He went inside again, wrote a message of condolence, and just then Lala Prabhashankar and Dayashankar arrived. Gyanshankar abhorred their arrival at this moment. Prabhashankar said, 'I just got to know about it. It was so shocking. Poor Rai Sahib had to bear this jolt in his old age. His house has been deprived of all joys.'

Gyanshankar – Strange are the ways of God!

Prabhashankar – It was not an age to go! He was just a boy. I saw him in your wedding; he was so attractive. I never saw a boy as popular as him.

Gyanshankar – This makes us lose faith in the justice of God.

Dayashankar – Your elder sister-in-law doesn't have any son; does she?

Gyanshankar said in a listless tone, 'No'.

Dayashankar – In that case, Maya will be the heir.

Gyanshankar said in a rebuking voice, 'How can you talk like this? Is this an occasion to discuss these things? This is not the time for such talk.'

Dayashankar also felt embarrassed. Gyanshankar felt impatient at the delay now. He took his bicycle, and leaving the two men in the verandah, set out for Dr. Irfan Ali's bungalow, who was a famous lawyer.

The barrister's bungalow was very well-decorated. It was evening time, and he was about to go for a walk. His car was ready but he was still surrounded by his clients. He was lying on an easychair in his office smoking a cigar and petting his little lapdog that was lying in his lap. The clients were sitting in the other room. They went to the doctor's cabin turnwise to narrate their woes. Gyanshankar kept sitting there till eight o' clock. His turn came and he started talking about his matter in the office. The clerk noted down everything. This cost him around five rupees. He was called the next day for Doctor Sahib's advice. The fee for his consultation was five hundred. If he still had some doubts after that, he would have to pay two hundred per hour for further advice.

Gyanshankar didn't know that the lawyer's time was so valuable. He started repenting about his decision to consult him. He paid the initial fees to the clerk and got out on the pretext of fetching the pending money from home. But on his way, it occurred to him that his consultation must be quite sound which was the reason it cost so much. 'Or else why would so many men clamour for it? Probably, that's the reason why he was called the next day, so that advice could be given after proper scrutiny of the case. Had he wanted to give a temporary advice, he could have finished the matter rightaway. This is the real, principled, British way of doing things; it costs you a lot, but you get true worth for your money. He would have to see many precedents, analyze Hindu texts, only then the true essence will be found; I must arrange for the money. I will get nothing if I just try to save it. By spending some money, I will acquire confirmed knowledge about the issue. It might happen that I keep following my assumptions and the matter is all lost along with my hopes. This legal profession really seems to be the best. If one wants one can build walls of gold. God knows what came upon me that I left it, or else my monthly income wouldn't have been less than two thousand. When foolish men can earn in thousands, then why couldn't I? May this zamindari be damned; it has not helped me in any way.'

When he reached home it was already nine. Vidya was lying sadly, alone in her room; the maidservants were busy in their work, and the neighbouring women had left. Gyanshankar kept Vidya's head in his lap and said in an emotional voice, 'You couldn't even see his face in his last moments.'

Vidya wept and replied, 'I cannot forget his face even for a second. It almost seems as if he is standing before me and smiling.'

Gyan – I have lost faith in worldly things. I feel like leaving everything and going somewhere.

Vidya – Let's go by the evening train tomorrow. We will have to take along some money. I wish to donate something on his sixteenth day ceremony.

Gyan – Yes, of course. This is the only means left with us to pacify his soul.

Vidya – He was very fond of horse-riding. I want to donate a horse in his name.

Gyan – Very well. We can get a horse in about two hundred rupees.

Vidya had suggested this proposal apprehensively. By accepting it happily Gyanshankar impressed her greatly.

Gyanshankar didn't wish to dismiss this expense at this crucial moment. The occasion was such that he couldn't afford to insult or ignore Vidya.

10

Rai Bahadur Kamlanand was a rich landowner belonging to Lucknow. He had an annual income of about one lac rupees. He had a huge mansion in Aminabad. There were other houses that he had in the city, but he usually spent his time in Nainital or Mussoorie. Although he had lost his wife in his youth, he had not married again. His friends and well wishers pressed him a lot but he refused to marry again. According to him the purpose of marriage was to have children, and when God had blessed him with a son and two daughters, where was the need to remarry? He had married his elder daughter to a rich Seth of Gorakhpur. He spent lacs of rupees on the event. But when Gayatri became a widow within two years of marriage – her husband had been poisoned by a family member due to greed for money - Rai Sahib decided to marry Vidya in an ordinary family where life was not haunted by such perils. That was the reason why Gyanshankar got the honour of becoming his son-in-law. Late Babu Ramanand (Kamlanand's son) was yet unmarried. Though he had crossed twenty years of age, Rai Sahib was not eager to marry him off. He didn't wish to hinder his mental or physical development. But alas, the workings of bad fortune! Ramanand had gone to Poona to participate in a horse race. He fell down from the horse and his vital organs got badly wounded. He expired two days after reaching Lucknow. Rai Sahib's aspirations related to his son were destroyed; the lamp of his hopes was extinguished.

But Rai Sahib was not a man who could be overwhelmed by the sorrow of grief. You might term it as detachment or a passive kind of love, or a stability of mind. Within a few days his grief for his son disappeared within the tireless stream of life and its activities.

Rai Sahib was a man devoted to the pleasures of materialistic life. He had a special interest in horse-racing, hunting, and in playing sarod and sitar. He was well-versed in literature and politics. He was about sixty years old, but his interest in these affairs hadn't lessened even a bit. In his stable there were twelve choice horses, various kinds of carriages, two cars and two elephants. Besides these, he had dozens of pet dogs and an ariel army of eagles and other birds of prey. The range of weapons in his sitting room gave the appearance of an artillery. In the field of horse-racing he competed with the best of jockeys. While hunting he rarely missed a shot. In the field of polo, his swiftness and alacrity of shot surprised one and all. In the pursuit of vocal arts, he was quite skillful. When he sat down to play sitar in the evening, then the best of musical experts were surprised at his sense of melody. His voice had a divine sweetness. He knew the deepest principles of music. After hearing him sing raag Dhrupad, the greatest of artists swayed with joy. His poetic sense and sensitivity put many a poets to shame, and his poems gave competition to all of them. Sanskrit, Arabic, Hindi, Urdu and English were part of his sound scholarship. He also had an excellent memory. He had memorized thousands of couplets, stanzas and passages and used them skilfully in his conversations. That is why people enjoyed listening to him. He had also entered politics since the past ten or twelve years. He sat in a premium position in the council house. His opinion was always fearless. He wasn't a slave of time or opportunity. Instead of serving the vested interests of the nation and the administration he always relied on his own strength of thought. This is the season why he was respected a lot in the council. Though he spoke very less and no one could hear his voice outside the house of politics, but whenever he spoke, he spoke very well. Gyanshankar was deeply amazed at his wisdom and knowledge. Had he not seen with his own eyes, he wouldn't have ever believed that a single person could be an apostle of so many qualities. His company was almost an eye-opener for him. Earlier he was quite proud of his own abilities and cleverness. Rai Saheb's achievements destroyed his pride completely. For the first two weeks, he was completely taken over by a sense of devotion towards him. Whatever Rai Saheb said appeared as a universal truth to him. He found faults with himself at every step, and felt ashamed about it. Even in the field of literature and philosophy, which were his main subjects, he found a lot to mull over Rai Sahib's thoughts. The biggest surprise lay in the fact that Rai Saheb stood straight in the face of such extreme sorrow. His pleasure garden seemed totally unaffected by this gust of pain.

But gradually Gyanshankar felt a kind of disillusionment with Rai Saheb's overwhelming sense of knowledge. It was unbearable to feel an inferiority complex all the time. In his opinion, Rai Saheb should not have devoted himself to any subjects of pleasure after the death of his son. 'Is there any limit to this craving? This is not any kind of liveliness, nor any kind of tranquility; it is just a form of patience. But patience never assumes the form of hyperactivity or lust. It paints the heart with shades of detachment, passivity and sorrow. The burning of heart is such a fire that turns even tears to vapour. That sorrow is also a sort of last stage. No ascetic or even the holiest of men can remain tranquil in the face of a young son's death. What Rai Saheb is pursuing is a naked strive towards pleasing the senses. His pride has destroyed his great soul and his materialism has annihilated the softest of the heart's sentiments.' Gyanshankar now started witnessing a kind of cheap materialism in every little aspect related to Rai Saheb. He started watching his actions with an eye of deep criticism.

But a complete month passed and Gyanshankar did not express any desire to return to Benaras. Though Vidyavati's refusal to go back with him was a good reason for him to stay back, but actually there was another reason behind it, which he wouldn't dare to admit even in private. Gayatri's soft demeanour and sweet talk had started attracting his heart. Her mature and alluring beauty pulled his heart in an unknown way and he was moving towards it unmindful of its consequences, just as an insect is pulled towards a lamp. To him, Gayatri seemed like an apostle of love's desires and aspirations, and this myth kept igniting his desire all the more. There was no elderly lady at home who could attend to his care hence Gayatri looked to the same, and with such love and affection that Gyanshankar felt in it a deep delight akin to the strings of love. Happy thoughts started dancing before his eyes, taking a most attractive form. He had never thought his life to be so comfortable. His heart had never experienced such strong currents of love. His mind was not just lost in love-related pleasantaries; it also envisioned a control over Gayatri's unlimited wealth. The house of his future progress was completely ready; if it could be decorated with a garden of love, what better adornment could be provided? 'That scene would be so extensive, and so pleasant!'

In Gyanshankar's eyes self-control wasn't a very important virtue. He thought tolerance and discipline to be impediments in the natural development of human character. 'Only that sapling can become a dense tree which can tolerate winds, cold and hot, rain and snow with equal strength. A blazing hot wind is as important for its growth as a cool slow breeze; dryness is as nurturing as humidity. A similar varied set of conditions is important for the development of human character. Why should one treat poverty as a black serpent? For an integrated character, it is far more essential than wealth itself. It engenders the feelings of determination, resolve, kindness and compassion in a man. Every experience strengthens some or the other aspect of character. This is a natural dictum. If one puts artificial hurdles in this, then the character becomes complicated. In fact, even in feelings like envy, anger, falseness and wickedness, there are seeds of invaluable learning. Till the time every string of the sitar is struck hard, no melodious tune can be heard. To stop the flow of natural sensibilities is to interfere in the divine set up. To destroy one's desires is a kind of suicide. It makes one's character low and impeded. This is not the age of fetters; rather, it's the time of unbridled, generous and great progress. Sacrifice and detachment were suitable for those times when people deemed the world as transient and dreamlike. This is the age of worldly progress; to think too much of right and wrong is an indicator of a narrow mind. Worldly progress is our true aim. Every means that can assist us in this achievement is fit to be imbibed.' These thoughts had made Gyanshankar mindless. Well, the present situation did make him a bit fearful of criticism and mockery, though these too, in his opinion, were signs of mental weakness.

Gayatri was not one of those women for whom men's hearts are an open page to browse. Her husband was of a loose character but Gayatri never doubted his actions; she never got to the crux of his feelings and though it was almost three years since he died, she still used to worship his memory with a divine respect. Her innocent heart was totally ignorant of the mysteries of a lustful love. But alongside this nature, a deep sense of honour was a prime feature of her character. She used to think herself to be far more wise and knowledgeable than she really was. Her thought process and its components were not like the stable rocks of a waterbed but shallow bubbles floating on the surface. Gyanshankar was a handsome, sophisticated and sweet-talking man. Gayatri had a simple liking for these qualities. She smilingly used to tell him, 'Your words are so magical; no one can feel satiated with your talk.' She often nudged Vidya in Gyanshankar's presence, 'You don't praise your fate even after getting such a husband?'

Though Gyanshankar was only a few months younger to her; being the husband of her younger sister, she thought of him as a younger brother. She herself used to make many delicacies for him and often called him to relish these during the day. She had a special interest in religious and scientific subjects. She got a heartfelt delight in discussing these with Gyanshankar. She also had fun with him as is apt for a sister-in-law; mocked him and laughed at him. To brood or sulk was not a part of her nature. She was a fun-loving, polite and simple-hearted woman whose heart had no place for fake pretences or playfulness.

But this simple, straight nature of hers became transformed in Gyanshankar's evil eyes into something else. He saw an attraction in her openness and complication in her equanimity. To him Gayatri appeared to be saying through indications, 'Come and revive this deserted heart. Come, light up this dark cottage.' It was impossible for him to ignore this call of love. But his heart had never invited Gayatri in any such way; he never devoted his love to her — often he got late in the club; he could not leave the game of cards midway; sometimes he was delayed by his outings, but he never grew impatient himself. He only thought that Gayatri must be sad for him. The fire actually burnt in Gayatri's heart; he only had to warm his hands around it. The happiness he derived in this endeavour was akin to that derived by a hunter in hunting; by a player in his victory. This wasn't really love; it was a desire to have full control over her. There's a world of difference between such a desire and love; desire pulls the heart towards itself, love gets pulled on its own. There's a sense of ownership in desire; a sense of surrender in love. These waves of desire kept playing their full part in Gyanshankar's heart.

Gayatri might have been ignorant or innocent but she was increasingly getting drawn towards Gyanshankar. If one consumes poison by mistake that doesn't lessen its effect. If Gyanshankar was delayed in coming back home, she felt restless; she couldn't concentrate on anything and started waiting for him on the terrace. She initially used to laugh and joke with him in front of Vidya but on meeting him alone, became quite tongue-tied. That stage was over now. She now used to look for solitude and privacy with him. Both used to turn silent in Vidya's presence. Nor were their discussions limited to scientific and religious topics. Often, they used to analyze the relations between a man and a woman and sometimes, it entailed the mentioning of such aspects that Gayatri lowered her head in embarrassment.

One fine day, Gayatri was sitting on an easychair in the garden during evening and was reading a letter which had just arrived through post. Though the hot winds of June had stopped blowing, the heat was still unbearable. A flame seemed to be rising from every object. She picked up the letter, and kept it back again, feeling oppressed due to heat. Finally, she called a maidservant to fan her and started reading the letter. Her general manager had asked her to come urgently to the estate. He had written, 'Many affairs are lying pending here which cannot be decided without your permission. There was no rain this year in Hariharpur, as you must be knowing already. It is getting very difficult to obtain rent from the tenants out there. They wish to be exempted from it totally. I requested the District Magistrate to intervene in this regard but to no avail. If you come in person and see him, then it might help our case. If honourable Rai Saheb can take the trouble of coming here, his influence might turn the difficult situation into a simple one. We are quite disturbed due to the rebellious movement of the tenants. I doubt that if we don't give them some exemption they might cause further unrest. That's why it's extremely essential for you to meet the District Collector.'

Gayatri started thinking, 'This zamindari is nothing but a pain in the neck. God knows how this spirit came upon the tenants that they seem prepared to revolt everywhere. The government should handle them with a tight fist. They tend to go out of control in the wake of a little concession. If they are given discount in the rent, I might run a loss of about twenty or twenty-five thousand. In the same way, if the rent is subsidised in other areas too for fear of revolt, then I will lose everything. If nothing is earned how shall I pay for my expenses? Even if the area's official payments are left out, there are various kinds of payments given under various heads which can't be avoided. Where will they come from? Even if the rent is subsidized, I will extract these expenses from the tenants only.'

'But how shall I spend my time there (Hariharpur)? I won't get to listen to any pleasantries there; I'll get bored lying alone. Till the time Gyanshankar is here, I won't go to Gorakhpur. Well, once he goes away I'll have to go as well. How far can I bother about the losses? Let them be. I am at least happy out here; I get to listen to discussions on religion and knowledge. Yesterday, Babu Sahib must have felt offended with me, but I find it hard to admit that marriage is just a physical relation and a sort of social arrangement. He himself says that human body undergoes a complete transformation in certain number of years. Perhaps he mentioned eight years. If marriage is just a physical relationship then it cannot exist after the said number of years. It almost implies that after eight years, both the husband and wife are released from the bond of this duty; they have no right over one another. I shall raise the same question today also. Well, there he is.' She asked, 'Are you ready to go somewhere?'

Gyan – A theatrical company is about to present a show here. I came to ask you if I should reserve a place for you. It's going to be very crowded today.

Gayatri – Did you ask Vidya; will she go?

Gyan – She says it would be difficult to take Maya along. I too didn't coax her.

Gayatri – Then I will not enjoy going there alone.

Gyan – If you won't go then I too wouldn't.

Gayatri – In that case, I would never go. Conversations with you are far more pleasant than theatre. Come, sit. Our yesterday's discussion is still incomplete. You were saying, women have greater powers of attraction than men; but you didn't cite any reason for it.

Gyan – The reason is quite clear. The life arena of women is limited, and that of men, quite vast. That's why their powers get focussed, and that of men gets scattered.

Gayatri – But had this been the case then men should have stayed subservient to women; why do they rule over them?

Gyan – Do you think that men really rule over women? That's not true. Actually, men are indeed subservient to women. The latter are the writers of their fate. Their bodies might be independent, but their hearts are indeed ruled by them.

Gayatri – Then why do men grow so ruthless?

Gyan – It is against a sense of justice to blame men with ruthlessness. They cannot raise their heads till the time a woman frees them totally or till another woman doesn't affect them with a powerful, electric kind of power.

Gayatri (laughing) – You have put the entire blame on the heads of women.

Gyanshankar replied in an emotional voice, 'They are the ones who do injustice; who shall listen to our pleas?'

Just then Vidyavati came and stood with Mayashankar in her lap. Maya was four years old now, but due to the lack of another sibling he still enjoyed the privileges of childhood.

Gayatri asked – Why, Vidya, will you come to the theatre today?

Vidya – If someone insists I can go but I don't really wish to.

Gyan – You may go if you please; I won't force you.

Vidya – Then I wouldn't.

Gayatri – I insist you'll have to come. Babuji, please get our seats reserved.

At around nine p.m. in the night, the trio sat on a carriage and set out for the theatre. Maya was also there. When the carriage had gone a few miles, he started craving for water. Gyanshankar asked Vidya, 'If you were getting a small child along, you should have carried a water jar with you.'

Vidya – I didn't know he would feel so thirsty right after getting out of the house.

Gyan – You didn't forget your paan-box?

Vidya – This is why I said I won't go.

Gayatri – We shall get ice and water in the theatre complex.

Maya grew all the more impatient on hearing this. He started howling loudly. Gyanshankar incited him all the more. He started crying in a loud voice.

Gyan – If this is his state now, God knows what will happen by two o' clock at night.

Gayatri – He won't be awake till then. As soon as we reach he will sleep.

Gyan – He wouldn't be able to sleep comfortably in the lap; he would wake up intermittently and cry. The whole crowd will be disturbed. People will say, 'Why did they carry such a tag along?'

Vidya – Why don't you tell the coach driver to return his carriage; I won't go with you.

Gyan – You should have thought about these things beforehand. If the coach goes to drop you, it'll take it ten p.m. to reach here. Half the show will be over. Once we reach there, either watch the show, or let Maya stay in the carriage or come back if you deem fit.

Gayatri – It doesn't look nice to return back once we reach there.

Gyan – I have left everything to her will.

Gayatri – Won't she get an easychair out there?

Vidya – Where is the need for these arrangements? I shall come back. I wasn't even willing to see the show; I had come just for your sake.

The theatre complex arrived. There was a huge crowd there. Gyanshankar got down. Gayatri asked Vidya to get down, but she didn't relent even after a lot of coaxing. She sent the driver to get water. Just then Gyanshankar hurriedly arrived and said, 'Bhabi, please hurry up, the show is about to begin. Till the time she gives water to Maya, you please go and sit, or else there might be no space left.'

Thus saying he took Gayatri with him and entered the complex. In the first class, there was just a cloth partition between the male and female sections. Gyanshankar sat outside the partition and made Gayatri sit inside. He had reserved those two places himself.

Gayatri had hurriedly got down from the coach and come with Gyanshankar. She was hoping that Vidya would arrive inside very soon. But many hours passed and Vidya didn't come. In the end Gyanshankar came and said, 'She's gone.' Gayatri felt very repentful. She understood that Vidya had got upset and left. 'She must have thought it rude and impudent of me. I should have gone back with her. There wasn't any harm in watching the show with her. People would have thought that I've come with her but my staying on after she has left is totally improper. Even the maid and workers of the house will laugh at me and rightfully so; what will my father think? For a widow like me, the right course is to go for pilgrimages, holy baths, worshipping and fasting. All this enjoyment is meant for a married woman. I must go back. But if I tell Babuji to return so soon he will be irritated with me and be upset at getting me here. I have been caught in a mess. There is no way out except sitting here for some time.'

Deciding thus she kept sitting. But when she happened to glance around at the crowd she felt it suffocating to sit there even for a second. The entire female section was full of prostitutes; all more beautiful than the rest; more colourful and vivid than all. Fragrant fumes of khus and henna were floating all around. Their dresses and make-up, their glamour and mannerisms; even their smiles seemed hateful to Gayatri. She too was proud of her beauty, but she seemed lost in this ocean of beauty like a small dewdrop. She felt her difference more keenly. 'These fallen women are so shameless,' she thought, 'I don't complain that they follow this sinful and hellish path. This is the fruit of their past deeds. Bad situations can harm anyone; but why this pride? On what basis do they flaunt themselves? They pretend as if they belong to a noble lineage. They should have hung their heads in shame. Their whole manner should have reflected shame and humility. But they seem so happy as if there is none more blessed than them in the entire world. Sin is a pitiable thing, and is a symbol of human weakness. One feels pitiful seeing it, but sin combined with shamelessness and proud intoxication is a dance of the devil; outside the purview of kindness and religion.'

Gayatri could not stay back even for a moment. She said to Gyanshankar, 'I am going out. I can't stay here; please send me home.'

She doubted that Gyanshankar would force her to stay back. Even if he returns, he'd be angry. But this was not the case. Gyanshankar got up gladly. He booked a carriage and set out for home. Gayatri apologized for leaving the theatre so soon. She discussed the shameful behaviour of the prostitutes, but Gyanshankar didn't reply. He had thought of a strong resolve today, and was now concentrating upon his powers to implement it; as if he was preparing himself to dive into a deep river. His heart was beset with the clouds of impure thoughts which had been gathering since months now. He was looking just for an opportunity like this. He had fixed up his plan. The symptoms indicated cooperation from Gayatri's side also. Her agreement to go to the theatre, her staying back without Vidya, her accompanying him alone with him in the coach, were all clear signs of this. Maybe she had returned so soon to give him a chance for there was a fear of getting impeded by using the private carriage. In his opinion, it was unmanly to hesitate in such a favourable situation and it would prove fatal for the achievement of the desired goal. He had read in books that a manly sense of rudeness is a sure means to hypnotize a person. That very moment his impure efforts were ignited all the more; his eyes started burning, his blood started boiling and his breathing became fast. He nudged Gayatri's leg with his knee. Gayatri immediately composed herself; she didn't smell a rat. But right after that Gyanshankar pressed her wrist with his burning hand. Gayatri was shocked and withdrew her hand as if she was bitten by a serpent and started looking at Gyanshankar with fearful eyes. Electric lanterns were lighting up the streets outside. In their light she saw a kind of burning impudence and a keen daring on his face. Her heart missed a beat, her eyes were taken over by darkness and her body was covered in sweat. She looked outside with helpless eyes. She couldn't understand where she was, and when she'd reach home. A helpless kind of anger ran in her veins and fell out as tears from her eyes. She couldn't dare to look again at Gyanshankar. She couldn't say anything to him. Her anger also quietened down. She became numb altogether. All her feeling came to a standstill. Only a sense of sorrow was cutting her heart like a knife. The thing that was most dear to her had been lost; that thing which was a protector of her mind, a nurturer of her self-pride, a basis of her patience and a reason for life itself. Her heart was sinking. Suddenly she realized that she couldn't show her face to anyone. Till now she hadn't thought about this external fact of her insult. She now understood that this wasn't just a fall of her soul; it had not just blackened it, but had also destroyed her public honour. This feeling caught her drowning heart. A bird which is about to die due to a bullet also shivers when it sees a knife hovering above it.

Gayatri gathered herself and looked at Gyanshankar with tearful eyes. She wanted to say, 'Whatever you've done God will punish you for that. But if there's even an iota of character left in you, then please guard my honour. My womanly credentials have been lost but please guard my public honour...' But she couldn't say a thing; her words were lost in the flow of her tears.

Gyanshankar too realized that he had been duped. 'My impatience spoiled everything.' Till now he hadn't felt ashamed of his degradation. But when he heard Gayatri's sobs, they fell like an assault on his heart. His inner soul got awakened and his head hung in shame. His lust disappeared. He realized the fallen nature of his sin. Words expressing guilt and repentance came to his lips but couldn't be uttered. He couldn't even dare to look at Gayatri. He could see his corrupt and evil nature with his own eyes. 'Oh! What an evil soul I am. My prudence, knowledge and good thoughts have been overtaken by self-violence. It's a pity that my high education and ideals should come to this!' The knowledge of his moral fall ignited a sense of deep pain and unhappiness in his heart. A stream of tears started falling from his eyes.

Both the creatures kept weeping, looking out of the window, till the carriage reached home.

11

When the first rush of a storm calms down, strong gusts of wind, the dazzle of lightning and the growl of thunder also stop and a heavy rain ensues. Gayatri's sense of peace had also got liquefied. A stream of tears was now flowing in her heart instead of blood.

Midnight came, but her tears didn't stop. Her self-pride had got destroyed today. After the separation from her husband, his strong memory was the very foundation of her peaceful life. That blessed imagination was the object of her worship. She used to guard this innermost treasure which housed the priceless gem (of his memory) from the eyes of evil desires. Doubtlessly, she adored good clothes and jewels, had delicious food and always kept herself happy but not due to any love for materialism; rather due to a pride in her strong sense of womanly attributes.

She hated to feign a pretence of restraint and discipline. She used to visit the theatre, and participate in merry gatherings too. She never felt any reason to abhor dressing up, style and entertainment for she thought she had a control over the state of her heart. She used to manage the affairs of her estate with a similar confidence.

When her tears receded, she started surmising on the reasons and origin of this accident and gradually it dawned upon her that she was not totally guiltless in the matter. 'Gyanshankar wouldn't have dared to do this,' she thought, 'had he been unsure of my own weakness. Why did he gain this confidence? I had started liking him a lot recently. This was just too improper on my part. Perhaps this is why he was deluded by this thought.' She now remembered the conversations she had had with him. He had always loved to discuss those issues which required privacy and restraint. At that time, such talk had seemed quite faultless, but now Gayatri felt ashamed at the very thought of them. She now realized that in her state of ignorance, she had been moving towards a fall and had this pit not arrived she wouldn't have felt the real extent of her deterioration.

She now understood that the love-strings that had tied her to her husband had weakened or else she would have remained immune to the attraction of these talks. She got up impatiently, and stood before a portrait of her husband. She used to hang this picture always in her room. She looked at it with guilty eyes, and then took it down with trembling hands; she kept crying for a long time clutching it to her heart. She felt a strange satisfaction at this soulful hug. It felt as if someone was applying a balm on her bleeding heart, and with absolutely gentle hands. She couldn't separate herself from the picture and lay on her bed along with it. Her heart was all lit up with love for her husband. She was almost in a state of trance. She felt as if the soul of her husband was in the room with her, though his body was not to be seen. Gradually, her imagination became visual. She almost forgot that her husband had died three years ago. She got up anxiously. She felt as if blood is flowing from his heart and her saying, 'This is the wound of evil perpetrated by you. Your purity and truthfulness were weapons for my protection. That guard was broken today and the knife of your unfaithfulness pierced my heart. I was proud of your womanliness. This pride got totally shattered into pieces. Alas! I was killed by the same hands that used to engulf me in the past with love. Today, our relationship is broken; forget that I was once your husband.'

Gayatri was pleading before this imagined persona in a dreamlike state with stretched hands. In this delusion, she lost all control and fell on the ground with a loud scream. She kept lying unconscious for many hours. When she returned to her senses, she saw that Vidya, the maids and all others were gathered around her and a person was being sent to call the doctor.

When Vidya saw her opening her eyes, she leapt to hug her and said, 'Sister, what had happened to you? It had never been so in the past?'

Gayatri – Nothing, I was just watching a bad dream. Give me a little water to drink, my throat is dry.

Vidya – You must have watched a frightening scene in the theatre.

Gayatri – No, I too had come back a little while after you. I just lost interest. Has the night just fallen? Babuji is singing the Dhrupad raga.

Vidya – It's been twelve since long, but what does he care about someone's life or death? He is just bothered about his own pleasures. The maid reported about your condition to him so he sent a person to call the doctor, and started singing again.

Gayatri – This is his old habit; what's new about it? Raman Babu was in a terrible state out here and he had gone for a dinner. When the next day I talked to him about it, he said he had given his word and going there was a duty. He said he wanted to keep personal issues absolutely separate from his public life.

Vidya – The year when there was famine in the region and an outbreak of plague as well; we had gone to the estate. You were in Gorakhpur. The tenants were unable to pay the rent, and there were dance parties at our place. When Babuji didn't get money to squander, he took out his anger on those tenants. He used to make a hundred odd men stand in a line and beat them with a hunter. Those people cried in pain but he didn't feel any pity for them. This beating has made him so ruthless. Life and death is in the hands of God, but still I would say that the untimely death of our brother is an outcome of the curses of these poor people.

Gayatri – You are being unfair to Babuji. He is not to blame. After all, how else could he have earned the rent? Ruthlessness is not good, but if there is no other way out, what can be done? Your brother-in-law was such a good man; he never sent a beggar empty- handed from his door. He spent thousands of rupees in charitable causes. Not a single day passed when he didn't feed about a hundred or fifty ascetics. He used to donate in thousands as well. But he too had to be strict with the tenants. I have myself seen him getting their hands binded and having them beaten. When he couldn't think of anything else, he used to put their houses on fire, and today I'm also forced to do the same. Back then, I too thought that he is being unkind and torturous. I used to debate with him about it, but when I was burdened with the estate, I understood that these lowly men do not pay unless beaten up. They have money in the house, but till the time they get a few blows or abuses, they don't feel like paying. It's their old habit.

Vidya – I cannot believe this. Nobody can get used to getting beaten up.

Gayatri – But nobody has an inborn habit of beating up also. This relationship is such that on one hand it nurtures feelings of fear, mistrust and inferiority complex in the tenants and on the other hand, makes the landlords proud, unkind and unbridled in their power.

Vidya didn't say anything in reply. Both the sisters lay on the same bed. Gayatri felt a repeated desire to describe the day's incident to Vidya. Her heart was feeling burdened in a way. She wanted to lighten it. She also wished to show Gyanshankar's true colours to Vidya. Though she'd have felt insulted in the process, she was willing to pay this price in order to shame and criticize Gyanshankar. Yet she couldn't gather enough courage to say anything. And she was incapable of thinking anything else. Suddenly she had an idea. She shook up Vidya and said, 'Are you beginning to sleep? I wish to leave this place by tomorrow or the day after.'

Vidya replied, 'So soon! Please stay till the time I am here.'

Gayatri – No, I don't feel like staying here. I have to look into the affairs of my area also.

Vidya – But you haven't spoken about it to Babuji as yet.

Gayatri – What's there to tell him? Whether I stay or leave, it's the same thing.

Vidya – Then I won't stay either; I'd leave along with you.

Gayatri – Where will you go? Now this is your own home. You are its queen. Tell Gyan Babu to manage its affairs. The two of you should stay here happily.

Vidya – I too had wanted this, but perhaps God has something else in his mind. Since many days, I am seeing the daily arrival of Pandit Parmanand. Chintaram also keeps coming and going. These people are surely conspiring something amidst themselves. Your going away will give them a further opportunity to do so.

Gayatri – So Babuji wishes to marry again?

Vidya – This is what it seems to me.

Gayatri – If he has thought it out then no one can stop him. He does care about me, but I wonder if he cares to consult me in the matter. He knows very well about my opinion on this.

Vidya – If you had stayed back, he must have hesitated a little.

Gayatri – I don't think so. If I go there at least I'd be able to take care of my estate. It's almost three months now; God knows what mess must have ensued in my absence. About a dozen relatives keep hankering at my door. One of them is an uncle in relation; he keeps fishing from morn till night. The other is a son of my aunt, he's been staying there since the days my father-in-law was alive. His chief pastime is to eve-tease the women in the neighbourhood and have fun at their cost. A third fellow is the brother-in-law of my husband's sister; he is an agent dealing in bribes of all sorts. Whatever time he finds spare, he uses it to drink and serve bhaang. The chief quality of these people is that they are epitomes of contentment. They should get food and clothing peacefully and they do not want anything else. Yes, they do take pride in being zamindars; they all want to boss over the tenants, and are most willing to throttle their throats. Poor farmers who eat bread earned out of hard labour, have to bear the tyranny of these idlers only because they happen to be my distant relatives. Free food has made them so lacking in self-respect that they won't budge an inch, however rudely you might treat them. Around ten families are such that are dreaming of my death all day. They could have poisoned me if they had been allowed to do so. Gifts arrive daily, but I just don't touch them. Their sole job is to make all kinds of squabbles and interrupt my work. Some conspire with the tenants, some incite my servants against me; some others want to award me a bad name. You will feel like laughing, but many of them have taken debts on a high interest in the hope of receiving money from my heritage. If nothing else happens, they end up fasting, but a fake pride of inheritance does not allow them to plan a livelihood. These people must have made a mess in my absence. Please let me go now. Babuji is also planning to go to the hills very soon. If you are in need of something, write to me; I'll surely come back.

Gayatri spent the next two days in great uneasiness. She didn't get a chance to talk to Gyanshankar again. The third day, she left. Rai Saheb went to the station to see her off. Gyanshankar was also with him. Gayatri boarded the train. Rai Saheb, bent on the window, was filling her coach with baskets of mangoes, melons, litchis and grapes. Gayatri was repeatedly protesting saying, 'What's the use of this fruit; it's not a long journey,' but Rai Saheb refused to listen. This too was a matter of prestige for him. Gyanshankar was sitting sadly on a bench. Gayatri felt pity for him. We happen to become kind in moments of separation. We might leave a debt for somebody while leaving but we never wish to carry a debt. When the guard gave the whistle, Gyanshankar got up suddenly and stood before Gayatri, watching her with shameful and pleading eyes. They were filled with tears. He seemed to be an icon of repentance. Gayatri too came near the window; she wanted to say something, but the train took off.

Gyanshankar's humble figure kept haunting her eyes for the rest of the journey.

12

After Gayatri left Rai Saheb's house, it became quite impossible for Gyanshankar to stay there. His good luck had been rapidly pushing him towards a heaven of fame and achievement, but in a single blow of fate, the bright stars on the firmament had disappeared; that life nurturing mild breeze, that vast universe and happy imagination had all been lost; and he was lying in the old darkness, depressed and hurt. All indications told him that Rai Saheb was hellbent upon getting married and this made his helpless anger even more helpless with each passing day. He felt increasingly irritated with Rai Saheb's love of worldly pleasures and mean nature. He sometimes reasoned with himself that he had no right to feel bad about it; 'Rai Saheb is the master of his assets; he is fully free to remarry; he is quite healthy and his age is also well within limits. Why should he try to sacrifice all this for my sake? It is so shameful for me that I should think ill of him due to my own selfishness and pray for the end of his lineage. It is absolutely too mean of me.' But the efforts to distract such thoughts from his mind became a kind of reaction which took away all his patience and contentment in its sway and broke the barriers of his heart. It then became anxious for that blessed moment when he would get the control of that boundless wealth; when he would not stay there temporarily as a guest, but as a permanent master. He used to be lost in this fake happiness almost daily. Almost every night he kept lying awake, and daydreamt about all kinds of pleasures. Many ideas of progress and improvement crossed his mind. He didn't enjoy his walks anymore; he usually lay in his room brooding about his desires. This went on upto an extent that a situation of hope and fear became intolerable. The month of June passed away in this state of confusion and July was here.

Rai Saheb's sojourn to the hills had been delayed by the sorrow of his son's untimely death. With the first shower of the monsoons, he started preparing for his journey again. Gyanshankar could bear this no more.

He thought, 'Who knows he might get married in Nainital to some modern lady, and no one shall get to know anything here;' so he decided to end all his doubts.

The evening had fallen. He went to Rai Saheb's room with a determined heart but he saw someone already sitting there. He was an agent of some company and was pressing Rai Saheb to buy its shares. But from the latter's response it seemed that he wasn't ready to do so. Ultimately the agent asked, 'What makes you so sceptical? Do you think that our base is not strong enough?'

Rai Saheb – If Seth Jagatram and Mr. Manchurji are involved in it, I cannot have any doubts about it.

Agent – Then do you think that the company won't be managed efficiently?

Rai Saheb – Absolutely not.

Agent – Then why do you object to being a partner? I had come to you with the hope of selling almost five hundred shares. If thoughtful people like you stay away from business enterprises, the progress of this unfortunate nation will always be a pleasant dream, nothing else.

Rai Saheb – I do not see such business organizations as the key to the country's upliftment.

Agent (with surprise) – Why?

Rai Saheb – Because Seth Jagatram and Mr. Manchurji's wealth cannot be the country's wealth. Your company will make the rich more rich, but there's little possibility of the profit reaching the poor public. Undoubtedly you will put thousands of labourers to work, but a majority of these will be farmers and I am strongly opposed to their turning into labour. I do not wish that due to a greed for money they leave their children and stay in the company's encampments and lose their character. In the villages, they enjoy a certain position. Their feeling of self-respect remains alive. The fear of society saves them from evil ways. In the employment of the company, they cease to be the masters of their homes; they become other peoples' slaves and being free from the fear of society, fall on the stray path. At least I don't want to put my farmers in such a moral tussle.

Agent – Pardon me, but you have looked at only one side of the picture. Please do examine the other side as well. We give the labourers best clothing, food and houses; the kind that they can never dream of in the villages. We also care for their medical needs, education of their children and their old age. We even manage their entertainment and exercise routines. They can play tennis or football, or roam in the parks if they please. Once in a week they are given an early off to sing and entertain themselves. In my understanding and the way I look at it, no labourer will care for farming after staying in the parks.

Rai Saheb – No, I just cannot approve of this. A peasant can never thank God for making him a labourer, in the same way that a man who has enjoyed the freedom of trade will never enjoy the slavery of employment. Possibly, poverty may force him to be a paid employee but I duly believe that once he gets a chance to be free of this slavery, he would immediately set out for his home and love to stay with his kids in his broken dwelling, spending life most contentedly. If you have any doubt about that, you can talk to the peasant labour privately and dispel your doubts. I am saying this due to experience that in this matter, you are destroying the qualities of our social life by blindly following the Europeans. If industrialism flourished in Europe there were special reasons behind it. At that time their peasants were worst than slaves, and were bonded labour of the landlords. The slavery of capitalists was far better than this erstwhile bondage. Our peasants might be in a sorry state of finances, but they are not anyone's slaves. If anyone terrorizes them, they can appeal in the courts. In the eyes of law, peasants and zamindars are on an equal footing.

Agent – I don't wish to argue with your learned self, but I am myself a small farmer, and I am well aware of the real status of the peasants. You call European farmers as slaves, but the farmers out here are in no better condition. Despite legal limitations the zamindars torture the peasants a lot, and had there been another means of livelihood available to the peasants they would never tolerate these atrocities.

Rai Saheb – When there are legal postulates available, then the peasants need education to be able to avail them and there's an increasing emphasis on the same. I agree that the zamindars do all kinds of tyrannies on the peasants. I myself am not totally blame free in this. I force them to do free labour, take penalties, do not let go any kind of opportunity to seize land or increase the rent, lick the feet of officers to impress my tenants; do all kinds of deeds by hook or crook but what for? Due to the same old convention; the ignorance of farmers and their lack of legal knowledge. As soon as education is promoted, the zamindars will lose all these chances. Man is a selfish creature and it's impossible that he abstains to profit from opportunities to throw his weight around. Your statement is quite true that the peasants have to bear these atrocities because the doors of all other livelihoods are closed at them. Certainly there should be other means of supporting their life or else their inner jealousy and struggle will forever make them slaves of the zamindar, however much the law might protect or assist them. But these means must be such that do not corrupt their behaviour and character. It must not drive them out of their homes to trap them in evil habits, and must not destroy their self-respect! And this can happen only in a situation when cottage industries are promoted and they keep doing their respective jobs under a sharp gaze of their families and society in their respective villages.

Agent – You mean the cottage industries? The newspapers are mentioning it here and there, but its strongest advocate too, cannot ensure that you can oppose the use of foreign goods through them.

Rai Saheb – For this, we must levy taxes on foreign goods. Europeans get raw materials from other countries, pay the rent for shipping, give high wages to the labourers; on top of it the capitalists want high profits as well. Our cottage industries shall be free from these hurdles and there's no reason why they cannot overtake foreign trade with proper organization. Actually we have never bothered about this issue. People who have capital are scared to get involved in the matter. They know that cottage industries shall end their monopoly so they keep opposing it.

Gyanshankar did not participate in this discussion. Rai Saheb's proposals were against the principles of economics, but he had no time to dispute them at the moment. When the agent found that Rai Saheb cannot be impressed, he left. Rai Saheb saw an anxious Gyanshankar and understood that he wanted to say something but was quiet due to hesitation. He said, 'Please say what you want to; I am free to listen.'

Gyanshankar could not open his mouth. He was slowly becoming aware that what he wished to tell Rai Saheb was totally improper and against good manners. Rai Saheb would feel so sad, and he would think of him as a greedy and lowly person. He said, 'Nothing much, I just came to ask you by what time you wish to leave for Nainital.'

Rai Saheb – You are trying to dupe me. Your eyes are saying that you have something else in mind; please be clear. I want nothing but truth in our midst.

Gyanshankar was totally confused. In the end, he said, 'I too, want the same but the topic is such that I am ashamed to raise it myself.'

Rai Saheb – It's okay, I understand. You need not say anything. I ensure you that the rumours that have caused these doubts in your mind are totally baseless. I am a straightforward man, but I cannot afford to ignore my old time well-wishers. But as I told you, these stories are totally hollow. You very well know that I don't believe in death rituals; nor do I think that my world will be empty without a child. As for sensual pleasures, I have so many other means to attain them that I can enjoy them without putting my feet in iron shackles. And I have never been a slave of physical lust, or else you wouldn't have found me so healthy. People can take me to be materialistic but actually I have led a life of restraint ever since my youth. I think these answers must have dispelled your doubts. But please don't mind, to get so disturbed hearing false rumours does not make you respectable in my eyes. Supposing I have really thought of remarrying, it's not necessary that I must have children, and even if I have then it must be a son, and even if it's a son, he must remain alive. Besides, Mayashankar is still an innocent child. You and I are unaware about what God has written in his fate. Even if you admit that he becomes my heir on achieving adulthood, it's not essential that he turns out to be so dutiful or righteous as you wish him to be. If he had been an adult and these doubts had arisen in his mind I would have excused him, but a sensible man like you forgetting to eat or drink behind a baseless possibility is truly a sorry state of affairs.

Gyanshankar had not been satisfied with the first part of this statement, and the latter part depressed him all the more. He understood that Rai Saheb hadn't liked the discussion and though he wanted to quieten him with his arguments, he had actually decided to get married. 'Not just that, he does not even like my staying here. Had he not thought of me as a dependent he wouldn't have talked so curtly to me.' His honour incited him to give an apt answer but he controlled his instinct. He decided to gulp this bitter medicine. He thought in his mind, 'You are playing out your double standards with me; I will prove that I'm not beneath you in this particular matter.'

He did not say anything in reply. Rai Saheb too, felt sorry for saying what he had. He started discussing mundane matters to keep Gyanshankar engaged. Nainital also came up in the discussions. He asked him to accompany him. Gyanshankar immediately agreed. He saw two benefits in this. On one hand he would be able to keep an eye on Rai Saheb; secondly he would be able to impress the higher officials with his abilities. Quite possible, Rai Saheb's good word could take him to a high post. He started preparing for the journey.

13

Although the villagers had protected Ghaus Khan with all their might, Jwalasingh's enquiry regarding his conduct was enough to make him lose his night's sleep. The peons, the munshi, and the other officers; all were surprised that this rustic lad had hypnotized the Deputy Sahib in such a way that he had emerged all new. 'He has now forbidden the free loading of fuel, fodder, utensils, milk, curd, meat and fish, and even vegetables. It cannot continue this way for long. We don't even get proper allowance. This chap is too smart. On one hand he got us reprimanded, and on the other, put this burden on our heads. Let's go and tell the Deputy Sahib. Today we are facing this ill treatment; in the next village the situation will be worse. We shall be craving even for water.' So as soon as Jwalasingh returned all the members of his entourage went and stood before him. Ijaad Hussain was again forced to become their spokesperson.

Jwalasingh gave them an angry look and asked, 'What are you people up to? Do you wish to say something? Mir Sahib, you have told them about my orders, I hope?'

Ijaad Hussain – Yes of course, these people have come to see you after hearing those very orders. Yesterday, there was an unfortunate incident in this village. The villagers became incited to fight with the peons. Had these people not run away to save their lives, criminal cases would have been lodged. These people didn't deem fit to report this yesterday and spoil you peace, but after listening to today's orders, they have lost their own peace of mind. It was already difficult to find men for labour; now if people get to know of these orders, they will grow all the more impudent. Yesterday's quarrel was incited by the same fellow who had appeared before you in the morning. He must be controlled in some way or the other.

Jwalasingh – From his version, it appeared that the peons had treated him roughly.

A Peon – He will obviously say so; but God's our witness, had we not run away, we'd have lost our lives. We had never faced such an insult. We are servants getting menial wages, but for the sake of our officers' honour, we don't care about big ruffians.

Ghaus Khan – Huzoor, that fellow is a prankster of the first order. We are fed up with staying in this village. He daily picks up one or the other squabble with us.

Second Peon – Huzoor, we've spent our lives in slavery, but we had never faced such a sorry state as now.

Ijaad Hussain – We do not doubt the benevolence of our sire. An officer must be so, but the truth of the matter is, that if labour is prohibited, these humble people won't be able to survive.

Jwalasingh – No, I just don't wish to trouble them. My only motive is that the common people must not be unduly tortured. Whatever orders I have passed, I have taken due care of these men and their needs. I wonder how these people start needing those very things in the village, without which they carry on comfortably in the city.

Peon - Huzoor, you can treat us the way you like; we are your slaves but such orders also harm your aura in the long run.

Ghaus Khan – Of course, these rural fellows do not think him to be a proper officer who treats them softly. They are trying to be so bold because they think it's the matter of an Indian officer. When the British officials arrive, nobody dares to even whisper a thing. Just two weeks ago, the church priest had arrived and stayed for a week, and the entire village kept standing with folded hands in his service.

Ijaad Hussain – You are absolutely right. They do not treat an Indian officer properly till he treats them strictly.

Jwalasingh had adopted a British lifestyle only to flaunt a good impression on other people. He did not count himself any less than a Britisher. When he went to call upon an Englishman, he used to take his cap in his hands. He was thus saved from the insult of taking off his shoes. He used to sit with the British during train journeys. People even termed him so, seeing his ways and style. To be called an Indian was almost an abuse to his ears. Ghaus Khan and Ijaad Hussain's comments hit him in the eye. He said with pride, 'Really, if this is the case, I'll show them that I'm no less than an Englishman. They will also remember what an officer they had encountered. Till now, I'd believed that all faults lay with us. Now I realize that it's a prank played by these rustics. Ahlmad Sir, please write a report to the regional sub-inspector that he must enquire into the matter and submit a report about it as soon as possible.'

The Peon - If nothing else, these people must be forced to pay a fine.

Ghaus Khan – It's very important to control this chap.

Jwalasingh – I don't wish to take any action before the report arrives.

The result of the discussion was that by evening, Babu Dayashankar, who had been appointed in the same region after reinstatement, came to Lakhanpur. Many constables were also with him. These people sat down in the chaupal. All the people in the village were called there. But Balraj was nowhere to be seen. He and Rangi had gone to chase away the neelgais. The daroga got upset and asked Manohar, 'Where is your son? He is the root cause of the whole matter; have you made him hide somewhere? Please make him show his face or else I'll issue a warrant against him.'

Manohar had'nt yet replied, when someone came and said, 'Here comes Balraj.' All the eyes were fixed on him. Two constables went up to grab him and two others tried to tie up his hands. Balraj looked helplessly at Manohar. His eyes were burning with a terrible feeling of retaliation.

They were reflecting that the insult was unbearable to him. 'I want to stake my life and teach them a lesson. What do you say?' When Manohar saw the state of his son, his blood started boiling. He almost turned mad. He couldn't decide what to do. He leapt like an eagle on to Balraj and pushed the two constables aside saying, 'Leave him, or else you'll regret.'

Struggling thus, his speech got strained and tears started falling from his eyes. Sukhu Chaudhary was rejoicing in his heart. He was already seeing the day when his ploughs would run over Manohar's ten bighas of land. Dukhran Bhagat was trembling with fear at this mess up. Dapatsingh was thinking that if people lay their hands on each other, these people will be taught a lesson, and Bisesar Sah was far too afraid; only Qadir Khan had real sympathy with Manohar. Manohar's rudeness had hit his heart. He thought, 'If people start manhandling each other, all will be lost.' He immediately went up to Dayashankar and whispered in his ears, 'Huzoor, you are our master. We are your subjects. Please restrain the constables or someone will lose his life. I will do whatever you say.' Dayashankar was one of those men who do not learn even after suffering a loss. But the charges levied on him had given him a nice moral. Earlier, he used to gobble up the entire bribe himself as much as he could. For this reason, the other officers of the department used to be jealous of him. He now learnt how to share and eat. Hence the entire police station was hands in glove with him. Besides, he didn't use abusive words as he used to do earlier. He had now realized that good manners were not just a matter of ethics; their economic value was also great. Thus his nature had become quite controlled and serious. He wanted to involve the entire village in this squabble and make a profit out of it. The rudeness of the constables could be an impediment in the success of this aim. Thus he calmed them down and started writing his report. The peons were asked to give their statement first. They all vented out their anger on Balraj. Ghaus Khan and his two followers also gave a similar statement. Only Binda Maharaj's evidence was a little weak. Now the villagers were asked to express their opinion. Initially, these people had thought that the whole village will be affected, but it was clear from the statement of the opponents that all efforts were on to trap Balraj. The entire village used to dote on Balraj due to his magnanimous nature. Internal affection and benevolence is also a positive feature of village life. On this occasion, just a reporting of truth could have saved Balraj's life; there wasn't any need for subtracting or adding anything. Therefore, they gathered courage and reported the actual incident; only hid away Balraj's rough words. The opposing party left no stone unturned to divide them but Qadir Khan's determination did not allow anyone to falter.

By eight o' clock, the enquiry had got over. There were no evidences found to take Balraj under arrest. Ghaus Khan could only lick dust. Darogaji went up from the chaupal to the inside room. The villagers started leaving one by one. Dapat Singh proudly declared, 'No one can harm us if the village stays united. Darogaji was arguing his best to mislead one of the witnesses.'

Dukhran – Godwilling nothing will happen now. Unity is a great force.

Manohar – Brothers, you have kept up my honour, or times weren't favourable.

Dapat Singh – The camp people had thought that they would be able to suppress us in the same way as they do to the rest of the villagers.

Dukhran – This village is protected by Lord Mahavir, who can dare to oppress it?

Manohar – Qadir Bhai, when the two constables grabbed Balu's hand I went mad with anger. Had they not left him, I would have surely killed one of them even at the cost of my own life.

Dapat – I'm surprised how Balraj controlled his anger.

Balraj – I had almost lost my senses. It seemed as if my hands had lost all their might. And when they started manhandling my father I just couldn't control myself.

Dukhran – All went off well with God's grace. There's nothing to worry now.

Talking thus, they all left for their homes. Manohar had sat down to smoke his hookah after dinner, when Binda Maharaj came and sat down.

He was a very generous man. He was the landlord's employee, but his sympathy was always with the tenants. On seeing him Manohar got up from his cot, Bilasi came out of the house and Balraj, who was cutting down the sugarcane into pieces, came and stood with his knife in hand. Nowadays, sugarcane was being processed to make jaggery. Sugar mills kept working till late night.

Manohar asked, 'Why Maharaj, what brings you here? What's going on in the chaupal?'

Binda – They are preparing to slice you throat. Darogaji has called the important people of the village and has asked them to change their statements. He is terrorizing them that if they don't do so, they'll have to pay fines. On top of it he's demanding a sum of hundred rupees. Everyone is scared to death. They are all ready to change their statements. I thought I should come and inform you. Even if I serve the zamindar, we are but one.

Manohar was shocked beyond belief. Bilasi stood dumbstruck, and Balraj too could not react. These poor men had thought that the worst was over. They had started their usual routine. This news came like a storm and upturned their life boats. No one could utter a word.

Binda said again, 'We had given such an apt statement. I thought, all would stick to what they had said, but all came out as cowards. They lost their balance in just a single threat.'

Manohar – I am overshadowed by bad stars; what else? God knows what all I'll have to bear for the sake of this lad.

Binda – It's quite late in the night, but do go to these people if you can. Please go and plead your case. Who knows, they might relent.

Balraj proudly said, 'No. There's no need to go to any coward. At worst, I'll be punished. May God save me from such cowards. People who have been scared to death in the name of fine are not to be trusted. I am a man; I'm least afraid of punishment. I have not stolen or robbed anyone; even if I lose my head after truth, I'll never be scared of them.'

Manohar – Oh! Please keep quiet. I know what a man you are! When I was your age, I too wanted to touch the skies; where should I find that spirit now?

Binda – These boys talk like that only. What do they know of the parent's heart? You please go, argue with them, and force them; they might side with you when they see you face to face.

Bilasi – Yes, do what you can. We'll have to bear what lies in our future.

It was nine at night. All nature was enwrapped in a sea of fog. The doors of all houses were closed. Fires had gonc cold. Only Sukhhu Chaudhary's mill was still on where jaggery was being made. Many people were warming themselves near the fire of the hearth. The poor women of the village were standing with their pots to get some warm sugarcane juice. Just then Manohar came and sat near Sukhu. The Chaudhary had just returned from the chaupal and was praising Darogaji's good nature with his friends. He changed his stance on seeing Manohar and said, 'Come Manohar, sit. I wanted to come to you myself. I just sat to test this juice. These people don't know anything. Yesterday an entire lot was spoilt. Darogaji is opening his mouth a bit too wide. He says he'll take fine from everyone. Moreover, he wants a hundred rupees extra. It's a life-risk to meddle with these officers. They have made a mountain of a molehill. People are trembling after hearing about the fine; they are preparing to change their statements.'

Manohar – Then there's no chance of Ballu's (Balraj's) escaping the gallows.

Sukhu – Yes, if the statements change he cannot escape. I hadn't given any statement due to the same reason. Khan Sahib kept assuring me but I said I'm neither here nor there. Neither will I spoil my terms with you or with the village. He felt bad about this; the entire village thinks I'm hands in glove with him, but can anyone tell me what bad I've done to anyone? Yes, I do sit with him. If a little friendship enables me to get other favours, why should I spoil it? The results one can get by good terms can't be achieved by spoiling all relations. Our head keeps lying below the zamindar's feet. It is best to keep such a God in good faith.

Manohar – What way out do you suggest to me?

Sukhu – What can I say; you know the condition of the village. Who will agree to pay the fine for your sake? No one. Now, you can either have faith in God or in your pocket.

Manohar didn't talk much to Sukhu. He understood that he wished to entrap him. He would give some of his money to the Daroga, and eat up the rest along with Ghaus Khan. These days he had no money in hand. He had bought a pair of new oxen and had spent everything on them. Khan Sahib had taken away some of his rented farms. Hence there was lesser hope of the rabi harvest also. He just had sugarcane to hope for but he had to pay off Bisesar Sah's debt and also the lagaan. Jaggery could not earn more than this. There was no other mahajan who could have given him any further loan. He went off to Dapat Singh's house but he hadn't yet thought about what to say to him. He was following his way like a lost traveller, absolutely unmindful of the destination, only because walking was perhaps more satisfying than remaining static at one place. 'What's the harm if people agree to pay the fine?' This solution was so far-fetched that his own mind could not devise it properly.

There was a solitary oil lamp burning in Dapat Singh's dalaan. Hay was strewn on the floor, and many men and boys were lying under a thick jute sheet squeezing themselves together. A bitch was feeding its pups in a corner. Dapat Singh hadn't slept as yet. He was hoping for sweet juice to arrive from Sukhu's mill so that he could have it before sleeping. His younger brother Jhapat Singh was trying to strain his eyes by reading the Ramayana in the dim light of the lamp. On seeing Manohar he said, 'Come Mahto, I see that you've got yourself embroiled in a bad mess.'

Manohar – I can be saved only if you people wish so.

Dapat – We didn't leave any effort in doing so. We had given such statements that Balraj could never have been caught, but we are quite helpless to pay the fine. We might pay the fine today, but if tomorrow Ghaus Khan reports falsely we can be punished also.

Manohar – No brother, I'll never ask you to pay the fine.

Dapat Singh was Manohar's well-wisher, but could not express those feelings presently. He said, 'God should not give a disobedient child even to an enemy. Had Balraj not exaggerated the matter yesterday, you wouldn't have been pleading before others like this.'

Suddenly Qadir Khan's voice rang aloud, 'Is this the justice you're implying Thakur! If Balraj was spoiling the matter, you should have scolded him there and then. You too kept smiling and approving of everything. Today when things have gone wrong you call it exaggeration. Initially you only had talked about your daughter, and I had narrated my woes. Balraj was already pent up due to all this. He lost his head at the first instance. You and I worked silently, but never opened our mouths. He is a man of courage; he couldn't bear all this. If he had got himself caught due to our sake, then isn't it unfair that we leave him to face the music just for the fear of fine?'

Dapat Singh said with surprise – Then do you suggest all of us should pay the fine?

Qadir – No, I am not suggesting that. I am just saying that we should stick to our original statements. Who knows whether the fine orders will comply or not? But even if it happens we should not turn our backs. Just think, how unfair it is that we should change our statement due to the threat of payment? And push our own child to drown in the well?

Manohar looked at Qadir Mian with tearful eyes. It seemed to him as if a God had arrived on the scene. Qadir's opinion which was based on ordinary sense of justice appeared divine to him. Dapat Singh also saw logic in what he said. His doubts about the fine were laid to rest. He was ashamed in his mind on his selfishness but he couldn't stop thinking that Balraj was responsible for the entire issue. He said, 'Qadir Bhai, your allegation that I instigated Balraj is not correct. When did I ask him to fight with the members of the camp? He himself started the quarrel. His nature is just like that. Today he's got into a mess with constables; tomorrow if he goes and beats up anyone, how will you go and save him?'

Qadir – I haven't asked you to save him. If he follows the stray path, he will fall himself. I just want to say that we should not change things seen with our own eyes and heard with our own ears due to fear from someone. We shouldn't attempt a fraud just to save our skins. What to talk of fines; it's our duty to stick to truth even if it entails going to jail.

Dapat Singh couldn't find a way to escape his words, but he still wanted that a way could be found which could enable them to follow this proposal in a practical manner. He said 'Well, suppose you and I keep firm on our statements, what will you do about Bisesar and Dukhran? They won't accept this.'

Qadir – Let me drag them here and talk to them, why won't they agree? If they fear God, they cannot escape us.

Qadir left after saying this, and returned after a while, bringing the two men along with him. Bisesar Sah looked at Dapat Singh with questioning eyes, as if asking him what he thought about it, and Dukhran Bhagat, who used to visit a temple twice a day for worship, and who was never tired of discussing God, sat with a bent head, as if some great trouble had befallen him or Qadir Khan was pushing him in a deep pit.

After making them sit, Qadir Khan took out a little tobacco from his turban, got some fire and after smoking a few shots, gave the hookah to Dapat Singh saying, 'Say Bhagat, what shall we do after seeing the Daroga tomorrow?'

Dukhran – I shall do the same as you people. But, I do not wish to pay the fine.

Qadir applied the same logic which had proved successful to impress Dapat Singh. Simple farmers are not complicated. Actually these people had never thought that changing of statements was a clear trap. When Qadir Khan explained the matter to them, their simple devotion to truth got awakened. Dukhran soon agreed with him. But his lecture failed to affect Bisesar. Sahji used to trade in sugar and foodgrains. He used to keep good profit margins, used to lend money, and had two ploughs; he had even taken a license to trade in various drugs like opium etc., but his external demeanour used to protect him from the trap of officers. He said, 'Bhai, if I side with you, I'll be left nowhere; I have trade worth a few rupees, I cannot manage without being strict with people. People become as good as brothers when they wish to borrow money and don't recognize me when it's time to pay back. This profession is such that after spending one's savings, one gets enmity from others in return. If a fine is levied, or if something else crops up tomorrow, there will be no witnesses left in the village, and how can one save oneself from fraud if one has to survive in the world? This whole universe is built on evil. One has to do all kinds of immoral deeds to serve one's own ends. If I start thinking about ethics today, tomorrow itself it'll cost me a hundred rupees; no one will pay me a penny and my whole trade will be destroyed. Whatever business is left nowadays is all based on fraud. None amongst us can come clean out of it; all of us mix mud and wood in bales of jute, and put sand and stones in oilseeds and grain. Isn't this immoral? You can slap me if I'm saying something improper. You can do as you please; I can never bring myself to pay the fine.'

A selfish principle works best on weak souls. Dukhran and Dapat Singh found these arguments quite justifiable. These very thoughts were in their hearts earlier but couldn't have been expressed due to some reason. Both looked at each other with emotional eyes. Dapat Singh said, 'Bhai, you say the truth, none can comply with this world by following a straight path. If you really wish to escape evil, you can go and rest in a forest. There can't be any escape here.'

Qadir Khan understood that no amount of religion or justice would be able to impress Sahuji. He will not relent until he can be made to understand what all hurdles can arrive in the way of changing one's statement. He said, 'Sahuji, whatever you say, you put it bluntly; of course how can one escape corruption while existing in the world? We are all involved in it day and night! But when we're ready to face the result of so many sins, let there be one more. And it's not just an issue of duty out here. The real risk is that we might fall into trouble by changing our statements. The police are not anyone's friends. Our first statement is secure with the Daroga. Our signatures and thumb impressions are all secure on it. If after taking a second statement they arrest us under charges of fraud, what will be our fate? We can be sentenced upto seven years. No brother, a fine is far better than this. How can we gobble a fly after seeing it with our naked eyes?'

Bisesar Sah's eyes opened up wide. Others too, got perplexed. Qadir Khan's logic worked its way out. People understood that they'd been caught on a wrong foot and could not escape the matter too easily. Bisesar made a long face, as if he had lost a bagful of money. He said, 'Darogaji does not seem to be such a man. He is our master after all; he'll do some concession to us, but only God can tell what goes on inside a man's heart. Who knows, evil might enter his mind. All of us will be destroyed then. Let's all resolve that we'll not change our statement nor shall we go to the Daroga. We are caught in a trap now. If we move mindlessly, the strings will tighten all the more. Let's keep still having faith in our God.'

They thus discussed everything and went to their homes. Qadir Khan's glib-talk had won over everybody.

Babu Dayashankar got up at eight, according to his routine, and started waiting for these people after the night's intoxication had spent itself out. When no one turned up till nine, he said to Ghaus Khan, 'Well Khan Sahib, won't they come here? It's so late.'

Ghaus Khan – God knows what transpired amongst them yesterday. Why Sukhu, Manohar had come to you last night?

Sukhu – Yes he did, but nothing was discussed about that issue. Qadir Mian was visiting people till late in the night. He must have taught something to them.

Ghaus Khan – It's indeed his very prank. Till nightfall yesterday, everyone was hellbent upon changing their statement. It seems when they went off from here they got a chance to woo them to his side. Had I known this I would have called everyone here. This fellow doesn't abstain from his evil ways. He always spoils a game.

Daya – If that's the case, I'll now write my report. I am not finding any evidence of any intemperance from the side of the villagers.

Ghaus Khan – Huzoor, for God's sake please do not write such a report or else they will become all the more impudent. Huzoor is not just an officer, he's my lord. This slave has eaten your salt since a long time. For me, you and Babu Gyanshankar are one and the same. I just want that Balraj should be sentenced for at least one month and the others should be made to pay the fine. This will actually be a great favour to me. They will see how powerful I am, and in future, the officers shall be served by the labour without any problem.

Dayashankar – What you say is indeed right, but at this moment, I'm neither your lord nor I am obliged to send labour for the officers. I have come to investigate and cannot be lenient towards anyone. You know very well that I haven't been trained to pick up my pen for free. I do not torture or trouble anybody, only want fees for my work, and whoever wants me to work happily should produce a renumeration. And I'm not bothered only about myself; I have many people working on menial wages under me.

How will they be able to survive? The village shall be in your awe, but how will it benefit me? You will rob the tenants; what about my concerns? I have no enmity with the villagers; those poor men are my loyal subjects. I am not a mosquito that I may roam about biting people. I have made a resolve that I will not look at any amount less than a hundred, whether you pay it or anyone else. I must see the amount before me. I cannot commit a crime without getting a feel of it.

Ghaus Khan kept pleading before him. He kept exaggerating his poor position, kept explaining his bad situation, but the Daroga didn't budge an inch. Khan Sahib had thought of teaching the people a lesson; only this could have benefitted him. He had no other option but to appease the Daroga. He thought that once he could have his way, he would be able to earn many a bagful of rupees. He took out some money from his trunk, borrowed some more from Sukhu Chaudhary and presented them to the Darogaji. He had saved this amount to build a mosque in the village. He was quite pained to sacrifice them, but the present problem had not left any other way out. When Dayashankar saw the heap of rupees, he was absolutely delighted. He said, 'Now you'll be victorious. I'll write such a report that it will shake up Mr. Jwalasingh as well. But had you hidden these rupees under the earth or what?'

Ghaus Khan – Please don't ask me huzoor. It's the earning of years. These rupees are marks of my sweat.

Dayashankar – (smiling) Well, not the marks of your sweat, I guess, but the marks of the blood shed by your tenants.

The report was ready by ten o' clock. For two days, the whole village was boiling with unrest. People were summoned. Then everyone was asked to give statements. In the end, everyone was asked to pay hundred rupees as fine. Qadir Khan couldn't face anyone in the village.

Evening had fallen. Babu Jwalasingh had gone out for hunting. The decision was about to be taken the next day. Ghaus Khan came and sat near Ijaad Hussain and asked, 'Hasn't the Deputy Sahib returned from hunting as yet?'

Ijaad Hussain – He will return late in the night. The real power of ruling lies in official tours. He will attend the court for a few hours, and keep roaming for the rest of the day. Just gave up the routine papers to be filled and kept enquiring about things.

Ghaus Khan – You must be knowing; Darogaji teased me a lot today.

Ijaad – These Hindus are just like that. They are far too selfish. Our Sahib is also quite judicious apparently, but whenever there is a vacancy, he always gives it to a Hindu. You must have heard about the peon Majid. Recently he has opened a shop for book binding, and has resigned from his post. In his place, Sahib has kept an illiterate milkman. This man is now a peon, but his real job is to milk cows and feed them. He has also kept two such servants in the entourage. They are now meant to serve him. When they can serve their ends by using such tactics, where is the need for extra labour? We, on the other hand, are ordered not to force anyone to do unpaid labour.

The sun had set. Khan Sahib remembered that the time to offer namaz was passing away. He washed his hands and feet and started reading namaz under a tree.

Just then Bisesar Sah came and greeted Ahlmad Sahib respectfully. He had a fat body, a thick vest, an old shawl, a dirty turban, bare feet, dirty face and a selfish look playing on his face. A peon scolded him saying, 'Where are you going just like that? Don't you have any respect for the officers?'

Bisesar Sah retraced his steps and folded his hands saying, 'Sarkar, I have a request. May I utter it if you please?'

Ijaad – What do you have to say? I don't have a moment's rest due to people like you. At all times; someone or the other keeps riding my head like a devil.

Bisesar – Huzoor, I've been standing since a long time.

Ijaad – Well, say what you want.

Bisesar – I only wish to plead that I may not be forced to pay the fine. I'm very poor, I'll be totally destroyed.

The ahlmad used to deal with such self-oriented, blind but rich men on a daily basis. He knew their tactics very well. He first turned his face and expressed his helplessness, but kept talking politely so that the prey might not escape his clutches. In the end he arrived at the real issue. He took the money with such a face as if he was himself paying it. He sent away Sahji after giving him adequate sympathy.

The peon asked – Won't he be asked to pay the fine?

Ijaad – Why not? The decision has already been made. He can pay a hundred or even hundred and twenty. I haven't assured him a bit that I will get the fine exempted for him. I just told him that I will try my best under the circumstances. If he was satisfied with just these words, what further headache is required? People defame the practice of bribery, but if I hadn't taken money from him, God knows what would have been his condition? God knows, who all he might have approached, and what not he might have done? He got relieved after giving the money and his heart was at peace. He will eat properly and have a sound sleep. I'll tell him tomorrow, 'Bhai what to do, I tried my best, but the Deputy Sahib did not relent.' If I get a chance, I'll play another game. I'll say the job won't be done without gifting something to the Deputy Sahib. If you pay a hundred rupees, I'll get your fine dismissed. If this is agreed upon, I'll be so happy. This is what is known as joint sharing and getting a joint credit. I haven't been unjust or cruel to anyone. This is a kind of divine charity. Possibly in my last birth, he must have owed me some money. Almost daily I get such men in my trap who seem to be hating their money. I laugh at their foolishness in my heart of hearts, and thank God for producing them, or else how would men like me survive?

14

Rai Saheb has arrived in Nainital since one month. His bungalow is situated near a picturesque lake in a conclave of green trees, which costs him about one thousand rupees as monthly rent. There are many horses, motorcars, and servants accompanying him. He stays here royally like a king. He sometimes roams amidst the mountains, goes out on hunts or for boating in the lakes, plays polo and golf, sarod and sitar, and keeps organizing picnics, parties and many such outings. Rai Saheb enjoys these excursions with delight and vigour. No party or gathering is complete without his presence. He is the bridegroom of all such celebrations. The organizing committee meets daily, but from the demeanour of the members, it is difficult to guess whether they give importance to outer pleasures, or to dispensing of their duties.

But Gyanshankar did not find any engaging attraction even here. Rai Saheb got him introduced to that society. He used to take him almost daily to dinners and gatherings, praised him before the officials and introduced him to the ladies. What more he could have done? It was up to Gyanshankar to raise a structure on this foundation, but he was like a plant which cannot thrive in unfavourable conditions despite the gardener's care and nourishment. It seemed as if he had lost his way in a deep valley. He used to feel embarrassed in front of decked-up ladies despite his being well-versed in social manners. Rai Saheb often used to preach to him about decent behavior in private. He used to present himself as an example, explaining why one must talk to men even without purpose or praise the good looks of women, but in all such situations, Gyanshankar used to become clueless and tongue-tied. He was surprised as to how Rai Saheb was able to mix with women despite his old age, and talked in a way that one could not sense any pretension, as if he had been brought up in this very environment.

Once he was sitting on a bench near the lake. Many women were enjoying water sports on a boat. They recognized him and called him to join them. Gyanshankar was nonplussed. He couldn't find words to refuse. He was scared lest he should be termed unsocial. He went and sat on the boat with a long drawn face; a living picture of guilt and embarrasment. His heart felt very heavy. The women, on seeing him in such a state, mocked him to an extent that he almost became unrecognizable. It seemed he had lost his original face. It was as if a little monkey had fallen into the hands of wanton boys. His eyes became full of tears and he kept sitting in a corner cursing his fate. Finally he got down from the boat and thanked his stars. He swore never to go near those women again.

Gradually Gyanshankar lost all interest in these outings and diversions. Jealousy, which is often an admission of one's own weaknesses, became a chink in his armour. He felt its sting day and night. His high desires had taken him to the foothills of a mountain but couldn't take him any further. He lost his courage and started criticizing the other courageous climber who was busy scaling the peak despite all hurdles. 'What kind of a madness is this! People deride the English lifestyle for no reason. For a little fame and power, these Indians adopt so much polish and paraphernalia that they've lost all touch with reality. All seem such imposters! The British might not say anything on their faces but must be mocking them among their own friends. What's more, they hanker after having a dance with the ladies. What shame, what impudence; it's something that stains our very race! Rai Saheb is also a strange creature. He feels like dancing even at this age. It seems as if he's lost all control and is making a mockery of himself. Dr. Chandrashekhar is a master of philosophy, keeps lecturing on dense topics like nature and man, but once he starts dancing all his scholarship seems lost. Then there's Raja Indrakumar Singh, whose belly's blown up like a pot but he too is intent upon showing his dancing skills, and the biggest surprise is that they all claim to be the devotees of society and the nation. Whosoever you meet pretends to be shedding tears on the country's misfortune. They mourn its destruction and poverty while having wine and lemonade in luxorious hotels. This has also assumed the shape of a fashion.'

This way Gyanshankar's jealousy made itself apparent in the form of a newly-found patriotism. His own inabilities turned him into a socialist. To him, all capitalists now seemed wolves and a gang of robbers. He thought, 'No one has any idea as to what is happening to poor people. No one has any kindness left in their hearts. Someone is a king or a landowner, or a moneylender; they all suck the blood of the poor, rob the huts of the weak and afterwards mourn the degradation of the nation. It is quite fitting that the officers don't bother about these people. If they fall a prey to their talk and hand over the reins of the nation to them, the whole race will be wiped out. They will eat up everything. Can someone go and ask them, what good is the country incurring by the millions of rupees they're spending on their outings? If they had spent this money on the people, the latter would've thanked and worshipped them, but as of now they have no idea who the former are and what they do. The suppliant won't be satisfied if one merely gives him something as a donation; he will feel content only if one can spare something of one's own to give him.'

These revolutionary thoughts started evolving in Gyanshankar mind. His tongue started getting anxious to express them at a suitable moment. He got into a tiff with Raja Chandrashekhar one day. In the same manner, he started a verbal tussle with Raja Indrakumar; and with Mr. Haridas, the barrister, he almost went up to the extent of starting a physical fight. The result was that people started boycotting Gyanshankar; in fact they stopped visiting Rai Saheb's bungalow. But when Gyanshankar got his opinion published in a famous English magazine, the whole of Nainital was forced to sit up and take notice. One who could initiate such excellent thoughts could not be easily dismissed as insane or a mere glib-talker. The style of the essay was so lively; expression so sharp, sarcasm so sweet and quotations so heartrending that people felt an untold pleasure even in their assaults. It was an extensive picture of the real Nainital. The artist had painted each face with its own particular character in such a way that people couldn't oppose the portrayal in any manner. The essay contained such satire that many a sentence became part and parcel of the common dialogue between people.

Gyanshankar was doubtful that on the publication of this essay, the entire Nainital would be after his life, but his doubts were dispelled very soon. Whereas earlier people kept insulting and ignoring him they now began treating him with respect. They also visited him to apologize for their rudeness. All seemed to be enjoying the sarcasm levelled at one another. Dr. Chandrashekhar and Raja Indrakumar were close pals, but the reference to the Raja as a two-faced serpent delighted the doctor to no end. Raja Saheb was also elated at Doctor Saheb's description as a middle aged lady. These assaults did not go futile. People lost their interest in outings and pictures. If not from a heartfelt desire, merely for the sake of appeasing Gyanshankar, they started seeking his opinion in public schemes. Gyanshankar grew all the more courageous. He started reprimanding people more openly. He almost became a moral preacher, from being a mere critic. He got a new sense of self-pride. He understood how easy it was to impress these officers and their subordinates. All this was achieved due to just one essay. The pure feelings of service and kindness that he had portrayed therein now had an effect on his own soul as well. But alas! this situation did not continue for long. By the end of rainy season people started fleeing Nainital, and gradually, the entire place became deserted. Gyanshankar again began the pursuit of his original vested interest. His heart became a miser day by day. He had derided the expensive ways of Rai Saheb in Nainital. Now in Lucknow, he openly expressed his opinion which was a reflection of his narrow- mindedness. He had only his own subordinates to express his anger upon. He often got into quarrels with the manager and other servants, saying, 'You people are bent upon robbing the estate; like master, like servant; all are full of pretensions about money. It doesn't hurt to spend free money. Had you earned it by your own sweat you'd have felt the pinch on the pocket.'

Rai Saheb was the President of the Ramleela committee. He used to spent thousands of rupees on the occasion; the servants got new uniforms, rich men were invited to dinner, and on the final day of Ram's ascension to the throne a lavish spread was laid out. Gyanshankar abhorred such mindless misuse of money. When he saw the preparations for Diwali in a similar vein, he got very upset and went on the tour of the region for a week.

It was Christmas time in the month of December. Rai Saheb was busy preparing for gifts to be given to the British officers. Gyanshankar saw him doing this and kept making faces, as if he was doing something utterly hateful. At times, he even commented on him in a low voice. He wanted to incite him into a discussion. But Rai Saheb was immune to all this. He seemed too aware of Gyanshankar's characteristics. Perhaps he was indulging in all this merely to make him jealous. This feeling was enough for Gyanshankar to lose his night's sleep. On top of it, when he came to know that Rai Saheb was under a huge sum of debt he was almost sick with depression. He anxiously approached Vidya and said, 'It seems he won't even leave a penny for his burial. I will talk to him today itself and tell him clearly that if he doesn't restrain himself I will also do what I please.'

Vidya – It's his property; what right do you have to raise any objections? He might go on spending night and day; there will still be enough left for us to enjoy. We cannot get more than what is due in our fate.

Gyan – One cannot see one's own destruction, sitting idly, waiting for one's fate to take charge.

Vidya – Suppose my brother had been alive; then what?

Gyan – Then it would have been a different case altogether. I wouldn't have had any concern with this property. Nor would I have been bothered about its preservation or destruction. The moment one finds a mark of ownership on something one develops an intimate relationship with it.

But alas! the workings of misfortune! The botherations of Gyanshankar were not just limited to a use or misuse of property. Till now, his position was similar to that of a revolutionary army. He had no trouble brewing back in his own house. But now, ill-luck started raiding his own territory. His elder brother Premshankar had been missing since several years. Gyanshankar was almost sure that he wasn't alive any more. It was the month of March. Suddenly, a letter from Premshankar arrived from America that he would be reaching Benaras on the first of April. Initially, Gyanshankar was delighted to receive this letter. The hope of meeting his brother after years of separation made his heart full of happiness. He ran to Vidya to tell her about the good news. Vidya said, 'It's our good fate! Bhabhiji's wish has been fulfilled by God! Where was he uptil now?'

Gyan – He was studying agriculture in America. He has even worked on a farm for two years.

Vidya – It's the fifteenth of this month today. We should leave this place in a day or two.

Gyanshankar only replied, 'Yes, of course', and went outside. His happiness vanished in a second and new worries started dancing before his eyes, as if a sick person gets rejuvenated due to the effect of a strong medicine, but lapses into the same sickness once the effect is over. Whatever ambitions he had nurtured till now; whatever life path he had paved, he had not kept any space for anyone except for himself. He wanted everything for his own self. But in the present arrangements, two families would be difficult to manage within a single estate. Lakhanpur would have to be divided into two. Gradually, as he started thinking more on the topic, the problem appeared more complicated, and his worries became all the more intense. It went on to the extent that by evening, he couldn't bear it any more. He was sitting sadly in his room, when Rai Saheb came and asked, 'You haven't dressed yourself; won't you come for a walk?'

Gyan – No, I don't feel like.

Rai – There's going to be a live band in Qaisarbag. A lovely breeze is blowing.

Gyan – Please excuse me today.

Rai – Well, even I won't go then. Are you writing anything these days?

Gyan – No, I haven't written anything recently.

Rai – Then write something now. I will give you the subject and the material for it. Write the first essay on this year's budget and the next one on Gayatri.

Gyan – I haven't read any budget-related essay; how can I pick up my pen on it?

Rai – Well, what's there to do in that? Who reads the budget these days? You can simply highlight a need for more funds for education, mention the significance of education, demand money for healthcare and make a few comments on some of its aspects. The police department must have received more funds; that's quite sure. You must insist upon a reduction in that, and end your essay with showing a need for building new canals. That would be a perfect critique of the budget. But all this should be put forward in such a polite way and the financial secretary should be praised for his efficiency in such a manner that he gets impressed and thinks that I have surmised on his objectives a great deal. Your style is already too lively; just try to make an effort that my knowledge and versatility should be evident from every single word. That's about all. I know that none of our proposals is going to be accepted ever, then where's the need to read other essays on the budget and try to critique them?

Gyan – And what should I write about Gayatri Devi?

Rai – Just a brief life-account. Write something about my family, some words about her husband's family and discuss a bit about her education. You can then mention her husband's demise and describe with detail her skills of management and welfare-plans for her subjects. In the past three years, whatever donations she has made for various institutions and arrangements for the upliftment of her people are there in my records. You'll get a lot of help from those. You will have to beautify that structure yourself. In the end you can write that such an efficient and learned woman must be given a prominent post, the absence of which says a lot about the skills of the administrators themselves. It is the duty of the government to award her suitably and encourage her for a better dispensing of social duties; but write quickly whatever you wish to write; delay will spoil everything.

Gyan – I will write the budget critique soon till tomorrow, but the second essay will take time. My elder brother, who had been missing since long, is arriving home on the first of the next month. We must reach home before he comes back.

Rai – I guess he had gone to America?

Gyan – Yes, he has written to us from there.

Rai – What kind of a man is he?

Gyan – What can I say? It's only when he actually arrives that we can see how much he has changed. As far as I remember, he was a very quiet and thoughtful person.

Rai – But are you aware that America's environment is not conducive to a feeling of brotherly love and compassion? Personal interest is the basic principle of their lifestyle and your brother too, must have been affected by that.

Gyan – Let's see, I will not give him any reason to complain from my side.

Rai – You may or may not; he will find a reason himself. It's quite possible that my doubts are proved baseless. I wish with all my heart that it happens this way, but it's my experience that a long stay abroad causes the strings of love to become lifeless.

Gyanshankar could not hide his feelings any further. He now openly said, 'I too fear the same. If he didn't bother to write to us for six years, then it's evident that he does not have any affection left for us. You are a father figure to me; what's there to hide from you? All my ambitions have been destroyed with his arrival. I thought my finances would improve after I separate from my uncle. It's me who insisted upon it; I divided the property myself, for which my uncle's children will forever curse me. But now every effort has gone down the drain.'

Rai Saheb – If he claims his share in the profit of these erstwhile years you'll be caught in a huge trouble. Please don't do anything in this matter without consulting proper lawyers.

What objective lay in Rai Saheb's mind by instigating Gyanshankar's doubts like this is difficult to ascertain. Perhaps he wanted to gauge his inner feelings or just wished to have a glimpse of his meanness and selfish nature. He just sparked off these thoughts in him and left for his walk.

Poor Gyanshankar started burning in a fire of jealousy. He was haunted by a stream of negative thoughts which he wanted to resolve immediately. 'Can Bhai Sahib really claim his share of the yearly profit? If he actually does, is there no means of escape for me? Does Rai Saheb have a right to keep burdening the estate with mindless debts? Can there be a legal way to stop his overspending?' These questions were causing deep unrest in his mind, and he was troubled greatly by such meanderings. He went to Rai Saheb's library and took out a book of law. But he could not find any answer to his questions. He took out another book, and soon enough, a heap of books lay before him. He kept turning one page after another, but no satisfactory answer could be found. He desperately started looking here and there. He glanced at the watch. It was almost ten in the night. He kept the books away. He had his dinner, and lied down, but there was no trace of any sleep. A troubled mind is the biggest hurdle to a sound sleep. Till now, he was his own safe harbour to the wild waves of his life-sea. All his desires were anchored safely in his mind. Premshankar came and destroyed this anchor, and made all his boats wary of their safety. 'Why will my brother relent? Will he understand flattery? That seems difficult, he's a clever man. With politeness and good manners? Impossible. Politeness can be returned with good behaviour, not with a sacrifice of one's own personal interest. Then should I initiate a fight? Absolutely not; it will further weaken my claim.' He finally jumped at an idea which occurred to him after all such meanderings. 'Oh!' he thought, 'What an idiot I am. The society will not even let him enter the house; what can he do to me? Surprising, I couldn't think of this basic idea uptil now. Nor did Rai Saheb think about it. Bhai Saheb would be attacked as soon as he enters Benaras; he won't be allowed to even set his feet properly. On the face of it, I will treat him with brotherly affection, keep mourning the narrow-mindedness and injustice of our social set up, but will keep churning the tide against him. He'll probably quit himself in a month or two. Perhaps Shraddha will also not cooperate with him. She will have to be incited. She is otherwise quite religious-minded. She'll definitely be affected by public opinion. Well, the road seems clear of all hurdles now. There's no need to be scared of this fellow. I can fearlessly exercise my show of brotherly love.'

This thought delighted Gyanshankar to an extent that he wanted to go and wake up Vidya, but he restrained himself. Once he got out of this sea of worries, he thought, 'Gayatri's anger is also a kind of doubt that's troubling me. I am totally unaware of the feelings of women. Possibly, I might have shown some impatience, but this is not a crime that Gayatri cannot excuse. It seems quite natural for her to get upset on my sense of daring. No honourable lady can be empowered in such an easy way. The consciousness of her womanly sense of purity suppresses the feeling of love. Even if that's not the case, she seems necessarily bound to put up a show of rudeness to express her detatchment and disinterest. Perhaps her purpose is to test my love. She is a coveted object, and does not wish to devalue herself. I got so oppressed with my defeat that I couldn't think of raising my head again. She was here for so many days. I should have gone and apologized to her. Had she been angry she could have scolded me. She wanted to come out clean of everything and blame me entirely for it. I should have tolerated this assault of words and in a few days, I would've ruled her heart. I just couldn't achieve that; rather got upset myself, and distanced myself from her. She must have thought me to be so immature, coward and foolish. Well, now I must make amends for all this. This is a kind of inspiration. Once her life-story gets published it will put an end to all her passivity and pride. She dotes on honour and fame. Rai Saheb has himself appeared in the form of a woman. If Gayatri's desire gets fulfilled she'd be delighted, and if she gets the title of a queen she'll forever worship me on a pedestal. Once I'm done with the affairs of my brother, I can start working on this objective. God know if she enquires about me in her letters or not. Let me go and ask Vidya.' This time he couldn't suppress this strong desire. Vidya was asleep in the adjacent room. He went and woke her up. She got up with a start and asked, 'What's up? Why haven't you slept till now?'

Gyan – I cannot bring myself to sleep today. I wish to talk to you. Rai Saheb hasn't returned till now.

Vidya – Has he ever returned before twelve that he will do so today? Sometimes it gets as late as one or two in the night.

Gyan – I had taken a short nap. I saw in a dream that Gayatri is standing before me, crying loudly so I just woke up. I have been tossing and turning since then. I hope you receive letters from her?

Vidya – Yes, I get a letter every week, in fact I get delayed very often in sending a reply.

Gyan – Does she ever enquire about me?

Vidya – Well, there's hardly a letter in which she doesn't ask about your well-being.

Gyan – I would have gone and met her if she'd have called me.

Vidya – She'll worship you if you go there. She has a lot of affection for you.

Gyanshankar could not sleep now; he soon became lost in daydreaming about his happy days.

15

It was morning time. Gyanshankar was waiting for the train on the railway station. There was still half an hour left in the train's arrival. He started reading an English newspaper, but soon got bored. The advertisements for medicines seemed far more interesting than ordinary news. He read out all those in just ten minutes. His mind was still not at peace. It was proving difficult for him to sit idle. It needs a lot of concentration to do so. Ultimately his mind found rest in eating chaat from a roadside vendor. It is the best option to divert one's attention during idle hours.

When he came to the platform again, the signal had been given. Gyanshankar's heart started beating fast. As soon as the train arrived, he started looking into the first and the second class coupons. But Premshankar was not in these. There were just two compartments of the third class. Premshankar was sitting here. As soon as he saw Gyanshankar, he went up to him and hugged him. Gyanshankar too, felt an upsurge of strength and affection. A real moment of brotherhood wiped out all the ill-feelings. His throat got full and tears started falling from his eyes. Both the brothers kept crying for sometime. Gyanshankar had thought that his brother would arrive with great pomp and show, but his clothes and luggage were quite ordinary. His body was appearing quite healthy, and though he was elder to Gyanshankar by five years, he appeared much younger to him and his face was glowing in the pink of health.

Gyanshankar was busy calling the coolies when Premshankar took his entire luggage in hand and started moving outside. Gyanshankar moved back in hesitation lest any known face should see him with a man carrying his own stuff.

Both the men sat on a tonga and Premshankar said, 'I have come back after six years and it seems as if it's been only a few days since I left the place. Hope all's well at home?'

Gyan – Yes of course; everything's fine. It's been so many days that you wrote to us; you seemed to have forgotten us totally. Babuji expired, mourning your absence.

Prem – I got to know of that tragic news through an Indian newspaper, but I couldn't come home due to some reason. The 'Hindustan Review' published your article on life in Nainital, after reading which I decided to come here. Your progressive thoughts have pulled me here, or possibly, I wouldn't have come for a few more days. Do you participate in politics?

Gyan (with hesitation) – I haven't got an opportunity for that as yet. But of course, I do keep studying about it.

Prem – What profession have you adopted?

Gyan – I am still engrossed in matters of the house. I needed to stay at home to manage our land affairs. You know what an imbroglio it is. Almost daily there are squabbles and conflicts. It might not earn you a profit but makes you inclined towards a lazy lifestyle. You lose the courage to dive into the real challenges of life. Had I not got caught into all this I must have been a lawyer today.

Prem – So you too have been trapped in the net of ownership, and are busy misusing your higher faculties? How long will our estate survive?

Gyan – It would have vanished long back had our uncle had his way, but probably it will survive for a few more days now. I now have a separate establishment of my own.

Prem – I am sorry to hear that; what have you done? He must be facing lots of financial difficulties now?

Gyan – Not really. Dayashankar has joined the police and he has an income of about two thousand from his share of the property.

Prem – But he must be quite unhappy at the division of the house. Actually his deep love was the main reason behind my elopement. You were probably in school at that time; I became active in the freedom struggle during my college days. Those days our old leaders used to tremble at the very mention of swaraj. Mostly, it was the youth who were leading the movement. I worked for a year with great enthusiasm. The police wanted to trap me. As soon as I found that they are planning to file a chargesheet against me, I thought it best to run away. If Babuji had seen me under the gallows, he would probably have borne it somehow, but our uncle would've surely committed suicide. It was due to this very fear that I stopped all correspondence with you, lest the police should get you in trouble. One cannot discover one's true state of slavery without going across the borders. The thoughts that made me a culprit of sedition here, are daily expressed by the Americans to their rulers even more bluntly; in fact, there, the more bold a critique of the administration takes place, the more it is respected. I guess there has been some improvement in freedom of thought here as well. You essay is a fine example of that. These emancipating winds have inspired me to come here and the real truth is that I increasingly became disillusioned with America. I saw such cruel aspects of money and autonomy there that I ended up hating them. Life in small towns and villages is far better out here. My plan is also to lead a simple life. I also wish to develop agriculture as far as possible.

Gyan – This secret has been revealed only today. Till now, I and other family members believed that you had gone there for higher education. But nowadays, the freedom movement has slowed down a lot. The swarajists have been forced to shut their mouths.

Prem – That's not a bad development, it will make people work, rather than waste their time talking. Almost an era has gone by in foolish talk. I too, have lost faith in mere words. We now need to unite, act with compassion and remove social injustice. I plan to modify the ways of farming. That's why I've studied agriculture in America.

Talking thus, both the brothers reached home. Premshankar found his house to be quite small. His eyes had become used to seeing the skyscrapers in America. He had never imagined his house to be so devastated. When he entered the room, he got all the more depressed seeing its condition. There wasn't even a proper floor. There were two or three chairs lying around, but they too were pretty old and covered with dust. There were some new paintings on the walls but absolutely weird and unnatural. Though in principle Premshankar detested things of pleasure, he still hadn't lost a natural interest in them.

Lala Prabhashankar had been waiting for them. He came and hugged Premshankar and started weeping loudly. Other people of the locality also came to see him. Premshankar kept narrating anecdotes of his life in America. No one was ready to leave him alone. None was brothered that he had come after a long journey; it was time for him to bathe and eat; they could talk later. Ultimately Gyanshankar had to ask them to allow his brother to have food; it was getting quite late.

Premshankar took a bath, said his daily evening prayers, and went upstairs to have food. He was hopeful that Shraddha would serve him there; he would be able to meet her and would talk to her a great deal. But his hopes remain unfulfilled. A mat was spread on a low stool, where his meal had been served, but Shraddha was nowhere to be seen to welcome him. Premshankar felt very sad at this lack of love that he encountered. His love for Shraddha was a major reason behind his return. Her memory had always haunted him and her lovelorn image always remained alive in his heart. He hated an outward display of love. He was still attracted by women's respect, devotion, shyness and affectionate nature. He had missed Shraddha's presence in the drawing room, but his heart became full of sorrow at not finding her here. He thought that this was not any feeling of shyness but a total lack of love. He felt so upset that he wanted to leave at once, but he still chose to act with patience. He sat down for his meal.

He said to Gyanshankar, 'Come brother, sit. Where's Maya? Please call him; it's been a while that I've had the good luck of seeing all of you together.'

Gyanshankar replied with a lowered head, 'You please eat first; I'll have my dinner later on.'

Prem – It's almost eleven; how much will you delay having food? Come and sit. How will I eat so many things alone? I cannot wait any longer. I have seen chapatis after so many days. I have almost forgotten the taste of halwa, samosas and kheer. There's no joy in eating alone. What kind of hospitality is this that I should eat here and you, somewhere else? In America, it would have been taken as a huge insult of the guest.

Gyan – Please excuse me at this hour. My digestion is quite weak; I stay with much restraint.

Premshankar had forgotten that the Hindu religion dissolves immediately once it enters the sea. While leaving America, Premshankar had never thought that his society will boycott him, and even his real brother will treat him like an untouchable. But now, when Gyanshankar did not sit with him for his meals despite repeated requests and kept making one pretext or the other, he suddenly remembered a forgotten fact. The utensils lying before him further confirmed it; there were no utensils of brass or any pure metal. All were made of china and the tumbler was made of glass. He asked with a tinge of doubt, 'Why is it that you are avoiding to sit with me? I hope you are not restricted by orthodox views regarding touch and all that?'

Gyanshankar replied embarrassingly, 'What can I say to you? You know Hindus quite well; how fanatical they are. Ever since the news about your return arrived, there has been a storm brewing in the society. I personally have no objection to going abroad. I consider it necessary for the emancipation of the nation and the race and admit that this restriction has harmed us a lot, but I still don't have the courage to oppose my social set up.'

Prem – Oh, I understand! Surprisingly, why did I remain oblivious to this issue uptil now? I will not force you anymore. I will eat but I'm sorry that you are still the slave of the society despite being so progressive;

especially when you admit the social restrictions in this case as totally unjustified. Education should enable you to reform the society, not make you sacrifice your principles at the altar of its pressures. If you had derided sea journey from an independent point of view I wouldn't have objected a bit. Your thoughts and behaviour would have been synchronized. But if you believe in something internally, and fail to practice it only due to a fear of criticism or mockery, it doesn't suit a radical person like you. If your religion does not prohibit you from believing the words of a traveller, I assure you that I haven't done anything in America that is out of the purview of Hindu religion. I lectured a lot on philosophical texts, kept upholding our traditions and caste system; and even praised the system of purdah, so I cannot admit that any one has a right to call me an agnostic. I am as much a devotee of my religion and faith as I was earlier; in fact, much more than before. I cannot justify myself more than this.

Gyan – There's no need for that, because the objection that these people have against foreign travel is not due to any logic or principle. But you will have to admit that the Hindu religion is dependent on some rituals and conventions, and you cannot follow them properly in an alien land. You can refute the Vedas, follow Jesus Christ or Hazrat Mohammad, but you cannot forego these conventions. Doubtlessly, these restrictions are loosening up day by day, and there are many people out here who call themselves Hindus without following anything, but a majority of people ignore them and criticize them. You can call it my weakness or idleness, but I think it's my duty to walk with the majority. I am not an advocate of violent revolution. I think we can reform the society more by staying within its limits rather than by growing independent of it.

Premshankar did not say anything in return. When he lay down after dinner, he started surmising on his situation. 'I had thought I would be able to work peacefully here, at least no one shall oppose me in my own house; but I see that I'd be facing great unrest in the coming days. Gyanshankar's benevolent essay put me in this state of confusion. Well, I should not worry. What worst can the society do to me? And what good I would gain by staying within its boundaries? If no one eats with me let it be; I would also refuse to eat with them. If people avoid me, it's okay; I too will do so. What sin have I committed by going abroad; no one even turns the real sinners out of society. People who sell off their faiths, their conscience, even their children keep thriving here; no one even stares at them with a harsh eye. Why should I destroy my own soul to stay close to such fallen and evil men?'

Suddenly he remembered, 'Is Shraddha too boycotting me for the same reason? Probably she too has been affected by these narrow views! My whole life will be spoilt, if this is so.' This doubt landed him in great tension and gradually this anxiety grew so much that he couldn't stay still. He asked about Shraddha's room from Maya and climbed upstairs. ,

Shraddha was standing at her door at this time, in a manner as if a traveller had forgotten his way. Her heart was trembling not with a sense of joy but with a kind of unexplained fear. She had worshipped hard for this blessed moment. This desire had been the lamp of her dark life; the anchor of her sinking boat. She had spent thirty days of every month and twenty four hours of each day, dreaming about it. The irony was that those desires were not meant to be completed but only appeared to torture her soul. That fire and that patience, was not willing to be culled peacefully. Premshankar was only a wishful dream for Shraddha. She used to offer the entire gift of her life to this imagined dream. Her devotion was only meant for his memory, which was too attractive, loving and full of feeling. His physical presence put an end to this happy imagination and pleasant memory. She who doted her very self on his memory, was now scared of his power, as the memory on its own was a nurturer of her womanly self, and the present power, its destroyer. Shraddha was moreover, acutely aware of the social arrangements and needs of the hour. She didn't have any freedom of thought or any divine inspiration that was required to break the shackles of tradition. She was a very ordinary Hindu lady, devoid of all traces of power. She could have sacrificed her life for the sake of her husband but it was far too impossible for her to ignore her religion or tolerate social indictments. Ever since she had heard about the arrival of Premshankar, her condition was that of a criminal, who was awaiting the fall of the sword. She had been shedding tears since Permshankar had come and sat downstairs. Her heart was trembling lest he should come upstairs; he must not stand before her or touch her in person. It was far easier for her to give away her life. 'How will I face him, how will my eyes be able to meet his; how shall I answer his questions;' she was lost in thoughts like these, when Premshankar came and stood before her. Had Shraddha been struck by lightning; had the ground beneath her feet slipped away, or had a lion come and scared her, she wouldn't have been so shocked and wouldn't have escaped to her room. She just went inside and stood in a corner. She was trembling with fear. Premshankar was totally shocked. Had the sky disappeared in front of his eyes, he wouldn't have been so dumbstruck. He stood still for a while and then went downstairs with a sigh. He couldn't muster enough courage to enter Shraddha's room or ask her anything. Her distancing had spoilt his enthusiasm, and even those poetic dreams which had been his companions in his days of struggle. Shraddha saw him going towards the stairs from an opening of her room. Alas! No one could guess what her heart was going through at the moment. Her dear husband, in whose separation she had spent seven years, weeping by herself, was going away with a devastated heart, and she was standing at a distance as if there was a deep sea in the front. Her religion did not allow her to step forward. The sway of love swept upon her like wild waves, but came back after banging across the rocks of religion. She almost went ahead to hold his hands and bring him back, but could not move forward. Religion seemed to challenge her and say, 'Love is transient and hollow. Who is a husband and who is a wife? All is a myth. I am transcendental, take care to protect me.' Shraddha was stupefied. She reminded herself of a husband who had travelled beyond the seven seas; God knows what he might have eaten or drunk, or stayed with whom; what relation could she have with him? But when Premshankar reached downstairs, Shraddha became unconscious and fell down. No amount of splashing waves could break the barrier; they instead ended up flooding the banks.

16

Premshankar stayed here for two weeks, as if he was a prisoner awaiting his release. He just couldn't bring himself to rest. Shraddha's religiosity had pained him in a way that he kept feeling the pain day and night. He repeatedly resolved to go back to America, and to never come back again. But a faint hope that the knowledge of the nation's real condition might spark a change in Shraddha caused him to rethink his resolve and stay back. He kept lying in the drawing room day in and day out, without meeting anyone and all his programmes of agricultural reform got postponed. On top of it, Gyanshankar kept troubling him by bringing all kinds of news about the conspiracies being hatched against him. One day, he informed him that people had passed a proposal to socially boycott him in a prominent meeting. The next day he brought news of a Brahminical Sabha, wherein it had been decided that no one should go to Premshankar's house for any kind of rituals. The following day, Shraddha's purohitji stopped coming to their house. Gyanshankar often indicated in his talks that he too was getting a bad name due to Premshankar, and it was quite possible that people might boycott him as well. He pretended one way in front of his brother, and used to criticize Premshankar in front of other leaders – 'He abuses our gods and goddesses; he also says that all flesh is the same whether it belongs to any living being. He doesn't even wash his hands and face after meals. According to him, even a scavenger can become a Brahmin if he performs such duties.' All these charges incited the society even more, to the extent that some daring youth wanted to beat up Premshankar if they could find him alone. 'Tilak' was a local newspaper. It reported all the venom being produced against Premshankar. Gyanshankar used to get that paper daily and narrate all the criticism to his brother so that he might run away and he would not be forced to give away his share in the property. Premshankar was a man of courage who was least bothered about such threats, but he could not tolerate Gyanshankar falling into trouble because of him. He was quite disillusioned with Shraddha's behaviour also. He wanted to end this worrisome situation by going away somewhere and fulfilling his life goals in peace. But where could he go? He had expressed a desire to Gyanshankar about staying in Lucknow, but he raised so many objections and painted such a gory picture of the troubles and inconveniences that Premshankar got a glimpse of his real intentions. He wanted some land near the city, where he could set up an agricultural farm. He used to roam around looking for such a place. But his hesitation did not allow him to express his desire to anyone. Lala Prabhashankar's fatherly love often made him express his heartfelt emotions to him. Whenever Lalaji found time, he used to sit with Premshankar and listen to the anecdotes of America with great interest. Premshankar was increasingly getting impressed with his goodness. Gyanshankar had always tried to dissect his behaviour, but he had never uttered a word against Gyanshankar. He did not agree with Premshankar's plans; rather he wanted him to take up a government job.

Once, on finding Premshankar sad and worried, Lalaji said, 'Aren't you feeling at home here?'

Prem – I think I should take a separate home and stay there. My staying here troubles everyone.

Prabha – Then you can come to my house; that too belongs to you. I am not a stranger to you. You won't have any kind of trouble there. We shall deem it our good fortune to serve you. Have you written for a job anywhere?

Prem – I don't wish to take up a job.

Prabha – Why do you abhor the idea of a job so much? Is it a bad thing?

Prem – Not at all; I don't call it bad but I cannot bring my mind to focus on it.

Prabha – Then you must make yourself understand. In these days, no other position is more respectable than a government job. On top of it, you get a good income, less to work, and more holidays. Trading is always haunted by the fear of losses; in the zamindari you have to appease the officials daily and there's also the fear of revolt by tenants. A job is best out of all these professions. One can still fulfill the hobby of farming while having a job. This is just a kind of entertainment for rich people. I don't know the situation in other countries, but here it is quite insulting for a rich person to do farming. I can afford to die of hunger, but not to take up petty trading or farming.

Prem – You are absolutely right, but I can't bring my mind to agree. I am looking for some land, but can't manage to find any.

Prabha – If you are so intent upon it, then try it out and see. What to do, I don't have any land near the city or you wouldn't have had to worry. If you wish to explore my village, you can have as much land as you wish, but it's far off from this place.

The month of April passed away in all these confusions. Premshankar published many scholarly articles in newspapers to insist upon the need for an agricultural farm and to attract the attention of the area's capitalists. These essays were very well received. Other newspapers quoted them, commented upon them, and they were also translated in many other languages. The result was that the Talukedar Association invited Premshankar on its annual function to read out an agriculture-related essay. Premshankar was delighted at the invitation. He wrote the essay with great research and labour and arrived in Lucknow. There was a huge tent erected in Qaisarbag for this function. Rai Kamlanand was chosen to preside over the function. It was the month of May. The weather was growing hot day by day. In the plains, the hot winds blew till late evening. It was too uncomfortable to stay locked up in the house. Premshankar reached Rai Saheb's residence at eight p.m. in the night. Rai Saheb called him inside. At this time, he was sitting in a small room behind his main drawing room. There was a dim lamp burning in the room. The heat was so great that the room seemed to be burning like a furnace. But in this hot environment, Rai Saheb was sitting wrapped in a heavy woollen blanket. His face was shining brightly and a divine light seemed to be emitting from his eyes. He seemed to be a live picture of intellect and sophistication. His physical fitness and huge built could shame even a wrestler. He had a rudraksh string in his neck and a silver bowl and jug were lying by his side. On one side of his bed two fat young men were having a bout of hand-wrestling and on the other side, three young and beautiful women were sitting decked up in beautiful clothes and jwellery. It was like the court of Raja Indra, where devils and fairies were all playing their prescribed roles.

As soon as Rai Saheb saw Premshankar, he got up and welcomed him. He ordered a chair for him and said, 'Please excuse me, I am engaged in worship at the moment, but was so eager to meet you that I couldn't bear the delay even for a moment. I am so glad to see you. This entire world is a reflection of God. Whosoever has seen the world has met God in his most real form. Travelling is the best means of acquiring knowledge. Shall I get you some refreshment?'

Prem – No, please; I have just eaten.

Rai Saheb – I got it, you have become an old man in your youth. To think too much about mealtimes and their suitability is a sign of old age.

A young man can very well eat even after having meals; can digest even bricks and stones. A person who cannot eat after eating once; who thinks pumpkin is heavy, bitter gourd too hot, and jackfruit too complex to digest, is really old in my opinion. I can eat everything, and it's due to this reason that I'm still young at the ripe old age of sixty.

After having said this, Rai Saheb took his jug and had many a draught out of it; he then ate many spoonfuls from the bowl and licking his tongue, said, 'Please don't think that I am a slave of my senses. I rather act as a master of my desires. This is just a means to vanquish them. A swimmer always loves to dive in deep waters. A warrior is he who goes out in the battlefield. One cannot escape troubles merely by running away from them. Such a person cannot save himself by falling in any trap. A real winner over life is he whose natural fire and inner flame burns up all the germs of a disease. This jug contains sparks of fire, but it seems like cold water to me. This bowl contains such an eatable that can intoxicate even an ascetic, but it's almost like a dry vegetable to me. Nowadays this is all I have for a meal. In summer time I consume fire as my food and drink; I worship Shiva and Shakti. I treat poison as good as milk and ghee. In winter times, I consume snowdrops, and enjoy the winds of the Himalayas. Our soul is a shining reflection of the eternal Brahma. I wish to keep it free from the worries of the nation and other desires and problems. There's no fixed time for anything I do; I do whatever I please. I hope you're comfortable enough; please sit with ease.'

Prem – I am quite comfortable.

Rai Saheb – You must be surprised to see this statue. But all these are as good to me as toys of mud. Lustful eyes dote over their outer beauty, but I look at that flame which shines in their innermost being. No amount of external beauty can lure me. Those who sit in caverns to worship and meditate are frauds in my opinion. They are cowards, escapists from the world of matter, and ones who save their skins from desires. What do they know about self- independence? They have never experienced a determination of heart and any kind of self-endurance. They are like dry leaves which fall on the ground due to just a single gust of strong wind. Yoga is not a physical activity; self-purity, self-strength and a destruction of the senses is true meditation. A real state of asceticism is to stay undisturbed while staying in the world of desires. You should have the best of food, enjoy good music, worship beauty, but not be a slave of these pleasures; only then you can be called a true ascetic. (To the two wrestlers) Panda ji! You are absolutely foolish. My guest has come from America; he's our son-in-law. Recite some of your poems to him; they should be very lively and entertaining stanzas.'

Both the wrestlers stood up and started reciting a passage together. The passage was a livid example of abuse and vulgarity. Any crude performer too wouldn't have been able to describe such a nude and hateful account of one's shameful parts. The poet had brought together the entire set of Holi limericks, the wedding songs of Kayastha society, the lewd abuses sung by women during weddings and the abusive language used by the police department; and this vulgar poetry was being uttered by those two fellows in a manner as if they were reciting something very beautiful. Rai Saheb was sitting absolutely still; no laughter, or even a smile could be witnessed on his lips. The three prostitutes hung their heads in shame, but Premshankar couldn't help laughing. He went rolling in streams of laughter.

As soon as these men stopped, the instrumentalists made their entry. They tuned their instruments, tapped the table, played the sarangis, and the three women started singing the Dhrupad raga. Premshankar was enjoying this melody in such a way, as if a rustic gets dazzled by the show of brilliant gems. There was no real talent in this joy, but the learned Rai Saheb was absolutely engrossed in the music and at times, even started singing himself.

The singing continued till midnight. When Premshankar started falling in the lap of sleep, the group was dispersed. He was quite surprised at Rai Saheb's versatility and talent. 'This man is so full of such miraculous wisdom; such confidence, such a sense of achievement, liveliness, and such a brilliant life goal!'

The next day when Premshankar got up it was already eight. He freshened up and started roaming in the verandah when he saw Rai Saheb coming on a horse. He was wearing his hunting clothes. He had a gun on his shoulders. Behind him came a pack of hunting dogs. When he saw Premshankar he said, 'I had seen a lucky face in the morning. None of my shots went empty. I had decided to come back by the time of breakfast. Can you imagine what distance I've covered? About twenty miles in all. I never sleep for more than three hours. I hope you know that the function will begin at three p.m. today.'

Prem – Of course; the delegates must have arrived?

Rai – I have no idea, nor am I the president of the welcome committee. My manager must have arranged for everything. I haven't yet thought about what to say there. I will just say whatever comes to my mind at that moment.

Prem – Your ideas must be very good.

Rai – Yes of course; there's none in my association who isn't a good thinker. There are many who are blessed with this quality. The treasurer has no idea of income or expenditure, but will explain everything in the meeting. Others are also the same. Life is so short that man keeps busy solving his own issues; who can take up the cause of the society?

Prem – What good can such organizations do to the nation?

Rai – Why not; do you think that leadership of society is a useless thing? Nowadays it is the main entry to the world of rewards and titles. Is it a minor achievement to become respectable in the eyes of simple devotees? Poor people, who sacrifice themselves in the name of race, come from far-off places to catch our glimpse. They pull our carriages, and apply our foot-soil to their foreheads. Is this a small thing? And there are many amongst us who keep all the accounts in their mind, and if you ask about it, they threaten to resign. The assistant secretary of this association has no proper legal practice, but he has bought a bungalow recently for twenty thousand rupees. One has to take one's upkeep from society in either way; you can take it on one pretext, or on the other.

Prem – When will I get the time to read my essay?

Rai – Not today. Tomorrow there's a garden party. His Excellency and other officials have been invited. The whole day will be spent in the arrangements. The next day all birds will fly away; a few will remain, then you can read out your essay at leisure.

They were talking about these matters when Raja Indrakumar Singh arrived. Rai Saheb welcomed him and asked, 'When will you come to Nainital?'

Raja Saheb – I have made all the arrangements. I will go from here with His Excellency. Hasn't Mr. Gyanshankar come here?

Prem – No, he didn't have time to come here.

Raja – I have seen your essays in the newspapers. It is quite clear that you are a scholar of agricultural science, but the proposal that you've given doesn't seem very practical for our region. Our government has not left any stone unturned for the development of agriculture. Many laboratories have been opened, seeds are being sold at low prices and agricultural inventions are being promoted through newspapers. Many inspectors have been appointed for this reason; many agricultural colleges have been opened, but to no avail. When they haven't been able to achieve much by spending crores of rupees, what can you achieve by wasting a sum of two lacs? No one will take your implements even for free. Your chemical manures will all rot away. At best, you will earn a profit of five or seven percent. What can this achieve? When we can do the same by getting a few wells digged, and appease the officials with the help of the patwari, why should we get into this mess?

Prem – My aim is not to open a business. I only want money for the development of agriculture. Possibly, some profit may be earned in future, but right now, I cannot ensure any such thing.

Raja – Oh! I got it; so it's just a means of charity.

Prem – Yes, this alone is my aim. I have clearly said it in my earlier and in this recent essay.

Raja – Then you've made a mistake right in the beginning. You should have first earned the approval of the Laat Sahib in this regard. You would have then got even ten lacs easily instead of two. Such endeavours cannot be successful without government help. Whatever associations you are seeing all around haven't emerged independently. This is the convention out here. If Rai Saheb can get you introduced to His Excellency and he empathizes with you, you will have no dearth of funds.

Rai – I am quite ready to do this.

Prem – I want to keep this organization away from government influence.

Raja – In that case, you should not expect any help from our association. At least this is what I think; what do you say, Rai Saheb?

Rai – There's no need to say that.

Prem – Then my reading of this essay would be a waste of time.

Raja – No, it won't be a waste. It's quite possible that you might get official help through it, sometime in future. Yes, Rai Saheb, are we arranging to take out a procession for our President? He is arriving by the afternoon train.

Premshankar was quite disheartened. To read his essay in front of such a gathering was to cry in front of blind people. He stayed in Lucknow for three days but he didn't read his essay; nor did anyone insist upon him to read it. All the members out there were busy in serving the officials as if they'd come in a wedding party. In fact his staying there was not deemed congenial by anyone. All thought that he was criticizing them in heart of hearts. People had somehow found out that he was a swarajist as well. That's why no one asked him to read out his essay; in fact he wasn't even invited to the garden party also. His swarajist status had been revealed to people only a day after his arrival, or he wouldn't even be invited to read his paper. Why would Premshankar have stayed there in such a situation? He came back home on the fourth day. He was quite upset for a few days, not because he hadn't got the desired success, but because he had killed his self-respect by begging before the rich men of that unsympathetic society. Though he was quite bored, lying alone the whole day long, but this condition was quite conducive for self-introspection. 'Selfless service is my duty', he thought, 'By setting up the laboratory I wanted to fulfill a personal interest as well. I would have earned some profit, and some fame. Perhaps God has punished me for this reason. Is this the only means of serving people? Why am I so hellbent upon setting up this lab? Agricultural ideas can be promoted through other measures also. Isn't medical service too a kind of service only?' These questions excited a feeling of enthusiasm in Premshankar. He often got out of the house and visited the nearby rural areas where he talked to the peasants about the issues related to farming. He now understood that the peasants who were generally taken to be ignorant and foolish were not quite so. He himself got to know of many new things from them. Gradually he kept staying out of the house for the entire day. Sometimes, he used to visit distant villages also, and didn't return home for quite a few days.

17

It was the month of June. Heat waves were ensuing all over. Government officers were holidaying in the hills, in cool climates. The touring officers had also taken a break but Premshankar had no respite. He often had to spend the afternoon under the shade of a tree; sometimes the whole day went without a meal, but the spirit of service had made him passive towards physical comforts. He used to hear all kinds of news at all times; about the spread of cholera in a village, or the destruction of sugarcane crop by pests, or some squabble somewhere between the villagers. Premshankar used to reach these places like a quick postman and resolve these issues to the best of his capacity. Sometimes he used to visit Lakhanpur also. When it started raining in July, he had to face a lot of trouble in fulfilling his mission. He wanted to promote a particular type of paddy for cultivation. He had also ordered some vegetable seeds for distribution among farmers. He had to tell them about their sowing and cultivation. For this, he decided to stay in Hajiganj, near the banks of Varna river, about five miles away from the city. People built a cottage for him outside the village. They also got a few charpoys. The villagers had great respect for him; they thought his arrival to be a great blessing for them. He was deemed as a great protector, almost like a God, and everyone was ready to lay down their lives for his sake.

Though Premshankar was quite at peace here but he was often troubled by the memory of Shraddha. He thought, if she too had accompanied him, it would have made his life ideal and complete. He had understood now that Gyanshankar had incited her against him, thus he felt more pity for her than any kind of anger. He really craved to meet her once and know about her innermost feelings. He tried writing to her many times, but kept postponing the idea thinking that she might not reply. Besides this, he was also troubled by a shortage of funds. Whatever money he had brought from America had been spent in the past four months, and his present situation demanded money on a daily basis. He felt hesitant about discussing his problems with the farmers. He did not like to burden them with the expenses of his meals, and nor did he wish to ask any rich person for any kind of donation. Finally he decided to demand his share of the land profit from Gyanshankar. 'What right did he have to eat up the entire amount falling in his share? He can at best take half of this amount for the upkeep of Shraddha. I would still be able to get at least one thousand. It will suffice for now; rest will be taken care of afterwards. Of course I haven't earned this income and have no direct right over it but I do not want it for my personal pleasures; only for spending it on charitable causes.' Initially Premshankar hadn't thought about it; he had deemed taking this money as totally improper. But necessity often becomes an impediment to various principles and considerations. He thought that he would write everything clearly to Gyanshankar in a letter, but he could only write, 'I am in dire need of money. I hope you will help me out soon.' It is a complex job to pen down our real feelings sometimes.

When Gyanshankar received the letter he lost his temper. He said to Shraddha, 'He does not think of doing any efforts himself; he rather wants to sit and enjoy the fruit of fame. He's thinking I'm rolling in the lap of wealth. I get lots of profit just by doing nothing. And the reality is that the expenditure on court cases is making my pockets empty. I have already taken a loan of one thousand rupees and the entire year lies ahead of me. If he sees the accounts even once he'll know what the reality is; zamindari is not an open feast. Thousands have to be spent only on gifts and appeasement of the officers.'

He then went downstairs in a fit of anger to write a reply to the letter. He was very upset on his condition and ill-luck. He was remembering what Rai Kamlanand had told him about the issue. Whatever he had said had come true.

It was evening time. A black sky was overcast with clouds. Premshankar was thinking, 'It's been so long; the servant hasn't returned with Gyanshankar's reply. If rain starts falling he won't be able to reach on time. Let me see what he says. He may not refuse directly, but will surely be irritated. I too must ask people for help without restraint as I cannot bear this burden alone. Had I got a bit of land, I would have produced something, and my finances would have improved. There's very little land here. There is this cultivable land of fifty bighas, but it's difficult to strike a deal with the zamindar. He will ask for a gift of two hundred rupees. Then there's other expenditure on making it even and digging drains for irrigation. What to say, Gyanu has destroyed all my ambitions, or else Lakhanpur is well within reach from here. If I had cultivated about fifteen or twenty bighas there I wouldn't have sought anybody's help.'

He was lost in these thoughts when he saw a cart coming in his direction. At first many people called out to its driver. 'Why are you getting the cart into the fields? Are you blind or what? Can't you see; the seeds have been sown?' But when the cart turned towards Premshankar's cottage, everybody kept quiet. Lala Prabhashankar and his sons Padmashankar and Tejshankar were sitting on it. Premshankar ran and welcomed them. Prabhashankar hugged him and asked, 'Has your servant returned with Gyanu's reply?'

Prem – No, not yet; it's been quite long.

Prabha – That means I came first. I started off an hour later than him. Take this, my daughter-in-law has sent this envelope and box for you. But tell me, why are you undergoing this exile? You have two houses, not one. If you don't wish to stay there, many of your houses are on rent; I'd have got any of them vacated. Stay comfortably in the city. I cannot bear to see you in this condition. Look at this grass hut, this deserted place, with no trace of any man or civilization! I cannot stay here for even a moment. You do not come home for days. I won't let you stay here. We stay in a palace and you are alone in this exile. (With tearful eyes) All this is my ill fate. My heart is broken into pieces. Till the time my brother was alive, I was so proud of myself. I thought that the family's unity is preserved due to me. But all our dignity went away with his going off. I couldn't even keep everyone together for even a few years. He was fortunate and I am stricken with bad luck; what else?

Premshankar opened the envelope with curiosity and started reading. He was not bothered as to what Lalaji was saying.

'Dear lord of my heart, please accept the regards of your slave. Till the time you were in America, I kept bearing the sorrow of separation with patience, but I cannot bear this exile of yours. In the house, I wasn't able to speak to you or meet you, but could see you with my eyes and had the opportunity to serve you. You have snatched this blessed job from me. I had the world's comments to fear; what were you afraid of? I am scared that if I see you some bad omen may befall us. Who can remain in peace by flouting the orders of religion? You are a liberated man; why don't you care about me?

People are talking about your re-initiation here. I know you're not afraid of the society, but I am also aware that you have love and kindness for me in your heart. Won't you do this much for me? Won't you keep up the faith for my sake?

The box contains some money and my ornaments. For whom should I wear them now? Who will see and appreciate them? This is my offering to you; please accept it. If you do not take them, I shall think that you've broken all ties with me.

Your unfortunate wife — Shraddha.

Premshankar first thought of returning the box and writing to her that he did not need her help. 'Have I become so shameless that I should accept help from a woman who has treated me with such rudeness?' he thought. But almost immediately, he changed his stance. He started thinking whether Shraddha had something else in her mind. 'Was this letter an indication of some dangerous resolve?' He started roaming about in a worried state of mind. Suddenly he asked Lala Prabhashankar, 'You must be knowing how Gyanshankar behaves with her?'

Prabha – Son, do not ask me anything about this. I can only say that she is very pained about your living here. You very well know how much she loves you. She has sacrificed a lot for you. Your indifference to her is totally unjustified.

Prem – I have no objection to staying there. But I feel sad at Gyanshankar's shrewd behaviour and moreover, I won't be able to do anything if I stay there. I can serve the peasants only by staying in their midst, not away from them. I request you to make her understand my mission. I may think her behaviour to be improper but I also know that she's innocent. All this is merely a result of conspiracy by others. But I fear if she has decided to end her life by taking some untoward step.

Prabha – But you must promise me that you will go there at least once a week.

Prem – I promise to do that.

Prabhashankar wanted to return but Premshankar insisted upon him to stay back. Thakur Bhavanisingh was a prominent person in Hajiganj. He arranged for Lala Prabhashankar's meals in his house. For dinner, thick pooris were served with a curry that wasn't really well-made, but milk was very delicious. Prabhashankar smiled and said, 'Are these pooris or thick chapatis? If I get to eat them for some days, I will probably go out of breath. But the cream on this milk is very good.'

Prem – I make my chapatis myself. I generally take milk in the afternoon.

Prabha – That's as good as following a yogi's life. If you can't get food to your liking, what's there to enjoy in this life?

Prem – What can I say; I am quite satisfied with chapatis only. Sometimes I don't even make any curry or lentils. Mere chapatis seem so delicious to me. I guess a plain diet is good for one's health also.

Prabha – All this is just a new-age fad. Actually people's digestive powers have gone weak. It is their way of pacifying themselves. I have consumed spicy food all my life, but I never had any health issues.

After dinner, they engaged in random conversation. Lalaji was tired so he slept early, but the boys didn't wish to sleep. Premshankar said, 'Why Tejshankar, aren't you feeling sleepy? I guess you are in tenth standard. What do you plan to do after matric?'

Tejshankar – What can I say? I will do whatever my father says.

Prem – And what will you do Padmashankar?

Padma – I have no interest in studying. I wish to become an ascetic.

Prem – (With a smile) So early in life?

Padma – Yes, I will roam about in the mountains. I will go to far-off places. Bhaiya also talks about being an ascetic.

Prem – So both of you will relinquish the world and leave the burden of the house on the shoulders of my uncle?

Tej – When did I talk about this Padmu? Why do you tell lies?

Padma – You talk about it daily, but are denying now.

Tej – You are a great liar.

Padma – Only yesterday you were talking about going to the hilly areas and learning some occult practices from the ascetics.

Prem – What shall you gain by those practices?

Padma – Well, these mantras have such powers that one can disappear at one's own will and even find treasures beneath the ground. There's even a mantra that can put life in a dead body. You only have to be a gifted practitioner. We shall always be in ease. Otherwise we'll have to put in years of study; only then one can hope for a job. On the other hand, if we can achieve even a single mantra, we'll be rolling in money.

Prem – Why Teju; you too believe in all these myths?

Tej – Not at all; Padmu keeps spreading such rumours, but I do think that a man can achieve a lot by getting hold over these mantras. But he shouldn't be scared in doing all this, or else there's a danger to one's life.

Prem – All this is just a fake story. I feel sorry for you; even after studying science you believe in all this. The best mantra to achieve worldly success is one's own enterprise, knowledge and determination; rest everything is false.

The boys didn't say anything in reply. The idea of the mantra had delved deep in their hearts and it was difficult to revert their opinion on this by any kind of logic.

After all had slept, Premshankar opened the box sent by Shraddha. The ornaments were all made of gold. He counted the rupees; they were one thousand in all. At this moment Shraddha appeared a kind of goddess to Premshankar. Her face seemed to be emitting a divine light. She appeared to be a great picture of sacrifice and love; one whose eyes were alight with the rays of devotion and empathy. Premshankar was overwhelmed. He felt very guilty about his rudeness. He found his own bitterness and self-centredness very hateful as compared to the devotion expressed by her. He closed the box, kept it under his bed and started thinking, 'What shall I do with these ornaments? The total wealth sent by her is no less than five thousand. If I take this, Shraddha will lose all her savings. But I hope my condition will improve very soon. I can take this as a debt, and will return this later with proper interest. I can buy twenty-five bighas of fertile land in about two thousand rupees. One thousand will be spent on adding manure and digging it properly. Another one thousand can get me a good pair of oxen and other implements. In ten bighas, I can plant a nice garden, and use fifteen bighas for farming. For the first two years, the produce may not be too much, but I can hope for an income of two thousand or more in the coming years. I can manage my own expenses with only two hundred a year and use the rest for fulfilling my life purpose. Possibly, I may be able to find a like-minded compatriot. But even if no one helps me in that situation, I shall be able to pull on. But I didn't consider one thing. If I buy this land, there will be no pastures left in the village. This plain fertile stretch is the only land available for cattle out here. No, I must not think about buying land here. Now I have funds with me, I can get some good piece of land anywhere. Well, if the land is good, this money won't be able to fetch more than ten bighas. How will I manage then?'

Premshankar was lost in all these thoughts. It was raining cats and dogs. Suddenly he heard a loud roar of the clouds, as if a train was passing through a long bridge. But when the sound kept coming, and was joined by the shouts and screams coming from the direction of the village, he got up and looked towards the village. There were people all over. Men were running with torches made of jute and arhar stalks. Some of them were going towards the river with those torches. Within a second he saw a streamed reflection of torches, as if waves of water were flowing all over. Premshankar understood that the flood had arrived.

There was no time to waste in any kind of delays. He immediately set out for the village. In just a few hours, water had come up to his knees.

There was so much force in the flow of water that his feet found it difficult to remain stable. Many a times he almost fell into deep pits. In his haste, he had forgotten to take a stick to measure the depth of water. He wanted to fly to the floodhit village and help the people, but it was difficult to keep up walking in the situation. It was pitch dark all over; heavy rain was falling, wild waves encircling the feet, and all roads were lost to the eye. He could only follow the torches that were lit by the people. Many a times he heard noises of houses falling off due to the flood. When he reached near the village he found devastation and cries all around. All the villagers, the young and the old, children and women were standing on the platform of the temple, watching the destruction wrought by the clouds. As soon as they saw Premshankar, they came and surrounded him. The women started crying.

Premshankar – 'Has the flood come only now, or has it come before also?'

Bhavanisingh – It comes every two or three years. Sometimes it even comes twice a year.

Premshankar – No efforts were made to stop it?

Bhavanisingh – There's only one solution. A dam should be built on the river. But it entails an expense of three thousand rupees. We cannot afford this much. We are sometimes hit by the floods; at other times by drought. Where can the money come from?

Premshankar – You didn't say anything to the zamindar about the issue?

Bhavani – We don't even get to see him; how can we discuss anything with him? Sethji had given this village to him in the name of his ancestors. He himself stays in Gaya for most part of the year. His munshi comes twice a year to take the land rent. If we say something to him, he only replies, 'We don't know anything, talk to Pandaji.' Whatever troubles we might have to endure, he's only bothered about his profit.

Premshankar – Well, what can we do about it now? Has anything been saved or everything's drowned?

Bhavani – One can't say anything in the dark, but I guess no house has been left intact. Clothing, utensils, bedding; all have been taken away. There was no scope or time to save anything. We ran out in the condition that we were sitting in. Such a flood was never seen before; it was almost like a storm. Even a storm sends some indication; this was totally unexpected.

Premshankar – Have the animals also drowned?

Bhavani – God knows; some must have broken their ropes, some may have been drowned, others might be standing in the water. If the water rises more, even they will not be found.

Premshankar – At least we must try to save them.

Bhavani – That seems next to impossible.

Premshankar – No, please don't lose heart. How many men are present here?

Bhavani (counting with his eyes) – About forty or fifty.

Prem – Then please make groups of five men each and take a round of the village. Gather all the animals you can and take them to my hut. The ground level is high there; water will not seep in easily. I will also accompany you people. Whosoever wishes to come forward for this task, please come with me.

Premshankar's enthusiasm inspired the people to rise to the occasion. About sixty people came forward; they had sticks in hand. They tried to stop Premshankar, but he did not agree. He took a stick in hand and walked ahead of the crowd. At almost every step, he banged into floating pieces of huts, fallen trees, and floating beddings and cots. There was no trace of a village anywhere. The villagers could not see any remains of their houses. The only voices that could be heard were groans of buffaloes and oxen. At some places, animals were also found floating. The rescue-party kept rescuing the animals the whole night. Their courage was relentless and efforts untiring. Premshankar used to help other groups also, along with his own group. Even the weak-hearted were encouraged to come foeward seeing his patience and efforts. When the day dawned and he reached home, he saw more than two hundred animals sitting there and clucking happily. But he had never done so much of physical labour ever before. He felt too tired to keep standing. His body was aching badly. By the time it was eight, he was burning with fever. Lala Prabhashankar came to know of everything and was very upset. He said to Premshankar, 'Son, it's very nice to do charity, but not at the cost of one's own life. You might count your life less precious than that of these animals, but we can sacrifice many such creatures for your sake. If Shraddha comes to hear all this, she'll be so upset.' Saying this, his eyes filled with tears.

For almost three days, Premshankar didn't have any relief from fever, and for these three days, Lala Prabhashankar kept sitting by his side. He sometimes read out passages from Vianaypatrika to him; at other times he recited Hanuman Chalisa. There were two Brahmins in Hajipur. Those two were asked to worship goddess Durga in Premshankar's hut. Others used to get many medicinal herbs and plants for him. Whosoever heard of his illness in the nearby villages came running to see him. The fourth day, his fever got over, the sky became clear, and the flood also relented.

It was early morning. Lala Prabhashankar had gone home after giving gifts and fees to the Brahmins. Premshankar was sitting on his charpoy, leaning by his pillows, looking towards Hajipur with worried eyes. About four days ago, there was a green and prosperous village out there, green fields stretching for miles, hordes of buffaloes grazing on the plains, flour mills churning in the huts and children playing about, but now there was a desert looming large. Majority of the villagers had left for other places, and others were lying before Premshankar's hut in small camps. They didn't have any food or clothing. It was a very heartrending scene. Premshankar thought, 'What a complicated problem has emerged! There's no one to help these people. They are often struck by these problems and they have no solution to it. Whatever they save by their frugal lifestyle they have to offer to the flood every year. So much of wealth and so many beings have been consumed by this turmoil, so many houses have been destroyed, so many families devastated and all this only because they don't have the courage to build a strong dam on the river bank. There's no money, no co-operation or unity that can achieve great goals even in the absence of money. If such a dam is built it will save not just this particular village but many nearby villages also. I have about five thousand rupees in hand. Why shouldn't I spend this on building of this dam? These villagers may not be able to give money, but they can very well do physical labour. One only needs to unite them. People from other villages will surely help in this mission. If this dam comes about, these poor people will be benefitted on all fronts.'

Though Premshankar was still feeling weak, these thoughts excited him so much that he immediately got up and despite being stopped by people, took a stick in his hands and went on to inspect the site of the dam at the river. He also kept a pencil and paper in his pocket. Many people also went with him. He kept standing at the riverside for quite some time and kept drawing a figure of the dam on the paper, estimating its length, breadth and depth. In his own enthusiasm, he thought the task to be easy; it was just a matter of beginning the project. He decided there and then that he would start the construction once the rains got over. Godwilling, the dam would be complete by winters. Along with the dam, he would also reconstruct the village. 'There wouldn't be any fear of the floods; I'll make strong walls, and install a roof of tiles instead of hay.'

Bhavanisingh said – Babuji, this work is not within our reach.

Premshankar – Why not, I'll make you people do it. You've thought it to be impossible, that's why you're facing so much trouble.

Bhavani – I fear there are not many men in the village.

Prem – People from other villages will help you; let the work begin first.

Bhavani – The kind of dam that you've planned will not cost less than five or six thousand rupees.

Prem – Don't worry about money. The month of Kartik is coming; just start with the work. The dam will be ready in a few months. I will arrange whatever money I can.

Bhavani – We have only you to count on.

Prem – Have faith in God.

Bhavani – If we get proper labuor, the dam will be ready by the month of Aghan.

Prem – I can assure you of that. This place will also ensure a fertile land of about sixty or seventy bighas.

Bhavani – Then we'll make your cottage here only. Your place is on a high level, but still gets flooded at times.

Prem – Please inform the people who have gone from here, and also send a message to other neighbouring villages.

18

Gayatri was one of those women whose character is an unusual combination of beauty and womanly attraction along with a sense of manly courage and patience. If she loved her comb and mirror, she didn't shy away from the dirt and dust of the village lanes. She loved the crude songs of the villagers with as much wonder as she played her piano. She enjoyed reading popular literature, and handled issues of agriculture with equal ease. It had been two years since she'd arrived from Lucknow but she had not sat in her huge mansion even for a day. She used to visit one village or another, stay in some camp, visit the district office, and went to see the officers repeatedly. She was slowly realizing that in order to rule others, one had to bend one's own terms a lot. The karindas in her region robbed the tenants to no end. She often thought, 'Shall I fire these managers and karindas? But who will do these jobs then? And where's the guarantee that the people who'll replace them will be more honest and hardworking? The real trouble is that I am more pained by their atrocities than the tenants themselves. No one complains or pleads against them; they are used to bearing this injustice in a way that they treat it was a normal condition of their lives. That there can be a way of getting free from this does not ever occur to them.'

This was just one part of the story. The other part was that the tenants looked at Gayatri's honest endeavours with suspicious eyes. They just couldn't believe that any zamindar could punish his servants for their benefit. The prevalent injustices were part of their known experience; they were not really afraid of those. On the other hand, the efforts of reform and upliftment made them scared, as these were totally unknown to them. They doubted that it was probably a new way of torturing them. Their experience also confirmed this doubt. Gayatri had ordered that the peasants should be given loans at nominal interest rates, but the karindas charged an interest even higher than the moneylender. She had also instructed that the tenants should be given foodgrains from the godowns at the rate of one eighth of their produce. But people used to get grain from other sources by giving more portions. She also wanted to make her area neat and clean. She had got special pits built outside the village for collecting cowdung. She had appointed sweepers for cleaning the drains. But the tenants thought all this as an unnecessary interference, and feared that the Rani Sahiba (Gayatri) was perhaps wishing to occupy their houses and reserves.

It was winter time. Gayatri was touring the villages near the banks of river Rapti. Many villages had drowned in the seasonal floods. The farmers had pleaded for a discount in the rent payment. The officers had written after a cursory enquiry that there was no need for a discount. Gayatri wanted to see the condition of the villages with her own eyes and decide about the concession. The evening had fallen. Gayatri was tired with the day-long journey, and was lying about sadly in the camp at Bindapur. The whole house was falling into pieces. She had given thousands of rupees for the repair works to the karindas, but the condition she saw betrayed that the roof hadn't been changed since years. The walls were falling down, and the roof was coming apart due to cracks in the supporters. Garbage had accumulated in the verandah. She had thought the karindas out here to be very honest. She was feeling very upset about their careless and dishonest behaviour. There was a mat kept on a low stool for pooja, but she didn't feel like getting up and worshipping; just then a peon came and informed her, 'Sarkar, the Kanungo Sahib has arrived.'

Gayatri got up and sat on the stool and fearing lest the kanungo should go away, finished her pooja quickly, and called him after arranging for a partition.

Gayatri – Well Khan Sahib! How have you been? Is the inspection of the flood going on?

Kanungo – Yes of course, these days I've been touring your estate.

Gayatri – How far has agriculture been affected in your opinion?

Kanungo – If you ask at an official level then just an annah in a rupee; if at a personal level, then about twelve annahs of a rupee.

Gayatri – Why do you follow these double standards? Don't you know that the subjects suffer a lot due to this?

Kanungo – Huzoor, please don't ask me the reason. If we do not follow double standards and write the real report we shall be turned out as idiots. We are not sent for inspection to know the real state of things, but to hide that. We have to do everything to keep up our livelihood.

Gayatri – You should avoid earning the curses of the poor in the process. If we cannot do anything good for the people at least we must refrain from doing any harm to them. What is the real condition of this area?

Kanungo – You will feel disheartened to know that. In Saran you have many bighas of fertile land which the tenants have cultivated. In the village of Jagraon, the Thakurs have turned your new orchard into fields, and have digged it into rows. Till the time it is measured again, one cannot know how much land has been encroached by them.

Gayatri – Is the karinda sleeping out there? I have become fed up of all such squabbles.

Kanungo – If you submit an application for re-measurement of land, I will take care of the rest. Well, the general kanungo will have to be appeased by some gifts. I am your slave; I won't give you any advice which harms you in any way. I would also request you to appoint a manager. Excuse my opinion, but the management of such a huge estate is not within your capacity.

Gayatri – I too want to keep a manager, but where to get one from? If he too starts conspiring with the karindas, my reputation will be further harmed. My husband's last instructions had been that his tenants should not face any trouble. I am engaged in this mission day and night only to fulfill his last wish. If you know of any honest and wise person who can take this load off my head, please do inform me.

Kanungo – Very well, I'll keep this in mind. I have a friend who's a graduate, and is very talented and experienced. He belongs to a reputed family. What's the order for me? Should I talk to the general kanungo?

Gayatri – Yes, that's what I am saying. Are you talking about Lala Sahib? But his expectations are too high.

Kanungo – Please have faith in me, I'll set him right. He might demand as much as he pleases from others but he won't be able to fool me. You will only need to spend five hundred rupees. I will get both the villages measured up within this amount.

Gayatri – (smiling) Obviously, you will pocket half of this amount.

Kanungo – God forbid, what are you saying? I cannot cheat you till my last breath. Well, if you give me something as a tip after the work is over, I'll be too glad to take that.

Gayatri – That means, I'll have to pay even more than five hundred. I won't make such an expensive deal.

They were still talking when Pandit Lekhrajji arrived. He was wearing a silk achkan, silk turban, and a silk shawl and dhoti. He had Delhi's famous embroidered shoes in his feet, a small tilak on his forehead, the redness of paan on his lips, and golden spectacles on his eyes; he was smelling of keora perfume, and came and sat on a chair.

Gayatri – I pay my respectful greetings to you, Maharaj.

Lekhraj – May God bless you! I guess you've been through a lot today.

Gayatri – What to do, had my ancestors too thought of farming without farming, zamindari without land and moneylending without money, I too would have been at ease like you.

Lekhraj – (laughing) Kanungo Sahib! Do you listen to that? She teases one in such a way that one just becomes speechless. You are actually a queen blessed by the lord; we are just as good as beggars at your door. You had asked me about an auspicious time for the foundation-laying ceremony of the guest house; I have decided upon that. On the morning of this fortnight's Ekadashi, you can lay down the foundation stone.

Gayatri – This fame is not meant for me. Have you seen any rich person laying the foundation of any public building with his own hands? People get the foundations of their own houses laid from the hands of officers. How can I break this tradition? I shall invite the district collector for the foundation ceremony. The guest house will be named after him only. Have you talked to any contractor as yet?

Lekhraj – Yes, I have appointed a contractor also. He is a very nice man. He wants to do this auspicious job without any profit. He will only take his own expenses.

Gayatri – Have you shown him the map? How much does he demand for the contract?

Lekhraj – He says that he should be given hundred rupees less than what the other contractor demands.

Gayatri – That means we must have another contractor. How much does he expect?

Lekhraj – According to him, this project will cost sixty thousand rupees. He will use best quality material. He will finish the work in six months.

Gayatri had got the map for this house made in Lucknow. There, its estimate had come to forty thousand rupees. She said sarcastically, 'Then your contractor is a great man indeed. A part of this money will surely be offered to your Thakurji.'

Lekhraj – I think you're joking. I get so much from you otherwise that I just can't think of fixing a commission with the contractor. If I desire anything I'll ask you for it; why should I betray my conscience?

Gayatri – I'll reply to this proposal in a week.

Kanungo – And what are the instructions for me? Punditji, you also must have seen, how much land has got eroded in the floods of Saran and Jagraon?

Pundit – Yes of course, it must be near about a hundred bighas.

Gayatri – I will inform you after inspecting the land. If things can be sorted with a common agreement, there's no point in increasing the expenses.

Both the fellows left her place disappointed. They were cursing Gayatri in heart of hearts. The Kanungo said, 'She's far too clever. It's very tough to fool her.'

Lekhraj said, 'She's very particular about her money; God knows what she'll do with it; she has no relative or successor to spend it on.'

It was already dark. Gayatri was thinking, 'How should I escape these robbers? They just want to dupe me in broad daylight. There are so many employees, but none who's bothered about the progress of the region. Where can I find an honest man? How far can I manage everything single-handedly?'

'If I give it on lease, I'll earn a far greater profit. I'll be relieved of all my cares, but my tenants will be destroyed. The contractor will crush them. If I give it in charity the result will be the same. If Gyanshankar agrees to be my manager, it will be the good fortune of my estate. He's such an experienced man; so knowledgeable and blessed with such a foresight. If he comes here, I will be relieved of these thieves. The whole estate will bloom like a garden. But the trouble is that after listening to his talk, my devotion and religious beliefs get all shaken up. Had I stayed with him in Lucknow for a few more months, I would have become a fashionable lady by now. He has a strange influence in his speech. I almost lose my senses in front of him. He used to treat me with such respect, even then I used to follow him like a shadow, and do all kinds of lighthearted mockery with him. God knows what kind of feelings must have arisen in his heart about me. Men have this deplorable quality that they cannot keep fun and laughter separate from other evil characteristics. They just can't enjoy its pure pleasure. If a woman speaks a little jovially to them, they think she's attracted towards them. If they are given a tiny space they want to take utmost liberty. If Gyanshankar is ready to come here, I'll keep him here only. He can manage the estate from here itself. If there's any particular reason he can visit the city. There too, I'll keep him at a distance. I'll never invite him home. No, he won't then get a chance to be so daring with me. Poor man, he was so ashamed that he couldn't even look at me. He came to the station to see me off, but kept sitting away and could not say anything.'

Gayatri was lost in these thoughts when a peon came and brought the day's post to her. The post office was three miles away. A man had to be sent daily to get the letters.

Gayatri asked – Where's that man? Why, did you get your wage?

Servant – Yes Sarkar, I did.

Gayatri – Is it enough?

Servant – No Sarkar, it's more than enough.

Gayatri – Will you go tomorrow also or do we need to find someone else?

Servant – Sarkar, when I am available, why would any other man go?

Gayatri started opening the letters. Most of them were about the advertisements of perfumed oil and other medicines. Gayatri threw them in the dustbin. One letter was from Rai Kamlanand. She opened it curiously and as soon as she read it, her eyes started shining with a happy pride and her face started resembling a blooming flower. She immediately opened the packet which she'd been ignoring as a catalogue of some pharmacy. On the first page itself she saw her own photograph. The tittle of the first essay was, 'Gayatri Devi'. The name of the writer was Gyanshankar B.A. Gayatri had little knowledge of English, but could understand ordinary words with her natural intelligence. She started reading the essay with great curiosity and though it was twenty pages long, she finished reading it in just half an hour and took a deep sigh with pride-laden eyes. She had never felt such an intoxicated sense of happiness in her life. She had never delighted in the celebration of her honour. Gyanshankar had described Gayatri's character, her qualities and good deeds with such an excellence that the essay spelt a kind of historical seriousness rather than mere appreciation. Undoubtedly, every single word of it betrayed a sense of devotion, but the reader found it a historical benevolence instead of mindless devotion. The style was further enhanced by the beauty of the sentences. Gayatri saw her image in the mirror and an extreme enthusiasm flowed in her heart, as if she was going to heaven sitting in an aircraft. It seemed as if high emotions were flowing in her veins instead of blood. If at this time, an army of beggars had arrived at her door, she'd have fulfilled all their demands. Had the kanungo arrived, he would have earned five thousand instead of five hundred and if Pandit Lekhraj had got a double estimate it would have been approved immediately. She had not talked to the karinda since many days; she was very upset with him. Now when she saw him standing like a defaulter, she addressed him with a happy face and said, 'Well, Munshiji, you must be having your native drink (wine) almost daily?' Munshiji slowly came forward and said, 'Sarkar,

I swear upon my sacred thread, ever since Sarkar has prohibited me, I haven't touched a drop.'

Saying this, he picked up a magazine to flaunt his literary interest and started turning its pages. When he saw Gayatri's picture, he was startled. He said, 'Sarkar, this is your photograph. How lively! It seems it will soon start speaking. Have they written something about you?'

Gayatri said carelessly, 'Of course, if there's a picture there would be some description also.'

Karinda Sahib ran out and told everyone about it. Many karindas and peons were making dinner, someone was grinding bhang, and another person was singing. All of them came and thronged over the picture. They started snatching it amongst themselves and many pages were torn. Usually Gayatri didn't let anyone touch her books, but today she didn't say anything.

A talkative peon said, 'Sarkar, please read out some of it to us.'

Gayatri – I won't be able to do it. It is so long, how far will I be able to read? Its translation will be published in a Hindi newspaper in a few days; then you can go through it.

But when all of them started requesting unanimously for it, Gayatri was forced to read. She translated a few parts for them. If she had had a good knowledge of English, she would have translated word by word.

One of the karindas said, 'God knows how these newspaper wallahs get to know these things!' The other karinda said, 'Their representatives keep roaming everywhere. Wherever anything happens, they get to know about it.'

Gayatri was delighted to hear this talk. The next morning she wrote a very polite letter to Gyanshankar. She did not discuss the essay, but only talked about her troubles and requested him to come and take over the management of her estate and rescue her drowning ship. Her heart had been cleansed of all the earlier malice. Praise often makes pride disappear. Gayatri was the epitome of self-pride. Gyanshankar had won her over with his devotion.

19

When Gyanshankar received Gayatri's letter his joy knew no bounds. Many pleasant thoughts started emerging in his mind. The goddess of good fortune was ready to welcome him with gifts of his dear life-purpose. He hadn't hoped that his beautiful dream would come true so soon. God had provided him with an opportunity to become the master of such a big estate. If he still couldn't profit out of it, it would be entirely his own ill-luck.

But before he started off for Gorakhpur, he wanted to be relieved about Lakhanpur. Ever since Premshankar had demanded his share of the profit, endless doubts had been arising in his mind. He also disliked Lala Prabhashankar's visits to his place. He doubted that the clever old man must be planning something against him. 'This fatherly love cannot be without any reason. Premshankar might be clever, but is just a child in front of a Chanakya like him. He must be wishing that by bringing Premshankar to his side, he would be able to get fifty per cent of Lakhanpur's property in the name of his boys or sell it to some other moneylender at a commission of about five or ten thousand. Of course, this is the reason behind this camraderie or else when he's short of meals himself, he wouldn't have sent delicacies to him. Now I only have Shraddha as my recourse. I must ask her to get half of Lakhanpur written in her name for her upkeep. I can tell her that Premshankar can't be trusted; he is all alone, if he again goes away somewhere she will have nothing to fall back on. If this shot hits the target, I can still hope to acquire all of Lakhanpur. I will send Shraddha on a pilgrimage. One fine day, she'll be no more. Even if she lives on, she can stay in Haridwar on the banks of Ganges. I will have nothing to fear about Lakhanpur.'

Deciding thus, Gyanshankar went inside. By chance Shraddha was sitting alone in her room. Maya was down with fever since many days; Vidya was sitting in her room fanning him by his side.

Gyanshankar sat on the cot and said to Shraddha, 'Did you see the cleverness of Chacha Sahib? I had already understood that he must be planning something. I have heard that talks are on to sell Lakhanpur.'

Shraddha – (with surprise) Who told you? I don't think him to be so mean. I am sure he goes there only out of affection for my husband.

Gyan – This is only a delusion. These people are not the ones who can love selflessly. They who have robbed others for a lifetime; how can they love after losing everything? He has some other motive in mind. It's my brother's wealth; he might keep it or sell it; he might give it to Chacha Sahib or in charity, he has all the right to do so; who am I to object? Well, this much is sure that you will not have anything left in hand.

Shraddha – Even if what you are saying is true, what control do I have over it?

Gyan – Why not? After all it's his duty to care for your upkeep. You can get fifty per cent of Lakhanpur written in you name. Bhaiya cannot object to it. If you are hesitant, I can go and decide everything with him. I'm sure he won't refuse and even if he does I can force him. When it's given in your name, he won't have a right to sell it, and Chacha Sahib's plans will also flop.

Shraddha was immersed in deep thought. When she didn't raise her head for a while Gyanshankar asked, 'What do you think? Is there any harm in it? The property gets lost; is that better, or it stays within the house, that's better?'

Now Shraddha raised her head and said proudly – I cannot do this. He can do whatever he feels like; he can keep or sell his share. He is a wise man; he'll do whatever he deems fit. Why should I put chains around his feet?

Gyanshankar angrily replied – Have you thought that if this property is lost how will you survive? If he goes to America again; then?

Shraddha – Don't you worry about me! He is my master; whatever he decides will be good for me. I cannot believe that he'll leave me without any assets.

Gyan – As you wish. I have told you about all pros and cons; if something happens after this, do not blame me.

Gyanshankar came out with a heavy heart. Shraddha's sense of contentment and devotion to her husband had landed him in a fresh confusion. He already knew that Shraddha would not accept his proposal easily, but she's endowed with such a spirit of sacrifice was a fact unknown to him. He had taken pride in his knowledge of human psychology;

Shraddha's sacrifice destroyed it completely. He thought, 'Alas! Women are such foolish beings. I tried to teach her these lessons for months, but to no avail.' He sat in his room and kept thinking for a while, 'How can I solve this issue? If he (Premshankar) wants to leave Shraddha's maintainence to me, he will have to write Lakhanpur in her name. I will force him to do this. I'll tell him everything openly.'

He got out of the house in this very confusion and left for Hajipur. All along the way he kept thinking about it. He was also hesitant that he was meeting his brother after so many days and that too, for a selfish motive. Ever since Premshankar had started staying at Hajipur, Gyanbabu had not taken the trouble to go there. He used to meet him at home only. But the two brothers had not seen each other for quite a few months now.

When Gyanshankar reached Hajipur, evening had fallen. It was the month of January. The fields were full of greenery. There was mustard, peas, and blue and yellow flowers of flax blooming all around. Parrots twittered at places, and naughty crows did the rounds of the place. At many places, silent pairs of crane stood peacefully, as if in a non-violent meditation. Some women were bringing pots of water from the river; some others were plucking greens in the fields, and others brought green fodder on their heads to feed the oxen. It was a pious picture of a simple and peaceful life. It seemed too comforting in the face of the noisy hustle and bustle of the city.

Gyanshankar reached Premshankar's hut with a man and was amazed to see its attractive ambience. It was built on a river bank, on top of a high expanse, and was decorated with creepers and flowers. It resembled the contented heart of a great soul. As far as the eyes could stretch, one could only see nature's blooming and scented imagery. Premshankar was feeding the oxen in front of the hut. On seeing Gyanshankar, he hugged him warmly and after enquiring about the family, said, 'You seem to have forgotten me. Have you decided not to come here?'

Gyanshankar felt embarrassed and replied, 'I was thinking since long to come here, but couldn't find time. It's my misfortune; what else? You are so close to me, but there's a difference of a hundred miles between us. This is my moral weakness and care for the family. The kind of troubles that I've been forced to bear due to the family are known only to me. This place is so beautiful. Whose fields are these?'

Premshankar – They belong to thc tenants of this village only. You must be aware; this region had been flooded during the monsoons. The whole village had been drowned, so many oxen were lost, even the huts of people had disappeared. Since then, they have felt the need for cooperative set-ups. All of them have built this dam, which has afforded us a fertile land of sixty bighas. We have built high fences around it. Whosoever had whatever bighas, will get land accordingly. People have made me the supervisor. This kind of functioning saves us a lot of expenses. The amount of work done by ten labourers gets done by only six or seven. The ploughing and irrigation is also done in an efficient way. You have written a beautiful narrative about Gayatri Devi; I was very pleased to read it.

Gyanshankar – She has called me to take over the management of her estate. It's a great opportunity for me. But how can I go? I can take Maya and his mother with me, but Bhabhi (Shraddha) will never agree. I don't wish to complain but these days, she's getting very friendly with our aunt. She and her daughter-in-law keep inciting her unnecessarily. Bhabhi is a simpleton. She gets swayed too easily. Nowadays both these women are advising her to get half of Lakhanpur bequeathed to her, saying, 'Who knows, if your husband again goes abroad, who will care for you?' Chacha Sahib is also a part of that group. Very soon, they'll get the proposal to you. Therefore, it's my polite request that please inform me whatever you wish to do about it. All my hopes are dependent on your decision. If you've decided to sell your share, I'll think of something else for myself.

Premshankar – The doubts that you have regarding Chacha Sahib are totally baseless. He has never complained to me about you. He is at peace, and though his finances are not good, he does not seem to be dissatisfied with them. And regarding my plans about Lakhanpur – I just don't want to listen that I am a zamindar of that village. Rest assured from my side. You can assume that I just don't exist. I want to eat the fruit of my own labour. I do not wish to become a middleman or an agent. If my name has been recorded in the government documents I am ready to resign. Your Bhabi's upkeep will be your responsibility. I will keep assisting you in whatever way I can.

Gyanshankar was amazed to listen to his brother, though he knew these thoughts weren't his own. He had seen such descriptions in socialist texts, but he had taken it to be merely an ideal set before human society. He was surprised to see this ideal in its practical form. If he wanted to debate on the topic, he would have silenced Premshankar with his strong arguments. But the situation demanded that he should agree with him at the moment; not impress him with his oratory skills. He said, 'Bhai Sahib, the unity of the society is a great ideal, and I am proud that you are committed to it not just in thought, but also in action. It is quite natural for these thoughts to emerge in an independent land like America. I never got a chance to get out of this place and think like that. I am also deprived of self-confidence and the power of wisdom. How can my resolves be so pious or excellent! In my narrow opinion, this institution of zamindari, which you (smiling) deem as mediation, is the best form of life. But it's quite possible that I too might cultivate these high ideals under your influence.'

Prem – Just think about it yourself. Is it justified that someone does all the hard work; his protection is the job of someone else, and we extort all the money?

Gyan – What you say is true, but this system has been followed conventionally for years. There seems no scope to modify it at present.

Prem – When do you plan to leave for Gorakhpur?

Gyan – First you must assure me that whatever you've said regarding Lakhanpur is full and final.

Prem – Count it as such. I did ask you once about my share of the profit. At that time I hadn't been able to decide properly on the issue. I was financially unstable. I am very sorry for that. Godwilling; you'll find me determined this time.

Gyan – In that case, I'll go to Gorakhpur by the festival of Holi. If it doesn't harm you, please come home. Maya asks for you a lot.

Prem – I am not free today; I'll come some other time.

When Gyanshankar left the place, he was in high spirits. He thought, 'My long-lost ambition has come to fruition after so many years. I am now the undisputable master of Lakhanpur. No one can stop me now. Whatever I wish to do I can do freely. Bhaiya is true to his word, he can't go back on it now. If he had resigned, the matter would have been closed, but to insist upon it would only reveal my mistrust. This much is enough for now; the rest can be handled as it comes.'

20

Gyanshankar had been thinking of increasing the land rent on Lakhanpur since two years, but he had always been impeded by one hurdle or the other. Some days were spent in the division of the house. When that was accomplished, he had to leave for Lucknow. After that, Premshankar's arrival had created a new problem for him. He now found a favourable opportunity to do what he wanted after many days. The papers had been prepared already. The applications were filed without delay.

The people of Lakhanpur were already upset about the fine. When they were encountered with this new trouble, they got all the more annoyed. The tenure for submitting the fine was ending with this month. They could now demand an explanation with a free mind. The whole village got united on the issue. There was a fire of revolt burning within them. Even old Qadir Khan, who was notorious for his patience could not bear this assault. In the panchayat, which had been called for launching a protest against the zamindar, he said, 'Everything grows on this earth, and ultimately gets absorbed in it. We too have been born out of the soil, and will be lost in it one day. Then why should be bear these attacks? The greatest of kings have lost their heads for the sake of land; we too will do the same. All the people of this village must contribute to this mission; all must lend a hand to it.' All responded in a united voice, 'We all are with you; we shall follow wherever you lead us, and sacrifice ourselves for this land.'

Undoubtedly, the villagers knew that the zamindar had every right to increase the rent but they also knew that this right could be exercised only in a situation when he tried to increase the productivity of the land by his efforts. This unjustified increase was deemed as a torture by everybody.

When Gyanshankar saw the village united he was surprised, but he still had little doubt in his success, due to his own pressure tactics and also due to his friendship with the district collector, Mr. Jwalasingh. But when the case for rent increase was put up in the court, Gyanshankar got to know that success was far too difficult than he had deemed. Jwalasingh sometimes questioned him in a strange way while expressing his own concern for the tenants, so that his real motives became very apparent. The situation was turning against Gyanshankar in a discreet way. He didn't go to the court himself but used to listen to the proceedings daily. He couldn't do anything but feel irritated with Jwalasingh. 'This man used to be my classmate', he thought, 'we have played together for years. We had jokes to crack, games, fights, did everything together. If today he's got a powerful position, he's started turning his eyes away, as if he never knew me before.'

In the end, when he saw that the matter might be spoilt without any particular effort he decided to see Jwalasingh himself. 'Who knows he might be spreading this net to trap me with his power.' Although he knew that Jwalasingh never met the petitioners during the hearing of a case, he didn't bother about it in his selfish mood. He went to his bungalow in the evening.

Jwalasingh had become fond of playing the sitar these days. He found this to be a particular lack in his education. He wanted to play a special composition; he tuned the instrument but the strings were all out of tune. He kept tuning its points but before he could start playing Gyanshankar entered the room. Jwalasingh kept the sitar aside and hugged him saying, 'Come bhaijaan, please sit. I was thinking of you since many days. Nowadays your literary reputation is on the rise. I saw your essay on Gayatri Devi. I just wanted to greet your pen. The entire court is abuzz with its popularity. Such an expression, such talent and flow is not seen in many essays these days. I had gone to see Sahib Bahadur yesterday. The magazine was lying on his table. He immediately stated discussing the essay. These people have a special eye for talent. God knows how they manage to quote such words and idioms, as if someone has brought together a bouquet of beautiful flowers!'

Jwalasingh's words of praise were coming from the mouth of a nobleman who had been charmed at the wonderful music of his musician. Gyanshankar asked, 'What was the Sahib saying?'

Jwala – At first he asked; 'Who's this man?' When I told him, 'He's my classmate and used to play with me'; he was all the more interested. He asked what you did, and where you stayed. I think that the remarks you had made with regard to rural banks had impressed him a lot.

Gyan (smiling) – Bhaijaan, what's there to hide? That piece was actually taken from an English magazine after some modifications. (Carefully) At least the thoughts were not mine.

Jwala – Then you should have given proper reference.

Gyan – I don't think anyone has any exclusive right on thoughts. The words were mostly mine.

Jwala – Gayatri Devi must have been very happy. Will she gift you anything in return?

Gyan – I have received a letter from her. She wants me to take over the management of her estate.

Jwala – Oh! That's wonderful! The salary will not be less than five hundred rupees.

Gyan – There wasn't any talk of salary as yet. Perhaps she won't be able to give this much.

Jwala – Brother, even if you get about three hundred you'll be far better than any of us. You can roam about freely, drive around the estate; what else would be there to do? You won't need to carry a heap of papers everyday home like us. When do you plan going there?

Gyan – I'm ready to go, but only when you resolve my case.

Jwalasingh interrupted him in between and asked – Will you take your family along with you? Please do so. I have also called my wife since one week. I was getting bored lying in this desert all alone.

Gyan – Oh, has Bhabiji arrived? That will be so good. During college days, you were a dire opponent of the purdah system?

Jwala – That I am, but the trouble is that she feels very disturbed if asked to face strangers. She talks freely to the servants but runs away from the very shadow of my friends. Even if I drag her forcefully, she would keep standing there like a criminal.

Gyan – I wonder if I am one of those friends?

Jwala – Right now she'd hesitate to see even you. Well, if you meet her a few times, and your family and wife start coming then possibly she'd lose this hesitation. Why don't you send Mrs. Gyanshankar here tomorrow? I'll send the car. I hope your wife won't have any objection.

Gyan – Not at all, she'd love to come.

Gyanshankar didn't get a chance to say anything about his case, but when he left the place he was very happy. He thought, 'If our women start seeing each other, I'll have a complete control of this fellow. I'll be able to have my way with him'. He didn't have any doubts about his success now. But when he came home and discussed it with Vidya, she said, 'I am embarrassed to go and visit them; I don't know them at all, nor am I familiar with their lifestyle. What shall I talk about? I'll just be forced to sit with my mouth shut. You didn't ask me about it; why did you promise on my behalf?'

Gyan – Mrs. Jwalasingh is very social. You will be glad to meet her.

Vidya – And what shall I do about Munni (her younger daughter)? If she starts howling there and they feel bad?

Gyan – Take your maid along with you. She will keep the girl engaged in the garden.

After much coaxing by Gyanshankar, Vidya agreed to visit Jwalasingh's house. His car arrived in the morning. Vidya went there with great pomp. She came back by ten o' clock. Gyanshankar was very curious to know about Jwalasingh's wife. He asked, 'How did she meet you?'

Vidya – Very nicely. She's as gentle as a goddess. I've never seen such a pleasant and affectionate woman. She wasn't ready to leave my side. I could come only after a lot of insistence. She had tears in her eyes when I was leaving. I couldn't help crying myself. She knows Urdu, English and other languages also. She is so simple that she doesn't even address her maids roughly. Her name is Sheelmani.

Gyan – Did she talk about me?

Vidya – Of course. She was telling me that you are an old friend of her husband's. She had seen you from behind the partition. She doesn't like your achkan. She said, 'Achkan is an attire of the Muslims. Why doesn't he wear a coat?'

Gyanshankar's hopes got a further push but when the next hearing of the case occurred he found no favourable difference in the behaviour of Jwalasingh. He repeatedly questioned the witnesses doubtfully and raised objections to the lawyers' questions. When Gyanshankar heard the news in the evening he was amazed. 'He's a strange man. He wants to tread both the paths together. He simply wants to make a fool of me. He has learnt how to double cross by getting this position.' He thought he should go and tell him clearly, 'It's not good to be shrewd with friends. Either be my enemy or remain a friend. It is terrible that you have one thing in mind and something else in your mouth.' A whole week passed in this confusion. The next hearing was approaching fast. Gyanshankar's heart was very anxious. He had decided that if Jwalasingh played a double game with him he would shift his case to another court. Why should he face this oppression?

But when Jwalasingh extended the date of the hearing in order to go and inspect Lakhanpur, Gyanshankar felt very irritated. He said to Vidya angrily, 'Did you see that? Now he wants to go and inspect the area! I cannot take it anymore. Let me go and talk it out clearly with him.'

Vidya – Why are you getting so impatient? Who knows he might be pretending to do this inspection only to fool others? Everyone is afraid of getting a bad name.

Gyan – How far can I keep sitting here waiting for his decision? It is costing me hundreds of rupees a month.

Gyanshankar had not yet discussed Gayatri's proposal with Vidya. He just happened to mention it by chance. Vidya asked with surprise, 'How can it cost you anything?'

Gyanshankar saw that he couldn't hide the issue any further. He said, 'I haven't mentioned Gayatri Devi's letter to you. She has offered to appoint me as a manager of her estate and has called me there soon.'

Vidya – And you've already agreed?

Gyan – Why not; what's the harm?

Vidya – If you cannot understand a simple thing what can I say? Just think; how will people react to it? They would only think that we relatives are out to rob a helpless widow. You will not be able to escape criticism even if you work with most selfless intentions. She's you elder sister-in-law; she has lot of affection for you; she has laid out a cot for you with her own hands many a times. You will lose this respect once you become her servant and I too will become a servant's wife instead of being a sister. Even if she appreciates and respects you, a genuine regard will be missing. People will complain against you in all possible aspects. Because of this special relationship, she won't be able to check you, but feel disappointed in heart of hearts. I will never advice you to take up this post.

Gyan – Is that all you wish to say?

Vidya – It is not a matter of opinion. I find your going there totally improper.

Gyan – Then you must first listen to me. After analyzing my present and future situation, I think that I must not let this opportunity slip out of my hands. When I'll work in the hardest possible way, spend lesser than usual, and increase her profits, Gayatri will have no reason to doubt my intentions. And I am not thinking of the job aspect; my real aspiration is something else.

Vidya cast a doubtful look at Gyanshankar and asked, 'What else do you have in mind?'

Gyan – I cannot bear to see this prosperous estate slip away in the hands of others. If after Gayatri, it has to pass into the hands of others; why not me?

Vidya asked with curiosity, 'What right do you have over it?'

Gyan – Even if none at present, I want to exert my future right on it. I'll leave now; let me sort it out with Jwalasingh.

Vidya – What will you sort out? Has he taken any bribe from you?

Gyan – Why does he show such a friendly attitude when he doesn't wish to favour me?

Vidya – This is his greatness. It is not necessary that he deals the rest with injustice only for your sake.

Gyan – I want him to admit just that. I have a solid answer to give to it.

Vidya – Then go if you please. Why do you seek my advice?

Gyan – I really don't; if you really had some grey matter, I wouldn't have had to bother so much. Women accomplish great deeds these days. You couldn't even discuss my case with Sheelmani; you are so scared of losing your dignity in the tiniest of issues.

Vidya – I cannot do all this. My nature is like that only.

Gyan – Why, what was the harm if you would have even jokingly told her, 'Your husband is making us lose thousands of rupees annually; why don't you drive some sense into him?'

Vidya – I cannot coin such phrases; what to do? I cannot say anything to Sheelmani in this regard.

Gyan – Even if my plea gets dismissed?

Vidya – Whatever might happen.

Gyanshankar came outside thinking of this new problem. 'How should I make Vidya agree to it?' he thought, 'I know that by serving one's relatives, one's dignity gets harmed, but not to the extent that one spoils all longlasting ambitions for it. Vidya has a bad habit of stubbornly sticking to her own opinion. If I go there (Gayatri's place) and she complains against me to Rai Saheb the whole matter will be spoilt. She is no longer a simpleton. She's increasingly getting conscious of her self-respect. This is not a good time to make her unhappy.'

He was lost in these worries when Sheelmani arrived. Gyanshankar decided to approach her himself and tell her about his problem. The women were exchanging greetings of well-being when he reached upstairs, and standing near the curtain at the door said, 'I pay my regards to Bhabiji.'

Vidya immediately understood his intentions. She turned red with embarrassment. She left the room, and looking at Gyanshankar with reprimanding eyes, went to the other room. Shraddha was left to mediate between him and Sheelmani.

Gyanshankar said, 'Bhai Sahib does not appreciate the purdah, and when we have entered this mutual friendship, this system must be removed amongst us. I have a lot to discuss with you. God has blessed you with qualities of compassion and humility that's why I've gathered the courage to speak to you about personal matters. I hope you will not ignore my plea. My case regarding an increase in land rent is being heard in Bhai Sahib's court since two months. I regard him so much that I hesitate to talk about it personally to him. Though he regards me as a brother; I guess he believes that my appeal is false, and I'm afraid he might dismiss it. Of course he will also feel bad about it, but he does not have a correct knowledge of my real situation. Zamindari these days is a big headache. Life's essential commodities are getting expensive day by day and my income is still what it used to be thirty years ago. What best can I do except to increase the rent on land? Foodgrains are selling at the rate of jewels. The peasants are earning twice, in fact thrice their usual income. If I demand a small share of their increased income what's so unjust about that? If I win the case my income will easily increase by one thousand. But if I lose, I'll lose my respect too, in the eyes of tenants. They will become unduly bold and will pick up daily fights with me. Then the only way out for me would be to resign from zamindari and become a burden on my friends. (Smiling) I'll land at your very door and even if you get me beaten up, won't leave your place.'

Sheelmani listened to his explanation carefully and said to Shraddha, 'Please tell Babuji, I am very sorry to hear this. Why didn't you mention this earlier? Vidya too didn't speak about it, or else you would have been relieved of all this. But please be relaxed now. I assure you that I won't leave any stone unturned to plead your case.'

Gyan – I had similar hopes from you. Bhai Sahib will arrive in a few days to inspect my area. So please discuss it as soon as possible.

Sheel – I will talk to him as soon as I reach home. Please rest assured.

21

It was morning time. The cool breeze of April was flowing peacefully. Babu Jwalasingh was lying on an easychair in the verandah, waiting for his horse. He had to go today for the inspection of Lakhanpur. But a great hurdle had come in his way. Yesterday evening Sheelmani had spoken to him about Gyanshankar's case and he had been quite confused since then. He had a difficult choice before him; justice or love; duty or the honouring of his wife's promise. He was thinking, 'I made a big mistake by keeping this case in my court. But how could I have known that Gyanshankar would play such politics. He's such a selfish man! He's started interacting with the ladies due to this reason only.'

'What does Sheelmani know about his tactics; she just made a promise out of courtesy. If I do not honour that she will cry her eyes out. How can she understand that this injustice will pain my soul to no end? The witnesses that have appeared till now all prove that Gyanshankar has filed this case only to oppress his tenants, and possibly this is true as well. He's such a pretentious man. He writes such essays as if he's all engrossed in the efforts of social upliftment but actually he's far too selfish. Once he becomes the manager of Gayatri's estate he will indulge in all kinds of fraud. No, I won't be able to bear this injustice; I can't know everything and still do nothing. If Sheelmani gets upset, let her be. She should have understood that she has no right to make any such promise. But the real problem is that she won't stop at only crying. She'll keep taunting me now and then. She might leave for her parents' house. She has this nagging habit of going to the extremes; she'll either be the epitome of love or the extreme end of torture. Gyanshankar has put me in such a tight spot that there seems no way of escape.'

Jwalasingh was lost in this very confusion when Gyanshankar arrived on his bicycle. Jwalasingh got up from his chair at once and called his syce loudly to get the horse. The latter was already ready with the animal. As soon as he got the orders, he brought the horse in front of his master. Jwalasingh got up to its back. Gyanshankar came close and asked, 'Bhai Sahib, where are you off to, so early in the morning?'

Jwala – I'm going to Lakhanpur. I wish to see the site of the case.

Gyan – It's going to be very hot.

Jwala – Doesn't matter.

Gyan – Shall I come with you?

Jwala – I know the way quite well.

Saying this, he kicked his horse and soon disappeared. Gyanshankar understood that the game he had played with Sheelmani was showing its effect. 'This rudeness is a clear sign of the same. Had this not been the case he'd have had his usual sweet talk with me. Let me go and see Sheelmani; she should not leave me midway.' He thus went inside Jwalasingh's house and sat in his room. The servant said, 'Sarkar has gone out.'

Gyan – I know. I had met him. Please inform someone in the house that I've come.

Servant – Sarkar has forbidden to do so.

Gyan – Do you recognize me or not?

Servant – Why not?

Gyan – Then why don't you inform about my presence?

Servant – I've been asked not to do so.

Gyanshankar had a firm belief now that his shot had hit the target; Jwalasingh has been behaving shrewdly only to prove himself unbiased. He was thinking of what to say to Sheelmani when a maidservant arrived and on seeing him, went and informed Sheelmani. Sheelmani immediately sent paan for him and made him sit in the drawing room. After a while she came and stood near the curtain and sent a message through the maid, 'I've pleaded your case with Babuji.'

Gyanshankar thanked her and said, 'I have no other option but to trust you.'

Sheelmani said, 'Don't you worry, I'll not let him rest till the matter is resolved.' Gyanshankar did not think it proper to stay long after this. He happily took his leave.

On the other hand Babu Jwalasingh rode his horse and stopped after four miles. He felt a desire to smoke a cigar. He took out his cigar-case; but he had no matchstick to light it. He was greatly addicted to the cigar. 'What to do now?' He looked here and there, and saw a palanquin going somewhere. He took his horse near it, and saw Premshankar sitting on it. Jwalasingh had been introduced to him earlier. He had gone to see his agricultural farm many a times, and had great respect for his simple and contented life. He asked, 'Say Sir, where are you off to?'

Prem – I'm going to Lakhanpur, and you?

Jwala – I'll also come with you.

Prem – That will be nice company. Is there a case going on?

Jwalasingh smilingly lit his cigar and narrated the case and its proceedings to him. Premshankar kept listening at first; then said, 'You didn't ask him to leave these poor people alone?'

Jwala – Why should I have asked him anything? Well, whatever transpired between the ladies indicates that he's helpless due to his expenses; he is not being able to manage properly.

Prem – Two thousand per annum is not less for a family of four.

Jwala – But half of this income is yours.

Prem – No, I don't have anything. I have told him clearly that I don't wish to take anything from this property.

Jwalasingh – (with surprise) Have you signed up everything in his favour?

Prem – Not yet, but you can call it done. My personal principle is that a man should eat from an income earned by his own hard work. Nobody has a right to make someone else's income a basis of his livelihood.

Jwala – Then say this clearly that you deem the profession of zamindari totally baseless.

Prem – Yes, I do not approve of it at all. Land belongs to those who till it. A ruler has a right to share the produce because he arranges for peace and protection in the country, in the absence of which, agriculture is not possible. Any third estate does not have any place in the society.

Jwala – Sir, your thoughts are capable enough of bringing a revolution in the nation. According to your principle, our great zamindars, talukedars and rich people have no place in the society. All seem to be robbers.

Prem – They are not to blame for this; it is the fault of our conventions. The kind of social and moral deterioration that the country is facing due to this cannot be truly estimated. That part of our society which is greatly attributed with physical valour, wisdom and education, which is decorated with best qualities of heart and mind, is trapped in the shackles of laziness, show and thoughtlessness only due to this convention.

Jwalasingh – Are you going to Lakhanpur to propagate these ideas; I might have to call the police if there's some unrest.

Prem – Well, if I can be charged with destroying peace, then please call the police.

Jwalasingh – I'll have to keep a watchful eye on you. I am also a small landowner. I ought to be scared of you. Will you go to Lakhanpur only or further ahead?

Prem – I plan to return from here only; rest is up to the situation. I've heard that plague has spread in the nearby villages. I've brought some medicines with me. I'll distribute them if the need arises; who knows I might be able to save a few lives.

Thus talking, the two men reached Lakhanpur. The village was nearly empty. People had put up their huts in the gardens. There was a lot of hustle and bustle in this small settlement. Yet, there was no sign of those heartrending sorrows that had torn apart the hearts of the people. The flowers of mahua were being dried on the roofs. The roar of the floor mills, churning of buttermilk, and sounds of pestle and mortar were indicating the signs of that self-struggle which doesn't even bother about that massive destruction that plague had let loose. The boys were pelting stones at mango trees. A woman sat about cleaning utensils; another was coming out with fire from a neighbour's house. No one could be spotted sitting idle.

Premshankar got down from the palanquin as soon as he reached the camp and sat on a cot near a house. Jwalasingh didn't get down from the horse. It seemed insulting to him to sit on a cot. He called out loudly, 'Where's the headman? Let him go and call the patwari; I want to inspect the site.'

As soon as they listened to this order many men left their patients in the huts and came out. Everyone started running around. A few men ran to the chaupal to get a chair; others went to find the patwari, and prominent people of the village came and surrounded Jwalasingh. No one bothered about Premshankar.

Just then Qadir Khan came out of his hut and said something in the ears of Sukhu. Sukhu consulted with Dukhran Bhagat and also with Bisesar Sah, as if they were discussing something important. After ten minutes, Sukhu Chaudhary came out with a plate. He was carrying some grains of rice, curd and some money in it. The priest of the village came and put a mark of curd-rice on Premshankar's forehead, and kept the plate in front of him.

Jwalasingh sat on the chair and said, 'Well, you've earned your first income of the day; it's me who's suffered a loss. Are you still against the profession of zamindari?'

Premshankar said, 'Even stones are worshipped in the name of the goddess.'

Qadir Khan – We are fortunate to have met both our masters together.

Prem – Has the epidemic relented here or is it still wreaking havoc?

Qadir – Sarkar, don't ask anything about it; it is still increasing instead of going down. There's hardly a day when some house or the other doesn't lose a life. The river is about six miles away from here. Sometimes we have to go there twice or thrice to immerse the dead bodies in it. On top of it, there's the danger of storm, or flood, or even fire. The foodgrains are rotting in the fields. Even if we cut the crops, there's no place to store them. In almost all the houses, the hearth is lit only once, at dawn. Thereafter, no one lights a fire to cook anywhere in the village. We don't even get a hookah to smoke. Huzoor, we don't even have the energy to cry about our woes; you can see our condition with your own eyes. Moreover, the masters have no sympathy for us. We have to run to the court, leaving behind hundreds of jobs. Sometimes, we have to go leaving a dead body behind in our homes. What to do, we have to bear what has been inflicted upon us. There was a poor subject of yours. He was quite healthy. He took good care of his family. He expired in a single day. He didn't even get any time to sigh about his pain. Sukhu Chaudhary's entire family has been destroyed. It's only he who is breathing alive. Poor Dapatsingh's younger son died yesterday; today his elder son has fallen sick. He can be saved only by the almighty. His speech has been lost. He is beating his hands and feet, lying on the cot with red eyes. What all can we tell you; we've been praying to our Hindu as well as Muslim gods, but no one seems to listen. We've been appearing for the case somehow till now. We aren't even sure if that can be done for long. For whom should we do all this? The masters don't take pity on us even in this situation.

Premshankar – I want to see Dapatsingh's son.

Qadir – Of course, let me take you.

Jwalasingh – Please be careful; this disease is said to be infectious.

Premshankar did not say anything in return. He took his bag of medicines and started following Qadir Khan. When he reached Dapatsingh's hut there was a huge crowd at his door. The patient's cot was kept under a mango tree. Dapatsingh and his younger brother Jhapatsingh were standing near his head, fanning him with their hands. Two women were standing at his feet, crying; when they saw Premshankar they went inside. Both the brothers looked at him with a helpless expression and stood aside. Premshankar checked the temperature of the patient which was 107 degree celcius. The symptoms of the disease were clearly evident. He understood that the patient will not live beyond a few hours. He was just taking out the medicine from the bag when the boy let out a scream and fell down with a thud. His eyes turned to stone. The women started beating their breasts. Dapatsingh was so taken over by grief that he gripped the dead body of his son, crying, 'My son! Oh! My son!'

His eyes grew red weeping like this. He was intoxicated with grief; just like a wet wooden stick steams with the first spark of fire, and with the next spark turns to ashes. Dapatsingh was overwhelmed with sorrow. He stood up and said, 'Why doesn't anyone set this house on fire? What's left in it? What is all this misery? The father is sitting and the son has left for his final destination. I had played with him with these very hands. How can I light a fire to his pyre with the same? He has left us as if he never had any relation with us. He used to say, 'Dada, you have grown old, now relax and pray to God, we will serve you now.' But both of them have gone (his sons). No one had any pity on me. I call upon you now. Now respond, or were those just fake promises?'

Thus saying he left the corpse and went and sat under another tree. After a while he again said, 'I will break this network of wordly bonds. It has trapped me for long; now I'll make it dance around my fingers. You both have gone; very well. You have made me free of this trap. Due to these worldly desires, I've done so many evil deeds, told so many lies, strangled so many throats and usurped so many fields. Now there's no reason to indulge in all this. There lies the cause, all dead. Who says he was my son? No, he was my enemy, the knot around my neck, and the chain around my feet. The knot has been loosened; the chain broken. Come, set this house on fire; burn everything down. Balraj, why do you stand shedding tears? Is there no fire anywhere? Come and burn it all.'

Everyone around was weeping. Premshankar was also quite sad. He went to Dapatsingh and said, 'Thakur, have patience. This is the way of the world. The women and the brothers are crying to see you in such a state. Go and console them.'

Dapatsingh saw Premshankar with lost eyes and said sarcastically, 'Oh, I see. You are our master. Have you come to extort the rent? Go and take it from one who's lying there; he'll pay every penny of yours. Tell Ghaus Khan to arrest him, tie him and beat him up; I will not say a thing. I have resigned from the matters of the fields and the house.'

Qadir Khan said, 'Bhaiya Dapat, strengthen your heart. Don't you see; this fire is burning in every other house? Even I have been struck by this disaster. You won't get anything by losing heart. You'll have to get up and think of the cremation; it's getting late in the afternoon.'

Dapatsingh came back to his senses. Along with his consciousness, tears also came afresh. Crying out he said, 'Dada, I do not have a strong heart like you. I cannot console myself. Alas! Both went away like that; none was to become my repose in old age. Looking at this corpse, I feel like slicing up my throat. Dada, you know what a gem this son of mine was. He was insisting to buy a pair of dumbles the other day. I abused him a lot; even raised my hand. The poor boy did not say a word. He kept craving for good food. None of his wishes could be fulfilled. He couldn't have a proper meal, or proper clothes ever. Curse on my life! I cannot bear to see this house anymore. Jhapat, take care of the family; I have only losses written in my fate. Brothers, Ram-Ram; Ram-Ram to my master; Ram-Ram to the government. This unfortunate man leaves his home; please excuse all my mistakes.'

Thus saying, Dapatsingh went up to a side. When men tried to catch hold of him, he ran away. Many of them followed him, but they couldn't gather anything except dust. It seemed he had disappeared in thin air. People started losing their breath; they started falling here and there. Balraj followed him till the end; even Dapatsingh couldn't escape him and fell on the ground. Balraj ran to hug him, and started fanning him with his hand cloth. When he woke up, he got him home.

Jwalasingh was also moved by the scene. He said to Premshankar, 'Babu Sahib, it's so sorrowful.'

Premshankar – What to say, my heart is full.

Many men started cutting the bamboo for cremation, but the body wasn't lifted till late afternoon.

Premshankar asked Qadir – Why's it getting so late?

Qadir – Huzoor, what to tell you? There's no money in the house. Poor Jhapat is running about for the expenses, but there's no one who can lend a penny. It's we alone who know our real situation. The case for rent increase has made us pawn even our basic utensils. This epidemic has taken a toll of whatever little was left. There's nothing left in any house.

Premshankar sighed and said to Jwalasingh – Have you seen their condition now? They don't even have a penny to buy a shroud.

Jwalasingh – I am feeling sorry about levying a fine last year. I had not known till then that their condition is so bad.

Prem – I am regretting that I too didn't carry any money with me.

Jwala – I do have money, but I'm feeling hesitant to give it. Perhaps they'll feel bad? You please take it from me and give them; it will save the situation.

Premshankar took the twenty rupee note and gave it quietly to Qadir Khan. One of the men ran to get a shroud. People started picking up the dead body. The women became unrestful. Till the time a corpse keeps lying in the house, the family members keep hoping for a miracle. The going away of the body is the sign of the final separation. It breaks away the last fragment of hope.

The body was taken away late in the afternoon. All the men of the village accompanied it. Qadir Khan was the first to lift it on his shoulders.

Jwalasingh had some official work so he returned after the cremation. But Premshankar decided to stay back in the village for a few days.

22

A fortnight passed away. It was evening time. The shops selling ice in the city were getting thronged by people. They had started losing interest in hookah and cigarettes. Jwalasingh had just returned from Lakhanpur after inspection and was having cool sherbet sitting on a chair when Sheelmani came and asked, 'Where were you held up in the afternoon?'

Jwala – I was with Babu Premshankar. He is still in the village.

Sheel – The epidemic has not relented as yet?

Jwala – No, it is going down slowly. He has been touring the rural areas since fifteen days. He hasn't taken rest for a single day. People in the village worship him like a God. Even the greatest of officers do not command so much respect. God knows how he stays there in such hot weather; without a fan, khus chik, ice or cold drinks. He keeps lying in a hut under a tree. I wouldn't have been able to stay there even for a day.

Sheel – He seems to be a true philanthropist. What happened in the Lakhanpur case; did you see the site?

Jwala – Yes, I did. All my doubts about it were true. Gyanshankar's appeal is totally baseless. His manager and peons tried their best to dupe me but I know their tactics very well. They only know how to serve their interests by cheating the officers. Look at this follow's conscience (Gyanshankar's); the tenants are fighting for their lives and he just wants his cup of blood! He can't even go and console the villagers. It is his very brother who has forsaken the zamindari to serve the poor selflessly; he is playing with his own life in the process. And this great man doesn't even refrain from killing the poor. In my eyes, he has lost all respect; he's a total sham.

Sheel – If you start criticizing somebody you drive him to nothing. I too have my own understanding of people. Gyanshankar is not a god, but he's as ordinary as any other man. He's not worse than any other of his like.

Jwala – You can take him to be as you please, but I only think him to be a cruel and evil soul.

Sheel – Then I guess you'll surely dismiss his case.

Jwala – Not at all; even after knowing everything, I'll give the decree in his favour.

Sheel – (happily) Yes, that's exactly what I want. Please do it in a way that my promise is also fulfilled.

Jwala – But think clearly that you're taking a burden on your conscience. Lakhanpur has been badly affected by plague. People have lost everything. They don't even have time to harvest their fields. There's no house from where you cannot hear cries of mourning. Those poor people don't have the means to appeal against the case. Gyanshankar will impose the decree as soon as he gets it. Someone will have to auction his oxen, some others would sell their houses and someone's ripe harvest will be sold off at the rate of pennies. Who will bear the curses of these poor? Who will take the responsibility of this torture? I am not afraid of a bad name, but my soul trembles at the thought of injustice and tyranny.

Sheelmani was shaken at this narrative. She hadn't thought the issue to be so complicated. She broke her silence and said, 'If this is the condition then please do whatever is the call of justice and truth. I cannot take the curse of the poor. How could I have known that such a minor case would bring such dire reprcussions?'

Jwalasingh felt very relieved. He had not understood Sheelmani completely. He said, 'How will you face Vidyavati now?'

Sheelmani – Vidyavati is not a mean lady and even if she gets upset I don't care. How can one ruin the poor just for the sake of friendship? I guess even she's annoyed with Gyanshankar. Whenever he's discussed this case with me she's always left my side. His hankering after material pleasures is quite hateful to her. If she hears about the dismissal of the case, she'll be happy in heart of hearts.

Jwala – On top of it he's planning to take over Gayatri's estate. She won't be able to tolerate him even for a day. She's too kind.

Sheelmani – If he appeals against the dismissal of the case?

Jwala – Quite possibly, he would.

Sheel – And can his case be reiterated after that?

Jwala – Yes, maybe.

Sheel – He will then absolutely crush the poor.

Jwala – Well, that's his very nature.

Sheel – Can't you help the farmers in any way?

Jwala - No, that's outside my purview.

Sheel – If the farmers can get monetary help from somewhere, then they won't lose the case?

Jwala – Losing or winning is up to the discretion of the officers. Well, if they do get financial help they'll be able to fight their case properly.

Sheel – Why don't you give them some money?

Jwala – Well, how can I do the same kind of injustice which I dislike?

Sheel – Premshankarji is very kind. If he has money he should help.

Jwala – I don't think he will strike enmity with his own brother for the sake of justice.

Just then, many of Jwalasingh's friends arrived outside. A famous jaltarang player had arrived from Gwalior. He was about to perform in the club. All of them left for the club.

In the next hearing, Gyanshankar's case was put up again. Jwalasingh gave his decision. His case was dismissed. Gyanshankar was himself present in the court that day. When he listened to it he was very angry. He came home and discussed everything with Vidya. He also went to visit Prabhashankar after many days and lamented about Jwalasingh's heartlessness. This routine continued for a week. There was no person left in the city to whom he had not complained about this betrayal. He even charged Jwalasingh with bribery, and didn't remain content with mere verbal slandering. He started attacking him with his pen also. He wrote articles against him in many daily newspapers. In almost every paper, he filled one column after the other talking about his unjust practices. The Anglo-Indian newspapers got a golden opportunity to comment on the inefficiency of the Indians. The noise went on for about a month. No aspect of Jwalasingh's life could escape insult and critique. An editor went on to describe his house as a rendezvous of the city's most vile and disreputable fellows. Gyanshankar's writing skills, joined with his ill-feelings painted Jwalasingh as a devil of oppression and evil. The poor man read all this and could do nothing. He had no right to give any kind of justification. Law did not allow him to open his mouth. There was no one among his friends who could have spoken in his favour. He was annoyed with the false reporting of the newspapers which just delighted in slinging mud at the officials, without any discrimination between the right and the wrong. He found it difficult to get out of the house. All over the city he had become a topic of open discussion. People used to comment directly on him off and on. The officers were also affected by all there developments. Once he went to see the District Collector. He refused to see him saying he wasn't free. The commissioner was a Bengali gentleman. Jwalasingh went to appeal to him. He listened to the entire story sympathetically but finally told him, 'It is impossible that this unrest won't affect you. I am afraid lest this topic is raised in the organizing committee. I will try my best to save you. But you must be ready to bear a loss in your mission to save justice; an honest path is not a bed of roses.'

Jwalasingh was lost in these very worries one day, when Premshankar arrived. Jwalasingh ran and hugged him. His eyes were full of tears, as if he had met some great well-wisher of his. After enquiring about his well-being, he asked, 'When did you return from the village?'

Premshankar – Today itself. It took me almost a month and a half. I had planned to stay only for a few days. If people from Hajiganj had not come repeatedly to call me, I would have stayed there for the entire month of June.

Jwala – What's the news of the epidemic?

Premshankar – It seems to be over now. You tell me, what is this mess being created by the newspapers? I saw it today only. I had no idea what was going on beyond the village. This group is all out to harm you.

Jwala – It's all his (Gyanshankar's) goodwill; what else?

Prem – As soon as I saw it, I understood that it's the result of dismissing Gyanshankar's case.

Jwala – I had never expected from Gyanshankar that he would punish me in such a way for following my duty. Had he only attacked my sense of justice and other related ideas, I wouldn't have bothered so much. He could have called me tyrannical, oppressive, and impudent; we are used to such charges. I am pained because he has maligned my character. If I have something to be proud of, it's my clean behaviour. Many of my friends call me an ascetic. I have never visited any theatre here, not even a fair or a performance. Babu Gyanshankar is well aware of all this. But he didn't hesitate to portray me as the leader of all types of loafers. I am so upset with these attacks that I cannot express my sorrow. I felt like taking poison many a times; but thinking that it will confirm these charges, restrained myself. I was also afraid lest Sheelmani would cry herself to death. Honestly speaking, it is her deep love for me which has saved my life; had she turned away from me even for a second, I would have certainly committed suicide. Gyanshankar knows my nature very well. We have stayed together like brothers for years. He knows where the soft spot lies within my heart. He targetted it with his pen, and has weakened my soul forever.

Prem – I would advise you to file a case of defamation against all these newspapers. There is no other way out to prove yourself innocent. I am just not bothered as to how it will affect Gyanshankar. He should be punished for his deeds. I am an advocate of tolerance but it's just impossible that someone should falsely malign my character, and I keep my mouth shut. You consult your lawyers and do file a case of defamation.

Jwalasingh thought for a while and said, 'I'll earn a further bad name.'

Prem – Absolutely not. You will get a chance to answer these false charges and you'll gain respect in the eyes of the public. In such a situation, your keeping quiet is not just unpardonable, but is absolutely atrocious. Please don't think that I hate Gyanshankar or love verbal slandering. I am just looking at the matter with an eye of principle. It is our duty to save our honour. Babu Gyanshankar will not have any escape then.

Jwala – I become helpless when I think of the repercussions. Possibly he might have to go to jail. That pain will be far more unbearable to me than this. The person who was like a brother to me for so many years; with whom I ate and drank; I cannot be so hard on him. I tremble to even think of him facing a hard time. These charges can only harm me to the extent that I might be transferred or at the most suspended, but Gyanshankar will be totally destroyed. I cannot harm his family only to avenge my losses.

Premshankar looked at Jwalasingh with appreciating eyes. His head bowed at such self-depreciation; his heart became full of compassion. He fell at Jwalasingh's feet, and said with tearful eyes, 'Bhaiji, God has created you as his own reflection. I had not known till now that such feelings of purity and divinity were hidden in your heart.'

Jwalasingh took his feet aside and said, 'Bhaiya, please don't do this for God's sake. I am not even capable of putting your feet-dust on my head. Please don't drag me to this condition.'

Premshankar – If you wish I can oppose these charges in the same newspapers.

Jwalasingh actually felt the need for opposing the charges on him, but he was scared lest his opinion should take him away from that high position which he had just achieved, so he refused. He said, 'No, I don't think that is needed now.'

After Premshankar left, Jwalasingh felt sorry that he had lost an opportunity to answer back. Had he answered on his behalf, this entire false network would have been destroyed. 'But whatever happened happened for the best. I got a place in the heart of an honest man.'

Premshankar had decided to visit home when he had left Hajipur. He hadn't got any news of the house since months, but when he got up from Jwalasingh's place, it was almost nine, and the hot winds of June had started blowing. It would have been difficult to go to Hajipur from home. So he decided to go there some other day.

But Gyanshankar was not at peace. As soon as he came to know that his brother had returned from the rural tour, he was anxious to meet him. It was very essential to bring down Jwalasingh's reputation in his eyes. It was evening time. Premshankar was watering the flower-pots in front of his cottage when Gyanshankar came and said, 'Has the labourer gone out somewhere?'

Premshankar – I am also a labourer. Is everything fine at home?

Gyan – Of course, all's well due to your blessings. You must be having many ploughmen. Can't they even water the pots? You have to unnecessarily take this trouble.

Prem – I have no right to make them labour for me. They are not my personal servants. I am just a supervisor out here, and in America, I have washed dishes with my own hands, cleaned tables in hotels, and swept the roads; I haven't become a great man by coming here. I haven't kept any servant also. I do all my work myself.

Gyan – You are really impossible. May I ask you why you give yourself so much trouble?

Prem – I am not troubled at all. In fact if I act in opposition to this, I will certainly be troubled. It has become my habit.

Gyan – I hope you admit that there are various levels of soul development.

Prem – I haven't thought about it and nor can I fix any principle on it. Have you appealed against that case as yet, or not?

Gyan – Yes I have. Did you see Jwalasingh's greatness? This fellow has been helped by me in so many ways. I made him finish graduation by revising all his lessons. I used to ignore my own work, but used to remove all his hurdles. This is the way I've been rewarded for my good deeds. I have never seen such on ungrateful man.

Prem – There were articles against him in the newspapers. Did you write those articles?

Gyan – Yes I did. If he behaves like this with me, why should I give him any concession?

Prem – Your behaviour was totally unjust. Whatever he did, he did for the sake of justice. His aim was not to hurt you. You attacked him with the sole intention of destroying him.

Gyan – When there's so much enmity between us, who can analyze the truth? This is no age for a principled fight.

Prem – Then you admit this is your false imagination?

Gyan – Yes, in front of you, but in front of others …

Prem – (interrupting him) If he files a case of defamation?

Gyan – It needs a lot of courage and he doesn't have an iota of it. All his power is only a matter of show. If the appeal is accepted in my favour then I will further attack him. Where can he go? Even if nothing else happens he will get transferred along with this bad repute. This time you travelled a lot in Lakhanpur; the tenants must have complained against me.

Prem – Yes, all seem to be complaining.

Gyan – I hope there isn't a danger of a fight or riots?

Prem – I don't think there's any chance of that.

Gyan – And if they come to know that we have our own differences on the topic, and this is but natural – because you cannot hide your inner feelings – they will grow all the more bold.

Prem (smiling) – Then what's the harm in it?

Gyan – According to your principles, there's no harm, but I'll have no recourse. It is important for my sake that you please reduce your visits to the area.

Prem – Do you doubt that I incite the tenants against you? Am I your enemy? I have my deepest sympathies with not just the farmers of Lakhanpur, but with the farmers of the entire nation. But that does not mean that I have some issues with the zamindars; well, if you don't want that I should go there, I won't. I will stop visiting the area.

Gyanshankar was satisfied but he was too embarrassed to express it. In the face of his brother's pious nature, he found his material cravings very mean and lowly. He kept roaming in the cotton and corn fields for some time, which had been sown here since a long time. He then returned home. Premshankar didn't ask anything about Shraddha, nor did Gyanshankar say anything on his own. Shraddha was no longer his brother's beloved; she was a goddess meant to be worshipped.

The next day, a postman gave a registered letter to him at ten o' clock. He looked at the envelope with surprise. The address was written clearly.

When he opened it, he found a currency note of five hundred rupees. There was also a letter in which it was written:

'This money is being sent to you for helping the people of Lakhanpur. Please give this sum to them for the defence of their appeal. Please excuse us for causing you this trouble.'

Premshankar started thinking, 'Who has sent it? Who knows me out here? Who is aware of my opinion on the topic? Who trusts me so much?' The answer to all these questions seemed to be only one, 'Jwalasingh'; but his mind refused to accept this answer.

He was now worried about the sending of the money. 'If Gyanshankar comes to know of it, he will think that I've helped the tenants. He would never believe that this money is someone else's doing. If I do not give it to the tenants, it would be a great betrayal.' Evening fell in this confusion, and someone announced the arrival of Lala Prabhashankar.

23

Gyanshankar was fully confident about the success of his appeal. He knew that due to lack of finances, the peasants were in a very weak position. But when he saw the farmers preparing seriously for their defence, he started having doubts about his success. He was surprised as to find them furnished with proper funds. He thought, 'Ghaus Khan had told me that the epidemic has destroyed everyone; no one will appear in the court, and I will have a clear win. Why has the picture changed? They must have got help from some source or the other. Perhaps some moneylender is backing them. There seems no one like that in the city; must be someone belonging to Lakhanpur. Well, the secret will be dispelled one day, and I shall find the truth.' He went to the court himself on the day of the final decision. The appeal got dismissed. Ghaus Khan was the first to come forward. Gyanshankar angrily took him to task, 'Why sir, you told me that these people didn't have a single penny; did this lawyer come for free?'

Ghaus Khan replied hotly, 'I told you the truth, but I didn't know that there was so much disunity among the masters. I have found out that a week ago, your elder brother has given one thousand rupees to Qadir for fighting the case.' Gyanshankar was shocked. He said after a moment, 'This is all lies.'

Ghaus Khan – Absolutely not. My peons have themselves heard Qadir Khan say this. If you ask him he'll tell you also, or else you can ask your brother yourself.

Gyanshankar was clueless. He took his bicycle, came home irritated and angry and said in a sharp tone to Shraddha, 'Bhabhi, did your see Bhaiya's doing! I came to know today that he has given one thousand rupees to Lakhanpur people for their defence. The result is that my appeal got dismissed; about a month of running about and thousands of rupees went down the drain. I lost one thousand annually and my honour is absolutely ruined. I never suspected such politics from him. Now please tell me if I should now count him my friend or my enemy?'

Shraddha said in a doubtful tone, ‘Someone must have tried to fool you. How can he get so many rupees?’

Gyan – No, I have confirmed news. People who have got the money are saying this themselves.

Shraddha – He had promised you that he won’t have any link with Lakhanpur; he would never go there.

Gyan – Yes, he did, and I had believed him but I got to know today that there are some people who are friends with the entire world, but enemy of their own family. Chacha Sahib must have had a hand in all this.

Shraddha – First go and ask him. I still cannot believe that he had so much money.

Gyan – His backstabbing has put an end to all my ambitions. When he has so much malice against me, I don’t think I can count him as my brother. The social boycott inflicted upon him was not totally unjustified. A stay abroad destroys all personal ties.

Shraddha – You have been deluded.

Gyan – You talk like small children. How can you tell whether he had money or not?

Shraddha – Why don’t you just go and see him?

Gyan – I cannot bring myself to do that. I cannot bear to see his face. If he has sided with the tenants I’ll also show him what all I can do. A zamindar has numerous hands. I will crush the people of Lakhanpur in a way that no bones will be ever found. I know what’s there in Bhaiya’s heart. You are a simpleton; you can never understand his deepest motives. All he’s concerned about is that I should be at unease, he should take over the village after duping the tenants, and both of us should lose everything. I have now seen his real face. He is a clever wolf – he has something else in mind and something else in his mouth. And someone who’s lost his religion can do the most unexpected of things. Jwalasingh is far better than him. Whatever he did, he did for the sake of justice; not to harm me in any particular way. I have been quite unfair to him, and have defamed him all over the country. I am pained even to think of those things now.

Shraddha – He has been transferred from here. Sheelmani’s maid came today. She was saying they will go from here in a few days. His position has also been demoted.

Gyanshankar was startled to hear this, andcould only say, ‘Really!’

Shraddha – Sheelmani is supposed to come tomorrow.

Gyan – I made a big mistake. I will forever repent this. I am forced to believe now that Bhai Saheb had incited him (Jwalasingh) also. The day he had gone to inspect the site Bhaiya had also reached Lakhanpur. On one hand, he duped Jwalasingh and on the other, he also instigated the villagers to unite against me. I could never imagine that he would think of such far-fetched plans, or else I would have been more cautious.

Shraddha looked at Gyanshankar with disrespect and got up from there.

The next day Sheelmani came and stayed for the whole day. As she left, she cried a lot, hugging Vidya and Shraddha.

Jwalasingh stayed for five more days. Gyanshankar daily thought of meeting him, but at the precise moment, lost all courage to do so. He was afraid lest he started discussing those critical essays; what would he do then? 'I can lie about the fact that I didn't write or publish any essay in my name, but this might demean me further in the eyes of Jwalasingh.'

On the fifth day, Jwalasingh set out to leave. Many of his friends had come to the station to see him off. Jwalasingh was meeting his friends and taking their leave. There were just a few minutes left in the departure of the train when Gyanshankar came rushing to the platform and stood in the back row. He lacked the courage to come forward and meet him. Jwalasingh saw him and got down from the train to hug him. Tears started falling from Gyanshankar's eyes. Jwalasingh was weeping at this lamentable end of their lifelong friendship; Gyanshankar was crying because he was sorry to have harmed such a true and simple friend.

When the guard gave the green signal, Gyanshankar said in a shaking voice, 'Bhaijaan, I am extremely sorry.'

Jwalasingh replied, 'Please forget about those things.'

Gyan – If God allows me, I'll try to compensate this loss.

Jwala – Please keep writing to me; don't forget.

People were intrigued at this gentlemanly behaviour between the two friends. They had thought the wounds of their friendship to be irreparable. The person most surprised at this scenario was Premshankar, who thought Gyanshankar to be far more wicked than he actually was.

24

After the appeal was dismissed, Gyanshankar started preparing for Gorakhpur. He thought, 'If I keep getting bothered this way, I'll never be able to leave Lakhanpur all my life; some trouble or the other will keep emerging. If I can strengthen my hold in Gorakhpur, many Lakhanpurs can be acquired in a few years.' Vidya too agreed to send him after thinking about the situation. She thought, 'If the brothers keep fighting like this, the assets will be divided very soon, and then we won't be able to manage with one thousand per annum. He (Gyanshankar) will not be able to follow any other means of livelihood. Let him take whatever is coming his way.' So Gyanshankar reached Gorakhpur after the festivities of Janamashtami. He did not see Premshankar before going.

It was morning time. Gayatri was sitting for her daily prayers when the guard informed her about Gyanshankar's arrival. Gayatri didn't call him in immediately, but her prayers which normally continued till nine, got finished by seven o' clock. She then came to her room, wore a beautiful saree, combed her hair, and sat on the divan with a sense of dignity. She instructed her maid to call Gyanshankar. She was now the 'Queen.' She had received this title recently. She thus wanted to meet Gyanshankar with appropriate pomp and show.

Gyanshankar was waiting to be summoned inside. He was amazed to see the glamour of the place. Two liveried guards were roaming at the door. A huge bell was hung in the open verandah. In the stable he could see many horses of a noble breed. On the other side two carriages stood under a tin shed. There were many cages too, housing birds like the myna, shyama and white parrots. Imported mules were also tied up on one side. In front of this building was Gayatri's bungalow, which was furnished with tables and chairs. This was her office. Though it was early morning, everybody was busy in their work. This seemed to be the meeting room. It was decorated quite tastefully. Such expensive carpets and huge mirrors had never passed through his eyes.

After passing through various halls and lounges, when he reached Gayatri's drawing room, he saw that incomparable figure of beauty and attraction which was lit up with rays of pride and honour. She did not seem to be the happy-faced, simple-minded Gayatri of yore.

Gyanshankar paid his regards with a bent head and sat on a chair. His embarrassed feelings didn't allow him to raise his head. Gayatri said, 'Welcome sir! Didn't Vidya allow you to come earlier? Hope everything is fine at home?'

Gyan – Yes of course, all are fine. Maya was insisting to come here; he wanted to see his aunt, but he's just recovered from fever, so I didn't bring him. He remembers you daily.

Gayatri – I too remember his innocent face a lot. I really wish to come and see you all, but the affairs of the estate don't let me. If you undertake this burden now, I'll find time to breathe. Your essay was appreciated a lot. (Smiling) One should learn the art of flattery from you.

Gyan – It was just a trivial part of my real respect for you.

Gayatri said in a tone of appreciation – When a little sin is sufficient to defame one, why must more be employed? His Excellency is due to arrive here in the month of Kartik. They have decided to organize a function for endowing me with the title. Till now, only a notice has been published in the gazette. Now, on his arrival, I will be decorated with appropriate pomp and honour in his court.

Gyan – Then the preparations for the court function ought to begin rightaway.

Gayatri – You have arrived at the right time. Please get involved in the preparations. The guests should be welcomed in a way that all should talk about it. Just don't worry about the money. You're the initiator of this act; you must organize its grand finale. I once talked about you to the District Collector. He asked, 'What are his political thoughts?' I replied, 'He's a man of a very thoughtful and tranquil nature.' He was very happy to hear this and said, 'When he comes, ask him to meet me in relation to this function.'

After this, Gayatri started talking about the management of her estate and her own plans about it. Gyanshankar was surprised at her experience and knowledge. He was afraid that he might not be able to administer these jobs in the best way. He had no knowledge about rural banking. He was unaware of the matters of construction or new inventions in agriculture but this was not the right time to express one's inability. He kept nodding at Gayatri's remarks with a pretence of intelligence and kept commenting in between, as if he was an expert in all these affairs. He was confident about his wisdom and cleverness. On this sole basis, he never hesitated to take charge of anything under the sun.

Gyanshankar did not find any time to sit back and understand the intricacies of his job. From the next day itself, he had to become fully involved in the preparations for the court. From morning till evening, he had no time to relax. He had to keep consulting the officers, and keep running to the prominent traders of the city to acquire expensive items. It almost seemed as if it was an official court. But Gyanshankar was a duty-conscious, enthusiastic man. He did not shy away from work. He did every job with full responsibility. His earlier hesitation and lack of trust which restrained him to take a frontal position in life was slowly vanishing. People were surprised at his spirit of hard work. After two months of untiring enterprise, the arrangements for the court were complete. The collector came and saw everything and appreciated Gyanshankar's alacrity and work-efficiency a lot. When he met Gayatri, he congratulated her on the appointment of such an efficient manager. It was also his duty to write the letter of appreciation. When the Sahib Bahadur read it, he was absolutely charmed and said to the prominent men of the city, 'I have never seen such a miracle in the pen of any Indian.'

The date of the court was fixed for the fifteenth of October. People kept awake the whole night. The guns started firing their salute since early morning; if the whole itinerary of the day is to be described even briefly it would assume an epic length. On such occasions, a novelist leaves his imagination to the service of the journalists of newspapers. If you need to enjoy the adornment of the ladies, the show of rich personalities, the taste of the delicacies served at the feast, and the adventures of a hunting expedition, you will need to have a look at the pages of a newspaper. You will find the entire description there in extremely lively and picturesque words. When President Roosevelt went to Africa for hunting, a whole group of journalists went along with him. When Goerge V came to India, an army of reporters walked in his procession. This court was not so significant, but the papers kept talking about it for months. We only need to clarify that the court ended as per schedule; there was no anomaly noted anywhere, everything happened at the ordained moment and no mismanagement was noted anywhere. This excellent success was attributed to Gyanshankar. It seemed as if all puppets were dancing to his instructions. The Governor thanked him before bidding farewell. He was applauded everywhere.

It was evening time. The function was over. Gyanshankar had come home after seeing off the Governor at the railway station with prominent men of the city and was relaxing on the couch, smoking a cigar. He had been running around for the whole day long, and had not found any time to breathe. He was feeling lazy, but had a heart full of such joy that is found after achieving an expected success. When he analyzed his actions, he was himself surprised at his ability. 'Where was I about two and a half months ago?' he thought, 'Just an ordinary zamindar; with an annual income of two thousand rupees! No one bothered about me in the city; I used to feel small before menial officers and kept appeasing them. Now the officers want to meet me themselves. The cream of the city count me as their leader. I could have spent a lifetime in Benaras, and still couldn't have acquired this respectable position. Today even Gayatri must be on the ninth cloud. I had never hoped that she'd come on the dias so confidently. When she arrived there, the entire court started dazzling. Her Agra saree was looking splendid on her golden complexion. The flame of her beauty had beaten the shine of the gems on her body. Vidya is far more beautiful than her, but she doesn't have such attraction, such self- pride and such taste. Before her, one finds it difficult to control one's eyes, heart and tongue. I want to draw her towards myself, and be the object of her craving, but some unseen power forcefully pulls me in her direction. I cannot stop myself now. Perhaps she retraces her steps when she sees me approaching and does not wish to have any other relation with me except that of a master and a servant. She respects me and wants to use me as a means of her craving for social honour. All she desires is respect. This seems to be the prime goal of her life. I have reached this point by fostering that, and will be able to plant the seeds of my love in her heart on this very basis.'

Gyanshankar was lost in these very thoughts when Gayatri called him inside and smilingly said, 'The credit for the success of today's gathering goes to you. I am heartily indebted to you. The Sahib Bahadur praised you a lot before leaving. Have you paid the labourers their wages? I do not wish to disappoint anyone by using free labour.'

Gyan – Yes, I had told the manager to do so.

Gayatri – Please give one rupee to every worker as a gift from my side.

Gyan – Their number is not less than five hundred.

Gayatri – Doesn't matter; such occasions don't come everyday. The overseer who made the pandal should be given a hundred rupees.

Gyan – He may not accept it.

Gayatri – This is not a bribe, but a gift. Why won't he accept? Something must also be given to those who laid down the carpets and who managed the fireworks.

Gyan – Then why should you leave aside the sweetmeat makers, chefs and butlers?

Gayatri – Of course not; pay them not less than twenty rupees each.

Gyan – (smiling) All my budgeting goes down the drain.

Gayatri – Oh no, it is your very budget that has allowed me to do all this. If a labourer is paid high wages, he doesn't feel as happy as on being bestowed with a tip. Please give something suitable to your servants also.

Gyan – Of course; when outsiders are having a riot; why should the family be ignored?

Gayatri – Of course; the family members have a right before everyone else who slave for me all day long. Please call everybody here; I will pay them myself. They will feel specially honoured.

Gyan – It will take hours. It may continue till twelve.

Gayatri – It's no big deal for me. It's my heartfelt desire. I have to accomplish many great plans. These are my studded bangles. These are for Vidya; please parcel them to her along with five hundred rupees.

Gyan – (with a bent head) What's the need for this? It's no big occasion.

Gayatri – Which occasion will arrive now? I don't even have children that I would celebrate to my heart's content in their weddings. Vidya liked these bangles a lot. I got them from Italy last year. You are younger to me. You should take what is rightfully yours, and with complete heartlessness.

Gyanshankar replied with embarrassment – Your goodwill is enough for me. Whatever fame I've earned on this occasion is a reward in itself.

Gayatri – Not at all; I will not agree to that. Please don't restrain yourself and be as ruthless as moneylenders. It is your pen which has bestowed me with this position, or else there are many women like me in the district, who stand nowhere. I won't be satisfied till I have suitably rewarded your pen.

Gyan – That would have been required, in case I had been less happy than you are.

Gayatri – I will not listen to these arguments. You won't ask for anything yourself so I'll have to specify it on my own. Please get a beautiful bungalow constructed for yourself adjacent to your house in Benaras. There should be four rooms and open verandahs all around it. They should be covered with imported tiles and proper roofs should be made over the rooms. There must be a special room on the terrace for the month of rainy season. Does that make you happy?

Gyanshankar looked at her gratefully and said, 'I am not just happy; rather feeling envious with my own self.'

Gayatri – Please start the work from Diwali onwards. Now tell me; what should I gift to Maya?

Gyan – Maya doesn't need anything at present. Let his gift remain as a future promise with you.

Gayatri – You forget; one should neither borrow nor lend.

Gyan – One often gets some interest on whatever is deposited.

Gayatri – That's alright; but as of now, please order a small carriage for him from a factory in Kolkata, and send my tonga to Benaras. For the little girl, get a necklace made of not less than five hundred rupees.

When Gyanshankar left the place he was in seventh heaven. He had craved for a bungalow since ages. He had also thought that it would remain a lifelong dream, but good fortune accomplished that dream in just a single stroke.

The beginning was quite enthusiastic; let's see what happens in the end.

25

A decrease in expenses and an increase in income; this was the result of Gyanshankar's efficient management. Though Gayatri too tried to use her money wisely, but her spending was similar to being penny-wise and pound-foolish. Gyanshankar changed the entire organization of funds and assets. The karindas had carelessly left huge chunks of land uncultivated in her estate. Thousands of bighas were under the plough but no foodgrains were ever found surplus; all was consumed by the constables and their flatterers. The patwari and the karindas conspired with each other to declare most of the fertile land as fallow. The entire income of the estate was used up to appease government officers. The servants were also far too many in number. When Gyanshankar went through the documents he found many grey areas. Since a long time, the rent on land had not been increased. The records of land had not been maintained under any rules or regulations. Thousands of rupees went away in yearly payments. Huge chunks had passed on to others by way of inheritance. Gyanshankar started investigating all these matters. The whole region was agog with rumours. Gayatri started receiving complaints and though she wanted to treat her tenants softly, when Gyanshankar explained the anomalies in the records, her eyes were opened. More than one thousand tenants were such, on whom there was a need to file immediate cases of disownment, or else they would have become too independent to control and would have cost a loss of twenty thousand per annum. The income was increased up to one and a quarter by an increase in land rent. The estate which had not even earned two lacs per year started giving a profit of three lacs without any extra trouble. In such a situation, it was but natural that Gayatri agreed with her efficient and able manager on all such issues.

For three years, the whole estate was full of disturbances. Gyanshankar was lured many a times; even threatened with death, but he did not stray from his path. Had he wanted, he could have used this situation to earn unlimited amounts of wealth, but respect and authority had purged him of such lowly emotions.

However, the ambitions which had brought Gyanshankar here showed no signs of getting fulfilled. Gayatri respected him a lot and took his advice on each subject, but she also remained distant from him in many ways. He got a chance to meet her almost daily. He used to come after inspecting far-flung areas of the region with her on a motor car, but these meetings were all work-related. There was no chance to express love here; some maid or the other kept surrounding her and he used to come back disappointed. The fire he had ignited to warm his hands was now burning his heart. His eyes remained hungry for a glimpse of her and anxious to listen to her sweet voice. If due to some reason he had to stay back in the rural areas or wasn't able to see her, he became like a drug addict who hadn't received his daily dose of opium.

One day Gayatri called Gyanshankar in the morning hours. Nowadays, the house was getting cleaned and painted. The festival of Diwali was fast approaching. Gayatri was sitting in the garden feeding birds. There was no servant around. Gyanshankar's heart started hopping like a bird. He had got this opportunity for the first time. Gayatri saw him and said, 'Do you have any important work today? I want to consult you regarding a special matter.'

Gyanshankar – I had to see some accounts, but it's not so important.

Gayatri – My husband had made a will in his last days that I should offer this estate in charity and make a trust for its supervision and management. I now want to fulfill his wish. Life is too uncertain. The final call can come anytime. If I die without making the legal papers, the estate will be divided amongst numerous men and the will shall disappear like a ripple on water. I want that you should solve this problem; a better chance will not arrive again.

Gyanshankar's eyes were enveloped in darkness. The basis of his tripartite ambitions was about to collapse. He asked, 'Was the will documented on paper?'

Gayatri – For me his wish is far more important than thousands of papers. If he didn't care about me, he would have donated this estate in his lifetime only; He just postponed this idea to keep my honour intact. If he used to regard me so much, I too regard his wish as the word of God.

Gyanshankar understood that it was time to be diplomatic. Even if one had to oppose, it had to be done in the garb of assent. He said, 'Of course, but one needs to decide first, the real nature of this charity.'

Gayatri – You can meet my father in this regard. You can even talk to your elder brother.

A mention of Premshankar brought frowns on the face of Gyanshankar. He had his own misgivings regarding him. He said, 'It's important to consult Rai Saheb; he's wise enough, but I don't consider my brother apt for asking an advice. A man who's so thoughtless that he abandons his wife, insults the society in the name of false principles and hides one's wickedness under dubious colours of social devotion to deceive his own brother, is not fit to be consulted about such a religious matter. Due to him I lost one thousand annually and the village is still unquiet after three years; in fact the unrest keeps increasing. Shraddha hates him due to these very misdoings.'

Gayatri – In my understanding this is unfair on part of Shraddha. If a woman is married to a man, she must keep up that relation like a dutiful lady.

Gyan – Even if the man turns agnostic and irreligious?

Gayatri – Yes, that's what I think. Marriage binds the existence of a man and woman together. Their souls become part and parcel of each other.

Gyan – People might have thought so in the older times, but the new age does not agree to that. It declares a woman to be completely independent. She's not subordinate to anyone in mind, speech and action. The deep relation that a man has with God is far superior to any relation concocted by man. In the West, divorces happen very often due to religious differences.

Gayatri – Please don't talk about those countries; there people think of marriage only as a social contract. You had yourself told me once that some people there take the institution of marriage to be totally fake. In their opinion, a mere consent between the man and the woman is as good as marriage, but such thoughts have never been approved in India.

Gyan – Our ancient texts have elaborated a lot upon this.

Gayatri – I know very well, but it was never propagated here and rightly so, as in our country a man and a woman can stay together and still worship God according to their respective faiths. At many places a man is a Vaishnavite, and the woman a Shaivite; somewhere else the man an Arya Samajist, and the woman follows the age-old Sanatan Dharma; someone else does not follow any god, and the woman worships even bricks and stones. But these differences do not cause a husband and wife to separate. May God never bring such awful days here when people get inflicted with the disease of free thought.

Gyan – The reason behind this is that we are cowards by nature; we refuse to face reality and hide our weaknesses under a false love of ideals.

Gayatri – I didn't understand your motive.

Gyan – I only mean to say that to hide one's love or hatred due to a fear of social criticism is to ruin one's ethical independence. I don't appreciate a woman who remains devoted to a characterless man only because he happens to be her husband. She destroys a life that could have been so meaningful. This can be said for men as well. We haven't arrived in this world to cry and feel frustrated and nor is self-destruction our life's goal.

Gayatri – The essence of your statement is that we must follow our feelings and move in the direction where our desires take us. We must not try to suppress them. You had expressed this opinion earlier also. I have thought a lot about it since then, but cannot accept it by heart. To make one's desires the basis of one's life is to build a wall of sand. In our religious texts, self-control and restraint has been celebrated; in fact this alone had been defined as a medium of redemption. Desires and lust have been proved as the main reason for the downfall of man and this is indisputable in my opinion. In such a state it is foolishness to follow the West. It is better to follow traditions rather than following desires.

Gyanshankar was enjoying this conversation a lot. It was revealing those known and unknown places in Gayatri's heart which would have later helped him in achieving his desired target. He wanted to give a suitable reply when a maid came and handed over a telegram to him. Gyanshankar opened it with surprise. It was written, 'Please come soon; there is a fear of criminal case being fought in Lakhanpur.'

Gyanshankar threw the letter passively on the ground. Gayatri asked, 'Is everything fine at home?'

Gyanshankar – It has come from Lakhanpur; a criminal case has been filed there. This village is troubling me a lot. All are such rogues there that it's impossible to control them. This is all a doing of Bhai Saheb.

Gayatri – Then you'll have to go. The issue must not be allowed to go out of hand.

Gyan – I'll resolve it forever now. Either I will resign from the village or will set it on fire. They will also remember who had set them right.

Gayatri – Please get Maya along with you when you return; I really feel like seeing him. If you can get Vidya also, it would be wonderful. I am tired of writing to her for a visit.

Gyan – This is a similar kind of slavery to tradition, which you applaud so much. There is no tradition of visiting a sister's house very often, so why would she follow it? Perhaps this is also the reason why you don't go there.

Gayatri – (embarrassed) I don't bother about such things, but you can see how busy I am.

Gyan – She can also make the same pretext.

Gayatri – Well, even if she doesn't come, do bring Maya and keep writing to me. Please come as soon as you are free.

Gayatri's last sentence was such an indicator of her desire that Gyanshankar was delighted. It had been three years now that he had been staying there; he had gone to Benaras many a times but Gayatri had never requested him to return with so much of feeling. His heart whispered, 'Perhaps my charm is working upon her.' He said outwardly, 'It will not take less than two weeks.'

Gayatri said in a worried tone – Two weeks?

Gyanshankar's thoughts were further confirmed. He left by the nine o' clock train and reached Benaras by five p.m.

26

The time when Gyanshankar's appeal got dismissed was one of trouble and tragedy for the people of Lakhanpur. Many houses were wiped away by plague. Many others were set on fire. Many thefts also took place. On top of it, divine calamities had also occurred. Storm and rainfall kept up their alternate arrival. In the month of March hailstones destroyed all standing crops. Now the villagers had nothing to fall back upon. Bisesar Sah refused to help them against the zamindar. The women had already lost their ornaments. There was none except Sukhu Chaudhary who could have fought the appeal. People were still relying on their fate. In this situation the money sent by Premshankar came as a divine rescue. It breathed life into dead bodies. Qadir Khan stood up with a new determination to fight the case. But the moral victory of peasants was just a prelude for their real defeat. Gyanshankar was craving to punish the tenants for their daring. The villagers were still in their huts when Ghaus Khan came with his three peons and set them on fire. The land of the orchard belonged to the zamindar. The tenants had no right to build their huts on it. Two new peons in this group were Faizu and Kartar. Both were efficient in wielding sticks, and had served a sentence many a times. Their hearts were totally bereft of kindness and compassion. In the older group, only Binda Maharaj was spared due to his wicked ways. The flames ignited by the earlier fine hadn't yet cooled down when people were forced to come back to their old settlement; the result was that the next day itself, Thakur Jhapatsingh was taken away by plague and Kallu ahir narrowly escaped death. Pleas and requests were made but the tyranny didn't relent. After Jhapat's death, Dapat was ready to die. He took his stick and said, 'I won't leave Ghaus Khan alive. Whom do I have to fear now?' But Qadir Khan fell on his feet and brought him home after much insistence.

There was a huge pond in Lakhanpur. The animals of the entire village used to drink water from there. It was also used for bathing and washing.

It was the month of June; all the wells had dried up to the last drop. All the nearby pits and ponds had dried up. Only this huge pond had some water. Precisely at that moment, Ghaus Khan prohibited the water of the pond for general use. Two peons stood on guard and sent away the animals by force. The villagers were shocked. 'Will the zamindar actually stop the water?' They had never thought in the wildest of their dreams that the zamindar would do such atrocities. They had an age-old right over the pond. But now they discovered that they did not own anything. It was the zamindar's benevolence that he kept quiet for so long, but a long tenure of benevolence is taken to be a right very often. The people of the village gathered near the pond and started arguing with the peons. Qadir Khan saw the tempers rising and thought it best to leave the place. He knew that many others would retreat after him, but he had gone just a few steps when Sukhu Chaudhary held his hand and said, 'Where are you going Qadir Bhaiya! You will not be able to leave till the matter is resolved. When we are to be oppressed in all matters, right or wrong, why do you assume our leadership?'

Qadir Khan – Do you want me to wield the stick?

Sukhu – What else is a stick for?

Qadir – On what basis can we do that? Who is left in the village? God has chosen to call all our strong lads.

Sukhu – What if there are no young men; the old are still there. When will our lives be utilized for our goals?

When Ghaus Khan came to know that the villagers have gathered near the pond, he too rushed to the spot and said in a loud roar, 'Beware! No one should approach the pond.'

Sukhu came forward and said sharply, 'Who can dare to stop the waters of the pond! We and our ancestors have been redeemed by this pond only. Even if Brahma comes in place of zamindar and asks us to leave we won't, even if we have to lose everything we have.'

Ghaus Khan looked at Sukhu Chaudhary with surprise and said, 'Chaudhary, you too will deceive me in this situation? Come back to your senses.'

Sukhu – Do you want that I should make myself handicapped for the sake of the zamindar? Should I cut off my legs under an axe? I cannot leave my right in the name of friendship.

The peon Kartar laughed and said, 'What do you bother about so much? There's no one to mourn for you. You will leave for your final journey empty-handed in a few days. This pond will not go with you.'

Old people cannot bear any satire related to death. Sukhu said with pride – 'How can you say for sure that we would leave first? Who knows you may have to go before us. Whatever happens; we will go, but the village will not come to an end with us?'

Ghaus Khan – Is this the return of our good deeds?

Sukhu – If you have behaved well with us we've done the same, and no one can leave one's rights for the sake of obligations.

Faizu – So do you wish to get into a legal fight?

Sukhu – Why should we do that; isn't there a rule of the Lord Governor? Well, if he doesn't listen then you can do whatever's there in your heart.

After saying this Sukhu came from the pond and sat on his bullock cart to go the court. The next day a petition was filed.

The final decision was dependent on the witness of Lala Maujilal Patwari. He gave evidence in favour of the villagers. Ghaus Khan tried to win him over, and even threatened him with dangerous repercussions. But Maujilal's only son had died in the sway of the plague. He considered it a result of his earlier evil deeds. He thus refused to stray from the honest path. He gave a clear statement. The case went in favour of Sukhu Chaudhary and though he had to spend a lot, his reputation was restored in the village. The entire village started worshipping him. They decided to celebrate this victory. Lord Satyanarayan was worshipped, Brahmins were fed and pucca ghats were to be constructed around the pond. Ghaus Khan lost a lot of money. He had got into the mess without consulting Gyanshankar. So he had to bear the repercussions all alone. Money earned through evil ways was spent in protecting an evil cause.

Ghaus Khan could not bear this defeat. Sukhu Chaudhary kept annoying him like a sore wound. Dayashankar had been transferred elsewhere. His position was now taken up by someone called Noor Alam. Ghaus Khan started fostering camaraderie with him. They became friends very soon and Lakhanpur was now beset with troubles on a daily basis.

It was the onset of the rainy season. The peasants had to guard the crops of jowar and bajra the whole day long. All kinds of sounds were floating in the air. People kept beating drums and tin boxes to frighten away stray animals. Groups of parrots descended on crops during daytime, and packs of wolves came at night; moreover, paddy stalks had to be planted properly. People had to work in standing water day and night. Mosquito bites caused their bodies to get swollen. Someone's hut broke down in rain; another lost his fields. Life and its struggles had put everyone to unrest. Precisely at this time, Noor Alam raided the village. Sukhu Chaudhary had never taken cocaine or seen its face but an ounce of cocaine was recovered from his house. A case was filed immediately. He was arrested as soon as the drug was found. He was sure that he won't be released now. He had himself got many people punished in a similar way. A moment before his arrest, he went from the house and returned with a pot. All the villagers were gathered there. He said to them, 'Brothers, I take your final leave. Who knows whether we will meet again or not! What's certain about the life of an old man? We'll meet if fate allows. This pot contains five thousand rupees. I shall entrust them to Qadir Bhai. Please get a ghat made near the pond. I relieve all who owed me any kind of debt. See, I'm tearing all such papers in front of your eyes. I don't have any account with anyone; all is squared now.'

Darogaji was present there. As soon as he saw the potful of money, his greed took over him. He called Sukhu and whispered in his ears, 'How foolish you are that you can't think of saving yourself even with all this money?'

Sukhu – What will I gain by saving myself? Who's there to grieve for me?

Noor Alam – You must be thinking the judge will have mercy on your old age and release you. Do not be deluded. I shall write such a report and produce such concrete evidence that no barrister will be able to open his mouth in your favour. What to talk of five thousand, even if you spend five lacs, you won't be able to get out of my trap. I am not Dayashankar; my name is Noor Alam. If I want I can even trap God.

Sukhu said in a passive tone, 'You can do what you want to. What do I have to look forward to in life that I should take another obligation on my head?'

Ghaus Khan's milk of muman kindness erupted afresh. Faizu and Kartar also got active and Binda Maharaj was staring continuously at the pot.

Everyone talked to Sukhu, collectively and later separately, but he refused to budge. Finally the people surrounded Qadir. Noor Alam took him aside and said, 'Just drive some sense into the old man; why is he hellbent on losing his life? He will not be sentenced for less than two years. The matter is still in my hands. Everything can be managed. If things go out of hand I won't be able to do anything. I feel pity for his old age.'

Ghaus Khan said, 'Yes, this is the time to feel pity for him. He lost everything in the fine payment and plague.'

Qadir Khan started pleading to Sukhu. He threatened him with defamation, described the troubles of custody, but Sukhu didn't relent. When

Qadir Khan insisted a lot and the villagers unanimously started requesting him, Sukhu said in a sad voice, 'What are you trying to tell me? I am not an innocent child. I am just a few days younger to Qadir. I have spent a lifetime harming my fellowmen. When my father died, there was nothing in the house. I have become the village headmaster by conspiring with the karindas. People know me and respect me, but now I have recognized the truth. Who will bear the results of those evil deeds? It's me who has to bear this, whether here or in hell. This pot contains my evil deeds, not money. This alone has destroyed my family. There's no one left to give me a single drop of water. If this money can be spent in charity, I'll be relieved. Get a ghat made, and if some other expenses incur, please spend from your side. If I remain alive, I'll return every single penny of yours.'

The next day, the chargesheet was filed against Sukhu. Faizu and Kartar gave evidence from the side of the police. The drug had already been recovered. The further recovery of thousands of rupees confirmed the charge against him. There was no lawyer to defend him. He was sentenced for two years. An innocent and blameless Sukhu was sacrificed at the altar of Ghaus Khan's enmity and jealousy.

The whole village was shaken up with fear. When the appeal for rent increase had got dismissed people had thought there's no cause to worry; it was as if God had given them a divine protection. But seeing these tyrannous tactics, everybody started trembling for life. If a powerful man like Sukhu Chaudhary could be destroyed in a few seconds, what couldn't happen to them? But Ghaus Khan was still not satisfied. His wish that the entire village should become his slave and dance to his instructions hadn't yet been fulfilled. Peasants who had inherited land were many in number. Qadir Khan was still there and so were Balraj and Manohar. All of them were thorns in the garden of his dreams. He could not roam about peacefully without picking them away.

Lakhanpur was just ten miles away from the city. The month of December had just begun when a huge encampment arrived under a police officer. The tehsildar came himself to arrange for the rations. There was almost an army of peons with him. The camp had about a hundred men. When the villagers saw this crowd they got worried. Manohar sent Balraj to his wife's place and asked them to retain him there for a few days. People started storing their wood and fodder inside then homes. But these were the days of sowing the fields; no one had much free time.

Bisesar had just opened his shop in the morning when ten or twelve peons came to him. Bisesar opened the sacks of flour and pulses; the rations started getting weighed. This continued till afternoon. Tins of ghee became empty. The rations which could have fed three camps were finished in an instant. Bisesar was dumbstruck. He sent his men to the wholesale market. The issue of labour was far more complex. It was not easy to cut grass for five huge horses. All the chamars in the village were forcibly put to this work. Some were filling water pots. Four men were sent daily to receive the post. Other lowly servants had no respite from jobs ordered by the officers. When at two o' clock, the Sahib ordered to clear the ground and prepare a tennis court; even those people were caught who had hitherto been spared due to old age or their upper caste. The peons caught Dukhran Bhagat first. Bhagat asked with surprise, 'Why am I being called?' The peon replied 'Come to the camp for cutting grass.'

Bhagat – It's the chamars who cut grass; we don't.

Just then a peon held him by the neck and pushed him saying, 'Will you move, or will keep explaining the law to us?'

Bhagat – How can you force me like that? I haven't fed my Thakurji as yet.

Peon – Your Thakur will not die without food in a single day.

Bhagat didn't deem it fit to argue; he escaped from the grip of the peons, went inside and locked up the door. The peons started beating the door with all their might. One of them said, 'Let's set this hut on fire; let him rot inside.' Dukhran replied from inside, 'Just wait, I'll come after feeding my lord.' The peons started breaking the tiles on the roof. Just then many peons arrived with Qadir Khan and others. Dapatisngh had left home the previous night. Qadir said, 'Bhagat, why are your hiding inside? Come, we are coming with you.' Bhagat opened the door and came out. Qadir smiled and said, 'Let's have a contest with each other. Let's see who cuts the maximum grass.' Bhagat didn't say anything in reply. Everyone reached the camp and started cutting grass.

Manohar said – We all became chamars due to Khan Sahib.

Dukhran – It's God's will. Today we had to do what we had never done before.

Qadir – Aren't you a tenant of the zamindar? Don't you plough his fields?

Manohar – If we plough his land don't we pay rent on it? No one leaves a single penny pending.

Qadir – What's the use of all this talk? If we have enjoyed for some days; we'll have to toil for the rest. Talk about something else. Kallu, you stayed in your in-laws' house for a long time. What all did you get from there?

Kallu – Are you talking about gifts? Put it like this that I saved my own life as a gift. When I left from here I had three and a half rupees. I bought sweets for a rupee, paid fifty paise as railway ticket, and kept two rupees with myself. As soon as I reached there my elder brother-in-law came and placed his son in my lap. I had to give him something as a gift. I gave him a rupee. At night, all the women in the village gathered and sang traditional songs. They too, had to be given something. I gave them the last rupee that I had. I would have been mocked if I hadn't given them anything. I thought I had nothing else to spend on, and they too will give me something when I leave. I stayed comfortably for eight days. When I started for home, they just gave me a pot of sugar, a basket of jowar cobs and some tamarind in a bag. They asked a man to accompany me. That's all. I got into a trouble as to how I'll reach home. 'I know no one; from whom will I borrow?' I came to the station with that fellow. It was very difficult to come home on foot carrying that entire burden. After much thinking I decided to sell off the jowar cobs. 'Even if they sell for fifty paise, I'll be able to manage.' I asked in the market, 'Will anyone buy these cobs?' One of the shopkeepers enquired about the price. I just uttered, 'I can't tell you the exact price, take it for fifty paise.' He thought I was selling goods of theft. He snatched all the cobs and threatened, 'Just run away, or else I'll call the guards and get your arrested.' So what could I have done? I left everything and ran for life. I reached home hungry and tired, after a day's adventure. I learnt a lesson never to go to my in-laws' house again.

Qadir – You still managed to save your life. Once I too had gone to my in-laws' house. I was young at that time. I kept walking in the sun, so I got night blindness by the evening. But I didn't tell anyone due to shyness. When it was time to have dinner, my sister-in-law called me in the hall and went inside. It was dark in the hall. When I stood up I couldn't find my way. I couldn't dare to call or ask anyone. I started touching things to find my way. A ram was tied in a corner. I landed upon him. He stood up and pushed me so strongly with his horns that I fell down. My sister-in-law came hearing this noise and took me inside. In the verandah my father- in-law and a few men were sitting. I also sat down. I could not make out what to do. Food was kept before me. Just then my mother-in- law came to put ghee in my bowl of dal with her bangles tinkling in her wrist. When I heard that tinkling noise, I was too scared. My knee was still paining. I thought the ram had been set free. I stood up and started knocking everyone down. I gave a knock to my mother-in-law also. She dropped the bowl of ghee. She ran away, shocked at the scene. People held me and asked, 'What happened?' I was too embarrassed to speak. I couldn't utter a word. My brother-in-law ran to get a maulvi. He looked at me and said, 'A devil is upon his head.' All kinds of prayers and amulets were tried on me. No one ate anything that night. My in-laws kept sitting by my bedside and wept the whole night but I was having a hearty laugh inside. Ultimately I went to sleep. As soon as I got up in the morning, I came back straight to home, without asking anything to anyone. Dukhran Bhagat, you too tell us something about your in laws' house.

Dukhran – I can't think of mockery at present. I just want to break my head and give away my life.

Manohar – Qadir Bhaiya, if Balraj had been here today, he would have let loose bloodshed. He couldn't have borne this degradation.

Qadir – You've started lamenting again. If God wanted us to live with honour, he wouldn't have made us a peasant. He would have rather made us a zamindar, a peon or a constable that we could have sat and ordered others around? Just see, we earn our own bread; we eat through our own labour but just about everyone tries to oppress us by force. We have to slave for everyone. All are out to torture us, be it the zamindar, the government or the judge, and perhaps even God. Or else aren't we living beings or is everybody wiser than us? But what is to be gained by crying? Who will listen or see our woes? Even the lord has shut his eyes towards us. Even if a kind man tries to support us, he too gets trapped badly. People think of various laws to trouble him and trap him. Can't you see, what kinds of things are reported in Balraj's newspaper? It's all a doing of one's fate.

While saying this, Qadir Khan broke into tears. That burning heart which he wanted to hide behind fun and amusement showed its flames. When Manohar saw it, his eyes grew red – like a statue of pride suppressed with force.

None among the four could speak. All kept cutting grass with a bent head till late evening. The ground was cleared. All kept their spades aside and lied down to take some rest. The poor men thought that they were free now but the tehsildaar arrived and ordered, 'Get some cowdung and cover it nicely to make it smooth, without any stones or anything. Where are you Nazirji; get them buckets and ropes.'

The Nazir immediately got the stuff. Qadir Khan picked up the bucket and went to the well, but Dukhran Bhagat set out for his house. The tehsildaar asked, 'Where are you off to?'

Dukhran replied rudely – I'm going home.

Tehsildaar – And who will polish the ground?

Dukhran – Whosoever's interested.

Tehsildaar – You'll get so many blows on your head that you'll lose all your heat.

Dukhran – You have all the authority; you can beat me with shoes or hang me, but I can't polish floors.

Qadir – Bhagat, you won't have to do anything. Go, keep sitting. I'll do your share of work also.

Dukhran – I'll now get beaten up only. Let everyone have his fill.

Tesildaar – This chap is doomed. Is there a peon around; just beat him up fifty times with a shoe, he'll cool down.

On getting this order a peon pushed Bhagat so hard on the ground that he couldn't get up; he then started beating him. Bhagat lay down stupefied. He lost his senses; there wasn't any sign of anger or guilt on his face. He didn't even let out a sigh. His poor state had robbed him of all his conscious powers. Qadir Khan came running from the well and bent his head before that ruthless peon, saying, 'Sheikhji, please beat me as much as you like instead of him, but enough has been done to him.'

The peon pushed Qadir Khan aside and picked up the shoe again when suddenly Premshankar and Dapatsingh arrived on a horse cart. Premshankar couldn't bear to see this heartrending scene and jumped down to face the peon, saying, 'Beware of raising your hand again!'

The peon was shocked. Kallu, Manohar and all the rest left their buckets to come and pay their respects to him. The chamars too had been waiting for their wages. They too came near. A huge crowd gathered around Premshankar. The Tehsildaar asked in a rough tone, 'Who are you? How dare you oppose official orders?'

Premshankar – I didn't know that beating poor men with shoes is part of official work. What was his fault, for which you devised this punishment?

Tehsildaar – He refused to comply with official orders. He was asked to polish this ground with cowdung but he misbehaved with us.

Prem – Didn't you know that he's a peasant belonging to upper caste? He's not supposed to polish floors or dispose off garbage.

Tehsildaar – Shoe-beating gets everything accomplished.

Premshankar's blood started boiling but he restrained himself and said, 'A responsible person like you should not speak thus; I'm extremely disappointed.'

Manohar came forward and said, 'Sarkar, only we know what we had to face today.' One of the chamars said, 'I have cut grass the whole day long, but no one has paid me uptil now. We all have been demanding money since hours.'

The Tehsildaar became mad with anger and said, 'Please go away from here or else it won't be good for you. Nazirji, what are you doing? Tell these peons to beat up these chamars. This will be their apt wage.'

The peons started surrounding the labour. The constables started attacking them with the butts of their guns. Many people were injured. Premshankar said loudly, 'Tehsildaar Sahib, I appeal to you to prohibit these peons to manhandle these people; or else they will lose their lives.'

Tehsildaar – You yourself indicated these men to become bold and revolting. You are responsible for this. I now get it; you seem to be related to some kisaan-sabha.

Premshankar saw that the faces of the people of Lakhanpur were becoming weird with anger. He feared every second that someone might react violently. Every moment the problem was getting more complicated. There was no expectation of any humanity or kindness from the Tehsildaar or any other officers. He decided upon his duty instantly. He faced the villages and said, 'Please obey the Tehsildar Sahib. No one should leave this place. All men will be paid their desired wages. Don't worry about that.'

All the men stopped at listening to this and looked at Premshankar with surprise. The official men were also surprised. Manohar and Kallu went to the well. The chamars started gathering cowdung. Dapatsingh too, started clearing the ground of all bricks and stones. The whole job started getting done at such a peaceful pace as if nothing had happened. Only Dukhran Bhagat did not stir from his place.

Premshankar said to the Tehsildar, 'Can this man go home if you permit? He is badly injured.'

Tehsildar said after thinking something, 'Okay, let him go.'

Bhagat got up stealthily and moved toward his house. On the other side, all men quickly cleaned and prepared the ground for tennis. Everybody was working with such enthusiasm as if they were preparing to welcome a wedding party at their home.

The evening had fallen. Premshankar was setting on the floor, thinking – 'How long will the poor be tortured like this? When will they be taken as human beings? When will our educated class learn to respect its poor fellowmen? When will it stop flattering its officers for its vested interests?'

Just then the Tehsildar Sahib came and said politely, 'If you're feeling uncomfortable here please come to my tent. Please excuse me, I hadn't recognized you earlier. I feel like praising you for your compassion with the poor. You're very lucky that God has bestowed you with such a kind heart. We unfortunate men spend their whole lives bothering about their own selves only. What to do? If I tell you clearly that I cannot get enough labour then people will think me to be inefficient. I can see with my own eyes that they get fifty paise daily as wages, but if I ask Sahib Bahadur for these funds, he'll never give them. The government has made very nice rules, but these officers just don't bother about them. If I start acting according to rules, I cannot survive even for a second, and what can I do alone? Not less than fifty rupees must have been spent on mud utensils. Huge amounts of wood, fodder and hay have been spent. Who pays for them? There are others like me. If you see their atrocities you will be shocked. Even if God has blessed you with frugal meals you should never take up a job like this. Come sit, I can tell you a thousand tales in which the Tehsildars have been sent to hell for following rules and regulations. I have myself gone through it once.'

Premshankar felt sympathy for the Tehsildar. He understood that he was helpless. He felt bad about arguing with him without any reason. He went with him to his tent. They kept talking for a long time. The Tehsildaar Sahib turned out to be a very simple man. When he stopped talking about power-related problems, he started discussing his family issues. His three sons were studying in college. Two daughters had become widows. One widowed sister and her children were also his responsibility. He managed his expenses with great difficulty in two hundred rupees. So wherever he found an opportunity or convenience, he did not refrain from taking a bribe. He narrated this matter with such simplicity and politiness that Premshankar developed a soft corner for him. When he got up from there it was already eight. While going towards the chaupal, he reached Dukhran Bhagat's door and saw a strange scene. Many villagers had gathered there. Bhagat was standing in their midst, with shaligram in his hands, muttering like a mad man – 'This is the great shaligram. He cares a lot for his devotees. He always protects them! He likes Mohanbhog a lot! He also loves the fragrance of kapoor and incense. Ask him, what all I did for him! I used to have sattu; my children only had chana to eat, but I fed him Mohanbhog. I used to travel miles to gather flowers and tulsi stalks for him. I may not have any tobacco, but I daily bought kapoor and incense for him. I used to worship him first before doing any other job. Even if anyone lay dying in the house, I never used to leave my daily rituals. There has been no single day when I haven't made charnamrit, haven't done aarti, or read the

Ramayana. Was this devotion and reverence for this result that I should be beaten with shoes, tortured in all ways, and degraded as a chamar? Curse on me if I call upon such a God, keep him in my house or worship him again! Yes, Curse on me! Wise men have truly said that He is an enemy of His devotees, gets them insulted, uproots them, and is pleased with those who insult Him. I was deluded till now. Say Manohar, should I throw Him in a well or upon a garbage heap, where He should be covered with tons of filth everyday, or throw Him on the road, where people should walk upon Him from morning till evening?'

Manohar – Bhaiya, you know everything and still act as ignorant. He is the master of the world; his glory is unparalleled.

Qadir – Who knows; what's there in His will? He does good to you in various ways. Don't lose heart.

Dukhran – (laughing) All these are fake ways of fooling yourself. Qadir Mian, this is merely a stone, an object of mud. I was lost in its false image uptil now. I thought that by worshipping it, I'll acquire the best position in the temporal as well as transcendental world. This whole myth was broken today. It is just a ball of mud. Go Maharaj, please go where you wish! This alone can be your worship. Whatever return you've given me for my thirty-nine years of devotion, I too return the same to you.

Saying this, Bhagat threw the image of the shaligram forcefully in one corner. God knows where it fell down. He then ran inside the house and came out with his worship basket. Manohar rushed to snatch it from him. But Bhagat saw him coming towards him and quickly opened the box, and threw it up in the air. All the things got scattered. Religious faith and soul devotion of thirty years got destroyed in a second. The wall of religious trust was shaken and its bricks fell all around.

It was a heartrending scene. Premshankar's heart melted on seeing this. 'O Lord! This unsophisticated, illiterate and poor man has so much of self-respect! This insult has hurt him so much! Who says, the poor don't have a sense of respect? What a henious assault is this that it has destroyed devotion, trust and honour all together!'

Premshankar was standing behind all men. No one had seen him. He went to the chaupal from there. A bed was ready for him there. Dapatsingh was getting the stove ready for cooking and Kallu was filling water. As soon as Ghaus Khan saw him, he greeted him by bending down, and said with some hesitation, 'Huzoor got very late at Tehsildaar Sahib's place.'

Premshankar – Yes, he was talking about random stuff. Why, isn't there a servant out here? Why are these people filling water? Call a servant; he'll be paid suitably.

Ghaus Khan – Huzoor, there were four families of water keepers, but all were destroyed. Not a single one is left now.

Premshankar – Why?

Ghaus Khan – What to tell you Huzoor; it's all due to our own tyranny. We have around three or four peons out here. All need a servant each. And for me, the more the servants, the merrier it is. The poor men were caught in the morning and were relieved only in the evening. Ultimately all ran away; some went to Kolkata, some others to Rangoon. They took their families along with them. Now we have to wash our dishes with our own hands; this is our condition.

Premshankar – Why do you torture these poor men so much? Just now, the Tehsildar Sahib was blaming you alone for all the atrocities of the camp people.

Ghaus Khan – Huzoor is an angel, but we have been ordered such by our young master. Nowadays, he keeps instructing us in the fields that no tenant should be allowed to exist in the village. If I eat his salt, I must obey his orders, or else how will I face God? That is why I have to be tough on those poor men. I trap them in false cases; I catch them for begaar or make them fight amongst themselves. According to the law, everyone who pays the rent must be given proper receipt, but I give it only to those who are alert; I send the other simpletons away. Our young master insists that nothing should be kept pending; even if a penny is left unpaid the tenants' land should be auctioned. Thus, many of them run away out of this fear. For me, you are as respectable as the young master. Why should I hide anything from you? We also manage to survive through such fraud ways, or else we couldn't have managed in so little salary.

Just then Bisesar, Manohar and Qadir Khan also came and started talking about the day's incident. Manohar got milk and Kallu fetched curd. All were eager to welcome and serve Premshankar. When he lay down after dinner, people decided that he should be welcomed by reciting the Ramayana. Bisesar Sah got dhol and manjiras from his house. Qadir sat with the dhol. Manjiras were played and passages from the Ramayana were sung. Premshankar was not very proficient in Hindi and could hardly understand a chaupai, but he was enjoying the pure religious affection of these rustic men. 'How pure, simple hearted and honest they are! They bear so many difficulties, take so many insults, but do not have any malice towards anyone. Everyone is lost in the intoxication of joy.'

When the Ramayana got over, Kallu said, 'Qadir Chacha, now you must present something.'

Qadir replied beating the dhol, 'You are there to sing; are you tired so soon?'

Manohar – No bhaiya, you must sing a nice song. We haven't heard you since so many days; God knows when we shall be able to sit together next. Sarkar, there's no singer like him in many villages out here.

Qadir – How will sarkar relish my rustic song?

Premshankar – Not at all; I'll listen to it with great interest.

Qadir – Huzoor, it's not singing; just a sort of crying, but how can we refuse you?

Saying this, Qadir beat his dhol to his song and sang a bhajan.

I am pleasing my Ram.

I won't go to the jungle, nor touch any bush, nor any branch,

In every leaf there's the unseen, I will see him in the glory of nature.

I am pleasing my Ram.

I won't take any medicine or herb, nor call any doctor.

My ultimate doctor is the unseen one; to him I'll show my pulse.

I am pleasing my Ram.

Though Qadir's voice had no particular beat or melody, but he sang in tune. Qadir was clever in this art. Premshankar was very happy to hear the bhajan. Every word of this song was steeped in devotion and sincere expression. Instead of the dry and harsh voices of professional singers, there was a feeling of deep love and emotion.

After the song got over, it was decided to present a mimicry. Kallu was skilled in this art. Qadir Mian became a king, Kallu a minister, and Bisesar Sah a rich man. Dapatsingh took a sheet on his head and became the queen. They needed to find a prince. They started thinking as to whom to allot this role. Premshankar said with a laugh, 'Make me the prince if you don't mind.' All were happy to hear this. The mimicry began.

FIRST ACT

The King – 'Alas! Alas! The doctors have given up, the vaids and hakims have lost hope, no one could guess the disease. All were robbers. There's no hope of life now. All this wealth and state will be left behind. What will become of my subjects after me! The prince is young and immature, he's into bad company. (Looking at Premshankar with scorn) He keeps company with the peasants. He fights with official men for their sake. He treats those patients, from whose shadow even doctors run away.

He has no care of his life or his money. How will he take care of such a big kingdom? How will he punish the tyrants? Alas! My dear queen, whom I married only a month ago; how will she live without me? Who will love her? Alas!'

The Queen – Swamiji, I will die of grief. How will I see these white hair, this wrinkled face; (with scorn) whom will I take in my lap? To whom will I show my wants and desires? I will not be saved anymore.

The King starts losing his breath, his eyes turn to stone; his pulse starts sinking. The queen weeps and beats her breast. The whole court is steeped in grief and mourning.

Suddenly a voice speaks in the King's ears - 'We give you an hour's time. If you can find three men who really wish you to be alive, you will be immortal.'

He is suddenly brought to his senses; the light of life starts shining on his visage. He wakes up happily and says to himself – 'Now I'll live forever, I'll rule without fear, and destroy all my enemies. Who's there in my kingdom who doesn't wish me to be alive? Not just three, but three lac men will come out in a matter of few seconds.'

SECOND ACT

(The King in the disguise of a common man)

'The time is very limited; I must go to those three men who were my ardent followers. First of all, I'll go to the rich man. He used to help me in all charitable causes. I have protected him so many times, and profited him a lot. Here's his house. 'Sethji, Please come out.'

Seth – What's up? What do you want so late in the night?

The King – Nothing; I just wish to sing the praises of my late king, and bring peace to his soul. What a great, honest and subject-loving man he was! With his demise, darkness has descended upon our land. People will never forget him. You and he were great friends; you must be too sad.

Seth – What benefits did I avail under his rule that I'll feel sad now? It's good that he died. I had to spend thousands on feeding holy men for his sake.

The King - (to himself) Alas! I trusted this Seth so much! He used to donate lakhs of rupees at just one signal from me. It's truly said that baniyas are no one's friends. I stayed with him for a lifetime but couldn't recognize his true colours.

I should now go to my minister; he's a very loyal and nice man. I have obliged him many a times. Here comes his house. Perhaps he's coming from the court. 'Mantriji, are you coming from the court? There must be mourning going on there. However much you grieve for the death of such a noble King, it isn't enough. There won't be any such king again. You must be very unhappy?'

Mantri – What happiness has he given me that I should be sad now? It's good that he died. I didn't have time to breathe because of his affairs. He used to kill himself after the good of his subjects, and forced me to kill myself too. Day and night, I had to be alert to his orders.

The King – (to himself) Alas! This well-wishing servant has also deceived me. The whole world has become my enemy as soon as my eyes were shut. People who were willing to offer their blood in place of my sweat are now openly defying me. There aren't even three men alive who want me to live. When these two have gone, what's there to expect from others? Now I'll go to my queen. She's a woman devoted to her husband. Even her friends used to dote upon me. My wish shall definitely be fulfilled there. Now just a little time is left. Here comes the royal palace. The queen is sitting alone in mourning. 'Maharaniji, please have patience, your lord was a man whose praises will forever be sung by the world. He has become immortal by leaving his physical self.'

The Queen – Immortal or a stone? The world might have benefitted from him, not me! I felt ashamed at sitting by his side. What praises can I sing of him? I became a widow the day I got married to him. I was a widow even when when he was alive, and also when he's dead. Look at Kunwar Sahib, how pleasing and handsome he is. He was fit to be married to me, not that old hag, who didn't even have teeth in his mouth.

As soon as the King hears this, he lets out a long sigh, and falls down on the ground, unconscious.

(The act is over)

Premshankar was amazed at the acting skills of these rustic people! There wasn't' an iota of pretence in it. Everyone completed their specific roles in a natural manner. There were no curtains or props yet the acting was entertaining and amusing.

In the morning when Premshankar went towards the camp, he found that all the men were preparing for departure. The tents were being uprooted. The luggage was being packed on the carts. Sahib Bahadur's motor car was ready and Bisesar Sah was standing before the Tehsildar with a sheaf of papers in hand. The oil-presser, tobacco-seller and butcher were all standing under a tree like criminals, waiting to receive their wages.

Premshankar shook hands with the Tehsildar and sat down to watch the proceedings.

Tehsildar – Where are the cart drivers? Call them; we want to account for the rations.

Hearing this, a driver said, 'Huzoor, have we got rations out here or life-threatening goods? In the flour, this dishonest shopkeeper has mixed such adulterated items that our stomachs have been upset since then. He even mixed oil in ghee, and now wants the accounts to be cleared. If we tell the higher officers, he'll have to pay badly for it.'

Many peons also said, 'This baniya ought to be shot dead. We have never eaten such bad flour. God knows what he's mixed in it that we just can't digest it. There was such an odour in the ghee that we just could not swallow daal. He must be fined for this. On top of it he wants money.'

One of the constables said, 'We know him very well; he's one of a kind. He gave us sugar full of sand, ghee full of tubers, flour full of husk and all kinds of filth in pulses. He should be beaten up at a place where he can't even get water.'

Many of the stable attendants said, 'The feed for the horses is all rotten; half gram and half husk. The horses did not even touch it. If we tell the Sahib he'll be beaten up with a hunter.'

Tehsildar – Why didn't you all complain earlier?

Many men – Huzoor, we've been shouting everyday.

Tehsildar – (looking at Premshankar) No one ever told me. I will not hear all this now. Whatever is their due, pay everyone. Sahji, get your accounts.

Bisesar – Maula Baksh ardali; flour three seers, ghee eleven seers, rice two seers, pulses one seer, spices one seer, tobacco one seer, betelnut one seer, sugar one seer – all come to three rupees in total.

Tehsildar – Where is Maula Baksh? Pay the price and take the receipt.

One orderly – No one's here by that name.

Bisesar – Who says there isn't? He's a tall man, has a small beard, has pox marks on his face and a few of his front teeth broken.

Many orderlies – There's no one having such an appearance also. Identify who he is.

Bisesar – He must have gone somewhere; what else?

Tehsildar – Take some other name.

Bisesar – Dhannu ahir; rice three seers, flour two seers, ghee one seer, husk four seers, grain eight seers, and tobacco - two rupees in all.

Tehsildar – Where's Dhannu ahir? Take out money.

One orderly – He went late at night, taking away the Sahib's goods.

Tehsildar – He went away without clearing the accounts. Okay Nazirji, write his name. Where can he go? I will extract every single penny from him.

Premshankar – This is really an atrocity on part of the camp people.

Tehsildar – Just don't ask, these rougues eat up and run away, and it's the Tehsildar who gets a bad name.

Bisesar Sah again read a similar account again. This was a paper for Jairam peon. Jairam was present there. He came forward and asked – Why! Did I take eleven seers of ghee or two?

Bisesar – It's written in the paper.

Jairam – It's all false; totally false.

Tehsildar – You can pay for two seers, or do you wish to give nothing?

This mess-up continued till nine or ten in the night. More than one third of the people had left without squaring the account. More than one-fourth vanished. Half of the men who were present had their doubts about the account being correct. Only five or ten men came out who paid their dues properly. When all the chits were finished, Bisesar Sah threw them in front of the Tehsildar and said, 'I don't know anybody; I know only Huzoor and gave the receipts on Huzoor's orders only.'

Tehsildar – Will I pay from my own pocket?

Bisesar – Huzoor can pay or make them pay. I have received only seventy rupees out of two hundred. I am a poor man; how will I bear this loss? The moneylender will sell off my house.

Tehsildar – Okay, you'll get your money. Nazirji, you take the peons with you, get his account books and estimate his yearly income yourself. Everything will come out clear. I'll pay all his money, but only after taking them from him. You wicked chap! You make a profit of two thousand rupees per annum, and now if you've incurred a loss of just hundred rupees you're making such a noise.

Till now Bisesar Sah was fuming in anger but as soon as he was threatened in this way, he got scared. He said, 'Yes Huzoor, please check all the accounts. Which profession can fetch one a profit of two thousand in this village? If one gets to eat, that's enough.

Tehsildar – And where does the produce grown in nearby villages get stored? You think the officers are ignorant about it. I can even tell you what's cooking in your house today. We are lenient only to maintain this position; not to see your stupid face.

Bisesar Sah quietly took his leave. The oil-presser and the tobacconist also understood that wages can't be got; rather they could be unduly caught, so they too went their way. The Tehsildaar looked at Premshankar and said, 'Did you see, how a very mention of texes takes their breath away. I know that his yearly income would be one thousand rupees at the most. But they can bear all losses, except showing their accounts. It's their old habit.'

Premshankar – Well, he was saved from any further loss due to his cleverness, but all the rest were put to loss for nothing; moreover they were insulted so much.

Tehsildar – Sir, I have no cure for that. Till the time you people make the nation aware of its rights, these frauds will continue without end. Where hearts are full of vested interests and the public is so naïve, nothing can be modified. (Smiling) We are actually your helpers. We torture and crush these people to make them incorrigible and pave the way for national workers like you.

27

It was morning time and the month of September was here. The rains had ended. Wherever one might go in the rural areas, smells of rotten jute were floating in air. Sometimes, a strong sun, rampant like the month of June came up, at other times, dark clouds, darker than those found in the rainy season were cast. Mosquitoes and malaria wreaked havoc, and herbs like neem bark and anti-fever drugs were used extensively. In the pastures, green grass was blooming in plenty. No one was free to cut it as yet. At this time Binda Maharaj and Kartarsingh came and stood under a tree, with sticks on their shoulders. Kartar said, 'This oldie keeps thinking of one issue or the other. You tell me, if animals are not allowed to graze here, where will they go, and people have been doing so since ages; why will they relent? If someone could beat him up, he'd get rid of this bad habit.'

Binda – I have been around in this region for thirty years. About ten karindas have come since then, but none stopped the grazing. The animals of the entire village kept grazing in peace.

Kartar – What do they have to lose by giving an order! It's we who are affected.

Binda – I am so fed up of all this that I wish to leave everything and go home. I've heard that the master has come. I just want to meet him once and go home.

Kartar – Faizu keeps lying on his cot the whole day long; no one says anything to him. Everyone keeps calling Kartar only, as if Kartar is their father's slave. And look under the peepal tree, where you and I offer water, they offer namaz, gargle their mouths, and take a bath. Tell me; isn't our faith polluted in this way? You can read the Quran daily but when I read the Ramayana I'm scolded; 'What's all this noise!' In the month of July they got a nazrana of three hundred rupees; I didn't get to see even a penny.

Binda – I got one rupee.

Kartar – Do you really call it an amount? Elsewhere, the peons get fifty percent of such gifts. They can at least pay us twenty-five percent. They don't know what to give but only how to order me around. You had gone somewhere yesterday. I was told, 'Kartar, fill up a pot of water.' I replied, 'I cannot do such service. You can ask me to wield my stick, I'll never refuse, but filling water or preparing the hookah is not my job.' They were very angry with me. Once they commented on the idols under the peepal tree, 'Why have you gathered these stones here?' I have decided now, if someone comes with a gift, I'll straightaway demand my twenty five percent. If they show even a little temper, I'll strangle their necks. I'll see what happens later. If Faizu interferes, I'll teach him a lesson also. They are just enjoying rich meals at my cost; I'll put an end to all this. See, the animals are approaching. Is that Balraj out there?

Binda – Even if he's there what's the reason to fear? He's had such a fever this time that he's thinned down a lot.

Kartar – He's such a strong chap. I got into a squabble with him once, where Sukhu Chaudhary's pond is getting constructed. I controlled him in one blow; but he escaped with such swiftness that I couldn't steady myself. His body is as strong as iron.

Binda – He's got a strong character as well. He never dares to eye anyone else's wife or daughter with a bad intention.

Kartar – See, even Ghaus Khan and Faizu are coming this side; it's going to be dangerous, it seems.

Binda – These cows and buffaloes seem to be Manohar's; Bilasi is getting them here.

Kartar said in a loud voice, 'Who's coming here with these animals? Please take them away; it's against official orders.' Just then Bilasi came close and said to Binda Maharaj in a carefree voice, 'Just listen to Maharaj Thakur!'

Kartar – It's officially prohibited to let the animals graze here.

Bilasi – What kind of orders? The ground does not belong to the government. Maharaj, you have been here since ages; has anyone ever prohibited animals to graze?

Binda – Don't talk about those old times, now fresh orders have been issued. Someone might take away your animals; or else Ghaus Khan is coming; he will catch them all and send them to the animal shelter.

Bilasi – How can they do that? Is there a misrule going on? Our animals have always been grazing here and will keep doing so. What kind of an order is this? Today they're telling us to leave the pastures; tomorrow they will say, 'leave your house; go and stay under a tree.' What is all this nonsense?

Just then Ghaus Khan and Faizu reached there. Bilasi's last words were heard by Khan Sahib. He immediately rebuked her and said, 'Take your animals away, or else I'll send them to the shelter home.'

Bilasi – Why should I take them away? The pasture land belongs to the whole village. When the village stops sending its animals here we'll also stop.

Ghaus Khan – Will you take away the animals or keep arguing about law?

Bilasi – Khan Sahib, you are trying to order me as if I survive on your charity.

Ghaus Khan – Faizu, this talkative woman will not obey us easily. Surround her animals and take them to the shelter home.

Faizu rushed towards the animals, but Kartar and Binda Maharaj got into a great confusion. Khan Sahib called out to them, 'What are you people doing there? Take these animals away. It's an official order, not a joke.'

Now Kartar and Binda Maharaj also got up and tried to enclose the animals on all sides. The animals grew alert, plucked up their ears and started running here and there. They understood the perilous situation. Bilasi said, 'I warn you not to drive them, or it won't be good for you.'

Faizu – Get out of our way. Do you want to invite trouble?

Bilasi stood in the way and said, 'How will you take my animals?'

Ghaus Khan - If she doesn't get aside beat her up.

Bilasi – I am telling you, streams of blood will flow because of these animals. People will lose their heads.

Faizu – Do you leave or not, you witch?

Bilasi – You get aside, O bearded rogue.

She had just said so, when Faizu came forward to hold her neck and push her so forcefully that she fell down near his feet. Her eyes became dazzled and she almost became unconscious. For a second, she kept lying still; then got up and limped away to narrate her insult to the men who were the guardians of her honour. Manohar and Balraj had gone to a nearby village to harvest paddy. It was about two miles away from here. Lakhanpur had no paddy fields. For this reason, people often cultivated paddy in that village only. Bilasi was crossing the paddy fields. Her feet kept slipping one way or the other. She was getting so anxious that she wanted to fly off to the place, but she was forced to slow down due to the injury in her knees. A flame erupted from her body. Her whole self seemed to echo – 'How could they dare to do this!'

She wasn't yet worried about any result or repercussion of her complaint. Who will lose his life? Whose house would be destroyed? She was not bothered about these things now. She had released herself from the bondage of thinking about all future possibilities.

But when she reached near the village and saw paddy fields blooming in the air, she thought for the first time as to what this rage would bring. 'Balraj is too short tempered, and Manohar even more than him; if they hear me crying they will be mad with anger. If they get into trouble; then what?' But a wounded heart replied, 'What's the harm? Why does a man have children? Why does he bother about a spouse? For such a day only. That black-faced Faizu will lose his pride once and for all! Ghaus Khan's haughtiness will also be destroyed forever!'

Still, when she reached her fields and saw Manohar and Balraj, her feet started shaking. In fact when she reached near them, the thought of future repercussions defeated her altogether. She started weeping bitterly. She knew very well that these teardrops were sparks of fire, but she just couldn't control herself. She stood in a corner and started weeping, hiding her face.

Balraj grew doubtful at once and asked, 'Amma, what happened? Why are you crying? How did your clothes become blood soaked?'

When Bilasi looked at her saree, she actually saw drops of blood. Her knees were also bleeding. Her heart started trembling. She could have given up her life to hide those bloodstains. 'Alas! What came over me that I came running over here? I didn't know that I had got injuries also. It's too bad now. I should have had some patience. In the evening, when these two would've returned home and all the villagers would have gathered, I should have told them everything. Whatever they'd have advised would have been followed.' In this upset condition, she couldn't think of a suitable reply which could have proved peaceful as well.

Balraj asked again – 'Why don't you say something? You just stand there crying. What happened; just tell me!'

Bilasi – (crying) Faizu and Ghaus Khan drove away our cows and buffaloes to the animal shelter.

Balraj – Why? Did the animals get into their fields?

Bilasi – No, they said that it's now prohibited to graze in the pasture.

Balraj saw that his mother's eyes were bent and her face was revealing an attack on her honour. He mistook the situation to be far graver than it really was. He didn't have the courage to ask anything else. His eyes grew red. He kept his stick on his shoulders and told Manohar, 'I am going to the village.'

Manohar – What for?

Balraj – I need to have a man to man talk with Faizu and Ghaus Khan.

Manohar – This is not the time for such talk. If you go now, the situation will grow worse and you'll gain nothing. People will criticize you only. This is not the way to avenge your insult.

Manohar's words were so full of a serious determination and such dangerous resolve that Balraj couldn't insist any further. He kept his stick down and said to his mother, 'You go home for now. When we return home we'll see what's to be done.'

Manohar – No, don't go home. Sit here only. We'll go together in the evening. Who's coming here running? Is it Binda Maharaj?

Balraj – No, it seems like Qadir Dada. Yes, it's him only. He's running like anything. It seems like there's been a quarrel in the village. Dada, what's up? Why are you running; is everything fine?

Qadir took a breath and said, 'We were coming to you only. Bilasi came here crying. I was scared lest you people might lose your temper. I came to stop you in the way, but couldn't find you anywhere. Whatever has happened has happened; take stock of the future. The zamindar has prohibited grazing in the pasture from today. Do you see this tyranny?'

Manohar – Yes, I can see it; there's nothing but tyranny all around.

Qadir – We'll have to approach the court again.

Manohar – Come, I'm ready.

Qadir – Yes, after you come, we'll discuss it together and file a petition. This time we'll go up to the High Court, even if we have to sell our houses. Only, we must contribute towards ploughing.

Manohar – Yes, that would be fine.

Qadir – I was offering the namaz; I heard that in the pasture, Bilasi was insulted by the peons and she has come crying over here. I understood that the unexpected had taken place. Thank God you acted with patience. God will reward you for this. So I'll go now and discuss the donations. Please come before evening.

Qadir Khan left after alerting them. He could not sense that something else had been resolved. He thought Manohar's balanced words to be a sign of mental patience.

Manohar got busy in his work with such a renewed vigour that it seemed his youth had returned. The sheafs of paddy got collected in heaps. He didn't bother to look in the front, nor at the back; he didn't say anything to anyone nor heard anything; his hands didn't grow tired, nor did his back ache any moment. Balraj prepared his hookah. The tobacco got burnt. Bilasi brought a sherbet of jaggery before him. He didn't even look at it; a dog finally drank it off. The September sun blazed hot; his body became red, streams of sweat started flowing, but he didn't raise his head. Balraj sometimes came into the fields, or sat under a tree, or smoked his hookah. The same fire burnt in their hearts, one slow; the other blazing. One was as swift as the speed of air; the other helpless and weak. The same feeling was there in their hearts; one was boundless and uncontrolled, the other, serious and stable.

It was afternoon. Bilasi came and said in a fearful tone, 'Come and have something to eat.

Manohar replied with a bent head – You go; we'll come.

After an hour Bilasi came again and said, 'Come and eat; the day is over. Will you cut the entire field today?'

Manohar replied in a rough voice, 'That's what I have thought. Who knows whether tomorrow comes or not?'

The way a stone hits a filled pot, and water starts flowing over, the same way, Bilasi's heart was hit and tears started falling. She started repenting badly. 'Alas! God knows what he's decided in his mind?'

She kept crying, standing there for quite some time. A fearful image of a horrible repercussion was dancing before her eyes. It seemed that the image would engulf her any moment, and alas! she had made this image with her own hands. Finally she sat before Manohar and looking at him with a most helpless expression said, 'I plead to you with folded hands; please eat something. Your silence is threatening me like anything. What are you thinking about; why don't you say something?'

Manohar – Go and sit quietly. I'll eat when I am hungry.

Bilasi – Oh God! What are you hellbent on?

Manohar – What can I do? If I had been able to do anything I'd not been insulted like this. Whatever's in my fate will happen.

After saying this, he again got busy in his work. No one said anything to anyone. Bilraj kept avoiding food, and Bilasi kept crying and cursing herself alternately till the evening fell. The three of them packed the paddy sheafs on the cart and went towards Lakhanpur. Balraj drove the cart, and

Manohar sang a traditional song of separation as he walked behind the cart. They met Kallu ahir on the way; he said, 'Manohar kaka, you seem too lost in yourself.' When Manohar's song got over, he too sang a similar song. When both reached the village together, there was unrest all around. There were discussions going on about the prohibition of the pastureland. At Qadir's door, a panchayat seemed to have gathered. But Manohar did not go to the panchayat. He went home and demanded food. His daughter-in-law had prepared the meal. He had his dinner tastefully and started smoking his hookah. After a while Balraj returned from the panchayat. Manohar asked, 'Say, what happened?'

Balraj – Nothing, they have just decided to appease Khan Sahib by giving him some gifts. Everyone's scared of the court.

Manohar – I knew this beforehand. Okay, go and eat something quickly. Today I'll also go with you to guard the fields. If I happen to fall asleep, wake me up.

After an hour, both the men set out for the fields. Manohar asked, 'Your axe is sharpened well enough?'

Balraj – Yes, I sharpened it today only.

Manohar – Take it with you.

Balraj – My heart is beating too fast.

Manohar – Let it be. I'll be with you. After striking one or two blows, you can run away, and I'll manage the rest. Come home and sleep, as if you don't know anything. Even if people ask you don't open your mouth. I would have gone alone, but firstly, I am sick with night-blindness; I can't see clearly; secondly my hands aren't so strong anymore that I can manage the show with just one blow.

Manohar was talking in a tone as if they were just discussing some mundane domestic issues. On the contrary, Balraj was getting anxious with doubt and fear. He could have jumped into fire in a fit of anger, but this planned murder was getting on his nerves.

After reaching the fields, both lay down on the guarding platform. It was a dark night of Amavasya. The sky had become a little cloudy. There was absolute darkness all around.

Manohar started snoring immediately, but Balraj kept turning on his sides. His heart had become a continuous stream of all kinds of doubts.

After about half an hour, Manohar woke up. He asked Balraj, 'Are you asleep?'

Balraj – No, I can't sleep.

Manohar – Okay, now remember God and get ready for action. No need to fear or worry. It's a man's job to guard his honour. How else can we answer such atrocities? It is better to die than to keep living even after getting insulted. Strengthen your heart. Come back after finishing your job. The night is dark. No one will be able to spot you. The constables will threaten you, but beware! No need to be afraid! If you stay united with the villagers no one will be able to harm you. Dukhran Bhagat is not a good man; be wary of him. But Qadir is trustworthy. Don't feel bad about his words. I will not return home now. You will be the head of the family. Leave your teenage tantrums; learn to tolerate others. Don't do anything that will bring a bad name to your ancestors. Don't spoil your wife. Keep instructing her to obey her mother-in-law. I won't be there to see anything, but if fights keep going on like this, our house will be destroyed.

Balraj said in a pent-up voice, 'Dada, just listen to me; have patience for now. I will break everyone's heads tomorrow.'

Manohar – Of course, if someone beats you, you should beat up the entire world. Do you think Faizu and Kartar to be balls of mud? Ghaus Khan has also served in the army. You will not be able to win over them in any stick-fight. See, there comes the Hiranyaksh constellation in the sky. Think of Mahavirji and get up to go. One must not think too much before such actions. We'll have to move along the border of the village, or dogs will bark and people will wake up.

Balraj – My hands and feet are shaking.

Manohar – Don't you worry. Once you take the axe in your hands everything will be alright. You are my son; you ought to have a strong heart. The kind of fear you're experiencing is the shivering one gets before an onset of fever. Once you keep the axe on your shoulders, take Lord Mahavir's name and move forward, your eyes will start emitting sparks of fire. You will have blood upon your head. You'll leap like an eagle on your prey. If I stop you then, you won't even listen to me. See, the wolves are howling; it's midnight now. Hold my hand and move ahead quickly. Glory to Lord Mahavir!

28

Premshankar's agricultural farm was one of city's main attractive sites nowadays. There was so much neatness and beauty all around that very often tourists came there for a stroll. Although Premshankar was only its supervisor, but the absolute devotion and trust of the tenants had made him their master. He tried new crops for cultivation and did all kinds of experiments, but no one intervened or stopped him. And why should anyone do so, for none of his experiments were unsuccessful. The fields that produced hardly five or seven man of foodgrains now produced upto fifteen or twenty. Plus there was the additional income from the orchard. In the last four years, mango, berries, orange and other trees had also started giving fruit. There were vegetables too, grown on spare land. Premshankar hadn't yet been touched by professional meanness. Whoever came for a visit was presented with a basket of flowers and fruit. Seeing Premshankar's modern methods the people of Hajipur had also devised such a livelihood that all their needs were met by that farm only. One-eighth of the land was reserved for growing cotton. High quality seeds were obtained from other states and sown there. The villagers spun their own cotton and the village weaver made their clothes. He was called Masta. He used to gamble earlier and had been caught stealing many a times. He was now counted as a respectable man of the village due to his hard work. Due to Premshankar's efforts, the nearby villages had also started growing cotton and this had brought prosperity to all the weavers in the area. People who came from other villages in pursuit of court cases often stayed at this place. They didn't have to spend any money on fuel, vegetable or spices. Premshankar chatted with them and took them on a round of the farm. It almost became a permanent abode of holy men. Few of them stayed all the year round. God knows how blessed the land was that despite spending so much on hospitality, there was no scarcity of any kind. The Hajipur people worshipped him like a god and praised their fortune that such a divine soul had come to stay in their midst to redeem them. His kind, generous and simple nature had reformed many fallen spirits besides Masta kori. Bhola ahir, who always stole grain from the fields and Damdi passi, whose sole profession was roguery, were now one of the most hardworking and honest farmers of the village.

Premshankar often surmised upon the economic degradation of the peasants. He didn't like to find its solution by blaming the latter for over-expenditure, laziness, illiteracy or ignorance of agricultural developments like other economists. He actually used to say that he could hardly tell the farmers about anything which they didn't already know. 'There's hardly any group more hardworking than them in the world. They are skilled in budgeting, self-restraint and domestic management. The responsibility of their poverty lies not upon them, but on those conditions under which they spend their lives, and what are these? Mutual distrust, selfishness, and an institution which lies around their feet like a chain. Think properly and you'll find these three stalks erupting from the same branch and this is that same institution which thrives on the blood of the peasants. Why do they have mutual opposition? Due to ill-arrangements, which have been created by the present rule. Why isn't there mutual love and trust among them? Because the administration deems these feelings fatal for itself and does not let them thrive. What is the most terrible result of this mutual opposition? The gradual division of land in extremely small parts and unlimited increase in land rent.' Premshankar deemed this administrative reform beyond the limits of human capacity, but he thought that the division of land could be controlled. And though he didn't want to lead any movement on it, he was so curious on the subject that he could not stop himself from expressing his motives in the newspapers. He simply wanted that by doing so, someone more experienced, efficient and talented than him should take up the question seriously.

Once, he was sitting with many of his liberal friends and discussing the topic, when one of them said, 'If you think that this custom can be stopped legally then you are surely mistaken. The poisonous roots of this plant are in a man's heart, and unless they are dug up and thrown away, it will keep blooming as before.'

Premshankar – One can modify the law in some way or the other.

The other friends responded forcefully by saying, 'Absolutely not. In fact, selfishness, if not allowed to exist naturally will become all the more dangerous.'

Hearing this, a farmer who had just returned from the court after submitting an application for division of land, and was staying on the farm said, 'Nothing can happen anywhere. We follow you people only. When you too cannot exist as brothers; how can we? God has given you everything, but still you live separately from your brother.'

These open words hit Premshankar's heart like an arrow. He lowered his head. His face lost colour. His friends looked at that farmer with anger. Their talk was a kind of social intercourse. Here, no one should have been pulled up personally, but how could that rude rustic know the intricacies of civilization? He uttered whatever came to his mind. One of them said, 'You are so unpolished; you don't know how to speak?'

Another friend said, 'If they knew that, why would they be called rustics? They don't care about the occasion, or the purpose; whatever nonsense comes to their mind, they mutter that.'

The poor farmer now understood that he had said something improper. He said in an embarrassed tone, 'Sahib, I am a rustic fellow. I don't know any manners. If I have made a mistake please forgive me.'

Premshankar – No, no, you haven't said anything out of context. I needed this blunt critique. You have actually taught me a lesson. Undoubtedly, there's as much opposition and enmity among the educated people as is between uneducated ones; and I am to blame in this matter. I do not have the right to preach to anyone.

The friends kept sitting for some time but Premshankar was subdued in a way that he couldn't open his mouth again. In the end, all went away.

The sun was slowly setting in the West. Premshankar was strolling in front of his hut in a state of great worry. His problem was how he could unite again with Gyanshankar. The more he thought, the more he found himself to blame. 'All this is my doing', he thought. 'When he was at conflict with the tenants it wasn't proper that I should have sided with them. True, Gyanshankar was trying to oppress them. In such a situation, I should have stayed away, or tried to make him understand in a brotherly way. I didn't bother to do that. On the contrary, I ended up fighting with him. I admit that there's a world of difference between his principles and mine. But why should an opposition of principles pollute love among brothers? I also know that ever since I've arrived here, he has ignored me; in fact deprived me of my wife's love, but I too never attempted to befriend him, forget his bitter behaviour or tolerate his unpleasant comments. If he moved away an inch I distanced myself by a foot. A love for principles does not mean that one should strike an opposition with your loved ones. It is unpardonable to place principles at a higher pedestal than man. It is a good opportunity to clear his heart from my side.'

The evening had fallen. Gyanshankar was sitting outside his beautiful bungalow and talking to Maulvi Ijaad Hussain. Maulvi Sahib had resigned from his government job not finding desirable success, and was now engaged in community service. He had established an organization called "Anjuman Ittehaad" (association for concord), the purpose of which was to promote mutual love and friendship between Hindus and Muslims. It survived on donations and Syed Sahib had arrived there due to that motive only.

Gyanshankar said, 'I am experiencing everyday that zamindari needs much strictness to be dispensed. A zamindar can leave the perks of gifts, free labour, fines etc., but he can't leave land rent. That too is not obtained without court cases these days.'

Ijaad Hussain – You are absolutely right, but I have seen such rich men who have never gone near the door of a court. Whenever someone revolts he gets beaten up, and the best part is, they never use a stick or a hunter to subdue him. A strong sun during summers, and cold, icy water in winters – this tactic gets all their taxes in place. Just a little heat of the May and June sun is enough to melt the pocket of a tenant.

Gyanshankar – God knows where such men exist. I have always encountered rogues who are ready to go to court at the drop of a hat. Just see my estate; what a great riot has ensued only due to prohibition of the pasture.

Just then Dr. Irfan Ali, Bar-at-law arrived in a motorcar. Gyanshankar welcomed him.

Doctor – This time you made me wait for a long time. I was about to come to Gorakhpur to see you.

Gyanshankar – The work of the estate is so widely distributed that however much I wind up, it refuses to finish.

Doctor – You must be knowing that there's a place vacant in the Economics department in the University. You have joined the Syndicate as well?

Gyanshankar – Yes, I was forcefully dragged in it, but I hardly get time from my estate work to devote it anywhere else. Some documents had been sent, but I had no time to look into them.

Doctor – That space is vacant after the going away of Dr. Das, and I am an applicant for it.

Gyanshankar said with surprise, 'You!'

Doctor – Yes, I've decided about it now. I am getting disillusioned with the legal profession day by day.

Gyanshankar – But why? Your legal income is no less than three or four thousand. Are you fed up with pleasing the officers, or are you more bothered about your conscience?

Doctor – No, only because in this particular profession, a person is forced to use unjustified force all the time. However righteous a lawyer might be, he's never happy with compassion or humanity in a way that an honest man should be. On the contrary he develops an interest in mutual quarrels and frauds which is devoid of all feeling. I have been lost in this confusion since months and have now decided to bid farewell to this profession at the earliest.

These talks were still going on when Faizu and Kartarsingh came and paid their respects. Gyanshankar asked, 'Hope all is well?'

Faizu – Huzoor, what to talk of well-being! Someone killed Khan Sahib last night.

Ijaad Hussain and Irfan Ali were shocked but Gyanshankar remained unfazed as if he knew about this news beforehand. He said, 'Where were you? Had you gone for merry making, or were you lying doped with opium?'

Faizu – Huzoor, we were in the chaupal only, but who could think that this could happen?

Gyan – Why, how could you remain ignorant to it? A person who's busy crushing a serpent must know that a serpent has poisonous teeth. Zamindari is as good as handling a serpent. That snake charmer is naive who lets a serpent bite him. Anyway, did you come to know of the culprit?

Faizu – Yes, it's the same Manohar ahir. He admitted his crime in the morning, after coming to the police station. The inspector came in the afternoon and is investigating the case. Did you receive Khan Sahib's telegram? The day Khan Sahib prohibited the public use of the pasture, all the villagers became one. Khan Sahib sent you a telegram as he was worried about the situation. I returned from the post office around three, and found the village people contributing money to fight the case. At night this incident took place.

Suddenly Premshankar came with Lala Prabhashankar. As soon as saw Gyanshankar he hugged him tightly and asked, 'When did you come back? Hope all is well.'

Gyanshankar replied roughly, 'Ask about well-being from these men who've come from Lakhanpur. The villagers have murdered Ghaus Khan.'

Premshankar was shocked. He could only say, 'Oh! When did this happen?'

Gyan – This very night.

Prem – What had happened?

Gyan – What else could have been the reason except the wickedness and revolt of the villagers? I had stopped common use of the pasture. I wanted to grow an orchard there. They just became intent upon bloodshed only on this pretext.

Prem – Did you come to know about the murderer?

Gyan – Manohar has just owned up in the police station.

Prem – Manohar is such a simple and serious man.

Gyan – (sarcastically) Of course, he's a god.

Doctor Sahib said emotionally, 'This is beyond the capacity of a single person.'

Gyan – I too think so. Manohar is not capable enough of doing this all alone. Undoubtedly the entire village has conspired together. Manohar is just a puppet in their hands. Let's see what the investigation brings out. Whatever happens, I'll make this region deserted. Why Faizu, what do you think? Can Manohar do this alone?

Faizu – No Huzoor, how can a sixty year old man dare to attempt this! And even if no one was there to help him; his son must have been there with him.

Kartar – What if he's old; he's a man of great courage. There's no one in the village as brave as him.

Gyan – You are a foolish rustic; what do you know about these things? You just need your daily dose of bhang. Doctor Sahib, in this case the plaintiff will be the government, but fight it from my side. I have decided that I'll not let any adult in this village go unscathed.

Premshankar said in a low voice, 'If you are sure that this is the job of a single man, it's not proper to sue the entire village. It's not right that the innocent should be crushed along with the culprits.'

Gyanshankar angrily replied, 'It would be better if you don't pretend to uphold your rules of truth and justice in this matter. These evil men have got this strength due to these rules only. You are forcing me to say all this openly. All of them are receiving this instigation from you. On every such occasion you have helped them against me and professed brotherhood with them. And you are always ready to support them in all ways. This kindness from your side has made them lose their senses. They have stopped being afraid of me. I respect your thoughts and principles, but you are trying to irrigate neem with milk and are hoping for a sweet fruit. To behave with rules and regulations with such evil men is to lend a torch in the hands of a madman.'

Premshankar didn't open his mouth now and didn't even raise his head. Lala Prabhashankar got so upset with this talk that he immediately left the place. But Premshankar kept sitting like a statue in self-introspection. It was a totally new experience for him that his concern for the poor villagers would bring such a horrible result. It wasn't just one man who had lost his life; there was a fear of many other men losing their lives. 'O God! Please have mercy on these men,' he thought, 'I don't think I served them with a pure heart. Jealousy and envy kept pushing me to do it. I wanted to defeat Gyanshankar. Was it just Lakhanpur which was suffering at the hands of its zamindar? Is there any region which is not shedding tears of blood due to the atrocities of its zamindar? Then why did my compassion grow so much for the people of Lakhanpur, or wasn't the situation as grave as before? It used to happen day in and day out, but the tenants never dared to open their mouths. Why did they become hellbent on violence and bloodshed?' All these doubts had just one answer, and that made the burden of responsibility all the more heavy. 'Alas! I have pushed so many lives in the fire of my jealousy. Now what is my duty? Should I just watch the repercussions from far, after lighting this fire? This is absolutely improper. I'll have to help these unfortunate men by all means, even if Gyanshankar feels bad. There is no other way out for me except this.'

Premshankar was lost in these thoughts when Mayashankar came and said, 'Chachaji, Amma is saying that it's got very late; how will you go to Hajipur now? Have your dinner with us and stay here for the night.'

Premshankar had forgotten in his depressive thoughts that he had to return to Hajipur. He petted Maya and said, 'No son, I will go back; it's not too late at night. If I stay here, my work will suffer.'

Thus saying, he got up. He looked at Gyanshankar with sad eyes and left without saying anything. Gyanshankar didn't even bother to look at him.

After he left, Doctor Sahib said, 'I had heard many good things about him, but right in the first meeting, I've had enough. He seems to be a little angry.'

Gyan – He's my elder brother, what can I say in his praise; he's stayed in America for some time and now thinks himself to be an apostle of rights and justice. Though even in America, these thoughts are far from achieving a practical form. The world has always been agog with such discussions, and so will be the case in future. We have to see how far they can be put into action. I am myself an advocate of these principles but I think this plant will take a long time to bloom in this land.

After this, they kept talking about the murder for a long time. When Doctor Sahib and Ijaad Hussain went away, Gyanshankar went home and said, 'Did you see, what Bhai Sahib has done in Lakhanpur? The news has come that Ghaus Khan was killed by the people there.' Both the women (Shraddha and Vidya) were shocked and started staring at each other.

Gyanshankar continued, 'He used to go and talk to the tenants since ages; God knows what he used to teach them that we had to see all this today. When I got the news of his visits there, I got concerned and requested him to stop meddling into those affairs. He also promised that he won't have anything to do with them. But he does not take anything seriously. I'm afraid that he might also get trapped in this matter. The police are harder than stone. They will try to catch a rich culprit. If the villagers are pressurized they will spill out everything and put the entire blame on Bhai Sahib.'

Shraddha looked at Gyanshankar with sad eyes, and lowered her head. She could not express her feelings openly. Vidya said, 'Why don't you go and see the inspector? Try to appease him in whatever way you can.'

Gyan – Yes, something has to be done indeed, but it's so insulting to plead before a lowly person. I never knew Bhai Sahib would turn out to be like this.

Shraddha said in an annoying tone, 'The police can charge him with whatsoever they wish; he's not a man who would lead the villagers astray; in fact if he had known that the villagers were planning any such thing, this incident would never have taken place. You need not plead to the inspector. He can protect himself on his own.'

Vidya – I had always told you not to increase enmity with the villagers. If a cat does not find a way to escape, she becomes as bold as a lion. But you never listened to me.

Gyan – What nonsense are you talking about? Should I feel scared of these chits of farmers? Am I a zamindar or a grasscutter? They never could have dared to stand against me. But if people from one's own family become traitors then anything can be expected. I will reiterate this a hundred times that if Bhai Sahib hadn't spoiled them they couldn't have mustered such courage.

Vidya – (in a low voice) A person who is worshipped by everyone in the city appears to be traitor in your eyes?

Gyan – This public adulation is the chief reason behind these riots.

Shraddha could not listen to all this anymore. She got up and went to her room. Gyanshankar said, 'I have no doubt that he'll be caught by the police.'

Vidya – You please leave no stone unturned to save him; this is your duty. Whatever is willed by God is bound to happen.

Gyan – Bhabi seems to be in a different state of mind.

Vidya – You don't know about her true nature. She might run away from Dadaji's shadow, but she can sacrifice her life for him; she still worships him in her heart.

Gyan – She seems to be riding two boats simultaneously.

Vidya – On one side she's afraid of public criticism, but her heart is on the other side, with her husband.

Gyan – Then I'll have to think of something else.

Vidya – For God's sake, don't talk to me in such a vein.

29

Gyanshankar grew doubtful after listening to Shraddha, but after thinking carefully, his doubts got dispelled, because it was absolutely certain that Premshankar would be chargesheeted in the case. In such a situation Shraddha's anger couldn't have harmed Gyanshankar in any way.

He decided that there was no need for him to do anything in the matter. The entire system was conducive to his interests. 'The inspector will forward the case due to his own vested interests; he will try to entrap the entire village and it's highly improbable that he doesn't prove successful in it. However much the village may be united, someone or the other will surely act as a police informer. The inspector must have raided the zamindari office of Lakhanpur. Some of my letters must have been found there which may prove Bhai Sahib's sympathy and compassion towards the villagers. I had written in many of my letters to Ghaus Khan that I dislike such behaviour on his part. But one thing is quite possible. The villagers might bribe the inspector to get away scot-free and he might chargesheet Manohar alone. But in such a serious matter he cannot dare to do that. He will prove the incident to be important by all means. The officers are already annoyed with Bhaisaheb due to his fearless profession of socialism. The sub-inspector would surely like to impress upon them by proving him as the instigator of this conspiracy. If the charge is proved, he too will be promoted and rewarded. The villagers can't offer him a huge bribe and he would not like to spoil his ambitions for the sake of a menial amount. It is a myth to think too much about brotherly opposition. Everyone lives for himself and dies for his own sake; it is laughable to hurt yourself for the sake of silly emotions.'

Gyanshankar's premonitions were absolutely right. Almost every adult in Lakhanpur was chargesheeted. Bisesar Sah turned a traitor due to fear of tax. The zamindari office was also inspected. After a week, Premshankar's hut was raided in Hajipur and he was taken under arrest.

It was evening time. Gyanshankar was taking Munnu for a walk when Doctor Ifran Ali came and gave him the news. Gyanshankar was shocked and tears filled his eyes. For a second, his love for his brother suppressed all selfish feelings. But as soon as the question of bail came up the rush of emotions cooled down. When the news reached the house, everybody was taken by a storm. Shraddha collapsed; the elder lady (Prabhashankar's wife) came to console her. Munnu also went inside and started weeping loudly, hiding himself in his mother's lap.

Premshankar stayed away from the centre of the city in a way that he rarely knew any influential men in the city. He also personally refrained to meet the rich. Some scholars had seen his agriculture-related essays in the papers and were impressed with his ability, but they too thought him to be idiosyncratic. His real well-wishers were actually college students, office workers or people in the rural areas. Hearing the news of his arrest, thousands gathered and followed him to the police station, but not a single one among them could make any efforts to pay his bail.

When Lala Prabhashankar heard of his arrest he came rushing madly to Gyanshankar and said, 'Son, you must have heard about all this. The honour of this family has been destroyed. (Crying) My brother's soul would be so pained to know that the honour for which we sacrificed all our wealth has been ruined today. Alas! He never saw the gates of any court all his life. We had thefts in our house, but never informed the police as enquiries would have been held and the police would have arrived at our door. Today his own son …; why son; can't he be released on bail?'

Gyanshankar got angry at his painful anxiety and said, 'God knows; all depends upon the will of the officers.'

Prabha – Then why don't you go and meet them? Are you bothered about the family honour or not?

Gyan – It's easy to say; difficult to accomplish.

Prabha – Bhaiya, how can you talk like this? You are respected so much in the official group out here? The seniormost officer too treats you with so much respect? On what occasion will these people help us? Will you keep waiting for some other incident?

Gyan – If you want that I should go and plead before these officers; beg them for concessions; I am sorry I can't do that. I cannot fall in a pit that's dug by him (Premshankar). On what surety can I pay his bail, when I know that he will not leave his beliefs and will cause my downfall too, along with his own?

Prabhashankar said with a deep sigh, 'Oh God! This is the state of real brothers! I never knew you had such a ruthless heart. Your real brother is in such trouble and your heart refuses to melt. Well, doesn't matter. If it's not beyond me, my brother's dear son will not be insulted before my eyes.'

Gyanshankar was feeling angry about his uncle's flood of kindness. He thought, 'He's getting so voluble only to ignore me. He wants to demean me in the eyes of the officers.' But Prabhashankar was not a man of fake claims. He could sacrifice his very life for the sake of his family's honour. He had such an allegiance to family pride that could make him fast and yet feel fortunate to entertain guests at his door; a feature which sadly enough has vanished from the country now. Wealth, in his opinion, was just a means to protect pride and honour, not to serve the senses. He immediately went inside to change; wore his robe, tied a special type of turban and went to see the magistrate dressed like a traditional rich man. It was already eight at night, but he didn't bother about it. The way he explained his position before the Sahib; narrated his tale of sorrow, pleaded in a lowly manner; the way he stood with folded hands, kept his turban in the feet of the Sahib and started crying; the tale he told about his family honour and produced such evidences of its loyalty to the state – any newly educated youth would have deemed it not just embarrassing but laughable as well. But the Sahib melted down. He agreed to release Premshankar on bail, but the proceedings couldn't be completed as night had fallen. Prabhashankar came back disappointed. His prime wish that Premshankar should not stay in police custody at night could not be fulfilled. He kept turning and tossing in worry all night. 'Bhaiya's soul would be in such sorrow', he thought, almost mistaken that his brother stood at the door crying. 'Alas! Poor Premshankar would be sitting in a sorry state. He would be lying in a narrow, smelly, dark room unable to control his tears. He wouldn't have been able to eat anything. The constables and guards must be torturing him. God knows how the police must be treating him? God only knows what they wish to listen from his mouth? A man becomes an animal in this department. My Dayashankar was such a well-mannered fellow; the day he joined the police he has turned into someone else. He doesn't even care for his wife. If I get caught in a case he won't even release me without taking a bribe. Premshankar must be refusing to tow the line of the police and therefore they must be troubling him all the more. Bhaiya used to love him so much; and today he's fallen in such hands?'

In the morning Prabhashankar went again to the magistrate's bungalow. He found that the Sahib had gone out for hunting. He went to the Police Superintendent from there. He was still asleep. There was no chance of meeting him before ten o' clock. He was disappointed here also and kept running here and there, till late afternoon, without food or drink, all worried and haggard. He ran continuously from one office to another. He was surprised to see that even low-grade officers were so selfish and unkind. What to talk of speaking properly, they don't even hesitate to speak ill and taunt you in all ways. In the end, the bail was accepted at four in the afternoon, but not for one or two thousand; in fact ten thousand, and that too, in cash. Premshankar was very depressed. He took a deep sigh and set out for home slowly as if his body had become lifeless. He fell on his bed when he reached home, and started thinking, 'How should I arrange for ten thousand? Who will give me such a big amount, only on goodwill? Should I mortgage my land? Yes, there's no other way out. But my family will not agree to this; there will be a big fight on the issue.' He was lost in this confusion for quite some time. Soon, it was time for dinner. His wife came to call him. Prabhashankar looked at her with a humble expression and said, 'I am not at all hungry.'

The elder lady – What kind of a hunger is it that doesn't seem to come back? You didn't eat anything last night nor during the day; will you give away your life for this matter? People who should have actually been worried; who eat up their brother's share, they are least bothered, and you are fasting for no reason; you are making all of us starve with you.

Prabhashankar replied with tearful eyes, 'What to do, I have lost all my appetite. What a well-mannered, soft-natured, peace-loving boy he is. His face is always before my eyes. How can I eat? When he was abroad we had forgotten him, and thought we had lost him, but after recovering a lost gem one cannot bear to see it in the hands of thieves.'

The elder lady – He's such a boy that I pray every couple should be blessed with such a son. An absolutely innocent boyish nature; the same sweet talk and a similar kind of loving attitude. One feels proud to see him. He hasn't been touched by a tinge of pride. But nothing can be gained by leaving food and drink; come and have something.

Prabhashankar – A bail of ten thousand has been demanded.

The elder lady – Why can't you tell Gyanu that he just cannot swallow all sweet things and spit out the bitter part? Does Premshankar's part of the profit get totally spent on Shraddha's food and clothing?

Prabhashankar – What to say to him; does he ever listen? He's been affected by the Western culture, which separates a son from his parents as soon as he achieves adulthood. He has received an education which is based on self-love as its founding principle. He has become devoid of all kindness, humility and manners. He is just a slave of his senses and desires now.

The elder lady – Then how will you arrange for all this money?

Prabhashankar – What can I say; I'll have to take a loan from someone.

The elder lady – It seems that whatever is left out of family property will also be ruined by you. I have never seen money being returned in form of money. It's always land which is returned in exchange of money.

Prabhashankar – The land is there for my sake; I am not a slave of this land.

The elder lady – I will not let you take any loan. God knows what situation might turn up for us. In the end, we'll have to bear this entire burden alone. My boys will not have anything to look forward to.

Prabhashankar looked at his wife with a stern eye and said, 'I am not seeking any advice from you nor do I think you to be capable of dispensing it. You can forget all past obligations; I can't. I am not an ungrateful man. If my boys have comfort written in their fate, they will enjoy; if there's trouble in their destiny, they will bear it. I am not their destiny. If Dayashankar too falls into trouble today, no one will refuse to sell even family jewels for his sake. I do not deem Premu any less than Dayashankar.'

His wife again requested him to have dinner and Prabhashankar started refusing again. Finally she said, 'I've got pumpkin cutlets made today. If I had known you won't be having dinner, I wouldn't have had them made.'

Prabhashankar's passivity vanished. He asked with curiosity, 'Who has made them?'

The elder lady - Our daughter-in-law.

Prabha - Fine, bring me a plate. I am not hungry, but I'll have a few bites.

After having food, Prabhashankar got consumed by his worries again. 'Where to get the money from? Poor Premshankar had to stay in police custody again for tonight. The elder lady has clearly said that she won't allow me to take a loan and there seems no other option but to take it.' Lalaji kept lying awake for the night. He decided that he would fulfill his duty at all costs, even if his family members protest by all means. As soon as the sun rose, he went to Seth Dinanath and narrated his tale of woe. He had a long-term relationship with Sethji. He had become a zamindar only due to him. He agreed to do what Prabhashankar wanted. The papers were made and by ten o' clock, Prabhashankar received a bagful of ten thousand rupees in his hands. He was so happy as if he had found a great sum of money lying accidentally. He said to the Seth happily, 'Sethji, how can I thank you enough; you have kept my family's honour. My brother's soul will sing your praises in heaven.'

He went straight to the court from here and submitted the money for the bail. At this moment his heart was as happy as if a child was going to visit a fair. He was delighted with just imagining how happy his brother must have been on his sense of family devotion.

It was eleven o' clock. At the hearing place, the chargesheeted men of Lakhanpur were standing wearing handcuffs. Thousands of city people had gathered there to have a glimpse of these strange creatures. Everyone was curious to have a glimpse of Manohar. Some were cursing him; another man said what he did was right. That's the right way to deal with tyrants. Bilasi was sitting under a tree depressed and sad. Balraj's face reflected fearlessness. Dapatsingh and Dukhran Bhagat seemed worried. Qadir Khan was a picture of patience as usual. But Manohar was getting anxious with embarrassment and regret. He couldn't bear to face his fellowmen. 'It's me who has put the entire village into trouble', this thought refused to leave his mind. A little farther stood Bisesar Sah; a perfect image of guilt and repentance. The policemen were surrounding him in a way as if street children were gathering around a monkeyman. Last of all stood Premshankar; serious and tireless. The magistrate announced – 'Premshankar is now released on bail.'

Premshankar came forward and said, 'I am grateful to you for this kindness but when my innocent brothers are standing in chains I don't think it proper to leave them alone.'

Thousands of men were standing in the court. Everyone was looking at Premshankar with surprise. Prabhashankar became emotional and said, 'Son, please have mercy on me. Think of my efforts, you family's honour and the sorrow of you relatives. My heart weeps at this decision of yours.'

Premshankar said with tearful eyes, 'Chachaji, I am grateful with all my heart for your fatherly love and goodwill. I came to know today only that a human heart can be so pure, generous and loving. But my going away will break the hearts of these poor people; they will be badly disappointed. Therefore it is very essential for me to be with them. I have no trouble here. I thank God that he's given me an opportunity to console and help these poor men. I have another request to make. There's no need of a lawyer for me. I can prove my innocence myself. Well, if you wish to help me, please appoint a lawyer for these dumb creatures, or else it's possible that they may be treated with injustice.'

Lala Prabhashankar came out of the court totally depressed.

30

The case created a stir in the entire city. Wherever one could see, its proceedings were being discussed. All were praising Premshankar's self-sacrifice with open mouths. Although Premshankar had clearly said that he didn't need a lawyer, Lala Prabhashankar did not pay any heed to him. He was afraid that things would go further wrong without a lawyer. That could not be allowed to happen at any cost. If something grave takes place people would say that a lawyer was avoided for the sake of money; that's why everything got spoilt. There would be nothing left except regret. Thus he went to all the famous lawyers of the city. But no one agreed to fight the case. Someone said he was not free; someone else made some other pretext. All believed that the officers were annoyed with Premshankar; to defend him legally was almost akin to going against one's self-interest. When Prabhashankar's efforts didn't bear fruit he didn't make any further efforts for the other accused. His sympathy was limited to his family members only.

The chargesheet was ready and hearings started taking place in the court of the magistrate. The inspector, Faizu, the Tehsildar, the peons and guards; all gave their statements. On the eighth day, Gyanshankar came to the court. Prabhashankar was so pained that he went out of the room and started crying under a tree. 'This is the state of enmity between real brothers! One brother is acting as a witness against the other to prove the police correct.' The audience was also feeling curious to hear his statement. Everyone was staring at him intently. The police were sure that his statement would be enough to trap Premshankar, but they; and the audience were quite surprised when Gyanshankar took out his anger on the people of Lakhanpur and did not utter a single word against Premshankar.

The government lawyer asked him, 'Do you know that Premshankar used to visit that village quite often?'

Gyan – He owns half a share in the village.

Lawyer – Do you know, when the Inspector General of Police came on a tour, Premshankar had tried to stop the use of Lakhanpur men as free labour and had tried to quarrel with the Tehsildar?

Gyan – I have no news about that.

Lawyer – You must be knowing that when you had applied for an increase in land rent, Premshankar had given five hundred rupees to the villagers to fight the case.

Gyan – I know nothing about the matter.

Gyanshankar's evidence was complete. The government lawyer was too disappointed. But the audience said in a collective voice, 'Brothers are brothers after all; even if they are thirsty for each other's blood.'

After this, Mr. Jwalasingh came to the hearing. He said, 'I was a collector there for many years. Lakhanpur fell under my jurisdiction. I went to tour the village many a times. I don't remember that we came across any more trouble about rations or labour, than we do in any other village. Babu Gyanshankar had once applied for rent increase in my court, but I had dismissed the appeal.'

Government lawyer – Do you know that Premshankar had given five hundred rupees to the Lakhanpur people for fighting the case?

Jwalasingh – I know that. But I think that this money had been given by someone else in order to help the villagers.

Lawyer – You must also be aware that Premshankar used to visit that village quite often.

Jwala – Yes, he used to go there during plague and other epidemics.

This account was also complete. All the questions of the government lawyer proved useless. Then Bisesar Sah arrived on the scene. His statement was very extensive, sequence-wise and summarized, as if a novelist had imaginatively created the situation. Everyone was amazed as to how such an illiterate rustic had acquired such an oratory skill? His narrative had such a tone of reality that it was difficult not to believe him. The enmity of the villages with Ghaus Khan, their opposition and fights during the hours of labour, their incitement at the prohibition of the grazing, and their collective conspiracy to kill Ghaus Khan – all these things were elaborated with great skill. Mainly the hatching of the conspiracy was described in such a lively and emotional manner that even Chanakya would have been impressed. 'At nine o' clock in the night Manohar came and said to Qadir Khan, 'Why are you sitting still? The grazing has been stopped, it won't pay to keep quiet, think of a solution.' Qadir Khan was sitting on a stool washing hands and feet, to offer namaz. He said, 'Come and sit; what can you or I do alone? If the whole village decides, only then something can be done, or the karinda will keep suppressing us like this. One day, even our fields will be taken away; go and call Dukhran Bhagat.' Manohar went to Dukhran's house. I too went with Manohar. Dukhran said, 'A thorn has pierced my foot, I can't walk. Call Khan Sahib here only.' I went and brought Qadir Khan; Manohar called Dapatsingh and Kallu. Qadir Khan said, 'We are foolish rustics; if we decide on our own it may or may not prove right; let's go and consult Babu Premshankar.' Dapatsingh said, 'Where's the need to go to him? I will go and call him.' The next day Babu Premshankar came in the evening on a horse-cart. I was almost shutting down my shop. Manohar said, 'Come, Babu Saheb has arrived. I went with Manohar to Qadir's house.' Premshankar said, 'Gyan Babu is my brother; so what? Such a brother should be killed rightaway.' Qadir said, 'We don't have any enmity with him; our fight is against Ghaus Khan. This killer has made it so tough for us to survive in this village. You only tell us, what should we do?' Manohar said, 'We can't bear these insults.' Premshankar said, 'Why do you tolerate this insult if you're a man? You can strike him off in single blow.' Qadir Khan said, 'We can do that but the whole village will be arrested.' Premshankar said, 'Why do you act with foolishness? All can put the blame on one man. One person is too unfit for the job anyway; there are three peons to tackle. Ghaus Khan is a strong man himself.' Qadir Khan said, 'What if the whole village gets trapped?' Premshankar replied, 'There isn't such misrule. What are lawyers for?' In the meanwhile, I went home to have food. Premshankar also went back on his horse-cart. At night, around twelve or one I heard some noises. I went to see around the house when I saw many people going somewhere. I understood they were our friends only. I called out Qadir's name. Qadir said, 'Get aside; do not stop us; go and lie down quietly.'

Qadir could not bear it anymore. He stared at Bisesar with stern eyes and said, 'Bisesar, God is seeing you from above; aren't you afraid of Him?'

The government lawyer said, 'Keep quiet or else you'll be charged with pressurizing the witness.'

In the evening, these people were sitting in the custody talking about random things. Manohar had been kept in a separate cell. Qadir said to Premshankar, 'Master, you have been caught in this trouble without any rhyme or reason. We are so unfortunate that whosoever helps us also gets caught in a net. We have spent a lifetime dealing with all this; we've seen thousands of educated men, but haven't seen anyone except you who hasn't tried to slice our throat. The whole world praises education. We rather think that a man becomes all the more wicked once he's educated. It teaches you how to torture a poor man. God had given you enemies precisely due to that.'

Dukhran – All this is Manohar's doing. He got the whole village in troubled waters.

Balraj – God knows what came upon him? We had also got angry, but he just went mad.

Dapat – What did a pasture matter? So much of scandal after that!

Qadir – Friends, don't talk like that. The poor man has done this for you; to protect your rights. Instead of praising his courage and daring, you are bent upon criticizing him. All of us are cowards; he alone is a true man.

Kallu – Bisesar has lost all sense.

Dukhran – His statement is like a lesson recited by a parrot.

Dapat – Who knows what he's scared of? There's no one after him to mourn his loss.

Kallu – If I am released from here I'll paint his face black and take him around the village.

Dapat – He's such a miser; if he sees a beggar, he goes and hides in his house like a shrewmouse.

Kallu – The sahuaain is a step ahead of him. Bisesar might even throw a penny at someone, but if she's alone in the shop, she doesn't give out anything except abuses. If you go to buy goods worth one paisa she'll give you only what's worth half a penny. She cheats in a way that no one can find out.

Balraj – Why Qadir Dada; do people cultivate land in the Andamans?

Qadir – I've heard there's a lot of sugarcane grown there.

Balraj – Then we can mint money. We'll plant a lot of sugarcane.

Kallu – But Dada, you won't live for another fourteen years. Your grave will be dug in the Andamans only.

Qadir – We want to come back so that our bones are cremated here only. God knows how you'll treat our dead bodies there.

Dukhran – Bhai, don't talk about life and death. Just pray that God brings us back alive in the midst of our children.

Balraj – They say the waters are very rough there.

Dukhran – This is all your father's doing. He has ruined the whole village.

Suddenly the door opened and the station inspector said, 'Babu Premshankar, the charge against you has been dismissed. You are now released. Your family's standing outside.'

Premshankar was enjoying the simple talk of the villagers a lot. He was surprised at the news. Gyanshankar and Jwalasingh had given statements in his favour, but not due to a motive that it might prove him innocent. He immediately understood that it was his uncle's doing and actually this was true. When Prabhashankar had lost all hopes of appointing a lawyer, he acted with prudence and sacrificed about two thousand rupees to get the desired result. Bribery, flattery, falsehood; all were pardonable in his eyes to escape custody.

Premshankar said to the jailer, 'If it's not against rules, please let me stay here for another night.' The jailer said with surprise, 'What are you saying? So many people are standing outside to welcome you.'

Premshankar thought, 'These poor men had so much of support in my staying here. Perhaps they were hopeful of getting released along with me. They all will be disappointed by my going away.' He consoled them saying, 'Brothers, I am being forced to leave you all, but my heart shall be with you. Possibly, I can serve you better by going out from here. I shall keep meeting you everyday.'

As soon as he took leave from his friends and reached the gate, Prabhashankar came to hug him. The peons of the jail gathered around him and started asking for a tip. Prabhashankar gave everyone two rupees each. Their carriage was about to leave when Babu Jwalasingh came on his motorcycle and hugged Premshankar. Prabhashankar wanted to take the two friends home and give them a feast, but Premshankar decided to return to Hajipur first. As soon as his carriage reached the farm, the ploughmen and gardeners all came and stood around him.

Prem – Why Damdi, is the ploughing going on properly?

Damdi became embarrassed and replied, 'Master, I can't say about others, but I didn't feel like working at all. I was always worried about you; (coming closer) Bhola has plucked a basket of guavas and has sold it.'

Bhola – Damdi, if you say something in the master's ears, it won't be good. Don't you know me well? I'm not afraid of the jail. Whatever good or bad you wish to say, you should say it on my face.

Damdi – You are getting angry for no reason. No one is saying anything to you.

Bhola – Why did you do all that whispering? If you didn't talk about me, it must be about someone else. Why do you tell tales about other people?

Masta kori tried to intervene – Bhola, you pick up fights for no reason. You have nothing to do with it. Whosoever wishes to say something to the master, he does. Why do you feel bad about it?

Bhola – Who are they to tell tales; they don't do any work themselves, they keep lying drugged the whole day long; how can they dare to complain against others?

Just then Bhavanisingh arrived, who was the headman. When he heard the debate he said – 'Why do you waste time in quarrels; won't you have time later for this? You didn't bother to ask about the well-being of the master or serve him in any way; you can only spend time fighting.'

This timely warning calmed everyone. Someone ran to sweep Premshankar's hut, someone else lay down his cot, another got stools, someone else got water, and some lighted up the lantern. Bhavanisingh got milk from his house. When the three men sat down, relaxed after dinner, Jwalasingh said, 'How do you make these people work? I find all of them worthless.'

Premshankar – Not at all, they might keep quarrelling, but they work with all their might. The amount of work I tell them for a day, they finish by afternoon itself.

Lala Prabhashankar was afraid in his heart that Premshankar might question him about his release. He wanted to keep the real reason a secret. He thus started talking to Jwalasingh. Ever since the latter had been transferred, he had not been at peace. His seniors were annoyed with him, so were the juniors, and so were the zamindars. He was questioned now and then. Once he also had to face suspension. He tried a lot for transfer to some other place, but couldn't be successful. He had become fed up of his job and was thinking of resigning from it. Lala Prabhashankar said, 'Don't even think about resignation; this is not an ordinary job. People go to the extent of licking the feel of rich and powerful men, and still can't get anywhere near it. Where else will you get so much respect and authority?'

Jwala – But one has to kill so much of one's soul for the sake of this respect and authority. If you try to do your work in an unbiased way, powerful men start bothering you. If you follow your principles independently, the higher officials get annoyed. Only that person can be successful out here who is a flatterer and is not bothered about any principles. I have never seen a generous man prospering here as yet. Only the clever and the politically smart fellows can move ahead. I have tried my best in all aspects. I cannot cope up in this environment. I am thinking of resigning and settling down in this farm with Babu Premshankar for the rest of my life, provided he does not have any objection to it.

Premshankar – Please do come, but make sure you are determined enough in your resolve.

Jwalasingh – Even if there are some loopholes, I hope they'll be covered up there.

Premshankar talked to his men abut some agricultural matters and left for Lala Prabhashankar's house around eight.

31

It was around ten o' clock at night. Jwalasingh lay down in Prabhashankar's sitting room after dinner, but Premshankar was attacked so much by mosquitoes that he couldn't sleep. He kept fanning himself for a while, but when it became impossible to stay inside, he came out and started strolling in the lobby. On the other side of the lobby was Gyanshankar's door. There was absolute stillness all around. The silence brought Premshankar's thoughts into focus. He started thinking, 'My life is so strange. Shraddha's room is right in front of me, but I cannot dare to even look at it. She must be reading some religious text at the moment, but I have no right to listen to her sweet voice.'

Suddenly he saw a woman coming out of Gyanshankar's door. He thought she must be a maid, going home after a day's work. 'But no, she's covered in a sheet from head to toe. Maids are not so conscious. Then who is she? She's walking like Shraddha; her height is also the same. But where will Shraddha go at this time of the night? No, she must be someone else. I am not sure. I must find out this mystery.' Though Premshankar did not find it proper to stalk an unknown and lonely woman, the curiosity to unlock the secret was so great that he couldn't restrain himself. After walking for some time in the lane the woman reached the main road and started going towards Dashashwamesh Ghat. Lanterns were burning on the road. The road wasn't closed, but very few people were around. Premshankar was now sure from watching her gait that it was none other than Shraddha. His surprise had no bounds. 'Where does she go at this time of the night?' He still had no doubts about her. He knew her to be absolutely devoted and loyal to her husband. But this trust further heightened his doubts about her true motives. He kept following her, till they reached the banks of the Ganga, with huge buildings all around. There was darkness in the lane, but some light came from the windows, as if a sleeping man was watching a dream. At every step, bulls could be seen lying about. At other places, dogs were licking empty plates strewn on the ground. Shraddha descended from the stairs of the ghat to reach the Ganga. Now Gremshankar became afraid, lest she had some dangerous resolve in her mind. His heart started trembling. He quickly moved down and stood at such a distance from Shraddha so that he could catch her in an instant if he wanted. The Ganga seemed asleep. At some places, water creatures could be heard making noises. Many beggars were sleeping on the stairs.

Premshankar was torn with guilt and pain at this moment. 'This is the result of my cruel nature – my hard-heartedness. I have always ignored her in the pride of my principles; I crushed her feelings and thought her religiosity to be below my standards. When the whole society has turned me out as a misfit, when so many misconceptions are floating around me, when I'm being considered irreligious, agnostic and an outcaste, then a religious woman can surely turn away from me. God knows how this poor woman has decided this terrible course after what kind of pain, soul-trouble and mental torture.'

Shraddha kept standing at the riverbank for quite some time. Then she slowly started entering the river. Premshankar knew there was no time to waste now. He took a leap and caught Shraddha on the last step of the ghat. Shraddha was startled; she grew doubtful and said, 'Who is it; go away!'

Premshankar said with guilty eyes – 'It's me; the unfortunate Premshankar'. Shraddha looked carefully at her husband, and said in a scared tone, 'You – at this place?'

Premshankar – Yes, the court released me today. There was a feast at our uncle's place. When I came out after dinner I saw you coming here. I followed you. For God's sake get out of the water. Have mercy on me.

Shraddha came out of the water, stood on the stairs, and looked at the Ganga with folded hands, saying, 'Mother, you've heard my prayers; how can I sing your praises with my humble mouth? You have redeemed this unfortunate woman.'

Prem – How did you come so far in the dark? Didn't you feel afraid?

Shraddha – I've been coming here since many days; what's there to fear?

Prem – Don't you know what kind of rogues roam about in this place?

Shraddha took out a knife from her waist and said, 'This is enough for my protection. When you have no other support in the world you become fearless.

Prem – What would the family members be thinking about your visits to this place?

Shraddha – They can think what they like; what control do I have on someone else's mind? Initially I was afraid of the society. But now I am not bothered about it; I have recognized its true feature. It's like a silken net, beautiful to see but very complicated in reality. Very often it makes the right as wrong, and the wrong as right.'

Premshankar's heart leapt in joy; he said, 'Oh God, will the moon of my fate start shining again? Shraddha, I tell you honestly that I felt like going back to America many a times, but a minute string of hope kept holding me back always. I find a halo of your love and devotion spread around me. This strong flame works like a lamp in the darkness around my soul. I feel your good wishes shading me like a benevolent tree always. I find kindness in your rudeness, a loving heart in your passivity and a deep affection in your devotion. I have now understood that you are doing this ritual for my redemption. If my own love had been selfless, I would have been satisfied with this soulful union, but I am a lover of beauty and pleasure; a slave of desires and wants; I cannot be satisfied with this love of the soul.'

Shraddha – I can never get rid of the doubt that my union with you is against religion and anything that goes against it makes me tremble in fear.

Prem – How can this doubt be dispelled?

Shraddha – You know very well; still you ask me?

Prem – I want to hear it from you.

Shraddha – By repentance.

Prem – That same repentance which has been devised in the religious texts?

Shraddha – Yes.

Prem – Do you really believe that by taking bath in multiple rivers, by burning various kinds of wood, by eating atrocious things, and by feeding the Brahmins, I will be able to get rid of my impurity? I feel sorry that you follow such false concepts despite being so aware and intelligent!

One of Shraddha's hands was in Premshankar's hands. As soon as she heard his last sentence she pulled her hand out and closing her ears with her thumbs said, 'For God's sake, don't criticize the scriptures in front on me. We must adhere to whatever our holy men have prescribed in these texts. It's not correct to find fault with them. We do not have the wisdom to understand their deep instructions. We can only benefit by following them.'

Prem – You ask me to do something which is against my beliefs and principles. I refuse to admit that travelling abroad is a sin of any kind. In such a condition, you are being very unjust to me by asking me to do repentance.

Shraddha said with a deep sigh – Pride hasn't yet left your heart. Till the time you purge yourself of it, you won't understand the true preachings of the ascetics.

Thus saying, she started climbing the stairs. Premshankar couldn't say anything. He didn't have the courage to stop her. Gradually Shraddha entered the lane and disappeared in the dark.

Premshankar kept standing there for a while; he then suddenly woke up from this semi-unconscious state, almost like a patient getting up after remaining unconscious for a while. He got to know his true condition. 'Alas!' he thought, 'I have lost this opportunity. I gave my principles a greater importance than man. Principles are for human beings; human beings are not meant for principles. I couldn't even understand that! Agreed, I don't believe in repentance, but it could have brought happiness to the lives of two people. This love of principles has ruined us both. Why not go and tell Shraddha that I am ready to follow repentance. She must not have gone very far. Her beliefs might be false in my opinion, but are so strong. How selfless is her devotion to her husband, and how deeply rooted is her faith in religion.'

Premshankar was lost in these thoughts when he saw two people descending from upstairs. A mind needs to rest after deep and engaging thought. He also started looking carefully at those men. 'Who are they? What have they come to do here at this point of time?' Gradually the two came down and stood at some distance from Premshankar. Premshankar listened to their talk and recognized their voices. These two were Padmashankar and Tejshankar.

Tejshankar said, 'You have a bad habit of discussing everything with everybody. All these things are meant to be kept a secret. If one opens them to all, they become ineffective.'

Padma – I haven't told anyone.

Tej – Why? Today only you were telling Babu Jwalasingh that we would become ascetics. Long back you had told Amma the same thing. What's the use of telling all and sundry about it? We shall definitely become ascetics, but not now. First achieve this knowledge, keep one or two lakhs in store, and then you can leave home without care. Bhaiya is not bothered about us at all. If we too leave the house, how will Lalaji take care of so many family members? I won't be able to sit for the exam this time. Who can learn all this massive geography and history and even if one passes the matriculation exam, it doesn't promise you a kingdom. At best, one would find a job for fifteen or twenty rupees a month. We have been failing in exams since three years; we won't be given any place to study as it is.

Padma – Okay, I won't say anything to anyone. If we achieve this mantra, then uncle will surely win the case?

Tej – Haven't you seen that as yet? Lalaji was giving twenty thousand as bail, but the magistrate was refusing to take it. We prayed for three days and he's been released today. There was no need to pay a single penny as bail.

Padma – Chacha Sahib is a very nice man. I love him very much. It's our younger uncle whom I really fear.

Tej – It's he who has trapped our elder uncle. I am scared of these things or I would have offered prayers for one week and taken away his life.

Padma – He never even talks to me. I respect the younger aunt, or I would have beaten up Maya properly.

Tej – This time even Maya is going to Gorakhpur. He's going to study there only.

Padma – Ever since they've got a motorcar, Maya is in airs. No one is dying after a motorcar here.

Talking amongst themselves, they sat on the stairs. Premshankar got up and came near them, wanting to say something when Padmashankar let out a loud scream and Tejshankar stood up and started muttering something. Premshankar said, 'Don't be afraid; it's me.'

Tej – Chacha Sahib! How come you are here at this time?

Padma – I thought that a ghost had arrived.

Prem – You are wasting your time in such fraudulent things. This is so dangerous and will bring you nothing. You cannot achieve any kind of success through these mantras. Study properly, do some enterprise and develop a good character. That is the only mantra for wealth and fame. Get up from here.

The three men left for home. On the way back, Premshankar kept discussing things with the two teenagers. After reaching home, he tried to sleep again, but instead of mosquitoes, he was now confronted with another problem. This was Shraddha's last sentence, 'You haven't yet got rid of your pride.' Premshankar started analyzing his actions ruthlessly. He was opening the layers of his consciousness and could feel every second that he was really an icon of pride. He couldn't find any of his actions; any resolve devoid of it. It seemed as if his kindness and devotion to the poor also had an element of pride. He was now beginning to doubt whether a love of principles was just another form of pride only. On the other hand, Shraddha's religiosity was totally untouched by any such feeling.

Just then Jwalasingh came and asked, 'Will you keep on sleeping? It's morning now.'

Premshankar saw the door with a start and found that the day had dawned. He said, 'I just couldn't sleep a bit due to the mosquitoes! I have been lying awake all night.'

Jwala – And I kept sleeping on a single side till dawn.

Premshankar got up and started washing his hands and face. He had to do a lot of work today. Jwalasingh also freshened up. The two men were dressing up when Tejshankar got freshly made halwa, apple marmalade, fried pistachios, almonds and hot milk for their breakfast.

Jawalasingh said, 'Your uncle is an excellent host. It seems as if he takes real delight in caring for guests, and here are we, who feel depressed even by looking upon a guest. Whatever we do is only to follow the convention; we actually pray for him to depart as soon as possible.'

Prem – Such pure souls are slowly disappearing from this world. Wherever you see, people are only engaged in serving their selfish interests. My uncle takes such meals that are not even thinkable for the richest of men. He is himself skilled in culinary arts. But he's more interested in feeding others rather than feeding himself. I often feel like learning this art from him if time permits.

Both the friends took their breakfast and taking their leave from Lala Prabhashankar left for home. Jwalasingh said, 'We must fix up a lawyer.'

Prem – Yes, that's most important. Let's see if we can find someone. All seem to have refused my uncle.

Jwala – I know Dr. Irfan Ali very well. Come, let's go to him first.

Prem – I don't think he'll agree. He has already talked to Gyanshankar.

Jwala – No authority letter has been issued as yet. Gyanshankar is not so foolish that he will spend thousands without reason. Whatever he wanted has been fulfilled by the police. The entire village of Lakhanpur has got trapped. Why should he appoint a lawyer now?

Doctor Sahib was roaming in his garden. On seeing the two men, he came forward to greet them and took them inside his bungalow.

Doctor – (to Jwalasingh) I have met you after a long time. Nowadays you are posted at Hardoi I guess? Your statement shut up the mouths of the policemen. But remember, you will have to bear its repercussions.

Jwala – There will be no chance for that. I have come to hate these double standards, and have decided to resign.

Doctor – The situation is such that no self-respecting man can bear it. Only those men can flourish here, whose conscience is dead. Take my profession for instance; it is said that it is a free profession. But Lala Prabhashankar (looking towards Premshankar) could not find any lawyer to defend you. I wonder why he didn't come to me.

Jwala – We have come precisely to atone for that mistake. You will have to have mercy on the poor farmers.

Doctor – I am ready for this service. I have an old enmity with the police. I am on the lookout for such cases. This will be my last case. I have also come to hate the legal profession. I have applied in the university. If it gets approved I too will wind up everything and go there.

32

Premshankar was much consoled after talking to Dr. Irfan Ali. He wanted some concession in the fees also, but was hesitant to say anything in this regard just then. Suddenly, our well-known persona, Syed Ijaad Hussain entered the room and after greeting Jwalasingh, stood in front of him. There was a Hindu youth accompanying him, who appeared to be quite rich from his demeanour.

Jwalasingh – Please come! Hope you are doing well. Which department are you serving now?

Ijaad – Ever since you left, I too bid farewell to this job. Life was getting spent out in serving the wants of the stomach. I have now decided to serve the nation. I have opened Anjuman Ittehad (association for concord) for this purpose. Its main motive is to promote brotherhood amongst the Hindus and the Muslims. I think it's a major issue facing our country. If you both agree to grace our organization with your blessed feet, I will think myself to be fortunate.

Jwala – You are doing true service to the nation.

Ijaad – Thank God, you have understood my real purpose. People otherwise make fun of me by calling me Mian Ittehad (Mr. Unifier). They often taunt my organization. I am called a selfish and self-oriented man. I take all these insults in my stride. When I find the two communities (Hindus and Muslims) separate and divided my heart breaks into pieces. The affection and virtuosity that's the basis of any race is slowly getting dissipated. If a Hindu professes faith in Islam, noises are afloat that the Hindu race is getting destroyed. If a Hindu gets a high position Muslims start protesting. Some say Islam goes down the drain; others find its ship drowning in deep waters. Curse on the devil! Religion is meant to redeem your soul; it's not a means to earn worldly pleasures. Our maulvis and priests further promote this racial enmity. My voice is a lonely cry in a noisy musical but my pain and respect for the nation doesn't let me keep quiet. I keep shouting at the top of my voice whether anyone listens to me or not. My organization has about hundred members at present. Around seventy of them are Hindus and thirty are Muslims. With their co-operation, I have set up a small school and a library. We have further thought of setting up a common prayer room, which should have a Shiva temple on one side, and a Masjid on the other. We have also laid down the foundation for an orphanage. We will admit orphans from both the communities. But no buildings have been made as yet. All these plans are dependent on money. This poor man has sacrificed all he had. Now it's up to the society; whether to continue it, or shut it down. Why, Doctor Sahib, did you get my gift deed ready?

Irfan Ali – I am waiting for a holiday so that I can do your work at leisure.

Premshankar said respectfully, 'People like Syed Sahib are a blessing for the nation. I donate a humble amount of hundred rupees to the organization, and fifty mans of wheat, five mans sugar and twenty rupees monthly for the orphanage.

Ijaad Hussain – God will definitely reward you for this. If you permit, should we add your name in the list of trustees!

Premshankar – I don't deserve this honour.

Ijaad – No sir, you will have to accede to my request. God has given you a compassionate heart. And why not, you happen to be late Lala Jatashankar's son whose kindness to the poor benefitted the whole city. The poor shall bless you and the organization shall be ever grateful to you.

Irfan Ali asked Jwalasingh, 'How long are you planning to stay here?'

Jwala – I can't say anything with surety. I came with an intention to spend the rest of my life in the service of Babu Premshankar. I have decided to resign from government service.

Irfan Ali – Great! You both are such lively men. Pray to God that I too am blessed with the wealth of contentment and am benefitted by your company.

Jwalasingh said with a smile, 'Get our people released; we shall pray for you day and night.'

Irfan Ali smiled and replied, 'This is a difficult condition, but I accept it. If Dr. Chopra gives a statement in our favour, we shall win the game.'

Ijaad – Please pay attention to this poor man now. He stays in my colony. He owns a big cloth shop. His elder brother is quite rude to him. He doesn't give him any pocket money, doesn't show him any accounts and eats up the entire profit. Yesterday he spoke very roughly to him. When he owns half the share, then why shouldn't he claim it? He is an adult, knows his right and wrong and does not want to live on his brother's charity. Say, Bhai Mathuradas, tell Barrister Sahib what you want.

Mathuradas stared at the ground and looking partially at Ijaad Hussain, said, 'I only want that you should make my brother patch up with me. Yesterday I had abused him. Now he says, 'You take care of the house; I won't be bothered about anything.' He has thrown away all keys and has stopped going to the shop.'

Ijaad Hussain looked at Mathuradas with an angry look and said, 'Why don't you state you purpose clearly?' You must have understood his motive. He is still inexperienced doesn't know how to talk; that's why he's suffering so much. He wants you to apply for his claim in the shop, but doesn't want to aggravate the matter; only wants a peaceful separation. 'Is that right?'

Mathuradas – (in a simple way) Yes, I just want to patch up with him.

Munshi Ramzan Ali was the steno in Jwalasingh's office. Ijaad Hussain took Mathuradas to his room. It was a big office. Many people were sitting and writing out papers. Ramzan Ali asked, 'How much is the claim for?'

Ijaad Hussain – About one lakh rupees.

Ramzan Ali wrote out the authority letter. Court fees, fees for the witnesses, wages and tips, all were written and demanded which Mathuradas gave white watching Ijaad Hussain with a distrustful eye, as if a peasant takes out money reluctantly to pay a priest. And then the two men left for their homes.

On the way Mathuradas said, 'You have actually made me fight with my brother. Thousands of rupees have been paid and the court fee is still pending.'

Ijaad Hussain said, 'You won't be grateful to me that I have paved the way for you to be independent of your brother? You will be the master of half the shop; on top of it you are complaining about it.'

33

Dr. Priyanath Chopra was a very generous, thoughtful and open-hearted person. He had a good knowledge of medicine and most importantly, his nature was very soft and polite. If a part of the patient's share of vegetables, milk, butter and fuel reached his home, it was only due to an old convention. This was followed even before he came here. He didn't find any reason to intervene into it. Therefore, no one could defame him, nor did he find any particular corruption in it. He used to charge only half the fees for employees having less salary, and took only a nominal fee for night visits as well. His government dispensary used to give free medicines, thus his practice was better than that of other doctors. His income was therefore quite good. When he came here three years ago, he just had a bicycle; now he had a carriage. Small prams were there for his children to stroll around. Furniture and carpets in his home also belonged to the hospital. He also escaped giving salary to the servants from his own pocket. But after all this budgeting, when he compared his situation with the district's sub-engineer or some important lawyers, he wasn't particularly happy. Though he did find many occasions to fulfill his financial ambitions, thoughtfulness never allowed him to go astray. After leaving college, he followed his duty fearlessly for many years, but when he had to suffer due to appearing as a witness against the police, he changed his stance. He used to decide his policy after seeing the leanings of the police, yet it disturbed him mentally to fix his diagnosis according to the wishes of the police. Thus, when Ghaus Khan's dead body was sent to him for inspection, he was caught in a great dilemma. The diagnosis said it was the doing of a single person; the murder had occurred in a single blow, but the police believed that a whole gang was involved. The poor doctor was very nonplussed. This was a serious charge. The police had left no stone unturned to prove it right. To refute them was to strike enmity with them and his experience told him it was a very expensive deal. It was a kind of unrewarded supplication. For many days, he kept arguing with himself but his mind refused to work. In the meanwhile, Gyanshankar saw him with a letter from Rani Gayatri and a reward of five hundred rupees. The Rani had recognized his prominence and fame after listening to public views about him. She wanted him to write a book on child care. Besides this, she had appointed him as her family doctor, with a promise of hundred rupees per visit. The doctor was highly pleased. He looked at Gyanshankar with grateful eyes and said, 'I have no words to thank Her Highness's benevolent sense of recognizing my abilities. Please take me to be your servant. This is all a result of your generosity, or else there are thousands of doctors like me lying all over the place.'

Gyanshankar replied suitably. The two men kept talking about issues relating to the nation and the times. The doctor claimed that he was far more able in medical knowledge than the I.M.S. people, and had treated many such terminal patients whom the former had refused to treat. But he still had no hopes of getting released from official slavery. His fate had decreed him to a subordinate position under newly educated men whose only credential was their foreign education.

In his reply, Gyanshankar only mentioned the political conditions of the state. While leaving he asked quite passively, 'What have you decided about the Lakhanpur case? The dead body must have been sent to you?'

Priyanath – Yes, the body was sent here. The signs indicate that it's just a single man's job, but the police wish to drag many people into it. What's there to hide; I cannot dissatisfy the police but it is hateful to my soul to trap so many innocent men like this.

Gyanshankar – It is quite possible that the inference you have reached after observing the signs, might be true, but actually this murder is the result of a conspiracy hatched by many people. Lakhanpur is my own village.

Priyanath – Okay, Lakhanpur is your village? So this karinda was your employee?

Gyan – Yes, he was and very loyal and efficient in his work. The villagers had a grudge against him that he never mingled with them. In every matter, he first thought about my profit or loss. This is the punishment he has received for his loyalty. But I do not view this incident from the police point of view. The murder has been done; whether by one person or many. For me, this issue is far more complicated. The question is regarding the zamindar and the peasants. If the murderers are not suitably punished, such accidents will keep occurring day in and day out, and it will be too difficult for zamindars to save their lives.

After lending this colour to the present problem Gyanshankar took his leave. Though Dr. Chopra persisted in his opinion about the state of the crime, now this opinion wasn't without a reward. A sum of five hundred rupees; hundred rupees per visit; a hope of earning around ten thousand a year and most of all the goodwill of the police. There was no need to think any more about it.

The only fear he had was regarding Dr. Irfan Ali's defence of the case. He was famous for it. So Priyanath studied many texts regarding the topic and found many points to favour his opinion. He didn't think for a second about the unjust repercussions of his diagnosis on so many innocent people. He couldn't afford to care about it. How narrow our point of view becomes on such important occasions?

It was ten in the morning. Dr. Chopra carried a bundle of books with him and left for the court. His heart was beating fast. He was afraid of losing his stand in the cross-questioning. As soon as he reached there, the magistrate summoned him. When he reached the witness box and saw the accused looking at him with helpless eyes, his heart became unstable for a second. But it was a momentary rush; it came and went off. He analyzed the murder with great seriousness and emotional feeling. 'The signs indicate that it's the work of only one man. But the murderers have tried to act very cleverly. They seem to be very skilled in it. The real reason behind death is not any assault by an axe or a weapon, but strangling of throat and it's quite impossible to suffocate a strong man like Ghaus Khan without the help of a number of men. Once he died they seem to have sliced his throat so that it might appear to be the work of one person.'

Irfan Ali started his cross-questioning.

'Which exam have you passed?'

'I am an L.M.S. from Lahore, and an M.B. from Calcutta.'

'What's your age?'

'Forty years.'

'Where's your residence?'

'Delhi.'

'Are you married? If yes, do you have children or not?'

'I am married and have many children.'

'How much do you spend monthly on their expenses?'

Irfan Ali was asking these questions with such a scholarly confidence as if the whole case depended on them. On each question, he looked at Jwalasingh with such pride as if he wanted applause for his brilliant sense of justice from him. But the magistrate objected to his last question saying, 'What's you motive in asking such a question?'

Irfan Ali said proudly – You will soon come to know my purpose.

He then started questioning Priyanath. Poor Priyanath was already scared in heart of hearts, 'God knows what trap this fellow is laying out for me?'

Irfan Ali – Please answer my last question?

'I do not keep a record of those expenses.'

'How much milk do you get monthly and on what price?'

'This account is kept by my servants.'

'How much do you spend monthly on ghee?'

'I cannot answer these domestic questions without asking my servants.'

Irfan Ali said to the magistrate, 'My questions must be answered satsifactorily.'

Magistrate – I don't understand what you mean by such questions?

Irfan Ali – My motive is to expose the real virtuosity of this witness. By these questions I want to prove that he's not a man of high principles.

Magistrate – I refuse to register these questions.

Irfan Ali – Then I too refuse to do all questioning.

Thus saying, the Barrister came out of the hearing place and said to Jwalasingh, 'Did you see how this fellow was taking such undue sides! God! I would have torn Doctor Sahib apart. I never do any purposeless questioning. I wanted to prove that someone who can be bought for menial amounts cannot remain unbiased in such a significant case. Still, nothing is lost. Let the case go to the civil court; I will see him there.'

After one hour the magistrate gave his decision – All accused be sent to the session's court.

It was evening time. These tortured souls had to leave for the jail once again. There was misery written on their faces. Priyanath's statement had disappointed the villagers badly. They could never imagine that such a high official could lean towards untruth due to temporary lures. All were going with their heads bent down. Only Manohar was shedding tears.

Just then Priyanath's carriage passed on the road. The accused looked at him with disrespectful eyes. They seemed to be saying, 'You had no mercy on our poor souls.' Doctor Sahib also saw them; his eyes too reflected a tiny feeling of guilt.

34

When the case was handed over to the session's court and Gyanshankar was assured that the accused will not be allowed to escape, he appointed Faizullah in place of Ghaus Khan and left for Gorakhpur. Gayatri had written many letters asking him to return. He also took Mayashankar along with him. Vidya insisted that she would be sad and forlorn without the child, but Gyanshankar refused to listen to her.

In the past one month Gyanshankar had arrived at a solution to the problem that had been engaging his mind for many years. He had decided upon a way to reach the inner doors of Gayatri Devi's heart. There were two branches of this way; one was oppositional, and the other, resolutional. Gyanshankar decided to follow the latter. This much he knew that it was far too difficult to remove Gayatri's religious beliefs, which were guarding her from desires like the unassailable walls of a strong fort. Gyanshankar had failed in this attempt earlier also and there seemed no reason that he would not fail again, if he tried the earlier way. In comparison to this, the other way was approachable and easy to follow. Instead of removing those religious beliefs, why not work upon strengthening them further? Instead of destroying a building, why not coat its walls further with the same colour? Instead of trying to make her his own; why not become hers, in the way that she desired?

After reaching Gorakhpur, Gyanshankar tried to work far more enthusiastically and earnestly on this project. The work on the guest house had been postponed. Now he started getting it done under his own supervision instead of appointing outside contractors. In front of it, he laid the foundation stone of a temple as well. Almost daily, he took his motorcar and went on a round of the region and came back by evening. No karinda or employee could dare to smuggle even a penny under his careful eye. No peon or servant could torture the tenants, and no tenant could delay paying the rent even by a day. The co-operative bank started running successfully. The farmers started getting free from the trap of the moneylenders and could now afford to sell the foodgrains on their own prices instead of those negotiated by the buyers. Seeing such efficient management on part of

Gyanshankar, Gayatri's goodwill had started assuming the form of deep respect. She tried to pay back the obligation in various ways. She sent many gifts for Vidya and doted upon Mayashankar to no end. He had two tongas to ride and two tutors to give him lessons. One came in the morning the other in the evening. He had two servants appointed for his care. Gayatri fed him personally in the morning. She used to cook many delicacies for him. She told him stories and listened to his childish tales. She often gave him gifts and rewards. Mayashankar almost forgot his own mother due to such lavish care. He was such a well-mannered, polite and simple child that within a short span, Gayatri started loving him deeply.

Gyanshankar's life also underwent a sea-change. He now started listening to the Bhagwat daily in the evening. Few holy men usually came around, some friends used to gather, some local religious men also came and a religious meeting of sorts used to happen. They talked about lord Krishna, his life and loves, and sang devotional songs. Very often, people started crying out of devotion and Gyanshankar was the one who wept the most. He seemed to have sold himself for love.

One of these days, Gayatri said to him, 'There is so much of Krishna devotion happening at your place; if you can arrange for a partition, I would also like to come.' Gyanshankar looked at Gayatri with respectful eyes and said, 'All this is a result of your blessed company. You have shown me this holy way and I see you as my Guru. Many months ago I was trapped in the net of wants, and was a slave of my desires, lusts and the material world. You told me why one should stay in this world with a sense of detatchment. You are an ascetic despite being so wealthy. Your life has been the ultimate instruction for me.'

Gayatri thought Gyanshankar to be the ocean of knowledge and enlightenment. 'This great man, whose skilful pen could endow me with the little of the 'Queen', whose quotes should impress the highest of British officials and whose administration has been applauded in the whole district – such a man should be my devotee' – this very thought overwhelmed her proud heart. On these occasions, she often remembered her late husband. She said politely, 'Babuji, all this is the grace of God. He has blessed you with this devotion or else people keep listening to these religious preachings all their lives and still remain distant from the ultimate knowledge. If you had met my husband you would have been pleased by his very encounter. He was an apostle of religion and love. Whatever I am today is due to his efforts. I try to follow whatever he has taught me; otherwise I am not so capable that I could have tasted the fruit of devotion.'

Gyanshankar – I am also sorry that I have been deprived from meeting that great soul. If his teachings are so powerful he himself must have been so talented! I am sometimes blessed by his appearance in my dreams. What a pleasing picture! A light of love seemed to be emitting from his face. He seemed to be an image of Lord Krishna himself.

From the next day onwards, the arrangements for a partition were made, and Gayatri started participating daily in the religious meeting held at Gyanshankar's place. The number of devotees started increasing every day. During the singing of songs, people started dancing, overcome with emotion. Gayatri's heart was also touched by these waves of love. Even Gyanshankar could not reamin stable in such an environment. The puristic love stories of Krishna lighted up his heart with love for a second, and in this light, he found his wickedness and meanness quite hateful. But as soon as the congregation ended, this momentary light faded away in the darkness of his selfishness. The childlike pranks of lord Krishna, his kiddish talk, Yashoda's divine motherly love, the affection of the milkmaids, the emotional secrets of love, the sweet tunes of the flute, and the stories of Yamuna soirees, all elated the people with a divine sense of happiness. In the eyes of the agnostics, these stories might have been embarrassing, but the hearts of these devotees were delighted with merely listening to them. As soon as the names of Radha and Yashoda were uttered, a stream of tears started flowing from their eyes. They could experience the magic that lay in Krishna's name.

One of these days, a Rasleela group come from Vrindavan and continued doing shows for a month. The whole city came over to watch them. Gyanshankar welcomed them wholeheartedly, assuming himself as the very image of love. He treated everyone equally. Special arrangements had been made for women. There, Gayatri welcomed them, met their children affectionately and distributed sweets amongst them. The day Krishna's departure for Mathura was enacted, there was such a rush of spectators that there wasn't any space to breathe. The heartrending dialogues of Yashoda and Nand moved the audience to tears. Many of them lost their senses crying and Gayatri too fell down unconscious. When she returned to her senses, she found herself in her bedroom. There was stillness all around, and only Gyanshankar was standing there, fanning her. Gayatri was overcome by a strange listlessness at the moment. When a man runs towards shade like a tired, impatient traveller, his heart overflows with a pure, unmaliced kind of love. She signalled Gyanshankar to sit down and kept her head in his lap with a childlike simplicity, saying in a desirous way, 'Please take me to Vrindavan.' The third day the Rasleela got over.

The same day Gyanshankar left for Vrindavan with Gayatri, with great pomp and show.

35

The case is going on in the court of the session's judge since a month. The accused have given a statement again. Today was Manohar's turn. The court almost resembled a small fair. Manohar narrated the entire incident from beginning to end with a fearless determination and had the public been given the authority to judge, the rest of the accused would have been definitely released, but the court was restrained under rules and regulations. Manohar's last words were very touching – 'Sarkar, the reality is that which I have just told you. I have killed Ghaus Khan with this very axe and these very hands. I had no one to advise or help me. Now you have the authority to either hang the entire village, or send it to the Andamans, or release them. Whatever Faizu, Bisesar or the Daroga have said, is all false. I can't say about the Daroga, but if you call Faizu and Bisesar at home, and assure them that the police will not threaten them, the veracity of my statement can be tested; what else can I say? Those people must be having a heart of stone who can put these poor men to gallows. God sees everything. Bisesar and Faizu are lowly men, and the Daroga is surviving on bribes, but how come a man like Dr. Sahib who is such a great scholar, could have spoken such lies; I am indeed surprised. What else can I say except that the poor are condemned to such a fate that they are punished without fault? I can only pray to the government and the judges that they are sitting on the seat of justice; they should separate the truth from falsehood, with their sense of judgement.'

The court was dismissed. All the troubled men went back to the jail. Most of them had told themselves that whatever's written in their fate is bound to happen, but Dukhran Bhagat was not at peace. He was repeatedly instigated to take Manohar to task. But he couldn't do anything as Manohar was kept separately from others. At best, he could only keep taunting Balraj as a consolation. When he heard Manohar's statement today he was all the more annoyed. 'When everything has been lost, he's trying to make amends. Why didn't he think rationally when he had picked up the axe on a minor pretext?' On the way to jail he found an opportunity to take out his anger on Manohar. He said, 'What nonsense were you talking about today? A man should think before shooting an arrow as to whom it would hit. When it has left the bow, what's to be gained by regret? Because of you the whole village has been ruined. Who will care for our orphaned kids and women? They must be starving for food. You brought the entire village to destruction.'

Manohar was tortured by the same guilt night and day. He was conscious of it even while murdering Ghaus Khan. That is why he had owned up his crime in the police station. He tried to do whatever he could to save the village and was sure that however repentant he might be feeling the villagers must have pardoned him and must be sympathetic towards him. The inner fire of guilt was enough to burn him; there wasn't any need to ignite it further. On hearing Dukhran's bitter words, he was hurt in a way a ripe wound is further attacked. But he couldn't say anything in reply.

Today, Premshankar had sent a few dishes for the accused after taking permission from the Daroga. He used to appease the small employees of the jail even against his principles, so that the latter would not torture the accused. Life's experiences had taught him that man is a far more precious and respectable entity than principles. The rest of the men ate tastefully, but Manohar's heart was burning with guilt. His hunger refused to be excited even by the tempting smell of those delicacies. The words that were earlier locked in his heart were now ringing in his ears – 'You have destroyed the whole village; you brought ruin upon everybody. Yes, this mark of shame is forever attached to my name, it will never be removed. Those who are yet children must be abusing me. Their children, when they come to know about me, will call me a traitor. When men can think like this, who are aware of everything, who know that I did everything I could to save the village and whatever is happening is a turn of fate; what must the women be thinking, who are simple and ignorant by nature? Poor Bilasi must be hiding her face from everyone. She must be finding it difficult to leave the house and why shouldn't people taunt her? They are bearing the brunt of my deeds so they have every right to do so. Right now they must be having the earlier produce to eat, but there's no one to sow the fields for the next season. When nothing will grow in April, children will cry for food, then who will come to their rescue? It seems there are bugs in this blanket, they are pinching me like anything, and this is not a problem of one or two years; if we all are sent to the Andamans, we will cry for the rest of our lives. Qadir Mian's son will take care of the house but the rest will be devastated, and all because of me.'

Thus thinking, Manohar fell asleep. He saw a dream that thousands of men have gathered in a huge ground. 'The gallows are ready and I am being hanged. All the eyes are staring at me with hate. All over, sounds are coming that he has ruined us all.' Then he felt as if he has died and many ghosts have surrounded him saying that he has made them starve; he is a sinner; he should be burnt in fire. A scream escaped his lips. He got up with a start. The room was dark, but even after waking up; the same ghostly figures seemed to be hovering around him. Manohar's heart was beating very fast. He wanted to escape and run away, but the doors were closed.

Suddenly, a thought occurred to Manohar, 'Should I remain alive only to listen to all this hateful criticism? The whole village; the entire countryside hate me. Balraj too must be hating me in heart of hearts. He tried to drive sense into me, but I never listened to him. People must be saying that after getting the whole village arrested, he's trying to be a hero. He has no shame; why doesn't he kill himself! Balraj too must be receiving taunts from all sides; his heart would be mourning my heinous deed. Oh God! What kind of a light is this! No, it's not light. These are reddish eyes of a ghost; they are coming towards me! Oh Lord! What to do?' Manohar's legs started shaking. Those red eyes seemed to be approaching him every second. He could neither see in their direction nor take away his eyes from them as if a devilish power had tied up his vision. After a second, Manohar found a group of eyes at a single place, as if it was a huge bunch of lighted, fiery, bloodshot eyes! No body, head or any other organ; only hurtful eyes, which seemed to be heading for him like broken stars. Another second passed, and this group of eyes started assuming a body and became Ghaus Khan's murdered image. A loud sound came from outside. Manohar ran towards the back wall, but in just one step, his head banged against the wall and he fell down. Then it seemed as if someone was opening the lock of the door. Someone called out, 'Manohar! Manohar!' Manohar recognized the voice. It was the Daroga. He came back to his senses. He loudly replied, 'Yes Sahib, I am awake.' From the hellish world he came back to the human world. He now knew the mystery behind the group of eyes. It was the light of the Daroga's lantern which was coming into the cell through the slit in the door. A small thing had caused such mental suffering. The Daroga had been doing his rounds of the jail.

After the Daroga went away, Manohar became somewhat cautious. His doubtful hallucinations became quiet, but he was again lost in the worries about his insults and curses. He started thinking, 'There are some who enable a village to prosper, and people sing their praises for eternity. And here I am who has made the village deserted. Now no one would like to take my name in the morning. It seems all will be banished for life, no one shall be spared. God knows how long the case will stretch. Either for one month, or two. For all these days, I will keep getting cursed and abused. Today Dukhran uttered his feelings; tomorrow someone else will do the same. Even Qadir Khan must be annoyed with this arrest. I fear, even Balraj might open up negatively against me. Alas! I didn't even care for his youth; my son has been tortured by my own hands … My young child … Oh God! I can't bear this sorrow anymore. Who knows when the hanging will take place! If I am also banished like all these people then I will be condemned to hear their curses for a lifetime. Balraj, how can I save you? Who knows, the judge may decide that he's a strong youth, he alone must have struck the axe. O God! What will happen then? Will I have to see all this with my own eyes? No, it's far better to die than to live like this. A handicapped man has no life worth a penny. Yes, there's only one solution - Yes!'

36

The appointment of Faizullah Khan on the post of Ghaus Khan was like sprinkling salt on the wounds of the poor villagers. Right from the first day, there was a sense of unease and Faizu did not feel any need to control the opposition. He was now the authoritative ruler of the entire village. His order was as good as law itself. No one could utter even a sigh of opposition. All the milk, ghee, fuel, fodder, vegetables, ploughs and oxen that were there in the village became his property. The rights which Ghaus Khan could not acquire in a lifetime became available to Faizullah from the first day itself by virtue of fate and its workings. In the open ground of injustice and selfishness, the unbridled horses of his greed had no fear of any fall. Initially, he had some doubts about Kartarsingh, but his political abilities soon defeated the latter's lack of devotion. He was now his loyal and obedient servant; his chief well-wisher. He now read the Ramayana on top of his voice. He gathered all kinds of stones in the village in front of the chaupal and offered them water and rituals. He rubbed sandalwood for hours, made bhaang; there was no one to stop him. Everyday, Faizullah took a round of the village on his tonga and Kartar and Binda Maharaj followed him with sticks in their hands. Whatever they could extort from people, they took it and came back. In the month of January, Bilasi was penalized for pending land rent and all her animals were seized. Faizu was sure that no one would be able to pay the rent in April. So he thought of dismissing everyone and acqire all land in one go. 'I shall disown the entire village, and my income will be doubled.' But he couldn't be satisfied only with this evil thought. It was difficult for him to exercise his authority without scoldings or abuses. Therefore this policy was regularly put to good use. Bilasi never left the house out of fear. Her rabi crops were drying up in the fields, but there was no one to water them. She didn't have any oxen of her own and did not have the courage to ask anyone for ploughing.

One of such evenings, Bilasi was sitting at her door, weeping at her condition. She could only do this nowadays. The news of Manohar's suicide had reached her many days ago. She did not mourn her own ruin so much as she mourned the fact that there was no one to console her. Almost everyone around used to taunt her. No one visited her or spoke to her. If out of boredom, she went to someone's house, there too she was insulted. She was treated like a serpent, whose poison had engulfed the entire village in the fold of death. What's worst, her own daughter-in-law used to taunt her. Suddenly she heard that Sukhu Chaudhary had come back and was sitting in the village temple. She set out for the temple immediately. She was craving for sympathy. She really wanted to know what Sukhu Chaudhary thought about the recent incidents. She was hopeful that Sukhu would express his opinion in an unbiased way. When she reached near the temple she found many women and girls gathered over there. Sukhu had a flowing beard, a monkey cap on his head, and a shawl around his shoulders with Ram printed all over. He seemed very sad and upset. The women were discussing Ghaus Khan's murder with him. They were gossiping about Manohar in their different ways. Bilasi stood near the temple when Sukhu saw her and said, 'Come Bilasi, come and sit. I was about to come to you myself.'

Bilasi – Were you alright?

Sukhu – I am still alive; that's all. When I got out of the jail, I went to Badrinath. From there, I went to Jagannathpuri. I met a Mahatma in Badrinath, and I became his disciple. I now survive on charity. I have become free from the trap of running a household.

Bilasi asked fearfully, 'You must have heard about our situation.'

Sukhu – Yes, ever since I came, those discussions have been going on, and after listening to them, I've gained such a respectful feeling towards you that I feel like worshipping you. You are a warrior though by birth you might be a dairy farmer's daughter. You have done precisely what warrior women do. Manohar is a warrior too; he has done what warriors do in such a situation. He was a brave soul. His tombstone will be built in this temple and he will be worshipped here. It doesn't have any idol as yet; it will now have a statue of that brave man. He died for the honour of the village, and for the honour of his wife. All these lowly souls are busy criticizing him. They say he has ruined the village. They do not have any shame or any sense of pride or honour. He hasn't brought ruin, but martyrdom to the village, and has redeemed it. It is the duty of men to protect their women. Manohar did his duty well. Only he can defame him who has lost his soul; who has turned shameless. Even if a few men in the village are hanged there's nothing to worry; in our history thousands have lost their heads after a single woman. Ravana lost his kingdom due to Sita. Eighteen lakh warriors were killed due to Draupadi. If a few lives are lost to protect one's honour, what's the big deal? Bless you Manohar! Blessed be your honour, your valour, and your brave heart.

Every single word spoken by Sukhu was echoing with brave feelings. Bilasi's heart was tingling with joy at these praises. She wanted to keep her head at Sukhu's feet, but other women were staring at him with curiosity at these strange words.

After a second, Sukhu asked Bilasi – What's the state of your crops?

Bilasi's fields were drying up, but she didn't want to upset Sukhu by telling him her tale of woe. She said, 'Dada, the fields are fine with your blessings; there's nothing to worry.'

Many other holy men arrived, who seemed to be Sukhu's comrades. They lit up a fire and started smoking marijuana. The villagers started leaving the place one by one. When Bilasi started leaving, Sukhu said, 'Bilasi, I will go from here late at night, and will come back after a few months. Then the idol will be put up here. We want to collect donations for it. If you have any problem please let me know.'

Bilasi – No Dada, there's no problem, by your grace.

Sukhu left in the morning, but Bilasi was deeply affected by his emotional talk. She now refused to listen to the accusations of the villagers like a downtrodden being, nor could anyone openly taunt her anymore. Moreover, her demeanour and way of talking started reflecting a deep self-pride. She sometimes used to boast about herself, telling her neighbours, 'You can sell your honour to save your skins; people like us can sacrifice our lives to save our honour. I became a widow; my house was destroyed, so what; I didn't have to cut a sorry figure in front of anyone. I kept my honour.' She didn't feel the separation from her husband and son so unbearably now.

Once she boasted about herself so much that her daughter-in-law couldn't bear it. She said annoyingly, 'Amma, do not sprinkle salt on our wounds by such talk. You have enjoyed all the pleasures of life; what if you have become a widow now? Ask those poor women who have a lifetime ahead and who have not seen any pleasant phase in their lives. Everyone loves his or her honour but it's difficult to bear a lifetime of widowhood for its sake. What's the big deal for you; it was natural for you to become a widow; now or a few days later. If you too had been young, I would have seen how much you had bothered about honour.'

Bilasi was hurt and shocked. She stopped talking to her daughter-in-law since that day; in fact even stopped mentioning Balraj. She started hating the son who was the apple of her eyes. Her daughter-in-law's rude words had ended that stream of motherly love, which had been the edifice supporting her life for the past twenty-four years. For some days, she expressed her anger by keeping silent, but when this experiment failed to produce any results she started criticizing her daughter-in-law. There were many such women in the village who disliked their daughter-in-laws. They were sympathetic towards Bilasi. Gradually, it so happened that all mother-in-laws used to gather in Bilasi's sitting area and vent out their feelings against their daughter-in-laws. One the other side, the latter also started associating to defend themselves. This meeting took place at Dukhran Bhagat's house. Bilasi's daughter-in-law was its chief perpetrator. Thus the opposition between the two started rising. Everything that was discussed at those two places used to be communicated secretly to both parties. They kept reacting and counteracting to each other and the process went on. This kind of cross-defence was far more enjoyable than shedding tears on one's deplorable condition. There was a lively kind of joy in this war of words. An envious interaction is probably far more capable of taking away sorrow than any kind of melodious music.

They were engaged in such petty wars, and on the other hand, the crops were drying out in the fields. Mian Faizullah was beaming at the sight of the dried fields. Eventually the month of April arrived. The demands for tax payments came up. The villagers now took stock of the situation. They had forgotten that taxes had to be paid on time. In a state of poverty, man becomes subservient to fate. Faizullah began his atrocities. He made people stand out in the sun and inflicted beatings on many others. An animal-like behaviour was ensued upon the poor women; their bangles were broken, and hair were pulled apart. Who was there to stop these tyrannies now? The saying that an insistence upon truth can destroy justice was proved to be wrong. Faizu knew very well that oil cannot be extracted from stones, but his chief motive behind these tortures was to destroy their self-respect. These evil deeds satisfied his animal nature to no end.

Gradually, the month of June also passed, but not a penny was paid as land tax. If the fields had foodgrains, any moneylender would have given them loans, but no one looks at a dry field. Finally Gyanshankar decided to file the case for disownment. Almost immediately, the tenants were penalized but the money could not be arranged by any means. No one was there to defend them; or object to these practices. Everyone believed that a decree would disown them from their land, and no one would be able to save them. Faizu and Kartar hopped around happily. 'Now we have won the game. Khan Sahib was lost, but we have acquired the whole village. There will be no tenant left now; we can increase the rates of land as much as we want. We shall extort two thousand in place of one. This miracle will be accredited to me. I shall be praised far and beyond.' These thoughts kept delighting Faizu Mian to no end.

Ultimately the day of the decision arrived. Kartarsingh took out his loose mulmul kurta and pink turban, polished his shoes with oil, rubbed his stick well, made his hair, and rubbed ash on his forehead. Faizullah got the saddle repaired, and took out his black achkan and white turban. Binda maharaj also wore a fresh vest and saffron dhoti. The labour was made to carry blankets and mats and the three men got ready to go to the court. The only delay was Khan Sahib's offering of namaz.

But the village was all quiet. Among the men, except for Qadir Khan's younger son, the rest were all people from lower castes, who had no notion of insults or honour, and he himself had no idea of legal formalities. Jhapat was so scared that he did not leave his house at all. The rest were women; those poor helpless beings had no knowledge of law. They were still divided into two camps which had been devised earlier. The old women said, 'Let the fields be gone, what do we have to gain from them? We are about to die. Even if the fields remain how are we to be benefitted? These queens should lose their pride.' Even Bilasi, who was the perpetrator of all these proceedings, was sitting in a carefree way. Their opponents now wanted a ceasefire, but they were being restrained partly by their pride and partly by the fear that their plea might be rejected.

Khan Sahib finished his namaz by eight o' clock. Binda Maharaj ate up his tobacco after breakfast and Kartarsingh ordered for his horse to be brought, when they saw Sukhu Chaudhary coming towards them. He had the same old attire; monkey-cap on head, sandalwood on forehead, shawl in the neck, and tongs in his hands. He came and sat down in the chaupal. The boys of the village who had been running along with him, stopped outside. Faizu asked, 'Say Chaudhary, how have you been? How long have you been released from jail?'

Chaudhary took the hookah from Kartar, took a deep shot and puffing out smoke from his mouth, said, 'Today is the date for disownment?'

Kartar – I can only say after looking at the papers. One or the other matter keeps going on here. How far can one remember?

Chaudhary – These poor men were already caught in trouble; this new problem has further toppled them.

Faizu – I was forced to do this. What else could I have done? I am tied up by the law. April, May, June – were the months I kept reminding them to pay, what else could I have done?

Thus saying, he looked at Chaudhary in a manner as if he was an incarnation of manners and kindness.

Chaudhary – If you get all your money today, the case will be dismissed?

Faizu looked at Chaudhary with surprise and said, 'It's the question of expenses as well.'

Chaudhary – Okay, tell me how much they owe you. Add up other expenditure also.

Thus saying, Chaudhary took out a bundle of notes from his waistband. He also took out some more money from a bag and started looking testfully at Khan Sahib. Faizu was dumbstruck; and Kartar's face lost colour, as if the news of a death had arrived. Binda Maharaj looked at the notes carefully. He was suspicious lest it might be the doing of black magic. No one could utter a word. The creeper of hope that they had been tending for years was about to be swallowed by a wild animal right in front of their eyes. For this single opportunity, they had planned so much, got into all kinds of politics, and done so many atrocities. And now when that auspicious moment came, a ruthless god was about to snatch it from them. Ghaus Khan's blood was about to show its colour, and now it was being proved worthless. Ultimately Faizu said on a serious note: 'Now the decision lies with the court.'

He wanted to scare the Chaudhary by naming the court.

Chaudhary – Very well, let's go there then.

Kartar said in a tone of moral wisdom, 'First these people should apply for an extension of payment period, then we shall respond legally to that application; after that whatever the judge will decide will have to be followed. How can we take money like that? It's against the rules.'

Binda Maharaj was busy thinking about a different problem – 'How has this fellow acquired so many rupees? He has just got out of the jail. The villagers can't give him a single penny. Whatever he had earlier he gave away for the construction of the pond and the temple. He must have found a magical potion which helps him make money. Holy men are capable of unbelievable deeds.'

Faizu understood that their fraud won't work with Sukhu. If he submitted the money in the court, all would be lost. He took off his shoes in a disappointed manner and started counting the expenses. The court fees, the bribes to various departments, the lawyer's fees, the gifts for the zamindar were added and then he said, 'There are seventeen hundred and fifty rupees in total.'

Chaudhary – Please see again, if any payment has been left. But do remember that if you charge a single penny over and above the account, it won't be good for you.

Binda Maharaj said doubtfully, 'Khan Sahib, please check everything again.'

Kartar – Everything has been counted; we do all this night and day; come and pay seventeen hundred and fifty.

Chaudhary – If you want seventeen hundred and fifty, take it in the court, here I will only pay one thousand.

Faizu – And the court expenses?

Suddenly Chaudhary picked up his pair of tongs and struck Faizullah's head with such a force that he fell down on the ground. He then said, 'This is the court expense; I can give more if you want. Dishonest man and a sinner; that's what you are. You call yourself a karinda. Yesterday's baniya calls himself a rich man today! You forgot your roots so soon. You too were a tenant of the zamindar. I have seen your house, your parents, family; everything. They are all toiling hard; engaged in unpaid labour out there. You read upto a few standards so you've lost your senses. You keep robbing the poor and the helpless. The case is for eight hundred rupees, and hundred rupees are the court expenses. I have gone and asked the court clerk. You are demanding seventeen hundred and fifty for it? And you Thakur; you too have forgotten yourself in the company of this Turk? You shout loudly reading the Ramayan, tell tales from the Bhagwat, and worship all kinds of stone idols; have you turned into a stone yourself? Why do you apply all this sandal on your face? What right do you have to do it? You have forgotten your religion after money? Do you want money? If money is there in your fate pick up this bag. (Thus saying Chaudhary threw the money bag towards Kartar). Just see if you have money written in your fate? Your heart is so sinful that even if you touch gold, it will turn to mud. Touch the bag and see, it will turn to stones.'

Kartar had initially spoken in a very rude tone. He wanted to show that he was not someone to be impressed by saffron robes. He wouldn't be fooled by all this but seeing Chaudhary's courage and listening to his harsh teachings, his passivity vanished. He now understood that this Chaudhary wasn't the one who used to tow the line of Ghaus Khan, but he did not wish to become a follower without testing him; in fact he wanted to expose his asceticism and take him to task. He looked at the money bag carefully; it was full of coins. He then picked it up reluctantly, but as soon as he picked it up, a most amazing sight was witnessed. All the coins turned into stones! Whether it was black magic or occult, who could tell? Whether it was a game show or an illusionist sight, no one could say except the Chaudhary. Only reddish stones could be seen in place of coins. The money bag fell from Kartar's hands. He folded his hands and fell at Chaudhary's feet with great devotion, saying, 'Baba, please excuse my sin; I am an impudent and evil sinner; please redeem me. I shall be in your service from now on; please take me out from the pit of greed.'

Chaudhary – Have kindness for the poor, and this grace will be your redemption. Kindness is the root of all mantras.

Faizu Mian had got up, dusting his clothes. The old Chaudhary was now appearing some kind of a demon in his eyes. He was also shocked to see this miracle. He too started pleading – 'Babaji, what can we do! We are caught in this knotty situation and have to do everything to survive. The officers, the departmental staff, orderlies, peons; all have to be taken into account. If we do not follow these tricks, how can we fill up their stomachs? We shall not be able to manage even for a day. Please accept me too in your service.'

Kartar kept the marijuana on the hookah and offered it to Chaudhary. Binda Maharaj had also got rid of his doubts. He said, 'Should I make some sherbet if you feel like having some refreshment?' Faizullah spread out his carpet for him to sit. Chaudhary was very happy. He took out a herb from his bag and gave it to him, saying, 'This is a sureshot medicine for epilepsy. Even if you have the disease since birth you'll be cured of it. Keep it safely and see, withdraw the case today itself. These are one thousand rupees; count them and keep. Give the receipts to all the tenants separately for whatever is pending. Now I'll take your leave. I'll come again after a few days.'

37

In the morning, when the news of Manohar's suicide came up, the entire jail was in deep turmoil. The Daroga, the staff, constables and guards – all were shocked out of their wits. When the police came to know about it, a group of big and small officials arrived on the scene. Everything was inspected and the statements of the jail officials were recorded. Within an hour, the civil surgeon and Dr. Priyanath also came. Then the magistrate, the commissioner and the city magistrate also arrived. The case was investigated for the whole day long. The next day also, similar crowds gathered and the same procedure took place, but the serpent had died; nothing was to be gained by beating its empty shell. But the jail officials had to face the music; the Daroga was suspended for six months, and the guards were fined heavily. The rules were modified, and the windows were strengthened with double grills. As soon as Premshankar heard the news, he came running to the jail, but the officials chased him from the gate itself. Till now, they had done all kinds of concessions with him. They had allowed him to meet the accused, and used to send the food that came from his house to the people in custody. But today they had a different stance. Premshankar was thinking what to do, when the chief commissioner of the police came out and said, 'All this is a result of your teachings; you alone have caused this suicide to save the rest of the criminals.' The Daroga of the jail also talked to him in a similar vein. Premshankar was very upset at these insults. Life almost seemed like a school affording new experiences everyday. This was the first occasion when his kindness and goodwill had been derided like this. He kept standing there for half an hour lost in deep worry, and then left for his cottage, as if he was returning after cremating a loved one.

After reaching home, he was again wrapped in these thoughts. He could not decide what to fix up as his life purpose. His heart hated wordly meanness, and following lofty principles brought opposite results. He had never experienced his helplessness in such a depressing way. He had also never received any clear evidence of how deluded human understanding was, and how narrow its vision. Though he avoided pride at all costs, it still reached the innermost chamber of his heart through a secret route. He became too happy when he saw his good efforts being successful, and a soft voice seemed to emerge from a minor corner of his heart – 'I have done such a good job!' But after every such moment he used to receive a warning in the very next second, which shattered his pride into pieces. 'Foolish man! You are proud of your love for principles! Just see how naive they are. You are proud of your knowledge and wisdom! See how misled it is. You are proud of you education and character! See, how incomplete and corrupt it is. Are you sure that your incitements were not the real reason behind Ghaus Khan's murder? Didn't your bitter teachings cause the death of Manohar? Didn't your wicked policies cause Shraddha to estrange herself from you?'

While thinking all this, his concern meandered towards his financial problems. 'God knows how long the case will go on. Irfan Ali has already taken three thousand, and almost an equal amount is pending as his payment. The sugarcane crop is ready, but won't fetch more than a thousand. How far can I keep pressurizing the villagers? Whatever was earned from the sale of fruit has also been spent. I haven't even shown the accounts to anyone. God knows what they might be thinking about me. There's no news of Lakhanpur as well. God knows what's going on in the lives of those poor men.'

Suddenly Bhola's wife Budhia came and said, 'Babu, we haven't eaten anything since two days and your ploughman is after my life. Tell me what I should do. Should I go and steal? I grind the flourmill all day and whatever I get I spend on the family and we still don't have enough to eat. Please don't pay him any wages. He loses everything in gambling. You neither scold him nor make him see any sense. You think he'll be reformed if you increase his wages. Even if you pay him a thousand per month, it won't be enough for him. Please give his wages to me from today onwards.'

Premshankar – But I thought he'd left gambling?

Budhia – Yes he did, but only for one or two months. He stops playing intermittently but he's still addicted to it. Please give his wages to me; then I'll see how he plays. You are a simpleton; you give him money as and when he demands.

Prem – He only tells me he has left gambling. Whenever he asks for money he says he doesn't have anything to eat. If I don't give him, what's the way out?

Budhia – That's why he doesn't see eye to eye. Has he taken any advance from you?

Prem – Go and ask him; he will tell you if he has.

Budhia – Don't you keep any records?

Prem – I don't remember anything.

Budhia – Then he won't bother to tell you. Do gamblers and drunkards have any honesty of their own?

Prem – Why; does wine wash away all honesty?

Budhia – What else? Just call him and I'll ask him in front of you. Oh Lord! The idiot blows up wage after wage; on top of it, he gambles after taking an advance. Let me see, how he pays off now.

Thus saying, she walked away irritated and came back with Bhola in a while. Bhola's eyes were red. He hung his head in shame. Budhia asked, 'Tell me, how much have you taken from Babuji as advance?'

Bhola looked at his wife with angry eyes and said – Who are you to ask? Doesn't Babuji know himself?

Budhia – Babuji is asking himself, or else why should I have bothered?

Bhola – I owe him a lakh, and I am his servant for life.

Budhia – Did you see that Babuji! Didn't I tell you, he won't disclose anything? Have gamblers ever been honest, that we can expect him to be?

Bhola – You think I am just telling lies. Lies are told to those who have an impure heart; who want labour for a rupee and pay for a penny. You cannot talk like this to gods. This life is his and so is the body; he just has to give a signal.

Budhia – Go away, you fraud! Babuji is tired of driving sense into you. You can't leave this damned game of gambling, what else can you do? People who sacrifice their lives for others are made of a different mettle.

Bhola – You liar, when have you seen me gambling?

Prem – Bhola, tell me the truth; do you still gamble? You have told me many a times that you have left it completely.

Bhola's throat became full. In an intoxicated state our emotions become melodramatic. He started crying loudly. When the rush of guilt cooled down, he said amidst sobs, 'Master, this is your only order that I've disobeyed. I haven't forgotten anything else. Please beat me up a hundred times with you shoes, only then this devil shall leave me. I daily pledge not to play, but as soon as the evening falls, someone seems to drag me by force to the gaming area. Alas! I told lies to you, I duped you; God will certainly punish me for it.' Thus saying, he again started sobbing.

Seeing this purity wrapped in a sense of shame, Premshankar's eyes were filled with tears. A drunkard and a gambler like Bhola, whom he thought to be a lowly fellow, turned out to be such a pure and clean soul! He hugged him and said, 'Why do you cry? I have not derided you in any way.'

Bhola – That's what is killing me at the moment. Please abuse me and cane me, only then this heady ghost will go away. We understand only the language of force, not of sweet talk.

Prem – Should I pay your wages to Budhia?

Bhola – Yes, please don't give me a single penny from now on.

Prem – (to Budhia) But if he picks up an addiction worse than gambling, then what?

Bhudia – The only thing worse than gambling is theft. The day I catch him stealing, I'll give him poison. I am ready to become a widow, than being called a thief's wife.

She caught Bhola by the hand, told him to leave for home and left behind a complicated problem for Premshankar.

38

Dr. Irfan Ali was thinking about the effects of Manohar's suicide on the rest of the accused. A heap of law books was kept in front of him. A thought occurred to him recurrently in the midst of all this; 'I took up this case without thinking properly. I am losing about hundred rupees daily and God knows how many days will be spent on it. Good God! I started thinking about money again. I really wish not to pay attention to it, but I just can't help it. It seems impossible to leave the legal profession. I have talked to Gyanshankar about professorship, but if I actually get that position, acceptance will be a big question. I cannot remain in this profession for very long; I'll have to leave it for the sake of my health if not for anything else. All I want is a sum of one thousand rupees every month. If I get this amount from professorship, it will be enough for me. No, it's not the right time to leave. I can think about leaving only after three years of solid hard work. But during these years, I should keep all kinds of concession and goodwill away. I should charge my fees properly; if I keep getting trapped like this, I'd never be able to relieve myself from this mess.'

'Oh, today the case will be argued. God! I haven't prepared myself as yet. I didn't have time to look at the statements of the witnesses. Well, nothing is lost. I do remember a few things. I'll gather enough matter from the arguments of the opposing lawyer. I'll spice it up further; hopefully a good argument will take place. This is my everyday job; what's there to worry?'

Just then, the king of Amouli arrived in his motorcar. Dr. Sahib came out and welcomed him. The Raja didn't know the English language but was well-versed in English lifestyle and principles. His clothes got stiched abroad. English ladies tutored his boys, and his estate manager was also an Englishman. He spent most of his day roaming about in English shops. He liked collecting ticket stamps and coins. He never missed a chance to go to the theatre. Since a few days, his manager had started mishandling the income of the estate. He thus wanted to remove him, but was scared of the wrath of British officials. The manager didn't bother about the Raja nor did he show him any account of the income. The Raja wanted to file a case in the civil court. But the manager was too friendly with the judge, so the rest of the lawyers had refused to take up the case. Disappointed, the Raja Sahib had approached Irfan Ali. He kept listening to him for long. He also kept consoling him from time to time. 'Don't you worry. I will make your manager pay back every single penny. The lawyers out here are a suppressed lot; a bunch of flatterers who defame or profession. Our arena is a free one. It's our duty to defend the right even if we have to oppose the emperor for its sake. Please don't hesitate one bit. I will fix up everything so beautifully that you will not be scarred at all.' Suddenly a peon came and gave a telegram to Doctor Sahib. Gyanshankar had called him to fight a case at a fee of five hundred rupees per day.

Doctor Sahib said to the king, 'This profession is very irritating. One can't sit in peace at any moment. It's Rani Gayatri Devi's telegram; she's calling me to Gorakhpur.'

Raja – I cannot postpone my case. It's quite possible that the manager plays some other trick.

Doctor – Please don't have an iota of doubt; I have taken charge of the case. Please send your administrative officer tomorrow; the authority letter will be ready. I will immediately file the case after seeing the papers. Even if I have to go to Gorakhpur, I'll take your papers with me.

The clock struck ten. The chef laid out the table. The kitchen was adjacent to this office. The fragrance of the spices filled up the room, but the doctor was busy laying down the trap for his prey. He was afraid lest the Raja should run away, if he went to have his meal. For about half an hour he kept talking to the Raja Sahib in relation to the case. After the Raja left, he sat down to eat. The food had grown cold. He had eaten only a few bites when it was already eleven. He left the food. He wore his clothes quickly and left for the court. He was regretting on his way that he didn't have food properly. 'The pulav seemed so delicious today. This profession is to blame; it doesn't even allow you time to eat. Well, what should I tell the Rani? Logically I shouldn't leave this place till the peasants are absolved. But how to bear the loss of five hundred per day? Then it's the matter of a big estate; it may give me thousands of cases every year. I must go and impress them.' The steno was sitting right there, he asked him, 'Why Munshiji, what should I reply to the Rani Sahib? Do you think it's right for me to go there at the moment?'

The steno – Huzoor is not subordinate to anyone's wishes. Please go for sure. All lawyers do the same! Don't let this opportunity go away.

Doctor – I'll be given a bad name.

The steno – Not at all. When this is the usual convention who will defame whom?

These words removed Irfan Ali's confusion. A person who was just yawning, got a pretext to sleep. As soon as his motorcar reached the court, Premshankar came running and said, 'I was so worried. The hearing has begun.'

Doctor – The Raja of Amouli came, that's why I got delayed; didn't even have time to eat. I wonder why people praise this profession so much. Actually it's the worst kind of job. In just a few days a person becomes a beast of burden.

Premshankar – Why are you going over to that side?

Doctor – Just to enquire about something in the court of the sub-judge. You go, I'll just come.

Prem – The government lawyer has begun his argument.

Doctor – Doesn't matter; let it be. I have prepared its reply already.

Premshankar went with him to the court of the sub-judge. Doctor Sahib kept talking to the office staff for about an hour. In the end he said in a very hesitant tone, 'I am sorry you had to keep standing here; please forgive me. I am regretful that I won't be able to defend the case for about three-four days.'

Prem – That's bad news. You can very well imagine that your absence in such a delicate situation will be disastrous for all of us.

Doctor – I am helpless; your brother has called me to Gorakhpur.

Prem – This is so depressing. You are leaving these farmers in a lurch. Just think what will happen to them. We won't be able to get any other lawyer at such a short notice.

Doctor – I am really sorry about it. But as long as I am keeping this shop, I'll have to entertain my customers. This profession is so damned that one cannot remain steady on any rules. I am myself concerned about these troubled men, but I can't afford to annoy Gyanshankar. And sir, the real fact is that if we profess to be atheists, why should we act with restraint? When we've decided to wear the black robes of law, why should we stain it with the white spots of honesty? When we are out here to rob; why shouldn't we do it with both hands? Why should a desire for wealth remain unfulfilled? We uselessly term the baniya community greedy. It's we who should be rightfully given that title. Wealth is our religion and our character. Don't think that the people who have reached the top in this profession are more enlightened than us. No sir; they are all tricksters. They keep quiet as if they have no concern with the world but as soon as they spot a prey you'll be surprised to see their alacrity and sense of catch. The way a butcher judges a goat by estimating its weight; in the same way, we estimate a person as to how far he's foolish and rich. People call it a free profession. I call it slavery of the highest order. A few months ago, my brother's wedding was about to be solemnized. The wedding party had gone to the district of Saadat. It stayed there for three days. I used to come here every morning and return by the night train. All rituals took place in my absence. I didn't miss the court even for a day. I myself find my lust quite offensive and will be ever grateful to the man who can cure me of this disease.

After saying this, Doctor Sahib came and sat on his motorcar and reached home in a second. The train was to leave at one. He started packing his luggage. Two leather boxes, one handbag, a box for his hat, office bag, food bag; all were loaded on the carriage. On each bag, his name was written. There was little time left, so he didn't go inside the house. He was about to sit in the car when a maid came and said, 'Huzoor, please come inside; Begum Sahib is calling you. Munira has got loose motions and vomitting.'

Doctor Sahib – Why don't you give her an essence of camphor? She must have eaten something indigestible. Where's the need to make a hue and cry about this?

Maid – Huzoor, we have given her the medicine; you please come and see. Begum Sahib wants to call the doctor.

Irfan Ali came in irritated and said to his Begum – Why have you created such a storm over a minor thing?

Begum – Munira seems to be too unwell. Please come and see her. Her hands and feet are getting stiff. I am afraid these might be symptoms of cholera.

Irfan – All this is your imagination. It's just a negligence of food habits; nothing else. Give her camphor essence every two hours; she'll be fine by evening. There's nothing to worry. I'm going to Gorakhpur by the next train. I'll return after three to four days. Keep informing me about your well-being. I'll stay at Rani Gayatri's bungalow.

The Begum looked at him angrily and said, 'The girl is so sick and you are leaving her alone. God forbid; if her condition deteriorates further?'

Irfan – Then what can I do by staying on? I won't be able to tend her and nor is her disease so friendly with me that it'll give me some concession.

Begum – You have left the girl to God's will but won't leave your money! Curse on this! A man may not have humanity, but at least love for his children! One craves after wealth for the sake of one's kids. If the kids are gone, will you make a bonfire of money?

Irfan – You're such a fool; who can argue anything with you?

Thus saying, he went outside, sat on his motorcar and left for the station.

39

Syed Ijaad Hussain's house was in a lane of Daranagar. In its verandah, ten or twelve shirtless boys sat on a torn jute mat and learnt Quranic precepts and pages from the Hindi-Arabic dictionary. Sometimes, in their enthusiasm they started learning their lessons in a loud voice, and no one could hear a thing. It all seemed like a noisy market. In the middle of all this mayhem, the boys abused each other, made faces, and pinched one another. If anyone complained all made such a hue and cry that the poor fellow lost his voice. In the middle of the verandah lay a low bed belonging to the Maulvi Sahib. A bearded Maulvi, wearing a loincloth, sitting against a dirty pillow kept smoking his tobacco, and took small naps even in the midst of this noise. He was addicted to his hookah. In one corner, a coal-stove kept burning, and a pair of tongs lay by its side. The boys loved to prepare his hookah; it was their chief entertainment. Their educational progress may not be a thing of praise; but all were trained in serving their teacher. This was Ijaad Hussain's orphanage run by his 'Association for concord.'

But in the room on top of this verandah the scene was quite different. There was a neat carpet on the floor, along with pillows and rugs. The betel-box, poppy-box, spittoons; all were arranged properly. A mat to offer the namaz was also spread in a corner. A beaded string hung on a peg. The roof was decorated with a frilled cloth, which was made attractive by colourful pots hanging down. The walls had large paintings hung on them.

It was morning time. Mirza Sahib was playing a harmonium sitting against a round pillow. Before him, three little girls were sitting, singing Dr. Iqbal's famous composition, 'Shivaji's couplets in their beautiful voices. Ijaad Hussain was singing with them, educating them about beat and rhythm. These girls were introduced as girls of the orphanage, but actually one was Ijaad Hussain's daughter and the other two were his nieces. This trio impressed the audience with their promotion of the Ittehaad. After one hour of practice, Mirza Sahib looked at the girls happily with proud eyes and relieved them. Thereafter, it was the turn of the boys. But they were not the boys belonging to the Islamic school; thin and clothless. They were only four in number but were an image of energy and liveliness. They were good looking, young, well-dressed; they came chattering from the house and sat on the floor. Mirza Sahib again tuned up his harmonium, and the boys started singing a proper ghazal which was composed by Mirza Sahib himself. In it, Hindu-Muslim unity had been compared to a beautiful garden and people had been requested to adopt this garden, enjoy its beauty and not get entangled in the thickets of envy and enmity. It was heart-touching in the soft and melodious voices of the boys. They were skilled in the expressions of emotions also. They were also introduced as boys of the orphanage but in reality, they were the sons of Mirza Sahib's two sisters.

Mirza Sahib was engaged in his musical practice when a man came from downstairs and said, 'Lala Gopaldas has sent me and has said that if you don't clear the account today, you will be taken to court tomorrow. One can give credit for only a few months in the cloth business, and it's been three years since you bought clothes from us.'

Mirza Sahib made such a face as if the burden of the entire world was on his head and said, 'Why file a case? Tell him to send me some poison; I will eat it and die. Some way or the other I'll be relieved from this cruel world. God has given him lakhs of rupees; there are heaps of notes in his house. How can he know what's going on with me? A large family, no source of income, the world is wicked, it doesn't listen to me; what to do? But Godwilling – within a month I'll come and clear all old and new accounts. Now I've got an idea which can never fail. People will give everything to listen to these boys and their songs. Go and tell Sethji; when he has kept up his patience for so long, he may do it for one more month.'

The servant laughed and said, 'Mirza Sahib, you always avert me like this, and I go and get scolded there. Munimji tells me, you must not be going there or else must be coming back after being shut up with a bribe.'

Mirza Sahib gave him a twenty-five paise coin. After he had gone, he called Maulvi Sahib and said, 'Why Mian Amjad, I had instructed you not to let anyone come upstairs. Why did you allow this servant? Was there curd set in your mouth? Couldn't you have said that I have gone outside? If you keep sending people like this then there will be a stream of people from morning to evening. What else have you been kept for?'

Amjad – I kept telling him repeatedly that Mian has gone somewhere, but he climbed the stairs forcefully. What could I have done; should I have manhandled him?

Mirza – Of course, you should have pushed him aside.

Amjad – Sir, dry chapatis and a watery dal do not have power enough to energise me; on top of it, these boys eat up my head. How can I find the vigour to beat people up? I never even find vegetables to eat. I keep lying at the door smelling spices and onions. The whole family enjoys pulao and sweet rice; I survive on dry rotis. I have never even seen a dining mat. Daily, I get to see only a mud bowl. Feed me rich dishes everyday. Then see; who dares to enter the house!

Mirza – Curse be on you; you are always lamenting your stomach and its woes. Mian, thank God that you are getting rotis for doing nothing, or else you would have been sitting somewhere coughing all day long.

Amjad – If I share my thoughts with you, you start abusing me. Well, I'm going; if you get to see my face again, take me to be a bastard. If God has given me a mouth, he'll also give me livelihood to feed myself. I will not starve in these days of swadeshi.

Thus saying, Mian Amjad started going downstairs with tearful eyes, when Ijaad Hussain called him again and said, 'You get upset over minor things. Can't you see how much I have to spend in the house? A bounty of kids is a beating from heaven; on top of it, a gathering of relatives is like a swarm of locusts which robs the trees of all their greenery. What can I do? It's my duty to bring up my children, and to be rude to relatives is not my habit. I keep thinking of various tricks, follow many disguises, and still nothing comes out of it. I will now give instructions that whatever is cooked in the house must be shared with you. But see to it that no one comes upstairs.

Amjad – I have sworn to go back.

Ijaad – Mian, how can you talk like that? People swear like that hundred times a day. Go and see; some devil has arrived again downstairs.

When Mian Amjad came down a real devil was standing there. Short statured, stout in appearance, black complexioned and wearing a tanzeb shirt. As soon as he saw Amjad, he said, 'Go and tell Mirzaji, Wafaati has come.'

Amjad said in a stern voice, 'Mirzaji has gone out somewhere.'

Wafaati – Mian, why do you tell lies? I just met Gopaldas's servant. He told me he's sitting upstairs. Did he go away so quickly?

Amjad – He must have duped you. Mirza Sahib has not been here since yesterday.

Wafaati – I might as well go upstairs and check him out.

Amjad – You aren't allowed upstairs. Women must be sitting there.

Thus saying he stood blocking the door of the stairs. Wafaati pulled him by the hand, and climbed up the stairs. Amjad caught him from the back. Annoyed, Wafaati gave him a push; Amjad fell down and toppled down the stairs. The boys started laughing at him. Wafaati went upstairs and saw Mirza Sahib sitting besides a long pillow. He said, 'Very good Mirzaji, you are so clever that you keep sitting in the house, and Mian Amjad tells people downstairs that you've gone outside. Will you pay me today or only on Doomsday? My feet have got blisters running after you.'

Mirza – Well, what can be better than that? On Doomsday; I'll pay every penny of yours; at that time I'll have income of a lifetime, there won't be any problem.

Wafaati – Please give me today itself; it's been years now. You get thousands of rupees in the name of the orphanage. Why don't you pay me back?

Mirza – Mian, how can you talk like this? The world is neither blind nor a fool. People's hearts are made of stone nowadays. No one melts down. If rupees fell on me like a shower I would never have let you remind me. This is my own helplessness that makes me guilty in front of you all. For God's sake, have patience for another month. Let the month of December arrive. The way October and November are months for doctors to flourish; in the same way, December is our month of harvest. Every city starts holding functions. This time I've thought of a ploy that can just not go unrewarded.

Wafaati – You have been making these pretexts for years. Today you'll have to give me something from the earlier account.

Mirza – Even if you slice me into pieces, you won't have anything except my dead body.

Wafaati went away disappointed. Mirza Sahib closed the door of the stairs from inside and picked up his harmonium when the postman called him out. Mirza Sahib remained very curious for letters. He went and opened the door and came upstairs carrying a bundle of newspapers and letters. The first letter was from his son who was studying law in Prayag. He had asked money for a suit and law books. Mirza threw away the letter annoyingly. 'All he wants is money; as if I have a tree giving out money.' The second letter came from an orphan boy. Mirzaji kept it in a trunk. The third letter came from a helping organization. It had promised to pay twenty rupees every month for the orphanage. Mirzaji was delighted to read it and kept touching his eyes with it many a times. Then came the turn of the newspapers. But Mirzaji was not bothered about articles or news. He only wished to read about the praises of his orphanage. But he was disappointed in this regard. None of the papers carried any report on it. Suddenly his eyes fell on a newsclip which made him jump with joy! In Gorakhpur, the convention of the Sanatan Dharma Sabha was going to be held soon. Gyanshankar was its organizing president. Scholars and holy men had been requested to participate and grace the occasion. Mirza Sahib started his preparations for the journey.

40

Gyanshankar's devotion towards religion increased so much that he felt disinterested in worldly affairs and gradually became disenchanted with everything. He still managed the affairs of the estate with the same old energy and diligence, but now he adopted a soft attitude in place of the earlier toughness. Besides the usual land tax, every tenant was supposed to pay donation for the temple and the guest house, but this amount was levied with such politeness, that no one had any reason to complain. He now used to file very few cases pertaining to aberrations, tax-increase and pending payments. He used to get loans for his tenants form the bank at nominal rates of interest and instead of extracting one and a half or one and a quarter above the original amount took only one-eighth of it. Whatever spare time he got from all these jobs, he spent it in the supervision of the temple and the guest house. He had invited skilled artisans from far-off places who were trained in the arts of making mosaics, painting, cutting and embossing stones. Loadfuls of marble arrived from Jaipur. Many kinds of stones were ordered from Chunar and Gwalior. It was Gyanshankar's deep desire that both the buildings should be exquisite and Gayatri was ready to spend the entire income of the state on the construction. 'I will manage with the income from cultivated land'; she said. But Gyanshankar used to devise such means of increasing the income that even after so much expenditure, there was no loss in the annual income of the estate. He organized bazaars in a few populous villages. Bridges were made on a few streams. At many places dams were constructed for water conservation. He got an irrigating machine and lent it out on rent. He also opened a huge mill for oil extraction. All these enterprises increased the profit of the estate instead of decreasing it. Gayatri was so overwhelmed with his managing skills that she never uttered her personal opinion on any subject.

Gyanshankar's lifestyle and attitude also went through a sea-change. He kept his hair long, wore wooden slippers instead of boots, and a loose ankle-length, saffron-coloured robe instead of a coat. This attire suited his soft demeanour a lot. His face was lit up with a divine light and his talk reflected a sweet simplicity. He was no longer interested in logic and justice. He talked as if he had achieved divine enlightenment. If anyone expressed any doubt regarding devotion or love, he answered him with a deep smile, which was far more effective than a thousand arguments.

Instead of chairs and tables, his sitting room now had a neat and clean carpet, which had bolsters and pillows kept on both sides. In the front, a child idol of Lord Krishna was seated on a wooden throne, studded with beautiful gemstones. The room had incense sticks burning all over. As soon as one came inside, one's heart became serene with the delightful fragrance. The neatness and simplicity of the room filled the heart with devotion and affection. Gyanshankar now followed the sect of Shri Vallabh. He was deeply interested in flowers, music, pleasant scenes and poetic thoughts, which are signs of spiritual development. The worship of beauty was the chief feature of his religion now. Nowadays he was learning how to play the sitar and while playing the couplets of Surdas, became totally enwrapped in them.

Gayatri was further influenced by this love and devotion. She bathed the Krishna idol, posing as Mirabai, decorated it with clothes and jewels, made various delicacies to offer as prasad, and sat in front of it, singing devotional songs for hours. Till midnight she kept talking about Krishna's antics and activities. She had stopped taking the purdah. She sat with holy men listening to talks on love and religion. But instead of deriving peace from this holy company her heart kept longing with a strange thirst, and an imagined fear of separation.

The instrument of her heart kept echoing an unknown desire. She couldn't decide what she really wanted. Actually she was incapable of understanding the deep truth about the love between Radha and Krishna. Her worldly vision could not go beyond the sensual form of that love and her heart could not be satiated with the imagined forms of such love and its manifestations. She wanted to experience those emotions in reality. She wanted to see the real form of separation and longing, sorrow and trouble, pleasure and enjoyment, happiness and revelry. Earlier, love for her husband was her complete self. That river flowed within the precincts of its banks. Now she found the image of that earlier love a bit erased, faded and contorted. The river had overflown its banks. The dam of devotion towards her husband that stood upon the foundations of family honour and self pride, stood broken in the flood of this new love. When does devotion bother about worldly ties? She now gave free vent to those feelings and dreams in her heart without any hesitation, which she earlier saw as flames of blasphemy. She wasn't satisfied merely with watching shows of Krishna's love-dances and plays. She wanted to create a pleasure garden herself.

She wanted to express those feelings in voice, action and thought which now flew about in her heart like restless birds. And who was her Krishna? She didn't want to admit that herself but the image had a close resemblance to Gyanshankar. She saw her Krishna in a temporal form in his physical self only.

Gayatri's heart had always been a generous one. She had become all the more charitable now. A constant stream of charity went on and no matter how many saints turned up; all were given food and clothing as per their desire. She also offered help to the nation's religious and charitable institutions. She was deeply affiliated to the Sanatan Dharma now. Therefore, when its annual function was decided to be held in Gorakhpur, the members appointed Rani Gayatri as their chairperson with a majority. This was the first occasion when a woman had been given such an honour. Gayatri had not been delighted so much with the title of Rani as she was with this position. She called Gyanshankar, who was the President of the association and handed over her box of jewels, saying, 'This box contains ornaments worth fifty thousand rupees; I donate them to the Sanatan Dharma Sabha.'

This news was flashed in the newspapers. Preparations began. The President now forgot the distinction between night and day, preparing for the convention. Such a huge meeting place had never been constructed earlier. There had never been such large scale preparations to welcome the guests. Never had the preachers been given such presents, nor had the public shown such affection towards the association. There had never been a better arrangement for the stay and welcome of guests. Groups of volunteers went running about, wearing flashy uniforms. Several shops were decorated in the space allocated to the tent. A circus company and two theatrical troupes had also been called. The whole city was agog with the celebrations. The markets were specially illuminated and decorated. On both sides of the roads, one could see streamers and flags.

One day prior to convention, the preachers started arriving. Motorcars kept waiting at the station to receive them. Many of these were ascetics. They thought the usual priests to be lowly and went ahead to board the cars. One of these, who was decorated with the title of Vidyaratna, got so upset about not getting a car that he didn't board a carriage even after much implorement. He came to the venue on foot.

But the pomp and show with which Syed Ijaad Hussain arrived was not destined for everybody. When he reached the venue, the function had already begun, and a scholar was lecturing on widow remarriage. He was making fun of this deplorable topic, finding it unfit for serious discussion, and was using much sarcasm, criticism and satire.

'Gentlemen, this is not an imagined incident but something I've seen with my own eyes. A babu sahib lives in my neighbourhood. Once he was praising widow remarriage in front of his mother. She was listening to him quietly. When he kept quiet, the mother said in a serious tone, 'Son, I have a request, please comply with it. Why not arrange my marriage with someone? When the widows of the country have become so lucky, why should I remain behind?' The audience started clapping happily and the entire tent echoed with their laughter.

Just then Syed Ijaad Hussain entered the tent. In front of him, four boys walked in a queue; two were Hindu, and the other two Muslims. Hindu boys wore yellow dhoti-kurtas; Muslim boys wore green kurtas and pyjamas. Behind them was a line of four girls; two Hindu and two Muslim. There was a similar difference in their attire. All had colourful flags in their hands, on which bright letters stated – 'Orphanage spreading concord'. Last of all came Ijaad Hussain. He had a fair complexion, white hair, green turban, black robe, white achkan, salimshahi shoes; and appeared as an image of sophistication and talent. He also carried a similar flag. Behind him walked his son Syed Irshaad Hussain – tall in height, waring golden specs, Albert-bearded, sporting a Turkish cap, a long achkan, and walking as a lively example of his association. Behind him came the instrumentalists. One of them had a harmonium, the other carried tablas, and the other two carried percussion instruments. All were dressed in a similar uniform, and their caps had the label of 'Union for concord'. There were thousands of people in the tent. All started staring at the promoters of the Union. The earlier lecture of the scholar faded away into the background. He tried to attract people by doing all sorts of antics, spent all his powers of comic art, recited vulgar poetry, even a crude song in a tuneless voice, but he failed to impress. All the audience was busy watching the Ittehaadis. Ijaad Hussain ascended the dias with great pretence. Many ascetics, holy men and preachers were sitting there on silver chairs. All watched Syed Saheb with envious eyes but stuck to their places. Only Gyanshankar was the one who welcomed him heartily and got a chair for him. His boys and musicians sat below the stage. The preachers were fretting in heart of hearts as if a crow had entered the gathering of swans. One or two of them also commented on him in a low voice, but Ijaad Hussain did not lose his temper. He was ready for this disregard. His face reflected a quiet determination that does not bother about difficulties and makes its way out of a bed of thorns.

When Punditji saw the audience disinterested he finished his lecture and came back on his seat. The audience thought that the Ittehaadis would begin their music; they pulled their chairs to the front and became alert, but the preachers could not bear that a Muslim could win the game against all of them. An ascetic soon began his lecture. He was a scholar of Vedanta and a yoga expert. He knew Sanskrit very well. He always spoke in Sanskrit only. People thought that Sanskrit was his mother tongue. People listened to him with the same attitude as they would listen to an ugly sparrow's song. No one could understand a thing, but all were taken over by his scholarship and hyperbole. He was known as a strange creature and this was the sole reason behind his popularity. However bored the audience might be; as soon as he came on the stage, people who were about to leave stopped and those who had got up to go sat down. The gathering gained its flavour back. He began his speech with the same pride but he too seemed to have lost his magic. The Ittehadis seemed to have taken his entire colour. He started a shower of Sanskrit words; he made much of it, but this was not a rain of August; just a minor April shower. Finally, he too left away tired and no other preacher had the courage to stand for his address. The Ittehaadis had won the game.

Gyanshankar stood up and said, 'Now, the coordinator of the Ittehaad organization, Ijaad Hussain will address you in his sweet voice. Please listen to him carefully.'

The meeting hall became quiet. People became alert. Ijaad Hussain picked up the harmonium and kept it on the table; the instrumentalists took out their instruments, and the orphan kids sat in a circle. Syed Irshaad Hussain took out the pamphlet containing rules of the organization. In just a second, voices of prayer started echoing in the pavilion. The voice of children has a unique attraction. Their singing together in rhythm along with the instrumental beats, all created a sweet atmosphere – the whole gathering was mesmerized.

Then the music stopped and Syed Ijaad Hussain started speaking – 'Dear friends, you will be surprised as to how this crow has entered a gathering of swans; how did a mere singer reach this group of learned men? This is a miracle of my destiny. The saintly men say that body is impermanent, the soul is permanent. But my experience is just the opposite. My appearance hasn't undergone any charge; my name is the same, long beard is as it is, my attire is also the same, but my soul has changed altogether. Do not be taken in by the appearance come and look into my heart; there it's written in bold letters, **'Hindi hain hum, Vatan hai Hindostan Hamara'**.

The boys and musicians started singing the famous song by Iqbal. The meeting was floored. Rays of pride started getting emitted from people eyes; some pulled up their moustaches, some gave out a sigh, some looked at their muscular arms, and many emotional men got tears in their eyes.

Especially when the stanza was sung –'**Hum Bulbulein Hain Iski, Yeh Gulsitan Hamara'**, the whole gathering flared up, people became full of feeling and shouts of "Vandemataram" filled up the hall. When the song was finished, the address began again.

'Brothers, religion is for the satisfaction of one's heart, not to achieve worldly desires, and to assume power in the nation. The fellow who wishes to acquire wealth and name in the garb of religion is an untouchable if he's a Hindu, and an infidel, if a Muslim. Yes; he's an unbeliever, a labourer, and a communist.'

The sound of applause thundered in the pavilion.

'We have been eating the grain of this land since seventy generations; this land has fostered us with its soil and water. Ash be on that Muslim who calls Arabia and Iraq as his country!'

People clapped again. The lecture continued for an hour. Syed seemed to have hypnotized the entire gathering. His proud politeness, his fearless outspokenness, his sweet jokes, his art of glib-talking, exciting sense of criticism; on top of it his smooth commentary, emotional outbursts and nationalist singing intoxicated the audience. Their hearts were awakened. Some thought, 'If I had a lakh of rupees, I would have donated them immediately.' Someone else thought 'If I didn't have kids to worry about, I would have gone and begged alms for my nation.'

Thus, by bringing forth racist feelings onto the surface, and by softening the ground for his spadework, Syed Sahib came to his actual motive, and started sowing the seeds.

'Friends, these are not the times to follow your religion blindly. Forget about old things. Long ago, foreigners ruled the natives of this place for ages; today those very natives have mingled with them. To make friends out of foes was an art that your ancestors possessed. The same art is there in you. You kept moving forward to hug us, but in the madness of religion we kept running away from you. But friends, don't be angry at our rudeness. You are a lively nation. Your heart is full of pain, courage and benevolence. Forget our meanness. A humble being of that alien race has some to you with the message of concord; please accept my request. This poor beggar is a mad promoter of concord; please encourage him. This tiny sapling of concord is looking at you with hungry eyes. Please satiate it with the rushing spring of your generosity. Then you will see how fast it grows into a strong tree and how many people enjoy the juice of its sweet fruit. Our heart has great ambitions and desires. We want to fill up every niche of this blessed land with the call of concord. Whatever has been done earlier has been done by you; whatever happens now will also be done by you. Look at the list of donations; it's full of your names only, and truly, you alone are its founder. Rani Gayatri Kunwar Sahiba's kindness is world famous. Is the patriotism of devotee Gyanshankar a hidden matter? What a minister; what a king! The land which houses such blessed souls is indeed fortunate. Today when I stepped on the blessed earth of this city, its people's affability and manners, hospitality and welcoming nature surprised me to no end. When I enquired further I found it to be a blessing of this religious fervour. This is the effect of Shri Krishna's love and devotion, which had made angels out of mere men. Sires, I cannot describe how much I revere Shri Krishna. People may taunt my Islamic faith for this, but I say fearlessly that the divine level which that pure soul achieved is beyond the reach of any ordinary saint or ascetic. In this gathering, I dedicate 'Anjuman Ittehaad' to that very divine soul. I am not just hopeful but sure that in front of his devotees, my call will not go unheard. The boys and girls of the orphanage are looking at you with helpless eyes. This nationalist beggar is standing at your door giving out blessings. Please see this white beard, and honour my white hair.'

The harmonium sang again; the tabla was struck, kartal started ringing and Ijaad Hussain's tragic song filled the air. The audience listened with a bated heart. When the appeal for donations was made, Rani Gayatri announced one thousand rupees; Gyanshankar donated a cow for the orphanage and people rushed to offer contributions from all sides. On one side the list of donations was making the rounds, on the other side, Irshaad Hussain started selling the pamphlets and medals of the association. The medals were very beautifully made. People bought them immediately. Within a few seconds, thousands of medals adorned the chests of the audience. Their hearts were stamped with the sign of Ittehaad from both sides. A total donation of five thousand rupees was collected. Ijaad Hussain was absolutely delighted. He thanked the people by singing another song and the programme ended. It was almost ten o' clock at night.

When Ijaad Hussain lay down after dinner, and started smoking a fragrant tobacco, his son asked him, 'You hadn't expected this much money.'

Ijaad – Absolutely not. I had expected one thousand rupees at the most, but now realize how foolish such people are. An Islamic function would have afforded not more than a hundred rupees. Praise these idiots. If it does not harm them, doesn't matter; extract however much you want.

Irshaad – Your lecture was excellent.

Ijaad – My life depends on that. I am nobody's servant or slave. All you need to be successful in the world is a clever policy. A man should be a glib-talker, perceptive of human psychology, and know how to change stances; that's all he needs to mint money. Wealth becomes his very slave.

Irshaad – Tell me honestly Abbajaan; haven't you ever thought that all this is just a kind of fraud?

Ijaad – Do you take me to be worse than ordinary human beings? All this is indeed a fraud; but what to do? My love for my family and children is far greater than the concern for my own salvation.

41

The function was organized very successfully. Rani Gayatri's lecture received a lot of praise all over the country. In it, she had described the historic origins of the Sanatan Dharma Sanstha, and had explained its rise and fall, reforms, its opposing and assistant powers with great deliberation. She had critiqued the present condition and the future goals of the association with great clarity. Those who read it in the newspapers were surprised, while those who had heard it with their own ears would never forget its heavenly impact. 'The sentence structure was so beautiful; so simple, effective and emotional! It was not just a lecture, but a melodious song!'

Three days had passed. Gyanshankar was sitting in his mansion and had a pile of newspapers before him. These days, all he did was to look for any news of the function in the newspapers and keep a cutout of it in a file. Gayatri now thought him to be a God. She had achieved nationwide adulation because of him only. She could return this obligation only by offering him her love-filled respect.

In the evening, Gyanshankar came with a bundle of newspapers and said to Gayatri, 'Just see; what is Rai Saheb up to?'

Gayatri pursed up her brows and said, 'Don't take his name in front of me. I had requested him so much to attend the function just for a day, but he never bothered. He didn't even reply to my letter. He's my father, so what; I cannot bear such an insult at his hands.'

Gyan – I had thought it to be his carelessness, but this letter reveals he's on a different project. Perhaps he couldn't find time due to this.

Gayatri – What happened; has he fought with an Englishman?

Gyan – No, he's preparing to hold a musical function.

Gayatri – Such functions keep happening at his place all the year round.

Gyan – No, this function will be held at a very large scale. All the prominent musicians of the country have been sent invitations. A world famous musical teacher has been called from Europe. Rich men and officers have also been invited. It will go on for a week. Its motive is to reform our native knowledge and style of music.

Gayatri – Our musical texts have been composed by ancient scholars. Who will dare to reform them? The raagas of Bhairav and Dhrupad came out of Krishna's flute. First people should learn to sing properly; then dare to reform anything.

Gyan – Rai Saheb has no liability, he keeps thinking of one or the other ploy; his debt is increasing, the estate is oppressed under it, but he doesn't listen to anybody! I think he has to pay around three lakhs of debt at present.

Gayatri – If he had spent so much money in the service of Lord Krishna his end would have been redeemed! Open the letters; he must have written to us.

Gyan – Yes, see, this envelope seems to be his. Of course, it's from him. He has invited me and you also.

Gayatri – I won't go. When he thinks it below his level to come here, then why should I go to his functions and fairs? You can take Vidya there if you wish but promise that you won't stay there for more than two days.

Gyan – I will think about it and then decide. These two letters are from the karindas of Barhal and Aamgaon. Both have written that the tenants are refusing to donate for the function.

Gayatri's face changed colour. The goddess of love turned into an image of ire. She said, 'Oh, have the winds of change started blowing in the rural areas as well? Write to these karindas that get the homes of these impudent men burnt and beat them with hunters. How can they dare to disobey my orders! Devkinandan, please excuse these human devils! Please send men from here today itself! I cannot bear this impudence. All of them are ungrateful. Had they been in some other estate, they would have known the real cost of things. I give so many concessions to them; am always ready to help them, bear losses for their sake, and this is the result!'

Gyan – This is a letter from Munshi Ramsanehi. He writes that the work on the temple has been stopped since three days. The labour is repeatedly asked to come, but they do not report.

Gayatri – Aren't they paid proper wages?

Gyan – Of course they are; but at the rate of the zamindari. The rate of zamindari is two annahs; whereas elsewhere it is six annhas.

Gayatri – If you think it proper, write to Ram Sanehi that the wages should be paid at four annahs a day.

Gyan – I can do that; actually two annahs aren't enough to feed a single mouth but if one shows kindness to these foolish rustics they think we've been suppressed by them. Tomorrow they'll start demanding six annahs, and stop listening to us.

Gayatri – Then write to him to get the labour arrested forcibly. If they don't come, turn them out of the village. We may treat them kindly according to our own will, but it's unbearable that a tenant starts acting willfully. One should keep up one's authority and fear.

Gyan – This letter has come from the market of Amelia. The contractor writes that people do not get their carts inside the circle. They sell their wares under the trees outside. They say they will sit wherever they please. In such a situation the contract should be cancelled, or else I will have to bear a huge loss.

Gayatri – The land outside the bazaar also belongs to me; what right do people have to set up shops there?

Gyan – It's just a kind of roguery. In the bazaars, one has to pay one paise interest on one rupee, no one can weigh in a false way, and some money has to be given for donations; outside one can do as one wants.

Gayatri – I am surprised that even in things that we do for the benefit of people, we are opposed like this.

Gyan – Nothing else, it's just human phycology. A human being naturally opposes any kind of suppression, and any regulation, even if it is meant for his benefit. A peasant will wash the feet of his foolish priest, but his karinda, even if he's a learned man he feels hesitant to greet. He might keep standing in the sun for whole day long, but cannot bear to get up from his charpoy on seeing a karinda or a peon. He does not want to remain burdened by his helplessness for the entire day. He might chew neem for his own happiness, but will hate to drink milk or sherbet forcibly. And we are forced to treat them strictly despite knowing all this.

Just then Mayashankar came from upstairs wearing a yellow cloth. He was just about fourteen years of age, but his face reflected a unique seriousness and thoughtfulness, which does not usually appear at this stage.

Gyanshankar asked, 'Where are you off to Munnu?

Maya looked at him with sharp eyes and replied, 'I am going towards the ghat to meditate.'

Gyan – It's very cold today. Whay don't you do it in the garden out here?

Maya – I am able to concentrate very well there in solitude.

When he left Gyanshnakar said, 'This boy is so strange. I just can't understand him. All kinds of vehicles are ready for him, but he'll always go by foot. He doesn't even take anyone along with him.'

Gayatri – The maids were telling me, he doesn't even allow anyone to touch his bedding. They keep waiting on him so that he might assign them some work, but he just doesn't bother about them.

Gyan – Sometimes, children behave like this in their teenage years. They know nothing about the world. Whatever rules are praised in the books one wants to follow them. But I find him somewhat dim-witted. He's so old, yet he doesn't know the value of money. If you give him a hundred rupees now, he'll not have a penny left by the evening. God knows where he blows up all that, but he never demands money as well. Till the time you give him yourself, he'll never ask on his own.

Gayatri – In my opinion, he must have been an ascetic in his previous birth.

Gyanshankar decided to go to Benaras by train, and from there to Lucknow taking Vidya along with him. Gayatri did not agree to go despite much insistence.

42

It's been seven years since we saw Rai Kamlanand, but this time-lapse does not seem to have left any impression upon him. His strength and vigour, lifestyle and attitude all are the same. As earlier, his hunting expeditions, polo and tennis, music and pleasure trips take up all his time. He keeps doing yoga also. He never hankered after money, and does not bother about it even now. Whatever he decides to do, he completes it at every cost. He just doesn't worry as to where the money will come from. He is still a member of the consultant organization. Elections have been held twice in the meanwhile, and both the times, he was elected with a majority. Though peasants and middle class people have also been given the right to vote, but who could have won against Rai Saheb? The peasant votes were in the hands of his brothers and himself and it wasn't difficult to overcome the middle class votes by giving donations to the communal organizations.

Rai Saheb remained a member for many days, but he was proud of the fact that he had never proposed anything in the council. He said, 'If someone delights in calling me a sychophant, he can; if anyone else is able to fulfill his goals by calling me a traitor, I have no complaints, but I cannot change my nature. If I can roam freely in the jungle by breaking my chains, I would break my anchor today itself. But when I know that even after breaking my shackles I cannot escape my cage; rather would be beaten up; why shouldn't I sit back quietly? If nothing else, the masters would see us with a benevolent eye. When the ruling powers are in the hands of officials and our non-cooperation and disregard cannot change it, why should we comment on their working for nothing and irritate them? We are just puppets set about for the purpose of entertainment; we should dance as the strings pull us. It is our wishful thinking that we are the representatives of the state. The state will never make us its representatives, whose very survival is dependent on its blood. The day this country is able to understand its profit and loss, we and you will be seen wielding the plough in the fields.

Our representation is entirely dependent on our selfishness and craving after honour. We are not the well-wishers of the state; we have merely made it an instrument of our selfish ends. We compare our salaries with those of the Britishers. Why? We should rather think that instead of coming to us, if this money can be spent on the progress and well-being of the nation it would be far better. If the British loot money with both their hands, let them. They have come here to do that only. They don't profess any love for our nation. We try to rob our countrymen even while claiming to be the nation's servants. We lament the downfall of our ancient professions. I tell you, you will further make the situation deplorable. We will open numerous mills, set up many industries, our peasants will become mill labourers and our nation will be destroyed. You deem this to be the highest point of national progress. I think it is an absolute destruction of our nation. Whatever it has suffered it's due to us. We are zamindars, moneylenders, lawyers, traders, doctors and officers; out of these who can claim to be a real advocate of the nation? If you think of benefitting the community, you propose a bill for compulsory education in the council. If you had been a true leader of the nation you would never have acted with such autocracy. No one wants heaven even against one's own wishes. Many people amongst us have got the highest of titles. But that education has given us nothing expect a love of pleasure, honour, selfish interests and a high sense of self-pride. We think of ourselves as an important part of society; but actually we are worst than insects and parasites. Why do we need two thousand a month, a motorcar, electricity, fans, carriage or servants to serve the nation? One can serve it far better by eating frugal meals.'

'You will say – Well, we have earned our education through hard work, that's why. If you have earned you education by hard work for your bodily comforts then how is the nation to feel obliged? How can you claim to be the leaders of you nation? You open a few mills and think that you have served the nation, but actually you have paved the way for the exile of about twenty people. You have prepared the atmosphere for their moral and social downfall. Yes, you and your partners have profited at the rate of forty-five per cent. So brothers, do this mish-mash till the time you can. You shouldn't criticize me; nor should I. Me and you, both are enemies of the extremists as well as the moderates. The only difference is that I understand my enmity and you still think yourself to be their friend in the intoxication of your pride.'

Listening to such talk, people used to call him an idiosyncratic. Along with age, his love for music had also started growing. He didn't bother so much about appeasing the officials now. But whenever he heard of a music expert he invited him and honoured him suitably. Seeing the present taste of the people he feared that if this state continued, the real form of music would fade away, and no one would know the difference between Desh and Bhairav. He thought musical arts to be the greatest wealth of any nation. Any degradation in that was the most deplorable form national downfall. His function was estimated to cost him four lakh rupees. Rai Saheb had not really asked anyone for monetary help, but many rich men had promised to give two lakhs each. Still, Rai Saheb was surely bound to bear a burden of around two lakh. Six famous musicians had arrived from Europe; two from Germany, two from Italy, one from France and another from England. Experts had been invited from Mysore, Gwalior, Dhaka, Jaipur and Kashmir. Rai Saheb's steno remained busy in correspondence the whole day long; still so many letters arrived that he himself had to reply to many of them. He had called Gyanshankar to dispense this job and he had just arrived along with Vidya. Rai Saheb was very sorry at Gayatri's refusal and said, 'She hasn't come only because I could not go for the Santan Dharm Sabha function. She's a Queen now! Won't she have a sense of honour? I didn't have time to die here; how could I have gone?'

Gyanshankar had been awake all previous night; he lay down after a meal and got up late in the evening. Rai Saheb was sitting in his drawing room and going through the letters. On seeing Gyanshankar, he said, 'Please come dear saint; you have donned a new avatar altogether. You are fortunate that you could achieve the ultimate knowledge in such a young age. I am approaching my last years, but am still caught in the net of wants and desires. Just see, Prof. Madhollkar has sent this letter from Poona. God knows why he's got a doubt that I wish to promote Western music in the country. He's very upset with me for this.'

Gyanshankar was getting impatient to come to his real motive; he got the opportunity and said – 'You called the European experts for nothing. That is why people are having such doubts. Have you decided their fees?'

Rai Saheb – Yes; that was the first step. Two experts are charging two thousand per day. Added to this are their travel expenses. The guests from Germany will cost one and a half thousand each. Only the Italian men have agreed to participate without any charges.

Gyan – Even if these great men stay here for just fifteen days one lakh is required only for them.

Rai – Yes, nothing less than that.

Gyan – Then the total expenditure might reach upto five lakhs.

Rai – The estimate was made around four lakhs, but it might exceed that.

Gyan – Have the rich gentlemen out here promised anything?

Rai – Yes, many of them. Possibly, I'll get two lakhs.

Gyan – Even if they fulfill their promise, you will incur a loss of around two or three lakhs.

Rai Saheb gave a sarcastic laugh and said, 'I don't think it to be a loss. Money is to be spent on pleasures of life. It has no other purpose. I deem wealth to be a slave of my wishes; I do not want to become its slave instead.'

Gyan – But your heirs too have a right to enjoy some of these pleasures?

Rai Saheb – Every creature in the world bears sorrow and happiness according to his or her deeds. Am I the devisor of anyone's fate?

Gyan – Excuse me, but these words do not suit someone who has spent a large span of his life already.

Rai Saheb said in a stern voice, 'You have no right to preach to me. I am the master of my assets; I can spend them according to my will and interest. If this destroys your dreams of prosperity, let it be; I don't care. It is not possible that after announcing this conference to the entire world I postpone or dissolve it. Even if I lose all my property I will finish this project to the very end. I can't understand why you are so bothered about worldly assets even after embracing Krishna's devotion and professing sacrifice and detatchment? One who has taken the road of Krishna; taken refuge in love and devotion; what does worldly splendour mean to him? After listening to you and seeing the leaning of your heart, I doubt that you have adopted that form, but haven't tasted the real flavour of love and devotion. A follower of Krishna can never be so narrow- minded. I am now having a doubt if you laid out this trap for the simple-hearted Gayatri; didn't you?'

While saying this, Rai Saheb looked at Gyanshankar with piercing eyes. His shot had hit the target so well that Gyanshankar's heart missed a beat. It was essential to dispel this doubt. It was very dangerous for it to stay within Rai Saheb's heart. Moreover, he needed to be fearless to remove it. It wasn't a time to be polite or well-behaved. He said, 'When I hear you criticizing fraud and disguise, I am reminded of an example, but I don't wish to quote it. A person who thinks pleasures and poison to be laudable in the name of religion; if he thinks others' religious devotion to be fraud he can be pardoned.'

Rai Saheb again looked at Gyanshankar with sharp eyes and said in a stern voice, 'You will have to tell the truth!'

Gyanshankar felt as if his heart was being uncovered. He almost became half unconscious. He said in a weak tone, 'Yes, I will.'

Rai – For whom have you laid this trap?

Gyan – For Gayatri.

Rai – What do you want from her?

Gyan – Her property and her love.

Rai Saheb laughed merrily. Gyanshankar felt as if he had just awoken from a dream. He remembered what he had just said. His anger died down. In its place, a kind of shame and humility had taken over which is usually seen on the face of an accused. He understood that Rai Saheb had hypnotized him and forced him to admit his evil plans. He seemed very dangerous to him at the moment. He wanted to return this tyranny of his in a terrible way, but was overtaken by a strange kind of fear. He found himself to be absolutely weak and helpless in front of this devil. He was getting so anxious in this situation that he almost wanted to commit suicide. The edifice that he had been building brick by brick since past seven years, was shaking badly and was about to fall down. It was not within his powers to save it. He thought, 'Alas! My ambitions are biting dust. I have lost even Rai Saheb's trust.' Suddenly Rai Saheb said – 'Son, why are you getting so angry with me? I am not so mean-hearted that I will insult you in Gayatri's eyes. If you happen to get her property I shall be most delighted. But if your efforts had remained limited to just her wealth I wouldn't have had any objection. After all, it's bound to go to someone or the other and those people cannot be dearer to me than you. But I consider her character to be far more precious than her property and cannot bear to see anyone coveting it with greedy eyes. I used to praise your strength of character; I was impressed with your efficiency and skills but I had no idea that you were so self-oriented. You deem me to be a fraud and pleasure-loving man, and I have no problem with that. Selfish people are naturally prone to have such doubts. But I assure you that I have never praised beauty with lustful eyes. I worship it, and think it to be a means of my self-chastisement. I derive soul-strength from it but do not use it as a means to gain what I want. And supposing, I am indeed a lover of comforts. So many days have passed like this; some more are left; I will remain what I have been uptil now. I cannot be reformed. But you have a lifetime ahead of you, therefore I request you not to become a slave of your desires and lusts. You are deluded under the impression that a man decides his own fate. This is a myth. We are toys of our fate, not its devisors. It makes us dance to our tune. How can you say that the goal for which you do not differenciate between truth and untruth, stay secure still your realization of it? Possibly, that heir who is about to inherit all this property is taken away by a little pimple right at that moment. Don't think that I am wishing ill for you. I just want to show you the hollowness of your hopes. I have seen many colours of fate, and have been teased by them a lot. One does not have the capability to turn it in your favour. I don't ask you not to worry about your own and your kid's future and not to earn money for it. No, earn a lot and prosper well, but do not sacrifice you soul and you conscience for it. Keep avoiding all fraud and conspiracy. My property is not less than twenty lakhs. Even If I incur a debt of three to four lakhs; you shouldn't worry. Isn't this wealth enough for Mayashankar? Your own ancestral wealth is not less than two lakhs. If you think it's not enough you may keep an eye on Gayatri's property; I don't call it improper. Become her confidante by your management, work-efficiency and goodwill, but do not take advantage of her innocence, simplicity and false devotion and try to capture her life.'

Just then, his private secretary arrived. Rai Saheb got involved with him. Gyanshankar was in tears. It was the sorrow of his exposure; of longstanding aspirations being destroyed, some guilt, some repentance of his evil nature and most of all a helpless anger. His argumentative powers could not counter so many assaults.

Gyanshankar got up and sat aside on a bench. It was the month of February, and evening had fallen. But he did not feel cold at all. His whole body was burning with the fire of an intrinsic fever. He had totally forgotten Rai Saheb's genuine advice. His only concern was to save the falling walls, and gather his scattered ambitions. 'This fellow says that he won't tell Gayatri anything, but he's not to be trusted at all. If he dares to utter a word to her, she will start hating my very face. She's a proud lady; and is proud of her womanly honour. Though she's in love with me, the basis of that love is religion, not emotions. What's the surety of her mental state? This evil man destroys not just his own wealth but is also trying to shut her doors for me, so that I may have no place to escape. I cannot bear the burden of so many disappointments. This life has no happiness left in it. When all ambitions are lost, why should one live at all? Alas! What all I had thought; and what all is happening?'

Rai Saheb went to the club in the evening and Gyanshankar kept deliberating on issues of life and death, sitting in that desolate place. His state was like that of a merchant whose everything had drowned or like that of a student who had failed despite years of hard work. When dewdrops started falling in the garden he got up and went inside his room. There, all kinds of worries surrounded him again. 'There's nothing left in life except insult and disappointment. I'll keep messing up my life like this. An end to this life is the only resort. Rai Saheb is not so mean that he'll defame me even after my death. He had truly said that man is a toy in the hands of his fate. I am in such a condition that death alone can relieve me of my woes.

People would naturally believe that I have given up my life after becoming disillusioned with the world; and have become free from the chains of desire. For a free soul like me, this dark world was not congenial. Vidya will respect me manifold and Gayatri will think I was an incarnation of Krishna. Quite possibly, she'd adopt Maya for the consolation of my soul. My uncle and brother are both upset with me. Death will soften their hearts as well. And what's so difficult about dying? I'll go to bathe in the Gomti river tomorrow. Even if I descend one step down, I'll be lost. The twenty thousand cash that I'd be leaving behind would be enough for Vidya's upkeep. Besides, there's income from Lakhanpur as well.'

Thinking all this, Gyanshankar was so caught in sorrow that he started sobbing loudly. 'Is this the final outcome of my life? Did I aspire for all this for such a resolution? This evil Kamlanand is hankering after my life. This ruthless man will end up killing me.'

Just then Vidyavati arrived and said, 'Did Dadaji have some altercation with you today? The manager was telling me he was quite angry. You unnecessarily comment upon his work. Whatever he does; let him do it. My mother died away driving sense into him; he never bothered. He doesn't think anyone's fit to advise him.'

Gyan – I just said that it's not proper to blow up two-three lakhs for nothing. He just got upset at this.

Vidya – This is his very nature. Whenever someone says anything opposite to his wishes, he gets out of control. I am also feeling bad, but do not dare to say anything.

Gyan – I am not bothered about his property. I am in the protection of Krishna; I do not desire anything else, but I just can't bear to see this injustice.

Vidya left the room. In a few hours, the cook brought Gyanshankar's meal. But he didn't feel like eating anything. He just drank a little milk and thought, 'Women are so narrow minded! That's why they get satisfied easily. They think, a man should get food and clothing with ease; some ornaments should be made, children should be born and nothing else is needed. As if human life is also meant to fulfill only natural needs like other creatures! How contented is Vidya! People appreciate this quality a lot in women. In my opinion, patience and contentment are proofs of their lack of wit. They are not wise enough to estimate their condition properly. Rai Saheb's expenditures irritate Vidya too, but she doesn't say anything, and is least bothered. She doesn't understand that this is her own loss; her own destruction. How has my condition overturned? If my ambitions had been successful I would have been earning around three lakhs every year, in a few years. In about fifteen years my wealth would have been immeasurable…, but nothing comes out of foolish dreams.'

Gyanshankar was blessed with a serious character. His resolves were often very determined. He never swayed in difficulties, or lost courage in the face of troubles. In Gorakhpur he had to face varied problems but he never bothered. But his toughness was of a kind that can touch the extreme of an ignorance of one's real state. He was not a gambler who takes pride in putting everything on stake. Small defeats and disappointments failed to affect him but a devastation of those motives on which he had based his life tests one's patience badly; and this was not just a case of depression or mourning. 'My evil plans have all been exposed! My devotion and religious faith, my high ideals; my refined behaviour has been revealed to be a sham! The world will now look for the real me. I had hidden my dark side by my logic, my words and my actions. Now they will all be under the sun.'

Gyanshankar couldn't sleep a wink. If he closed his eyes even for a moment, scary dreams started appearing. Sometimes he saw, 'I am drowned in the Gomti and my corpse is being burnt.' Sometimes he saw his huge mansion destroyed, and Mayashankar sitting on its debris and crying. Once he even saw Gayatri looking at him with rueful eyes and saying, 'You are a wicked fool; get out of my sight.'

When Gyanshankar got up in the morning his heart was quite disturbed. He was tired as if he had come after crossing a few milestones. He didn't talk to anyone. He picked up his dhoti and went to the Gomti. The sun hadn't risen as yet, but the tobacco shops had opened. Gyanshankar thought, 'Is tobacco so important in life that these shops open up so early?' In a short while, the dairy-seller gave his call. 'The smart fellow twists his tongue so much! He thinks that these irritating calls will please the customers. Had he sung properly, it would have been better still. Oh! 'Chai garam' has also arrived. It must be hot enough to burn your tongue but the taste must be like hot water. Who's this; riding a horse so fast? If the horse trips this fellow will break his bones.'

When he reached the banks of Gomti, he saw a crowd of devotees there. A dark tinted river was overcast by a dark foggy cloud. The golden rays of the sun were curious to break through this dark cover. A few boats were tied, trembling in the river.

Gyanshankar kept his dhoti on the riverside and entered the water; suddenly his eyes were full of tears. He waded through the water till his waist, but couldn't dare to move forward. The feelings of insult and depression which had excited his thoughts until now suddenly grew listless. Many of those who are dying to fight run away in the battlefield. Death doesn't seem to be a ghastly reality from far, as it seems to be at close quarters. One can understand how terrible a beast a lion is, only on seeing him closely. On seeing mountains from a distance, they seem to be high hills, which seem quite accessible; it's only when you go closer that you become afraid of their sky-high peaks. Gyanshankar had thought dying to be an easy act but he found it much more horrifying in reality. He thought, 'How foolish I am that I am willing to die for a minor issue. Admitted, I have fallen in Rai Saheb's eyes, Gayatri will boycott me and Vidya too would hate me; still can't I do anything about my life? Can't I make my life successful? The arena of this world isn't so small. I am in a far better condition than I was about six or seven years ago. I have a bank balance of twenty thousand rupees, an income of two hundred a month from the village, a bungalow and a motorcar; if I give this house on rent I'll get around sixty thousand a month more. Even if I do nothing, I can live like a gentleman. If Rai Saheb chooses to expose me, I too can take him to task. I can use my pen against him to such an extent that he won't be able to show his face to anybody. Gayatri is also under my authority; if she ignores me I can make her fall from her high position. I have made her earn a good name and can defame her if I choose. There is no end to the scope of politics. All that I have achieved till now is due to this, so why should I leave its arena? Why should I be disillusioned with it? If this broken boat has taken me along half the river; why should I desert it now?'

Gyanshankar took his bath and came out of the water. His face was shining with the light of victory.

But the manner in which a victorious army rejoices after removing the enemy from the battleground, and makes the latter weak and helpless to erase the chances of its return; Gyanshankar's courage also soared. He thought, 'Why should I allow a possibility that I am blamed from all quarters and I keep justifying myself? I wanted to be redeemed after death, why shouldn't I achieve that by making someone else die? This is my manly calling at the moment. It's easy to kill another than to kill oneself. Oh God! Your doings are so strange. You have saved me from the jaws of death! I had a narrow escape! I can still fulfill my ambitions. Wealth, fame, adulation, all is waiting for me; only a little courage is required. There's nothing to fear God; he is omniscient. It's the eyes of men that need to be covered, and I am skilled in the job.'

Gyanshankar came home in a tonga. On the way, he kept ruminating on what had just gone by. It was only Rai Saheb who was an obstruction in the path of his achievements. It was very essential to remove this hurdle. Initially Gyanshankar had thought of returning back from that path. He wanted to give away his life and be absolved of this problem. Now he decided to sacrifice Rai Saheb himself on the altar of his ambitions. 'The world might call it violence; it's a kind of heinous sin in its eyes – absolutely inhuman and unpardonable. But if you philosophize it, it has no relation to sin of any kind. What will anyone lose by Rai saheb's death? He has no children who'll be orphaned. He's not doing any great job that will lie incomplete in his absence; his property will be saved; rather it will be conserved under a proper arrangement. This cannot be called a murder from social or economic point of view. Even ethics would not be able to find fault with it. It can be called a sin only from a religious point of view. And from a worldly angle, it's not just laudable but actually very essential. This is a battle for life. No one can survive it through reason, religion or logic. It's not a matter of religion! It's proper to follow fraud, dupery and corruption if it fulfills your ends. It allows raiding and use of weapons to achieve victory. The decision of propriety or impropriety is subordinate to our success. If one succeeds, all frauds are called opportunities and people praise your skill. I just have to remove this boulder and my way is clean.'

Gyanshankar employed all kinds of logic to encourage his latest feelings in the same way in which a pigeon-flier lures his stray pigeons by offering them fresh bait. Finally his violent resolve grew determined. 'The world trembles at the mention of violence; a violent man is attacked unabashedly from all sides. He's an evil soul, punishable; it's a sin to see his face. But this endless world is a camp of idiots. To follow its rules and to respect its feelings is like walking on a bed of thorns. There is nothing called a rule, or a principle, or justice out here. There is just one way to shut its mouth. Bring a cover over its eyes and it won't object to anything. Not just that, you'll be able to deserve social honour in this way.'

After reaching home Gyanshankar immediately went to Rai Saheb's library and taking out an English text on chemistry, started analyzing the pros and cons of poisonous elements.

43

Two days passed and Gyanshankar did not see Rai Saheb. The latter wasn't one of those heartless men who first wounded someone and then sprinkled salt over it. When he got angry with anyone, it was taken for granted that his stars were ascending, and the moon of his fortune was shining, for as soon as his anger cooled down, he atoned for his anger with great generosity. He once beat up a servant as he had spilled water on the floor. The very next day, he gave him five bighas of land as an act of pardon. He was very upset with a karinda for doing fraud and even beat him with a hunter, but in the next few days, also increased his salary. Well, all that was required was that his bitter words should be tolerated quietly, without any arguments. As soon as he derided Gyanshankar he started regretting it. He was scared lest he might go away, hurt. 'Who's so great in this world who does not kill his soul for selfish ends? I am not altogether guiltless there. When this is the way of the world I shouldn't have humiliated him. At least I shouldn't have blotted his character. He's a thoughtful man; he would have understood my hints, but I abused him openly.' Thus when he sat down for dinner, he told the cook, 'Call Babuji here and get his plate also. If he refuses, tell him that I won't eat if he doesn't come.' Gyanshankar wasn't ready to go but Vidya said to him, 'Why don't you go! When he's calling you despite being an elder then he'll feel bad at your refusal. It's his habit that he speaks without thinking but later on, realizes his mistake.' Gyanshankar could not refuse anymore. He went with a long face, and sat a little away from Rai Saheb. Rai Saheb said, 'Why are you sitting so far away? Come near me. See, today I have got many English delicacies made for you. Maharaj, keep his plate here only.'

Gyanshankar said in a low voice, 'I am not at all hungry; please excuse me.'

Rai Saheb – You will feel hungry once you smell the food. I have decided to reward the cook. He must have spent all his skill today.

The Maharaj brought the plate and kept it before Gyanshankar. Gyanshankar's face changed colour. His heart started beating fast. Fear had overtaken hope. He just wanted to escape from there. He didn't want to be a part of that terrible scene. Every organ of his body was shaking; even his voice had become unclear. He was now experiencing that it's far difficult to kill anyone else than to kill oneself.

Rai Saheb had just eaten a few bites when he suddenly pulled his hand away from the plate and stared at Gyanshankar with poignant eyes. Gyanshankar lost his breath. Even if Rai Saheb had shot him with a bullet he wouldn't have been so hurt. He became somewhat unsteady. It seemed as if a mesmerizing power was taking away his life. No one would have been so afraid or careless even while watching his boat drown in a storm. Rai Saheb's sharp gaze proved that the secret was unveiled; all efforts and plans went waste. 'O misfortune! I have been left nowhere! How could I know that this fellow is so self-knowledgeable?'

Just then Rai Saheb said in an insulting tone, 'I had told you that wealth is not in your destiny; whatever games you'll play will all go wrong. You'll only get shame and guilt in the end.'

Gyanshankar feigned ignorance and said, 'I don't understand what you're saying.'

Rai Saheb – Absolutely false. You know very well what I'm trying to tell you. If I say more it won't be good for you. If I want I can make you spill the beans yourself but that's not needed. You were duped again. I thought you to be very clever, but I now know that you do not have a clear vision. You were in my company for so long, and still could not recognize me properly. You want to kill a lion with bamboo sticks, so if you are caught in his claws, it's entirely your fault. Don't take me to be a man; I am a lion. If I show you my real teeth and claws you'll shake with fear. Although this meal is enough to kill almost twenty-five people and after taking one bite they won't need any other, I can still digest the whole meal and you won't see a frown on my face. I am a worshipper of Shakti; such things are like milk and water for me.

While saying this, Rai Saheb picked up many bites from the plate and ate them up hastily. Suddenly Gyanshankar rushed forward; threw the plate on the floor and fell on Rai Saheb's feet, crying loudly. Rai Saheb's yogic powers had defeated him. He now understood it was a fight between a lion and a mouse.

Rai Saheb made him stand and said, 'Lala, I am not so soft-hearted that I will melt at your tears. I have now discovered your true self today. You're trapped in a most vile kind of self-interest. This is not your fault, but that of your unethical education. You were trained in materialism from the very beginning. Your heart was suppressed under it. Your teachers were selfish themselves. They never posited an ideal of a simple and contented life before you. All over, in your house, your school and the world around, you saw that only wisdom and strength are applauded. You got prizes and awards, you were praised in your class, and on each occasion, you were put up as an example before others. No one bothered about your spiritual development, and no efforts were made to take your feelings towards an honest path. You have never seen the light of religion and devotion, which is the only means of destroying the darkness of the heart. Whatever you are; you are a product of your education system. Your intrinsic values had sown the seeds, and education made it a dense tree. It's not your fault, but rather of the nation and the times. I forgive you and pray to God that He might bless you with good sense.'

Rai Saheb's lips turned blue, his face grew pale, and his eyes started turning into stone. Sweat covered his forehead, his body became damp and his breathing became fast. Gyanshankar grew anxious seeing him in such a state, and started fanning him with shaking hands but Rai Saheb indicated him to leave, let him be alone and shut the door from inside. Gyanshankar stood like a statue at the door, as if someone had buried his feet in the ground. He was repenting his act so much that he wanted to eat a poisonous bite from that very plate and end his life. Initially, after listening to Rai Saheb's proud words, he was hoping that the poison would not affect him, but now he was feeling scared that he had not calculated the real powers of his yogic exercises. 'What to do! Should I call a doctor? That desire for wealth be cursed which has inspired me to do this murder. Alas! My selfishness! You made me a devil out of human! Why am I becoming his enemy? For his property, his estate and his wealth! When I acquire all this, won't others become my enemies? Who can say that I wouldn't meet a similar end?'

Gyanshankar put his ears close to the door and tried to listen. It seemed as if Rai Saheb was beating his hands and feet. His fear made Gyanshankar unstable. He had never repented his heinous meanness and his terrible devilish characteristics so much. He was not worried about his own condition. He was only scared about Rai Saheb's torturous state. Even if someone had tried to remove him forcibly, he wouldn't have budged from there. 'God knows what might happen in a moment.'

Just then, the cook got some more eatables in a plate. On seeing him, Gyanshankar became pale with fear. He thought he would not be able to escape now. 'This evil fellow will soon make a noise seeing the situation. People will enquire and arrest me.' The cook seemed to be death himself.

He didn't allow him to come near only said from a distance, 'We have had our food; don't bring anything else now.'

The cook saw the shut doors with curiosity and tried to move forward, but Gyanshankar leapt on him like an eagle and pushed him saying, 'Didn't I tell you nothing is needed here; why don't you listen?' The cook stared at Gyanshankar, shocked. Gyanshankar was in a state when a man picks up a weapon, listening to a rustle in the leaves. He was no longer bothered about Rai Saheb. He thought him to be out of the purview of what worry could do. He was more worried about his own life now. His entire willpower was being spent on keeping this incident a secret.

Suddenly the door opened from inside and Rai Saheb came out. His face had turned a crimson red. His eyes were also bloodshot. There was so much sweat on his body as if an ironsmith had just left his furnace. Both the plates had been kept aside. The bowls were also clean. All the food was burning in a stove. Fire was consuming those eatables hungrily.

In just one second, Gyanshankar's thoughts turned upside down. Till the time he was worried about Rai Saheb's death, he was praying for his life to be saved. When he was assured of his death outside his door he became worried about his own life. Now upon seeing him alive, he got angry as to why didn't the old man die! So much of torture and mental torment had to be borne uselessly. His condition was like that of a tired ploughman whose oxen were about to run away after returning from the fields, and the possible trouble of chasing them the whole night long broke all his patience.

After coming out, Rai Saheb took loud and deep breaths many a times as if he was feeling suffocated, and then said in a shaking voice, 'I didn't die, but have entered a state worse than death. Although I have released all poison by Yogic procedures, but it seems as if instead of blood some molten lava is running in my veins. This heat shall destroy me in a few days. I will never be able to play polo and tennis again. The endless grace of my life is over. There's no longer that joy, which had little scope for sorrow or worry. I have forgiven you in words, but my soul would never forgive you. You are my son, I am like your father, but we'll never see each other's face again. I know it's not your fault, but that of our present worldly situation, but knowing this cannot console my heart. All this tragedy is a result of this property. We are thirsty for each other's blood due to it only. Wherever you see in the world, there's an empire of envy and jealousy, attack and counter-attack. A brother is an enemy of his own brother; father of his son, husband of his wife, all because of this! The kind of catastrophe, that it has bred, and will breed in future, should make us delete this convention once and for all. This is that field where saplings of deception and pretence bloom, and which has turned the world into a battleground. This has actually made human beings worse than animals.'

While saying this, Rai Saheb's eyes got closed. He came to the sitting room, supporting himself by the wall and fell down on the floor. Gyanshankar was after him, but he lacked the courage to hold him. When the servants saw his condition, they ran after him and made him lie down on a couch. They started sprinkling rose and keora water on him. Someone started fanning him; someone else ran to get a doctor. There was mayhem in the house. A big crowd gathered in the sitting room. After ten minutes Rai Saheb opened his eyes and indicated the people to leave. But when Gyanshankar started leaving with the rest Rai Saheb asked him to sit and said, 'This is not property. It's a mistake to call it an estate. It is just a kind of brokerage. What right do I have on it? I haven't earned it by my hard work. In the times of the Nawabs, some officer had appointed my grandfather to collect the land rent from here. The officers had a soft corner for my father also. After that the Britishers arrived and this right was taken away from my father. But during the revolt, he helped the British wholeheartedly. When peace was restored, my father got his rights back. This is the reality of this estate. We have been kept only to extort land tax. We wash our hands with each other's blood only due to this brokerage. This massacre of the poor is called authority, and we delight in this karindagiri. The government calls us the masters of our land only to serve its own purpose, but when we are made to pay taxes twice a year, how can we call ourselves masters? All this is a pretence of deceit. You will say, this is sheer nonsense; if estateship is so bad, why don't you leave it? Alas! My lament is that it has made us a lover of luxury; lazy and handicapped. We are good for nothing now. We are like pet birds, whose wings have been clipped. We cannot fly anymore. Our gaze is limited to the feeding bowls of our cage. We have sold our freedom for the love of a sweet bait.'

Rai Saheb's face started reflecting signs of a terrible intrinsic pain. He was lying down but he suddenly got up with a groan. His face became contorted. He kept his hand on his aching heart and said, 'Ah! Son, you have given me such poison that it's breaking my heart into bits and pieces. I will not live now. If a dying man's curse has any power, then you'll never be able to enjoy the wealth of this estate. Go away from my eyes. Possibly, I might strangle you with my hands in this angry state. I am not in my senses. I am like a mad serpent at the moment. Get lost from my sight and never show me your face. Once I die, you have the right to come back. And do remember that if you ever go to Gorakhpur now or have any relation with Gayatri it will not be good for you. My spies will keep chasing you like a shadow. If you disobey this warning, you won't be left alive. Alas!

My body is burning! Sinner, crooked man, why haven't you gone yet! Sher Khan … Is anyone there? … Get my revolver, (screaming) get my revolver … Is everyone dead?'

Gyanshankar got up and ran away from there. He went to his room and shut his door. He dressed up quickly, got his motorcycle and went straight to the railway station. He didn't even get a chance to meet Vidya.

44

It was evening time. In the court of the session's judge of Benaras thousands of men were gathered. The public had developed a special concern for the Lakhanpur case. Manohar's suicide had made him a topic of discussion in the entire city. On every hearing, people of the city came to the court. They had a strong belief in the innocence of the accused. Manohar's suicide was analyzed in various ways and all came to a conclusion that he alone was the murderer; the rest have just been trapped, and people attacked the selfish behaviour of Doctor Priyanath and Irfan Ali openly. All praised the selfless service of Premshankar. This case had made him the apple of the eyes of the public.

Today the final decision was to be taken so the crowd was larger than usual days. Not just people from Lakhanpur, but villagers from nearby rural areas had also reached in big numbers. At four p.m., the judge read out his verdict – Bisesar Sah was released, Balraj and Qadir Khan were sent to the Andamans, and the rest were given a term of seven years imprisonment with labour. Balraj saw Bisesar with angry eyes that seemed to be saying, 'Even if I get free for a second, I'll drink your blood.' Qadir Khan was very sad and upset. After hearing this verdict, many teardrops fell from his eyes on his moustaches. Life had come to an end. They had been waiting for justice, and what they got was a jail term in the Andamans. There was a loud uproar on all sides. The audience rushed to the accused, but the guards did not let them say or meet anyone. The car was ready. The seven of them were made to sit in it; the windows were shut and they left for the jail.

Premshankar seemed like an image of worry and sorrow, staring at the motor with tearful eyes, just like village women who stand on the border looking at the palanquin of the leaving bride with tearful eyes. When the car went out of sight, the people surrounded him and started asking all kinds of questions. Premshankar looked at them with hurtful eyes, but couldn't say anything. Suddenly he remembered something. He went towards the jail. People started following him. All were hopeful of seeing the accused or getting the good fortune of listening to them. They had just got out of the boundary of the court when they saw Dr. Irfan Ali coming on his motorcar. He had returned from Gorakhpur today only. He was going on a stroll. On seeing Premshankar he stopped his car and asked, 'Tell me, was the verdict announced today?'

Premshankar replied rudely – 'Yes, it was.'

Just then many men surrounded the car and a huge man came out and said, 'He's the one responsible for the murder of so many innocent men.'

Thousands shouted in one voice – 'Pull him out of the car; let's teach him a lesson. Let's make him spit out whatever money he has swallowed.'

The same stout man pulled the rim of Irfan Ali's pants with such force that he fell out of the car. Till the time he was inside, he was getting angry. As soon as he faced the music outside, he got mortally scared. He looked at Premshankar with pleading eyes. The latter was confused as to what he should do. He had never faced such a problem before, nor did he have any idea of the respect people had for him. But the only feeling that he had for the service of the poor, became alive again. He pulled Irfan Ali by the hand and said angrily to the man, 'What are you doing; leave him.'

One of the stronger men said, 'He's responsible for killing the whole village.'

Premshankar – That murder is not on him; it's due to his profession.

The man – Tell him to leave it then.

Many voices echoed, 'He'll have to taste reality, only then he'll be reformed.'

Others replied – Of course; let's treat him properly!

Premshankar roared loudly – Beware of raising your hands, or else you'll have to see my dead body here. Till the time I am standing here, you cannot touch him.

This warning had the desired effect. People left Doctor Sahib alone. But they were still lamenting the loss of an opportunity to make him lick the dust. As soon as the doctor saw the way being cleared, he looked at Premshankar gratefully and sped away on his car. All the men started clapping, 'There he runs! See how he runs!'

Premshankar was in a great dilemma. Every second he feared any kind of outburst from the crowd. If he saw any carriage, his heart started beating lest these men should stop it. He wanted to get rid of them but could not find a way. It was too difficult to control a mob of angry men. He thought, 'My threat has worked at present, but who can tell it will work the second time also. If the police come; all would be lost. A few might even lose their lives.' He walked ahead thinking of all this. Dr. Priyanath's bungalow was on the way. He was roaming in his verandah with a tennis racquet in his hand. Perhaps he was waiting for his car. When he saw the crowd, he came to watch from his gate.

Suddenly someone said, 'Let's have a word with him also. Actually it's he who has sliced their throats.'

Many men agreed with him – 'Yes, yes, let's catch him; don't let him go.'

Before Premshankar could go near Doctor Sahib, thousands of men had surrounded him. The same old man snatched his racquet and said – 'Tell us, how much bribe have you received in the Lakhanpur case?'

Many resounded – 'Why don't you speak up? How much did you get?'

Doctor Sahib started shouting for his servants but they didn't bother to show up on the scene.

One of the men said - He will not tell unless asked properly.

Priyanath – I will send everyone to jail; rascals!

Doctor Sahib tried to scare them off, but could not understand that people, who ordinarily fear a glare of the eyes, do not bother about bullets during times of revolt. He had just uttered these words that people lost their cool. A huge noise ensued, 'Don't let him escape; kill him, let's see what happens.'

Just then Premshankar went and stood near the Doctor. Many sticks, umbrellas and twigs had been raised. On seeing Premshankar, all were left hanging in the air; only one came and hit Premshankar's shoulder with a force.

The same strong man cursed Doctor Sahib and said, 'Why are you hiding behind him like a thief! Come forward and face the music.'

He had not even completed his sentence when people saw Premshankar falling on the ground. No one said anything to anyone, but all came to know about the ominous happening. There was silence all over. People's arrogance got converted into doubt. They started asking, 'Whose stick was it that struck him? Break his hands and strangle his neck! Why doesn't he come out open? Is Babuji hurt a lot? Is he injured badly?'

Suddenly Dr. Priyanath said loudly, 'Why did you leave him half-dead? Why didn't you strike another blow that the work could be complete? Idiots! I was your culprit; what wrong had he done to you?'

Thus saying he sat near Premshankar on his knees and examined his wound properly. His shoulder bone had broken. He took out his hankey and bandaged the shoulder. Then he got a cot from the hospital and took away Premshankar. All the men stood there, lost in worry. All were worried lest the injury should be serious. But when Doctor Sahib came after treating it and said, 'The injury is deep, his bone has broken, but he'll hopefully recover soon;' their hearts were at peace. They left the place one by one.

As soon as Lala Prabhashankar came to know about the tragic incident he came running in a bewildered state and kept crying at the bed of Premshankar. He was conscious now, but was in extreme pain. The doctor had forbidden him to speak or move, so he was lying quietly. But when he saw Prabhashankar getting too anxious, he said in a low voice, 'Don't worry, I'll be okay very soon. I just have a little pain in my shoulders. Apart from that I have no problem.' Prabhashankar was relieved on hearing this. While leaving, he said to Dcotor Sahib politely, 'Babuji, this man is the solitary lamp of my family. Please take good care of him. If he remains alive, I will serve you in every way I can. Though I am not capable enough, yet I'll offer you whatever I have.'

Priyanath said – Lalaji, what are you saying? If I do not devote myself to his care, there won't be a more ungrateful person than me in this world. He has been injured only because of me. Had he not been there, no one would have found even my bones. He saved my life by risking his own. His obligation can never be returned by me.

In about three-four days, Premshankar was well enough to sit by the support of a pillow. He started walking by a stick in the verandah of the hospital. Lots of people came everyday to enquire about his health. Premshankar praised Doctor Sahib a lot in front of them.

Priyanath's spirit of service had impressed him greatly. He used to come many a times during the day to see him. He used to read out newspapers to him and got special food made for him in his kitchen. Premshankar felt very guilty that he had doubted the intentions of such a godlike man. He was trying to compensate for his earlier disregard by showing him unmitigated respect now.

One week had passed since the assault. Premshankar was lying in bed, thinking about the state of the accused. 'God knows what condition they must be in. I am caught up here. Nothing has been decided about the appeal; how will it be filed? Where will so much money come from? Nowadays, justice has become out of reach of the poor. At every step one has to shell out money. And one still can't be sure that the result will be in one's favour. If these punishments are upheld, the appeal would go waste; but still we must do it. Money can be arranged somehow or the other. If nothing else happens, I will go from door to door, begging for donations. People have a natural sympathy for the poor. We might get sufficient money. If Gyanshankar feels bad, let him; I cannot help it. Wouldn't he have been informed about this accident? Leave alone coming to see me, he didn't even write any letter of consolation.'

He was lost in these thoughts when Priyanath came to him and said, 'You seem to be very worried. Have some tea; your mood will lift up.'

Premshankar – No, please, I just don't feel like it. When will you relieve me from here?

Priyanath – I guess you will have to remain in this house-arrest for another week, the bone is yet to heal; and what's the hurry? This is also your own house.

Premshankar – You keep burdening me with so many obligations that I find it difficult to bear them. It is the result of your kindness, affection and manners that I never really felt any pain. I have never felt so peaceful anywhere. Your heartfelt compassion has taught me that God can exist in this very world. I had lost my faith in civil society. You have restored it again.

Premshankar's meekness and simplicity kept enamouring the doctor's heart everyday. To become an object of respect of such a pure, holy and humble man, was like purging oneself of all lowliness and meanness. This light dispelled all the darkness of his inner self. He was so happy to acquire his prized company as if a poor man suddenly acquires untold wealth. He was always worried lest he should lose him. He wanted that he should clear his position regarding the Lakhanpur case but could not find any opportunity for it. Today, he got a chance and said, 'You are embarrassing me a lot. Had anyone else said these words, I would have thought he's trying to fool me. You are taking me to be far more wise and virtuous than I really am. Just like ordinary men, I am a slave of greed, want and my senses. I have committed great sins in my life. If I describe them to you, you will start hating me despite your generosity. I am hiding my evil deeds by my outward pretences, but the bad name that I have earned in this case is not something that I deserve. I tell you honestly that all the accusations levied on me are baseless. It's possible that in the analysis of the murder, I may have erred, but I am not so heartless or indiscreet that I would kill so many innocent men only for my selfish end. It is my sense of slavery that has put a mark of infamy on my forehead.'

Premshankar said in a guilty voice – Bhai Sahib, the fault of your disgrace is upon me. I am your culprit. I alone doubted you improperly, swayed by others. I can't tell you how sorry and sad I am about this. God knows what punishment I will receive for treating a holy man like you so unfairly? But I pray to you to consider my ignorance and forgive me.

Priyanath's heart became light on hearing this. Premshankar returned to Hajipur after a few days, but the doctor came to see him daily in the evening. He had become far more duty-conscious than before. He went to the hospital daily before ten in the morning, saw the patients carefully, and consoled them. Not just that, he didn't budge earlier without getting proper fees; now he went to see poor patients for free. He charged only half his fees with small workers. He also inspected the sanitary conditions of the city. Wherever he went, people greeted him respectfully. In a few months, the whole city started praising him. Kashi's famous newspaper 'Gaurav' was his old enemy. It used to comment negatively on his functioning. That too, started lauding him. It wrote in one of its articles, 'It's a matter of great fortune for Kashi that after so long, the city has got such a people loving, generous and duty-conscious doctor. The goal of medical science should be the earning of fame instead of money and Mr. Priyanath has proved by his behaviour that he deems the upkeep of this high ideal as his ultimate duty.'

Dr. Sahib now tasted the fruit of fame. The happiness which he received now in the service of the poor was something he had never derived through the increasing numbers of his wealth. Although he was not yet free from materialistic lures, the inspiration to acquire fame had defeated the desire for money. In Premshankar's company, his heart became as clear and pure as flowers washed with dew drops. In the wake of the former's simple, contented and wantless life, his own desire for money seemed very small. He even stopped bothering too much about his children. He thought that if in a state like Premshankar, one can remain content and happy, acquire a good name, help others, and become object of respect, then it's futile to hanker after money. He was slowly realizing that money is not an essential means for a successful life. He was sorry as to why his needs were so many; why he had slaved after pleasures despite being a doctor, and had run after good clothes! 'I was infamous in the city due to these only, and was deemed greedy, selfish and unkind. People doubted that I might prolong their disease, so no one called me quickly.' These thoughts started affecting his lifestyle also.

One of these days, he was returning after seeing a patient when he passed by the agricultural farm run by Premahankar. It was ten in the morning. The sun was blazing hot. The gleaming rays of the sun seemed to be piercing the sky like arrows. Doctor Sahib thought of meeting Premshankar. 'Let me see what he's doing?' When he went inside, he saw him scattering wheat bundles under the tree of his cottage. Many laboureres were laying down the roof. On seeing Priyanath, Premshankar got inside the hut and said, 'The sun is very strong today.'

Priyanath – But you are so engaged in your work as if there's no sun around.

Prem – Look at those labourers! They do not bother one bit about the sun.

Priyanath – This artificial life has spoilt us, or else we would have been like them and wouldn't have abhorred physical labour.

Premshankar wanted to say something else, when two old women came in, carrying bundles of wood on their heads, and asked, 'Sarkar, please buy our wood.' After the women came their boys; also carrying wood. All were drenched in sweat. The bones of their chests and ribs were showing out; their lips were dry, bodies covered with dirt, and lines of sweat could be seen all over. Premshankar asked the price and made them put down their bundles, but when he saw his box there was no money in it. He made the steward run for money. Both the women sat in the shade of the tree and the boys started eating the scattered bits of grain. Premshankar felt sympathy for them. He gave a few peas to all of them. The women blessed him saying – 'Babuji, may God always keep you happy. They didn't have any breakfast today.'

Presmahankar – Where is your home?

One of the old women – Sarkar, you must have heard of Lakhanpur.

Priyanath – You didn't see the bundles, all have cut down a great deal of wood.

Premshankar – Poverty makes one do everything. (To the old woman) You people come so far away to sell wood?

Old woman – What to do master, there's no human settlement in between. We have been travelling since night; it's already afternoon, we shall rest under a tree and reach home by the evening.

Prem – How's everyone in the village?

Old woman – What can we tell you; the zamindar became averse to our well-being, the whole village went under arrest; someone was banished; the others were sent to jail. Their children are starving for food. I had two sons. Two ploughs were used on my fields. One son was banished, and there's no news of the other since a year. The oxen broke down due to lack of fodder. Who can grow anything now? My daughter-in-laws cannot go anywhere to work. I sell cowdung cakes and feed all of them. I had grandsons, whom God took away early on. I had to bear all this in my old age.

Prem – Aren't you Dapatsingh's mother?

Old Woman – Yes Sarkar, how do you know?

Prem – In the days of the plague, I was there when your grandsons were sick. I have been there many a times. Didn't you recognize me? My name is Premshankar.

The old woman pulled a slight veil on her face. Instead of humility, a light colour of embarrassment came over her. She said, 'Yes, son, I now recognize you. I can't see properly. Bhaiya, may you live for many years. Today, the whole village is singing your praises. You did whatever you could, but how could our fate be overwritten? Son! The whole village is crying out in pain. You must be knowing about Dukhran Bhagat? This old woman is his wife. She used to eat the old produce, and preserve the new. Nothing is left in her house now. These boys are one of our kin. One is Rangi's son and the other two are Qadir Mian's grandsons. God knows what happened, but all homes became desolate once their men went away. We used to hear that Qadir Mian has a lot of money, but in just a few days we got to know that if the boys don't work, they won't have anything to eat. May god destroy this evil Faizu; he has spread all sorts of violence. He would have evicted the entire village, but God bless Sukhu that he paid every pending penny. But now, even he has failed to turn up and how can a single man take the responsibility of the whole village? He may manage for a year or two, but this is a lifelong issue. The karindas are threatening to disinherit everyone. Till last year we had cultivated jointly on half our fields. If we lose them altogether, what will become of us?'

Thus saying, the woman started crying. Premshankar also became tearful; he asked, 'How is Bisesar Sah?'

The old woman – I don't know Bhaiya, I haven't been to his door since one year. No one goes there now. It's a crime to see his face. People buy grocery from other villages now. He too doesn't get out of his house. He has shut his shop now. God knows what all he keeps doing inside? Whosoever will dig a pit for others will fall in a well himself. I haven't seen myself but have heard that from the time this incident took place; no one has had any rest in his house. One or the other member is overtaken by a ghost. Day and night, occult practioners keep lining at his door. They do all kinds of rituals and worship. One day he met Bilasi on the way. He started crying. He was regretting a lot that he did evil to us as he was misguided by others. Manohar seems to be after his life. He shuts his doors well before evening, and does not get out at night. Manohar keeps standing at his door day and night, and engulfs whosoever he finds. I have heard, he's about to leave this place and settle in some other village.

Premshankar started thinking deeply on these issues. 'I am so careless. These poor men have been suffering since the punishment was awarded a year ago, and I didn't bother to find how they were faring. What all they must be thinking in their hearts? I have been belittled before Gyanshankar. But I will have to go there now. Should I allow these people to die after my useless resolve? This cannot be. Their lives are far more precious than my promise.' Suddenly the old woman said – 'Tell me Bhaiya, can't anything be done now? People say, we can still appeal to a higher judge.'

Premshankar did not reply to this. It wasn't too difficult to arrange the money, but he wasn't much hopeful of benefitting from the appeal. The lawyers had a similar opinion. He thus used to avoid this question. He had never discussed the issue even with Doctor Priyanath. The latter was looking carefully at Premshankar. He understood his inner feelings and to remove his confusion, said – 'Yes, an appeal can be filed; we are preparing for it, be patient, we will soon put it up.'

The old woman – Son, may you prosper in all respects. I've heard there was a big doctor who took a bribe from the zamindar and had these poor people caught. If you deem fit, please go and plead to that doctor; who knows he might listen to you after all. He must be having children of his own. Why does he trouble us unnecessarily? It's not good to invite someone's curses.

Premshankar was feeling very embarrassed. 'Doctor Sahib must be feeling so bad; he must be getting so ashamed over this. This woman may start abusing him; how to stop her?' These thoughts were making him too anxious, but Priyanath's face was only reflecting kindness; and his eyes emitted a feeling of motherly love. He said smilingly, 'We went to that doctor, and drove sense into him. He is greedy, but has now understood what is right; he'll give a true statement now.'

Just then, Masta arrived with the money. Premshankar paid for the wood. The old woman left leaving her blessings along with the wood. At the door, she again said – 'Bhaiya, don't forget about us, it's a moral duty; you'll be rewarded with a good name for it.'

After they had gone, Premshankar and Priyanath kept sitting quietly. The former due to hesitation; the latter due to embarrassment.

Suddenly Priyanath stood up and said in a decisive tone – 'Bhai Sahib, you must file the appeal. Please go to Allahabad today itself. This scene has moved my heart today. Godwilling, only truth will triumph this time.'

45

Dr. Irfan Ali could not go for a walk after that day's incident; he went straight to his house. On the way, he was too wary of an attack by those rioters, as his life would have been endangered. He thought, 'It was a good fortune that Premshankar was present on the scene or those rougues would have certainly manhandled me.' When he reached home safely, and lay down on his easychair, he started thinking about the matter. Till now, he was taken to be a fearless advocate of justice and truth. His sword had always pointed at the workings of the police. This was the main reason behind his success. He was not a very studious, analytical or logical kind of a lawyer, but his fearlessness used to cover all these faults. The Lakhanpur case revealed his selfish nature for the first time. Earlier, even if he lost to the police, he was always victorious in the sense that the public kept up their faith in him; rather it increased his trustworthiness. This time, he had to face a real defeat. The people lost their faith in him. The public opinion openly condemned him now. His ears were echoing with the words of the rioters, 'The murder of these poor men is upon him.' Irfan Ali was not one of those men whose soul becomes dead under the burden of aspirations. He always used to lament the difficulties of his profession with his close friends and undoubtedly these laments came from the deepest throes of his heart. He used to pledge repeatedly to leave this profession, but like the resolve of a gambler, his decision was never fulfilled; rather he became all the more submerged in the sea of his greed. His condition was like that of a traveller who wants to reach his destination before evening and thus walks too fast. Irfan Ali wanted to earn enough before leaving the legal profession, so that he could live comfortably afterwards; he was thus walking on his path of greed too fast.

But today's incident had hurt him deeply. Till now, his state was akin to those rich men who take medicine simply because of their notion of an illness. They sometimes take a tasty dish or a sweet essence and consume it according to their will. But today he discovered that he was seized by a chronic disease, which would not be cured by any essence or cream. This could only be treated by a strong injection and harsh medicines. 'I used to pretend that I am a server of truth. Actually I am no more than a slave of my wants. Premshankar should not have saved me. Had I received a few blows my eyes would have opened.'

'O my great Lord! How selfish I am? I don't even bother about other people's lives to safeguard my interest. I treated this case deceitfully from beginning till end. I never read the precedents carefully; never pondered over the questions to be argued, didn't listen to the statements of the witnesses properly; I sometimes used to go for some other case, and talked to my friends during the hearings. Had I done even a little bit of research, I could have exposed Priyanath without much effort. The police informer could have been blown away in a few arguments. The statement of the inspector was also not very credible, but I never really bothered about my duty. I used to sit in the court as if I am sitting amongst a gathering of friends. If I call this profession bad, it's actually my own wickedness. It's our immorality which has given it a bad name. It is expected that we should aim at the truth, but instead of that we aim only for money. If God so wills, I will do what I ought to from now on. I will make Premshankar the ideal of my life; I'll follow the path of contentment and service.'

Till the time Premshankar stayed in the hospital, Irfan Ali used to go daily to ask about his well-being. Doctor Sahib too, was surprised at his patience and courage. His respect towards Premshankar increased day by day. His behaviour towards his clients became all the more polite. He used to look into their matters carefully, did not take more than one case at a time and and pledged against leaving a case in the court and going out to defend another. He wanted to urge Premshankar to file an appeal but used to hesitate thinking of his earlier dishonest behaviour. Finally he decided to go and consult Babu Jwalasingh in Sitapur, but the latter seemed to be caught in his own confusions. He had written to Premshankar that he would soon join him after resigning from his post. But something or the other cropped up which kept stalling his plans. The real reason was that Sheelmani wasn't ready for him to resign. She said, 'Your officer might be unhappy with you; you may not be promoted; let it be. You have the power of justice in your hands. If these people remove you from your post you should appeal against them and fight with the greatest of officers. It is highly improper that you should decide to resign out of fear of your seniors. This conduct on your part will discourage many of your just and self-respecting colleagues, and they too will start thinking of running away. This department will be deprived of all honest men, and only flatterers will be left to dance around the tune of the seniors.'

Jwalasingh had no reply to this argument. When Dr. Irfan Ali went and saw him, he could not abrogate himself by blaming Sheelmani for his own laziness and love of authority.

Sheelmani understood that it was difficult to detain him now; he would not listen to her. As soon as she got a chance, she asked Jwalasingh – 'What did you reply to the Doctor?'

Jwalasingh – What's there to reply; I'll now give my resignation. There won't be any scope to make excuses now. Till the time I go there, Babu Premshankar won't be able to do anything. Unfortunately, he trusts me a lot more than I actually deserve. If the tenure to file the appeal lapses, we won't be able to do anything. There are strong chances of it being successful and if my efforts can save the lives of so many innocent people I should not delay even for a second.

Sheelmani – Why don't you take leave for a few days?

Jwalasingh – You talk as if you don't know anything. I will have to do so many things which cannot be done till I am chained by the liabilities of this service. I'll have to ask for donations, meet the lawyers and do all kinds of things to relieve the Lakhanpur people of their troubles. The police will have its eyes on me; the officers will scorn me, so why shouldn't I cut off this chain myself? I am fully confident that the kind of service I can do on being free is not possible within the present circumstances.

Sheelmani kept arguing with him for a while; finally she said angrily, 'Ugh! Do whatever you feel like. How am I bothered? I am used to all kinds of situations. You will repent yourself. All this respect is there only till the time you're an officer. When you become one of the social workers, no one will bother about you. Are all men honest out there? Bad and good persons are everywhere. I cannot say about Premshankar, he's a holy man, but amongst the social workers you'll find so many people who are images of self-love and enjoy all pleasures in the garb of service. They cannot tolerate innocent and pure souls in their midst. You will find it arduous to survive among them. You will be irritated with their unjust, deceitful and narrow behaviour, but won't be able to stop them. So whatever you do, do it after a lot of deliberation and thought.'

These arguments were the same that Jwalasingh had once given to Sheelmani himself. Probably she had become opposed to the idea of his resignation after listening to them, but at the moment, Jwalasingh could not bear to hear these depressing words. He came out, and in the same state of rush started writing out his resignation.

46

Many months passed away, but Presmshankar could not decide whether to file an appeal or not. Any task which he had to finish without anyone's help; he did with all his alacrity, but when someone lent a hand, he was taken over by a strange listlessness. Apart from that, lack of funds was also a hurdle to be crossed. The expenditure on the civil case had burdened him so much that he couldn't afford to approach the High Court now. Although people respected him a lot and he could have easily got many contributions of money for this social cause, his natural simplicity and meekness did not allow this solution to emerge in his consciousness.

One day, he was looking at the newspaper in the evening. He saw the news of Gorakhpur Sanatan Dharma Mahotsav printed in bold letters. He had taken Gyanshankar to be an idol of deceit and self-love in his mind. He now felt sorry for it when he read about his religious devoutness and faith. He thought, 'I have been so unwise. I doubted such a divine and pure soul.' He felt great respect for Gyanshankar. He felt such an anxiety to praise him before others that he called out for Bhola and Masta many a times. When none of them responded, he went towards Masta's hut, where he found Durga, Masta and many workers of the farm dragging a man forcibly with them. Everybody was abusing him and Masta repeatedly whacked him now and then. Premshankar went ahead and asked in a sharp voice, 'What's the matter Bhola; why are you beating him?'

Masta – Bhaiya, God knows who he is? He was clinging to our gate. When I went to close it I saw him. He tried to hide when he saw me. I came back, took the others with me and caught hold of him. He must be a thief.

Prem – He might be, but has he stolen anything from you? Then why do you beat him?

Thus saying, he came and sat down in his verandah. The workers brought the thief before him. As soon as his face became visible in the light of the lantern, Premshankar let out a scream and said, 'Oh! It is Bisesar Sah!'

Bisesar wiped his eyes and said, 'Yes, sarkar, it's me Bisesar.'

Premshankar said to his servants in a stern voice, 'You people are so foolish and rude. God knows when you'll gain some sense.'

Masta – Bhaiya, we kept asking who he was. He didn't say a word; how could we have guessed.

Prem – Just shut up, you fool!

When the servants saw that they had made a mistake, they disappeared one by one. Seeing Premshankar in anger made them tremble with fear. Although Premshankar treated them like brothers, they respected him a lot. They never smoked in front of him. When they had gone, he made Bisesar Sah sit on a cot and said, 'Sahji, I am really sorry that my men behaved so roughly with you. All of them are uncivilized idiots.'

Bisesar sighed and said, 'No Bhaiya, they have not treated me wrongly. I very well deserve it. Even if you have me tied to a pillar and get me whipped, I won't feel bad. I am a traitor. Whatever punishment I get is little. I destroyed the entire village to save my skin. God knows where my wisdom had fled! I succumbed to the lures of the police. They all talk in such a manner, threaten you so hard that a simple man falls into their trap. They must be knowing some godly magic that whatever they want is uttered by one's mouth. God knows, I had no idea about Ghaus Khan. I came to know of his murder only late in the day, when I came to the shop after my daily prayers. But when the Daroga took me to the police station and started torturing me, something else took over me. I started repeating whatever he said. When I was giving my statement in the court, I couldn't lift my eyes with shame. No one in the world must be as evil as I am. I sliced the throats of those with whom I had my daily intercourse; and who were a part of my joys and my sorrows. When Qadir said to me, 'Bisesar, fear God;' that moment I wanted that the earth should split and I should be buried inside. I felt like saying aloud, 'All these are made-up facts', but when I looked at the Daroga, my heart lost courage. Ever since Manohar hanged himself, I have lost my peace. I start up and wake at night, as if Manohar is standing at my bedside. As soon as evening falls I shut my doors. When I go out I find him coming towards me. My wife has fallen sick ever since. My house is suffering thus, and on the other hand, the whole village is going through a horrible phase. Everyone's kids are dying of starvation. Faizu and Kartar keep devising new ways of torture every day. May God bless Sukhu Chaudhary; he sympathized with us and paid taxes pending since two years, or else the whole village would have been evicted by now. Faizu is annoyed precisely due to this. When Sukhu comes, he becomes meek but as soon as he leaves, he starts his atrocities again. I cannot bear to see these poor people suffering. He scolds and beats whosoever he pleases. Once, he got Qadir Mian's house burnt. And now he has an evil eye on the dignity of the village women. In Manohar's house, his wife and daughter-in-law keep fighting. They live separately. Day before yesterday, Faizu and Kartar got into the daughter-in-law's house at night. The poor woman started screaming. Her mother-in-law reached there with other people. Both of them ran away. But they took their revenge in the morning. Kartar beat Manohar's wife so much that she's lying in pain, having turmeric milk to cure her wounds. All this sin is upon my head. I am the root cause of all this tragedy. I wonder how God will treat me! Tell me bhaiya; can't anything be done now? I've heard, you're about to appeal against the decision, so why not do it at the earliest? If the duration for it lapses, we would regret it. You can invoke me again as a witness. Even if I am penalized for telling lies earlier, let it be. Now I will tell everything truthfully. At worst, I'll be punished, but the village will be saved. I can even help you with about a thousand rupees.'

Premshankar – The high court decides only after seeing the precedents; no one is called to give any statements out there.

Bisesar – Bhaiya, if they want money give them; don't worry about a thousand rupees even. You can tell me whatever you need. I was thinking of it since many days, but could not find enough courage to show you my face. When I went to buy something today, I met Faizu near the chaupal. He told me – 'Please go and give this amount to the master's family.' I took the money and reaching their gate, sent it to the younger mistress. When I was about to leave, the senior lady called me in the sitting room. She gave me such a lesson that I can't tell you. My eyes were opened. I decided to come to you and ask you to appeal, so that I too am redeemed of this guilt. But I came back after visiting your door two or three times. I was feeling very reluctant to face you. At sunset, I came again but was standing at the gate thinking as to what I should do. Just then your men saw me and brought me to you. How can anyone trust a false and treacherous man like me? But I now swear upon myself that if I am made to give a statement again, I'll tell each and everything truthfully. I'll then bear whether it harms me or benefits me. Please do file an appeal.

Premshankar thought Bisesar Sah to be an extremely fallen, deceitful and sinful man. In his opinion he wasn't even fit to be called a human being. But his guilty talk pulled him out of the category of devils and established his place in heaven. 'O God!' he thought, 'the man whom I thought to be so evil has such a feeling of remorse in his heart! This power to sacrifice himself, godfearing values and such pure feelings! How deluded

I was! People always defame others, but I have discovered goodness in every so-called evil person. It's my good fortune; what else? O God, please forgive me for this mistrust. His eyes became full of tears. He said, 'Sahji, your words have given me the same happiness that I would have got upon listening to a holy man's teachings. I am about to appeal very soon. The only hurdle is; how to change the statements of the witnesses? It is possible that the high court orders a re-examination of the case and it is heard in the same court; but as soon as you change your statement, both you and Priyanath will be caught. Priyanath has thought of a way out, but your escape seems difficult. Please think about it carefully.'

Bisesar – I have thought about everything, don't worry.

Premshankar – If God wills, you too will be saved. I'll consult the lawyers about it tomorrow.

Thus saying, he went to arrange some food for Bisesar.

47

Gyanshankar went straight to Benaras from Lucknow, but remained sad and upset. He stopped going for a walk and even avoided meeting people. His condition was like that of a bird whose both wings had been clipped or like a woman who had lost her husband and kids due to some natural calamity. All the ambitions of his life seemed to be licking dust. Just one week ago, the creeper of his hope was blooming under a happy breeze. In its place there was just a heap of burnt leaves now. He fully believed that Rai Saheb must have written everything to Gayatri. He had clamoured after the whole estate; he wouldn't even get half of it now. The biggest pain of his life was that his innermost feelings were now exposed before the world. His only patience came from the philosophy that in the given condition, there was no other way left for him to reach the desired goal. He actually had no guilt or shame for his deeds. His only regret was that all his conspiracies went down the drain.

He had written many letters to Gayatri from Lucknow, but he couldn't dare to write to her from Benaras. He even opened the letters that came from her very apprehensively. While opening the newspapers, his hands would start shaking. Vidya's letters arrived daily. Reading them was a task as thrilling for Gyanshankar as reading his fortune. He used to read every line in such a fearful manner as if he was stepping into a dark cave. He was afraid lest he might find any mention of that day's tragedy. Very often, he kept analyzing very simple sentences as if they might reveal some hidden meaning, some secret, or some quote. On the tenth day he received a long letter from Gayatri. When Gyanshankar held it in his hand, his heart started leaping out of bounds. He opened it with great difficulty, and the way one gulps a bitter medicine in one sip; he read it in a single glance. His heart was at peace to find no discussion of Rai Saheb. He then read the letter again in a relaxed way. Gayatri had expressed her anxiety on the absence of his letters in very touching words, and had requested him in an extremely polite way to come to Gorakhpur. Gyanshankar let out a careful breath. Gayatri had tried to hide the true state of her heart but every word that came from her was like life-giving nectar for Gyanshankar's dying hopes. He felt hopeful again; he felt satisfied that all was not yet lost; he might be proved innocent in her eyes if given a chance, he may prove Rai Saheb's allegations as false, and convert falsity into truth. Quite possibly, his tearful eyes may still assure her of her innocence. In the same surge, he wrote a letter to Gayatri, the greater part of which he devoted to the pain of separation and then indicated about Rai Saheb's false allegation. His last words were – 'You are well versed with my nature and thoughts. If I have an ambition in life, it's just that I should depart from this world listening to the tunes of (Krishna's) flute. When I die, I want the face of Krishna before my eyes and my head in the lap of Radha. Apart from this, I have no other want or desire. I can sacrifice the wealth of this entire world on Radhika's one slight glance, one sweet smile, one sweet comment and one unique presence. But till the time I am there in this world how can I escape its blackness? I had expressed my thoughts clearly to Rai Saheb regarding the Sangeet-Parishad. The result is that he is hankering after my life now. How to narrate my tale of woe to you; you'll feel unhappy about it. He had taken out his revolver to shoot me. Had I not run away, I would not have remained alive to write this to you. I have been ordered not to show my face again. Not just that, I have also been asked to stay away from you. If I disobey these orders, such a cruel punishment has been devised for me that I don't wish to hurt you by mentioning it. This is the chief reason behind my silence. Possibly, some letter in this regard has also reached you, advising you to shun me away from your life. You are free to do as you deem fit. It's your duty to obey your father. Please do so. I will always be close to you even from a distance; no power in this world can separate me from you. Who can dare to break a spiritual bond? This lover of Krishna shall always be attached to Radha's lap. I only beg you that please do not keep any disaffection in your heart for me, and keep my memory alive in a corner of your benevolent heart.'

After Gyanshankar had gone, Gayatri was finding it terrible to pass her days every single second. She now discovered how deeply she had entered the sea of Gyanshankar's attraction. Till the time she was with him, she had no idea of that depth. As soon as he left, she started slipping away. She wanted to stand firm, but the waves of love did not allow her to stabilize herself. This time Gyanshankar had left Gorakhpur after a year. She used to see him and talk to him daily and though it happened only once or twice in a day, her heart was content to have him near her. She now remembered the bird ardently on seeing the empty cage. She was simple and honour-loving, but there was a boiling spring of love in the crevices of her heart. It was covered with a huge boulder of pride, and getting no way to flow out, was in a sleepy state. This was actually her womanly honour. But devotion and affection had removed that boulder and that spring was now overflowing with a ferocious speed. She had almost lost herself in a trance; like an unconscious person. She had no idea that this devotion was pulling her towards a lustful state. In this intoxicated state of love, she said and listened to many things which could have made her kill herself; which were earlier quite abhorrent to her, but now she was a milk-maiden, and an image of pure love. In this spiritual commentary, where was the space for lust? Or for a gratification of the senses? The name, devotion and the maniac following of Krishna had drenched her soul in a holistic stream of love. When she stared at Gyanshankar with sweet glances or submerged his thirsty eyes with the nectar of her soft smiles she took herself to be a maiden who was having a funful engagement with Krishna. Her looks and smiles reflected a true state of affection. When Gyanshankar looked at her with love-lorn eyes and complained about her rudeness or passivity; she saw only pure feelings in them. This addiction to be involved in unspoken love mysteries increased day by day. She did not find peace without them. In this state of anxiety, she sometimes went to Gyanshankar's sitting room; upstairs, downstairs and in the garden, but she couldn't pacify her heart. She compared this unrest to the sorrow of separation which the milkmaids must have felt for Krishna. She sang those poems of Surdas which have a description of this pain. Her garden had a kadamb tree. She lay down in its shade; singing, crying, or roaming in an edgy and nervous state. Sometimes she thought, she should go to Lucknow; sometimes she thought of calling him back urgently; and decided that she'd never let him go again. His face kept appearing before her, and his talk echoed in her ears. 'What a mesmerizing image, and what pleasant talk! He is like Krishna himself.' She was surprised as to why did she let him go alone. 'Couldn't I have accompanied him?' She wrote to Gyanshankar and lamented his unkind nature and hard-heartedness. When his letters arrived she read them repeatedly. No kind of hesitation or shyness impeded her profession of love now. In listening to the separation tales of the milkmaids, she found a poignant delight. She would have hardly read a few passages from Premsaagar, that streams of tears started flowing from her eyes.

But when Gyanshankar went to Benaras and his letters almost stopped Gayatri started feeling as if she no longer existed in this world. 'It's a deserted, lifeless and soundless world.' She wasn't aware that he had already arrived in Benaras from Lucknow. She kept sending daily letters at the Lucknow address, but when no reply came, she was deeply annoyed with herself. She cursed herself like the milkmaids as to why she was hankering after a cruel, heartless and rude man. Why couldn't she become ruthless like him?

'If he has forgotten me why can't I?' But just in a second this annoyance dissipated and she again roamed about; lost and worried.

But when on the tenth day, Gyanshankar's letter arrived, Gayatri's heart became impatient. She rushed towards him with the same helpless gusto. This was the first test of her love. Till now, there were no thorns in the bed of her love. This was the first that had pricked her feet. 'Will this first hurdle remove me from my love path?' she thought. 'It's because of me that Gyanshankar is suffering. I am the root cause of his troubles. If my father is unhappy with him let it be; I don't care. Why should I turn away from love? The relation of love is only between two indivuduals; any third person has no right to intervene into it. How can my father order him to stay away from me? What does he think of me? All his life has been spent in the lap of luxury. How can he understand the deep mystery of love? How can he know this pure feeling? Had God given him true enlightenment, he would have known Gyanshankar's self-elevation, and understood the significance of his soul. Then he would have realized that he has been so unfair in blaming such a pure being. It's my duty to obey my father's order, but what is the value of a father's instructions before the true feeling of love. This fire is a gleam of the eternal light; this fever a mantra of the endless peace. Who can relieve me of this?'

The next day Gayatri telegrammed Gyanshankar, 'I am coming,' and went to Benaras by the evening train, taking Mayashankar along with her.

48

It had been more than two weeks since Gyanshankar came to Benaras. The Sangeet Parishad had been over and the local newspapers were still discussing it. Although Rai Saheb had not been able to participate in it enthusiastically due to ill-health but his administrative skills had ensured that it proves successful. It was evening time. Vidyavati was sitting inside and mending an old shawl. Rai Saheb had provided a nice carriage for her outings and had instructed the driver to keep it ready for her on all occasions, but she had never gone out since many days. Her heart felt much more satisfied in doing household work. She had no liking for theatre, for walks, or for music. Compared to these, cooking and stitching made her far happier. This life of solitude had taken away the colour of her face. She often suffered from headaches. She was an extremely beautiful, soft-hearted lady, and she didn't have an iota of pride. She didn't even bother to make her hair or do up her face. She was rather surprised that Gayatri spent a large part of her time dressing and adorning herself. The room was getting dark, but she was so busy in her work that she didn't even bother to switch on the light. Just then Rai Saheb came and stood at her door, saying – 'God really made a mistake in not making you a seamstress. It's dark all over; eyes can't see properly, but you have no respite from your needle and thread.'

Vidya winded up the shawl and said in an embarrassed tone – 'Just a little part of it was left; I thought I would first finish it and then get up.'

Rai Saheb sat on the bed and wanted to say something but a loud cough erupted and a little blood came out of his mouth; his eyes became lifeless and his chest started aching badly. His face became crooked. Vidya was shocked to see this and asked – 'Should I get you some water? You never had any such disease. Should I call for a doctor?'

Rai Saheb – No, there's no need. I'll get well soon. All this is the result of my efficient, scholarly and talented son, Babu Gyanshankar's kindness.

Vidya looked at him in a questioning manner and started staring at the ground in a meek way. Rai Saheb gathered himself and letting out a sigh of pain, said – 'I don't feel like telling you what has transpired between me and Gyanshankar, but to hide it from you is not just improper but unpardonable. You will be pained to hear that, but possibly the present sorrow would save you from those future troubles which destiny is arranging for you. Perhaps you may resolve them with your wisdom.'

Vidya's heart was overtaken by several kinds of doubts. She started flitting like a bird from branch to branch. She thought of Mayashankar; perhaps he has fallen sick. Was Gyanshankar caught in some trouble? She looked at Rai Saheb with apprehensive and tearful eyes.

Rai Saheb said, 'Till now, I thought Gyanshankar to be a devout, honest and truthful man. I was proud of his abilities and never tired of praising him before my friends. But now I have discovered that a devil can very well reside in a human form.'

Vidya's face was full of frowns. She looked at Rai Saheb sternly, but did not say anything openly. It seemed as if she didn't want to hear all these things. Rai Saheb got up and switched on the light and saw the dislike on Vidya's face clearly, but he didn't bother about it and said – 'This is my seventy-second year. I have dealt with thousands of men in my life, but my knowledge of human character never failed me. This is the first time in life when I have been duped in this manner; I have never seen such a selfish man.'

Vidya grew impatient, but still didn't say anything. She just couldn't understand the background that Rai Saheb was building, and the reason why he was using such abusive words.

Rai Saheb – 'I had complete faith in the character of this man. Due to my advice, Gayatri made him the manager of her estate. Had I been aware of his true nature I would never have allowed his shadow to fall upon Gayatri. I could never imagine that there could be such a rift between knowledge and actions. A man who has such a gifted pen, whose words emit a stream of clean and clear thoughts; could be so blackened and dark in his inner self was totally beyond me.' Vidya could not bear it anymore. Although she was well-versed with the selfish nature of Gyanshankar which had been proven to her many a times, her self-respect could not tolerate his insult. She didn't want to hear any critical word about him with her ears. In her opinion which was greatly coloured by her wifely faith, it was a great sin. She said in a sharp voice – 'Please do not criticize him before me.' While saying this, her throat became full and the feelings which words had failed to communicate started falling from her eyes as tears.

Rai Saheb said in a hesitant tone – 'I do not criticize him; I'm only telling you the truth. I have now discovered why he has disguised himself as a holy man, and why he's so involved in religious activities. I made him spill out everything with his own mouth. This colourful trap has been laid out by him for Gayatri and most probably, she's even got trapped in it.'

Vidya's brows stiffened, and her face became red. She said in a proud voice – 'Pitaji, I've always respected you and I can't describe how pained I am to disobey you, but it's impossible for me to listen to these allegations about him from my ears. I have spent the last seventeen years serving him, but have never found him getting attracted towards evil lusts. A man who has acted with restraint even in his youth, should not be doubted like this, and by doing so, you are being equally unjust to him as well as my sister. This will surely degrade your own soul.'

Rai Saheb – Don't worry about my soul. Go and drive some sense into that evil man, or else it won't be good for him. I'll never let Gayatri fall a prey to his lustful efforts. I can bear to see you as a widow but can't tolerate the honour of my family being destroyed like this. I had instructed him before leaving not to have any relation with Gayatri but her letters are arriving daily which inform me how caught up she is in his bonds. If you can save her you must; or else, these very hands which offered flowers and garlands at her feet, will sacrifice her on the altar of family honour.

Vidya said crying – You are insulting me in this way after calling me here; this does not befit you. You heart has become so hard. When you have all these thoughts bothering you, I won't stay here for a second. I cannot spoil my afterlife by doubting my own husband. He can be a characterless, evil and a strayed soul in your opinion, but is divine and fit to be worshipped in my eyes. Had I known that you would insult me so much, I would never have come here. If you think that I come here with an eye on your estate and want to trap you, you are highly mistaken. I don't care a bit for your estate. I swear upon God that I am totally content with my situation and I'm fully confident that Mayashankar is also a contented child. If he comes to know of your thoughts, he won't even care to cast a single glance on your property. You have been misled from the beginning to end in this matter.

Rai Saheb cooled down a little at this outburst. He said in an embarrassed tone – 'Yes, it may be possible because I am an old man now. I see something else, and hear something quite the opposite. I have become far more greedy and sceptical than before. I didn't want to defame you husband in your eyes more than what is required to save his life but your fake devotion is forcing me to narrate his heinous deeds in detail. You had seen me before also; was I ever like this? Was I so weak, sick, and ragged?

Did I find it difficult to take even a single step as now? Did I spit out blood like this? All this is his doing. He has given me so much poison with food that it was enough to kill almost twenty people. This is not just an aspersion. I am a living proof of his crime. He has himself admitted this. I found the entire act on eating the first bite itself. But only to show him that it's not that easy to kill me as he had thought, I finished the entire meal. I was confident that I will purge myself of this poison by Yogic procedures, but in a second only, the poison entered every corner of my body and I couldn't take it out. I have done whatever a man could for my health and long life, as a result of which I was more strong and courageous than a twenty-five year old man, even at seventy-two. I wanted to live my life to its utmost capacity. For this, I acted with so much restraint, did so much of Yoga, served the holy men, went to all kinds of places in search of herbs and roots, wandered till Tibet and Kashmir but this devil spoiled all my plans! I had sacrificed all my wealth upon achieving the best of human abilities. I had practiced Yoga and occult in order to enjoy eternal and untainted youth. My only objective in life was to enjoy luxuries. I always derided worry as a black serpent. My servants tortured the subjects in various ways, but I never allowed their pleadings to disrupt my comforts and pleasures. If I ever toured my region, I did it not for resolving their but for my own leisure and hunting, but due to this ruthless devil, all these sins lost their flavour. I am just a skeleton now – lifeless and powerless.'

Thus saying, Rai Saheb moaned with a terrible pain. He coughed loudly and vomitted many clots of blood. He kept lying unconscious for a few minutes. Suddenly he leapt up and said – 'You go to Benaras tomorrow morning and if possible, save your husband from falling into this furnace. Your devotion towards him has calmed me down. I give him the boon to live. But you must take the responsibility of saving your simple-minded sister. If her character is blemished even one bit, your family will be destroyed. This is my last warning. The only way to atone for this sin is to save Gayatri's chastity. There is no other way to redeem you.'

After saying this, Rai Saheb got up slowly and left. Vidya lay down on her bed, hurt with guilt, shame and depression and started sobbing uncontrollably. She had reacted and opposed the first allegation levied by Rai Saheb, but she couldn't resort to ignorance in the case of the latter crime. She was well aware of the selfish policies of her husband but she could not ever imagine that they could be so terrible and dangerous. Till now, his evil tendencies had remained hidden from the outer world. Whatever pain or resentment was caused, remained limited to herself, but now everything was revealed. She fell in the eyes of her father; her face was blackened. It was natural for Rai Sahib to think that Vidya too must be a participant in this evil deed. Perhaps he had come to warn her thinking in this manner only. How could she absolve herself by putting the entire blame one her husband? In this entire dilemma, when Vidya thought about the result of this crime, she trembled with fear. 'O God;' she thought, 'I am so unfortunate, have mercy on me; I have come to take refuge in you.' All kinds of doubts started visiting her heart. Mayashankar's face appeared before her eyes. She almost wished she could fly to her son. Repeatedly, she lamented all these happenings and her mind became anxious, thinking of a possible mishap.

Within a second, this guilt and doubt turned into a fierce anger. All the scattered sparks of fire became a terrible flame and rushed towards Gyanshankar to engulf him. 'You are so fallen, cruel and weak! You have left me in a lurch. It's because of you that I'm suffering so much and God knows how much I'll suffer in future. You are so wicked. God knows what ill deeds I had performed in my past life that I had to deal with you now.'

She decided to write a letter to Gyanshankar and started thinking about its tone. While thinking about it, she fell asleep. She kept lying for a long time. When she felt cold, she startled and woke up; the room was quiet, and there was pin drop silence in the whole house. The maids had also fallen asleep. Her refreshment was kept on the table and a pet cat was hiding near it, waiting for those mice who came out, lured by those delicacies and went back halfway through due to a strange fear. Vidya kept watching the scene for some time. Sleep had quietened her mind. She felt kindness for the mouse who would soon be gulped down by the cat. But just then, she started comparing Gyanshankar's situation to that of the mouse. 'Isn't it the same as this animal's? Why should I be angry with him? He is worthy to be pitied. He is rushing into the claws of death, overtaken by his senses, and is dancing like a wooden puppet in the hands of worldly desires. I will go and talk to him and request him that I have no desire for this wealth which is asking for a sacrifice of my soul and reason. I want to shun away this property. My son will remain poor, will eat the earnings of his sweat, but till the time I can ensure, I will not let him wander near this property.'

49

On reaching Benaras, Gayatri felt like a fish, who, after years of yearning on sand, had suddenly found it's way into water. Gyanshankar was so overtaken by the fear of Rai Saheb's threats that he became all the more doubtful of Gayatri's arrival. But her consolations gradually made him aware of the real situation. She told him clearly that her affections were not subordinate to her father's orders. She thought Gyanshankar to be a victim of injustice and wanted to pacify him with her loving talk. When Gyanshankar was relieved from her side, he took her on a tour of the temples and ghats in Benaras. He used to take her for a bath in the Ganga in the morning, and during the evening, showed her the bustling crowds of the ghats. His door was always crowded by priests of all kinds. The whole city was agog with tales of Gayatri's charity. One day, she went to see the Hindu University and donated twenty thousand there. The next day she inspected the "Ittehaadi orphanage", and gave two thousand to its building fund. The leaders of the Sanatan Dharma came to ask donations for their gurukul. She gave them four thousand rupees. Once she went to Gopal Mandir for prayers, and gave two thousand to the head priest. She kept enjoying the devotional songs there till midnight. She wanted to participate in the singing herself but Gyanshankar did not deem it proper. She had never heard such songs before.

One week passed in these activities. Evening had fallen. Gayatri was sitting in her room, inspecting a lot of sarees. She wanted to buy one of them, but couldn't decide the colour. She took the sarees to see herself in the mirror, and kept them back again. She couldn't make up her mind as to which colour suited her the most. Just then, Shraddha came and stood there. Gayatri said, 'Sister, it's good you came. Tell me, which of these sarees I should buy? I find them all the same.'

Shraddha replied with a smile – How can a rustic like me advise you?

Gayatri – Don't try to fool me. I leave the decision to you. Choose one for yourself and one for me.

Shraddha – You take it, I don't need any. This blue saree will look very nice on you.

Gayatri – Please take one for my sake.

Shraddha – What shall I do with it? It will be kept aside and be eaten by moths.

Shraddha said the last words in such a poignant tone that Gayatri felt the hurt hidden in them. She said, 'How long you'll remain like an ascetic? Why don't you patch up with Babu Premshankar?'

Shraddha smiled and said with tearful eyes, 'What to do; I don't know that art.'

Gayatri – Shall I do it for you?

Shraddha – That will be an obligation on me, but I have no hopes of your success. He has his own mind, and I cannot stray from the religious dictums. Then how can we come together?

Gayatri – Through love.

Shraddha – The love that I have for him cannot be expressed; I can even jump into fire if he signals me. And I believe he too has that kind of love for me, but such love can only make the hearts meet; it has no control over our physical selves.

Just then Gyanshankar came and said to Gayatri, 'I had gone to the Gopal temple. Some devotees think that in the honour of your arrival in Benaras, a Krishnaleela should be organized. I have told them to hold it in the front compound of this bungalow.' Gayatri's face became lit up with delight. She said, 'Will the space be enough?'

Gyan – Yes, it's quite spacious. They also want that you should enact a role in it.

Gayatri – (smiling) I will agree if you too agree to act.

Gyanshankar became involved in the construction of the stage from the next day itself. A huge canopy was erected. Many days were spent on its decoration. Caprets, chairs, glassware, flower-pots, paintings; all were placed on their proper places and started gracing the stage. Pamphlets were distributed outside. Printed invites were sent to the prominent men of the city. For almost four days, Gyanshankar didn't have time to sit back and relax. His one foot remained in the sitting room, where various actors rehearsed their roles, and the second foot in the stage house, where countless labourers, carpenters and painters were doing their jobs. The stage looked uniquely beautiful. There was beauty and greenery all around. As soon as the curtain was raised, a scene from Vrindavan appeared right here in

Benaras. The groves on the banks of the Yamuna, the cows resting in their shades, the hordes of deer, peacocks and cuckoos sitting on the branches of kadamb; the entire scene seemed to be seeped in a poetic colour.

It was eight at night. The entire tent was lit up with electric bulbs. At the main gate, an artificial sun was lit up with electricity, in whose light one could even see tiny ants and insects clearly. The audience had started gathering since seven o'clock. Lala Prabhashankar was welcoming the guests, wearing a black robe and a saffron turban. For women, a partition had been created on the other side. Though Shraddha didn't have any particular interest in such plays, she had agreed to look after the women audience upon Gayatri's request. By eight o'clock, the tent was so full of audience that it seemed as if trains had got crowded up in a fair. Mayashankar had not agreed to participate despite everyone's insistence. He was guarding everyone's shoes at the entrance of the tent. The tenthouse resembled a marketplace at the moment; some laughed, someone pushed the people standing in front, some were debating political issues, and at other places, people were fighting each other for space. Outside, the weather was biting cold, but the tent was very warm on the inside.

At nine p.m. sharp, the curtain was raised. Radhika was standing under a kadamb tree, singing a passage from Surdas, and playing a veena in her hands. Though she wasn't fit for Radhika's role; her pride, middle years and talent were not suitable to play a wanton milk-maiden, the pomp and show surrounding her had hypnotized everyone's critical faculties. The whole audience was submerged in marvel and affection. They thought, 'She seems like a heavenly nymph.' Her sweet voice, her song, her dress and jewels, her attitude and beauty – how to praise all these! She was one in a million, there was no comparison to her; she was unique and incomparable.

After Radha came her three friends; Lalita, Chandravali and Shyama. All started narrating their tales of separation. They started discussing the rudeness and wickedness of Krishna. On top of it, they were troubled by their family's controlling spirit, scoldings and restraints. One said, 'I have been forbidden to go to the well'; the second replied – 'I can't even stand at my door' and the third said – 'When I go to sell curd my old woman accompanies me.' Radhika said with tearful eyes, 'I have got a bad name, now I can't even discuss him with anyone.' Lalita said – 'He is himself not bothered, or else was there no way to meet you?'

Chandravali – He finds pleasure in our yearnings and cries.

Shyama – No, it's not true; he's actually afraid of our family members.

Radha – You keep taking his side in vain. He thinks himself to be so clever! Can't he dupe these idiotic people? The truth is that he is least concerned about us.

Lalita – Let's test him about this.

All agreed to this. They started looking here and there with alert eyes, and moving their brows and hands, discussed about it with each other. They soon finalized their plan. All the four left the stage singing a song. The curtain fell. It was raised again. A small village was visible among a grove of trees. There were many grass huts all around, but very clean and decorated with flowers and leaves. At some places cows were tied; at others, calves mood, and noises of milk being churned were audible. It was a very beautiful scene! In one house Chandravali lay on a bed, sighing in pain. Many men were sitting by her bedside, fanning her, and many women stood at her feet. Cries of 'Doctor! Doctor!' could be heard all over. In the next hut, Lalita also was sick. Near her too, many women were trying to do all kinds of medical remedies. Some said, 'It's a ghost' and another called it a doing of witchcraft. They wanted to call an occult practitioner. One of the young men said, 'All this is your delusion; she is struck with the disease of the heart, call a wise doctor.' In the third hut, Shyama's bed was put up and similar cries could be heard. The fourth house was rather big. Huge cows stood at the door. On one hand heaps of foodgrains were piled and on the other side, milk was stored in pots. There was cleanliness all around. Here, Radhika was lying sick in an anxious state. Near her a priest was sitting, saying his prayers on a mat. Beggars were being given alms. The family members stared at Radhika with worried eyes, and cried for the doctor.

Suddenly, a call came from outside – 'Here comes the doctor, healer for all maladies, for lust, anger, passion, greed; also for duty, deeds and redemption. He can purge the heart of all darkness, of all ignorance; he can give you knowledge, and put the heart to peace!' 'Doctor, doctor!!' The people came out and called him. He had a bag on his shoulder, a round red turban on his head, and a decorated coat of rich green woollen fabric. He had black kajal in his eyes, the reddish tint of betelnut on his lips, and a smile on his face. His gait suggested a gay abandon; as soon as he came on the stage, he kept his bag aside and started singing on his flute –

I am the one who takes away the pain of separation.

I cool the fever of love, just as water cools off fire!

I am the one ……

I give the herb of eternal knowledge, and patience to the heart.

I am the one .....

Radha's family members took him inside. Radha smiled upon seeing him and hid her face. The doctor pressed her fair wrist on the pretext of checking her pulse. Radha took away her hand hesitantly; then they started conversing in the secret language of love.

Radha – There water in the river is very deep.

Doctor – If one has a boat why should he fear the waters?

Radha – There's a storm there; dangerous waves and terrible water creatures.

Doctor – But the boatman is a clever one.

Radha – The sun god is there, but why are stars still shining?

Doctor – When the sunlight shall cover the sky, they will disappear on their own.

He then asked the family members to leave. When they were alone, Radha smiled and said, 'How strong is the bond of love?'

Gyanshankar did not reply to this. Gayatri said again – 'Fire burns the wood, but when the wood burns off, the fire also cools down.'

Gyanshankar still did not say anything. Gayatri looked at him with surprise, 'Why this silence? Have you forgotten your lines? People will laugh at you.'

Gyanshankar's lips were shut, but his breath was beating very fast. His feet were shaking; his eyes reflected a terrible resolve and his face transmitted a dangerous thought, as if a violent animal was gathering his powers to attack his prey. Actually Gyanshankar had decided to take the final leap. In this single leap, he wanted to reach the peak of his fortune, and for this he had been preparing since months; for this very motive he had enacted this play, and taken this disguise.

This was the right moment to take the plunge. It was a sin to let the chance go. He had lured the parrot by offering him grain to his side; it now went about pecking on it in a carefree manner. He was confident that it could be now easily brought to the cage. He had opened the doors of the cage. As soon as the parrot saw it, he opened its wings and flew to the nearest balcony. The lure of food had not been able to destroy its independent spirit. Gayatri was in the same situation at the moment. She hesitated when she saw this mute intention on Gyanshankar's part. This was not what she had desired. She had tasted the fruit of love, its cold fever and its pleasing pain; she had been hypnotized but had not yet lost the inner desire to safeguard her character. She hesitated, and got up in a way in which our hands are raised to avoid a sudden calamity. She quickly went behind the stage in a rush. A cot was lying there, and she fell on it. She felt dizzy and unsteady, like a wolf that listens to the roar of clouds on a quiet night and falls down howling. All she knew at the moment was fear.

But if she had a parrot-like natural apprehension; she also possessed a similar kind of belittled self-respect. The way a parrot falls again on the bait and finally gets caged; in the same way, Gayatri also felt ashamed of her fear and hesitation. Her spiritual purity had been lost long back. Now she also lost hold of the power to retaliate. Her mental horizon had become too wide. The love for her husband could have rested in one of its corners, and had no authority over her heart. Within a second, she returned to the stage, feeling shy as to what Gyanshankar must be thinking of her. 'Alas! I couldn't forget my own self in the rush of devotion. I still couldn't get rid of my pride. What must the audience be thinking about it?' When she reached the dias, Gyanshankar was singing a song to entertain the people. The curtain fell as soon as Gayatri came up.

After half an hour, the curtain was raised for the third time. The same kadamb tree was there, and the same dense grove. The four friends were discussing the healer image of Krishna. 'He's so loving, a mother to his devotees; the biggest devotee of all.'

After this conversation, Ramayana was sung out in passages where love and devotion were compared and finally the feeling of devotion was lauded. The four friends sang the final prayer of worship and the act came to an end. The curtain fell. Everyone was praising Gayatri's depiction of emotions, the sweetness of her voice and her acting prowess.

Many simple devotees believed that she was actually blessed by goddess Radha. The civil society was not so voluble, but the magic of Gayatri's talent, her seriousness, and her divine persona had impressed everyone. Gyanshankar's act was also praised. Though no one had liked his song, his voice lacked all twists and turns but people still couldn't find fault with his playing of the healer.

When Gayatri came inside her room and sat on a couch it was already one at night. She was far too delighted and was being praised on all sides; the city's learned men had praised her knowledge of human psychology before leaving, and even Shraddha was surprised at her acting skills. Her proud heart was getting delirious at the thought that the whole city was agog with her discussions, and her impression. And whose company and inspiration had brought it about? Gayatri's every pore started echoing with music of respect towards Gyanshankar. She cursed herself for doubting him unnecessarily. 'I must apologize to him, and fall on his feet to purge his heart of this sorrow. I am just the dust on his feet; he has made me sit on the highest sky, from the lowest place on earth. I had the ill-sense of doubting him! Who would be more ungrateful than me?' She was lost in these thoughts when Gyanshankar came and stood near her and said – 'Today you bowled over the entire gathering.'

Gayatri said – This entire magic is a result of your training.

Gyanshankar – I had heard that a man imbibes the same qualities that his name indicates, but I never used to believe that. I am now experiencing that this dictum is not without weight. I have also felt it twice that when I start playing my part, I enter a completely different world. A strange delight encapsulates my heart; I almost start feeling that I am Krishna myself.

Gayatri – I was about to say the same thing. I almost tend to forget myself.

Gyan – It's possible that I may have erred in that state of self-delusion. Please forgive me for that.

Gayatri said hesitatingly – When in love, one's inner self becomes pure, there's no scope for lust of any kind.

Gyanshankar kept reminiscing on the meaning behind these words for a minute and then went outside.

The next day Vidyavati reached Benaras. She had not informed about her arrival and had come along with a servant. As soon as she reached the gate she saw a huge tent. Shraddha rushed forward to hug her. The maids came running to her. They all were looking at Vidya with sympathetic eyes. Gayatri had gone for a dip in the Ganga. In Vidya's room Gayatri's set up had been established. All over the place, her trunks and other luggage could be seen. Vidya felt like throwing them out angrily, but chose to keep quiet at the moment. Many maids had also come along with Gayatri. They used to bully the old maids of the house. When they saw Vidya, they just disappeared and didn't bother to wait upon her. Vidya was judging the situation like a police officer, who has come to inspect the proofs left behind after an incident. Whatever doubts had been implanted in her mind by Rai Saheb, now seemed to come true at every step. As soon as they were alone, Vidya asked Shraddha – 'What is this tent for?'

Shraddha – Krishnaleela took place there last night.

Vidya – Did my sister also participate in it?

Shraddha – She became Radhika and Babuji played Krishna.

Vidya – My sister couldn't have acted properly.

Shraddha – Well, she seems quite skilled in it. The whole gathering was bowled over. She must be coming soon; hear it from her.

Vidya – Does she go to the Ganga daily for a bath?

Shraddha – Yes, she goes to the Ganga in the morning and listens to devotional songs in the evening.

Just then Mayashankar came and touched his mother's feet. Vidya hugged him and said, 'Why son, were you alright?'

Maya – Yes, I was very comfortable here.

Vidya – Sister, just see how much his voice has changed. How is the temperament of your aunt? Does she love you?

Maya – Yes, she loves me a lot, she has a very nice temper.

Vidya – Did Krishnaleela take place there also?

Maya – Yes, it took place almost daily. Also, the singing of devotional songs. Raas players were called from Mathura and Vrindavan. Babuji also plays the role of Krishna. His hair has grown very long. He looks like a priest now. You must have seen?

Vidya – Yes, I have! Does my sister still remain sad?

Maya – I haven't seen her sad at all. There isn't a happier soul in the entire house.

Vidya was asking these questions as if a lawyer was cross-questioning a witness. Every answer that came strengthened her doubt. At around ten the noise of a motorcar came. The whole house jumped into action. A maid started laying Gayatri's bed, someone started wiping her slippers, another dusted the carpet and someone else washed her bowl and tumbler. Just then Gayatri came upstairs. Behind her was Gyanshankar. Vidya didn't get out of her room, but Gayatri went and hugged her, saying – 'When did you come? You didn't even write to me about it?'

Vidya took herself aside and said rudely, 'What could have been the use of a letter? Who was free here to have come to receive me? I just came with Damodar Maharaj.'

Gyanshankar looked at Vidya with questioning eyes. The answer was written there in bold and clear words. Vidya wasn't skilled enough to hide her emotions. The whole story was written on her face. She didn't even bother to look at Gyanshankar; leave alone asking about his well-being! She looked like a drawn sword. Her temper clearly betrayed that she was full of anger and would spill over in the first given opportunity. Gyanshankar's heart became anxious. The doubts and the worry about repercussions that had been suppressed under Gayatri's arrival emerged again and started pricking his heart like thorns. He knew for sure that Vidya had come to know everything and would take Gayatri to task as soon as she gets a chance. 'I cannot stop her in any way. All kinds of scares, threats, prayers or pleas would go waste. The only way to save my life is that she shouldn't get a chance to talk to Gayatri now. I should either go to Gayatri with Gorakhpur today itself by the evening train, or else cause such an antagonism between the two sisters that they aren't able to talk to each other openly. What's the big deal in making women fight? Their moods change at the drop of a hat.' Gyanshankar had no idea that Vidya had reached the very crux of her love and devotion for him. He was only thinking that Rai Saheb's incidents were the only reason for her disaffection.

Vidya stepped aside from Gayatri and gave a sharp look to her dressing and style. She had seen her six years ago. Her face had been of a pale colour then, and she was as sad, dark and listless as evening time. But now she had a face as fresh as a blooming lotus. She was full of a developed, glowing and energetic vigour like a newly risen dawn. Vidya seemed like a lonely lamp in front of this glaring electric gleam.

Gayatri asked – 'You must have enjoyed the musical conference very well.'

Gyanshankar's heart started beating fast. He looked at Vidya in a humble way, but her eyes were glued to the ground; she said – 'I never went to the function. All I know is that it did not go off too well. Lalaji fell too sick, and could not participate in it even for a day.'

Gayatri – He must have been very upset at my not going there?

Vidya – Why do you worry about that? What harm can he do to you by getting upset?

Though this answer was enough to suggest a discord, Gayatri was so eager to discuss her Krishnaleela that she did not bother much about it. She said, 'What to tell you; you should have come yesterday, and seen the excellent Krishnaleela. With God's grace, the act was praised in the entire city. There was no fault of any kind. I'll show you the stage in a while, but yesterday's decoration was so attractive that I don't have words to describe it. Thousands of rupees were spent only on the curtains. The tent was glowing with electric bulbs. I was scared to face such a crowd but due to Krishna's blessings my part turned out to be the best. Ask Babuji, how the city people are talking about it! People made me sing a single passage many a times.'

Vidya said sarcastically – It was my misfortune that I didn't come yesterday.

Gayatri – We want to do the play again. I will keep a role for you also.

Vidya – No, please excuse me. I do not wish to aspire for heaven by acting in a play.

Gayatri stared at Vidya's face dumbstruck. But Gyanshankar was delighted in his heart of hearts. The enmity that he wanted to sow in the hearts of the two sisters was getting implanted on its own. He said to Gayatri – 'I think you'd be discomfitted out here. Why don't you shift to a room in the bungalow? You will be far more comfortable there.'

Gayatri looked at Vidya and said – Why Vidya, should I shift there? Wouldn't you feel bad about it? I guess my staying here will disturb you. I often sing religious songs.

Vidya – Do not worry about my comfort; I am not so delicate. Well, if you think that you'll be discomfitted, please do go to the bungalow.

Gyanshankar got Gayatri's luggage shifted to the bungalow. Gayatri too didn't say anything else to Vidya. She understood that jealousy was killing her. And is there anyone in this world, who doesn't want to enjoy the workings of jealousy? She looked at Vidya with proud eyes and went towards the stairs.

50

It was one o' clock at night. Gayatri was singing at her veena when Gyanshankar entered the room. He had decided to ask his boon from the goddess today. The iron was red-hot; there was no chance to think of any pretexts; the only need of the hour was to strike it with multiple blows. The delay of even one day could spoil the tireless enterprise of years, and could destroy all the hopes gathered till now. One improper comment from Vidya's side could turn the tables negatively and her single envious sign could demolish all the fortresses built by Gyanshankar. Perhaps no commander could have thought of such an important and decisive moment in the battlefield as Gyanshankar was anticipating now. His condition was that of a soldier, who sees a spark falling on the arsenal and rushes madly in order to save it. That speed is so important and so precious! The delay of just a second can be the cause of the defeat of the army, the destruction of the fort, loss of the kingdom and devastation of the community. Since today afternoon, Gyanshankar had been busy in finding a solution to this problem. 'How do I begin the topic with her? My style should be such that my selfless tendencies remain on the fore, and shouldn't be exposed.' He had devised such a sequence of discussion that Gayatri should herself propose to adopt Mayashankar and he should delineate his qualities and failings in an unbiased way. 'My position should be that of a third person; none of my words should betray any kind of bias.' He had never employed his wisdom, thought, foresight and deliberation to such an extent. All the hurdles that could impede his success had been planned for in advance by him. He had determined every single word, every hint and every feeling in his mind. He was wearing a saffron-coloured, silk shawl, and his long hair was strewn on it. His eyes were full of a devotee's delight and his face glowed with the divine light of love.

He threw a loving glance at Gayatri and said – 'Your passages are magical in effect. They make the heart seeped in waves of love and the mind intoxicated with devotion.'

Gayatri replied with a smile, 'The magic is not in my songs, but in your soft heart. The dull, lifeless noise of the outside becomes melodious and pleasant once it enters your being. A small earthen lamp also becomes an electric bulb once it is covered by a thick glass.'

Gyanshankar – 'My heart is in a strange condition these days. I am now realising that a man cannot house two different tendencies together; a single soul cannot adopt two forms.'

Gayatri looked at him curiously and keeping her veena on the table, started staring at him.

Gyanshankar said – 'Whatever image we adopt affects our conversation and lifestyle so deeply that our original self is almost lost. I am now experiencing why people object to boys enacting roles of women, and their dancing and enamouring on stage. A kind man becomes rude and rough by staying in the army. His circumstances destroy his kindness. All I can hear now is the sweet tune of the flute and my eyes can see only the lovely scenes from Gokul and Barsana. My whole being is getting united with Krishna, and I cannot stop thinking of Radha even for a second. I can't understand where my heart is trying to take me?

While saying this, a strange light started getting emitted from Gyanshankar's eyes; his face was seeped in love and his voice got submerged in a pleasing tone. He said – 'Gayatri Devi, you might call it my impoliteness, but I need to tell you that in this state of self-renunciation, your high position, your wealth, your real relation with me; all is disappearing before me and you seem like the same Radha to me; the Radha of Vrindavan, who has a sweet smile, soft feelings, a flitting heart and a mesmerizing disposition. I want to erase these feelings from my heart; I make countless efforts but my heart doesn't listen to me. I want to think of you as Rani Gayatri to whom I'm a humble servant but I keep forgetting it. Your one call, one glance, a single noise of your footsteps; in fact your lone memory is capable enough to lift me out of this outside world and take me into another. I completely forget myself. I had kept this feeling a secret from you till now, but the way in which a sitar breaks into music at a single strike of the ring, in the same manner, the heart starts speaking when struck by love. I have told you now the condition of my heart. I am at peace now. Who can tell about the final culmination of this love, except the one who has lighted this flame in my heart!'

The way in which a man suffering from thirst is satiated after drinking cold water; its every drop creates a light in his eyes and a colour on his face - in the same way listening to this love narrative made Gayatri's face lit up, her eyes drunk, and she felt a new energy in her life. In her opinion this was a spiritual kind of love devoid of all lust; Krishna was its main inspiration. He was sitting in Gyanshankar's heart himself, singing these love-notes in his voice. She had herself felt similar feelings but had not been able to express them due to shyness. She used to become Gayatri again after playing the part of Radha but listening to these words made her all intoxicated. She felt as if Radha was seated in her heart, and her voice became free of all shyness. She found her whole world, and her entire life small in front of this spiritual gem. Her eyes started shining with a self-pride. She said – 'Dearest, I am too in such a state. I am also burning in this fever. This body and mind is now offered to you. After getting the jewel of your love I have no more desire for any want or ambition. This self-light has removed the darkness of all greed and passion; I am now satiated with worldly things. My only aspiration is that this forehead should be at your feet and my life is spent in singing your praises. I am neither a queen, nor Gayatri; I am just your lovelorn beggar and disciple, Radha. You are my master, my life-basis, my God. I will wander in the lanes of Barsana with you, and sing your love songs at the banks of Yamuna. I know that I am not worthy of you and my heart is still caught in worldly pleasures. I haven't yet been able to break the bonds of religion and society but accept me whatever I am. Your divine company has made me taste this heavenly pleasure; won't it calm the perversions of my heart?'

While saying this Gayatri's eyes became full of tears. She fell at Gyanshankar's feet in a surge of devotion. He made her get up and hugged her tightly. Suddenly, the door of the room opened and Vidya stepped in. Gyanshankar and Gayatri both startled to see the door and stood aside in a hesitating way. Their eyes bent down, and their faces became pale. Gyanshankar took out a book from an almirah to read, but Gayatri kept standing like a mute, still and stone statue. Her face was covered in sweat. She wanted that the earth should split and engulf her. She couldn't make any excuse or pretext. Her guilt had left no scope for daring of any sort. She was seeing these words printed on the floor in bold letters, 'You have been left nowhere; your face is all blackened now.' This thought was moving her heart, and this voice echoing in her ears. She started sobbing loudly. Just a second ago, her eyes were reflecting self-pride, but now there was no one more meek and downtrodden than her in the world. In a single moment, her devotion, love and knowledge stood exposed. She found that under the clear waters of her devotion, there was a muddy pit, and under the peak of her love, a pitch dark cave. 'As soon as I stepped into the waters, I got stuck in the mud, and when I ascended the peak, I fell in the cave. Alas! I was duped by the clear, golden and overflowing water; these pleasing, white mountains and now, I have no way of escape.' She felt so upset at her weakness and lowliness, the feelings of shame and curse hurt her so much that she started screaming and crying. 'Alas! Vidya must be thinking that I'm so deceitful! She used to respect me so much; regard me in high esteem and now I am a wanton lady in her eyes, who has stained the good name of her family. I used to boast of my truthfulness and restraint and praised service and good deeds. I used to pretend as a highly devoted and honest woman; was proud of my love for my husband, and I can't show my face to her now. Alas! She must be thinking that I have relations with her husband. I'm a stone in her way and a thorn in her heart! I am the fire that has burnt her home; a bitch who has tasted the food meant for her. O lord! How blind I had become. She's my younger sister and just like my daughter.' This thought pained Gayatri's heart so much that she held her chest and sat up. Suddenly she got up crying and went and fell at Vidya's feet.

Vidyavati had happened to come to that room only by chance. She was sitting in her room upstairs and thinking, 'What has happened to my sister? How can I make her understand that this great man (Gyanshankar) is only luring her by means of love and devotion? All this drama is being enacted due to her property. God knows why he's become so blind that for wealth and property, he's crushing all ethics and reason under his feet. How wicked, greedy and blind this man is that he's not bothered about someone's life or honour to fulfill his own interests. He talks as if his eyes have opened to enlightenment, and there's no one more holy, scholarly or benevolent than him in the world, but his inner self is full of animal nature, deceit and evil. His only concern is that Gayatri should somehow adopt Maya, the papers should be done and his authority should be established in this area with a total finality. It's for this purpose that he has cast this net of knowledge and devotion; has donned the robes of a devotee, grown his hair; and he dances and sings as if he's Krishna himself. How terrible is his wickedness; how hateful his behaviour and his devilish nature!'

She was lost in these thoughts when she had heard Gayatri singing. She was singing a passage from Surdas on the veena. The tune was so melodious, her voice was so full of poignancy and desire, the effect was so beautiful that Vidya became lured to listen on and on; she almost became helpless before that polite ardour. She thought, 'It's impossible to have such an effect in music without true love and heartfelt pain. Her devotion is true indeed. She has been hypnotized. I should relieve her, and try to save her from falling into that pit, and awaken her true senses. Of course my husband would be angry with me and think me to be his enemy; he might even threaten me with life but I don't care. Even if I lose my life in this task, I shouldn't delay it. A man, who's such a killer; so dangerous and such a sham, is not fit to be kept in touch with. It's a sin to see his face, to stay in his house and to be called his wife.'

She descended from the stairs and came slowly to Gayatri's room but she'd just taken the first step, and she recoiled back. In front of her, Gayatri and Gyanshankar stood in an embrace. She had come with quite positive intentions, but on seeing this shameless scene, her blood started boiling, her eyes started emitting sparks, and her heart yearned to insult and curse them. She looked at her husband with fiery eyes. If her curse had a power to burn them to ashes, she would have indeed cursed them. If her hands had power enough to kill them in a single blow she would have certainly struck them. But all she had within her power was to flee from the scene. She couldn't have stayed there in such a dishevelled state. She wanted to return immediately. The fields were on fire, the bird had been sliced off; there was no use trying to save her. The sympathy that had just emerged for Gayatri disappeared; she was no longer an object of her compassion. We try to save our white clothes from dirty spots, but once they are soiled we throw them away, and feel hateful to touch them. In her opinion Gayatri should now be left to bear the consequences of her acts. 'I was under the delusion that this evil creature has swayed you, your inner self is pure, but I have lost this belief now. Krishna's devotion and love can't be so intoxicating that they do not allow a person to differenciate between good and bad. One can become so shameless only in a condition of one's downfall. Alas! You unfortunate woman, you thought of all this at this point of your age. The husband whom you treated like a god, whose pure memory you had worshipped, and upon taking whose very name your face blushed with pride, has been defamed by you in such a way; you insulted his dead body itself.'

But when she saw Gayatri screaming and crying, her heart melted, and when she fell on her feet, she sat up with a feeling of affection towards her and kept Gayatri's head on her shoulders. Both the sisters started crying; one with guilt; the other with a surge of love.

Till now Gyanshankar was in a state of perplexity; he was angry with Vidya but could not dare to say anything to her. He was dreading that his prey might run away breaking its chains. He was very annoyed with Gayatri's crying and wailing as well. Till the time she stood alone crying, he was hopeful of a remedy, but when she fell at Vidya's feet and both the sisters started crying together, he lost his patience. To remain quiet anymore was to lose an already won game, and to release a precious prey. He said in a rude tone to Vidya – 'What right do you have to enter someone's room without permission?'

Vidya didn't say anything. Gayatri held her neck tightly as if it was the sole means to save herself from drowning.

Gyanshankar became all the more angry and said, 'There's no need for you to come here and for your own good, you should leave or else I'll hold your hand and show you the way out. You have become the hurdle in my path many a times, but now I want to remove you forever.'

Vidya frowned at him and said - I have come to my sister; till the time she tells me to go, I won't.

Gyanshankar roared and said – Get lost, or it won't be good for you!

Vidya replied fearlessly – Never; I won't go if you say so!

Gyanshankar sped towards Vidya, shaking in anger and wanting to hold her by his hand when Gayatri stood up and said proudly, 'Why are you getting so angry? She has come to see me and I won't let her go right now.'

Gayatri's eyes were still full of tears, her throat was still shivering, and she was in sobs, but there were signs of waters relenting down; the sun was shining again. She had gained back her senses, and her natural sense of honour was again trying to wake up.

Gyanshankar said, 'Gayatri Devi, you are again forgetting who you are. I am really sorry that even after offering yourself on the altar of devotion and love for years, you are caught in the chains of attachment. Please remember who you are. Think who I am. Think of your true relation with me. Are you taking this pure bond to be so ragged that it should be saved even from wind and light? It is a spiritual relation; strong and undeterred. No temporal power can break it down. It's such a mournful state that despite being well-versed with our spiritual oneness, you are choosing to ignore me so much. Should I infer that for all these days you were just playing a game of dolls? If this is the case, you have not left me anywhere. I have offered all my body and spirit, duty and action to my love for you. I was thinking that you have stepped on this path after much deliberation, and know its difficulties. The path of love is difficult indeed; tough and endless. There's defamation here, and ill-words. There's social criticism and insult; stains and sarcasm. Only he reaches the ultimate goal who turns away from the world, and breaks all relations with it. On this path worldly bonds are shackles of the feet; it's impossible to take any step without breaking them. If you just stepped on it for fun, without thinking of the consequences you did great injustice to me. This crime will be upon you.'

Although Gyanshankar was skilled in the art of hiding his feelings, his embarrassed face exposed his brief exposition of love and its problems. The gilted ring had started glowing due to heat.

If Gyanshankar had said these words on an earlier occasion, Gayatri would have started crying and would have apologized by falling on his feet; rather, these words would have been uttered by her own mouth at Gyanshankar's disaffection. But now that intoxication had died down. She threw a flying glance at Gyanshankar. There seemed no devotion there now. The long hair and gaudy clothes of the actor had been taken off. That face which had mesmerized the audience and which was welcomed with loud applause on the stage had lost its shine. The way in which a simple rustic, once duped by the gamblers, does not even stand near them so that he's not lured again, Gayatri too wanted to run away from the spot. She didn't say anything to Gyanshankar and walked to the door, holding Vidya by her hand. Gyanshankar understood that his mantra had failed. He felt angry, but not on Gayatri; on his defeat and ill luck. 'Alas! My sacrifices of the past seven years are going in vain. The hopes of my life are turning their back on me – what to do? How to save them? I tortured my soul so much; devised so many conspiracies? I sacrificed my conscience upon this sole ambition. I did everything that I shouldn't have done. I learned to dance, to mimic, to act, but all efforts were futile. Rai Saheb had truly said that this property isn't there in my destiny. I will never fulfill my hopes. This aspiration will burn along with me on my pyre.'

Gayatri's rudeness was no less heartrending. Gyanshankar may not have loved her truly but he was charmed by her beauty and disposition. Her talent, generosity, affection, wisdom and simplicity drew him towards her. If Gayatri had been on one side and her property on the other, and if Gyanshankar had been asked to choose one of them, it was certain that he would have rushed to the latter, but divorced from her being, her wealth was like a saltless meal. The same Gayatri was now going away, turning her face from him.

These repentant thoughts pained Gyanshankar's heart so much that his eyes became tearful. He sat on the chair and looking towards the wall started crying. He had never felt so sad at his helplessness, nor so mournful ever in his life. He had never felt so guilty at his selfishness and lowliness. The way a man remembers God during illness, in the same way, he remembers his ill deeds after doing them. The spiritual significance of defeat is far more than that of victory.

When Gayatri saw Gyanshankar weeping, she stood still at the door. She couldn't step out. The tears of women are like water; they are signs of a destroyed patience and confidence. Gayatri felt sorry for her rudeness and disaffection. The fire of self-protection which had blazed a second ago, cooled off by meeting this water. Those feelings became revived which had beem tingling her heart for seven years; those pleasant talks, those activities, those singing sessions, love-talks and thoughts of separation started visting her eyes again. The clouds of shame and guilt dispelled, and the clear moon of love started shining. She came and stood near Gyanshankar and started wiping his tears with her handkerchief. Overwhelmed with love, she kept his head in her lap. In his tear-filled eyes, she saw a deep sea of love overflowing with its waves. His face was lighted with the rays of a sun which was love itself. She looked at him with thirsty eyes which were full of apology, as if she was saying, 'Alas! How weak; how heartless I am. How dumb have I been that I couldn't differenciate between appearance and reality. My lack of devotion must have hurt his pure and soft heart. You took me to the sky from earth, you sowed the seeds of power in my heart and I got a taste of the supreme pleasure of love through your inspirational teachings. How could I be so blind? Undoubtedly lord Krishna was trying to test me, and I failed miserably in it. He tested me on the touchstone of love, and I proved tainted. Alas! My seven years got spoilt today. I doubted a man whose heart is the home of Krishna and whose throat echoes the tune of the flute. Radha! Why did you dispel your magic from my heart? Please come, sit in my heart and feed me the nectar of you devotion.'

While thinking of all this, Gayatri's eyes became enamoured. She said in a shaking voice – 'O lord! Your maid is standing before you with folded hands apologizing for her sins.'

Gyanshankar looked at her with piercing eyes and understood that his tears had had the desired effect. He startled as if he'd just woken up from a sleep and said - 'Radha?'

Gayatri - Please forgive me.

Gyan - You are asking forgiveness? This is your injustice to me! You are a goddess of love, an image of affection, absolutely faultless and stainless. It's my ill-luck that you are so fickle–minded. What peace is there in the life of lovers? Your instability has robbed me of my senses. I am still doubtful whether I'm talking to Rani Gayatri or to Radharani? I have forgotten myself. My heart has had such an assault that I can't say if this wound can ever be healed. The love and devotion that I took to be so steady proved softer than a wall of sand. The creeper of hope that I had planted on it; the garden that I had planned upon it was submerged in water. Oh! What a pleasant dream I had harboured! I had thought this pleasure-garden will one day bloom with flowers; you and me will tear away the worldly net and enjoy the peace of devotion, sitting in some grove of Vrindavan. We shall fill up the tree-groves with the sounds of our love. The waves of Kalindi will echo our love-song. I will become a servant of Krishna, and you will cook delicious things for him. We shall build a cottage of love far from this world and its aberrations and spend our days devoted to Radha-Krishna or else give away our lives at the feet of Radha-Krishna in our own temple. It's with this very motive that I came and arranged everything in your estate. But now it seems that all those pleasant desires will be locked in my heart and soon, I'll depart from this world, depressed and devastated.

Gayatri was overwhelmed with love and said – 'My lord! Do not utter such words from your mouth. I am a poor, helpless woman, lost in the darkness of ignorance, I get deluded often; but I have caught your arm, I am your suppliant, and you'll have to forgive my lowliness and weaknesses. I also have an aspiration to spend my life at your feet. I will turn away from the world, break my ties with everyone, and will wander in the lanes of Barsana and Vrindavan. The only worry I have is that after me, my estate should be managed by able hands, my subjects shouldn't be tortured, and the income of the estate should be used for charitable causes. You and I will manage our lives in just ten or twelve thousand. I don't need anything else. Yes, I do wish that people should remember me, my name should be immortal, and so should be my fame and good deeds. This sole worry has chained my feet till now; please cut it off. I place this burden upon you. As soon as you arrange for these two things, I'll be assured and then we will never separate for all our lives. I suggest that you build a trust for my property. My husband also wanted the same.'

Gyanshankar – It's easy to form a trust, but I doubt if your objectives can be fulfilled by it. I have expressed my opinion regarding it earlier also. You can appoint various stoical and truthful trustees, but as soon as they get a chance, they will start filling up their own coffers. Human character is very strange. You cannot say with surety about someone that he will never be unsteady, or stray from the honest path. We shall be sitting in Vrindavan, and subjects will be tortured out here. Who will listen to their pleas? The income to be used for social welfare will be lost upon dance parties, that to be spent on Rasleela would be spent on garden-parties, the pieces meant for the temple will adorn the trustees' sitting rooms, friends will be entertained more than holy men, and all you will get is a bad name. I can get your orders implemented immediately, but I have no faith in the trustees. Your motive can be fulfilled only in a condition when the estate is in the hands of a man who respects you like his own, who is obliged to you, who cares for your wishes deeply; who is of the same inclination as you, whose heart is replete with kindness and love and all these qualities can only be in a man who has a childlike love for you and who deems you to be his mother. If you are aware of such a fellow, I would suggest that you adopt him. I cannot think of a better arrangement than this. Possibly we'd have to look after him for a while, but in the longer run, we shall be free of all responsibilities. Then our days of peace and free living will arrive. I will place a garland of love upon my dear Radha, and sing songs of love to her;

no kind of worry, doubt or threat from the world shall be able to disrupt our tranquility.

Gayatri was very pleased. The picture of that ideal life came alive in her imagination. Her temperament soared. She could not remember that will of her husband which he had done regarding the estate and one she had tried to protect even by opposing Gyanshankar. She couldn't think about the pros and cons of the trust herself. Gyanshankar's analysis seemed too decisive. She lost faith in the trust. She said – 'What you say is true. How can we believe the trustees? No one can tell what goes on in the mind of another; how can one decide the internal qualities of someone else?'

She kept thinking for a few minutes. She was thinking about the child she could adopt. She tried to think of her own family and relatives, but the problem remained the same. There were many boys, but due to one reason or the other, Gayatri couldn't decide in their favour. While thinking thus, she startled, and was about to take the name of Mayashankar when she stopped. Gyanshankar had hidden his desire so well and had spread an aura of his self-respect to the extent that initially Gayatri couldn't think of Mayashankar, and even when she did, she hesitated to express her opinion lest Gyanshankar's honour might feel hurt. Although his indications were too clear, Gayatri was under an intoxication which doesn't allow one to differenciate between wine and water. She thought of discussing the matter many a times, but Gyanshankar always had such a self-renouncing attitude that she could not open her mouth. She started remembering many of Mayashankar's qualities such as thoughtfulness, honesty, wisdom and good sense. She couldn't think of a better heir than him. Gyanshankar saw her confusion and asked – 'Did you think of any boy?'

Gayatri hesitated and said – Yes, I did, but I can't say whether you will like him or not. I can't choose better than that.

Gyanshankar – Let me hear who he is.

Gayatri – First promise me that you'll accept him.

Gyanshankar's heart felt a tickle. He said – How can I promise without knowing?

Gayatri – I know you'll object to it and Vidya will never agree, but I can't think of anyone except him.

Gyanshankar hid his delight and said – Let me hear whose sun of fortune has risen?

Gayatri – Should I tell? Hope you won't feel bad.

Gyan – Not at all, please say.

Gayatri – Mayashankar.

Gyanshankar started as if a bullet had passed by his ears. He looked at her with surprise and said in a tone as if she had joked, 'Mayashankar!'

Gayatri – Yes, you've promised; you'll have to agree now.

Gyanshankar – I had said that I'll give you my opinion after I hear the name. Now I know and I tell you that I just can't agree with you.

Gayatri – I knew this beforehand, but you shouldn't object, seeing the relation that's between me and you.

Gyanshankar – I don't have any objection myself. I have sacrificed my whole self to you and that includes Mayashankar, but you know very well the status of my family. Despite all kinds of downfalls, its honour is still intact. My uncle and other relatives will never approve of it, and Vidya may resort to poisoning herself. Apart from this, I will also be looked down upon. Possibly people will think that I've taken undue advantage of your simplicity and generosity and your family members will be after my life.

Gayatri – Please rest assured about my relatives; I will make them fight and kill each other. You will have to bear social criticism for my sake. Only Vidya is left; I'll make her agree somehow.

Gyan – No, don't harbour such hopes. If you are thinking of persuading her, it's far more difficult than you can imagine. You haven't seen her true colours. She is burning with wifely jealousy at the moment. Even if you give her nectar she'll deem it as venom. Till the time all legal formalities are done and all rituals are completed as per tradition she shouldn't come to know of it at any cost. Our hopes will be realized, but who will be the receptacle of those curses which will be given by people who had coveted your property for years? Their houses will be swept with unrest. All will rush for my blood. Though I don't fear them, but an enemy must never be thought as weak. We can never remain carefree about one from whom we've snatched money or land.

Gayatri – Don't worry about these evil men. They are dogs; they'll fight and kill themselves for a few bones.

Gyanshankar kept staring at the ground for a few minutes, as if he was doing a great sacrifice. Then he said with tearful eyes, 'As you wish; your orders are my command. I pray to God that this boy may prove lucky for you and whatever you expect of him may be fulfilled. May God bless him with good wisdom so that he realises your ideals. He is your boy from today, not mine. Though in separating my only child from myself, I am undergoing an agony only I can understand, but Krishna has opened the doors of devotion for us by putting this thought in your mind. He is calling us towards his feet. This is our great fortune.'

Gayatri held Gyanshankar's hand and emotionally and said – Please ask about an auspicious time from some priest tomorrow itself.

51

It was eight at night. Gyanshankar's sitting room was filled with many prominent men of the city. In the centre of the room, there was an iron cauldron kept, and sacrificial offerings were being made in it. On one side of it, Gayatri was seated; on the other side, Gyanshankar and Maya. The priest was chanting prayers from the vedas. Gayatri's fair complexion seemed like gold heated up with the flames of the fire. Her blue sari was suiting her perfectly. All eyes were fixed on her beautiful face. This was the ceremony of Maya's adoption; he was becoming Gayatri's foster-son. Some men were whispering to each other, 'What a lucky boy! He's being made the master of millions; and we never found any penny, lying anywhere.' Some others were saying, - 'Gyanshankar is a vicious fellow; he duped Gayatri so much that it ended with his taking away of her property. Now one knows why he had enacted all this drama. He had grown his hair long for this very day.' Some people thought that Gyanshankar was far more dark-hearted than it seemed on the surface.

When Lala Prabhashankar first heard of the proposal, he was very angry, but when Gayatri explained the entire situation to him politely, he too became almost half-ready for it. After the prayers, the feast began. It was arranged totally by him. There was no better way to bring his half-agreement into full for Maya's adoption. He had been given full authority to spend as he pleased, and to get whatever delicacies he wanted, cooked. Thus, on this occasion, he had exhibited all his culinary art. He was too delighted at the moment, and enjoyed the praises of food from the mouths of the people. Among the guests, there were many who had a temperamental dislike towards food; who actually thought participation in feasts to be an injustice to them. There were some who never ate anything without measuring or weighing it. But today's tasty delicacies had not kept any distinction between a strong and a weak digestion. Taste had strengthened even the latter.

After the feast, the musical function began. Alahdin was a seven year old boy, but a scholar of vocal music and well-trained in the art. He was divinely blessed. He had a unique mastery over instruments such as jaltarang, taus, sitar, sarod, veena, pakhavaj and sarangi. People were amazed to see his marvellous achievements at such a young age. The scholars who had spent a lifetime mastering a single instrument were also floored at the skill of his hands and their musical feat. His knowledge shamed their specialization. At present, his fame had spread in the entire country, as if he had won the entire universe. Gyanshankar had invited him from Calcutta on this function. He was very weak, crooked and ugly in appearance, but his qualities outshone his outer image. His voice was as sweet as a koel's melody. The entire gathering was mesmerized.

These festivities were going on in this side of the house, and on the other side, Vidya was sitting in her room crying at her fate. Every single beat on the tabla struck her heart like the blow of hammer. She was an honourable, religiously devout, contented lady and a follower of sacrifice as an ideal. Though she hated the selfish nature of her husband, she didn't allow this feeling to be an impediment in her spirit of service. Ever since she had heard the narrative of Gyanshankar's moral downfall from Rai Saheb, her respect for her husband had suffered a lot. Whatever was left dissipated after witnessing the shameful scene of the last night. When on seeing Gyanshankar, Gayatri again went to him; Vidya couldn't bear to stay there. She rushed upstairs in a state of anger and fell on the floor in her room. It was not a feeling of jealousy, where the prime feeling is of untowardness; nor of love, which thirsts for the opponent's blood. It was a fire that burns oneself; a self-destructive anger, which bites its own lips, pinches its own skin and bites its organs with its own teeth. She kept lying on the floor and wept the whole night. 'To whom should I attach my affections now? My husband is not my own, nor is my house. I am an orphan now; no one is bothered about me. O God! For which sin of mine have you punished me thus? I have never hurt anyone intentionally. Why did you destroy me in this manner? Why did you take away my husband? It was my sole wealth; I was proud of this only, and derived all my strength from it. You broke my pride, and took away my strength. When there's no fire, what is that use of ashes? This is my vanity box, my vanity bottle; what to do with them now?' Vidya took the box down from the shelf and threw all its components in the garden below in that state of pain and depression. What a piognant scene it was! Tears were flowing from her eyes like a stream and she was breaking her bangles and throwing them away. This was the highest extent of her weak anger! She was a wealthy man's daughter, but she didn't even have those comforts here which her father's maids enjoyed; still she was content and patient. She didn't mind her position too much. Gyanshankar was selfish, greedy, rude and irresponsible, and she did feel sorry about it. He was still her own, and she had all the right to curse and deliberate with him. After listening to the extent of his evilness, lowliness and hankering after luxuries, she was burning in a fire. She had come from Lucknow like a lightning. She wanted to strike Gyanshankar and burn away his vicious tendencies and pierce him with her sarcasms and bitter words. Till now, she was proud of her wifely status. Till about eight o' clock that night, she had thought of Gyanshankar as her very own; and she thought she had the right to be angry with him and burn him with her remarks; insult him as she pleased because he belonged to her. We cannot see our own house burning away. The house may be built of debris, or might be already ruined, but we cannot see it in flames of fire. But if, due to some reason, that house ceases to belong to us, then the flames might reach the highest of skies; we don't mourn its loss. The deplorable scene of the last night had removed this sense of belongingness and love from Vidya's heart. Her only sorrow now was about her misfortune, and her lack of a strong support. Her state was that of a kite whose string had been broken, or like that of tree whose roots had been chopped away.

Vidya kept lying in that dishevelled state the whole night. Sometimes she thought of going to Lucknow and spending her life there; sometimes she thought why she should live; what's wrong in dying rather than living like this? The whole night was spent in these confusions. Morning came, but she did not feel like getting up. Just then Shraddha came up and looking at her face, said, 'Did you keep awake for the whole night? Your eyes are all red!'

Vidya replied with downcast eyes – Yes, I couldn't sleep last night.

Shraddha – Weren't you able to talk to Gayatri Devi? I find her somewhat different today. You used to praise her a lot.

Vidya – Why, did you see anything new?

Shraddha – I see a new thing daily. But the scene I saw yesterday night and the things I heard, I am too ashamed to recall. It must be around eleven. I heard some noises, lying in my room. I was scared lest some thieves may have come. I slowly went downstairs. A lamp was burning in the sitting room. When I looked through the glass, I was shocked. What to tell you; I never thought Gayatri to be so wanton. She pretends to worship Krishna, but look at her frivolousness. I had sensed something wrong as soon as I saw her, but still couldn't sense that she was so deeply involved with him.

Vidya – I too had seen a similar scene. You had gone long after I'd left. I had got to know the entire story in Lucknow itself. I had come running from there only to stop its dire consequences, but have lost all hope seeing the situation here. These two have reached the middle of the waters; it's too hard to save them now. But I will still insist that Gayatri is not so much to blame as this fellow who is going around with long tresses and yellow robes. Poor Gayatri is a simple-minded woman. She is particularly inclined towards religion, so this man became a devotee and tried to influence her by donning this disguise. There won't be a more vicious soul in this world. Sister, I tell you something from my heart; I have come to hate his face. I have suffered such a blow that it's difficult for me to survive this. He will surely be punished for this heinous sin. May God forbid that I see the ruin of this family with my own eyes. It will be a golden moment when my bond with this world gets broken.

Shraddha – It's not good to speak ill of anyone, and I remained quiet uptil now even after seeing everything, but I can't restrain myself anymore. If it was in my power, I would get the heads of such evil women chopped off. This is not innocence, this is shamelessness. She pretends to be simple only to show off. A man might be too clever, too vicious, too entrapping, but women of a strong character can never be lured. What's the use of those eyes who cannot judge a man's intention by his outward style? Fire is there to burn everything, but has anyone seen a green twig burning? Shame is the soul of women; without it they are like dry wood, which can be burnt by a mere spark into ashes. She didn't even think about her husband's dead soul? How pained it must be? My house has been turned impure by her coming. From what I heard at night, I could guess that Gayatri wants to adopt Maya.

Vidya said in a scared tone – Maya?

Shraddha – Yes, these arrangements seem to be made for that only. Invites are being sent out in the city.

Vidya's eyes were filled with huge drops of tears as if they were peapods filled with peas. She said, 'Sister, my boat seems to be drowned now. Whatever had to happen has happened. Now I know the whole story. This wicked man had cast this net precisely for this; he has adopted this disguise for that only, and came to slave for Gayatri with this hidden motive in mind. I was scared about it beforehand. How much I talked to him, and forbade him, but he just didn't listen to me. Now I know what he had planned. He has been hankering after it for the past seven years. Till now, I thought that he has been impressed by Gayatri's beauty, style and way of talking. She is not fit to be hated even after this odious act. A person who can love, cannot be devoid of duty, kindness, and politeness; his heart keeps alight with the flame of love but a person who fulfills his vested interests by donning a disguise of love, and who hunts from behind a partition; none can be more low and fallen than him. He's worst than a robber who takes away people's lives for money. He insults a pure sentiment like love. His sin is unpardonable. I still take Gayatri to be innocent. Sister, the fall of this family now seems imminent. Where there is so much of sin, deceit and dishonesty, how can anyone survive? Now I remember my father's warning. He had told me before coming here - 'If you don't put down this fire, your family will be ruined.' Oh! My pores are tingling with fear! What will be the fate of poor Maya? This evil wealth and property will make him lose his life also; and will sting him like a serpent. Sister, my heart is wailing, how can I save Maya from this fire? He's the apple of my eyes and the sole basis of my life. This heartless devil, this butcher is putting a knife on my son's throat. How to hide him in my lap? How to cover him in my heart? He's giving him poison despite being his father. He's lighting a sinful fire and pushing my son into it. I cannot see this destruction with my own eyes. Sister, I can tell you that after my daughter's birth, he made me unfit to be a mother by giving me some strange potion and doing some horrible ritual upon me. Now I wish he had done all this much earlier. It's far better to remain without kids than to face a day when your child will be snatched from you. Alas! Who will save my son now? I can't protect him now. The flames of fire are rushing towards him. Sister, go and talk to that ruthless man. Please save my Maya if you can. No, I don't think you can do it, this Satan will not agree to anything. If he has resolved to do it, he'll do it at all costs.

Thus saying, she got up and looked down from the window. The area before the drawing room was being cleaned up, and carpets were being dusted. Her eyes were looking for Maya; she wanted to hug him tightly to herself. She couldn't see him. In a split second, a car arrived, and Gayatri and Gyanshankar came and sat on it. Maya too got out of the drawing room and sat in the car. Vidya called impatiently – 'Maya, Maya! Come here!' but either he didn't listen or did not bother. She kept calling out and the car sped away. Vidya felt as if her feet had slipped into water. She fell down unconscious. But Shraddha caught her, and avoided an injury.

For some time, Vidya kept lying unconscious. Shraddha kept crying, putting her head in her lap. 'I used to think that I am too unfortunate. This poor woman's trouble is far worse. If he (Premshankar) could have been informed somehow, he would certainly have requested Gayatri to see sense. She respects him a lot. Perhaps she would have relented, but due to the workings of this great man (Gyanshankar), he cannot meet Gayatri. They have left home precisely to avoid all hurdles. I think it's all Vidya's fault. As soon as I had told her about the adoption, she should have gone out and scolded them both, and should have dragged Maya inside with her. Could anyone have dared to snatch my son from me!'

Suddenly Vidya opened her eyes and said in a feeble voice - 'Sister, what will happen now?'

Shraddha – Everything can happen, if anyone wills it to happen. One only needs to sit up and act.

Vidya – No, nothing can be down now. All arrangements are taking place; God knows how our uncle became ready for it!

Shraddha – I will go and ask servants, when they have decided to return.

Vidya – They will not return before evening. They have thought of this ploy to remove Maya from this house. Whatever they have decided will now take place for sure. Our father's curse is before my eyes. This untoward incident is bound to happen and it will.

Shraddha – If this is your condition, any tragedy can take place.

Vidya asked her with curiosity – What control do I have upon anything?

Shraddha – Why not? When they return in the evening, go downstairs and get Maya with you forcefully. If he refuses, tell him everything clearly. He's a sensible boy; he'll surely turn away from them.

Vidya (thinking) – And if he refuses to believe me? These people must have filled his mind with all sorts of things.

Shraddha – Then wait for the people to gather, and tell them, that all this is taking place against your will. I do not wish to give away my son for adoption. The tables will be turned upon everybody. If I had been in your place, I would have caused such an uproar that they would have been defeated for life. What to do, I don't have any right to say anything, or else I would have taught them a lesson!

Vidya said in a hopeless tone – Sister, I can't do all this. I neither have such ability, nor such courage. If nothing else, Maya himself rejects my proposal then I will die of sorrow. It's impossible for me to address a crowded gathering. My feet will refuse to go there. Even if they do, my tongue will be tied once I reach there.

Shraddha – God knows where they have gone. If I could see Gayatri even for a second, I would have tried to make her see reason.

52

The celebration was taking place in Gyanshankar's sitting hall. Master Alahdin's miraculous performance was delighting the audience. The audience was crowding at the doors. All kinds of beggars were gathered in the porch. Mayashankar suddenly remembered his mother at the close of the day. He was very happy today. His feet were bustling. He was doing many jobs wholeheartedly. Gyanshankar repeatedly told him, 'You sit and relax. There are many men to work, what's the need for you to slog?' But he just couldn't sit idle. He picked up a lamp to clean, or the khus container for refilling. He kept strolling in the motorcar the whole day. When he returned, he narrated everything to Tejshankar and Padmashankar; 'We went here, and there, and saw many things.' He loved this exaggerated account. When he got bored, he sat on the offerings. Thereafter, he participated in the feast. When the singing began, his flitting heart became peaceful. Everybody was lost in the recital, and no one was willing to hear his talk. He now remembered, 'I didn't go to pay respects to my mother! Oh! She will hug me as soon as she sees me and bless me. She will praise my silk dress a lot.' Thinking about all this, he smilingly went to Vidya's room. There was stillness in the room, and a dim wall lamp was burning. Vidya was lying on her bed. Her maids had gone downstairs to listen to the music. The women of Lala Prabhashankar's house had not been invited and they hadn't come on their own. Shraddha was reading something in her room. Maya went near his mother and saw that her hair were all strewn, tears were falling from her eyes, her lips had turned blue and her face had become all lifeless. He called out, worried – 'Amma, Amma!' Vidya opened her eyes and kept staring at him for a minute, as if she couldn't believe her eyes. She then got up. She hugged Maya and covered his head with her sari end, as if she was saving him from an assault and said in a harried tone – 'Come, my dear son! Let me see you properly. I was thinking about you only. People were pushing you into a furnace. My heart was pounding loudly! I called you again and again, but you never listened to me. God has saved you. He is our saviour. I will not let you go again. Sit before my eyes. I will keep seeing you – See, see! He's coming to hold you, I'll shut the doors. He's your father. But he has no pity for you. I'll close the doors. Keep sitting here.'

Thus saying she rushed to the door, but became unstable, and fell on the floor unconscious. Seeing her condition and listening to her unsteady talk, Maya became dazed. He couldn't stay there for a second, out of fear. He fled the room like an arrow and came to the hall. Gyanshankar was busy looking after the guests. There was no scope to tell him anything. Gayatri was sitting behind a partition and thinking, 'I should keep this Alahdin in my service for singing devotional songs. My temple will be famous all over the country.' Maya came in and said – 'Mausiji, please come with me and see to Amma. God knows what has come upon her. She seems to be in a delirium.'

Gayatri's heart stood still. She knew Vidya's nature very well. On listening to this news, she got far more worried than she would have been in any other condition. She was seeing Vidya's changed stance since the previous day. She remembered last night's incident also. She went towards the stairs. Maya too followed her. Many things were scattered there at that time. Gayatri said –'You sit here, or else we won't find anything left out here. I'll just come. Don't you worry; I guess she's got fever.'

Gayatri reached Vidya's room. Her heart was leaping wildly. She could sense the real situation in an intuitive way. She stepped into the room very slowly. The faded lamp was still burning, and Vidya was lying near the door, on the ground, having lost her senses. Her face had turned deathlike, her eyes were closed, and her breath was beating fast. Although it was very cold, yet her body was covered in sweat. Drops of sweat lined her forehead, as if dewdrops had fallen on a stale flower. Gayatri increased the light of the lamp and saw Vidya's face in it. Her lips had turned blue and her legs and arms were trembling slowly. She kept her head in her lap, and took out her perfumed handkerchief. She started fanning her with it. Her heart became anxious with a pain caused by extreme love. Her throat choked and she asked - 'Vidya, how are you feeling?'

Vidya opened her eyes and seeing Gayatri, said – 'Sister!' She couldn't say anything else except this. She tried, to say something repeatedly, but failed. An extreme poignancy spread on her face. She looked at Gayatri helplessly. Her eyes were red, but they didn't have any anger in them. They reflected a kind of self-light. They were full of plea, pardon and peace. Our last reflections are the essence of our life; pure and devoid of maligned feelings like envy and jealousy. Vidya's lips were quiet, but her eyes were saying – 'Please excuse my crimes. I am a guest of a few hours now. Please purge your heart of all ill-will from my side. I have no complaints against you; whatever was destined in my fate, happened. Whatever is destined in yours, will also happen. I am entrusting you with all I had. Please protect it.'

Gayatri said, crying – Vidya, why don't you speak? How are you feeling, shall I call a doctor?

Vidya looked at her disappointingly and folded her hands. Her eyes became shut. Gayatri went down in the sitting room and said to Maya, 'Take your Babuji upstairs. I have to go; Vidya is not too well.'

In just a second, Gyanshankar and Maya came upstairs. Shraddha too came, listening to this noice. Gyanshankar called out to Vidya twice or thrice, but she didn't open her eyes. Then he took out a bottle of rosewater from the almirah and sprinkled it on her face many a times. Vidya's eyes opened, but as soon as she saw her husband, she gave a loud scream. Though her hands and feet were stiff, but it seemed as if an electric current ran in them suddenly. She got up immediately. She closed her eyes with her hands and moved to the door. Gayatri took to her and asked – 'Vidya, don't you recognize him, he's Babu Gyanshankar.'

Vidya looked at him with doubtful and fearful eyes, and moving backwards, said, - 'Oh! He's come again. For God's sake, please save me from him!'

Gayatri – Vidya, please gather yourself. Have you eaten anything odd? Should I call a doctor!

Vidya – Please save me, for God's sake; please save me from him.

Gayatri – Can't you recognize him; it's Babuji?

Vidya – No, no, he's a Satan. He has long hair. Look, he's rushing towards me with teeth protruding out. Oh! Please shoo him away; he'll eat me up. See, see he's about to catch me. He has horns, big teeth and huge nails. No, I will not go. Leave me you devil, leave my hand. Alas! He's throwing me into the fire. Oh see, he's caught Maya. He says, 'I'll sacrifice him'. You wicked; don't you have even a little pity? Please leave him, I'll go with you, push me into fire but leave him for God's sake.' While saying this, she again fell down unconscious. Gyanshankar said in a worried and embarrassed tone, 'She has consumed poison. I'll just go to Dr. Priyanath. Perhaps he can still save her life. I couldn't imagine that she'll be so upset at my giving away of Maya to you. I did not understand her true nature till now. She was a pure soul, a goddess, and didn't deserve a greedy and selfish man like me.'

After saying this, he went away with tear-filled eyes. Shraddha took Vidya in her lap. Gayatri started fanning her. Maya was standing there, weeping. The room was silent; it was a kind of silence which is nowhere except the venue of death. All the women were trying to bring back Vidya to her senses, but no one uttered anything. Everyone was taken over by the fear of death.

Vidya's eyes opened after half an hour. She saw pairs of scared eyes all around her, and then asked for water.

Shraddha mixed rosewater and water in a bowl and took it to her lips. She opened them to drink, but could not quench her thirst; her will could no longer control her organs. Her eyeballs turned in a second.

Shraddha understood that it was her last moment. She said – 'Sister, do you wish to say anything to anybody? Maya is standing before you.'

Vidya's listless eyes turned towards Shraddha, a few teardrops fell on the ground, her body trembled and the lamp was extinguished.

After a week, Munni also fell sick, clamouring for her mother. She kept calling for her day and night. She stopped eating and drinking, and when it was time to take medicines; she shut her mouth so tightly that no one could make her open it. Shraddha kept luring her in many ways, but didn't prove successful. Poor Maya took her in his lap, looked at her dull face and cried. Gyanshankar did not find time very often, but Lala Prabhashankar went to the doctor many a times, brought medicines, got many toys to entertain her, but Munni didn't even bother to look at them. God knows what grudge she had towards Gayatri. She started crying whenever she saw her face. Once when Gayatri took her in her lap, she bit her with her teeth. On the fourth day she was overtaken by fever and after three days of illness, the girl, hungry for the love of her mother, expired.

After Vidya's death, it was soon discovered how popular and decent she was. The women of the locality came to Shraddha and wept in her memory. They kept queuing the whole day long! The elder lady and her daughter-in-law too were mourning for her with a true heart. 'That goddess of a woman never called anybody in a rude manner; she even talked to her maids politely. Her fate may have been unfavourable, but she was too kind. She couldn't bear to see anyone in pain. She was so charitable that she never let any poor beggar go away empty-handed; she could give a rupee in place of penny, and a kilo where a gram was needed.' Gayatri used to shy away from these women. Whenever she came on the scene all of them kept quiet and ignored her. To earn their respect, Gayatri used to give sweets and toys to their children, and discussed Vidya in a woeful manner, but nothing came out of these efforts. Though none of them said anything openly, but their sarcasms were far more piercing than mere satire. One day, the elder lady said in front of her – 'God knows what kind of a thorn pricked her heart and took away her life. God had blessed her with husband and son both, but she just couldn't bear that thorn.' What was the thorn that she was referring to was reflected far more clearly in the eyes of those women than through her voice. Gayatri could do nothing except bear the insult.

In reality, Gayatri was far sadder at Vidya's death than any woman in the family or the village. Dr. Priyanath had said clearly that she had consumed poison. All the symptoms had also proved it! But Gayatri thought the murder to be upon her. Her honourable soul shuddered at the very thought of it. She hesitated to discuss Vidya even with her personal maids. She could never forget the night of her death. Vidya's apologetic image always visited her eyes. 'Alas! Had I known that she had been so deluded with me, I'd have never let it happen.' But when she analyzed the incidents of the previous night, her mind told her that it was natural for Vidya to have doubted her intentions. Besides, she could now remember many of her trivial acts which she had done merely to make Vidya jealous and to cause her pain. Although at that time, she had done all that under the influence of her lover, and could have done the same before the entire world, but the drops of blood had taken her out of that intoxicated state. Her heart admitted in private that this was not pure love, and lust had entered it by some unknown route. 'Vidya had turned soft upon seeing me, but on seeing Gyanshankar, her stepping back, screaming and shouting was revealing clearly that she died because of us. It was her supreme generosity that she thought me to be innocent.' This great obligation crushed her soul under its burden. By and by, this feeling became so strong that she became disillusioned with love and devotion. In her opinion, this tragedy had proved that they had fallen from the high ideals of devotion, and while wading through the clear waters of love, they had got caught in the weeds of luxuries; as if this incident was a divinely induced warning to waken up their souls. Now when Gyanshankar came to see her, she didn't talk openly to him. He had not done the last rites of Vidya himself, and hadn't even lit up her pyre. He had made a Brahmin do everything. Gayatri saw this as his dishonesty and hard-heartedness, and did not approve of it. She wanted that Vidya's death rituals should be performed according to tradition and with the honour she deserved. It was the sole means to lend peace to her soul. She hinted about it to Gyanshankar, but he avoided it. Therefore, she turned away whenever she saw him, and did not allow him to influence her with his words. She was scared lest his rampant behaviour would defame her further. She wanted to remain free of the blame of this murder, at least in the eyes of the world.

Gayatri came to know about other feats of Gyanshankar as well. He had criticized his family members so much to her that she had thought him to be an idol of patience and tolerance. But truth seemed to be totally different. He hadn't even informed Premshankar about this tragic incident. But as soon as the latter heard about it, he came running and participated in every ritual continuously for sixteen days. Lala Prabhashankar was so busy in arranging the death rites, the feast of the community and everything else as if there had never been any kind of discord with his nephew. His wife also expressed genuine sympathy. But Gyanshankar's attitude clearly revealed that he didn't like the participation of these people. He remained at a distance from them, and talked to them roughly as if all of them were his enemies, and wanted to harm him by coming there. On the day of the Brahmin feast, he had a great quarrel with Lala Prabhashankar. The latter was insisting that the sweets should be made at home. Gyanshankar thought it to be quite impractical. Possibly, the sweets would be far better in taste, but they would prove too expensive. One could get ordinary sweets form the market. Prabhashankar said, 'If you wish to feed somebody, feed him in such a way that those who eat should remember that they had eaten a feast somewhere.' Gyanshankar got angry and said – 'I'm not such a fool that I'll spend a fortune on this false praise.' The result was that cheap sweets were ordered from the market. The Brahmins had their fill, but criticized the family in the entire city.

The most hateful thing that Gayatri felt now was her state of house-arrest. Gyanshankar even opened her letters and read them, fearing that Rai Saheb may have written to her. If she started conversing with Premshankar or Lala Prabhashankar, he used to come immediately and sit there, and talked in such an improper way that ordinary talk turned into a debate. His attitude clearly revealed that he couldn't bear anyone's sitting with or talking to Gayatri. Not just that, as far as he could ensure, he didn't even allow Gayatri to see any women. A self-respecting attitude thinks public opinion to be dispensible in religious matters, but respects it a lot in worldly matters. To be free of the culpability of Vidya's murder, Gayatri deemed the sympathy of the family and the community women as essential. She wanted to fulfill this motive with her own behavior; by praising Vidya and even by criticizing Gyanshankar. After the sixteenth day ceremony and the Brahmin feast, she went on an inspection of the city's girl schools and instituted an award in each of them in Vidya's name; and this was not just a pretence; she had great love for Vidya, and she mourned her death truly. She used to cry in solitude, thinking of her, and her face never left her eyes. When the elder lady and Shraddha talked about Vidya, she often sat near them reluctantly to listen to them. She could not bring herself to mind their sarcastic comments. On these occasions, when Gyanshankar tried to divert her attention to the affairs of the estate, she felt very bad. She sometimes used to say irritatingly – 'Go and tell him I am not free. What's the need for consulting me regarding such minor things? Hasn't God given him any kind of sense? Estate! Estate!! He's not bothered about anyone's life or death, but everyone cannot have the same attitude.' Sometimes she used to keep sitting with Shraddha for hours only to annoy Gyanshankar. She didn't want to remain as a puppet in his hands now. Her proud temperament was now craving to be free of his control. She wanted to break this bond now. Once she went to Premshankar's farm without informing Gyanshankar and stayed there for the whole day. One of these days, she called Lala Prabhashankar and Premshankar for a meal and did the entire cooking herself! Lalaji too had to accept her culinary skills!

Two months passed away. Gradually, the women started believing Gayatri. The outward covers of envy and malice started receding. She now came to know many things that she had no inkling of earlier. In fact, she became a prominent part of this social group. The character of Gyanshankar was discussed almost daily out here, and as a result, Gayatri started losing all respect for him. The elder lady and her daughter-in-law told her the story of Gyanshankar's enmity which refused to end anywhere. Shraddha was not so voluble, but it didn't need any extra intelligence to understand that she too didn't have any particular affection for Gayanshankar. His narrow-mindedness and selfishness became evident to Gayatri almost every day. She now understood that her father had told her to beware of Gyanshankar not without undue reason. She became disillusioned with his love and devotion. She started doubting whether he had donned that cover to fulfill his goal. She could now remember many things that confirmed this doubt. As this doubt started increasing, her heart started turning away from Gyanshankar. He himself got very perplexed upon seeing this tendency in Gayatri. In his opinion, the only way to remove this grudge from her mind was to drag her to Gorakhpur in some way or the other. But he was afraid of proposing it to her. She was required to be alone for the fulfilment of his motive. There was no special benefit only by giving away Maya to her. Gayatri's present age was thirty-five and there was no reason why she shouldn't stay alive for another forty-five. Such a long wait was unbearable for impatient men like Gyanshankar. Therefore he wanted to woo her again by trying out the ploy of love and devotion upon her.

One day, he came to Gayatri with a letter and said, 'This important letter has arrived from Gorakhpur. The manager has written that these are the days of the harvest. It's important for us to be there, or the cultivated produce will be all lost, and servants will eat it up.'

Gayatri replied angrily – I will answer your question later, but first tell me why do you open my letters?

Gyanshankar was shocked, and understood that he had fallen far below in her eyes than he actually anticipated. He said reluctantly – 'I thought that after such intimacy, this formality was not needed amongst us. But if you find it improper, it shall not be repeated again.'

Gayatri said in an embarrassed tone – I didn't mean that. I only wanted that my personal letters should not be opened.

Gyanshankar – The reason behind this daring was that I thought our souls to be united, but it seems that the envious environment of the house has created a rift between us as well. Such audacity will not occur in future. It seems my bad days have arrived. Let' see what all I'll have to tolerate.

Gayatri changed the topic and said – You can write to the manager that we won't be able to come right now; he can begin collecting the taxes and all.

Gyanshankar – In my opinion, we must go there.

Gayatri – Then you can go. Where's the need for me to go? I wish to stay here for some more days.

Gyanshankar said in a disappointed way – As you wish. But without you, I will find every second like a year. The Krishna temple is ready. The pleasure that we will have in prayers and songs out there is unthinkable here. I wanted that we should spend the rainy season in Vrindavan this year. This hope has been slashed. You are the lamp of my life-path, and the centre of my love and devotion. Without you I'll find darkness all around me. It's quite possible that I may go mad.

Had Gayatri heard this loving talk two months ago, she would have been delighted but by staying here, she had got a complete insight into his character. The instrument which used to convert a tuneless rhythm into a melodious song was now out of order. She had now learnt to counteract the evil mantras of Gyanshankar. She said – 'My condition out here will be far worse, and I'll roam about in a lost condition, but what to do? It's very important to clear people's hearts from one's side. I'm ready to bear the sorrow of this separation for this very reason, or else you know that there's nothing to engage my attention here. I can only keep my body here. As far as my heart is concerned it will never leave the company of my Krishna. In the arena of love, a distance of a thousand miles too means nothing; one enjoys the bliss of meeting even in a state of separation. Well, you must write to me daily, or else I'll be as worried as death.'

Gyanshankar looked at Gayatri deeply, as if he wanted to understand her true motives. She didn't seem to be the simple and innocent Gayatri of yore. She had acquired the unfathomable artfulness of women; she had now learned to return fraud in exchange of fraud. He understood that he won't be able to have his own way with her now. His gilted coins will not fetch anything in this market now. A new play will have to be devised to win this game and new forts will have to be built. To leave Gayatri here was to lose one's prey. He decided to take up the topic on some other occasion and left. Suddenly Gayatri asked – 'So when do you plan to go? I think the morning train will suit you fine.'

Gyanshankar stared at the ground meekly and said - Very well.

Gayatri – Yes, when you have to go, then don't delay it. Till the time we're caught in this worldly net, we must sing according to its tunes.

Gyanshankar – As you please.

After saying this, he went away with a hurtful face. When he left, Gayatri felt the same unhappiness that one feels on hurting a friend, but she didn't stop him.

53

The friendship between Shraddha and Gayatri started increasing day by day. Gayatri now came to know how sacrificing, gentle, kind and chaste Shraddha was. Friendship led to further intimacy; one started sharing one's secrets with the other and soon there was nothing hidden between them. Shraddha's story was a poignant tale of love and separation where there was nothing to hide from beginning to end. She narrated her pain of separation in a tearful way, lamented the ruthless love of principles that Premshankar had, and also repented her own stubbornness. She used to feel a peaceful contentment in telling her story and expressing her feelings. On the other hand, Gayatri's tale began with love and ended with self-guilt. She had to be careful about expressing her feelings, and was often forced to hide something or the other. She had some dark spots in her heart which she couldn't dare to reveal; especially to someone like Shraddha whose mind and utterings were one. She used to shy away from discussing love and devotion in front of her. When she remembered the daring act of Gyanshankar on the night of the theatre outing, she realized that till that moment, her mind was pure and clean, though certain lusts had started raising their ugly heads. 'Whatever took place afterwards was a result of Gyanshankar's lust and my weakness, which I termed devotion. Gyanshankar spread out this colourful net of devotion before me to satisfy his evil interests. His articles about me, and pushing me ahead in religious and social fields, his tireless loyalty, alertness and self-offering were means of realizing his life-goals. My own pride caused my fall, and my love of fame devastated me. My religious devoutness, my fake and unreasonable devotion, my pleasures, and that rash gratefulness upon which I never hesitated to sacrifice even my restraint and purity, were all aspects of my pride. This hunter targeted the most sensitive part of my nature. He ruined my whole religiosity, and spoiled me for his love of wealth.' A woman always loves to blame a man for her failings, and deems herself to be downtrodden and hurt. Gayatri's heart now felt Gyanshankar's love-talk, soft behaviour and thirsty eyes like piercing arrows. She sometimes got so excited with sorrow and anger that she wanted to ruin him in the same way that he had ruined the purity of her life.

One day, she was sitting, lost in such perturbing thoughts when Shraddha came and sat near her, and looking at her face, said – 'Why is your face getting red? Are there tears in your eyes?'

Gayatri – It's nothing; just a matter of the heart.

Shraddha – Isn't it fit to be shared with me?

Gayatri – What have I hidden from you that you ask such a question? I might have tried to hide but you know everything. Who doesn't know it out here? When I remember those things, I feel like chopping off his throat and mine with a single knife. My blood starts boiling. I could never imagine that he's so vicious and such a rogue. My values tell me that I should also have poison and kill myself like Vidya, but this will be precisely what he wants; he'll praise his fate and openly enjoy this wealth. No, I will not be so foolish. I will cause him to die hankering and craving after this property. I will crush his head in the same way that a serpent's head is crushed. Alas! There won't be anyone as unfortunate as me in this wide world.

Thus saying, Gayatri started sobbing loudly. After taking a breath, she said in the same surge, 'Shraddha, you won't believe me, but this man is a hardcore magician. He had cast such a spell on me that I completely forgot my true self. I am not justifying myself. There are many germs floating in the atmosphere. Their poison affects only those creatures who already have the tendency to be affected by them. A mosquito bite does not cause fever and delirium to everybody. That outward effect only heightens the internal aberration. Had this not been the case, there wouldn't have been any healthy person in the world. I housed this crooked element within me. I was proud of my self-strength. I derided pleasures of the senses. This evil soul burnt my house with the same lamp that lighted it, and sliced my throat with the same sword which used to protect me. I will now cut him with that very sword. He must be thinking that I am weak and baseless, and cannot harm him in any way. But I'll show him that a weak woman can scatter away the mountains even if she seems as fluid as water. My respected father is blessed with foreknowledge. He had come to know of his ill-intentions, so he had warned me to stay away from him. He must have told Vidya too about it. That's why Vidya had come here to warn me. But alas! I was so intoxicated that I didn't bother about my father's warning. This rogue has made me fall in his eyes as well. He will not like to see my face again.

After saying this, Gayatri again became mournful. Shraddha couldn't understand how to console her. Suddenly Gayatri got up. She took out a pen, inkpot and paper from her box and said, 'Sister, whatever had to happen has happened. We shall mourn it for the rest of our lives. Vidya was a goddess; she thought it better to die than to live a life of insult. I am a devil; I am scared of death. But from now on, this life will be dedicated to sacrifice and atonement. I am resigning from my estate; I have no right on it. I have lost it since three years. For so many days, I was enjoying it without any authority. This estate was a gift of my devotion to my husband. I had inherited all this wealth and splendour so that I could guard the family honour, and my husband's memory should stay permanent. How significant that honour must be, for the protection of which I was given this property worth crores. But I disrupted its sanctity, and offered that precious gem to my love of luxury. I have no right to hold that estate now. I have no authority to enter that house now, and every grain of that coffer is fit to be sacrificed by me. I kept ruling a treasure earned out of corruption.

Thus saying, Gayatri started writing something, but Shraddha took away the paper and said, 'Please think carefully about it; it's not good to be so impulsive.'

Gayatri – I have thought of everything. I will take off these borrowed clothes right away and sit at a place where no one will be able to see my face.

Shraddha – Just think what will people say? They will imagine all sorts of things. Supposing, you do resign, then too, how will you ensure that people who will take over your estate will run it properly? Now the only way to improve your present and transcendental life is to spend the rest of the years in the service of God, going to pilgrimages and serving the holy men. Possibly, you might meet some great soul, whose teachings might bring peace to your heart. God has given you money. Do good deeds with it. Care for orphans and widows, get rest-houses made, and follow the path of knowledge instead of devotion. The latter is straight, but full of thorns, the former is complex, but clear.

Shraddha's lecture had not yet ended when a maid came and said – Bahuji, the Deputy's wife has arrived, who used to live here earlier. Should I get her here only?

Shradha – Is it Sheelmani?

Maid – Yes indeed; she's the one, somewhat wheatish in complexion! Earlier she used to be loaded with ornaments, but today she's not even wearing a ring. These rich people get tired of jewellery also.

Shraddha – Yes, get her here.

In just a second, Sheelmani came and stood there. She was just wearing a clean sari. What to talk of jewels, even her lips were devoid of any reddish tint of betel-leaf. Shraddha got up and hugged her lovingly, then asked – 'When did you come from Sitapur?'

Sheelmani – Today only, and for the reason that I wish to have a clear word with Lala Gyanshankar. Ever since I've heard of Vidya's consuming poison and killing herself, my heart is burning in pain. All this is the doing of that sister who's going around as a queen. She alone must have poisoned her.

Sheelmani had not looked at Gayatri, and even if she had, she did not recognize her. Shraddha bit her tongue, and touching her chest, indicated Gayatri with her eyes. Sheelmani startled and looked to her left, and saw a woman sitting with bent head. Seeing her glow, her beauty, dress and ornaments, she understood that it was Gayatri herself. Her heart missed a beat, but she had already uttered some words which were difficult to revert or keep up. She had already swallowed a burning morsel and there was no other option but to gulp it down. Although her anger was quite justified, she wouldn't have spoken such words on the face of Gayatri. But the arrow had already left the bow, so her anger now converted into haughtiness, and she became rude instead of getting embarrassed. She faced Gayatri and said, 'Oh! The Rani Sahiba is present here only. Whatever I've said regarding you must have sounded bad in your ears, but I can't apologize for it to you. I would have said the same to you directly and not just me, the whole world is saying just the same. People might not open their mouths, but this is precisely what's there in their hearts. Whosoever has dealt with Lala Gyanshankar even once, will not deem it impossible. My husband has studied with him and is well acquainted with his character.'

'When he was the magistrate here, Gyanshankar had filed a case for rent increase. He kept appeasing me for months so that I could get the verdict in his favour. I didn't know the truth, so I believed his false ways. My husband kept refusing at first but when I insisted he became ready for it. The only saving grace was that in the meanwhile, I became aware of his tyranny, and the verdict was avoided, or else many poor tenants would have paid for it with their lives. The plea was dismissed. He got so angry with this that he wrote in the newspapers against my husband. When he read in the papers about his religious fervour, he used to say that this fellow is upto some new conspiracy. The pomp and show that took place in Gorakhpur during the Sanatan Dharma function and the Krishna- leela that took place in Benaras, made my husband feel sorry, and according to him, it was a lure put forward by Gyanshankar for Rani Saheba. There has to be some other motive behind it. If I had met Lalaji, I would have taken him to task and he would have remembered it for life.'

Gayatri was staring at the window; in fact her vision lost hold of the window by and by. The waves of regret and guilt errupted from her conscience and struck her throat, but returned after giving a few jolts to the boat of her eyes. She had become devoid of all consciousness. All her life faculties had become still. Shraddha looked at her face and could not stop her tears. She had never felt so much pity for this unfortunate woman. It was unjust even to sit there. She couldn't do anything except take Sheelmani with her in the other room. The two ladies kept talking there for a while. Shraddha put the entire burden of Vidya's death on Gyanshankar's head. Sheelmani thought Gayatri too as a party to it. Both tried to prove their respective points. In the end, Shraddha scored over Sheelmani. After that, the latter narrated her story. How much she had tried for childbirth, and how many midwives and doctors she had consulted. In fact she made Shraddha believe that she'd even got pregnant once, but alas! a miscarriage occurred in the seventh month and all her hopes were destroyed! Shraddha consoled her with a true heart. Then they talked about random things for some time. Shraddha asked – 'What has the Deputy Sahib planned now?'

Sheelmani – He has resigned and wants to stay with Babu Premshankar. He has great faith in him. Initially when he used to talk about resigning, I thought that he doesn't wish to work, and didn't agree to it, but in the past three years I've realized that one cannot save one's self-respect in this service. Whatever plans the social leaders derive for the benefit of people; the government tries to hamper and disrupt them. It seems wary of the fact that if people progress and become aware, they may not follow its authority. Therefore, it keeps bringing in new laws to suppress the feelings of the people and to shut their mouths. The leaders have arranged for charkhas and looms to take the people out of the clutches of poverty. The government is trying to pose hurdles in that. It has declared the propagation of swadeshi cloth among shopkeepers and customers as a crime. In order to stop the sale of wine and drugs, it's again a crime to picket against addicts and contractors. In the past years, when there was a war in Europe, the government levied taxes on the people. It was deemed as a loan in words, but was actually a tax. The officers tortured the poor people, and forced them to pay in various ways; in fact many had to sell their ploughs and oxen to pay the government. Whosoever refused was either beaten up or caught under false charges. My husband did not apply any force in his district. He said clearly, 'Whosoever wishes to pay he can; anyone who doesn't, can refuse.' The result was that other areas got lacs of rupees, but his area didn't contribute much. Due to this, the district collector got angry and complained against him. He was forced to give away his post, and was demoted. When I witnessed all this, I myself forced him to resign. When we eat the money of the people, we must work for their welfare. It is improper that we strangle those who give us our basic earnings. This is a kind of traitorship; an extreme viciousness. This can be done only by those whose souls are dead, and who do not have any thought about the veracity of their deeds except filling up their stomachs. A person who has even an iota of love for his community, cannot do such injustice. It's the government who gets the maximum profit; it gets all authority, the British traders fill up their pockets, and all sin goes to poor servants who have their own stomachs to fill and that of their selfish officers. And why should we bother to get a job? There's enough to eat in the house. We can in fact feed a few others, besides ourselves. Now we have resolved to stay here with Babu Premshankar and try to serve the people as far as we can. But you tell me, for how long will you stay like this? Have you decided to spend the rest of your life in tears?

Shraddha – How can anyone erase the workings of fate?

Sheel – That's not the case; it's your useless stubbornness. I will now drag you with me. I won't be able to stay in that wilderness alone. If we both stay together, we can pass our days happily. I will also take your husband to task as soon as I get a chance. He goes about sacrificing himself for the world and is not bothered about his own family. Does he risk losing his honour in atoning a bit?

Shraddha – You don't know him as yet. He can do everything except atonement. He will not break his principles! He is, moreover, quite worried about me. Ever since Gyanshankar started staying in Gorakhpur, he often comes here daily. If needed, he can even stay here, but his rules are dearest to his heart.

Sheelmani looked towards the sky and found that the clouds had gathered. She said in a worried tone – 'It might start raining. I'll go now.' Shraddha tried to stop her a lot, but she didn't agree. Finally she said - 'Please come and wipe her (Gayatri's) tears. The poor woman must be crying since then.'

Sheelmani – It's written in her fate. These tears are nothing! Such a person should have this kind of punishment only. What can she do to me by getting upset? She might be a queen, but only in her own home.

After seeing off Sheelmani, Shraddha came to Gayatri feeling embarrassed. She was afraid lest Gayatri had stated doubting her intentions. She stepped in the room, scared like a criminal. Gayatri looked to her like a suppliant, but didn't say anything. She was writing something. Her face was reflecting a determined resolve along with sorrow. For quite some time, she kept busy in writing as if she hadn't noticed Shraddha. Suddenly she said – 'Sister, if you don't mind; would you please call Maya, and my maids too.'

Shraddha understood that there was something transpiring in her mind. She couldn't dare to ask anything. She went and called Maya and the maids. Maya came and stood before Gayatri in a second. The maids were playing on a swing in the garden. It was the month of August; there were clouds in the sky, and the rain songs sounded very pleasant.

Gayatri looked at Maya from head to toe, and asked – Do you know whose son you are?

Maya replied with surprise – Don't I know even that?

Gayatri – I wish to hear that from your mouth so that I can know what you think of me.

Maya hadn't understood the question before. After getting this indication, he became alert.

He said – I was Lala Gyanshankar's son earlier; now I'm yours.

Gayatri – That's why you must respect my wishes in each subject, after God.

Maya – Of course.

Gayatri – Babu Gyanshankar has no concern with your upbringing and education; it's in my purview now.

Maya – You need not worry, I want to stay away from him myself. Ever since I saw my mother screaming upon seeing his face in her last moments, I have lost all respect for him.

Gayatri – That means you are far more intelligent than I thought you were. I am leaving for Badrinath today. I don't know when I'd return. I am thinking of leaving you in Babu Premshankar's care till then. I want that you should follow him and treat him as your father. I have written this letter to him. You take it and see him. He will arrange for your proper education. He will also devise for your rest and needs according to your position. You will know in a few days that you are in far able hands than your real father. Possibly, Lala Pramshankar may not have that much affection for you as a real father can, but there's no doubt that the skills you will learn from him for your future responsibilities and the way he can consolidate your life, thoughts and character, cannot be done by anyone else. I hope he'll undertake this burden gladly. We both shall be bound to him for this. This second letter is for Babu Gyanshankar. He will be the manager of my estate till I return. I have instructed him to send two thousand every month to Babu Premshankar. Send this letter to the post-office.

Just then, all the four maids arrived. Gayatri said to them – 'I am going on a journey of Badrinath today. Who will accompany me from you all?'

All said in one voice – We all shall go.

'No, I just need one of you. Gulabi, will you come?

'As you wish; But I haven't seen my kids since one month.

'Then you can go home. Kesari, will you come?'

'When will you return?'

'I can't say.'

'I have no problem in going, but I've heard that the water on the mountains is very hard.'

'Then you can also go home. Will you come Anusuya?'

'Sarkar, there's no one back home. My house is getting ruined. If I go there, I'll have no foodgrains left when I come back.'

'You can also leave. Now only you are left, Radha; I've to ask you also, will you come with me?'

'Yes, Sarkar, I will.'

'We'll have to go today only.'

'Whenever you wish, we can go.'

'Your taxes will be excused on twenty bighas.'

All the other three maids were embarrassed and said – 'Sarkar, we all are ready to go. When we survive on your alms, how can we stay without you?'

'No, I don't need you. Only Radha will stay with me. All of you are an ungrateful lot; I'll have nothing to do with you from now on.'

Thus saying, Gayatri started preparing for the journey. Radha was standing there looking at her, but couldn't dare to say anything. In such a condition, a person becomes somewhat perturbed. A little thing can annoy him, and a little can please him as well.

54

Babu Gyanshankar came to Gorakhpur, but in a manner in which a girl comes to her in-laws' house. He often remained lost in sorrow and worry. He may not have had true love for Gayatri, but did possess that kind of love for her which drunkards have for their wine. Without her, he just didn't enjoy anything here. He kept reading or thinking something, lying in his room the whole day long. He stopped going for walks, and stopped seeing people also. He never stepped near the Krishna temple also. He regretted again and again as to why he didn't stop Gayatri from going to Benaras. 'All this is the result of that mistake only. Shraddha, Premshankar and the elder lady have poisoned her against me. They have influenced Gayatri and have maligned her heart towards me.' Sometimes he also got angry with his confusing lusts and in this state of depression; he started admitting the power of fate. 'The will of God is certainly a strong factor, or else why should all my plans get spoilt? No effort bore any result? My love of money made me do all kinds of things. I killed my soul, my duty, principles, and washed my hands with the blood of a virtuous woman, but could not gain victory over fate. I can see the road towards my goal, but God knows whether I'll be able to reach it or not.' In this hopeless situation, he remembered Gayatri repeatedly; her glowing figure kept haunting his eyes, her affectionate talk echoed in her ears, and he let out many sighs.

Gyanshankar now feared daily that Gayatri may separate him from herself. He was scared to open his letters lest any letter from Gayatri should shock him. He had written many letters to her, but she hadn't replied to any of them. He got all the more confused at this. Mayashankar's letters did arrive, but they didn't lend any peace to his heart. He was anxious to know what was happening in Benaras, but they there was no such being who could have provided any detailed news of the place. Sometimes he thought of going there himself, but was afraid of the repercussions. 'I am away from her eyes out here, and it's possible that her anger might cool down after a few days. If she gets all the more offended on seeing me, I'll lose all the remaining hopes also.'

About three-four months passed in this manner. It was the month of September. The festival of Janamashtami was approaching. The preparations to celebrate the festival were going on in the city. Since many years, this festival was celebrated with great pomp and show at Gayatri's place. Musicians came from faraway places, troupes performing Rasleela were invited and rich and prominent officers were given a feast. Gyanshankar thought that it was a good pretext to call Gayatri there. He wrote a long letter to her and requested her to come. The Krishna temple was ordered to be decorated, but on the third day itself a reply came, stating that no festival would be celebrated, so no preparations should be made. 'This is the year of mourning; I cannot celebrate at any level, even if it's a religious event.' Gyanshankar's heart was struck by a lightning. He understood that it was time for him to leave. His depression increased. His doubts grew so ferocious that as soon as he saw the postman, his heart would start beating rapidly. If he happened to hear the noise of any carriage or car, his head started rotating, fearing that it might be Gayatri herself. Daily, about four cars arrived from Benaras. These were moment of great anxiety for Gyanshankar. When the cars arrived he used to get up on his own. For about four days, his condition remained like this. On the fifth day, he received Gayatri's letter from registered post. As soon as he saw the topic, he lost his senses. He almost believed that it's a sign to remove me, or else why should she send a registered letter? He opened it with shaking hands. It was written – 'I am leaving for Badrinath today. You keep taking care of the estate properly. I have complete trust in you and due to that I've been inspired to take up this journey.' After that, those instructions were written about which it has been mentioned above. Gyanshankar's heart was somewhat at peace. He kept the envelope and started thinking, 'What I wanted has taken place. Gayatri has left after leaving everything to me. The journey is tough, the way is inaccessible; the water is bad,' all these thoughts made him worried for a while. 'Who knows what will happen?' He got so anxious that for a moment he thought, 'I might as well go to Badrinath myself. I might meet her on the way. There, nobody would be able to incite her against me. I might be able to restore my lost faith, and light up the extinguished lamp of love; this doubtful situation might come to an end.'

Without Gayatri, he had lost interest in everything. If this extensive wealth was a sea of comforts, Gayatri was the boat needed to swim in here. How can one enjoy the waters without a boat? But soon enough, this surge receded. He thought, 'She is full of doubts about me; she'll be angry if she sees me. How hard her heart has become from my side. She wants to snatch away Maya from me. In her opinion, she has punished me enough. In this situation, it's best for me to please her through my devotion, my management skills and welfare of her subjects. Premshankar has hit the right target. He's a real rogue; he got hold of two thousand a month without doing anything. Poor Maya has not been left anywhere. Premshankar will make him a skilled farmer, but not a clever landlord. He has no idea of what a rich child's education should be. Well, whatever might be, my condition is not as grave as I had thought.'

Gyanshankar had not opened the other letters as yet. He picked up the other letter after all other deliberations and found that it was from Rai Saheb. All that Gynashankar knew about him was that after Vidya's death he had gone to Mussoorie to get himself treated. He opened the letter and stated reading -

'Babu Gyanshankar, blessings from my side. About two months ago, I wouldn't have blessed you but I am in a different state of mind now. The holy men have said that good comes out of the bad. In my case, this axiom has proved absolutely true. You proved to be my greatest friend despite being my enemy. I got a golden opportunity because of you. I came to Mussoorie for treatment, but I got such a thing here, upon which many lives can be sacrificed. I was a servant of luxury. All my senses were devoted to an enjoyment of life's pleasures. I never allowed worries about present or future life to come near me. Here, I had the good fortune of meeting a divine soul and I am now discovering that my whole life has been wasted. I practised Yoga, worshipped Shiva and Shakti and increased my powers of attraction to the extent that my soul almost became electric, but the motives of all these exercises was only to satisfy my lusts. Sometimes, lost in the love of pleasure, I thought that this is the peaceful state of soul, but I now find that I was caught in a net of delusions! I would have departed from the world in the same state of ignorance, deeming myself to be knowledgeable, but you pushed me out in search of a doctor, and by God's will I found a doctor of soul diseases, instead of a physical healer. My heart blesses you but remember, Gayatri's woeful sighs will harm you far more than my good wishes can benefit you. Vidya's suicide has alerted her. Other women might have been happy in such a situation, but Gayatri's soul hasn't become lifeless as yet. She therefore made your spell useless. Your inner self has been made open to her like an open book. You cannot escape the fire of her curse. You will have to leave this world soon, along with your lusts. Therefore it's better that you spend the rest of your days in purifying yourself. This is the only way for your redemption. I am giving a part of my property to Mayashankar. He's a promising child and will bring name and fame to the family. You can keep managing the affairs of the estate till he becomes an adult. I have no concern with it now.'

After reading this letter Gaynshankar felt a strange sense of doubt instead of joy. He didn't believe in astrology, but to listen to the news of his future loss from such a man whose sacrifices had made him so knowledgeable, made his heart sorrowful. At this moment, his lifelong ambition had found fulfillment. He had never imagined, even in his dreams, that he would become the master of Rai Saheb's wealth so soon. In fact, he had lost all hopes regarding it. He was sure that Rai Saheb would hand it over to a trust. But all these hopes and doubts turned false. Yet, this letter caused the same ill-omen which a woman fears on the flitting of her right eye. His condition was like that of a man who is first captured by dacoits and is then fed sweets by them. Who will not be surprised at a dry trunk spluttered with flowers? He was lost in worries for about an hour. After that he went to the Krishna temple and then started preparing for Janamashtami celebrations with great enthusiasm.

In the life-drama of Gyanshankar, a new scene was inaugurated, which was far pure, beautiful and blissful than the earlier ones. Just ten minutes ago, the boat of his hopes was swirling in mid-waters but gradually the waves calmed down. The winds became favourable and the boat reached the shore, where a wide and magnificent garden of treasures could be seen, as far as the eyes could reach.

55

It was the second day of Babu Jwalasingh's arrival from Benaras. The previous day, he kept lying in bed due to fatigue, but now he took up the question of the appeal for Lakhanpur victims right in the morning. Premshankar said – 'I was waiting for you only. Earlier, I had confidence in myself in every task, but having a compatriot like you, I wish for your support at every step. I have lost faith in myself. In your opinion, how much money would be needed for the appeal?'

Jwalasingh – If not more, at least four or five thousand would be needed.

Prem – And I do not have even four or five hundred.

Jwala – There's nothing to worry. People can give about twenty thousand in your name.

Prem – I'm not a leader of the community that people should trust me so much.

Jwala – People think that you're far greater than that. I will start collecting donations from today itself.

Prem – I don't think you'll be successful. It's possible that you might get a few hundred, but people will think that I've thought of this trick to earn money. People start doubting as soon as they hear of donations. You can very well see how donations have defamed many of our respected leaders. There must be rare man who has got out of this network without a stain. I still have some of Shraddha's ornaments. If we sell all of them we may get around one thousand rupees.

Just then Sheelmani brought breakfast for the two of them. She heard their discussion. She said – 'Do you ever enquire about her well-being or only wish to take up her ornaments? If there's such a dire need, you can take mine.'

Jwala – Why not, you are so charitable indeed! You keep sulking for months for one particular piece; why should one take them and endanger one's life?

Sheel – The fire that is used to warm one's hands is also used to cook food if needed. Women love their jewellery like life itself, but can give them away if the situation demands.

Mayashankar was sitting in a corner with his books, but his attention was towards them only. He was thinking of something repeatedly, but could not express it due to hesitation. He decided many a times to utter it, but when he looked at Premshankar, he couldn't open his mouth. His eyes bent downwards! After hearing Sheelmani he grew impatient. He saw Jwalasingh with poignant eyes and said – 'Can I say something with your permission?'

Jwala – Yes of course, be open.

Maya – Please spend my stipend for this month on the appeal. I do not need the money for any particular reason.

Sheelmani and Jwalasingh thought this proposal to be a childish brashness and looked smilingly at Premshankar. Mayashankar thought he had done something wrong. 'Chachaji will be angry with my audacity.' His eyes became full of tears and a sob escaped his lips. Premshankar startled and looked at him, and understood his inner feelings. He hugged him lovingly and said in a reassuring tone – 'Why do you cry, son? I cannot express how happy I an on seeing this kindness on your part. You are like my child, but I really wish to keep my head on your feet. Your heart has benevolence and wisdom, and I'm confident that that your life will be for the good of the others, but the arrangements that I've made for your education, the cost of those is a bit more than your stipend.'

Maya felt a bit more courageous. He asked – 'Where's the need to spend so much on my education?'

Prem – Why, won't teachers be needed at home to teach you? One will teach you English and Maths, one each is needed for Hindi and Sanskrit, one for Urdu and Persian, one for French and German; another will train you in exercise, horseriding, rowing and hunting. I will myself teach you History and Geography.

Maya – The best students of my class do not study under a personal tutor. I don't deem them any less than me.

Prem – You need a carriage for outings. Also, two horses for horse riding.

Maya – Please excuse me; I really don't need so many tutors. I think carriages, cars and polo to be useless. Well, if a horse can be brought from Gorakhpur, I can practice riding on that. In order to row, I'll go and sit on the boat of seamen. The joy that I'll get on moving the oars with them can't be had with a single teacher. People are already saying that I'm a snob.

Padmu has taunted me many a times. I don't want people to make fun of me like haughty rich people. They would just say that till yesterday, there wasn't a single teacher for him, and now I've turned so proud after inheriting someone else's wealth.

Prem – One has to mind one's honour.

Maya – I have found that you are respected a lot even without these things. Everybody respects you. The students in my school take your name with dignity, thought they laugh upon other rich people of the city. Why should I need any special things for my upkeep?

Premshankar's heart swelled with pride at every sentence that Maya spoke. He was surprised as to how the feelings of contentment and sacrifice had emerged in this boy? In this age boys often run after outward glamour, do not have their fill of good clothes, and get wooed by glittering things. This must be the effect of his deeds in his past life; what else! He said – 'It was Rani Gayatri's wish, or else why should she have spent so much money?'

Maya – If she had wished that, wouldn't she have sent me to the school meant for landlords? The real reason behind keeping me in your care was that I should follow your footsteps.

Prem – Then how shall we spend this money?

Maya – The decision has been left to you by Rani Amma. Please keep me as you'd have kept your son. Please don't give me an education, or inculcate such habits in me that I am not able to participate in the troubles of my poor subjects in future. Do you really think this is the best way to educate me?

Prem – No, I do not think that way, but we'll have to do this to show off to the people. Or else they will say that I'm misusing your stipend.

Maya – Then you wish to educate me through a method which you yourself don't find much useful. You have arranged all this only to escape allegations from people.

Premshankar said in an embarrassed tone – Yes, I think that's the real reason.

Maya – But I've thought of other ways to spend my money. Can I tell you if you don't mind?

Prem – Of course, do tell me. I feel happy listening to you. I hadn't known that you are so thoughtful.

Jwalasingh – I have never seen anyone so aware at this age.

Sheelmani looked at Premshankar and smiled – He has been influenced by you only.

Maya – I want that my stipend should be spent to help poor boys. If 199 scholarships are given, of ten rupees each, there would still been ten rupees left for me. I can manage very well with that.

Premshankar said happily – Son, God bless your generosity; you are a divine soul. How rare this sacrifice is! What contentment! May God strengthen your pure feelings, but I cannot be so unfair to you.

Maya – Then reduce a few scholarships, but give this only to those boys who come here to learn farming and weaving.

Jwala – I favour this proposal. I think you must keep at least five hundred rupees for yourself. The rest of your money should be spent according to your will. Seventy-five scholarships each for weaving and farming should be given. Bhai Saheb is skilled in agricultural science and general sciences. I will teach weaving myself. I have practiced it a lot.

Premshankar rejected Jwalasingh's propositions saying, 'I cannot do anything in this matter without Rani Gayatri's permission and will.'

Mayashankar looked at Jwalasingh in a disappointed way and started seeing his books again.

Dr. Irfan Ali's sitting room was abuzz with discussions on a similar topic during the same time. Dr. Sahib used to criticize his profession quite openly. He sometimes thought of becoming a teacher of justice or philosophy. But his thoughts were not steady, nor did he have enough mental strength to put these thoughts into practice. On the contrary, the worst part was that the faults which he criticized, he never hesitated to adopt, as if an old patient, sick of all medicines, starts taking even the forbidden foods. He hated the money-mindedness of his profession, but he squeezed his clients to pay as much as they could. He lamented the lack of principles in the lawyer fraternity almost daily. But he never adopted any principles himself. He was just bothered about his own payments, whether his client lived or died. Lakhanpur victims had been destroyed due to his very selfishness and ill-polices.

But ever since Premshankar had saved him from the rioters his policies and behaviour had witnessed a kind of awakening. His greed for money was not ruthless anymore; he treated his clients politely, listened to their stories carefully and prepared the cases with all his heart; not just that, he often left the poor clients after taking a token amount of thanks. The reason behind this generous behavior was not only this that he wanted to recover his lost respect, but he'd actually been inspired by Premshankar's contented, selfless and stoic way of life. Whenever he found time, he went to see Premshankar and every time he returned mesmerized by his simple and pure ways. Till now, there had been no holy man in the city who had been able to impress him in such a manner.

Out of his colleagues, he found none to be more reasonable, honest or generous than him. In that condition, he had thought of his own self as the best and consoled himself by criticizing the legal profession. This much was enough to make his selfish nature proud, but now, a man was present before his eyes who was as learned and skilled in oral and written arts as himself, but was so much more polite, benevolent, kind and peaceful! Also, someone who did not ignore him despite being aware of his dishonesty. Therefore Doctor Sahib now repented his past deeds. He wanted to atone for them and get rid of the stains of defamation and corruption. He was shy of suggesting to Premshankar that an appeal should be filed but had decided that he would not leave any stone unturned to get the accused released. He even wanted to bear the monetary burden of the appeal. He had been preparing for it since months, had seen the versions of the case, decided the questions for the agreement and had written out his defence. He knew that the appeal would be filed after Jwalasingh's arrival. He was thus waiting for him quite enthusiastically. It was morning time. Doctor Sahib had got the news of Jwalasingh's arrival. He was going to meet him when Ijaad Hussain arrived. His black robe suited his soft demeanour very well. After the exchange of greetings, Syed Saheb looked at Irfan Ali doubtfully and said – 'Did you see how these two brothers have managed to dupe the Rani Sahiba? One brother got the whole estate and the other inherited a sum of two thousand a month so easily. Hardly four or five hundred would be spent on the boy's education, what else? This world is full of such tricksters!'

Ijaad Hussain suffered from a disease of suspicion. Ever since he had heard the above news, his heart was clamouring, as if the money was being spent from his own pocket. How unfortunate was this that Premshankar should get two thousand every month without lifting a finger and this poor man should keep worrying for morsels even after deceiving just about everyone!

Doctor Sahib said sarcastically – You lost this chance. If you had taken a deputation in her service, she might have given a stipend of one thousand for the Ittehaadi orphanage.

Ijaad Hussain – You seem to be joking. I am not so lucky. But the world is full of people who spread the golden net of sacrifice and trap golden birds.

Doctor Sahib cast a look of anger and said – 'You can think whatever you please regarding Lala Gyanshankar, but it's highly improper of you to doubt an honest man like Babu Premshankar, and when he's among your helpers, it doesn't suit you to be so suspicious of him. I know him since long and can vouch that such a soul cannot be found easily in this city, rather in this country. He doesn't boast about it, but the way he's serving the nation; had other people done so, this nation would have become the envy of heaven. A man who lives on ten rupees a month, treats his labour equally, is always ready to help the downtrodden with all his might and sacrifices his property for the sake of his principles should not be doubted in this unjust manner. Even if you wish to employ his workers on hundred rupees a month, they won't come, because they aren't his servants, but equal partners in his produce. Gayatri seems to have a great faculty for recognizing the true nature of men.

Ijaad Hussain said with surprise – Does he really survive on ten rupees a month? Why so?

Irfan – By reducing his wants. You and me have included the items of luxury in the list of our needs and remain worried about procuring them day and night. This is a slavery of the senses. He has controlled it. We spend our free time in complaining against society and fate. All the time, we keep hankering after hoarding more and more. And do not bother about just and unjust in our lust for more. I have never found him lamenting his fate. He seems to be always happy as if there's no sorrow anywhere.

Just then Babu Jwalasingh arrived. Doctor Sahib got up and shook hands with him. After usual exchanges, he asked – 'I hope you wish to stay here permanently now?'

Jwala – Yes, I have come with this very intention.

Irfan – Tell us, when will the appeal be filed?

Jwala – I will talk about that later. At present, I need to talk to Syed Sahib. I had just visited your place. I got to know that you'd come here. Babu Premshankar wants to know if you could teach Urdu and Persian to Mayashankar.

Irfan – Why not, what do I do sitting at home all day? Functions hardly take place around five or ten times in a year and I've to worry for food the whole year long. What has he decided about the salary?

Jwala – At present you'll get hundred rupees a month.

Irfan – That's very reasonable. Why Mirza Sahib; is it fine? You won't get such a chance again.

Ijaad Hussain said gratefully – I am ready for it wholeheartedly. My voice lacks the power to thank this obligation. I am surprised that I met him only once and he got so concerned about my livelihood.

Jwala – He's not a human being; he's an angel. He has discussed your orphanage many a times. He wants to fix up some scholarships for the orphans. How many of them do you have at present?

The recent obligation had filled Ijaad Hussain's heart with pure feelings. He could not exaggerate. For a second, he was confused, but finally, his true emotions won over him. He said – 'Sir, had you asked me this question on some other occasion, I would have answered differently but the goodness and compassion of you all has affected even a trickster like me. I have two types of orphans with me. One are the permanent types; the other are temporary. In the times of need, they both exceed fifty in number but if you remove the temporary ones, only ten are left. Possibly you may not count them as orphans, but think that a poor man's loved boys are the real orphans.'

Irfan Ali said with a smile – Then say that you've actually put up a farce of an orphanage. At least you shouldn't have hidden it from me. That's why you had willed you entire property in the name of the orphanage.

Ijaad Hussain bent his head in shame and said – 'Sir, the factor of need makes a man do everything. I'm no lawyer, barrister or landlord; just a man of simple abilities. My father was a high ranking nobleman in the estate of Tonk. He earned in thousands, and also spent in thousands. As long as he was alive, I kept roaming free and kept enjoying contests between trailing kites and patridges. After his death, the burden of the family fell on me; that too a family that was used to a life of luxury. My conscience didn't allow me to turn away from those upon whom my late father had provided his shade. I may not have been talented, but had a sense of family pride. My bad company made the qualities of fraud and constancy into an art. When I found nothing to survive in Tonk, I joined government service and came here after moving across many districts. My income was less; expenditure far more. In a few days all my savings were finished. There was no other option left for me; I could have either starved or found a way for livelihood. After much thinking, I could only think of that which I am doing at present.'

Irfan Ali – At an estimate how much do you get annually?

Ijaad – Won't you let anything remain under cover?

Irfan – One must not leave a tale half-finished.

Ijaad – So sir, there's no fixed income, and I'm not in the habit of maintaining any accounts. I get whatever is destined for me. Sometimes I get almost thousands in a month, and at other times don't get to see any rupee for months. But more or less this income has no scope for prosperity. The devil's eye is always on us. However rich food you may eat, however richly you may dress and live in pomp, you never find that satisfaction which you find in dry chapatis earned out of your sweat and in rough cloth similarly acquired. Sometimes I feel so upset that I start wishing for death. For me these hundred rupees are equal to lacs. Godwilling, if Irshaad too finds a job soon, I'll be free of the worry for food. The rest of my life will be spent in atonement and prayers. I'll keep serving the Ittehaad, but from now on, it will be true service, free of all selfishness. God will reward Babu Premshankar for this.

After discussing about the appeal for some time, Jwalasingh left for Hajipur with Mirza Sahib. Doctor Sahib also accompanied them.

56

As soon as the High Court opened after the Dussehra holidays, the appeal was filed, and newspaper columns started getting filled with its proceedings. The problem was very complicated. Out of the people who had been awarded a sentence, those witnesses were pleaded to be summoned again on whose basis the sentence had been given. The government lawyer opposed the plea strongly, but Irfan Ali strengthened his case with such points and expressed the injustice done to the accused in such a poignant manner that the judges allowed a re-examination of the case.

The subordinate court had to call the witnesses again. Bisesar Sah, Dr. Priyanath, Daroga Khurshid Alam, Kartarsingh, Faizu and the Tehsildaar appeared in the court. Bisesar Sah's statement continued for three days. It was rather an extensive and educative description of the strategies and gimmicks of the police. This was not a Bisesar who was weak, scared of income-tax, and a puppet in the hands of the police. The guilt, repentance and divine calamities of the past two years had transformed him completely. On one hand, his statement was total revelation and the rest of the task was accomplished by Irfan Ali's arguments. The government lawyer initially threatened Bisesar for going back on his earlier statements; the judge also scolded him, but Bisesar did not sway the least. Irfan Ali said very politely – 'A witness's going back on his account is indeed punishable, but the position of this case is unique. This entire storm has been created by the police. Considering the lives of so many innocent people, the court should not consider the law of the witnesses too strictly.' These soft words calmed down the judge. The old judge had been transferred; in his place a new officer had come.

The government lawyer also debated a lot on his side and wanted to prove that the witnesses had been influenced by the threats of the villagers; upon insistence from Premshankar and other such possible reasons, but Bisesar escaped all traps. The English and the local newspapers started critiquing this incident. The English ones felt that the change in the witness was the result of an influence of the nationalists. They have played this game to defame the police. The court has committed a grave error in accepting this statement. The informer should be suitably punished. The Indian papers got a chance to poke fun at the police. The case was going on in the court, but they started pleading that the police officers should be cross-questioned. A paper wrote, 'This incident is a brilliant proof of the fact that the Indian police has been formed not to guard, but to destroy the people. If one investigates properly, it will be fully established that eighty-seven per cent of the tragic incidents take place due to its irresponsible nature.'

Some papers found the tyranny of zamindars as the reason behind police injustice. They got a chance to spit venom on the former and their unjust practices. Some other papers started shedding tears on the deplorable conditions of the zamindars. A sort of movement began where it was proposed that they must be given such rights by the government that they may keep their tenants under control, or it seemed quite possible that the strong winds of impudence might uproot the foundations of the social structure.

After Bisesar Sah, Dr. Priyanath was called. The police officials had complete faith in him, but when they heard his statement they were shocked. Their curiosity was boundless, as if a new world had appeared before their eyes. That person who had once been the right hand of the police; a puppet in its hands, and who had earned thousands due to their connections, should deceive them in such a manner, and crush the law beneath his feet!

Dr. Sahib said clearly that the earlier statement was not according to medical texts, and the inference he had drawn after seeing the heart and the liver of the dead body was not textually supported. He had not found a chance to consult his books before giving that statement. The clots of blood in these places proved that they suddenly stopped functioning. If the victim had been strangled before being struck, these organs would have stopped gradually and so much blood would not have clotted there. To support his point, he mentioned the opinion of many famous doctors. Dr. Irfan Ali had also referred to many authoritative texts on the matter. His arguments further proved Priyanath's point. On the third day, the government lawyer began his examination. When he found Priyanath escaping all medical questions he started questioning his intentions.

The lawyer – Is it true that on the first day when the verdict had been announced, some rioters had surrounded you at your bungalow?

Priya – Yes.

The lawyer – At that time Babu Premshankar had saved you from their attacks?

Priya – Yes, if he hadn't come, I might have lost my life.

The lawyer – This is also true that he himself got injured while saving you?

Priya – Yes, he got badly wounded. His shoulder bone had broken.

The lawyer – You will also admit that he's a kind hearted fellow and has sympathy for the accused.

Priya – Yes, he does.

The lawyer – In such a situation, isn't it natural that he may have inspired you to save them?

Priya – There was no dialogue between us on this issue.

The lawyer – Isn't it possible that his obligation may have forced you to take it up?

Priya – I keep my personal feelings separate from my duty. Had this truly been the case, Babu Premshankar would have been the first one to dissuade me.

The lawyer kept flitting from one point to another, but Priyanath bit the bait like a clever fish and swam away. After arguing for two days, the lawyer had to sit back in defeat.

The statement of Daroga Khurshid Alam began next. This was just a reiteration of his earlier statement, but on the next day, Irfan Ali's arguments uprooted him completely. He struggled a lot but could not escape the net of his arguments.

Irfan Ali was now sure of his success. When he came out of the court, his happiness knew no bounds. He had defended many important cases before and had gone home with pockets full of money, but his heart had never felt as delighted as it was now. Premshankar was as happy as if his son was getting married.

After this, the Tehsildar was called. He kept lamenting the impudence and evil nature of the Lakhanpur people but Irfan Ali tore apart his narrative within ten minutes.

Irfan – Do you agree that all these accused are amongst the prominent men of Lakhanpur?

Tehsildar – They might be, but are actually dairy farmers, weavers and low-caste peasants.

Irfan – If a scavenger turns a millionaire, won't you hesitate in asking him to mend your shoes?

Tehsildar – There's no millionaire amongst them.

Irfan – But all of them are peasants, not labourers. What right did you have to make them cut grass?

Tehsildar – For official needs.

Irfan – Couldn't these needs have been fulfilled by paying wages to the labourers?

Tehsildar – There aren't many labourers in that village.

Irfan –Weren't there any dairy people, weavers or farmers among your peons? Why didn't you make them do this job?

Tehsildar – It's not their job.

Irfan – And is it the job of the peasants?

Tehsildar – If the need arises they too are made to do these jobs.

Irfan – Do you know which caste of people polishes the floors?

Tehsildar – This work doesn't belong to any particular caste.

Irfan – But you cannot refute that normally, dairy people and thakurs do not do it?

Tehsildar – They can, if need be.

Irfan – You too can give fodder to your horse if need be. Would you like to be called a syce due to that?

Tehsildar – My position cannot be compared to those peasants.

Irfan – At all costs, you'll have to admit that people who aren't used to a certain kind of work deem doing it as an insult, and to make them do it forcibly is unjust. A Brahmin can even wash your utensils happily. Yet, if you make him do it by force, he might do it out of fear but his heart will be wounded. He will complain against you as and when he gets a chance.

Tehsildar – What you say is true, but sometimes, officers are forced to do things under pressure.

Irfan – Then in these conditions, you should be ready to hear harsh things. On top of it, you blame the Lakhanpur people; this is just a fault of human nature. Now I hope you will admit that the impudence of these peasants was a result of your extremities?

Tehsildar – For the convenience of the officers…

The judge stopped him midway, understanding his motive.

When Irfan Ali reached home in the evening, he got an urgent telegram from Babu Gyanshankar. He had called him to fight an urgent case. There was a promise of one thousand rupees daily. Dr. Sahib tore away the telegram and immediately replied through another text message – 'I am sorry I'm not free. I am defending the Lakhanpur case.'

57

Gayatri's condition at this moment was like that of traveller who had been robbed by dacoits dressed up like ascetics. She repented like the same traveller as to why she had left home at an inauspicious time. 'Why did I leave a peopled road? Why did I trust those disguised ascetics and showed them my bag of money?' Like that traveller now, she saw every pedestrian on the road with suspicious eyes. This tragedy proved far more effective on her than thousands of teachings and warnings. She now remembered that a sadhu had fed her some holy offering. After walking a while when she felt thirsty he had offered her a cold drink which she had heartily drunk due to her thirst. She could now guess that the thirst was also a result of the eatables given to her earlier. The more she dwelt upon the incident, the more she found its mystery, cause and effect all tied up in a sequence. Gayatri had already given away her ornaments to Shraddha in Benaras; she now left wearing coloured clothes. She loved eating betel leaf. She left that also. She drowned her mirror and comb in the Triveni. She left eating delicious food. She experienced that these very addictions had made her heart unsteady. 'I was so proud of my womanly character that I thought my love of luxuries to be ineffective upon it. I could not fathom that lust doesn't merely win over one's senses; it gradually makes one's mind too subservient to it.' She just wore a white sari now, walked barefoot and ate frugal meals. She was fighting her desires and wanted to crush them. As and when a glass becomes clear, the faults in it become all the more apparent. Gayatri could now see the negative tendencies of her mind clearly. Sometimes, in a rush of sorrow and guilt, she contemplated suicide. She now saw her late husband in her dreams very often. His poignant talk pierced her heart, and his sharp gaze wounded it altogether.

From Benaras, she went to Prayag, and for many days stayed in an inn at Jhusi. She met many holy men here, but couldn't find any peace in their teachings. All of them were men of the world. Initially they didn't even talk to her, but when they discovered that she was Rani Gayatri, they all became images of knowledge and renunciation. Gayatri understood that their sacrifice was just a kind of lack of enterprise and their attire a means of wooing the simple-minded devotees. Disappointed, she went to Haridwar on the fourth day; but here too she saw a whole lot of pretence in the name of religion, and lack of true feeling. Tourists had come from faraway places, but not for a pilgrimage; only for enjoyment. At all times during the day, luxuries and glitter abounded on the banks of the Ganga. Gayatri left for Rishikesh, annoyed with all this. She didn't give her true introduction to anyone there. Everyday, she used to wake up at night and after taking a dip in the Ganga, read Gita for two-three hours. For the rest of the day, she read other religious texts. In the evenings, she listened to the preachings of the holy men. Though she met some sacrificing souls there, none was so enlightened that it could make her peaceful and detatched. Even after so much of restraint and sensual sacrifice, she was often haunted by worldly affairs. 'God knows what's happening back home? God knows whether the charitable works are going on or Gyanshankar has stopped them? What must be the condition of the floors? The servants must be looting away my household. My sitting room must be all covered with dust. If the roofs haven't been repaired, they will have cracks all over. Cars and carriages must be going to people on rent. Whosoever would have come and flattered him, Lalaji would have obliged him. He must be thinking he's the master now. The garden must have turned into a jungle. God knows if anyone has bothered about the birds and animals in it. They must have starved and died. The two mountain canaries had been bought by me after so much running about. They must have died or someone must have taken them. I have given the keys of my trunks to Shraddha, but an evil man like Gyanshankar can do anything.' Very often these worries came to her while reading religious texts or while chanting her prayers. The way in which a broken pot lets out water on being filled from the other side; in the same way, Gayatri was becoming eager to purify her soul, and yet was surrounded by all kinds of worries. That peace and concentration was out of her reach which is the basis of self-elevation. Surprisingly, she welcomed all hurdles and made them sit lovingly in the abode of her heart. She had left Benaras with a resolve that she'll not have any connection with the world, but she now discovered that no renunciation is needed to achieve self-knowledge. 'Can't I stay detatched even while staying in my house and caring for my estate;' but her heart got irritated with the idea. She debated with herself, 'What concern do I have with the estate now? I have enjoyed it enough. Now I must walk on the path of renunciation; this birth has gone waste, why should I waste my next birth?' Lost in these arguments, she couldn't go to Badrinath. About three months passed in Rishikesh, and winters came about; the journey now became too arduous.

It was the month of January; it had started snowing in the mountains. In the golden rays of the morning sun, the beauty of snow-laden peaks was beyond description. One day, Gayatri heard that a holy man had arrived from Chitrakoot whose very encounter makes the soul eternally happy. 'He does not preach much, but his gaze is far fuller of the life-giving nectar than his teachings. His face has such a glow as if it's beaten gold. His only meals are of milk; that too not more than a glassful, but his built and strength are such that he climbs even the highest of peaks rapidly; he neither loses breath, nor do his legs shake, and he does not sweat at all. On seeing his valour, even the greatest of ascetics become shocked. In the melted waters of Pasooni he keeps standing at night for two-three hours, and prays. There's such an attraction in his eyes that even wild animals follow his instructions.' When Gayatri heard of his powers, she felt very eager to meet him. She left for Chitrakoot the very next day, and on the fourth day, she was sitting in an inn on the banks of Pasooni.

Here just about everyone was talking about the fame of the same swamiji. Devotees had come from far away places. Some said he knew about all the three time periods together; some called him self-enlightened. Gayatri was so overwhelmed upon listening to these stories that she wanted to go and keep her head on his feet that very instant, but was helpless as night had fallen. She kept tossing and turning the whole night and kept thinking that on the break of dawn, she'll go and fall on his feet and say, 'Maharaj, I am an unfortunate woman; you know everything, my condition is not hidden from you, I am getting submerged in deep waters, you alone can rescue me. Please give me such a teaching and lend such power to my weak soul that it gets released from the network of worldly bonds. There's darkness in my heart; please light it up with your all-pervasive light.' She kept crying with this meek image for hours. It became so heightened that swamiji's reassuring words started echoing in her ears. 'When I fall on his feet, he'll put a loving hand on my head and say, 'Daughter, a great trouble has befallen you, but God will redeem you.' The long night of winter took a long time to get over. She repeatedly got up to see if it was morning, but got disappointed when she saw stars twinkling in the sky. When she got up the fifth time, dawn was about to break. The stars were about to disappear like the last notes of a melodious tune. The sky seemed like an ascetic clad in yellow robes whose face was bright with an internal delight, and the earth seemed like a never ending mystery. Gayatri took bath in the blue waters of Pasooni and went to meet the swamiji.

His cottage was on a steep hill. He was sitting there under a tree. Devotees used to come and sit on a floor around the tree. The way was difficult, but reverence used to take the people uphill. Strengthlessness and weakness had also bowed before a true feeling of affection. There was a queue of men from downwards to upwards. Gayatri started climbing the hill. After some time, she started panting for breath. Her feet became too heavy; she couldn't lift them properly, but she went upstairs crawling on her hands and feet, and breathing intermittently. Her whole body was drenched in sweat and darkness was engulfing her eyes but when she reached up, her heart became so happy as if a thirsty soul had found water. Gayatri's heart started beating fast. She had never felt such a crucifying pain of guilt. 'What face can I show to this light of wisdom?' She couldn't dare to face swamiji as if a man fears handing over a fake coin to a jeweller. She was lost in this confusion when she heard a voice – 'Gayatri, I am waiting for you since long.' This was Rai Kamlanand's voice, seeped in love and affection. Gayatri startled and saw that swamiji was coming towards her. His glowing face was beset with kindness and his eyes were full of tears of love. Gayatri's eyes bent down. She felt as if she was getting drowned in strong waves. 'Alas! I am this great soul's daughter.' Guilt said, 'Alas! You fallen woman;' shame said, 'Alas! You defamed your family;' depression said, 'Alas! You unfortunate soul,' sorrow said, 'Curse be on you. You are not fit to show your face to the world. How much more will you fall, for which you wish to live! God has not written knowledge and renunciation in your destiny.' All these ill-thoughts hurt Gayatri so much that all feelings of atonement, redemption and the ultimate goal disappeared. She looked downwards with her eyes, and like a wounded bird who falls from the tree by opening both his wings, she fell from the peak with hands wide open. There was a deep lake downhill. It hid her ashes in its deep and dark crevices, in order to save them from the ruthless sarcasms of the world.

58

Lala Prabhashankar had not learned the lesson of future planning. He was never bothered about anything called 'tomorrow'. His whole life had been spent in luxuries and in protecting the family honour. 'Feed, eat, and die after your name' – these were the sole motives of his life. He had always worshipped this tripartite image and did not feel like amending his practical rules even after wasting a large part of his ancestral wealth; and even if he did, it was now too difficult for him to tread a new path. He was a generous and an honourable man. In his view, wealth was just a means to protect one's honour. That it can be a means of increasing prosperity, or the fact that wealth can attract more wealth, never came to his imagination. He deemed worries as useless, perhaps because to be relieved of them, he had to visit his moneylender at the worst. Whatever time or money he could spend on welcoming and entertaining his guests was counted as best by him. On the occasions to show charity, his courage seemed to touch the skies. In that intoxicated state of mind, he didn't bother as to what would happen next; and how he'd manage his affairs. It was his wife's job to make this wild river relent. She used to save money from his eyes in a way someone saves a burning lamp from the winds. She used to say fearlessly, 'There's nothing left out here.' Lalaji used to start cursing her; calling her 'evil, unfortunate, mean-hearted,' but she refused to budge. It she could have followed this policy at all times, perhaps their property could have been saved, but Lala Sahib used to trick her in a different way sometimes. He wasn't unaware of the significance of politeness. His wife could have borne his anger, but was defeated by his soft words.

A large part of the loan which Lala Prabhashankar had taken for Premshankar's bail was still left with him. He did not return that money to the moneylender. Perhaps he counted this money as his own income. He didn't know of any other means to acquire it. He had seen a lump sum of money after many days; it seemed as if the sun of his fate had risen. Presents and gifts were now sent to his relatives and friends; dinners were also held for them. Lalaji was skilled in the culinary arts. He had composed a text which included his various recipes. This art had been learnt by him after spending a lot on sweet-makers and chefs. He could make such a tasty dessert out of neem-fruit that one could be deluded of it as an almond sweet. He could make another delicacy with bitter red chillies which could appear as Mohanbhog. He had duped many of his gourmet friends by making cultets of mango stones. His marmalade of gooseberries used to win over the grape one also. Although much money was wasted in the preparation of these delicacies; much effort had to be made, and an original touch kept missing, but Lalaji resembled a poet in this matter, for whom the praise of his listeners was the biggest reward. This year, he celebrated the anniversary of his late brother with much pomp and show after many years. The Brahmin feast and the community lunch were praised all over. There were many prominent men in the city, but none could dare to compete with him on such issues.

His wife knew that till the time there was money in the house, he would not stop spending and would finish every penny within a year, so why not make hay while the sun shines. As soon as she got a chance, she discussed the matter of the wedding of her two daughters. Though the girls hadn't yet reached a marriageable age, it was better to relieve oneself if the situation so permitted. The day Jwalasingh went to file the appeal, that very day Lala Prabhashankar started the first day ceremony of the weddings. From the next day onwards, he became busy in entertaining the guests in the wedding parties. In such auspicious works, he thought budgeting to be unpardonable. His plans were too great, but fortunately, Premshankar used to come daily to help him out. Prabhashankar respected him a lot so his suggestions weren't altogether ignored. The date of the wedding fell in December. The two months falling in between were spent on the preparations.

Premshankar often took his dinner here in the evening, and after chatting for sometime, used to leave for Hajipur. The real surprise was that even Gyanshankar seemed happy with his uncle. He sent many bags of rice, sugar and ghee tins from Gorakhpur. He arrived a day prior to the wedding with many liveried soldiers. He got so many carpets and rugs with him that many a wedding could have been adorned with them. He gave a gold watch each and a gold chain to both the grooms. He gifted a gold coin each to the guests during dinner. He had got gold necklaces for his nieces and gifted a decorated palanquin to their in-laws. He gave five rupees each to the servants, palanquin-bearers and barbers at the time of leaving. The entire house was amazed at his generosity and Prabhashankar almost started worshipping him like a god. The whole city was agog with his praise. People said – 'Even if an elephant dies, it would fetch nine lacs. The brothers were upset with each other but their courage and grace is the same. This can only be a feat of the genuinely rich! How can anyone else compete with them? Even if there are lacs in your house who will come and see? This courage is the real proof of richness.' But no one knew at what cost Lala Sahib had bought this fame.

After the weddings, some days were spent in enjoying the leftover delicacies, but gradually, this door also shut down and Prabhashankar had to revert back to simple, tasteless meals. After the earlier rainfall, this drought annoyed him very much. He just couldn't be satisfied without tasty dishes. Simple meals refused to go down his throat. Very often, he left his plate half-finished in the kitchen, but felt hungry the whole day. Opening his book, he looked for something that could be easily made, but he couldn't find any such dish. The poor man shut the book disappointedly and used to roam in the verandah to please himself. He went inside the house repeatedly; saw the almirahs and shelves with eager eyes that he may discover something. Some navratna chutney was left still. If he couldn't find anything he licked a spoonful of it. The worst part was that there was none to share this sorrow or sympathize with him. If he ever told his wife fearfully to make some good dishes, she either avoided him or said irritatingly – 'Your tongue keeps craving for delicacies like boys; all the time worried about eating. The whole property was spent on halwa and pulao, and you are still not satisfied. What's left in the house now?' Poor Lala Sahib used to feel embarrassed on such reprimands. Lovers find peace in discussing the features of their beloved, but the sorry state of affairs did not afford any such companion to Prabhashankar.

In the end, the situation became so worse that he called the street vendors and got chaat bowls from them; and used to go and sit in a corner and eat it with pleasure. Earlier, he never even looked at chaat, but now he had lost that pomp. This continued till one or two months, but the poor vendors couldn't have survived for very long on mere promises. They started pressing for their money. Lalaji used to wait for their strange calls earlier, but now when he heard their voices, he used to look for niches to hide himself. His promises didn't sound reassuring now; there was more a content of pleading and mistrust in them. God knows how long he'd have had to hide his face from them, but a solution soon appeared to pay them off. Shraddha gave him some money to get her two saris from the market. He got the saris on debt and paid that money to the vendors. He didn't fear any such reminders from the cloth dealer. He could have been avoided for years, but from that day onwards, all the vendors stopped visiting his house.

But chaat is a bad addiction. In one's good days, it's an ornament to be worn in the neck, but in bad days, it becomes a sharp knife which doesn't leave a strip of self-respect and honour intact. It was the month of February; it was so cold that blood froze in one's veins. Lala Prabhashankar went daily to Premshankar on the pretext of an outing and heard the news of the times. As soon as he got a chance, he started talking about a tasty dish; he told him the story of how he got to eat it, and what all his friends had commented on it. Premshankar understood the hint and got that dish made from Sheelmani, but he had no idea of what how severe Prabhashankar's greed for good food was. Therefore, Lalaji's desire remained unfulfilled there also. Thereafter he never took a straight route to home. The thirst for taste took him to the street of bakers. His hungry soul got quenched with the smell of onions and spices. What a poignant scene it was! A seventy year old man; someone who could sacrifice his life for family honour was roaming in that street only to find pleasure of taste through smell; always wary that someone might not see him there. The smell of a fresh cutlet filled water in his mouth; in fact he didn't even bother about what to eat or what not. At that time, only an unexpressed doubt and a fake hesitation used to gather his slippery feet.

One day when he went to see Premshankar he told him about the decision to file the appeal. Prabhashankar said happily – 'This is indeed very good. God had rewarded your efforts. Poor innocent farmers were rotting in the jail. God is very kind. Let's have a feast to celebrate this joy.'

Maya said – Yes, I was also saying the same. I will invite all the boys of my school.

Premshankar – Let those poor people arrive here first. It will take them months to reach; someone is in some other jail, the others are somewhere else. The judge had wanted to favour the police, but Dr. Irfan Ali did not allow him any chance.

Prabha – These judges are like that only. Their sole motive is to impress the government, not to do justice. If you hadn't ran about so much who would've listened to them? So many of such innocent people bear their punishments only due to the feats of the police and evil nature of the lawyers. When I see these lawyers arguing I feel as if singers are reading out poems. No one is bothered about justice. Both parties just wish to defeat each other by oral strength. Whosoever is a glib-talker wins. The decision of men's life and death takes place not on the basis of truth and justice; rather on the strength of a person's skill of deceiving the power of justice.

Prem – Till the time the plaintiff and the accused get their respective lawyers in the court, this condition will not be improved; because a lawyer is simply a mouthpiece of his client. He has no concern with the delineation of truth or untruth; his duty is only to prove the claim of his client. One can hope for true justice only when the lawyers are appointed by the court itself and is free of other political influences and corrupt practices. In my opinion, the government should appoint able and honest men in the police after choosing them properly. Till now, no one has bothered about the significance of character in this department. Only those men are taken in who can oppress the people and can scare them with their authority. No one is bothered about justice.

Prabha – Please read out the verdict; let me see what's written there.

Prem – Yes, please listen; I'll translate it for you. See, how sharply the police have been criticized. 'This case is a brilliant example of the working of the police. In order to decide the truth or untruth of a topic, it is necessary to deliberate upon the witnesses in an unbiased manner, and to establish an inference on that basis, but the police officials move exactly opposite to it. They first establish a notion and then search for witnesses and proofs to prove it. It is obvious that in this condition, they move from effect to the cause; and instead of modifying their imagined notion try to fit the evidences into the framework of their imagination by distorting them. Why is this reverse game played? It's difficult to anticipate this, but not quite impossible in the present case. The burden which a group can easily bear is impossible for a single person.'

Prabhashankar said in a worried tone – This is an open allegation. Won't the police be asked to account for it?

Prem – Who listens to these allegations? If people had bothered about them, the police would have been reformed much earlier.

Just then they saw Jwalasingh coming. Premshankar said – 'Chacha Sahib wants that this victory should be celebrated.'

Jwala – I too wish the same.

59

After childhood a stage comes when one wishes to refute just about everything. It lacks the determined goals of the youth; there is a huge hopefulness instead which deems the difficult to be simple and the impossible as an easy morsel to be gulped. Various kinds of pleasant thoughts keep visiting the mind. There's a mad spirit of tourism. Sometimes one thinks of boarding the train only to see where it reaches in the end. On seeing a corpse one walks till the cremation ground to see what happens there. When one sees a monkey-player going around, one gets curious to fling a bag in one's neck, and to go from place to place showing such tricks. One is so sure of one's capabilities that no sort of hurdles cross one's imagination. One is taken over by a simplicity which wants to look out for Alladin's lamp. In this stage, their no limit to what one thinks of one's abilities. We leave behind Tilak in the field of academics and move ahead of Napoleon in the battlefield. We sometimes become an ascetic, and at other times far more rich than Jamsetji Tata. We have so much faith in beggars and holy men that we deem their ash as all-encompassing. Tejshankar and Padmashankar were both travellers in spirit. There was no one at home to look after them and to keep them away from useless excitement; or turn their liveliness and boundless imagination towards intelligent thoughts. Lala Prabhashankar did not think much beyond getting them admitted in a school. Both left home to go to school; but on their way, roamed on the riverbank, listened to the band, or watched the parade of the soldiers. Both had a dislike for books and after failing in a single standard for many years, had lost interest in studies altogether. They now felt as if they were not meant for an education. They once found a book on black magic in Lalaji's almirah. They read it with interest and tried to learn its mantras. They often went to the riverbank and listened to the talks of holy men. On listening to tales of occult achievements; they too felt a deep desire to acquire them. This thought filled them with a proud pleasure that they too, could do anything with them, find hidden treasures, win over their enemies, and woo all terrible fiends. They had even tried a few tricks and though they hadn't got a chance to test these, they were fully sure of their success.

Ever since Gayatri had adopted Mayashankar, they both were burning with jealousy and hate. The fever refused to relent even for a second. The boy who was their playmate till yesterday should suddenly reach such a high position! Both kept thinking of achieving a power before which, wealth and splendour should become meaningless; and by which they could demean Mayashankar. Finally, after much deliberation, they decided to invoke the Bhairav mantra. They found a text on occultism in which the procedures for its invocation were written in a detailed manner. Both learned the mantra by heart for many days. When they had learnt it they started discussing as to when they should begin invoking it. Tejshankar said – 'Come, let's begin the auspicious job today itself.'

Padma – Whenever you say. Let's go to the Assi ghat.

Tej – If we can do it forty times, we'll become immortal. No guns, swords or tanks would be able to affect us.

Padma – O boy! It would be great fun. We'll live for thousands of years.

Tej – Thousands! Say millions! Such holy men are still lying about in the Himalayan caves who are about four hundred years old. They too must have invoked the same mantras. They are not affected by death at all.

Padma – Maya has turned too boastful. The boy will die one day; all shall be left here. Who's bothered about it here? We'll not even fear the guns now.

Tej – But it's not easy to invoke it. If you get scared you'll lose everything; if you startle you'll die immediately. You have read in the book; how terrible are the faces that you see! How fearful are the voices one hears! Ghosts and devils come to you with a drawn sword. At that time, you shouldn't doubt your strength at all.

Padma – I'll not at all be scared; they won't be any real ghosts. The gods must be sending them to test us.

Tej – What else! All is just a delusion. Please keep your heart strong.

Padma – And in case you become scared?

Tejshankar laughed proudly and said – I have roasted my fears and eaten them up. They cannot come near me now. I won't be afraid of real ghosts now; what to talk of fake ones.

Padma – So we'll definitely become immortal.

Tej – Of course, what's the doubt in that?

Both started invoking the mantra after this discussion. When everyone slept in the house, they stealthily left the home and sat near the Ganga at Assi ghat to chant the mantra. They did this exercise for thirty-nine days. How they cleared this awful test, would require a whole text to describe. They saw all those terrible images and heard all those exciting words which the book had mentioned. Sometimes they felt as if the sky was tearing apart, sometimes a wave of fire seemed coming near, sometimes a devil came to swallow them, emitting flames from his mouth, but the extreme end of all fears is courage. Both the boys kept setting quiet and tranquil, with closed eyes. The chant was just a farce; all their real energies were spent on keeping these doubts and fears at bay. Their main fear that if they startled, hesitated or deterred even one bit, their lives will come to an end, kept them tied to their spots. The trust that a brother is sitting close was a major reason behind their determination, though it did not assure Tejshankar as much as it did Padmashankar. He (Tej) did not have the same faith in Padmashankar as the latter had in him. Therefore this test was far more crucial for Tejshankar, but the fear that his unsteadiness would cost Padma his life, used to compensate for that little trust. Both had turned very weak these days; pale-faced, eyes flitting and lips dry and cracked. Both lied around listlessly the whole day; had no interest in games, wandering about or entertainment; their mind was distressed the whole day, and they didn't even enjoy their meals. Thirty-nine days passed in this manner; the fortieth day arrived. They started getting anxious from morning itself; their doubts became aggravated, and so did their hopes. Sitting in a state of hope and fear, they sometimes became delighted thinking of immortality; sometimes they trembled thinking of the day's awesome tests, but their hopes triumphed over their fears. 'The city will be abuzz with our news; we shall jump in a blazing fire and emerge alive, without a stain. We shall jump from that high altar and not be wounded in the least. People will be amazed to see us.' They didn't eat anything the whole day. They kept going upstairs and downstairs; cried, laughed and danced at intervals. If some other person had seen them thus, he'd have thought they had gone mad.

When it became dark, Tejshankar brought a sword from the house which Lalaji had just got from Jaipur. Both shut the door of their room, cleaned it with kerosene oil, and sharpened it on a stove to the point that it started emitting sparks. Thereafter, hiding it under the bed, they went to the market. When they returned it was already nine. At much insistence of their mother they had little food and started waiting in their room for other people of the house to go to sleep. As the time went by, the lamp of their hopes began to diminish in the darkness of fear. Their condition at present was like that of a criminal, whose time of hanging was approaching every second. Various kinds of ill-thoughts and doubts were emerging in their mind, but even in this heavy storm they could clearly see a sign of a boat from afar, which gave them courage to persist. Tejshankar was worried and serious, and did not care to answer Padmashankar's simple, hopeful talk.

When the appointed hour arrived, both came out of the house. It was the month of February; snow-laden winds pierced their bones. Their hands and feet stiffened. Tejshankar hid the sword under his shawl and both walked off in a manner as if a poor-witted student walks towards the examination hall. They stopped at every step, overwhelmed with fear, but again moved ahead, strengthening their heart. In fact they even contemplated returning many a times, but to lose courage after thirty-nine days of persistence, right on the day of the reward was unpardonable weakness and frailty. Now what ever might happen, this last test was essential. Scared and hesitant, they reached the ghat. None of them had spoken a single word on the way.

It was the dark night of Amavasya. Whether one had eyes to see or not, it was all the same. The stars were hiding their faces in the clouds. Darkness had made water and wind; earth and sky all seem similar. One came to know of the Ganga only by the sweet voice of its waves. There was so much stillness that even the sound of the water dissipated into it. It almost felt as if the earth was still lying in the womb of a vacuum. The worshippers of an eternal life reached the banks of the river, bearing jolts and hurdles at every step and got down in the waters. The water was as cold as ice. All their organs became languid. After taking bath, they sat on the sand and started chanting the mantra. But the surprising thing was that they didn't see anything today which they hadn't seen before, nor heard any voices which they hadn't heard before and no untoward incident happened. Cold had quietened all doubts. All complicated hallucinations too had become lifeless. Both were scared as to what all terrible images they'd encounter that day, and God knows how the ghosts would attack them. God knows whether they'd remain alive or not? But actually they came out quite easily today.

When the night ended and the two worshippers opened their eyes, they saw the reddishness of the dawn in the sky. The earth gradually started leaving the cover of its darkness. The trees and sand on the other side of the horizon became clear as if an unconscious patient was slowly coming back to life. The dark flow of water seemed as if it was carrying away the darkness with it. The trees afar stood with their heads bent down as if a mourning party was going after cremating someone with heads bent down.

Suddenly Tejshankar got up and said – Glory to Bhairav.

Both had a unique gleam in their eyes, and a strange shine on their faces.

Tejshankar – Take the sword in your hands, I will bend my head.

Padma – No, you weild it first, I'll bow down.

Tej – Are you still afraid? We have crushed death, won over time; now we're immortal.

Padma – No, you inaugurate it first. Make such a blow that the neck falls away in a single strike. But tell me, won't I feel any pain?

Tej – What pain? You'll feel as if someone has hit you with a flower. That's why I tell you to strike first.

Padma – No, I'll bow down first.

Tejshankar took the sword in his hands, weighed it, changed stances a few times, and then struck Padmashankar's neck with a cry – 'Jai Bhairav ki'. His hand was heavy; the sword was sharp, Padma's head was thrown away from his body in a second and a fountain of blood effused out. Tejshankar stood smiling, as if a sparkler was glowing brightly. His face had a bright shine of peace. No hunter could have remained so steady upon looking at a captured bird on the ground. No practised butcher could have remained so stable after slicing the neck of an animal; he was standing with such a determined faith as if a pigeon-flier was waiting for his pigeon to come home after letting it fly off.

The dead body kept wriggling for a while, and then became still. The drops of blood stopped; only a few streaks came out as if streams of drops fall after a spate of rainfall; but no signs of any reversal of life could be seen. One minute passed. Tejshankar had a doubt; but his faith quietened him. He took some Gangajal in his palm and read out the Bhairav mantra; he then threw it on the dead body after blowing it; but the exercise failed. The head that had been cut off did not stir, and there was no sign of any movement in the dead body. The life-giving powers of the mantra had no effect.

Now Tejshankar lost his confidence; the basis of his faith started shaking. It was written clearly in the book that the head comes back immediately after getting separated from the torso and if the process takes time, then a splash of the mantra-infused water is enough to revive it. Much time passed, and nothing happened. 'What was the reason? It is impossible that the mantra should have failed. So many people have achieved it successfully. No, there's nothing to worry; the body will be revived soon.'

He waited for a few minutes, but the dead body kept lying quiet and still. He again sprinkled Gangajal on it, read out the mantra, but the body didn't rise. He shouted – 'O God! What to do now?' The lamp of his faith got extinguished. He looked at the river, disappointed. He found the waves weeping and wailing. The trees seemed to be mourning the death. A scream came out of his throat, and he started crying. He now discovered what disaster he had committed. How fake and deluding was the alleged power to achieve eternal life. 'Alas! How blind, how foolish and uncivilized I am. Alas! Dearest Padma, I struck you with a sword with these very ruthless hands, only for the sake of a false power. Alas! I took your life! Who will be more sinful and luckless than me? How can I go home now? What face will I show to the world? Life is a waste now. You were dearer to me than life itself. How will I see you now; how will I get you back?'

Tejshankar kept crying for many hours, overwhelmed by these mournful thoughts. Just a second ago, what all hopes and aspirations he had? Were they all lost in dust? 'Alas! Which wicked devil has written this book; if I could get him, I would have cut his throat with this very sword. I destroyed myself by falling in his false trap.'

'Alas! There's no life in the body till now'; he felt scared to look at it.

The sorrow of depression, the fear of result, love and guilt – all these emotions crushed his heart! Still, his hopes hadn't died as yet. He looked at the corpse with scared, half-closed eyes, but there was no sign of life visible in it, so the last thread of his hopes also broke, and patience left his side.

He looked at the sky hopelessly. He cast a last look at his brother's dead body; became little alert, and then cut his own throat with the same sword. Fountains of blood came out, the body started wriggling and the eyeballs inflated. The sacrifice was complete. A false belief crushed two blooming lives under its feet.

The sun god was watching this complex game of life with his red eyes. His quiet yellow rays were falling on the mantra-hit boys in a way as if some creature, overwhelmed at their tragedy was hugging them and crying at their misfortune!

60

The painful death of his two sons made Lala Prabhashankar listless and senseless. Two weeks had passed since then, but he hadn't yet got out of the house. He lay on his bed the whole day long and kept tossing and turning at night. His life seemed empty to him now. He got averse to seeing people's faces and if anyone came to console him, he turned his face away. Only Premshankar was the one who was acceptable to him, perhaps because he never let out a word of consolation from his mouth. Real consolation is always silent.

One day, Premshankar came and found Lalaji dressing up, and a tonga waiting at the gate as if he was preparing to go somewhere. He asked – 'Are you going anywhere?' Prabhashankar turned his face towards the wall and said – 'Yes, I'll go to that heartless Dayashankar, and get him home somehow. Someone needs to be here. I cannot take care of the family now. My back is broken, and I have lost all my strength. I had resolved never to see his face, but God doesn't want my resolve to stay intact, so I'll have to fall at his feet. My lineage is about to end. There must be someone to take my name after death, offer water to my soul, and to keep the lamp of the family name burning. Who's left beside Dayashankar now; I'll plead before him, and request him to come and make this house alive. It seems like an abode of ghosts without the boys. Both the girls have gone to their in-law's place; the boys were sacrificed to Bhairav, now whose face should I see and console myself? I might have kept sitting, keeping a stone on my heart, but how to make your aunt understand? It's been two weeks that she ate anything. She weeps day and night. Son, if you ask me the truth, I am myself the killer of my two boys. They stayed the way they liked, and went wherever they wanted. I never tried to show them the right path. I never bothered as to how one should raise one's children!'

Premshankar grew sympathetic and said – The tonga ride will tire you out. If you say so, I can go; I'll be back by tomorrow.

Prabha – He won't come easily; he'll have to be dragged here. He's not rude; he just refuses to come here due to shame. He must be lying there crying. He loved his brothers too much.

Prem – I will get him forcefully.

Prabhashankar agreed. Premshankar started off immediately. The police station was about twelve miles away. He reached there by nine. There was silence in the station. Only the clerk was sitting on the floor and writing something. Premshankar said to him – 'You will be discomfitted, but please inform Darogaji that a person has come to see him.' Munshiji looked at Premshankar from head to toe, and then got to his feet. He pulled a chair for him and asked, 'Is your name Babu Premshankar?'

Premshankar – Yes, it's my name only.

Munshi – It's good that you came. Darogaji was just mentioning you. He often talks about you. Come, I'll go with you. All the constables are attending him. He's ill since many days.

Prem – Ill? What's the matter?

Munshi – Apparently it's fever, but who knows the internal story? His condition is deteriorating fast. Ever since he heard of the untimely death of his brothers he got fever. He didn't come to the station after that. He stopped coming out of the house also. Earlier too, he rarely came to the station; if not more, he used to drink around three to four bottles of wine daily. But he hasn't had a drop in the past fifteen days. He has stopped even looking at food. Either he lies unconscious in fever, or if he's a little better he starts crying. It seems as if he's struck with paralysis; he cannot even turn on his sides. There's a stream of doctors attending him, but to no avail. I've heard that you too know about medicines. See if your treatment can cure him. He's such a precious man. We are as sad as if our own dear one is dying. He was never bothered about money. He got thousands every month and distributed it in all departments. He just wanted his daily wine, and had no other addiction. Even if a junior erred somewhere, he never complained against him, rather took all the blame on himself. Which officer could have dared to look at his sabordinates with a crooked eye; he used to face everyone bluntly. He participated in their celebrations and mourning just like a close relative. He got many daughters of his constables married, gave fees for the education of their sons, and was still infamous for his strict behaviour all over the region. The whole area was against him, but the police was at peace. We won't find such a compassionate and poor-loving officer again.

Munshiji sang these praises with such affection that Premshankar was delighted to the core. He had thought Dayashankar to be a greedy, wicked and selfish man whose atrocities troubled the whole population in his region.

He seemed a traitor to him; a bad son and a characterless man who had turned away from his parents, brothers, sisters and even his wife due to his love of luxuries and lustfulness. In his opinion he was a shameless, fallen and heartless character. When he listened to this eulogy, he felt very sorry for his narrow-mindedness. He again felt his soul to be in pain – 'Alas! How proud I am! How easily I forget that this huge world is lit up with an eternal light. Every atom of this world is resonant with the same inner clarity. To think of any man to be low or fallen here is such a sin that cannot be atoned.' He asked the Munshi – 'Haven't the doctors diagnosed him properly?'

Munshiji said in a passive tone – Don't ask anything about the doctors; some say this and some say that. Either they don't know anything or they don't check him properly. They are just bothered about their fees. Come; let's go inside, this is his house.

When Premshankar went inside, many constables were crowding out there. Some stood crying; someone else was sad or down-faced, and some others fanned him. The room was very quiet. On seeing Premshankar, everyone greeted him and started looking at him with pleading eyes. Dayashankar was lying on his cot; his face had turned yellow and his body had thinned down a great deal. It seemed as if a green field had been eaten away by locusts. His eyes were closed; drops of sweat covered his forehead and there was a strange stillness in his respiration. Premshankar was pained to see this terrible sight; he went near the cot, kept his hand on Dayashankar's forehead, and asked – 'Bhaiya?'

Dayashankar opened his eyes and looked deeply at Premshankar, as if he was trying to recall a forgotten face. Then he said peacefully – 'You are Premshankar? It's so good that you came. I really wanted to see you. I decided to meet you many times, but could not dare to come as I felt ashamed. Hasn't Lalaji also come? It would have been good if he had; God knows whether I'll be able to see him again or not?'

Prem – He was ready to come, but I only stopped him. I didn't know anything about your condition.

Daya – That's okay. He'd have had trouble travelling on a tonga for such a distance. And moreover, what happiness will he find on seeing me?

After saying this, he kept quiet; he didn't have the energy to go on; he took a breath and continued, 'Why, Prem, who would be more unfortunate than me in this world? All this is a result of my evil deeds. I am a traitor of the family. I didn't know that the punishment for a sinner's sins is so great. If I ever loved anyone, they were my two brothers. My sins took the form of Bhairav and ...'

His eyes were full of tears. He almost became unconscious. He kept lying in that dubious state for half an hour. His breath was moving very slowly. Premshankar was regretting, 'If I had known about his condition, I'd have got Dr. Priyanath along. Should I telegram him to come? He won't take any fees, thinking it's my personal matter; this is the only trouble. Let it be, I must call him.'

Thinking thus, he started writing the telegram, when suddenly Dr. Priyanath stepped into the room. Premshankar looked at him with surprise and then hugged him saying, - 'Come Bhai Sahib, I am now reassured that God listens to the prayers of the poor. I was just sending this telegram to you. Please save his life.'

Priyanath assured him saying – 'Please don't worry, I'll just see him. What to do, no one informed me earlier. There's an outbreak of fever in this region. I was touring the villages when I came across the police station and Munshiji told me about the situation.'

Thus saying, Dr. Sahib took out an instrument from his handbag and applied it on Dayashankar's chest; after examining carefully he said – 'His lungs have got mucous, but don't worry. I am giving him medicine. If God wills, he will be better by evening.'

Doctor Sahib gave him the medicine and sat nearby on a chair. Premshankar said – 'I won't leave you before evening.'

Priyanath smiled and said – 'Even if you chase me off I won't go. He's my old friend. I have earned lacs due to him.'

An old guard said – 'Huzoor, please make him alright. It's not much, but we all promise to give you our wages for a day.'

Priyanath smiled and said – I won't leave you so easily. You'll have to promise that you'll not torture the poor, won't make them do unpaid labour, and give proper price for the goods you take.

The watchman – Sarkar, how shall we survive then? We too have children; nothing can be managed in ten or fifteen rupees.

Priya – Then why don't you ask your officers to promote you? All of you should go and plead to them. You are meant to protect the people, not to torture them. Do some other jobs in your free time so that you can increase you income. If you do that for two or three hours daily you can get ten-twelve rupees extra.

The watchman – What kind of a job Huzoor?

Priya – There are many jobs, but you'll have to leave your hesitation. You'll have to get rid of this feeling that you are constables so you can't do manual labour. A labour of hard work proves much more prosperous than an income of injustice and torture.

Munshiji said – Huzoor, the government rules are very strict in this regard. An employee in the police is not allowed to do any other work. If we do some other job we'll be kicked out.

Priya – This is your own fault. No one can stop you from weaving cloth, cotton or other things in your free time. Of course the official work should not be hampered. You people should explain your position to your officers.

Munshi – Huzoor, someone has to be there to listen to us? Our robbing of the public is not so much a crime in their eyes, as our appeals. We'll immediately be charged with conspiracy and groupism.

Priya – Then it would have been far better if you had learnt some skill and earned an independent income. An ordinary artisan too earns a lot more than you.

Munshi – Huzoor, it's all a matter of destiny. A person who has slavery written in his fate can never be free.

It was afternoon; Priyanath gave the second dose of the medicine. Just then the cook come and said – 'Sarkar, food is ready, please come and have it.' Premshankar didn't want to get up from there, but Priyanath assured him, saying – 'It may not be evident as yet; but the first dose has proved effective. You will see that he'll start talking by evening.'

Both the men went to have their meal. The cook had made it very spicy. Dayashankar was used to very heavy meals. All the items were so heavily spiced that Premshankar could not eat more than a few bites. His eyes and nose became watery. Priyanath laughed and said – 'You had a real feast today. This cook has defeated even the South Indian cooks. These heavy spices weaken the digestion. Listen Maharaj, do not make such things till Darogaji is well again; do not put spices at all.'

The cook – Huzoor, I've put very little spices today. If this food had been served to the Darogaji, he'd have said how bland and tasteless the food is.

Premshankar ate plain rice, but Priyanath didn't bother about the chillies. Both came to sit near Dayashankar after having their food. At around three p.m. Priyanath massaged an ointment on his chest, and gave two more doses by the evening. Dayashankar was lying quietly, but it wasn't an unconscious state; he was sleeping. His respiration came back to a natural rhythm and his face started gaining colour. When it became dark, Priyanath said, 'Please give me your leave now. If God wills, his condition will improve further in the night. There's nothing to fear now. I will come again by eight tomorrow.' Suddenly Dayashankar woke up; his eyes didn't have that awkward gleam of the past. Priyanath asked, 'How are you feeling now?'

Daya – It seems as if someone has picked me from the burning sand and put me in the shade of a tree.

Priya – Are you feeling hungry?

Daya – No, I am thirsty.

Priya – Then you can have some hot milk. I'll go now, and come by eight tomorrow.

Dayashankar looked at Munshiji and said – Open my trunk and bring whatever is there; keep it on Dr. Sahib's feet. Babuji, it is just nothing, but please accept it.

Priya – You get well first; my account can be cleared later.

Daya – I am alright, and have come out of the jaws of death. Till yesterday I only wished to die, but now I want to live again. This is not your fees. I am not capable enough to pay it. That can be paid for a physical treatment, but I am discovering that you have cured my soul. The only fees for it is the obligation that I'll bear lifelong and if God so wills, you'll never regret saving this sinful life from the clutches of death.

Priyanath still didn't take his fees, and left. Premshankar kept sitting for a while. When Dayashankar slept again after having milk, he went outside for a walk. He suddenly saw Lala Prabhashankar coming on a tonga. When he reached near him, he got down and asked in a trembling voice – 'Son, how's Dayashankar? After you left, a watchman came to me from here. He told such me a bad news that I lost my cool and immediately came here. The whole house is wailing. Please tell me the truth; what's the situation?'

Prem – He's much better now; there's nothing to worry, but when I came he was really very sick. It was good that Dr. Priyanath came here. His medicine worked like magic. He's sleeping now.

Prabha – Son, come, I want to see him, I am very anxious.

Prem – He might start crying if he sees you.

Prabhashankar said politely – Son, I won't utter a word; I'll just see him and leave. My heart is extremely worried.

Prem – Come, but please calm yourself. If he hears even a little noise, our day's hard work will be lost.

Prabha – Bhaiya, I swear, I won't talk at all; only see him from a distance and go. My heart is very restless.

Premshankar was helpless. He took Lalaji to Dayashankar's room. Prabhashankar looked inside from the threshold as if a child looks fearfully at the clouds; lest the lightening may befall him. But as soon as he saw Dayashankar, he screamed out of love loudly – 'Alas! Son!' and went on to hug him.

Premshankar held him annoyingly by the hand and dragged him out of the room. Dayashankar asked with surprise, 'Who's that? Has Dadaji come here?'

Premshankar – You relax. If you talk now, you'll be at unrest.

Daya – No, please make me sit for a second. I want to keep my head at his feet.

Prem – Not now. You can meet him properly tomorrow.

Thus saying, Premshankar went out. Prabhashankar was standing in the verandah crying.

He said – Son, please don't be angry with me. I stopped myself a lot, but my heart went out of my hands. At this time, my condition is like that of a traveller sitting on a broken boat, for whom even a small gust of wind is like a slap of death. Please tell me the truth; what has the doctor said?

Prem – In his opinion, there's nothing to worry. The symptoms also indicate this.

Prabha – May God bless him, but I'll be satisfied only when he sits up. This year his stars haven't been favourable.

Both men came out and sat under a shade. Both were lost in their own thoughts. After some time, Prabhashankar said – 'How unjust we are that upon seeing the same evil tendencies in our children which are there in us, we become their enemies. I was annoyed with Dayashankar precisely because he never cared for the family. Why does he waste his income in bad habits? Why doesn't he help me out? But ask me as to what I have done in my whole life? All these years have been spent in enjoying luxuries only. If he wasted, it was his own income; I actually finished off the wealth of my ancestors. I had no right to ruin that.'

Many officers and guards came from the police station and sat with them, praising Dayashankar's generosity and goodness. Prabhashankar was too delighted to hear them.

At eight o' clock, Premshankar again went and gave him medicine, and lay on an easychair near him. He didn't let his eyes wink even for a second.

When Priyanath came and checked Dayashankar, he was very happy. He said – 'There's nothing to worry now, he's absolutely alright. In a week's time he'll start doing all his jobs. More than medicine, it's the result of Babu Premshankar's care. I guess you didn't sleep at all last night?'

Premshankar – Why not? Yes, I didn't have a sound sleep.

Prabhashankar – Dr. Sahib, I am a witness to the fact that he didn't bat an eyelid the whole night. I came to check many a times, and always found him setting or reading something.

Dayashankar said in a respectful tone – If I remain alive I'll spend the rest of my life in his service. My life will be reformed under his guidance.

A week passed in this manner. Dr. Priyanath used to come daily, and after sitting for an hour, used to go to the rural areas. Prabhashankar went home the very next day, but Premshankar didn't budge for even an hour. On the eighth day, Dayashankar was able to leave for home on a palanquin. His leave had been approved.

It was morning time. Dayashankar was leaving the police station. Though he was only going on three months' leave, the employees of the station felt as if he was leaving them forever. The whole staff came running after his palanquin for about a mile. People were just not ready to go back. Finally, they left after getting much assurance from Premshankar. All were sobbing aloud.

Premshankar was feeling guilty in his heart as to why he had hated such a popular and respectable man for so many days. 'After all, how many honest, kind and soft-hearted men can the world boast of, who have the hearts of so many people attached to them, and whose separation can make so many of them unhappy!'

61

It was the day of Holi. Abeer and gulal were being thrown around all over the city; people were singing Phag and Chautal, but in Lala Prabhashankar's house the air was heavy with a sense of mourning. Sitting in her room, Shraddha was gathering Gayatri Devi's clothes and ornaments to hand them over to Gyanshankar. After Vidya's death and Gayatri's departure, she used to remain in an unsteady frame of mind. She used to sit with the elder lady of the house the whole day long, but ever since the two boys died, she further lost interest in everything. Sometimes, when Sheelmani came to visit, she used to feel happy for a while. The news of Gayatri's death had arrived here only the previous day. Shraddha kept remembering her and crying the whole night. At this moment also, Gayatri's image was moving before her eyes and she was thinking of her soft, simple and deceitless words. 'How generous, polite and loving she was. No amount of pride at all but alas! what a terrible end she had!' In the same state, she happened to remember the two boys. 'Alas! Both were so gay, talented and beautiful! There is no surety of one's life; a man plans so much; has so many ambitions, but nothing can be saved before the God of death.'

'He devastates everything in a spate. Five people left within a span of three months. Likewise, I'll also leave everything one day and all will remain unresolved in my heart. Since eight years, both of us are adamant on our own decision; neither does he relent nor do I. If he hasn't atoned for so many days, he'll not do it now. His soul is satisfied with its good deeds; it doesn't feel the need for it neither its significance; I myself will have to bow before him. Should I now ask a learned priest if I can do some ritual for his atonement or not? Will my prayers, Ganga baths, rituals and sacrifices all go waste? Admitted, he did many a thing abroad against the religion, but ever since he's arrived here he's constantly been doing beneficial works. He keeps busy in helping the poor and the downtrodden. He doesn't even care for his life. The greatest of men would not have kept so busy in social service. He has erased out his own personality. Whatever symptoms of a religious life have been mentioned in the scriptures are there in him. A man who has won over his mind, his senses and lusts by the strength of his knowledge needs no atonement. Isn't his range of actions equal to it? There is no text that has described any arrangement for it clearly. There seems no scholar who can solve my doubts. O God, what should I do? I will die one day, lost in these dilemmas and the desire to serve him will be lost with me. My life would have found its resolution in staying with him or else I'm just wasting my life in these four walls.'

Shraddha was lost in these very thoughts when she heard some noise at the gate. When she looked down from her window she found a crowd of men gathering near the door. Just then a maid came and said, 'Bahuji, all the people who were caught in the Lakhanpur case have been released. They are standing at the door and are blessing Babuji. Just listen, that bearded old man is saying, 'Allah! Keep Babu Premshankar alive till the day of judgement!' There's an old sadhu with him. His name is Sukhdas. He has been showering money over them all the way here from the market. It seems he's a rich man.'

Just then Mayashankar came running and said – 'Badi Amma, all the accused in the Lakhanpur case have been freed. Their procession was taken out in the market. Dr. Irfan Ali, Babu Jwalasingh, Dr. Priyanath, Chacha Sahib, Chacha Dayashankar and many men of the city were accompanying them. Come; give me the keys of the sitting room. I will make everyone sit there.'

Shraddha gave him the keys and started thinking, 'How should I welcome them', when she heard a sky-high noise – 'Glory to Babu Premshankar! Glory to Lala Dayashankar! Glory to Lala Prabhashankar!'

Mayashankar came running again and said – 'Badi Amma, please give me the drum and cymbals; Baba Sukhdas will sing a devotional song. See there, that bearded old man is Qadir Khan. That tall and stout man is Balraj. His father, Manohar had killed Ghaus Khan.'

Shraddha's face was shining with delight. Her heart was so delighted as if a wedding party had arrived at her door. All kinds of thoughts were emerging in her being. 'Should I make these people stay here today, should I feast them; or rather I should hold a Satyanarayan Katha today.' She was feeling such a respect for Premshankar that she wanted to hug his feet. She gave the drums and cymbals to Mayashankar.

Sukhdas hung the drum in his neck, the others took the cymbals; they all stood in a group and started singing this song-

'Satguru has held my hand, or else I'd have drowned.'

Maya was too happy. He came in and said, 'Qadir Mian sings so well.'

Shraddha – We should welcome them properly.

Maya – I want to feast everyone. You invite them from your side. Whatever you need you can tell me. I'll send the men to get it. All these appear so simple and poor that I find it hard to believe that they would've killed Ghaus Khan. Balraj is like a wrestler, but even he seems to be so simple.

Shraddha – It will take time to arrange a feast. Things will have to be bought, and cooking will take up the afternoon. Get some sweets and give them. Do you have money or should I give?

Maya – I have enough money. What to do; I didn't think of it before.

The singing continued till afternoon. Thousands of men in the city participated in the celebration. Premshankar welcomed everyone respectfully. Just then, sweets arrived from the market; people ate and left after praising Premshankar but the Lakhanpur people weren't allowed to leave. Shraddha sent a word that they should go only after having their meals in the evening. Although everyone was anxious to reach their homes, they could not refuse this invitation. Lala Prabhashankar started the preparations for the feast. Till now, he had only impressed rich guests with his culinary skills. Today even these rural men had the good fortune of tasting his food. Lalaji wanted to serve such tasty food to them which they would remember for the rest of their lives. All kinds of delicacies were being made. Things were hurried up; still it was eight by the time everyone finished eating. Priyanath and Irfan Ali had sent their vehicles. The people sat in them and left for Lakhanpur. All of them blessed the family openly. The family members were yet to eat; it took them almost ten o' clock in the night to finish. When Premshankar was about to leave for Hajipur, a maid came and said slowly, 'Bahuji says that you should sleep here for tonight. It's very late in the night.' This unusual concern surprised Premshankar. He could not get to the crux of it.

Jwalasingh joked with the maid – We can also stay or should we go away?

The maid was alert. She said – No Sarkar, you can stay; even Maya bhaiya should stay; the house has enough for everyone.

Jwala – Go away, you're just having fun!

When the maid left he said to Premshankar – It seems that your stars are favourable today. You're about to have another victory.

Premshankar said in a passive tone – I'll have to hear a new sermon; what else?

Jwala – Absolutely not, I think that your goddess will give you a boon today. Your sacrifice has borne fruit.

Prem – My goddess is not so loving towards her devotees.

Jwala – Okay, we'll know that tomorrow. Please give us your leave.

Prem – Why don't you too sleep here?

Jwala – My goddess takes even lesser time to get annoyed.

Thus saying, he left with Mayashankar. The maid had laid down a cot for Premshankar. When he lay down to sleep, his mind felt naturally curious about Shraddha's sudden kindness. 'Is the maid making a fool of me? No, she doesn't seem to be so light hearted. If she has really played a trick I might have to cut a sorry figure. God knows what Shraddha will think of me?' Finally, to dispel his doubts, he took out a book from Gyanshankar's almirah and started reading it.

Jwalasingh's prediction was true. Today, his sacrifice had indeed come to its completion. His fame had overwhelmed Shraddha. Today, when she saw thousands of men shouting his glory at the door, she was forced to think – 'Are all these good wishes, coming from the inner hearts of people less significant than atonement? Absolutely not. The importance of philanthropy cannot be any less than atonement; rather it is the most real form of atonement. So many blessings can redeem any great sinner. What can a mere atoning do? And these blessings won't end here. When they go home, their families will further bless us. Till the time they are alive, their hearts will keep wishing well for him. Such a famous and respectable man does not need any atonement. This shower of nectar has made him pure forever.'

It was eleven p.m. Shraddha came from upstairs and stood at the door of the sitting room shyly. A lamp was burning and Premshanakar was flipping through a book. Shraddha saw a divine light of self-pride on his face. Her heart was leaping out of bounds, and her eyes were full of tears of joy. Today, after fourteen years, she had got a chance to serve her husband. She was no longer that old, love-pained Shraddha whose aspirations had died. At this moment, her heart was jubilant with all sorts of desires, but there was no thirst in her eyes, and no smile on her lips. She had not come in a way in which a bride comes to her husband; she had come as if a devotee comes to his God; full of reverence and love.

She kept standing at the door for a second. Then she went and fell upon Premshankar's feet.

62

Human character is neither absolutely black nor totally white. It is a strange combination of both these colours. If circumstances are favourable, a man becomes as respectable as an ascetic; if they are unfavourable, he turns into a devil. He is just a toy in the hands of his situation. If Babu Gyanshankar was selfish, greedy and mean hearted till now, it was a result of his circumstances. A hungry man does not offer a bite to a dog till the time he's satiated himself. Gyanshankar's unhappiness had further aggravated his dark side. He had been born in a household which had spent its entire splendour on the upkeep of its honour. In this condition, the only way to find peace was to be contented but his higher education had taught him that life was a vast battleground. The ideals of men which had been kept before him had also achieved success only by taking resort to the policy of struggle. It's undoubted that his education had made him skilled in speech and writing, trained him in logic and reasoning and made him clever in behaviour, but along with it, it had also made him selfish and a slave of vested interests. This was not an education which teaches you to keep the doors of your cottage open, or to feed others before feeding yourself. Gyanshankar could not dream of giving shelter to anyone till he had made a mansion for himself; he could not give even a handful of grain to others, till he had filled up his own godown.

Fortunately, his mansion was now complete. He was now ready to give shelter to others; his coffers were now full. He didn't hate beggars now. After becoming wealthy, he had turned generous, kind and dutiful. He had helped a lot in the weddings of Lala Prabhashankar's daughters and had come to condole the death of his sons from Gorakhpur. He also felt compassionate towards Premshankar now; in fact he had congratulated him on the release of the Lakhanpur accused. When he got the tragic news of Gayatri's death, he did her last rites with great pomp and spent thousands on rituals. He got a pucca pond dug in her memory. Till the time he stayed in a grass hut, he was afraid of the sparks of fire. Now he had a proper mansion, and could see the show of fireworks from a safe distance.

Gyanshankar now remained eager for fame and goodwill. Lucknow's prominent men used to remain cut off from him, thinking him to be a usurper. And though he had achieved a high position in Gorakhpur, people were jealous of his new authority. Gyanshankar started increasing his contacts with the rich men in both the cities. Initially he thought Rai Saheb's unorganized expenditure as unnecessary and fit to be curtailed. He wanted to remove many horses, cars, and carriages from his itinerary. But now, he deemed to keep up the same pomp and show for his honour, and rather increase it so that people may not make fun of him. He invited other rich men to feasts, behaved politely with the young and the old and donated liberally to charitable causes. He already knew many editors of newspapers and now strengthened his relations with them. The papers started praising his generosity and character. In fact, a year had not yet passed and he was chosen as a minister in the association of Lucknow's talukedars. He was skilled in oratory; he often spoke gloriously at community functions. The newspapers showered praise on him. Thus, on one hand he started getting counted among the community's leaders, and on the other, his honour increased among the officers as well.

But his attitude towards his mute and poor subjects was not so kind. Those trees lacked any thorns, so there wasn't any harm in picking their fruits. The claims of expenditure, pending taxes and increased rent were being levied with full force; their bases were being changed and gifts et al were being extorted very ruthlessly. Rai Saheb had left the estate in a debt of five lacs. About twenty-five thousand came to be the annual interest on it. Gyanshankar compensated for the loss of interest through these efforts. Still, after so many atrocities, the subjects weren't unhappy with him. He used to administer bitter medicines by making them sweet. On the occasion of Gayatri's death anniversary he distributed a thousand blankets in the estate and feasted the Brahmins. Likewise, in Rai Saheb's region, he organized functions on Holi and wooed the simple subjects by giving them as much bhaang as they pleased. He established grain-markets at many places so that farmers could sell their produce easily and the estate could also profit well.

Two years passed in this manner. Gyanshankar's sun of fortune was now in its hours of noon. He had paid off Rai Saheb's debt to quite an extent. He was respected among the officers, honoured by the rich men, revered among the scholars; and was counted as a learned writer and excellent orator. He had everything to make life comfortable. The ambitions of his life had been achieved. When during leisure he thought about his past life, he was surprised at his success. 'What have I become from the position of my past? Just three years ago, I wanted to get the whole village hanged for an increase of a thousand rupees in the yearly profit. How narrow-minded I was! For a minor issue, I separated from my uncle, in fact wished ill for my real brother also. I didn't leave any stone unturned to trap them. But now I donate many such amounts. Whereas earlier I couldn't afford a tonga; now I give motorcars to those who wish to borrow. Undoubtedly I had to change many guises for this success, soil my hands; do all kinds of sin, deceit and roguery, but one can't find precious gems without delving in a dark mine. Yet, it would be a mistake to take it only as a result of my own efforts. If it hadn't been for a divine plan, none of my efforts would have borne fruit! At that time I used to think that my shots had failed; I had lost the target, but fortunately, those very empty shots and crooked ways made me win the game.'

Gyanshankar used to visit Benaras every two months and stay with Premshankar to enjoy his simple lifestyle. He asked him many a times as to why he stayed in a cottage, that too in a deserted place. He said, 'Come home with me and enjoy God-given wealth. If that is not acceptable, come with me and I'll give you a tract of land comprising of one or two thousand bighas; you can live a farmer's life there.' But Premshankar used to say, 'This much is enough for me; nothing more is needed.' But Gyanshankar's request had this effect that he agreed to increase his cultivation. About fifty bighas of land adjoining his fields belonged to another zamindar. He got its lease and instead of a grass hut, got houses made of tiled roofs. Gyanshankar used to propose all this, but was unaware of the significance of his contented, simple and hurdle-free life. After being infested with various types of worries and impediments, a relaxed and peaceful break on Premshankar's farm made his heart happy. He didn't feel like going away from there. This place was not like the old deserted place, where a man lay alone in his hut like an ascetic. It was a small, bustling settlement now, where all political and social matters were discussed and deep, complicated questions of life and death were analyzed! This was a company of scholars free of scholarly bias and haughtiness. Actually it was a holy ground of simplicity, contentment and positive thoughts. There wasn't any pain of jealousy, any surge of greed, any disaster of craving. Money wasn't worshipped here and poverty wasn't crushed under the feet. No single person sat on a throne here and no other stood with folded hands before the former like a criminal. No threats ensued from the master's mouth; no pleas came from the side of the servant. Here, all were each other's servants, friends and well-wishers. On one side was Dr. Irfan Ali's bungalow, decorated with flowers and creepers. Dr. Sahib now took up only those cases about which he was sure that they were true, and took only that amount of fees that was necessary for his daily expenses. He had emerged free of the worries of hoarding and saving. In the mornings and evenings he did gardening with Premshankar, which he had liked doing earlier also. At that time, he had merely felt happy looking at the plants; the real work was done by the gardener. Now he did everything with his own hands. Dr. Priyanath's bungalow was adjacent to his house. A dispensary was in front of his home. Now he often toured the villages and treated patients, and had left his job. For his livelihood, he had opened a dairy which had many cows and buffaloes. Milk and butter was sent to the city for sale. He didn't take any fees from his patients. Babu Jwalasingh and Premshankar stayed in the same house. Shraddha and Sheelmani got along rather well with each other. As soon as they got respite from the household chores, they either sat on the charkha or made socks. Premshankar worked regularly in the fields and Jwalasingh used to weave clothes on the latest type of looms, and even taught weaving to many a youth of Hajipur. He had become quite skilled in this art. Syed Ijaad Hussain also came to stay here. His family still stayed in the city, but his orphanage had come to Hajipur. It now housed real, not fake orphans. Syed Saheb still maintained his Ittehaad and gave lectures on it, but he stopped asking for donations and putting up shows. He was now a true promoter of Hindu-Muslim unity. Near his orphanage stood Mayashankar's Mitr-Bhavan. It was a small hostel. Irfan Ali's two boys, Priyanath's three sons, Durga Mali's son and Masta's younger brother all stayed here together. All went to the school together and had their meals together. Mayashankar paid for their expenses from his stipend. Food was cooked by Shraddha. Gyanshankar tried many a times to transfer Maya to the Talukedar School in Lucknow, but he didn't agree.

Once when Gyanshankar came from Lucknow, he got a fine silk suit for Maya, but he didn't wear it till the time such suits were stitched for the rest of the students of Mitr-Bhavan. Gyanshankar felt very embarrassed and despite a lot of restraint, he ended up telling Premshankar, 'Bhai Sahib, I cannot agree with you on this principle of socialism. It is an unnatural principle. We can praise it theoretically but it is impossible to follow it in a practical form. I know many socialists in Europe who stay like rich men, go about in motorcars and for six months a year, holiday in Italy or France. When they can still call themselves socialists, there's no reason for us to kill ourselves for the sake of this unnatural policy.'

Premshankar said politely – We have never discussed socialism here.

Gyan – Then it must be effect of the environment of this place. Though I do not have any right to say anything to you, but as a father, please excuse my saying that such education will not benefit Maya.

Prem – If you wish so and Maya agrees, you can take him to Lucknow; I don't have any objection. It's beyond my control to change the environment out here.

Gyan – I hope you know that there's a world of difference between Maya's position and that of his friends.

Premshankar said seriously – 'Yes, I know it very well, but I can't understand why this difference should be flaunted so much. All the boys know that he will be a big Talukedar in a few days. Isn't that enough to make them lament their misfortune, that a projection of this difference should be used to hurt them further? You may not know this, but I can say this for sure that Teju and Padmu's deaths occurred due to Maya's adoption. After seeing Maya in that exalted position, they were urged to achieve those occult powers. Maya kept boasting and exciting their urge further, and hence this terrible result …'

Just then Maya came and Premshankar had to leave his sentence unfinished. Gyanshankar too left the place in a disturbed state of mind.

63

According to Gayatri's instructions, Gyanshankar used to give two thousand rupees every month for Mayashankar's expenses. Premshankar wanted to keep many tutors for him, cars for his outings and servants to attend him, but he didn't agree to spend so much on himself. Premshankar was forced to agree to his proposals. Only two tutors came to teach him. Ijaad Hussain taught him Persian and a priest taught Sanskrit. There was a horse for him to ride. Premshankar taught him English himself. Maths was the responsibility of Jwalasingh; Priyanath taught music twice a week, in which he was trained and medicine also twice a week. Dr. Irfan Ali knew economics very well. He taught law twice a week and lectured on economics for two days. Many college students came from the city to listen to him and Priyanath's musical society was famous throughout the city. All the savings from there were spent on Mitr-Bhavan, Ittehadi orphanage, and Priyanath's dispensary. Ten scholarships of twenty rupees each were instituted in Vidyavati's name. Even after all this expenditure, a lot was saved every month. About twenty-five thousand rupees had accumulated in three years. Premshankar wanted to send Maya on a tour of Europe and America with Gyanshankar's permission. There couldn't have been a better use of this money. But Mayashankar had something else in his mind. He wanted to go on the tour, but did not wish to spend more than thousand rupees a month on it. He had thought of a better way to use this money, but was afraid of expressing it to Premshankar. Fortunately he found a good opportunity for it.

The loan which Lala Prabhashankar had taken to save Premshankar in the Lakhanpur case had to be returned in a period of three years. The time had lapsed, but even its interest had not been paid. Initially Premshankar had no inkling of the matter, but when the Mahajan dragged it to the court, he got to know of it. He also came to know why the money had been borrowed. Since then, he was worried as to how to repay the debt? Although only a small portion of it had been spent on the case, and the larger part on feasts and weddings this was not the time to account for all that. Premshankar wanted to bear the entire burden of the debt. But where to get the money from? He kept thinking about it for many days. Sometimes he thought of asking Gyanshankar or Priyanath, but could not ask any of them out of hesitation.

One day he was lost in this worry when Bhola came and stood near him. Seeing him worried, he said – 'Babuji, you remain very sad nowadays; what's the matter? If there's something that we can do, please tell us. We'll try to do it to the best of our capacity.'

Premshankar had great affection for Bhola. He had left drinking and gambling due to his influence. He thought of him as his redeemer and respected him a lot. Premshankar too trusted him. He said – 'There's some issue but what can you do?

Bhola – What else? Well, I can give my life for it.

Prem – That won't solve my problem, think of some other solution.

Bola – Tell me, I'm ready to do it. I won't stop pestering you till you tell me.

Finally, Premshankar said helplessly – I need some money and don't know what to do about it.

Bhola – If you can manage with one or two thousand, I can give them to you. If more are needed, I'll think of something else.

Prem – How will you manage even one or two thousand? You won't be having the money; you'll have to borrow from someone.

Bola – No Babuji, with your blessings, I'm not so ragged now. I have about more than a thousand. Another one thousand have been given by Masta. Durga and Damdi also wanted to give their money, but I didn't take. Why to bother oneself by keeping someone else's money? If something untoward happens they'll think I've eaten it up.

Prem – How did you get so much money?

Bhola – You only have given us; where else it could have come from? I swear upon my youth that since three years I haven't touched any dice or drink. If I had done such evil deeds even after staying with good people like you, how could I've shown my face to anyone? I can even say with surety about Masta that since two-three years, he has not eyed anyone's goods. Just a few days back, five guineas fell down from Bhavanisingh's pocket; Masta found them lying in the fields and went and gave them to him. Earlier, he used to pick fruit from this very garden and sell it, but now he has left all bad habits. Durga and Damdi do smoke some drugs, but very rarely and apart from that I haven't seen them following any bad habit. We all eat simple meals of chapatis, lentils and vegetables and save about two-three hundred every month. So tell me; should I get the money?

Prem – I am glad to know that you could also achieve some standing in life. All this is a result of your good planning. But my need is greater. I need about twenty-five thousand rupees.

Suddenly Mayashankar came and stood there. His eyes were full of tears and his face reflected a meek curiosity. Premshankar signalled Bhola to go and asked Maya – 'Why are you crying? Sit.'

Maya – It's nothing. I just remembered Teju and Padmu. Had they been alive I would have called them here. At that time I was very unkind. I wanted to make them jealous by flaunting my riches. After listening to me they too used to say, 'We shall invoke such a mantra that no one will be able to kill us. We shall acquire such mantras that we'll order the riches anywhere in the world!' At that time I could not understand their talk; I thought they were joking, but now when I think of it I feel as if I am their killer. My heart gets anxious and I feel so angry with myself that I can't tell you! I had just gone to see my granduncle. He was very upset. Some moneylender has filed a case against him, so he was all the more worried. If this trouble had not befallen him he wouldn't have been so sad. In times of trouble, sorrow becomes all the more unbearable. It's impossible to relieve him of the boys' tragic death, but this new problem can be resolved. I feel hesitant to say this to you but excuse me this time. Chacha Dayashankar was telling our uncle, 'We are not bothered about the land; let it go. What can you do now? Whatever befalls me, I'll see.' But uncle wanted that we should ask for some time from the moneylender. If you permit me, should I go and talk to him? He'll feel somewhat oppressed before me.

Premshankar – I'm trying to arrange the money, but God knows how much he needs. He has never discussed it with me.

Maya – From their talk, I could sense it's a matter of fifteen or twenty thousand.

Prem – That's what I had thought. Something will be arranged in a few days. Either I'll make the moneylender relent or take some time after paying him two or four thousand.

Maya – I want that my uncle shouldn't come to know and the money should reach the moneylender so that nothing is spoiled. When we do have money why should we plead before him?

Prem – Those rupees are your legacy. I have no right to touch them. I have kept them aside for your Europe tour.

Maya – My Europe tour is not so essential that I should leave my family in trouble and go.

Prem – They should be spent in the task that they were assigned for.

Maya went away upset, but he had grown close to Shraddha. He went to her and said – 'If Chacha Sahib doesn't give the money to my grandfather I will never go to Europe. What will I do with thirty thousand there? Only five thousand are enough for me to leave. Please get twenty-five thousand from him.'

Premshankar gave the same reply to Shraddha. She took Maya's side. They started debating. Nothing could be decided. The next day she took up the same question. Finally when she saw that even after being defeated verbally he doesn't want to give money, she said with a little anger – 'If you won't give money to Dadaji, Maya will not go to Europe.'

Prem – He can never disobey me.

Shraddha – He can't disobey other things but won't obey this one.

Prem – You must have taught him this lesson.

Shraddha didn't say anything. She felt hurt at this comment. She kept sitting quietly for a second. Then she got up to go. Premshankar had uttered these words in an impulse, but was now repenting his rudeness. He said – 'If Gyanshankar objects to it, then?'

Shraddha replied irritatedly - Then say clearly that you're afraid of Gyanshankar. Why are you taking refuge under things like rights, duties and legacy?

Premshankar was confused, and replied – It's not a matter of being afraid. I have full authority in the matter of money, but I do not wish to spend it like this without Gyanshankar's permission.

Shraddha – Then write a letter to him and ask. I am confident that he won't have any objection. He's not that same Gyanshankar who gave his life after every single penny.

Premshankar came out and sat down to write the letter. But then it struck him, 'What if Gyanshankar gives permission! What's his harm in allowing this? Then I'll have to give the money by all means. But this money is neither mine, nor Maya's; not even Gyanshankar's. This is meant for Maya's education.' He did not write the letter. He talked about it to Jwalasingh. He also could not decide anything. They decided to consult Dr. Irfan Ali. He advised that the money shouldn't be spent on anything else apart from Maya's education.

When Mayashankar heard about this decision he was very annoyed. He felt like going and debating with Dr. Sahib, but was afraid lest he finds it an impolite act. 'Why not go and ask the moneylender about all those rupees? I am a minor, he might object, but if I agree to repay double the amount, he would agree.' But then he grew doubtful that Premshankar may not say anything openly, but will really be angry with him. The poor boy lay down sadly lost in these worries; sad and depressed. Evening came and he did not come out of the room. Dr. Irfan Ali called him to study. He sent a word that he was down with headache. It was time for dinner. All the students of Mitr-Bhavan went to eat. Maya again refused, saying he had a headache. Shraddha came to see him. Maya burst out crying on seeing her.

Shraddha wiped his tears with love and said – Son, come and have some food. I'll talk to him again in the morning. Dr. Irfan Ali spoiled the whole thing, or else I had made him agree to our proposal.

Maya – Chachi, I don't feel like eating anything. (Crying) I killed Teju and Padmu and now I can't even help grandfather. Curse be on such a life!

Shraddha too became helpless due to a surge of emotions. She wiped Maya's tears with the end of her sari and cried herself as well.

Maya said – Chachi, you tire out yourself for nothing; I am so luckless, let me cry.

Shraddha – You come and eat something. I'll talk about it tonight only. Maya's heart was very upset, but he could not avoid Shraddha's request. He ate a few bites but it seemed as if every bite was falling out of the mouth. He washed his mouth and hands, and lay down in his room.

The whole night, Shraddha kept thinking as to how to make Premshankar agree. She consulted Sheelmani also, but could not think of a solution.

In the morning, Budhia came for some work. She said while talking – 'Bahuji, everyone sees money; no one's bothered about the hard work involved. A man earns just one or two rupees in a day and thinks so high of himself; a poor woman keeps slogging in the kitchen night and day, and is still called worthless.'

Shraddha suddenly leapt with joy. The way a smouldering fire burns quickly on being given a blow of air, this talk suggested a new resolution to her. A lost traveller found his way. Something that she had been searching for hours was suddenly found by her. As soon as Budhia left, she came to Premshankar and said – 'What have you decided regarding giving the money to Chachaji?'

Prem – I am worried about it. Something will be arranged in a few days.

Shraddha – Money is lying at home only.

Prem – I don't have the right to spend it.

Shraddha – Whose money is it?

Prem – (surprised) It has been given for Maya's education.

Shraddha – So the two thousand you get aren't spent every month?

Prem – Don't you know? Only eight hundred are spent; the remaining twelve hundred are left every month.

Shraddha – Why are they left? Can't you understand that? How much salary should Dr. Irfan Ali get for teaching Maya? If you had hired Dr. Priyanath and Babu Jwalasingh, you'd have to pay them properly. In your opinion, Irfan Ali's salary comes to nothing? Won't you give five hundred rupees as his daily wages? Priyanath never earned less than hundred rupees a day. He wouldn't have gone anywhere to teach in the first place, and even if he did he wouldn't have taken less than five hundred a month. Babu Jwalasingh is reasonable even if he costs a hundred. The only one left is you. Maya's your nephew; you teach him out of love but why should others slog for free? You think this money to be a saving; that's pretty unfair. You can either take it was a reward for your goodness or the cost of their obligation; they have every right to spend it.

Premshankar said doubtfully – You and Maya will not relent till I give the money; it's okay, let it be as you please. Your arrangement is fair, I admit that but my soul cannot be satisfied. I am giving you the money now but I will always deem it a debt and try my best to repay it.

64

When Lala Prabhashankar got the money he almost cried. The village had been saved, but who was going to inhabit it? Dayashankar's mind was again getting detatched from home. He had become a follower of many ascetics. Day by day, he was getting attracted to the path of renunciation.

On the other hand, Gyanshankar didn't agree to Mayashankar's Europe tour. In his opinion, the journey couldn't have benefitted Maya at present. It was far better that he toured his own areas. After that he could see the famous places in India, so by the month of April, Mayashankar went to Gorakhpur and after touring his region for two months reached Lucknow. He kept touring the villages there for about two months. He used to write whatever he saw in his daily diary. He studied the conditions of the farmers deeply. The farmers of both the regions were impressed a lot with his affection, politeness and manners. He found a place in their hearts. Love proferred instead of fear. People thought him to be their well wisher. They came to him with their tales of woe. He couldn't have come to know of their real state through any other means. Ruin was rampant everywhere. There was hardly a house which had metal utensils. Most houses didn't even have iron girdles. There was nothing in the huts except mud utensils. There was no bedding or beds in them and they couldn't be called proper houses even. They just comprised of one or two small rooms. One for men; the other for animals. In a single room, eating, sleeping and sitting – all took place. The settlements were so dense that no open spaces could be found in the village. There were no compounds in any houses; even the city localities would not be so lacking in air and light. The peasants who were thought to be very rich also didn't have proper clothes on their bodies, and they too had meals only once a day. Even these men were neck-deep into debt. One craved to see a breed of healthy animals. Wherever one could see, one could only find thin and weak oxen who crawled in the fields and yawned at their bins of fodder. Many of the villages didn't even get a drop of milk. Seeing this all-pervasive poverty and helplessless, Maya's soft heart shook in pain. He was very sensitive by nature; very soft, kind and generous. Education and music had further heightened these feelings. 'Premashram' was full of the discussions of service and social welfare. Maya's simple heart had absorbed that spirit completely. He used to write to Premshankar again and again, aggrieved at these scenes; described his experiences and asked about the resolution of these troubles, but either Premshankar did not answer or simply took up the old story of the peasants' foolishness, laziness and other characteristic frailties.

Maya was touring his regions, when the local Rajsabha elections were held. Gyanshankar was an old aspirant of this respectable post. He jumped into the contest enthusiastically, and though he was a minister in the Talukedar Sabha, he didn't have faith in the help given by the Talukedars. Many big Talukedars wished to become the representatives of their village. Before them, Gyanshankar had no hope of his success. So he decided to contest from the side of the Gorakhpur peasants. There, the battle was not so tough. His workers started going from village to village singing his praises - 'Babu Sahib is so kind and godfearing; you'll be blessed if you choose him. he will fight for you progress and benefit in the Rajsabha; he'll get the land-tax decreased, arrange for pastures in every village, ban the system of gifts, oppose the provision of rent increase, and uproot all unnecessary expenditure.' The whole region was up and about. The way in which days of the wedding season echo with drums and beats, in the same way, talks of community-love abounded everywhere. Dr. Irfan Ali stood from the Benaras University; Babu Priyanath chose Benaras Municipality. Jwalasingh belonged to the rich community of Etawah; he took the side of Etawah peasants. Syed Ijad Hussain also became excited. He got up to defend Muslim identity. Premshankar did not wish to enter this field, but Bhavanisingh, Balraj and Qadir Khan started propagating him amongst the peasants of Benaras. For about three-four months, the market of rumours was busy; the press people had no respite from printing election tracts. Feasts and plays were put up all over the city. Every contestant was beating his own drum, as if he alone had taken up the mantle of the welfare of the world.

Finally the Election Day arrived. On this day the enthusiasm of the leaders, their alacrity, their manners and politeness was over-evident and opinion-makers were on an all-time high. They ate sweets and dry fruits and roamed in motorcars. From morning till night, letters of opinion were read.

After this, seven days passed in great anxiety. They were somehow spent. On the eighth day, the mandate was declared. Many homes lit up lamps of ghee; and many others mourned. Gyanshankar won, but the success which Premashram residents achieved was amazing; every warrior in this arena came out with a victory flag. The biggest success belonged to Premshankar. He had reached this high seat without any particular enterprise or intention. When Gyanshankar heard the news, his spirits abated. He didn't feel much interest in sitting in the Rajsabha. Many a times, groves are full of the noises of birds at evening, but as soon as it gets dark and birds sit in their nests, stillness ensues there; in the same way the community representatives became quiet after reaching the decorated halls of the Rajsabha. They forgot all high and mighty promises that they had made. Some became busy in entertaining their clients, some looked after their accounts, and some were lost in tourism and hunting. All the spirits of community service vanished. People came to Rajsabha in a spirit of mockery and left after asking some futile questions or demonstrating their oral skills. What were those inspiring powers which had made people attached to this seat of power – it's difficult to determine this, but they had no intention of serving anybody, this is absolutely clear. Cause and effect, means and result – all vanished in that air of authority.

But Premashram was not so detatched from its aims. Here, people were already following the path of service. They now got a chance to extend their scope of work. They thought about new proposals of reform, analyzed the positive and negative aspects of government proposals, and inspected official reports. They asked questions on official atrocities, and wherever they found justice being trampled, they drew the attention of the council towards it. They were not just satisfied with asking questions, but tried to get to the core of the problem. They opposed not just for the sake of opposing, but for analysis. Their honest effort and dutifulness soon made them popular in the council. People saw their doubts, proposals and reactions with respect. The officers could not take their talk lightly. Although Dr. Irfan Ali was the mouthpiece of this group, it was an open secret that Premshankar was its backbone.

Two years passed in this manner, and though the 'Mitr-Mandal' had impressed the Sabha to quite an extent, Premshankar had yet not dared to present that proposal there, which was simmering in his heart since long, and according to which the right to dismiss the tenants from the land was to be usurped from the zamindars. He belonged to a family of zamindars; Maya who was dear to him like a son, was now a big talukedar. Jwalasingh was also a zamindar. Lala Prabhashankar who was a father-figure to him would not have tolerated even a little curtailment in his rights; for all these reasons, he shied away from proposing such a bill in the council. Though the latter had landlords in a large number and there was much pressure, but

Premshankar did not fear them as much as he did his own relatives, and besides that, his soul was pained at getting deviated from the path of duty.

One day, he was sitting in this very dilemma when Mayashankar came with a letter to him and said – 'See; Babu Deepak Singh is trying to wreak such havoc in the council? He's trying to get a bill passed whereby the zamindars will be given the right of arbitrary dismissal to extort the land rent. In his opinion, they will be able to collect the rent more easily upon getting this right.' Premshankar said in a passive tone – 'I have seen this letter.'

Maya - But you haven't replied to it?

Premshakar looked towards the sky and said – Not yet.

Maya – Do you think it will be accepted in the council?

Prem – Possibly, yes.

Maya – Then the zamindars will absolutely crush the tenants.

Prem – Well, what else?

Maya – We must cut away the roots of such a movement. If you reply to this letter, Babu Deepak Singh will not dare to present this proposal.

Prem – What will Gyanshankar say?

Maya – As far as I think, he'll not approve of it.

Prem – Yes, I am also expecting a similar response.

Mayashankar understood what his uncle had in mind.

Ever since he had returned from the tour of his region, he had been thinking how to improve the condition of the peasants. He had read many books on the topic, and also questioned Dr. Irfan Ali about it. Premshankar's confusion disheartened him a lot. He couldn't say anything further, but became impatient to react to that letter. He had never written any article in the newspapers till date. He was scared as to whether he'd be able to write or not, or anyone would publish it or not. He spent a few days deliberating on it. Finally he wrote an answer, and took it to Dr. Irfan Ali with some hesitation. When Dr. Sahib read the essay, he asked with surprise – 'Have you written all this?'

Maya – Yes, I have, but I don't think it has come out properly.

Ifran – Wow! I cannot write any better than this. You have inherited this quality from Babu Gyanshankar.

Maya – So should I send it for publication?

Irfan – Why not? I will send it myself.

Premshankar used to look at the papers carefully to see if anyone had replied to Deepak Singh's letter, but many days passed and his hopes were belied. Many a times he wished he could answer by taking a pseudonym, but either he couldn't find time or kept undecided, so he couldn't write. On the twelfth day, when he opened the newspaper he found Mayashankar's essay. He read it in one go. He found a proud delight in reading it. He immediately went to Shraddha and read it out to her. Then he went to Irfan Ali.

He asked – Do you have some news?

Prem – Didn't you see, Maya has written such a logical reply to Deepak Singh's letter?

Irfan – Yes, I did. I was coming to ask you if he has written it all by himself or have you helped him out?

Prem – I didn't have any inkling of it; he alone must have written it.

Irfan – We must congratulate him, should I call him?

Prem – No, we must suppress his enthusiasm. Gyanshankar will be very upset on seeing this essay. He'll put the entire blame on me. He will say that I've misguided his son but I assure you that I didn't even give him a single hint to write this letter. I didn't write myself precisely due to this fear of misunderstanding.

Irfan – You can put the blame on me. I will accept it very gladly.

Prem – Very soon, his missive of anger will arrive. Maya has not behaved well with me!

Irfan – What does Bhabi Sahiba think of it?

Prem – Don't ask. She wants to arrange a feast to celebrate it.

Premshankar's anticipation was absolutely true. The third day, Gyanshankar's letter arrived. His motive was expressed as feared – 'I did not expect this from you. You have done great injustice to the simple child by teaching him the lesson of socialism. His eighteenth year is about to be complete. He will soon get the ruling rights of his region. I will be coming by the end of this month of make the preparations. His Excellency, the Governor will himself arrive to give him the reins of government. That melodious tune has been spoilt by this odd music. You have misused your authority of education. Please send Maya to me now. I don't want that he should stay there even for a second. I'll keep him with me till his ascension. I'm afraid he might indulge in some unwanted incidents out there … that's all.'

Mayashankar left for Lucknow by the evening train.

65

Babu Gyanshankar's mansion is illuminated like the imagination of a poet today. This is the day for which he had been waiting almost since an age. The pleasant dream of authority and wealth has now been realized. The auspicious occasion of Mayashankar's ascension has arrived today. There is a huge, strong tent in front of the bungalow. For its decoration, clever workers have been called from Lucknow. Multicoloured chairs are adorning the dias. There's an incomparable splendour everywhere. Prominent men of Gorakhpur, Lucknow and Benaras are present. The sitting room, the house and the bungalow are all full of guests. There's an army band on one side, and on the other, skilled shehnai players of Benaras are sitting. In another tent, rehearsals for a play are on. The students of Mitr-Bhavan will show their talent today. Dr. Priyanath's musical society will also charm the audience. Lala Prabhashankar is busy in welcoming the guests. Many officers and headmen from the rural areas of both the estates have come. Lakhanpur has also sent its representatives. All these villagers are Premshankar's guests. Qadir Khan, Dukhran Bhagat, Dapatsingh are all wearing saffron robes today. They will put up an act on their life spent in jail. Syed Ijaad Hussain has written an impressive eulogy. The boys of the Ittehaadi orphanage are standing with green flags to welcome Mayashankar. The place for the English guests is separate. They are also coming one by one. Dr. Irfan Ali has taken the responsibility of looking after them. For their entertainment, Prof. Richardson has been called from Calcutta, whose musical skills are unparallelled. Babu Gyanshankar is busy in preparations for the Governor's welcome.

It was evening time. The pleasant, clear air of spring was flowing. People went to the station to welcome the Governor. Gyanshankar's elephant was right in the front. A band was playing behind him. The station had already been covered with piles of flowers. As soon as the Governor's special bogie arrived and he alighted from it, he was showered with flowers.

He was made to sit on a decorated carriage. The procession started moving. In the front there was a chain of elephants. After that, came the Rajput regiment. Behind these, came the Governor's carriage, which had an embroidered umbrella over it. After that, there were the vehicles of city's rich men. Then came the police, riding on horses. The bands were walking behind them. This procession covered the main roads of the city and then reached Gyanshankar's house by late evening. His Excellency, Maharaj Gurudutt Rai Chaudhary came down from the carriage, and sat on the special chair meant for him on the stage. In the sharp electric lights, his huge talented persona seemed as if a divine soul had descended from the sky. A saffron turban and simple white clothes further added a gleam to his presence. The rich men sat on the chairs. For the rural guests, a clean carpet was laid on one side. Premshankar had already seated them there. After everyone had sat down, Mayashankar, shining with silks and gems, came out of the sitting room and came to the tent with the students of the Mitr-Bhavan. The gun salutes were fired, and the Brahmins started their welcome-song. Everyone stood up to greet him. Maharaj Gurudutt Rai got down, hugged him and made him sit on the throne. There was no sign of joy or gaeity on Mayashankar's face. He seemed lost in worrisome thoughts. The condition of a groom on the day of his wedding could well be compared to his. Such a huge burden of responsibility was to be kept on his head! From today onwards, he would have to take charge of the upkeep of so many men, their welfare and protection; will have to watch the areas of religion and justice, and if his officers terrorize the people, its blame will be upon him. He will have to remain wary of the curses of the poor and the tears of the weak. Besides these inner feelings, the task of facing such a distinguished audience and becoming the centre-point of so many eyes was no less daunting.

The procedure began. After the auspicious song, Pdt. Srinivas Vedacharya did the ritualistic prayers. Then Syed Ijaad Hussain read out his eulogy which was praised a lot by the audience. As soon as he sat down, the boys of the orphanage sang a praiseful song for the Governor. People were charmed by their sweet voices. Then Babu Gyanshankar got up and read out his impressive welcome address. Its language and content were both faultless. Dr. Irfan Ali translated it in Hindustani. Then the Governor stood up to reply to it. He first thanked Gyanshankar and other rich men, praised the work-efficiency and abilities of Gyanshankar in a few sentences, and then mentioned the good name of Rai Kamlanand and Rani Gayatri and also their love for their subjects and self-sacrifice. He then addressed Mayashankar and expressed happiness at his good fortune. In the rest of his speech, he preached about duty and good policies to Mayashankar, and in the end expressed a hope that he'd become an ornament of his society, and a servant of his country, community and state.

Now Mayashankar got up to reply to this. His feet were trembling and his heart was beating fast. He was afraid lest he should sit down in trepidation. His heart was recoiling back in fear. Gyanshankar had already prepared him. He had made him learn his speech, but Mayashankar had other feelings. The sequence that he had built of his thoughts had got scattered. For a second, he kept gathering his thoughts; 'What should I say; how should I begin?' Premshankar was sitting in the front, anxious at his dilemma. Suddenly Mayashankar's gaze fell on him. This gaze worked on his psyche in a way a halted train is pulled up by a call of challenge. His voice became alive. After thanking God and the present guests, he said –

'Maharaj Sahib, I am deeply indebted to you for those priceless teachings that you've given me regarding my forthcoming duties. And I assure you that I'll try to transform them into reality to the best of my capacity. You have said that a talukedar is his people's friend, philosopher and guide. I very politely wish to add that he's a little more; he's also his people's servant. This is the motive and purpose of his existence or else he was not needed in the world; the social structure would not have been lacking without him. He's not there to spend the hard-earned money of his people in luxuries and sensual pleasures; to erect a high palace in front of their ragged huts, to insult their humility with his gem-studded clothes, to shame their contented simplicity with his temporal splendour, and to mock their pain of hunger with his tastebuds. He shouldn't be one who's bothered only about his own concerns, but unaware of his duties. The sooner the subjects are freed of such anarchic creatures; the sooner their burden is taken off the heads of the people, the better it is.'

'Learned men, I do not have any fake pride that I'm the master of these regions. My values and fortune has given me a chance to be profitted from the valuable company of such pure, progressive and divine souls, and if any such pride would have entered my mind even for a second, I would have deemed myself fallen and unpardonable. Land belongs either to God who has created it, or to the peasant who puts it to use according to godly inspiration. The king protects the nation, so he has a right to collect taxes from the farmers, either directly or through a less complicated system. If any other class or category is given the liberty to make the peasants their means of pleasure in the name of contract, authority or property then this convention can only be deemed as a blot on the present social system.'

Gyanshankar's face started losing its colour. The Governor also changed stances unhappily and the rich guests started signalling to each other. People were surprised as to what was his motive behind saying such things? Premshankar was feeling utterly embarrassed. However, Dr. Irfan Ali and Jwalasingh were absolutely delighted!

Mayashankar took a pause and continued –

'I'm afraid that my talk will be variously deemed as somewhat improper or against the times; or even anti-community and revolutionary, but this fear cannot stop me from expressing those thoughts which are the fruit of my experience and and to execute which I've got this golden opportunity. I am of the opinion that I have no right to burden the peasants with my load. It would be my moral weakness and frailty if I sacrifice my principles for my love of luxury. Who would like to live after being fallen in one's own eyes? In front of this esteemed gathering, I today give up all those rights and authority that convention, law and the social system have given me. I liberate my people from the chains of my right upon them. They are neither my subjects, nor am I their talukedar. All these good men are my friends. They are my brothers; from today onwards, they are the zamindars of their cultivable land. They will not have to tolerate any injustice or tortures from my karidnas due to my selfish interests. They have been relieved from the tragic burdens of rent-increase, expenditure and unpaid labour. Please don't think that I have made this decision in any rush of emotions. No, I decided to do this when I completed the tour of my region. I have freed myself by making you free. I am now my own master; my soul is liberated. I do not need to bend my knees before anyone. Due to this brokerage, I would have had to torture my own soul, and I have a little experience of it. I thank God that he has saved me from such self-annihilation. I request all my brothers here that within a month, they should ask my manager about the official tax that they need to pay and deposit it in the royal treasure. I request honourable Dr. Irfan Ali to help me in this matter and solve the complex issues of law regarding this. I hope that my entire fraternity will stay in peace and love and won't run to the court for deciding trivial matters. May God fill your heart with tolerance, compassion and wisdom; and enable you to fulfill your new responsibilities. Well, I also wish to warn you that you won't be allowed to further lease your land on profit to other tenants. If you do that, it will be very unfair to me, for by doing that, you will promote those very evils that I wish to eradicate. You will have to pledge that you will never profit from this practice, and deem any income from tenancy as illegal and improper.'

As soon as Mayashankar completed his speech and sat down, thousands of men came and surrounded him from all sides. Some fell on his feet; some were crying, some were blessing him and others were jumping with joy. They had got that precious thing today which they had never imagined in their dreams. How can a poor peasant dream of becoming a zamindar? Thousands of men fell on the feet of the Governor, and many others hugged the feet of Gyanshankar. The whole tent-house was filled with hustle and bustle. People hugged each other and praised their fate. Premshankar was standing with a bent head, as if lost in deep thought, but this other friends were extremely happy. Their proud eyes were saying that it was a result of their company and teachings; they must be given some credit for it. The rich men had their lives in trouble. They looked at each other in amazement, as if they couldn't believe their eyes and ears. Many scholars wanted to express their views on the topic, but now there wasn't any scope for it.

The Governor was quite perplexed as to how to answer the speech? In his heart of hearts he was praising this great sacrifice by Mayashankar but he was afraid to express it lest other talukedars and the rich feel bad. At the same time, keeping quiet would have been an insult to Mayashankar. He had got a loving respect for him now, which is often a due of pure souls. He stood up and said softly:

'Babu Mayashankar! Although a majority of men amongst us would not approve of the principles that have inspired you to adopt this unique policy of contentment, but a man who isn't heartless will surely deem you as a God. It is possible that a person becomes detatched after spending a life of luxury; but someone who has just entered a pleasant, comfortable space of authority and splendour cannot be expected to make such a sacrifice. But if Babu Sahib doesn't feel bad, I would say that no social system can be deemed faultless only on the basis of principles; however high or pure they might be. A system can progress only under a high human character. We have seen gods among autocrats, and devils among democrats. People would have benefitted a lot from a generous, thoughtful and kind master like you. You could have become their guide. Now those subjects would be deprived of the means of their welfare; but I do not wish to delude you by these opinions. Good things always occur due to the inspiration of God. This too is His very desire, and we should hope that its result is favourable. I pray to God to bless these new zamindars and make your fame immortal.'

On one hand, the Mitr-Bhavan group was putting up its play; the stage was echoing with the tunes of Mastana and Priyanath's sarod; and on the other hand, Babu Gyanshankar was rushing to the banks of the Ganga in a spate of depression, as if a broken boat was being taken away by the surge of waves. Today fate had defeated him totally. Till now, he had always proved victorious over fate. Today the tables had been turned, and in a way that he hadn't found any time to make himself steady. Just a second ago, the edifice of his fortune was lit up with so many lamps, but a single gust of wind had extinguished them all. Now there was only a deep, dense, fearful darkness surrounding him on all sides.

He went on thinking, 'Did I offer my entire life only for this goal? Did I load my boat only to see it getting drowned?'

'Alas! This craving for wealth! What all didn't I sacrifice on your altar? I have given away even my religion and my soul. Alas! What all didn't I burn in your furnace? My mind, thought, duty; everything was burnt in it. Only for this that I shouldn't get anything except black dirt in returned?'

'It's not the fault of Mayashankar or Premshankar; it's the fault of my fate's complicated games. I thought that I was the devisor of my fate. Scholars have said the same, but I now know that I was a toy in its hands. I was a puppet dancing to its tunes. The way a cat makes a mouse dance or a fisherman lures a fish; this fate too kept deceiving me. When I got out of its clutches for a second, I thought I had won over it, but today that game came to an end; the cat strangled the mouse, the fisherman pulled out his hook. Man is so meek; so subservient to the other! Destiny is so strong and so tough!'

'The three-tiered mansion that I built in an age with tireless enterprise was devastated in soil in a second, as if it never existed, and no sign of it is visible now. Was that huge house just a fake creation of destiny?'

'Alas! Life has proved so worthless. O craving for luxury, you have left me nowhere! I just kept following you and you put me in this terrible whirlpool!'

'I cannot show my face to anyone now. Wealth, respect, authority – all are meaningless. A man can be happy without them; in fact, the truth is that happiness lies in liberating onself from them. The sorrow is that I cannot participate in this movement even in one tiny bit. People will think it to be the tragic outcome of my love of luxury. They'll say how horribly the son has destroyed the father's pride; how he has reprimanded him? Who will bear this sarcasm and insult? Alas! Had I known such an end beforehand I would have been deemed worthy of worship today; and would have been termed as a devout father of a sacrificing son. How fatal and secret was destiny's assault! Why should I remain alive now? Only for this that fate should be happy at my sordid state and insult, and applaud my heartrending pain! No, I have not yet turned so shameless and so undignified.'

'Alas! Vidya! How much did I tyrannize you! You were a chaste woman; I crushed you under my feet. How much did my good sense falter! O Goddess! Have mercy on this fallen spirit!'

Lost in these painful thoughts, Gyanshankar reached the river bank. Bulls could be seen sitting here and there. The still, medium sound of the river was heightening the stillness of the environs.

Gyanshankar saw the river with poignant eyes. His whole body trembled; he started crying. His sorrow was far greater than that of the river.

The events of his life started moving before his eyes like stills of a movie. His wicked deeds were more bright and clear than the stars in the sky. His mind questioned him, 'Is there no other way out except dying?'

Depression replied, 'No, there's no other way!' He went and stood at a yellow plank of the ghat. He raised both his hands, as if a bird opens its wings, but couldn't lift his feet.

His mind said, 'Why don't you too go to Premashram?' Guilt replied, 'What face whould I show there? I do not wish to die, but how to live? Alas! I am being killed forcefully.' This thought made Gyanshankar sob loudly. Tears started falling in streams from his eyes. His sorrow became even deeper. All the senses of his heart became submerged in this deep sea of pain. The earth and the sky; water and ground – all were absorbed in this mournful ocean.

He rose in an unconscious, empty state of mind and jumped in the Ganga. Cold waters of the river calmed the burning heart.

Epilogue

Two years have passed. It's evening time. Babu Mayashankar entered Lakhanpur, riding on a horse. He saw great beauty and cleanliness there. Almost every door was covered with a shade. The houses had big platforms built in the front. Most of the houses had been painted. The earlier grass huts had disappeared. Now all the houses had tiled roofs. On the doors, pucca bins of fodder had been built and many of them had horses tied near them. In the old chaupal, there was a school, and in front of it, there was a well and a guest house. On seeing Mayashankar people left their jobs and ran to him, and in just a second, hundreds of them gathered there. Mayashankar stopped at Sukhu Chaudhary's temple. It was very crowded at the moment. Various types of flowers were blooming in the temple compound. On a high seat, Chaudhary was sitting, reading the Ramayana and many women were listening to him. Mayashankar alighted from the horse and went and sat near him.

Sukhdas startled, stood up and asked - 'Hope all is well. Are you coming just now?'

Maya - Yes, I thought I should come and see you all.

Sukh - It's all your good grace. We are lucky that our master comes to see us in our own houses.

Thus saying, he rushed inside the house, got a woollen carpet for him, and got water from a pot to make some sherbet. Mayashankar washed his face and hands; drank the sherbet, and was unsaddling his horse when Qadir Khan came and greeted him. Maya said - 'Say, Khan Sahib, is everything well?'

Qadir - It's all the blessing of the Almighty. We keep praying for your life and belongings. Hope you'll stay here today?

Maya - That's what I had decided.

In just a while, all the young and old in the village arrived there. People started talking amongst themselves. Qadir asked -'Son, what's going on in the council these days? Will anyone bother about the tenants or not?'

Maya - Why not? Chacha Sahib and his friends are making great efforts. Hopefully, something will be achieved very soon.

Qadir - May God make them successful. How else can we bless them? Our every pore is blessing them. The condition of the peasants has improved a lot. Son, look at me alone. I was a farmer having twenty bighas, and had to pay hundred rupees rent on it. Ten or twenty rupees were spent on gifts. Now just twenty rupees is my land tax and no gifts have to be paid. Earlier, no foodgrains reached the house. Your peons and karindas strangled us and weighed away everything. Now we have our produce in our homes and sell it at our own convenience. In two years, we must have saved about four hundred. I got a pair of oxen for hundred and fifty, got the house repaired, got a shade built, and bought brass utensils instead of mud ones; the biggest advantage is that no one can oppress us now. We come home peacefully after depositing the tax. Otherwise, we were always walking a tight rope. We also say our prayers in peace, or earlier, even offering of namaz appeared to be burdensome.

Maya - How are you doing, Dukhran Bhagat?

Dukhran - Bhaiya, everything is fine with your blessings. Now it feels that we are also human beings, or else we were worse than oxen. Those creatures can relax after coming back from the fields; we had to come back and worry about them. When those worries were over, we went to appease the karinda. We used to return around twelve from there, and have our meals. I had fifteen bighas. Of these, ten were mauroosi. I paid fifty rupees tax on them. Five bighas were shikmi. Sixty rupees had to be paid for them. Now, I just pay thirty rupees for all my fifteen bighas. All unpaid labour and gifts have have been stopped. In just two years time, I've saved about four hundred. I've got a buffalo for a hundred rupees. I had some debt on me which I've paid off.

Sukhdas - And you've also bought a tabla and a harmonium; why don't you tell him that? You have got a pucca house and a well dug up; why are you hiding that? Bhaiya, he was a great devotee of Thakurji. Once, on being caught in forced labour, he took out all his anger on him. He broke his idols and threw them. Now he's again become respectful towards Him! He's even got all the musical instruments for singing devotional songs!

Dukhran – Why should I hide? Where's the need to hide anything from our master? It's all due to his blessings.

Maya – Had my uncle got to hear this, he'd have been too happy.

Kallu – Bhaiya, if you ask me, it's me who has profited the most. I've turned into a king from being a beggar. Earlier, I was a tenant of six bighas, all shikmi; I had to pay seventy-two rupees as tax, and always plead Ghaus Mian not to take away my fields. Around fifty rupees went away as gifts only. The peons had to be appeased separately. Now I only give nine rupees as tax. I became a respectable man in these two years. I stayed in a grass hut earlier; now I have got a pucca house made. Earlier, I used to be always scared lest anyone should complain against me to the karinda. Now I sleep in peace and sing your praises.

Maya – (to Sukhu Chaudhary) Your fields must be cultivated by labourers only? You must be busy with your religious affairs?

Sukhu – (laughing) Bhaiya, what do I have to gain by farming? I only aspire to go to the next world singing the praises of my lord. I have given all my forty bighas to those poor men who didn't get any land (after your renunciation). This way, the seven-eight families who did not have any job and couldn't even do labour due to the system of begaar, have now become men of dignity. I myself am able to survive on charity alone. Well, all I need is acquired here only; I don't have to go to any other village to beg. Some holy men keep coming off and on. They too are taken care of in the same way.

Maya – One doesn't see Bisesar Sah today?

Sukhu – He must have gone out for some work. He too is in a comfortable state now. He has added on to his stock a lot and does not indulge much in moneylending. Earlier he didn't take less than an annah as interest on a rupee, and what could he have done? He still couldn't retrieve a penny from many tenants. His money was often lost. He used to compensate for that by the interest he levied on loans. Now we give a rupee as interest on a hundred. There's no fear of losing any money. The shop is also doing well. Earlier, the official tours used to make him bankrupt. Now the village is strong; no one can suppress us, and moreover, even if there's any loss, the villagers make up for it together.

Just then, Balraj was seen coming on his horse, clad in a saffron turban and a vest. When he saw Mayashankar, he jumped down from the horse and touched his feet. He was now a member of the Zila Association. He was returning from their function.

Maya smiled and asked – Say Member Sahib; what's the news?

Balraj – I am fine with your blessings. Hope you too are fine? I had gone to attend a function of the board. It was evening by the time it got over.

Maya – What was the function about?

Balraj – The same question of begaar or unpaid labour. Heated arguments took place. My proposal was that no officer of the district should go to the village and force the villagers to do jobs like filling up water, cutting grass or sweeping. Whatever rations are needed should be informed to the village headman and it must be paid for, there and then, at market rates. Many Tehsildars and officers got annoyed at this. They said it would make government work suffer. I too argued openly. No government work should be accomplished by torturing the public and by insulting them. If it suffers let it be. The mockery is that many zamindars were also on their side. I took all of them to task. Finally my proposal was accepted. Let's see what the District Collector decides. My other proposal was that a sub-committee should be constituted for writing the inspection report, which should have a majority of traders. It shouldn't be the case that the Tehsildar takes a pen and writes whatever he pleases. This proposal was also accepted.

Maya – I congratulate you on these achievements.

Balraj – All this is nothing but a result of your great goodwill. Earlier, no one even knew the name of any newspaper here. Now we get many good papers. I'll show you my reading-room tomorrow morning. The villagers give a donation of ten or twenty rupees as per their capacity, or else, when we used to get the papers earlier, all of them abhorred it. When any officer came on a tour, the karinda used to complain to him against me. Now, with your blessings, there's Ram-rajya in the village. You won't find Pusa or Muzaffarpur wheat in any other village. We have got seeds from those centres and are hoping for almost a double produce. Earlier, no one sowed cotton out here. I got seeds from Malwa and Nagpur, and distributed them in the village. A wholesome cotton crop was harvested. All these jobs cannot be accomplished by poor tenants who don't get enough to eat and whose entire produce is gobbled up by the moneylender.

While talking about these matters, it was soon time for dinner. Peole left for their homes to have the night meal. Mayashankar ate pooris mashed in milk; drank some more milk and lay down to rest. After some time, people gathered again. They decided to sing and entertain themselves. Kallu sang a song. Qadir also sang a few passages. The Ramayana was read out. Kallu also put up an act of mimicry. They enjoyed themselves for two-three hours. Maya was quite amused. He too recited some nice passages. People were charmed by his sweet voice.

Suddenly Balraj said – Babuji, have you heard? The case that was going on regarding Mian Faizullah was decided today. He had committed a theft in his neighbour's house, who's an old woman. He has been sentenced for three years.

Dapatsingh said – Very well. If he'd also been caned a hundred times it would have been all the more better. Our curses have fallen upon him.

Maya – Do you know anything about Binda Maharaj or Kartarsingh?

Balraj – Yes; Binda Maharaj stays here only. He keeps a watchful eye on the village, which also serves as a means of his livelihood. Kartar has joined the police.

All the people left by ten o' clock. Mayashankar was as happy as if he was sitting in heaven.

People who are caught in the self-serving net of worldly desires cannot think of enjoying such peace, such happiness, and such self-contentment. It's just not there in their destiny!

Glossary

Aarti : A rhythmic prayer-song offered to a particular deity; usually after the completion of a ritual.

Abbajan : Father

Abeer : Literally meaning, 'smell of the rose'; rose-scented powder used during the festival of Holi.

Achkan : Long, buttoned coat, reaching upto the knees.

Aghan : The ninth month of the Hindu calendar; (December/January in the European calendar)

Ahir : A cattle-herding caste of India; usually engaged in the selling of dairy products.

Ahlmad : A keeper of court records; also responsible for issuing summons.

Amavasya : The lunar phase of the new moon in Sanskrit; a dark, moonless night.

Amma : Mother

Anjuman-e-Ittehaad : Association for concord

Ardali : Helper, assistant.

Arya Samaj : A monotheistic Indian Hindu reform movement that promotes values and practices based on the belief in the infallible authority of the Vedas. The Arya Samaj was founded by Maharishi Dayanand Saraswati on 10 April 1857. The followers of Arya Samaj, the Arya Samajists believe in one God and reject the worship of idols.

Badrinath : Literally meaning Lord Vishnu; a religious place in north India, at the foothills of the Himalayas. Also regarded as one of the four sacred *dhams* or places of pilgrimage outlined in Hinduism, along

		with Jagannathpuri, Dwarikadhish and Rameshwaram.
Bahuji	:	A colloquial word for addressing elder brother's wife.
Bakrid	:	The Muslim festival of sacrifice; also known as *Eid-al-Adha* or *Eid Qurban*, it honours the willingness of Ibrahim to sacrifice his son as an act of obedience to God's command. It entails the sacrifice of a sheep, goat, buffalo or camel followed by prayers.
Benaras	:	Also known as Varanasi or Kashi; a city in the state of Uttar Pradesh in north India, famous for the holy river Ganga and its *ghats*.
Baniya	:	A shopkeeper who deals in grocery items
Bazaar	:	Marketplace.
Begaar	:	Unpaid labour; usually forced.
Begum	:	The title of a married Muslim woman.
Bhaang	:	A mild preparation of marijuana; made from young leaves of cannabis sativa, mixed with milk or water.
Bhabi	:	Brother's wife.
Bhagwat	:	One of the eighteen puranas dealing with *Bhakti* or devotion.
Bhairav	:	A Hindu tantric deity; said to have been vanquished by goddess Durga.
Bighas	:	A term of land measurement; almost five-eighths to a quarter of an acre.
Brahma	:	The Creator in the Hindu Trinity; the four-headed God who is said to have created the temporal aspects of the universe.
Chachaji	:	Uncle; father's brother
Chai Garam	:	'Hot tea'.
Chamar	:	Name given to a caste involved in shoe-making and scavenging.
Chanakya	:	An ancient Indian teacher, philosopher, jurist and royal advisor. He assisted the first Mauryan emperor, Chandra-gupta in his rise to power. Widely accredited for playing an important role in the establishment of the Mauryan Empire.
Chanas	:	Gram (grain).

Chapatis : Light pancakes of wheat, usually round and fluffy.

Chaprasi : Peon

Charas : Marijuana

Charnamrit : A mixture of five elements: milk, Ganga-water, honey, tulsi leaves and curd; offered first to the deity and then to the worshippers; literally meaning, 'nectar of the feet.'

Chaupai : A quatrain; usually two lines of a verse.

Chaupal : Village assembly or hall.

Chautal : A musical term denoting "four claps"; also called Dhrupad *taal*.

Chitrakoot : A famous pilgrimage centre, situated in the Bundelkhand region of the Indian state of Madhya Pradesh. Lord Rama (the hero of the epic, *Ramayana*) is said to have spent a large part of his exile there.

Dada : Elder brother; a senior person.

Dalaan : Central hall of the house.

Daroga : General term used for a police officer; usually implied to denote a police inspector.

Dashashvmedh Ghat : "Dashashvmedha" literally means 'Sacrifice of ten horses'. It is the series of sacrifices performed by Lord Brahma to test the king Divodasa. Dashashvmedh Ghat is the main ghat in Varanasi, located on the Ganga, close to the Vishwanath temple; probably the most spectacular of the ghats in Varanasi.

Devkinandan : Another name for Lord Krishna; literally meaning Devaki's son.

Duryodhana : The Kuru prince in the epic *Mahabharata*; he was the eldest of the Kauravas; the 100 sons of the blind king Dhritarashtra and his queen Gandhari. An extremely courageous warrior, yet his greed and arrogance were the two qualities that allegedly led to his downfall in the battle of Mahabharata.

Ekadashi : Literally meaning number eleven; a spiritual day in Hinduism and Jainism that occurs twice in every lunar month; a day for fasting and praying in many Hindu communities.

Ganga : A major river of north India; counted extremely holy by the Hindus.

Gangajal : Waters of the Ganga

Ghat : A broad flight of steps leading down to a river.

Ghazal : Traditional lyric poetry in Persian or Urdu; usually having a fixed number of couplets.

Ghee : Clarified butter

Gulal : Traditionally used coloured powders during Hindu rituals; especially during the festival of Holi

Gur : Jaggery

Gurukul : A type of school system in ancient India with the student and teacher living in the same house; said to have been the usual norm of education in Vedic India.

Haakim : A man of authority; variously referring to a ruler, judge, master or chief.

Hakim : A medical practioner of the Unani system of medicine.

Halwa : A sweet made of semolina or vegetables like carrot or gourd; enriched with milk, sugar and dry fruits.

Hanuman Chalisa : A Hindu devotional poem addressed to Lord Hanuman; part of Tulsidas' version of the *Ramayana*, '*Ramcharitmanas*'.

Havaldar : A soldier or police officer corresponding to a sergeant.

Hiranyaksh : A notorious devil; said to be the brother of Hiranyakashyap; Lord Vishnu killed him during his Varah Avatar.

Holi : A festival of colours, celebrated during the spring season or the month of *Phagun*.

Hookah : An oriental tobacco pipe with a long, flexible tube which draws smoke through water contained in a bowl.

Huzoor : Sir

Jagannathpuri : A place in the Indian state of Odisha; with a famous Hindu temple dedicated to Lord Krishna and his siblings, Balram and Subhadra.

Jaltarang : A unique musical instrument; literally meaning "waves in water". Sound is created using waves in bowls of water.

Janamashtami : The birthday of Lord Krishna, usually falling during the months of August-September.

Jarasandh : According to the Hindu epic *Mahabharata*, Jarasandh was a descendant of king Brihadartha, the founder of Magadha. A great and powerful king, he was also known as Magadha Samrat, and was finally killed by Bhima in the battle of Mahabharata.

Jhusi : A town in the Allahabad district of the Indian state of Uttar Pradesh.

Jowar : Millets.

Kachories : Crisp savories usually stuffed with vegetables like peas and potatoes.

Kadamb : An evergreen, tropical tree; native to South and South-east Asia.

Kanungo : A person dealing in land measurement; one who holds all revenue records in duplicate.

Karinda : An agent appointed to work on someone else's behalf.

Karindagiri : The gamut of work done by a karinda.

Kartaal : A percussion instrument made of wood or copper; also called *manjira* in Hindi.

Katha-supari : Ingredients to make *paan*; catechu (a vegetable dye) and betel nut.

Keora : A fragrant plant, the leaves of which are used to flavour rice and curries.

Kheer : Rice pudding

Khus : An aromatic grass whose especially fragrant roots yield an oil used in perfumery and are also made into mats in tropical India.

Koel : Cuckoo

Kori : An Indian caste, whose traditional occupation was weaving.

Krishna : Literally meaning 'black' or 'dark'; it is the name of an extremely popular Hindu God believed to be an incarnation of Lord Vishnu.

Krishnaleela : Enactment of scenes related to lord Krishna's life.

Kurmi : A Vedic Kshatriya caste that has adopted agriculture as their profession.

Laat Sahib : Governor General.

Lagaan : The tax levied on land.

Lalaji : A senior, well-to-do; usually rich and respectable person.

Mahajan : A moneylender.

Maharaj Thakur : A respectable term used for anyone having a high social status and religious learning.

Mahatma : A great soul; for example, Mahatma Gandhi.

Mahavir : Lord Hanuman, the chief ally of Lord Rama in his battle against Ravana.

Mahto : A surname used by several castes and communities in India and Nepal. In the Oraon tribal society, a Mahto or Mahato originally referred to a secular chief of a village, who held administrative authority along with Pahan, the religious priest.

Mahua : An Indian tree with fleshy edible flowers; yields oil-rich seeds.

Man : A unit of weight equal to 40 kg; generally used to measure agricultural output.

Mantra : An oft-repeated word or phrase; usually expressing a strong belief.

Mantri : A minister.

Manusmriti : Literally translated as the 'Code of Manu', it actually means 'Reflections by Manu'. It is the oldest surviving document that compiles and organizes the code of conduct for Hindu society.

Mathura : A city in the state of Uttar Pradesh in north India; revered as the birthplace of Lord Krishna.

Maulvi : A Muslim priest.

Mauroosi : That which is capable of being inherited or of passing by inheritance; used as adjective for land.

Mirabai : Meera, also known as Mirabai was a 16th century Hindu mystic poet and devotee of Krishna. Born in a Rajput royal family of Rajasthan, she is a celebrated Bhakti Saint, particularly in the North Indian Hindu tradition.

Mitr-Bhavan : Literally meaning, a house of friends.

Mitr-Mandal : An association of friends.

Mohanbhog : A sweet made of gramflour, ghee and dry fruits.

Myna : An Asian/Australian starling; usually having a dark plummage and a loud call.

Namaz : Ritualistic offering of Quranic precepts as prayers.

Nazir : A native court official who assists higher officers, acts as treasurer and performs similar other duties.

Nand : Foster-father of Lord Krishna; a dairy farmer of Mathura.

Navratan : Nine gems, an allusion to nine artists in Akbar's court; also used to qualify nine ingredients in culinary terms.

Neelgais : A large Indian antelope, the male of which is bluish-arch and short-horned while the female has no horns.

Paan : Betel-leaf

Panchayat : A village council; usually comprising of five panchas or judges.

Pakhavaj : A barrel-shaped, two-headed drum.

Passi : A prominent Kshatriya clan in north India.

Patwari : A government official who keeps records regarding ownership of land.

Peshkar : A court reader; official who produces documents before the judge.

Phag : Songs sung during the festival of Holi.

Phagun : The 12th lunar month of the Hindu calendar; (Feb-March in the European calendar)

Pooris : Deep-fried, small pancakes, made of wheat and its derivative flours.

Prayag : The place in Allahabad, Uttar Pradesh where the three rivers - Ganga, Yamuna and Saraswati meet.

Pulav : A rice preparation with vegetables or meat.

Purohitji : A Hindu priest.

Raag Dhrupad : The oldest surviving classical style of Hindustani (or North Indian) vocal music; its major emphasis being maintaining the purity of the *swaras* or sounds.

Raagas : A melodic composition; considered a means in the Indian musical tradition to evoke certain feelings in the audience.

Rabi : Winter crop; grown in the Indian subcontinent in autumn or early winter and harvested in spring.

Radha : The consort of Lord Krishna.

Raja Sahib : A respectable term of address for the king.

Ram : Lord Ram, the seventh incarnation of Lord Vishnu; also known as Purushottama or the best of men; one of the most commonly adored God of the Hindus.

Ramayana : A Sanskrit epic traditionally attributed to Valmiki; concerns the banishment of Rama from Ayodhya, abduction of his wife Sita by Ravana and her rescue, and Rama's eventual restoration to the throne.

Ram-rajya : A system where the society is run by the principles of Lord Rama. The term was popularized by Mahatma Gandhi during the nationalist struggle, as against the all-exploitative British rule.

Rani Sahiba : A respectable term of address for the queen.

Rasleela : The term '*rasa'* meaning 'aesthetics' and '*leela*' meaning 'act', 'play' or 'dance'; the term usually denotes the dance of love between Krishna, Radha and the milkmaids.

Ravana : The devil emperor of Sri Lanka; described in the Hindu epic *Ramayana* as a follower of lord Shiva; a great scholar and a capable ruler, but someone who wished to overpower the Devas. He abducted Rama's wife, Sita and was defeated in the battle that ensued for her rescue, leading to his final death and downfall.

Rishikesh : Part of the legendary Kedarkhand; the Ganga flows through Rishikesh, a small holy town in Uttar Pradesh, India at the foothills of the Himalayas.

Roti-Saag : *Chapatis* and a curry of greens; a term denoting basic, rustic food.

Rudraksh : A seed used as a prayer-bead in Hinduism, especially in Shaivism; literally meaning 'fierce-eyed'; part of Lord Shiva.

Saag : Spinach or any green leafy vegetable.

Sadhu : An ascetic; someone who has renounced the world.

Sahib : A polite title or form of address for a man. For example, Doctor sahib.

Sahuaain : The female counterpart of 'Sahu' or 'Sah'; generally denoting a caste involved in business and moneylending.

Samosas : Triangle-shaped crisp savouries; usually stuffed with potatoes or peas.

Sanatan Dharma : In Hinduism, a term used to denote the 'eternal' or absolute set of duties or religiously-ordained practices incumbent upon all Hindus regardless of class, caste or sect.

Sangeet Parishad : A musical council, assembly or seminar.

Sarangi : An Indian musical instrument about two feet high, with three or four main strings and upto thirty-five sympathetic strings.

Sarkar : A man who is in a position of authority, especially one who owns land ploughed by the tenant farmers. Nowadays, the term is used as a general Hindi term denoting government.

Sarod : A lute used in classical North Indian music, with four main strings.

Sattu : A type of flour consisting of a mixture of ground pulses and cereals (usually seven). The dry powder is used in various ways as a principal or secondary ingredient of dishes.

Satyanarayan Katha : A prayer ritual concerning the worship of Lord Vishnu. Satya means 'truth' and 'Narayana' means 'the highest being', so Satyanarayan means 'the highest being who is an embodiment of Truth'.

Seer : In India, the seer was defined by the standards of weights and measurement Act (1956) as being exactly equal to 1.25 kilograms.

Seth : A respectable, rich, well-to-do person.

Shakti : The female principle of divine energy, especially when personified as the supreme deity, the Hindu goddess Durga.

Shaligram : Refers to a fossilized shell used in south Asia as an iconic symbol and reminder of Lord Vishnu as the universal principle by some Hindus.

Sherbet : A drink made of sweetened fruit juices diluted in water and served with ice.

Shikmi : A person who holds land from an occupant and is, or but for a contract, would be liable to pay rent for such a land to that occupant, but does not include a mortgagee or a person holding land directly from the Government.

Shivaji : Shivaji Bhonsle was a sixteenth-century Indian warrior king and a member of the Bhonsle Maratha clan. He was widely known for his guerilla warfare tactics. He gave a solid opposition to the Mughal Empire, organizing the Marathas into an independent kingdom in Maharashtra. For his achievements, he was endowed with the respectable title of 'Chatrapati Shivaji Maharaj'.

Shiva : The great Hindu God; also known as the Destroyer in the Hindu trinity that includes Brahma and Vishnu.

Shaivites : The followers of lord Shiva

Shri Vallabh : A sect founded by Vallabhacharya (1479-1531 CE); an Indian Telugu Philosopher, centered on Krishna and the Vaishnavite precepts in the Braj region of North India.

Shyama : A white-necked singing bird of India noted for the sweetness and power of its song.

Sitar : A large, long-necked Indian lute with movable frets; played with a wirepick.

Surdas : A sixteenth-century blind Hindu devotional poet and singer; known for lyrics written in praise of Lord Krishna; especially in celebration of his childhood antics.

Swadeshi : An adjective referring to goods manufactured in India from Indian raw materials. Also refers to a political movement started in the 1920s by Mahatma Gandhi to encourage domestic production of goods and oppose the economic exploitation of Indian raw materials and labour.

Swaraj : Self-rule or self-government; a term popularized during the nationalist struggle.

Swarajists : Nationalists demanding and struggling for 'Swaraj'.

Tablas : A pair of small hand drums, one of which is slightly larger than the other; used in Indian classical music.

Talukedar : An Indian landholder in the Mughal Empire and British Raj; responsible for collecting taxes from a district.

Tanzeb : A fine fabric; light as muslin

Tehsildar : A person appointed to collect '*lagaan*' or tax levied on land.

Thakurji : A term used variously to denote God or a specific deity

Thakurs : Members of the *Kshatriya* (warrior) caste among the Hindus of North India.

Thanedar : A police officer in-charge of the '*thana*' or the police-station.

Tonga : An Indian carriage usually driven by a single horse.

Triveni : A confluence of the three rivers, the Ganga, Yamuna and Saraswati.

Vaid : A medical practitioner; usually following the ancient Indian system of medicine, the Ayurveda.

Vaishnavites : Followers and worshippers of Lord Vishnu.

Vande matram : An ode to goddess Durga as the Mother goddess, it was written both in Sanskrit and Bengali script in the novel *Anandmath* (1882), written by Bankim Chandra Chatterjee. Literally meaning "I praise thee, O Mother", independent India adopted it as the national song of the country.

Veena : An Indian stringed instrument with four main and three subsidiary strings; especially used in Carnatic music.

Vidyaratna : Literally meaning, 'A gem in the field of education'; a title accorded to a highly-educated person or a scholar.

Vrindavan : A holy town in the north Indian state of Uttar Pradesh; lord Krishna is said to have spent a large part of his childhood here; famous for the Banke Bihari temple.

Yagyavalakya : A Hindu Vedic sage who proposed and debated metaphysical questions about the nature of existence and impermanence, and expounded the epistemic doctrine of 'Neti-Neti' ("not this, not this") to discover the Universal self and Atma or the soul.

Yamuna : A north Indian river; tributary of the river Ganga.

Yashoda : The foster-mother of Lord Krishna.

Yoga : A Sanskrit word literally meaning 'connection' or 'union', it refers to the spiritual discipline that includes meditation, exercises and breathing techniques to improve the overall health and well-being of an individual.

Zamindar : Landowner; especially one who leases his land to tenant farmers.